MALUS DOMESTICA

A Horror Novel

S. A. HUNT

Malus Domestica
Copyright © S. A. Hunt, 2015
Cover: S. A. Hunt

This book is dedicated to my mother Kathy, who fights harder than anybody in this story and who inspired the protagonist's wise, feisty mother in *Ten Thousand Devils,* volume three of my Outlaw King series.

The character of Robin is named after the lady-sai Robin Furth. We are well met along the Path, gunslinger.

LOCAL WOMAN MURDERED IN DOMESTIC VIOLENCE INCIDENT
Hysterical Daughter Claims 'It Was Witches'
Blackfield Times-Register, Oct 2009
Blackfield, GA

BYSTANDERS PURSUE ARSON SUSPECT
Investigators Find Body of 84-Year-Old Neva Chandler; Attacker Still at Large
The Birmingham News, June 2012
Birmingham, AL

CARJACKING ENDS IN MYSTERIOUS CRASH
Stolen Car Found Abandoned; Carjacker 'covered in blood'
The Chronicle, Jan 2013
Willimantic, CT

BODY OF LOCAL MAN FOUND
Allegations of Child Abuse Arise on Identification of Family
Clearwater Gazette, Mar 2013
Clearwater, FL

DEAD ANIMAL DUMPING GROUND
'Hundreds of Cats' Found Illegally Discarded
Breckenridge Daily News, May 2013
Breckenridge, MN

SUSPECT SOUGHT IN VIOLENT ATTACK MONDAY AFTERNOON
'He Was Screaming & Yowling Like a Cat,' says Witness; Victim in Critical Condition with Bites to the Face and Neck; Investigators Suggest Drug Abuse
Bangor Daily News, May 2013
Bangor, ME

ORACLE OF THE SANDS CASINO DESTROYED BY FIRE

Fire Chief Blames Over-Capacity Crowd, Fire Code Violations; 3 Killed, Dozens
Injured by Flames and Smoke Inhalation
Today's News-Herald, June 2013
Lake Havasu City, AZ

SUMMER CAMP FIRE POSSIBLY ARSON

Site of 2006 Molestation Case Burns Saturday
Herald and News, August 2013
Klamath Falls, OR

MYSTERY WOMAN RESCUES 2 MISSING CHILDREN

Boy, 4, and Girl, 6, Kidnapped by Babysitter in October Found
Gridley Herald, Nov 2013
Gridley, CA

SUSPECT SOUGHT IN BREAKING & ENTERING CASE

Police Seeking Caucasian Female Between 18-25 Years Old
Oelwein Daily Register, March 2014
Oelwein, IA

YOUNG WOMAN SAVES 2 FROM HOUSE FIRE

Heroine: 'I happened to be filming nearby and smelled smoke'
Fairmont Times West Virginian, May 2014
Fairmont, WV

NATIVE GEORGIAN FILMS GONZO HORROR
SERIES ON YOUTUBE

3.5 Million Viewers Strong, 'Best job I ever had,' says filmmaker
Atlanta Journal-Constitution, July 2014
Atlanta, GA

TWO YOUNG MEN STOOD on the shoulder of a sunny highway, bicycles between their knees.

Three or four hundred yards of gravel road led out to a Spanish mission house on top of a hill, baking in the sun. The front of the house was a tall pink facade with a run-for-the-border church bell hung in the peak. An adobe privacy wall obstructed their view of the front porch.

A single word was handpainted on a nearby mailbox, CUTTY, and the whole thing tilted slightly as if some drunk had walked up and jammed the pole into the dirt, there, job done.

"That might be the coolest place I've ever seen." Sweat trickled down the small of David's back, turning his white dress shirt a damp gray. His necktie danced in the wind. "Now I kinda feel like we were meant to come out here. Maybe this long-ass bike ride was worth it after all."

Greg unbuckled his helmet and ran a hand through his sweaty hair. "It looks like a church. Y'know, like one of those Catholic convents down south around the border."

"Exactly."

"It also looks like it could be where some notorious Mexican drug lord lives."

"In Georgia?" David scoffed. "Not unless there's such a thing as a meth lord. This ain't Tijuana."

"Ehh." Greg checked his watch. "It's about time for lunch. I guess we'll head up there and give it a try, then head back to town."

"You don't want to hit all these houses on the way back down?" David asked, flourishing a hand at the trailer park in a magician's reveal.

"Do *you*?"

"I wouldn't be—" He almost said *a good little Witness if I didn't,* and at the last second thought it was a little too self-deprecating. "—doing my duty if I didn't."

1

To their left, an expansive trailer park flanked the driveway. Greg chewed the corner of his mouth, staring at the mobile homes, and the car parts and toys strewn across their lawns. The trailer park exuded a feeling of quiet, lonely despair only rural poverty can adequately express.

"*Everybody* is worthy in Jesus's eyes," said David.

Greg sighed and put his helmet back on, kicking off. "Race you to the top," he called over his shoulder.

The drive dipped before it made a precipitous climb again, and the chalky gravel rattled David's bones. He rose off the seat and stood on his pedals, driving them deep, cleaving the wind with his face. Fire coiled in his thighs and he downshifted to first gear.

By the time they reached the plateau approaching the house, they were both walking alongside the bikes, panting, sheets of sweat pouring down their backs.

He winced as the burn drained from his legs. "I'm thinking of buying one of those Camelbak things. Y'know, the rubber water bladder things you wear on your back. With the drinking tube." The damp breeze did little to leech the heat, but it was just enough. Several days in July, David had sweated so hard it actually soaked through his bookbag and ruined a sheaf of tracts. Few people are amenable to receiving Jesus into their heart, but when Jesus is suspiciously damp even the country folk won't talk to you.

"That's a good idea," said Greg, laying his bike down and taking off his bookbag. "Glad I thought of it."

Inside their bags were rubberbanded sheafs of *The Watchtower*. Greg took one out and left the bag with his bicycle. David did as well and lingered for a moment, savoring the chill of his shirt drying in the sun.

As they always did, they shook fists at each other.

"One, two, three." Greg pointed two fingers, David opened his hand out flat. "Scissors beats paper."

David took the *Watchtower* out of his hand and approached the house. The privacy wall completely enclosed the front porch, so there was no access to the front door except through a wrought iron gate secured with a padlocked chain. On the other side of the gate, he could see a quaint garden and a little pond.

"Is that a real hitching post?" asked Greg, pointing at a long wooden trunk on two stumpy legs.

A canvas awning jutted from the side of the house, shading a white screen door. The inner door was open, and a sweet, bready aroma wafted through the screen. David knocked on the aluminum frame.

After an interminable silence, someone stepped close to the heavy antique screen. Their face was only a pale smear in the shadows, and they carried some large white object.

He couldn't see the person's eyes, but he could *feel* them.

Greg gave him an anxious glance.

An elderly woman opened the door, wiping her hands on a dishtowel. She was tall, taller than beanpole David even, and lean, broad-shouldered, with feathered gray hair. That and her hawkish nose made her resemble some sort of dour gray Big Bird.

Or a bird of prey. "Hello there," she said.

"Good morning," said David, even though it was after twelve. "We'd like to talk to you about Jesus."

The woman regarded them with a slow smile.

"I just finished baking a pan of brownies. You boys look like you could use a pick-me-up. Why don't you come in and have a snack, and we'll talk. I made a pitcher of tea, too."

Warmth welled from the travertine floor and flooded the air as they stepped inside. David scanned the black marble countertops and stainless steel appliances, appreciating the tasteful decor and the leaded glass billiard table lamp hanging from the ceiling. "What a gorgeous house you have here, ma'am."

"Thank you," said the woman. She shook their hands. "I'm Marilyn, Marilyn Cutty."

"David Hansford."

"Gregory Tell."

"Very nice to meet you." She directed them to the island in the center of the room, donning a quilted mitt.

One brick wall was dominated by two ovens. Marilyn opened one, sliding out two dark pans and depositing them on the counter. Swirled with blonde ribbons, the brownies smelled amazing.

They took a seat at the island and David rolled *The Watchtower* in one hand like a diploma. The ministry could wait. It had been a long trek out here and Jehovah was everlasting; a few more minutes wouldn't hurt. "Me and my friend here were talking about your house…it sort of reminds me of, like, the Alamo, y'know, and those Catholic missions you see out west."

Marilyn sat opposite them and poured two glasses of tea, sliding them across. "Would you be surprised to know that it used to be a whorehouse?"

Heat flashed across David's cheeks. "A whorehouse?"

"Well, I suppose the more tactful parlance might be *brothel*. It's called the Lazenbury House, after its original builder and owner, William Lazenbury. He was a nineteenth-century coal baron from Virginia."

Greg's forehead scrunched, his eyebrows bobbing. "Wow. That's pretty crazy, ma'am."

As they waited for the brownies to cool, Marilyn told them about her house.

Established in the lawless days of Wyatt Earp and Jesse James and Doc Holliday, the Lazenbury House was a popular 19th century brothel and saloon, drawing customers from miles around. In its hey-day, the house had seen its fair share of murders—gunfighters having a row over a

3

card game, drunken brawling, jealous lovers a little too attached to the working girls.

"The murders, of course, had everyone convinced that the house was haunted," said Marilyn, sipping her tea. "But then you get that with any old house with historical value like mine."

"Mmm," grunted David. "I don't know if I believe in ghosts. We're— our religion doesn't really, ahh, entertain the idea of eternal spirits."

"Interesting." Marilyn opened a drawer on her side of the island and rummaged around in it. "What happens when you die, then?" she asked, sliding a butcher knife from it.

The blade scraped on the way out with an eerie *sssssshink!*

Daylight glossed over the sharp steel edge. She laid it on the counter and removed a smaller knife, a plastic thing that looked like a spatula. Cutting into the brownies, Marilyn peeled a generous helping from one of the pans and served it to them on little china plates.

David stared at the butcher knife. He couldn't help it. He tried to peel his eyes away, but the next thing he noticed was the bamboo cutting board set into the end of the island surface.

Deep grooves made a hashmark across the wooden board. They were stained with old blood.

"Nothing. There *is* no immortal soul," said Greg. "Nobody goes to Heaven or Hell when they die—those are all more or less different words for what we call 'the common grave'. Death is just a state of non-existence." He chewed a bite of brownie. "I like to think of it as going back to the same non-existence you were in before you were born."

"Wouldn't that be awfully close to the concept of reincarnation?" asked Marilyn. "Or do we only get one trip to the physical plane?"

David started to speak, sought a quick inspiration in Greg's face, found none. "We definitely don't do reincarnation. That's all up to the Hindus and Buddhists and whatnot."

"That's a shame."

A white-patched tabby cat padded into the room and leapt up onto the kitchen island.

Marilyn kissed the cat on the forehead and stroked its back, moving the butcher knife out of the way. The blade reflected an arc of sunlight across the ceiling. "I don't believe in reincarnation myself, but if it were true, I've always wanted to come back as a bird. Preferably a hawk, maybe, or an owl. Such majestic creatures. Wouldn't it be nice to be able to fly?"

David glanced at the blood-stained cutting board.

"It'd certainly take a lot of the challenge out of going around talking to people," grinned Greg. "I bet people would be a little more ready to believe if the word of Jehovah came from a talking bird."

Marilyn cackled. "Perhaps!"

"Hi, kitty-kitty," David said anxiously, polishing off the rest of the brownie. He was almost stunned with relief to see the cat here, such a normal thing, and he realized that he was nervous, and had been increasingly so since he'd walked into the kitchen.

The cat sat on its haunches, staring at them with brilliant green eyes as if it were about to address them.

Why was he nervous? There was nothing to be afraid of.

"Ma'am," he said, rambling to make himself feel better, "these have got to be the best brownies I have ever had in my life, hands down. Were you a bakery chef in a past life?"

"Oh, I thought you didn't believe in reincarnation?"

"Ma'am, if you told me the Keebler elves made these brownies, I might have to start believing in elves."

Marilyn gave him a coy smirk.

"So what do you do?" asked Greg.

"Oh, I'm semi-retired. I write these days, mostly romance. I have a mystery series, too: *Deirdre Poplin and the Broken Warrior*, *Deirdre Poplin and the Strange Hitchhiker*, that kind of thing. I don't imagine you've read any of them."

They shook their heads regretfully. "I'm sorry, I'm afraid I haven't," said David.

The pan of brownies was calling his name. He reached out and touched the still warm pan with a finger. "Ma'am, do you mind if I have another one? I hate to eat all—"

"Ohh, pssh." She cut and served him another. "Have all you like. You've earned no less than this, out there doing the Lord's work." She served Greg another one as well.

"Thank you," he said, breaking it in half (as much as one could 'break' something so soft and fudgey and wonderful).

He slipped it into his mouth. "So...are you religious, at all?"

Marilyn screwed up her face, squinching one eye. "I guess it depends on what you consider religious." The ice in her glass tinkled as she picked it up, swirled it demurely, and raised it for a sip.

Her red lipstick had smeared on her teeth. It made David think of snow and starving wolves.

"What do you mean?" he asked.

"I've been here in the States for a very long time, but I moved here with my family from Europe when I was young. Our family has always been part of an obscure European faith as far back as anyone can remember, and I guess if I had to consider myself religious, I would claim that one."

"Is it a Christian religion?"

"Not quite. Ahh..." She became pensive, then shook her head dismissively. "You wouldn't believe me if I told you. Let's just enjoy each other's company, shall we? And you can tell me all about Jesus and the Witnesses."

Sounds like a rock band, thought David, fighting a smile.

"I've never really paid much attention to the American religions," Marilyn noted, "Except for a peripheral interest in the Mormon…Mormonism? Mormonic—"

David giggled. "The Moronic faith?"

Marilyn laughed again, her head tipping back. Her gums were black, as black as coal, as ink, as night.

"The Book of Moron." Laughter bubbled up out of him and David huffed brownie crumbs into his hands. "Oh, that's great." *Are these pot brownies? Did we eat pot brownies?* The idea was terrifying and exhilarating all at once. They weren't allowed to smoke cigarettes, much less marijuana, but who could blame them for being tricked into eating it?

Confusion spread across Greg's face, but he was smiling. "That's horrible."

"Speaking of horrible," said Marilyn, picking up the butcher knife. "Check this out."

Pressing the tabby cat against the counter, she raised the knife and with one swift motion decapitated it, the edge thunking against the marble. Both boys jerked in surprise, kicking the back of the island. The old woman cackled. Greg got up so fast he almost knocked his stool over.

"Holy shit!" he squawked. "What'd you do *that* for?!"

Vivid red blood squirted across the marble, that once Comet-sterile countertop in that clean, gleaming kitchen. The cat's body flopped and shuddered under Marilyn's spotty hand like a trout in a boat, kicking and flexing its claws.

Oh god oh god, make it stop, please make it stop, David thought, slowly getting out of his seat. His hands were shaking.

Marilyn tossed him the cat's head. Hot potato! It bounced off his shirt (off the backboard) and he instinctively caught it (nothing but net). Blood left a huge watercolor kiss in the middle of his chest, divided down the middle by his necktie.

David fumbled the cat's head back onto the counter. "What is *wrong* with you, lady?!"

"There's nothing wrong with *me.*"

Marilyn got up and rinsed the knife in the sink, rubbing it down with a washcloth. She dropped it into the silverware compartment of the dish drain. "Your friend Gregory seems a little out of sorts, though."

Greg made a weird creaking noise, like he was trying to do an impression of a squeaky door hinge. His eyes had gone from their customary deep deer brown to an insidious pea green. The pupils were thin vertical slits. As David turned to look at him, Greg's lips peeled back in a snarling grin, revealing clenched teeth.

"RrrrrnnnnNNNOWWWL."

His fingers were hooked into claws, so tight the tendons stood out across the backs of his hands.

"What—" David started to ask, and Greg flew at him.

Thumbs collided with his eyes and the stool slid out from under him. The travertine floor slammed into David's back, driving the breath out of him. Sharp, frantic fingernails raked down his face and neck and Greg was shouting, *screeching*. He'd lost his freaking mind.

David hit him in the side of the head with the rolled up *Watchtower*.

Greg flinched, scrambled backwards.

"What the hell are you doing?!" David demanded, and kept hitting him, *whap whap whap*. Standing over his cowering, incoherent friend, he touched his stinging face and found blood on his fingers.

"What did—" he started to ask Marilyn what just happened, but she was gone.

A skinny arm hooked around his shoulder, steel flashed in his right eye, and a line of pain seared across his throat as it was flayed open. The wound gushed decadent crimson down his shirt.

He spun around to face his attacker, and his elbow caught the edge of the counter. He leaned against it, blood coursing down his chest.

The old woman stood on a slowly tilting floor in a merry-go-round kitchen. "It looks like you've had an accident," she said, her voice muffled by his cotton ears. She waved the bloody carving knife to and fro like the slow swish of a cat's tail. "You *did* let your folks know where you were going to be, didn't you?"

David lost the strength in his knees and he fell, sliding down the back of the island, coming to rest on the floor.

Some subconscious caveman thought told him he could keep the blood in with his hands, so he cupped them under his neck, but it ran between his fingers. He furiously undid his necktie and whipped it out of his collar, stared at it in his hand, wondered what the hell he thought he was going to do with it (you can't put a tourniquet around your neck, you moron, you Mormon, hahaha), and threw it on the floor.

Marilyn crouched over him. "Take solace in the knowledge that you won't be going to Hell, at least. As you said, after all, it doesn't exist."

David's vocal cords didn't seem to work.

"Why, you want to ask—why? Why?" She smiled sadly, flashing those hideous black gums again. "Blood for the garden, young David," she said in that smoky, patronizing blackbird voice of hers. "We always need blood for the garden."

THURSDAY

One

ROBIN AWOKE TO BIRDSONG tittering through the windows of her tiny cupola bedroom. The first breezes of June came in through the open screen. Outside, green trees flashed the pale undersides of their leaves as if they were waving dollar bills.

A blue creature lay crumpled in a heap of legs at the foot of her bed. She dragged the stuffed animal over. "Look, Mr. Nosy," she squealed, "it's the first day of summer vacation!"

Mr. Nosy was a felt mosquito the approximate size and style of a Muppet, with big white ping-pong ball eyes. At the back of his open mouth was a sort of voicebox, and when you pinched one of his feet he whined like a kazoo. In her tiny hands, he came alive. "Yes, Miss Robin," she said in a high, growly giant-mosquito voice. "It's very warm today and I think I'm going to go down right now and find someone to bite for breakfast!"

Robin giggled. "Okay. Wait right here."

She sat him up very carefully on top of the quilt and wriggled out of her nightshirt, putting on a sundress and a pair of sandals. Cradling the puppet, she clomped down the twisting stairway and opened the door at the bottom.

The smell of bacon and biscuits were waiting to roll over her in a warm wave. Robin danced along the second floor landing and down a flight of switchback stairs to the foyer, skipping into the kitchen. Her mother sat at the kitchen table, reading a newspaper and sipping a cup of coffee.

Robin stared at the back of the newspaper and tried to read it again, but as always, it was just a grid of black squiggles.

"Goo morvig," said her mother.

"Good morning, Mama."

Mrs. Martine—Mama to Robin, Annie to everybody else—talked as if she had a mouthful of water. She had a speech impediment that made her difficult to interpret, but Robin had grown up with it and found her as easy to understand as anybody else.

She smiled, scooping bacon and eggs onto her daughter's plate. "Did you sleep good?"

"Yep."

Robin arranged her pet mosquito on the counter in front of the bread box and hopped into her chair.

"Your birthday is at the end of the month." Annie cut a biscuit open and knifed grape jam into it. "Have you decided what you want yet?" Annie Martine wasn't the loveliest of women, but her petite Audrey Hepburn frame and heart-shaped face gave her an ethereal, elven quality that people couldn't seem to resist.

In that brutally honest fashion of curious children, Robin had asked her several times over the years why her tongue was the way it was.

Annie gave her a different tale each time. "I stuck it out at a crab and he pinched it," she'd say, or "I was running with scissors and tripped and, well, *snip snip!*" and sometimes, "I tried to kiss a turtle and he bit me," and the last time she claimed she'd stuck it in a light socket. Once Robin had even hauled out her toy doctor bag and asked to examine Annie's tongue with a magnifying glass. A jagged red scar about an inch long bifurcated the very tip, twisting it.

Most strangers who heard Annie speak assumed she was deaf and spoke loudly to her, carefully enunciating their words. But she was never offended. She dryly looked up at whoever was speaking to her and said, "I'm not deaf," and then stuck out her tongue. Robin hated the way they would recoil in horror at her twisted scar, but Mama always laughed gaily and carried on as if it were nothing but a bawdy joke.

"No. What about a book? I like books."

"Books are the best. Even better than toys and videogames, I think. Definitely better than videogames."

"I want a Harry Potter book."

Annie sneered in mock disgust. *"Harry Potter?* What do you want to read about Harry Potter for?"

"Harry Potter does magic." Robin rolled her eyes. "I want to read about magic. And swords and kings and dragons and wizards." She waved her fork around as if it were a wand, touching her eggs, her orange juice, the table. "I love wizards. I wish I could do magic."

As she always did when her daughter spoke of magic, Annie smiled bitterly, as if the word dredged some long ago slight from the water under the bridge. "No, you don't, honey."

"But I do."

"You *know* there's no talk of magic in this house, ma'am." Annie folded the newspaper and set it aside, cradling her coffee in both hands. The steam curled lazily against her face. "Magic is wrong. Magic goes against God. And in this house, God's rules come before man's now. We've been over this."

10

"Yes, Mama."

"You're more than welcome to read your Harry Potter book, but I won't have any talk about magic. Okay? A book is just a book. It's not real."

Robin sucked on her lip for a moment. She summoned a little courage and asked, "If magic isn't real, why does God not want it in our house?"

Annie gave her that exasperated don't-be-a-dummy scowl from under her eyebrows. "I didn't say *magic* wasn't real. I was saying that Harry Potter isn't real. You can read them as long as you understand the difference between reality and fiction. Harry does 'good magic', and that's okay—he's a good little boy—but in real life, good magic doesn't exist. In real life, honey, *all* magic is bad."

The little girl sighed. "Yes, Mama."

Tick. Tick. Tick. The clock on the kitchen wall chiseled away at the morning. The short hand and the long hand were racing each other around the dial as though reality were in fast forward. The numbers were unintelligible sigils.

Annie had finished her coffee by the time she spoke up again, cutting through the droning of the lawnmower. "Hurry up and finish, and we'll go down to the bookstore in town. You can pick something out."

After breakfast, they went out the back door, marching down the little wooden stoop. Their back yard was huge, occupied by a stunted oak tree and a lonely gray shed fringed with ragged weeds. A board swing twisted and wobbled in the breeze. In the distance, out by the treeline, Robin's father Andy Martine bumped and roared along on his gas-stinking Briggs and Stratton.

"We'll go tell Andy we're going to town," said Annie, referring to Daddy by the secret identity all superhero Daddies had. She started off across the grass. "Don't want him to come in and find us gone without telling him where we went." *You know how he can get.*

Robin clutched Mr. Nosy to her side, the Muppet mosquito flopping around with every step.

Daddy was apparently doing a bad job at cutting the lawn, because there were long thin tiger stripes of unmowed grass every ten or twenty feet. Annie walked through them, kicking up drifts of chewed-up lawn that looked like canned spinach. Robin plowed through it, making soft explosion noises with her mouth as she went.

"You shouldn't strew the grass around like that," said Mr. Nosy. "You know he doesn't like it."

Robin's heart lurched. "Oh, right." She laid the mosquito on top of her head like a hat, so he could see better. "Buzz buzz buzz." His soft legs flopped against her face like blue dreadlocks.

The back yard was so big. Why was it so big? It seemed like the farther they walked, the bigger it got. The sun bounced up off the dry, prickly grass with a hard, walloping heat, and the tufts of lawn got taller

11

and thicker until they were wading through a thicket of crabgrass, clover, and wild onions.

"Hold on, Mama," Robin said, stopping to search the ground, "I want to find a four leaf clover."

Annie stopped, took a knee, and swept her hand like a beachcomber with a metal detector. Easy as pie, she plucked a lucky four leaf and held it up for her daughter to count the leaves.

It never failed to amaze Robin that while she could wander the yard for hours stooped over like an old woman and never see a single one, her mother never seemed to have any trouble finding them. "You're so lucky. But you're not as lucky as me." She inserted the clover's stem behind Robin's ear so that it flowered against her temple like a hibiscus in a hula girl's hair. "You're not as lucky as *me*, because I have *you.*" Annie grinned. Instead of their usual eggshell white, her teeth were made of wood, brown and swirly dark. "I'm the luckiest mommy in the world, you know that?"

Robin stared at her mother in horror. "Why is your teeth made of wood, Mama?"

"What?" Annie threw her head back and laughed. "You're so silly. Such a silly-billy. Come on, we'd better get going. We don't want to be late for the market, we'll miss all the best veggies."

Veggies? "But I thought we was going to the bookstore."

Annie said nothing. She kept trudging across the endless back lawn in her delicately inexorable way.

Shuff, shuff, shuff, their feet plowed across the interminable lawn, breaking up clumps of mulch. Robin squinted into the heat. Beyond an invisible motion swirling in the air, she could still see her father on his red-and-black riding mower. He didn't seem any closer, but somehow she could smell his briny dungeon aura of Old Spice and Budweiser. He always smelled faintly of alcohol, even when he hadn't been drinking, that cold dank funk of old nickels and wet dirt cellars.

For some reason Annie seemed to be slowing. Not all at once but gradually as they walked, as if each step were a centimeter shorter than the last.

Her mother seemed to be the only one succumbing to it, though, like a peat bog, because soon Dear Mama was up to her ankles in the turf. Ripples bobbed outward from her toes, lapping over her instep. "Don't want him to come in and find us gone without telling him where we went," she said, the grass welling around her shins.

"Mama?"

"Not as lucky as me." Now Annie was positively forging against the grass, the sun breaking over her glossy tresses. She reached with every step, leaning forward, steaming across the yard. Robin looked the way they came, hugging Mr. Nosy against her chest. She wiped her hair out of her eyes.

The house was a brick of blue clapboard behind them, as faraway as Christmas, the swingin'-tree and woodshed tiny and model-like as if they'd been made of popsicle sticks and reindeer moss. "We've come a long way," said the mosquito. His real voice sounded nothing like the one Robin did for him—it was rumbly, friendly, *sandy*, the best word for it, sandy, rough but warm. Grandfatherly. "Why aren't we any closer to your father?"

"It's always like this."

"Don't want him to come in and find us gone," said Annie. The lawn had swallowed her up to the knees. Her fists pistoned in and out like a boxer working a belly, as if she were walking in treacle. "Not as lucky as me." Her mother was walking so slowly now that Robin could overtake her.

Polished cedar. Annie's eyes were made of wood. The sclera were a pale alabaster with streaks of pink, and ragged black knotholes gaped where her irises and pupils should have been. Goatish eyes. "Don't want him to come in and find us."

"What do you mean?" asked Robin, standing in front of her mama, clutching Mr. Nosy. Annie was no longer driving forward, but halted mid-stride. Her feet were rooted in the earth as firmly as any fencepost and her arms were at kung-fu angles, one punched forward and the other's elbow jutting out behind her. She was a statue locked in an action pose.

"What do you mean?" Robin repeated, her voice climbing. Now she was shrieking. "What do you mean? *Goddammit why don't you ever tell me what you mean?*"

"Language!" said Mr. Nosy.

"Fuck language!"

She reached out and slapped her mother's motionless face with a six-year-old's hand.

Annie's cheek came loose like a deflated blister, a sag of translucent candle-skin, and the wind flaked a bit of it away, revealing dark brown underneath.

Then more came away, and Annie Martine's face began to peel as easy as old paint, spiraling like burning paper into the breeze. Below the flaking skin was bark, smooth black-brown bark, studded with jagged wooden teeth. A lovely wooden skull lurked behind that ivory Annie mask, intricately-carved, beautiful, horrifying.

Robin's lungs refused to inflate. Stepping back, she watched as the outermost layer of her mother deteriorated inch by inch, crumbling off and blowing away. Scrolls drooped from her shoulders, breaking off at the elbow; waxy-green leaves spotted with worm-rust sprouted from her hair, and uncurled from her knuckles and the tips of her fingers.

Annie's arms and wrists lengthened, reaching out in front of her, and over her head, and her legs thickened, elongated, becoming like those of an elephant, covered in cobbly flesh. The terrible sound of rending muscle-fibers whispered underneath Annie's bark as she stretched,

13

reaching for the sky, and then she was a tree, she was a goddamn *tree* towering over her daughter, her skull-carving face buried in her trunk so that only her sightless eyes and maniacal Jolly Roger grin were visible.

She had become a Titan's arm, reaching up from the crust and grass clutching a handful of leaves.

Then the tree that had been Annie burst into flames, all that foliage going up in a bonfire *WHOOSH* of hot light, and the woman-thing inside screamed in pain and terror, and

Little Robin screamed,

and

old women cackled, ceaselessly echoing back on themselves,

and—

❂

—a twenty-one-year-old Robin woke from a nightmare of trees and flame. She gulped a deep breath as if she'd surfaced from the ocean and lay staring at the carpeted ceiling, breathing hard and fast, trembling.

Condensation dribbled down the curve of the van's rear windows, refracting stony gray light.

Her cellphone told her it was a few minutes after ten the morning of October 23, 2014. She sat up and lifted a camcorder from its customary place in a tub lined with soft black foam, then wriggled out of her sleeping bag and dug through a tub full of rolled clothes.

The smell of burning bark still floated among the dust, as if the smoke had permeated her skin and hair. She wore nothing but a pair of gray panties and even inside the van, warmed by her farts and body heat all night, the air was graveyard-clammy, so she knew the late autumn morning outside would require something a little more substantial than usual.

Damn Georgia humidity, she thought, pulling on a pair of moss-green skinny jeans and a light jacket over a band T-shirt. *Makes the summers hotter and the winters colder.*

The entire back half of the van was lined with rails, shelves, and wire frames in which nested dozens of small plastic bins containing all manner of things:

- packets of trail mix
- electronics parts still in their blister packs
- condiment packets from just about every restaurant under the sun
- barbers' clippers
- toiletries and shaving razors
- USB cables
- name-brand double-A, triple-A, D-cell, and tiny dime-like watch batteries

14

- a rats'-nest of power adapter cables.

One tub held Gerber baby-food jars emptied of their contents and refilled with water. Another tub contained handfuls of stacked twigs, another was full of something that might have been ginger root, or perhaps bits of wild mushroom.

A large pegboard occupied one half of a wall directly behind the driver's seat. Several edged weapons had been mounted on pegs and held in place with little clips—a broadsword, a short-sword, a kuhkri knife like a boomerang with a handle, a wicked black tomahawk, a Cold Steel katana painted matte black, a gilded silver dagger that looked like something that belonged in a saint's tomb.

A fifteen-year-old stuffed mosquito peeked over the edge of a tub, his own personal plastic sarcophagus.

Mr. Nosy's proboscis was a lot more limp these days; both of his glassy wings and four of his six legs had been stitched back on at some point, but he was still whole and had both of his big white Kermit eyes. Robin leaned over and gave her oldest friend a kiss on the nose.

Once she was dressed, she put the camera on a screw-mount in the corner, facing her. There were several mounts around the van, including two on the dash and two clamped to the wing mirrors.

Tucked into the pocket of yesterday's jeans was an orange prescription bottle. She transferred it to today's jeans. Taking a moment to screw the heels of her hands into her eyes again to grind away any remaining sleep, she slapped a bongo beat on her cheeks to redden them, then turned the camera on and started recording.

"Good morning," she said, her whiskey-and-cigarettes rasp exploding like a hand-grenade in the silence.

She put on her socks and boots as she talked, long green Army socks and a pair of comfortable combat boots. "Malus here. You might be able to hear I've got a bit of a sinus thing right now. And I think I might be getting a sore throat. I guess that's what I get for not eating enough oranges?" She paused, glanced down at the van floor as if to screw up her courage, then went back to cramming her feet in her boots.

The black Army boots were like big sneakers, with a padded ankle, an Air Jordan profile, and soles like tractor tires. She'd bought them at a PX in Kentucky earlier that year for almost two hundred dollars, and they had earned the nickname 'shit-kickers' before she'd even paid for them. Postmodern punk-rock couture.

Her jeans were snug enough that the boots fit over them. "If you've been watching my channel, then you'll know what I've been through. Who I am. My purpose. Well, I'm here. ...Back where it all started." She tied the laces into a big floppy knot, then looked directly into the camera. "Home," she said, as if the word were a hex. "Blackfield."

Crows razzed at each other outside the van, chittering and muttering dark gossip.

Moisture on the windows made a swimmy, crystalline netherworld of the overcast day outside, where several black birds marched back and forth across the gravel in their bobble-headed way. She tucked the laces into her boots and turned the camera to point through the rear window.

"As you can see, the day is shit. And I feel like shit."

She swiveled the camera back around, filling the tiny viewfinder screen with her pale face and the dark circles around her eyes. Instead of giving her the tough rock-chick look she'd been going for, her wavy mohawk and shaved scalp made her seem otherworldly and delicate, fuzzy with a week and a half of chestnut stubble.

The bar-bell piercing through her tongue clicked against her teeth, a tiny silver ball like a pearl in an oyster. "So *this* girl is going to go find a cup of coffee."

Big black crows took flight in every direction when she opened the back door, complaining in their harsh voices. She stepped down out of the van and unscrewed the camera, then grabbed the vinyl messenger bag. As the doors met in the middle with a slam, a blue-and-red logo reconstituted itself: CONLIN PLUMBING.

She took some B-roll footage of the area. The van was parked at the edge of a large graveled clearing, and mild white-gold sunlight was trying to break through into the day. Several tents had been erected in the grass along the periphery some thirty yards away, and beyond them was a two-story cinderblock building reminiscent of a poolhouse, with doors labeled MEN and WOMEN.

From inside came the white-noise rush of hot showers running, and steam poured from PVC pipes jutting out of the roof. Simple black graffiti was spraypainted on the walls as if God had stepped down with His Mighty Sharpie and written it Himself: BITE MY SHINY LIBERAL ASS. ST. VINCENT. YEE-THO-RAH. Doodles of a monkey taking a shit and a robot on a motorcycle.

To her right, a sprawling split-level cabin lurked in the shadows of the woodline, pumping out the constant smell of cooking food. The back of the restaurant opened up in a large hangar-like seating area with five trestle tables.

As always, the hallucination waited for her.

A hulking figure stood half-visible behind the angle of the restaurant wall, seven or eight feet tall.

Her camera was oblivious to her private delusions.

She went around front, climbing a hill, and clomped across the front porch, where a smiling gray fireplug of a dog was leashed to the banister.

"Hello," she said, pointing the camera at him.

The Australian sheepdog licked his chops, regarding her with one icy blue eye.

Miguel's Pizzeria was dimly-lit and claustrophobic, with clumps of ropes and climbing gear hanging from the ceiling, and stacks of shoeboxes by the door. A half-dozen booths filled the room, all of them empty.

16

Robin went to the counter, a glass case containing mementos and historical knick-knacks, but nobody was there. A tip jar and a charity jar stood by the register, and A4-printed photographs postered the wall behind the counter.

The photos were of semi-famous people posing in their climbing accoutrements with the owners of the restaurant, and panoramic shots of the mountains around the valley. She thought she recognized Les Stroud of the TV show *Survivorman* in one picture, and maybe Aron Ralston in another, his prosthetic arm around Miguel's shoulder.

A man came out of the kitchen, wiping his hands on a bar towel. He was a dark, ruddy sienna and looked like he could handle himself in a fight—but he was wearing eyeshadow, a silk do-rag covered in purple paisley, and under his apron was an eggplant halter top embroidered with curlicues.

Eyeing the camera in her hand, he tucked the towel into his back pocket and leaned invitingly on the counter. "You a bit early for lunch." The nametag on his apron said JOEL.

"That's okay," Robin told him. A glass-fronted mini-cooler stood on a counter behind Joel. She pointed at cans of Monster coffee inside. "I'll have one of those. I'll stick around and wait for lunch time, if that's cool with you."

Joel regarded her with a tilted head, rolling a toothpick around and around his mouth. "You look supers-familiar. Where do I know you from?"

His weary tone and his delicate mannerisms were somehow masculine, yet...at the same time stunningly effeminate. He smelled like citrus and coconuts, strong enough to even overpower the burnt-bread smell of pizza crust coming out of the kitchen.

"I have a YouTube channel." She indicated the camera as he took a coffee out of the cooler and put it on the counter. "Called 'MalusDomestica'. Maybe you've seen it?"

Joel rang up the coffee and gave her the total, then inhaled and said, wagging a finger, "No, no, I think...I think I mighta went to school with you. Where you go to school at? You go to high school in Blackfield?"

"Yes, I did." She swiped her debit card and put in her PIN. "Do you have wi-fi here?"

"We sure do."

Joel printed out her receipt, operating the register in a bored, almost automatic way, not even looking at his hand as he tugged an inkpen out of his apron pocket, clicked the end, and gave it to her. "The password is on the receipt."

"Thanks."

Sliding into a booth, Robin took a Macbook out of her messenger bag and turned it on. She hooked up to the wi-fi with the password on the receipt *(sardines)* and went to YouTube, where she signed in and started uploading the week's latest video to the MalusDomestica channel.

17

While it processed, she perused the thumbnails of the videos already posted. Almost three hundred vlog videos, most of them no more than twenty minutes long, a few stretching into a half-hour. Her face peeked out from most of them, as if the webpage were a prison for memories, for tiny past-versions of herself, as if she continuously shed prior selves and kept them around as trophies. A packrat cicada, a collector-snake dragging around a suitcase full of old skins.

She enjoyed browsing through the grid of tiny pictures, each one representing a day, a week, a month of her life—seeing all those chunks of time, those pieces of creative effort, fulfilled her, made her feel accomplished. Three million, seven hundred and twenty-two thousand, six hundred and fifty-nine subscribers. 3,722,659 viewers' worth of video-monetization ad revenue and MalusDomestica T-shirt sales.

Their patronage was what funded her travels, was what put food in her mouth, clothes on her back, and gasoline in her CONLIN PLUMBING van.

She clicked one of the thumbnails, opening a video from a year and a half ago. Past-Robin's hair was dyed pink and she was slightly heavier, a spattering of blemishes on her cheeks and forehead. Now-Robin clicked to the middle of the video.

A pumpkin sat on a picnic table in a quiet park somewhere. The day was overcast and wind coughed harsh and hollow against the camera's microphone. Past-Robin turned and flung a hatchet with one smooth lunging movement.

The weapon somersaulted thirty feet and planted itself neatly into the rind of the pumpkin with a morbid *splutch*.

❂

She was reading the news when Joel slid into the seat on the other side of the table, startling her. His tropical aura of perfume swept in behind him, pouring into the booth.

"Hello," he said.

"Hello, Joel."

"You looked like you could use some company. And by the by, it's not *Johl*, it's… *Joe-elle*." he said, poetically pinching the syllable at the end with an A-OK gesture. "You know, like Noel? Or 'go-to-hell'?"

She smiled tightly. "Nice to meet you, Joe-elle."

"Likewise." Joel turned in his seat, throwing a leg over one knee and his elbow over the back of the bench. "I think I know you."

"Oh yeah?"

"You think ain't nobody gonna recognize you with that shaved head," said Joel, flourishing fingers at her. His fingernails were polished, glittering in the fluorescents. "Which looks really good on you, make you look like

18

Demi Moore n' shit. Very Amazonian. I likes. And you got the cheekbones fo it." He leaned in close, talking over the Macbook's lid. "Your name is Robin Martina, ain't it?"

"Martine. Yes." She took him in with tightened eyes now, assessing him fully.

"Your mama used to babysit f'*my* mama when we was little kids." He sat back again, smiling like a satisfied house cat. His eyes were almond-shaped and guileless, in spite of his sly tone. "You and me, we used to play together. If you had hair, it would be jet black. I knows you, yeah, I do. We didn't really ever talk much after that—"

"My father wasn't too keen on having other kids in the house in addition to—"

"—No, honey, he didn't like *black kids* in the house."

She felt transitive shame, even though she had no such prejudice herself. "Well, he's dead now. So...."

"Oh, yeah. I know."

Joel took out a pack of cigarettes and packed them against his palm. They were some brand she didn't recognize, with a logo in flowery script she couldn't read. "You mind if I...?"

She didn't mind. He took one out, but paused, waggling the pack offeringly.

"No." She waved him off. "Trying to quit."

Joel cupped the cigarette in one hand with a lighter, lit it and drew on it, then dragged an ashtray over and blew a stream of menthol smoke into the air. "Break a leg, bitch," he mused, tapping ashes. "I've quit *many* a time. Not as easy as it looks."

Robin studied her keyboard and decided to pay more attention to Joel than the computer. As slow as the internet was, it would be useless while the video was uploading anyway.

"So," said Joel, kicking a toe to an unheard beat, "What does 'Malice Domestic' mean?" He smiled evilly and feigned a shiver. "It sounds so *sinister*. Ooooh, *Mufasa.*" He shivered again.

"*Malus domestica*. It's the Latin scientific name of the common apple tree."

Joel stuck out his bottom lip and nodded as if to say *fair enough*.

She opened the can of coffee with a discreet *snick!* and dug the orange pill bottle out of her pocket, tipping one of the tablets out. Cupping the tablet with her tongue, she swallowed it with a swig of Monster and savored the sinking of the hard little pill, to be assimilated into the constant swamp-light still humming in the marrow of her bones from yesterday's dose.

Joel took another draw off the Newport and french-inhaled it up his nose, then blew it back out.

"What's it about?" he asked, studying the cherry at the end of the cigarette. "Your YouTube channel." She couldn't tell if she were being interrogated, flirted with, or patronized, but she had a distinct suspicion that there was nothing behind Door #2.

"It's sort of like…a travel journal, I guess."

"Whatcha travelin around doin?"

"Just, ah…trying to appreciate America." Robin fumbled for the words, wishing Joel would take a hike. "Roadside attractions, restaurants, that kind of thing."

"Kind of like a homeless Guy Fieri."

Robin chuckled. "Well, I live in my van—but, heh. …Yeah, I guess you could say that."

"You is *so* full of shit." He shook his head, the do-rag's ties rustling behind his head like a ponytail. "Look at this thrift-store Lizbeth Salander over here, talkin about highways-and-byways. You ain't Jack Kerouac." He leaned in conspiratorially again. "Whatchu *really* up to?"

Robin hesitated, glancing down at the camera. It was still rolling. "Well…I hunt witches."

"Really." Joel ashed his cigarette. *"That* is fascinatin." He reached over and turned off the camera, surprising her.

"Hey!"

"You needs to stop playin. I assume *huntin* witches means *killin* witches, and there ain't no way you're videotapin *that* shit. And I want to talk to you without this camera here. Backstage, so to speak. Off the record. Cause I can tell you just puttin on a show for the people at home. But I want *real* talk." He smiled darkly. "I *know* what you doin. You lookin for *them,* ain't you?"

Her breathing had become labored without her realizing it. She felt cornered. "Them who?"

"The ones that killed your mama."

"I don't know what you're talking about."

Joel squinted in the murk of smoke hovering over the table. "When it happened, *my* mama lost her shit. I remember this *vividly*…because she scared the *hell* outta me.

"This was about… sophomore year? Junior year, of high school? She was out of her mind freaked out about it. Shakin, wide-eyed, lockin-all-the-windows freaked. Like she thought the sky was fallin, like she was afraid the Devil himself was gonna get in the house. She asked me all kinds of weird-ass questions about this and that—wanted to know what kind of person Annie was, what kinds of things she did. Did she hurt animals, did she do anything to *me* when me and Fish was little…."

"She never would have." Robin felt her brow knitting together in defensive anger. "Mom wasn't like that—"

"Oh, I know." Joel traced imaginary hearts on the table with a fingertip. "She was a good woman. A good-hearted woman. I told my mama that. I still remember the way she cooked her bacon when me and Fish came over in the mornings. I cook mine the same way—" He illuminated each point with his hands, forming invisible shapes in the air, snapping and wagging invisible bacon. "—crispy, damn near burnt, but still floppy, fatty but not gristly."

Trying to visualize this, eating bacon for breakfast with her mother in their little kitchen, Robin saw two other little faces sitting at the table. Two quiet brown-faced children, wide-eyed

(my name is fisher and his name is johl but mama calls him jo-elle)

and spooked like baby owls. The knot inside her loosened, and her jaw tipped open in surprise. "I *do* remember you. It was the bacon that made me remember."

Joel smiled and made a *Halleluah!* raise-the-roof motion with his hands. "Ain't nothin in this world that good bacon can't make better."

"I'm sorry. They made me forget a lot. ...The shrinks the state made me talk to."

Joel glanced toward the kitchen—or perhaps it was the clock—and back at her, giving the pierced, scruff-headed woman an assessing look. Finally, he said in a tentative way, "That's why I believed it when the rumor was goin around you said *witches* had something to do with it."

Robin winced at that, but Joel was either oblivious or didn't care. "Yeah. I told people that. But they didn't believe me. That's why I had to talk to the shrinks. They thought I had PTSD or something. They thought losing my mother drove me crazy."

"You ain't found em, has you? That's what you been doin ever since the shrinks let you out. You been lookin for them witch bitches."

She squinted out the window at the noonday sun.

Joel put both feet flat on the floor and stubbed out his cigarette, leaning on his elbows. He clasped his hands together and spoke around them. "So you for *real*, then. You doin this shit for real. How you make YouTube videos about this shit? Ain't this incriminatin evidence?" He licked his teeth and pushed the ashtray back toward the wall, folding his arms and regarding her with narrow eyes.

Robin's fingernails dug into her palms. "You ever heard of Slender-Man?"

"Ain't he that skinny dude with no face, wears a black suit and a red tie, got long arms, creeps people out?"

"Yeah."

She did a search on YouTube for it and found the TribeTwelve channel, turning the Macbook around so Joel could see it. "There are half a dozen YouTube channels devoted to this guy Slender-Man. Each one chronicles a different group of people trying to figure out the mystery surrounding him...they're all set up as if the events happening in the videos are real.

"But, of course, everybody knows they aren't—wink-wink. They're each a scripted and acted horror series made to look real. Like, you remember the *Blair Witch Project?* How it was designed and shot to look like somebody found it on a camera in the woods, basically started the found-footage genre?"

21

Joel nodded. "Yeah. And you doin somethin like that, but theirs is fake and yours is actually real? But you make it *look* like it's as fake as theirs. Ah ha-ha. Reverse psychology up in this bitch."

"Yes."

"And instead of lookin for Slender-Man, you lookin for the witches that, uhh—"

"Yes."

Another man came out of the kitchen. His hair was going gray and his drawn Latino face was a hash of wrinkles, but Robin recognized Miguel from the photograph behind the register. "Hey," he called. "We got to get ready for lunch."

"Untwist them panties, hero," said Joel, grabbing at the air in a *zip-it* motion. "I'm just doin some catchin up." He slid out of the booth and stood up, stretching. Up close in the window's light, she could see that he was exquisitely chiseled.

"Who's your friend?"

"Her mama used to babysit me and Fish when we was kids." Joel coughed into his fist and took a bottle of hand sanitizer out of his apron pocket, squirting it into his palms and wringing his hands. "Robin Martine."

Miguel's brain seemed to hang like a busy computer program and then he subtly crumpled. "Oh."

An awkward silence lingered between them, and then one corner of his bushy mustache ticked up in a wistful half-smile. "I remember hearing about, uhh…" His belly bobbed with one hesitant breath. "I'm sorry about your mother."

Robin tried her best to be gracious, but didn't know what to say, so she echoed his expression and dipped her head appreciatively.

"I didn't really know her, but I heard she was a good person."

"She was." Robin's hand had found its way around the can of coffee while she wasn't paying attention, and now she drummed soft fingers against the aluminum. The two men watched her with expectant eyes, the quiet pause only scored by the sound of furious washing and banging in the kitchen.

Robin looked down at the Monster can. "Five years ago. I decided this year I would finally come back to Slade and visit her. This year I've decided I feel like I can finally…finally push through the dark and say the things I need to say to her. I guess."

"Well," said Miguel. "Welcome back, Kotter. Mi casa es su casa."

Joel followed him back into the kitchen. "What he said."

"Thank you," she called after them, and put the prescription bottle back in her jeans pocket.

Two

THE HOUSE WAS A two-story Queen Anne Victorian, an antique dollhouse painted the muted blue of a raincloud. A wraparound porch encircled the front, and the whole thing was trimmed in white Eastlake gingerbread. It was streaked with black like mascara tears, as if the house had been weeping soot from its seams. Empty sashed windows peered down at them like eyes, darkness pressing against their panes from inside.

"What did I tell you?" asked Leon. "Cool, right?"

The boy unbuckled his seatbelt and leaned up, pushing his glasses up with a knuckle. He gazed up through the U-Haul's windshield at their new base of operations. "It looks like the house from the Amityville Horror or something."

1168 Underwood Rd cut an impressively Gothic silhouette against the stark white afternoon sky. The neighborhood stretched out to their right, a mile and a half of red-brick Brady Bunch ranch-houses, double-wide trailers with toys peppered across their lawns, white shepherd-cottages, a few A-frame cabins lurking deep in the trees.

Across the road from 1168 was a small trailer park, eight or nine mobile homes marching rigid lockstep toward a distant treeline. Since his window was rolled halfway down, Wayne could hear the faraway mewling-seagull-cry of children playing.

His eyes broke away from the watchful windows, coins of white reflecting off his lenses. A grin crept across his dark face. "It's *awesome.*"

Leon beamed.

They got out of the box truck and clomped up the front steps. The porch was wider than he expected, four lunging steps across—wide enough to ride his bicycle up and down the length of the porch if he wanted to. Wicker chairs lined the wall underneath the front windows, and a swing was chained to the ceiling where the porch angled around the corner.

Click. The portentous sound of his father unlocking the front door made him twitch. "It even locks with an old-timey key," said Leon, showing Wayne the long, thin skeleton key. He pushed the door open with his fingertips.

Disappointingly, it didn't creak open in that spooky, melodramatic way, but the doorknob did bump against the opposite wall. Leon winced and stepped inside, checking behind the door for damage.

Wayne went in behind him and stood there, turning in a slow circle, taking it all in. The thick, astringent smell of fresh paint cloyed the air. The front hallway was interminably tall—the ceiling looked like it was fifteen feet high—but it seemed cramped, with only enough room for maybe three men to walk abreast. He felt like he could lie on the floor and touch the walls with his feet and hands.

To his right, a doorless archway led into a small den. To his left, a stairway climbed to the second floor and a dark bathroom yawned at the foot of the stairs, dim daylight glinting from the teeth of its chrome fixtures. Dead ahead, the foyer hallway went on past two closet doors and opened into the kitchen, the floor turning into turtle-shell linoleum.

An intricate red carpet runner had been laid down by the real estate agent, new and clean. Regardless, every shuffling footfall, every little noise they made and word they spoke reverberated in short, hollow echoes throughout the house.

"Hello?" called Leon. With the lights off, his Jamaican complexion was dark enough that he melted into the shadows—a business suit and a grin. He was wearing a blue two-piece suit and a cranberry tie.

For a terrifying second, Wayne almost expected to hear an answer from upstairs.

He *loved* it. "Do you think it's haunted?"

Leon tucked his hands in his pockets. "Who knows?"

The den was a cozy space, unfurnished as of yet with anything other than empty bookshelves and a cushioned reading nook in the front window. The walls were unpapered, painted the same rainy blue as the outside. A modest fireplace occupied one wall.

"I think I need to see if one of our neighbors might be able to give us a hand with the sofa."

"I can help you."

"I don't know, it's big. I don't want to see you get hurt. We barely got it out of the apartment."

They passed into the kitchen, where the walls had been wallpapered, and had been done so in yellow sunflowers that probably should have looked cheery, but were more forlorn and drab than anything else. The fridge was a new side-by-side slab of black humming efficiently in the corner, and the countertops were malachite-green marble over dark cherrywood cabinets.

Wayne decided that the kitchen would not be his favorite room. Leon went around to all the windows, parting the curtains and letting sunlight in. Dust satellited in the soft white beams.

The pantry was surprisingly large, a narrow ten-foot space lined with three tiers of shelving. He started to climb them to see what was on the top shelf, but his father shut him down with a hand on his shoulder. "Nope. Come on, let's go look at the bedrooms."

The stairs were steep and creaked as if they were made of popsicle sticks, groaning and cracking and thumping.

1168's second story seemed somehow more spacious than the first. As soon as they stepped up onto the upper landing, a narrow T-shaped hallway led some twenty or thirty feet toward a window at the bottom of the T, flanked by a pair of doors. The right one opened onto the master bedroom, unfurnished, with a walk-in closet that stank of mothballs. The left went into a bathroom, with a claw-foot bathtub and a porcelain sink.

The bathroom's wainscoting was done in rose-pink and teal tiles, but halfway up the walls and ceiling became painted sheetrock. Leon touched the wall. "I just realized—that sheetrock's gonna be a bitch to keep mildew out of. I am *diggin* this pink, though."

Wayne screwed up his face. A ring of metal was bracketed to the ceiling, and a diaphanous plastic curtain hung into the tub. "What kind of bathtub has *feet?*"

Back in the hallway, he stood dejectedly with his hands in his pockets. "Where's *my* bedroom?"

"Ah." Leon searched the hallway, even looking out the window and peering into the master suite again. "I thought I forgot something. I guess you'll have to sleep in the garage, chief."

Wayne's heart sank. "You're full of crap."

His father rubbed his goatee, then thrust a finger into the air and hustled away as if he'd suddenly remembered something. "There's one last place we haven't checked. There's a closet out here on the landing you can sleep in, if you can fit."

"A *closet?*"

"Yeah, like Harry Potter."

"Harry Potter lived under the *stairs.*" Wayne followed him in a daze back out to the end of the landing, then traced the banister down to a window that cast out onto the back of the house. From here, he could see a rickety tool shed and a huge back yard.

Next to the window was a door, which Leon opened to reveal a set of stairs leading up into soft sunlight and around a spiral, climbing out of sight.

Leon shrugged. "After you."

Wayne set off up them, hitching his knees high, almost clambering up them on all fours. The stairs spiraled once and a half, opening onto a small room inside a dome of windows that made him think of the belfry in a church steeple. The room wasn't a perfect circle but an octagon like a stop sign, with eight walls.

The ceiling was just high enough that his father didn't have to stoop, but he stood there with his fingertips pressed against it as if he were trying to hold it up.

"It's called a *cupola*," said Leon. "What you think?"

The 'cupola' seemed small, but as Wayne went from window to window assessing the view, the room proved to be larger than he initially gave it credit for. Plenty of room for his bed and at least two dressers besides, and each of the four windows stood atop a small nook bench that folded open to reveal storage space.

Across the street, a long gravel drive snaked between a trailer park and a series of cottages, climbing a hill to a building that looked like pictures he'd seen of the Alamo. Mud-pink walls topped with Gothic wrought-iron teeth, a triangular facade front, brown clay roofing tiles. A man drove a riding lawnmower up and down the hill out front, cropping dull green grass.

"I like it," said Wayne. To the south, he could see the tops of buildings in distant Blackfield, rising over the trees behind the house.

"Then welcome to your new Batcave, Master Wayne."

"The Batcave is underground."

Leon continued his Atlas impression, hands against the ceiling. "Work with me, here. I'm old and out of touch."

"Batman's older than *you* are."

"Keep it up and I'll make you sleep in the garage anyway!"

○

As the afternoon wore on, Wayne and his father managed to get most of the boxes and furniture into the house, with the exclusion of the sofa and dining-room table. The most troublesome items by far were Wayne's mattress and box-spring, which Leon could handle well enough by himself (with Wayne pushing helpfully from behind) until they got into the spiral stairway to the cupola. That became an arduous trial of swearing, sweating, and banging around in the stuffy space that left them flustered and irritated with each other.

To get the dining room table in, they carried the table up onto the front porch, then turned it on end like a giant coin and rolled it through the house. Leon ushered Wayne in ahead of the table, confusing him at first, but when his father started humming the Indiana Jones theme and pretending the table was the boulder from *Raiders of the Lost Ark*, he couldn't help but run away from it in slow-motion.

Their steel-blue Subaru already sat in the gravel driveway, in front of the U-Haul; Leon had brought it down before the move. They took a break to run to town in the car for hamburgers at Wendy's, and they came back to failing light as the evening came over the trees to the east.

"Damn, I hate to bug anybody this late. These rednecks givin me weird looks," said Leon, unlocking and opening the U-Haul. "But I'd really like to get this truck back as soon as possible. I guess we'll finish tomorrow afternoon."

"Hey," said a husky voice behind them.

A chubby white kid with brush-cut hair was making his way up the driveway, his hands buried in his hoodie's pockets. He seemed to be about Wayne's age, if several inches taller. Wayne thought he looked like Pugsley Addams gone mainstream, or maybe the older brother from *Home Alone*.

"Hey," said Leon.

Pugsley's voice was the high-pitched rasp of a boy accustomed to shouting. "You guys movin in?"

"Yep."

"Cool."

A weird silence settled over them. "Nice to meet you," Leon offered, smiling. "Anything we can help you with?"

Pugsley seemed to snap out of a trance. "Oh! I, uhh, I wanted to say hi, and...maybe see if you needed any help. But it looks like you're pretty much finished." He stepped forward and held out a stubby pink hand. "I'm Pete." Pointing across the street at the trailer park, he added, "Pete Maynard. I live over there. With my mom. I go to school over in Blackfield. Fifth grade."

Leon visibly relaxed, shaking the offered hand. "Nice to meet you, Pete. Leon Parkin. This here's my son Wayne."

Pugsley-Pete shook Wayne's hand and said to his father, "Welcome to Slade. Anybody ever told you you look like War Machine from *Iron Man*? What's his name—"

"Don Cheadle?" Leon had memorized his answer.

"Yeah. That's it."

"Only once a week." Leon stuck his hands in his pockets. "Well. I reckon since we got you here, you can help if you want."

"Sure."

With much grunting and swearing, the three of them got the sofa down out of the U-Haul, up the front stairs, and into the den. To get it out of the foyer and through the den door, they had to turn it sideways and angle the armrests around the doorframe. Wayne mashed a finger and Leon got pinned against the wall, but they finally managed it.

Once they'd gotten it into the room, screwed the feet back onto the bottom of it, and pushed it against the back wall, the boys sat on it to rest. "So what are you guys doin out here?" asked Pete, watching Wayne buff his glasses with his shirt. "I don't think I know anybody that dresses up to go to work."

Leon had taken off his jacket and loosened his tie. "I took a teaching position at Blackfield High School."

"Yeah?"

"Gonna teach Literature."

"That's cool. Maybe I'll be in your class one day. I like to read."

"Maybe. That's good. More kids your age should read. Hey, you had dinner?" Leon took the tie off. "I got us ice cream for when we got done with everything."

"No," said Pete, "but I don't eat dinner most days."

Wayne's head tilted. "Why not?"

"Just…not really hungry. My mom says I eat like a bird."

He couldn't imagine that. "Birds eat their own body weight in food every day. That's what *I* heard, anyway." Pete's hoodie was straining at the sides under his love handles, and he had two chins. The slope-shouldered boy was taller than the short, gangly Wayne by several inches and outweighed him by a dozen pounds.

The ice began to settle again.

Wayne broke it. "You like *Call of Duty?*"

Pete rubbed his forehead. "I don't know. I guess it depends on which one you're talkin about. I only have the first one for the Xbox. I haven't, uhh—haven't really played any of the new ones."

"Sounds like you guys have your evening figured out," said Leon, standing up. "Pete, does your mom know you're over here?"

"*Oh* yeah. Yeah—she's cool."

Leon rolled up his tie like a giant tongue, giving Pete the teacher stink-eye. "That sounds suspiciously like a *no.*"

"She knows I came over here. She doesn't really care when I come back, as long as she knows where I went and I stay out of trouble." Pete sounded non-committal, lax. Wayne got the feeling he was accustomed to being autonomous. "And I'm not like my dad. I stay out of trouble." He jerked up straight all of a sudden and put up his hands as if to ward off a blow. "Oh, I can head out of here if you guys—"

"Oh *no,* no-no, you're *fine,* man." Leon picked up his suit-jacket and beat the dust out of it, laying it over his arm like a sommelier with a towel. "You look like a good kid to me. And Wayne needs friends. He's the F-in' New Guy, remember?"

Pete smirked, but Wayne gave his father the side-eye.

"So yeah, hell. Hang out, by all means, this creepy-ass house is gonna need some cheerin up anyway. Me and him, we can't fill it up all by ourselves. We're from Chicago, we're not used to this kind of quiet, you know?"

"Okay," said Pete, in obvious gratitude.

Leon pointed at Wayne. "Why don't you head upstairs and start on putting your clothes up and make your bed? When you get done with that, feel free to play Playstation to your heart's content."

Wayne feigned belligerence. "Do I gotta?"

"How are you gonna sleep in a bed if you ain't made it? At least make the bed. We'll worry about unpacking when that's out of the way."

The two boys got up and left, creaking and crackling up the stairs to the second landing. They sounded like two colonial Redcoats marching across bubble wrap. "I can hook up the TV and Playstation while you make your bed and stuff, if you want," offered Pete.

"You got a deal."

Wayne led his new friend down the landing. When he opened the closet door to reveal the steep second set of stairs, Pete seemed impressed, if confused. "Wait, your dad's got you in the tower?"

"Yeah. It's the only other bedroom in the house. If you can call it a bedroom." They started up the almost ladder-like stairs. "Why? What's wrong with it?"

"*Nothin,* man, nothin. I think it's freakin awesome. I'm surprised, is all."

With the dressers and the bed in it, the cupola was a lot less spacious. Wayne and Pete had just enough room to sit on the floor between the bed and the television, a modest flatscreen set up on one of the windowsills. There weren't any power outlets in the cupola, so his father had bought a dropcord on their dinner trip and run it up from an outlet on the landing. The cord draped down the stairs for now, but they'd use nails to pin it out of the way later.

A lamp was plugged into it. Wayne turned it on.

To get them out of the way, he had already pinned up his posters on the narrow strips of wall between each of the cupola's windows.

One of them was a movie poster for a *Friday the 13th* movie, with a full-body shot of the hockey-masked Jason Voorhees coming at you with a machete. Another depicted the cast of the TV show *The Walking Dead,* with the character Rick standing on top of a schoolbus aiming his giant revolver. Romero's original black-and-white *Night of the Living Dead.* The popular zombie game *Left4Dead 2.*

The mattress was naked and had four cardboard boxes on it. Wayne opened a box and found it full of clothes. The next one had the videogames in it: a Playstation 3, a tangle of wires, and a handful of disc cases. "Here we are."

Pete carried the box over next to the TV and went to work on untangling the adapter and video cords. Wayne opened another box to find his bedclothes.

He was on his hands and knees trying to pull the fitted sheet over a mattress-corner when something occurred to him. "Hey," he said over his shoulder. Pete looked up. "Uhm. Do you know if this house is…. Do you know if it's haunted?"

Pete stared at Wayne as if he hadn't said anything. His eyes were flat in the arcane honey-glow of the lamp, but he slowly reached up and rubbed his cheek as though he had a toothache. The gesture seemed self-comforting, as if he were petting his face.

It took him a full seven seconds to answer. "I don't know. I've never been in here. But some people say it is."

"Why's that?"

"Well." Pete got to his feet and pulled the TV cart out, examining the connection jacks on the back. "You really want me to tell you?"

Wayne's curiosity was a bonfire in him, straining for secrets. "Are you serious? Of course I want you to tell me." He turned over and flopped down on his butt at the edge of the bed, the sheets forgotten. "Let me guess—what is it, there's an Indian burial ground under the house? They never moved the bodies! *They never moved the bodies!*'"

"No, there's—"

"A serial killer used to live here?" The more he talked, the more animated he became. He was clenching his fists in anticipation. "And he buried his victims in the basement?" That made him wonder if they even *had* a basement, and what it looked like. He made a mental note to go check in the morning.

"No, dude, somebody *died* in this house."

"Is that all? Man, *tch*...people die in houses all the time. Somebody died in the apartment next to ours back in Chicago. If people dying in a place made it haunted, nobody would be able to go into a hospital because of all the ghosts."

Pete grinned a creepy grin. "Why do you think hospitals creep people out so much?"

Wayne deadpanned at him and went back to making his bed.

"Anyway, this one, people say she was a witch."

"A *witch.*" Wayne was incredulous. "You're *shitting* me."

Both boys looked down the stairwell to listen for Mr. Parkin, then Pete continued. "No shittin." He sat down on one of the thin-cushioned windowsill seats. "The cops and the newspaper said it was an accident at the time, but I hear she was pushed down the stairs by her husband."

"A witch with a husband?"

Pete shrugged.

Wayne made a face. "I didn't even know witches could *have* husbands. Anyway, maybe it *was* an accident. Maybe he didn't mean to push her. I can't *believe* Dad didn't tell me about this."

"I don't know," said Pete, going back to untangling the controller cables. "My mom says he used to beat her and her daughter."

"So what happened to the husband?"

"He died a few months later in prison."

"What killed him?"

"Nobody knows. I heard it looked like tubber—ta-bulkyer—"

"Tuberculosis?" Wayne asked helpfully.

"—Yeah, that. But they never could find anything. What's this?" Pete held up the tangle of cords so he could see underneath them. He laid the tangle down on the floor and reached into the box, lifting out a Nike shoebox. Wayne abandoned what he was doing and politely took the shoebox, putting it on the bed.

"It's, ahh...just some old stuff."

30

Inside was a pile of photographs, a bottle of perfume, a gold ring with a simple ball-chain through it, the kind of necklace that usually has dog-tags on it. Wayne took out the ring and reverently lowered the chain around his neck, letting the wedding band rest on his chest.

"Nice ring, Mr. Frodo."

Wayne looked up. "It was my mom's." He picked up the photographs and shuffled through them with delicate hands.

The photos depicted separate events and locations—one seemed to be a very young Wayne celebrating a birthday in a dark kitchen, everything washed out by camera-flash, his face underlit by the feverish glow of a birthday cake; another was an older but still juvenile Wayne with his father and a pretty, small-framed woman. She was in all of the photographs, always smiling, always touching, embracing, or pressing against her son.

Presently Pete came out of the funk and went back to pulling at the knot of cables. "What happened, if you don't mind me asking?"

"She died a couple years ago. In Chicago. Cancer. Throat cancer, I think. It wasn't really the cancer that did it. Dad said, like, 'complications' or something. I don't really know what that means. Something got infected."

Wayne lifted the ring to his eye as if it were a monocle and gazed through it, the gold clicking against his right eyeglasses lens. "A couple of months ago, Dad was like 'man eff this shit, we need to get out of here, there's too many memories here, we need a change of scenery,' so he got a job down here and we packed up and left."

"Damn, dude. I'm sorry."

The eye inside the ring twitched toward Pete. Suddenly the soft brown eye seemed a decade older. "When I miss her, I like to look through the ring like it's a peephole in a door. I pretend that if I look through it I can see into a—uhh...."

"Another time? World? *Dimension?*"

"Another world, yeah." Wayne tucked the ring into his shirt-collar and took off his glasses, buffing a smudge with his shirt. Emotion etched a sudden sour knot at the base of his skull. "I feel like I can see into another world where she's still alive. You know, like Alice in Wonderland, lookin' through the lookin'-glass."

Pete seemed as if he were about to say something, but cut himself off before it could get out of him. Wayne thought he knew what he was about to say. He had thought it himself before, hundreds of times.

What if you look through that ring one day and she actually is there? What then, wise guy?

Three

ROY WAS OUT GASSING ant-hills when the sun went down. He slipped a Maglite out of the pocket of his jeans and took a knee, watching the gasoline soak into the grainy pile. Hundreds of ants percolated up from the tunnels, scrambling over each other in the pale blue-white glow of the flashlight beam.

They had found a grasshopper somewhere and dragged it back to the nest, and they had been in the process of cutting it into pieces and pulling it down into the dirt when he'd interrupted them. He liked to imagine the jackboot tromping of their tiny feet, the sound of a klaxon going off as the gasoline washed down into the corridors of the nest, little panicked ant-people running to strengthen levees, hauling children to safety, swept away by the stinking flood into dark confines.

Roy enjoyed watching videos on the internet of riots and fights, natural disasters, and sometimes people falling off of bicycles and skateboards. Fights were fun as long as they were street-fights. Ultimate Fighting was too structured—he didn't watch fights for the gore or brutality, the unpredictability was what drew him, the chaos and incongruity, the panic and frenzy that was almost slapstick in a way. Aimless beating, kicking, the rending of shirts and slipping and falling and flopping around, reducing each other to meaningless ragdolls.

If he were a decade or two younger, he probably would have enjoyed playing videogames like the *Grand Theft Auto* series.

As it was, behind the wheel he often fantasized about driving off the highway and tearing through back yards and flea markets, plowing through birthday parties and bar mitzvahs. Not so much for the violence of it, but for the strange sight of a car tear-assing through a place you didn't expect to see it. You just don't *see* things like that, and that's what he enjoyed: things 'you just don't see'.

When he was a kid, he'd gotten his hands on a smoke bomb and set it off in the gym showers after sophomore phys-ed, when he knew it would be full of unsuspecting people. Waiting until the smoke had almost filled the room and was beginning to curl over the tops of the shower curtains, Roy had shouted, *"Fire! Fire!"* and ran outside.

His father had whooped his ass for it, but seeing thirty butt-naked high-schoolers storming through the gymnasium had been the highlight of his freshman year.

He tipped another pint of gasoline into the ants for good measure and got back on the lawnmower, starting it up and climbing the sprawling hill toward the adobe hacienda. A garage stood open out back where the driveway snaked up out of the darkness and curled around the house like a cat's tail. Roy drove the lawnmower inside, filling the space with a deafening racket.

When he cut the engine off, the silence was even louder. He sat in the dark stillness beside the girls' Winnebago, packing a box of cigarettes.

Outside, the evening was tempered by the faint murmur of Blackfield's fading nightlife, an airy, whispering roar washing over the trees. In close pursuit was the constant drone of cicadas and tree frogs.

Southern cities don't necessarily have nightlife. You go up north or out to Atlanta, maybe, or Birmingham—Roy had been to Atlanta twice and didn't care to ever go back, that traffic was horseshit—and yeah, the cities don't sleep. Life runs around the clock. Out here in the sticks, though, a city of six thousand, seven thousand like Blackfield, there's a few creepers after dark (meth heads, winos, that sort of thing, sometimes hookers) but for the most part the main boulevard is a clear shot from one end of town to the other after dark.

He lit up, wandered back up the driveway and around the house sucking smoke out of the Camel as he went. Standing at the top of the drive, he was treated to a horizon swimming with the red cityglow of Blackfield, and under the jagged rim of the treetops glimmered the windows of the blue Victorian on the other side of the trailer park, a tiny hive of glowing elevens in the night.

As he blew the smoke into the night, multicolored lights flickered in the cupola. Someone was watching TV up there. "Looks like somebody's moved into the old Martine place."

An old woman stood by a barbecue grill crackling with flames. The ice in her glass tinkled as she took a sip of a Long Island Iced Tea. Cutty always started dinner with one to whet her appetite. "Know anything about them?"

"Black fella from up north, I expect."

Roy ashed his Camel and spat a fleck of tobacco. The wind rolling across the top of the hill pushed at his copper hair. He'd once let her make him a Long Island, but it was so strong he could barely finish it. No idea how she could manage it, with her scarecrow figure. "He brought the car down couple weeks ago and the real estate agent showed him around the place."

"Have you spoken to him?" Cutty threw another handful of *Watchtower* tracts on the fire. The smoke stank, and the ink turned the flames green.

"No."

She wore enormous shirts and patterned sweaters and dressed in loose layers, so that she always seemed to be wearing wizard-robes, even in the heat of summer. Roy was rail-thin and the jeans he wore draped from his bones, but even so he still sweat right through his shirts when he worked.

"Have you got anything for supper?" she asked the flames.

"No, ma'am."

Cutty closed the grill lid and started off toward the back of the house. "Why don't you stay and eat with us, then? Theresa is making porkchops."

"I might just do that," said Roy. "Thank you."

As soon as the door came open he was bombarded by the aroma of pork rub and steak fries, corn, green beans, baked apples. Theresa LaQuices bustled around the spacious kitchen, buttering rolls and stirring this or that.

Theresa was a solid and ruggedly pretty iceberg of a woman, a few years younger than Cutty. Her raven-black hair was dusted with gray. Spanish or maybe Italian or something, because of her exotic surname and olive skin, but Roy never could quite pin down her accent and it never really struck him as appropriate to ask. She was given to dressing like a woman twenty years her junior, and today she had on a winsome blue sundress roped about with white tie-dye splotches.

He couldn't deny that she wore it well. Against the well-appointed kitchen, she looked like she belonged on the cover of a culinary magazine. Reminded him of that Barefoot Contessa chick, only a lot older and a lot heavier.

"Well hello there, mister!" Theresa beamed. "Are you gonna be joinin us for dinner?"

Roy realized that Cutty had disappeared. She had an odd habit of doing that. "Yes, ma'am. And it smells damn good. I wasn't even hungry before I came in here, but now I could eat a bowl of lard with a hair in it."

Theresa made a face and gave a musical laugh. "I didn't prepare any lard, handsome, but you're welcome to a pork chop or two."

"I'll be glad to take you up on that."

Roy passed through a large dining room, past a long oak table carved with a huge compass-rose, and into a high-ceilinged living room with delicate wicker furniture. On a squat wooden pedestal was a flatscreen television that would not have been out of place on the bridge of a *Star Trek* spaceship.

Behind the TV were great gaping plate-glass windows that looked out on the front garden inside the adobe privacy wall, a quaint, almost

34

miniaturized bit of landscaping with several Japanese maples and a little pond populated by tiny knife-blade minnows.

The downstairs bathroom was one of many doors in a long hallway that bisected the drafty old house. The slender corridor, like the rest of the house, was painted a rich candy-apple red, and as the light of the lamps at either end trickled along the wall Roy felt as if he were walking up an artery into the chambers of a massive heart.

He washed his hands in a bathroom as large as his own living room. It was appointed with an ivory-white clawfoot tub, eggshell counters, white marble floor, gilded portrait mirror over a sink that looked like a smoked-glass punchbowl.

The vanity lights over the oval mirror were harsh, glaring. Roy was surprised a house occupied by three elderly women would have a bathroom mirror that threw your face into such stark moon-surface relief. Every pit, pock, blemish and crease stood out on his skin and all of a sudden he looked ten, twenty years older. And he had a lot of them for being in his forties.

His lower lids sagged as if he hadn't slept—which he hadn't, really, he didn't sleep well—and his red hair was fine, dry, cottony, piled on his head in a Lyle Lovett coiff. The lights made his normally attractive face look sallow, made him look melty and thin, like a wax statue under hot lamps.

Junk food, that was probably it. Slow-motion malnutrition. He ate a lot of crap because he didn't cook.

He *could* cook, no doubt—he could cook his ass off, learned from his mother Sally—but he never really made the effort. Not because he was lazy, but because he could never find anything in the cabinets that enticed him enough to cook it, and he never had anybody to eat with. So he really appreciated the chance for a proper home-cooked meal that left him out of the equation and gave him company to eat it with.

Back in the hallway, Roy passed an open door through which he could see a headless woman in a crisp new wedding dress.

"Hi there," said a woman's voice.

"Hello, Miss Weaver."

An elderly flower-child came flowing around the mannequin to him, decked out in a busy, psychedelic dashiki. "How many times do I have to tell you?" she said, wagging a knurled finger. "Call me Karen. Are you staying for dinner tonight?"

Locks of silver-blonde hair tumbled down from underneath a green knit cap and a long curl of yellow tailors' measuring tape yoked over the back of her neck, draping over her bosom. Karen Weaver had the open, honest face of a grandmother, and eyes as blue as a Montana sky. A silver pendant on her chest twinkled in the light, some obscure religious symbol he didn't recognize. It could have been a pentagram, except there were too many parts, too many lines.

"Yes, ma'am."

35

She playfully slapped him on the shoulder. Wisps of Nag Champa incense drifted through the open doorway behind her, accompanied by the sinuous, jangling strains of the Eagles. "Don't ma'am *me*, young man."

"Yes, ma'am," grinned Roy. He flinched away before she could slap him again.

Dinner was excellent. The four of them ate at the compass-rose dining table under the soft crystal glare of a chandelier, Cutty hunched over her plate like a buzzard on roadkill, Theresa with a napkin pressed demurely across her lap. Weaver ate with the slurping-gulping gusto of a castaway fresh off the island.

In the background, the vinyl turntable in the living room was playing one of those old records the girls liked so much—Glenn Miller, Cab Calloway, one of those guys, he wasn't sure which. Roy was a golden-oldie man himself, dirty southern rock. Skynyrd fan through and through.

"Cuts like birthday cake," said Weaver, flashing Theresa an earnest smile. "I've been cooking for ages, and somehow I still don't hold a candle to you."

"You get a lot of practice, cookin for a long line of husbands."

Cutty said in a wry tone, "I wonder why you outlived them."

Theresa feigned hurt at her and went back to feeding herself dainty bites of pork chop with the darting, practiced movements of someone steeped in Southern etiquette.

Roy interjected, "That's a nice dress you're working on, Karen. Where's this one going?"

The old hippie's smile only broadened. "Oh, it's going to a very lovely couple in New Hampshire. They're planning on a November wedding. No expense was spared."

"Too bad it won't be a Halloween wedding. That'd be interesting."

Cutty shook her head. "Ugh. I can't think of anything that would be cheesier than a bunch of youngsters decked out like extras from the *Rocky Horror Picture Show* or something, exchanging their vows in front of Elvis and a congregation of monsters."

"A congregation of monsters!" said Weaver, bright-eyed and smiling. "What a wonderful thought."

"Only you." Cutty eyed the voluptuous Theresa. "And what are *you* doing tomorrow?"

The dark-eyed Mediterranean straightened in her seat. "I'll have you know I'm volunteering at a soup kitchen tomorrow evening. The one in Blackfield. I'll be there all evening."

"You? *Volunteering?* At a soup kitchen?" Cutty huffed in disbelief and pushed her food around her plate. "The only thing *I've* ever seen you volunteer is your phone number."

As sullen and stormy as Roy could get, he enjoyed watching the sisters banter. They weren't biological sisters, or at least he didn't think they were. Never talked about where they came from, other than to swap stories and anecdotes about long-dead husbands. They never mentioned children.

"So, it looks like we've got new neighbors. Down the hill, in Annabelle's house."

The other two looked up from their dinner. Weaver was the first to speak. "Oh yeah? Well, are they nice? I think that house deserves someone nice."

"I haven't talked to em," offered Theresa. "I saw em when I was comin home from the grocery store earlier today...I was behind them on the road comin out of Blackfield. Looked like a man and a little boy. Colored folks. They was drivin one of them Japanese cars."

Sometimes Weaver could be a little eerie, but when she smiled, the old woman could light up a room. "Oh, that's nice—this gray old neighborhood could use a splash of color, I think."

At that, Cutty dipped her face into one hand and rubbed her forehead in exasperation.

"Say," Weaver added, "why don't we invite them up for dinner one night this week?"

"Like a welcome wagon," said Theresa.

"Yeah!"

"We'll have a barbecue out back and invite the whole neighborhood, and dance around the maypole and sing songs and tell stories," Cutty growled flippantly. "It'll be a regular bacchanalia."

Picking up her goblet, Weaver swirled a splash of wine. "That's the spirit! We'll even have a bonfire!"

Cutty gave her a shrewd glare.

"You *know* how I *feel* about bonfires."

"Oh, right."

"Still," said Theresa. "It would give us a chance to get to know them. After all, they're going to be livin in Annabelle's house. Like that bunch in Nebraska, they're gonna be askin questions sooner or later. We might as well lay the groundwork. Establish a little rapport."

"Redirect their curiosity. Yes." Cutty forked a piece of porkchop into her mouth and chewed thoughtfully. "Yes, good idea. Curiosity killed the cat, after all."

❁

After dinner, Cutty stood at the island in the kitchen and cut an extra porkchop into pieces, then put it in a food processor and chopped it into a dry, grainy paste. Then she used the processor to chop up a cup of green beans, and then a cup of corn.

She assembled all this processed food on a plate with two steak fries and took it upstairs, along with a glass of tea. She put the plate on a sideboard in the hallway and pulled a rope set into the ceiling, hauling down a hinged staircase behind a hidden panel. She took the plate up into darkness.

A pullchain dangled against her face. Cutty pulled it and a soft yellow bulb came on, revealing an attic.

Years of accretion surrounded her, most of it dusted. Victorian-style lounges and parlor tables with baroque mahogany scrollwork and silk cushions. Steamer trunks full of foxed books, scrolls of paper, yellowed newspapers, movie posters plastered with the faces of long dead actors. Bookcases with broken glass windows set into them. A clown marionette hung from the rafters, face forever frozen in a loopy laugh. A coin-operated weight scale from 1936. Shelves and shelves of bricabrac—toys, coins, bayonets, flintlock pistols.

Cutty walked a meandering path through the labyrinth to a door at the far end.

This she unlocked with a skeleton key.

Inside, a bed faced an old tube television in a dark room. The only window was a tall gothic rectangle that looked out on the back garden, and it simmered with Tyrian purple light.

Playing on the TV was the History Channel, which she never failed to find ironic, considering who was watching it. The TV's glow traced the contours of the room with a thin film of blue, but the shape under the thick quilt was only a suggestion in the soft light. The light of the attic's bare bulb filtered through the open door and fell across the foot of the bed, bisecting the bedroom with dirty gold.

A gray cat lay curled up by the footboard.

The bedridden shape stirred in the shadows. "Evening, cookie." Its genderless voice was a dry croak. Folded up in it was the hint of a sarcastic Brooklyn accent.

"Evening, Mother," said Cutty.

"It *is* evening, right?"

The old woman slept more often than not these days, and often woke in the wee hours of the night. The bedroom was timeless; there was no clock here, digital or analog, which is how she liked it. Mother hated counting down the hours alone in her rare moments of wakefulness, and the constant ticking was maddening, a torturous metronome out of a Poe story.

"Yes," Cutty said. "It is evening."

She put the plate on a vanity and took a bendy straw out of the pocket of her sweater, slipping it into the tea. Sitting on the bed, she helped her mother sit up and drink some of it. The sound of her slurping was like the slow tearing of paper.

"When is it?"

Cutty traded the tea for the plate. "It's October. October 2014."

She gathered up a spoonful of ground porkchop and fed it to the shape under the quilt. The spoon rattled against her mother's twisted

38

grimace as the meat slid inside. Mother mashed it against the roof of her mouth with her tongue and swallowed.

"2014?" wheezed the shape. "Shut the front door."

"Time flies."

"Time flies like an arrow, but bees like a fruitcake."

These garbled aphorisms had long ago ceased to concern Cutty. Considering the crone's state, it was a wonder she could even communicate. She eased some of the chopped green beans into her mother's hard mouth as if she were feeding her through a kabuki mask.

Mother sighed. "Will you hand me the television remote controller thing, cookie?"

"Where is it?"

"I dropped it. It's on the floor."

The shape's shriveled eyes followed Cutty as she put the plate aside and stooped to gather the remote. She put the batteries back in it, put the cover back on, and sought her mother's hand.

"Here you are," she said, putting it in the stiff claw.

Fingers curled around the remote with a subtle crackle. The TV changed channels at a stately pace as Cutty continued to feed her antediluvian mother pureed pork. The gray cat on the quilt looked up, yawned, stretched, went back to sleep.

"I think we're getting close," said Mother, when dinner was almost over. "Finally, finally, finally. After all these long years."

"Yeah?"

"Yeah. Maybe once it's done you won't be keeping me in the attic with the rest of the antiques."

Cutty gave her a wry look.

"What?" asked the shape.

"You *know* you're only up here to keep you safe. Safe from those nasty murdering men and their stolen heartstones."

"Bah. You don't care about me."

"How can you say that?"

"You hardly ever come up here to visit with me anymore." Her mother coughed softly into one dry fist. "You're always downstairs with your friends and that weird Irishman that cuts the grass."

"I've told you before, he's not Irish."

"He's ginger as hell, he does all the lawn work, he drinks, he's Irish until proven otherwise."

"No habeas corpus for you, huh?"

Her mother chuckled, though her face didn't move. "I'm corpse enough for both of us."

Cutty spooned the last of the green beans into her mouth and set the plate aside. Reaching into one of the deep pockets of her wizard-robe cashmere sweater, she brought out an apple. It was the size of a softball and its skin was the liquid, recondite red of a ruby. Rare striations of peach and gold curved down its sides.

Her mother sighed with relief and contentment at the sight of it, like a castaway seeing civilization.

"It's almost time for another harvest," said Cutty, handing her the apple. "I think this weekend I'll see to that. Roy and Theresa can help me carry them to the house."

Mother clutched it in her bony hands, and lifted it to her lips. Her mouth opened, the corners creasing and flaking, the joints of her jawbone cracking, and she pierced the fruit's skin with her teeth. A soft groan of delighted pain escaped her throat as she bit into the fruit.

Instead of juice, vibrant arterial blood dribbled from its rind and ran down her arms, dotting the quilt.

As the rich carmine ran down her throat, Mother's skin loosened, her fingers fulling and flushing. The corded veins snaking down her neck and across her shoulder plumped, throbbing, and fresh life trickled throughout her body.

"An apple a day," she gurgled.

Four

KNUCKLES BANGED ON THE side of Robin's van, waking her up with a start. She squirmed out of her sleeping bag and opened the door. Joel stood outside, sidelit by the pizzeria's security lights. He squinted into her flashlight beam. "Hey. I thought that would be you, out here in this sketchy-ass van." He had put on a light windbreaker, and had his hands tucked deep into the jacket's pockets. "You got any free candy?"

"No, fraid not."

"Damn." Joel glanced over his shoulder. "Hey, I wanted to come tell you...my brother Fish, he owns a comic shop in town? And he does this movie-night thing every Friday. He gonna start it up in about—" He checked his cellphone. "—Twenty minutes. You know, if you want to get out of that creepazoid van for a little while."

"I don't know. I—"

"Miguel usually lets me bring over a bunch of pizza from the shop. Employee discount."

Robin paused. The Sriracha-pineapple-pepperoni slice she'd had for lunch had been amazing, and she was more than ready for Round Two. "Jesus, why didn't you say that to begin with?" she asked, flicking on the dome light so she could find her clothes.

"What in the *hell?*" asked Joel, peering into the back of the van.

He reached in and took the broadsword down from its clamp on the wall and struck Conan poses with it. "What is all *this* now? This part of your witch-huntin YouTubes channel?"

Robin wriggled into her jeans. "Yep."

He put the sword back and tipped one of the plastic bins so he could see into it. Batteries. "You loaded for bear, hooker."

"Witch-hunting is a resource-intensive business."

Shrugging into a sweat-jacket hoodie, Robin clambered out of the back of the van and locked it up. She had the video camera in her hands, and as Joel led her out to his car, she turned it on and aimed it at her face, holding it at arms' length. "Hi everybody. It's Malus. I was getting ready to settle down for the night with a good book and a bowl of staple-food ninety-nine-cent Ramen when my new best friend Joel—"

She aimed the camera at Joel. "What up, internet." He blew a kiss.

"—came to invite me to Movie Night. Complete with more of that goddamn fantastic pizza from the pizzeria. Lady Luck smiles on me for a change."

Joel drove a beautiful jet-black Monte Carlo with bicycle-spoke rims and whitewall tires. She opened the passenger door and slid into the plush black interior to find an eight-ball gear shift and an armrest wedge with a picture of Elvira embroidered on it, and the words BLACK VELVET in cursive.

"All black." Robin buckled up as Joel tossed himself into the car. "I bet this thing is a bitch in the summer."

He turned the engine over with a cough and a beastly, deep-throated *grum-grum-grum-grum*. "Honey, it's a bitch all year," Joel said, throwing it into gear and pulling out of the parking lot.

The subwoofers in the back howled "Crazy On You" by Heart as he piloted Black Velvet down the twisting highway out of the canyon, his headlights washing back and forth across the trees. The backseat had a stack of vibrating boxes in it, filling the car with the tangy-savory smell of hot pizza, and her stomach twisted into knots immediately. As they came into Blackfield proper, the headlights spotlighted familiar sights that brought back a flood of nostalgia.

Much of the town was different—there was a new Walgreen's, and the Walmart had become a sprawling co-op—but underneath the shiny new veneer of change were old landmarks saturated with memories.

There was the bridge she used to play under when she was a kid walking home from school.

Jim's Diner, where she had her first piece of cheesecake.

The funeral home with the giant sloped parking lot that she'd sledded down one winter and crashed into some spare headstones at the back, leaving a bruise on her ass.

Walker Memorial, where she'd gone to church a few times under the instruction of her therapists in her junior year of high school. That lasted about a month, but she could still hear the vaulted echoes of footsteps, smell the varnish on the pews, the dusty carpet, the faint piss-reek of ancient hymnal books with stiff pages.

"Been a few years?" asked Joel, turning down the stereo so he could talk. He took out an iPhone and texted someone, typing with one thumb.

"Yeah." Robin spoke to the window, the world wheeling past her face like a diorama. They passed the Victory Lanes alley on 7th and Stuart, the neon sign out front showing a bowling ball knocking two pins into the rough shape of a V over and over. "It has. I didn't think I'd ever be back here. Lot of bad memories. I said I wouldn't come back."

"You said this morning you wanted to pay your respects to y'mama?" He attached his phone to a magnetized ball on the dash, *click,* where it perched above the radio like a mounted GPS.

"Yeah. I might visit my old house too, if I think I can handle it."

Joel sniffed, tugging his nose. He glanced out the window and then back at her as if he were about to give her nuclear secrets. "Ay, you want me to go witchu? You know, moral support? I don't know when you wanna go, but I got some time off comin."

"I don't know yet. Maybe some time this week."

"Lemme know. I'll be there with bells on." He flicked the tiny disco ball hanging from his rearview mirror and sun-cats danced around the interior of the car. "Jingle jangle."

Fisher's comic store wasn't quite on the main drag through town, but it was tucked into a homey little street one block over, a narrow slice of old-fashioned Americana. Knick-knack shops, drugstores, a pet shop, boutiques, barber shops, a bar, lawyers' offices, a Goodwill, a soup kitchen. They passed a looming gray courthouse and a redbrick police station.

The Monte Carlo slid into an angled parking spot on the street next to eight or nine other vehicles and Joel got out, taking half the stack of boxes out, leaving the rest for Robin. "Did you say Miguel donates these pizzas?" she asked, picking up the boxes and pushing the car door shut with her hip.

"He sees it as advertising." Joel said, suggestively tossing out a hip. "Give em a taste, they gonna come back for more."

Robin chuckled awkwardly.

She felt for the curb with her toe and stepped up onto the sidewalk. The windows of the comic shop were painted with intricate images of Spider-Man and Batman in dynamic poses, Bats in his blue-and-gray Silver Age colors. Over their heads was FISHER'S HOBBY SHOP in flowing cursive.

A man came out of the comic book store and held the door open for them. "You trying to hurt me, man," he told Joel, eyeing the pizza. He was brawny but slender, with a V-shaped torso and a round face.

"Fish, *you* the one doin it to yourself, don't blame me. *I* eat like a human."

The comic shop was dimly lit by bar fluorescents. Comics were only a fraction of the wares on the shelves—there were scores of rare, niche, and run-of-the-mill action figures still in their blister packs, board and card games, Halloween masks cast from various horror movies and superheroes, film props, videogame keychains, themed candy.

A life-size Xenomorph creature from the Alien movies lurked behind a shelf, motionlessly waiting to snag any customers unfortunate enough to step into range of its throat-jaws.

In the back of the store was an open area with booth seats and folding-chairs. Arcing over the heads of two dozen people and a small squad of children was a cone of light casting the opening sequence of horror classic *Evil Dead* on a projection screen.

"Fish on that keto diet." Joel put the pizza boxes on a booth table and squirted some sanitzer on his hands, wringing them.

The kids immediately got up and came to the table, standing at his elbow quietly like hungry hounds. "He try to tell me it's good and good for ya, but I see that look in his eye when I bring in these pizzas."

"What's the keto diet?" asked Robin.

"Zero carbs. None. Zero, zip, zilch." Joel made that *zip-it* gesture across his face and started putting pizza on paper plates, handing them out. "He don't hardly even eat fruit. He's always been a fitness nut, but this year he's goin balls to the wall. I don't know how he does it."

He gave one to Robin and she slid into the booth, sitting against the wall. "What *does* he eat?" she asked, placing her camera against the wall to capture the table and its occupants.

"Meat. Vegetables." He wagged his hand. "Bacon all day erry day. He cobble together regular food outta irregular bullshit. And the man fry *everything* in coconut oil. I tell you, one time he talked me into comin down to his place, and he made pizza with this dough made outta pureed cauliflower."

"Was it good?"

"As good goin down as it was comin up."

She made a face.

Fish, his tiny girlfriend Marissa, and a big white biker-looking guy named Kenway came to sit with her in the booth. She helped them destroy the pizza and an army of craft beers while they ignored the movie and played a game of Cards Against Humanity.

Kenway held up a black card in one tattooed hand. A riot of color and lines ran down his huge arms in sleeves. "We never did find *blank*, but along the way we sure learned a lot about *blank.*" His Sasquatch frame was crammed into a black T-shirt and he had a massive beard that made him look like a lumberjack having a mid-life crisis. A piercing in his eyebrow twinkled in the projector's glow.

Robin smirked and plucked two white cards—*the tiniest shred of evidence that God is real,* and *tripping balls*—from her hand, putting them face down on the table next to the others.

Marissa's cards won the round. "We never did find passable transvestites," Kenway recited out loud, and a huge grin gleamed through the dark cloud of his beard. "But along the way we sure learned a lot about Grandma."

The table roared with laughter, and a couple of the people watching the movie glanced at them.

As the evening progressed toward midnight, Robin became more and more glad that she'd agreed to come. Several dozen hands into a *Halloween* marathon, she looked up from her beer and realized that all the movie-watchers had disappeared. Michael Myers stared blankly out of the screen at a roomful of empty chairs.

"I think it's about time I head home," said Kenway, and Marissa let him out. Robin was taken aback at how tall he was as he unfolded himself from the booth and stretched six feet of broad muscle.

She polished off her beer. "Got work in the morning?"

"...No, ahh—"

Fish stiffened. Robin scrunched her brow at him in confusion.

"I don't really work," Kenway said, jamming his fingers into his jeans pockets. "Well, I *do*—" He gestured with a big craggy hand. "—But it's not really your usual nine-to-five."

Marissa smiled. "Kenny is Blackfield's local *artiste.*"

"Is that so?" Robin beamed. The smile felt alien and uncomfortable on her face even after laughing at the card game, and as usual it faded quickly. "What kind of art do you do?"

"A little of this, a little of that." The hulking man folded his arms. It should have looked authoritative, menacing even, but somehow it seemed protective, bashful. "I did the big mural on the wall at the park, and I did the superheroes out there on the windows. I have vinyl equipment too, and I make leather stuff."

"Maybe I can commission you to paint my van."

"That skeezy-ass candy van?" asked Joel.

Robin pursed her lips at him. "Yes, my skeezy-ass candy van. It needs a little style, maybe."

Kenway rubbed the back of his neck. "I'll take a look at it, then." He started gathering up the cards and shuffling them, sorting them into clean stacks and putting them into boxes. "What'd you have in mind?"

"Do you do a lot of vans?"

"A couple. Mostly pick-up trucks and hot-rods from out of town. I do a shit-ton of motorcycles for guys out of Atlanta and Chattanooga. I did a big-ass snake on a dude's truck a few years ago. It was pretty freakin' sick, took forever. Went all the way around the back from one door to the other."

Robin tried to picture the van with a new paint job. "It'd have to be something black, with stylized artwork. Nothing cheesy."

"I'm sure I could figure something out."

"I think you should take the lady back over there and let her show you her skeezy-ass candy van," suggested Joel, with a devil's grin. "I live on the other side of town, and it'd be out of my way, but your studio is between here and there."

A rush of cold heat shot down Robin's neck in embarrassment. She narrowed her eyes at him. *You planned this all along, didn't you?*

Kenway rubbed the back of his neck. "...Yeah, I *guess* I could."

After taking down the projector equipment and cleaning up the mess from the pizza, the five of them regrouped on the sidewalk and said their good-nights. Turned out the *artiste* drove a rattletrap Chevy pickup, an antique land-yacht with a bicycle lying in the back. The paint job was the tired Dustbowl-blue of the sky in old photographs, wistful and cool.

Climbing into the cab, Robin pulled her hoodie's sleeves down to cover her hands and pushed her hands into the muff pockets. She wasn't cold, but it made her feel better. Safer.

A set of dog-tags dangled from the rear-view mirror, twinkling in the light.

She rolled the window down and sat back to listen to the cicadas buzz and whisper in the distance. Kenway got in, filling the driver's seat with his muscular bulk, and turned the engine over with an oily, exhausted *chugga chugga chugga*. He fiddled with the radio, producing a static-chewed gabble.

"What kind of music do you like?"

"Any kind." She smiled as warmly as she could.

He settled on a classic rock station—*Revved up, like a deuce, another runner in the night*—and looked to her for approval. It was the clearest signal on the band, so she pursed her lips in an agreeing smile. "That's fine."

The gearshift was a twenty-sided die as big as an apple. As he went to put the truck in gear, he noticed her eyes on it. "I won it playing Trivial Pursuit at Fish's shop one night." He chuckled and pushed it across the gearbox, and the engine dropped in pitch. "First time my encyclopedic knowledge of TV shows has ever come in handy. It's actually not a real gearshift, I had to drill a hole in the back of it."

The Chevy swung out of the parking spot and lumbered down Main Street, passing a tremendous Gothic church that looked as if it were made of sandstone blocks.

The hallucination stood under one of the stone buttresses, in an alleyway.

Luminous green lamp-eyes gleamed in the darkness of its broad face, strobing between the bars of the churchyard fence. A yellow security light on the church wall illuminated it from behind, making a halo of the reddish hair covering its lumpy shoulders and long arms. Years ago, she had pegged it for at least eight feet tall, but next to Walker Memorial it almost looked delicate.

I must be late for my medication, Robin thought, making a mental note to take it as soon as she got back to the van.

"So what do *you* do for a living?" Kenway asked. "It must be pretty interesting—"

"Cause of the way I look?"

She glanced at herself in the wing mirror and suddenly she seemed outlandish, like an extra out of a *Mad Max* movie, all dark-eyed and gray-scalped. For the first time in a long time—maybe the first time *period*—she wished she were wearing more make-up. Her fingernails had been black earlier that week, but now they were only mostly black, chipped away.

Kenway scoffed, grinning. "You said it, not me."

46

"I make YouTube videos." She remembered that she was holding her camera, and she waggled it indicatively. It was not filming.

"Really. Huh." Kenway stopped at a red light, waiting for cross-traffic that never came. "I didn't even know you could make money doing that. What do you do in em?"

I bet you thought I did porn, she thought. *Or worse. You wouldn't be the first to make that assumption.* The radio was turned so low that Robin could hear the traffic light clicking softly in the breeze. Lyrics squirmed at the edge of her hearing like voices on a telephone.

"Vlog."

"Gesundheit."

"No, it's like a video journal. I… 'document' things."

She hesitated. Kenway was good-looking, and she didn't want to jeopardize whatever tenuous thing she could sense hovering in the cab between them with the goofy truth. The elephant in the room was a flighty one. "Ahh…I don't know, it's nothing. Not really that great. I just talk to the camera a lot. Drive around, visit places. Joel says I'm a homeless Guy Fieri."

"Cool, cool," he said, and laughed as the mental image sunk in. The light turned green and the truck grumbled across the intersection. "Anyway, I wanted to tell you, I really dig that mohawk."

She instinctively brushed a hand across her bristly scalp. "Yeah?"

"Yeah. I'm—I'm really into rock chicks. Biker chicks. That kind of thing. I guess." He rolled his own window down and laid an elbow out of it, leaning away from her. He shrugged. "I don't know. I just…wanted to say it, say something. You look good. It's a good look for you."

"…Thank you."

"Suits your face."

Kenway's smile was a tight, polite one. It didn't reach his eyes.

Robin summoned up her curiosity. "So…you don't really look like a local. I don't remember you from when I was a kid."

"I moved out here a couple years ago. I was visiting a friend of mine and decided to stay. I like this town. It's quiet, and I, uhh…I guess I had some baggage I needed to get rid of. And this place is a good place to lose it." He glanced at her and back at the road. "The baggage."

"I know what you meant." Robin stared through the windshield. "I think I brought some back here myself."

At night, Blackfield was a dead city, an abandoned town painted in shades of rust-orange. They only saw two cars, and both of them turned down side streets, heading home.

"Y'know, I guess it must not be 'nothing'—" Flicking the turn signal, *tick tock tick tock tick tock,* Kenway eased into a turning lane and boated left. "—I mean, if you can make a living at it, that whatever-it-is you do on YouTube must be good enough to pay the bills. Right?"

Robin sighed. "Yeah, I guess it's all right."

"So come on. Out with it, Miss Mysterious. What do you do?" He smirked at her, lip curling in one corner, white teeth glinting in his beard.

They crossed a small bridge over a canal running parallel to the main drag, and she could hear the faint gurgle of rushing water. On the other side, Kenway turned right and carried them up a street of quaint two-story buildings like some kind of historical business district.

"Do you watch a lot of YouTube videos?" she asked.

He shook his head. "No, not really. I don't even have a smartphone. I have a computer at the shop, but I only use it for work. My laptop in my apartment, I don't use it much at all except for watching movies or checking email. Reading the news."

She squinted. "What about that movie *The Blair Witch Project?*"

"I remember that, yeah. Came out in like, 1999 or 2000, something like that, didn't it?"

"Something like that. I do—my channel is sort of like that. Fake real-life footage of supernatural events in my life. There are...actually a lot of channels like mine, but not. Not exactly like mine. Most of them are people dealing with ghosts. Haunted houses. And monsters. Extra-dimensional monsters?"

Coming out of her mouth, it sounded stupid as hell. "Mm-hmm." Kenway nodded.

They slowed to a crawl, level with a dark shopfront. The plate-glass windows were painted with a gryphon in rampant red, and underneath was lettering in Olde English: GRIFFIN'S ARTS & SIGNS. "This is my place. I live upstairs from my shop in a drafty studio apartment. Yep, I'm the stereotypical starving artist."

They drove on. He took them to the end of the median and did a U-turn through the turning lane, going the way they came.

"Do you do a lot of business?" she asked.

"Not really. But I like it that way. I might have one or two big projects a month. The rest of the time I paint." He tugged his jeans leg up, revealing the sheen of a metal rod. His lower left leg was a prosthetic foot. "VA disability," he said, knocking on it with a hollow *tonk, tonk.* "Gives me a lot of free time."

"I *was* wondering if you were in the Army." Robin's eyes flicked to the dog tags hanging from the mirror. She caught one of them and turned it to the light. SFC GRIFFIN, KENWAY. BLOOD TYPE AB. RELIGION NONE.

"Used to be."

"Do you mind if I ask what happened?"

He didn't answer right away. His eyes were fixed on some point a thousand miles in front of the Chevy.

"I'm sorry," Robin said. "I shouldn't—"

"It's okay. I was uhh...collecting my thoughts." He tipped down the visor and caught a pack of cigarettes, pulling one out with his lips.

He didn't light it, but he put the box back in the visor and drove with his lighter in his wheel hand. "I was part of an escort for a Provincial Reconstruction Team convoy. They're the ones that...they have a lot...*women,* we brought female soldiers out to the villages where we were building schools and shit, you know, to talk to the Afghan women and kids. They don't really talk to the men, I guess." The wind played with his hair. His temples were shaved but the top was long, and it whipped in the breeze coming through the window.

A wincing expression had slowly come over his face as if he'd developed a headache. "Anyway. I stopped our vehicle when I shouldn't have. Ka-blooey. End of the line."

"I'm sorry."

Kenway lit the cigarette and took a draw, shrugging. "Oh—do you mind?" he asked, indicating the cigarette.

She smiled wanly. "It's your truck."

"You smoke? You want one?"

"Trying to quit."

The night blurred past them for a few more moments as they passed lightless storefronts, dead barber's shops, dark alleyways yawning in brick throats. They startled a cat that had been peering into a storm drain and it bounded away, leaping into a hedge.

"You're staying over in the hippie-village next to Miguel's, right?"

"Yep."

A silk sheet of silence settled over the truck as the town tapered away, the buildings rolling into darkness until they coursed along a narrow corridor of trees.

Robin became more and more at ease as they rode. Kenway had a calming, languid, ursine presence that reminded her of Baloo the Bear from that old *Jungle Book* cartoon movie. He seemed to operate on a different wavelength; everything he did was slow and lazy, as if he had all the time in the world. The night vacuumed his smoke away as he drove, his elbow out the window.

The trees fell away as well, the blue Chevy bursting into the open, the night sky unfurling above them in a dome of stars. Shreds of gray cloud sailed west under a nickel moon. Hills around them narrowed, enclosing the road in washboard crags of granite, then widened again.

BLACKFIELD CITY LIMITS, said a lonesome green sign. A bit beyond that was a turn-off leading east into the treeline. Kenway flicked the turn signal and the ancient truck slowed.

"What are...." Robin began to ask.

He looked over at her. "Shortcut? I *always* go this way when I go to Miguel's."

"Oh." The truck angled onto Underwood Road. "Do you like to hike?"

She knew from experience that the mountains around Miguel's were honeycombed with hiking trails, paths that trickled through the forest

49

toward Rocktown. Rocktown was a clifftop strewn with huge limestone boulders, the local hotspot for college kids, rock-climbers from afar, and anybody looking for an out-of-the-way place to burn a bag of weed with their friends. If there's anywhere safe from the prying eyes of Joe Law, it's at the top of a fifty-foot vertical rock face.

"I like to climb." He smiled. His eyes were the same tired blue as his truck. "Yes, in fact, I *can* climb with this foot, in case you were wondering."

Underwood Road.

She'd hoped Kenway would keep going. She wanted him to keep on driving to the far end of the four-lane where the freeway overpass arced above their heads, where the Subway restaurant, the bait shop, the Texaco, and the road to Lake Craddock clustered around a secluded rest stop in the wilderness.

She didn't really want to come out here yet. Not yet. She wasn't totally ready. She needed a few days to pump herself up.

Now the forest surrounded the truck in a claustrophobic collar of pines and elms, the tree-trunks shuttling past in a picket-fence flicker of columns and shadows. She stared out the window at them, the late-summer wind buffeting her face.

"I used to live on this road when I was a kid."

Kenway took one last draw on the cigarette and ashed it in the dash tray, then flicked it outside. "Yeah?"

The trees kept barreling toward them, counting down, becoming more and more familiar. She kept expecting the houses and the trailers with every turn, the memories leaking in like water under a door. There was the NO TRESPASSING sign, shot full of .22 holes. Just there, a faint patch of grungy Heathcliff-orange, the armchair someone had dumped in the woods when she was twelve.

Then, there it was: the forest opened up again and there was the trailer park on her left, all lit up with its sickly white security lights, trailer windows haunted by the honey-red glow of lamps and the epileptic blue stutter of TV shows. A large aluminum sign out front declared CHEVALIER VILLAGE, or at least that's what it seemed to say, under a coating of graffiti.

On top of the angular Olde English gibberish was a tiny spraypainted crown.

Suddenly she was sixteen again, she was thirteen, she was nine. Robin sighed, sitting up against her best judgement, and tried to see if there was anything—or anybody—she could recognize. But the night was too dark, and the cars were all too modern, and the yards were strewn with toys, and everybody was inside and had battened their hatches against the dark.

On her right, a double-wide by itself, with a hand-built porch and naked wooden trellis, chintzy aluminum birds with their pinwheel wings, a deteriorating VOTE ROMNEY sign by the culvert. A wooden-slatted swing dangled by one chain from a rusty frame, the end jammed into the dirt.

Next door, looming on the other side of a stretch of grass, was the monolithic 1168.

"Slow down," Robin blurted.

The Chevy downshifted and the neighborhood lingered around them. The engine protested. Materializing from the deep night like the hull of some sunken ship was the gingerbread Victorian farmhouse she'd grown up in, her childhood home.

All the lights were off, but the security lamp on a nearby power pole threw a pallid greenish cast across the front so that the black windows were more like eyes in a dead face.

"This was my house," she said, as if in a dream.

Familiarity wreathed the window-frames and eaves of the house in mistlike echoes as she studied it from afar. Her memories were stale, and far from her groping mental hands. The house was a different color (she knew it as green, the pale green of dinner mints, with John Deere trim), but it was her house. She could feel the splintery porch railing in her hands, the words her mother had carved deep in the windowsills and that her father had painted over.

"Nice place," said Kenway. "Looks like somebody else lives there now. Or they're about to move out." A U-Haul truck and a blue car sat in the driveway, the car tinted black by the watery light. She didn't recognize them.

Something drew Robin's eyes back to the trailer park across the street, and she traced the long gravel drive snaking along the east hip of the park to the old mission-style manor lurking on top of the hill. The Lazenbury House cut a tombstone silhouette against the Milky Way. All of the lights were off except for one window on the topmost floor. She'd never been up there, but she knew the rest of the house. She knew the blood-red walls, the piano, the Japanese-style front garden with its fish-pond. The sprawling, Eden-like garden out back. She knew the dirt-floored cellar, with its fire-blackened casks of wine and cramped dumbwaiter-style elevator.

She'd practically grown up in that house. She remembered stories her mother had told her when she was a teenager, losing sight of little two-year-old Robin and searching the house for her, only to discover that she'd wandered over to Granny Mariloo's house for cookies and apple juice. A few times, she'd cried for hours, banging on the door of an empty house. Robin had vague memories of her mother Annie marching resolutely up that long gravel drive barefoot, the wind pulling at her dress, to come fetch her daughter.

Those were the days when her father had been his worst, and her parents had fought with each other the hardest. Disturbed by the shouting, Baby Robin would creep out and seek solace with sweet, maternal Marilyn.

51

But she'd never been allowed on the top floor. Did the Lazenbury have an attic? She wasn't sure.

A shadow moved behind the window's lacy curtain.

"Okay," she said, startled out of her reverie, and Kenway took that as an indication to keep on trucking.

The forest swallowed them up again, and they followed their headlights down a long, winding two-lane under oppressive branches. Whenever there was a break in the trees, farmhouses sailed past in the cool twilight, surrounded by empty gray pastures tied to the earth with barbed wire and driftwood stakes.

Underwood came out at a lonely T-junction watched by a grove of birches, where a single cabin peered through the trees with one yellow eye. Kenway pulled left without his turn signal and the Chevy roared north. A few minutes later, the headlights scraped across the belly of the interstate overpass and a little beyond, in the crook of a long, shallow curve, was Miguel's Pizzeria, a single security lamp standing vigil by the shower building.

Kenway pulled up onto the gravel drive, weeble-wobbling across the jagged ground. The bicycle in the back thumped in time with the truck's creaking suspension.

"That's me." Robin pointed at the plumber van.

Kenway erupted into laughter. "Aha ha ha, Joel wasn't kidding. That is truly sketch." He must have seen the look on her face, because he immediately stopped grinning. "Oh, I'm sorry. I didn't mean—I mean...shit. I wasn't trying to hurt your feelings. I'm sorry."

She waved him off. Cool indignity rested in her belly like a stone. "It's okay. I know how it looks."

"If...if you don't mind me asking, why are you living in an old panel van?"

Opening the door, she started to get out but something seemed to press her back into the cab of the truck. Reluctance? Robin slid to the edge of the bench-seat, the fabric of her jeans buzzing across the tweed upholstery, but she just sat there. *To hell with it,* she thought, her eyes fixed on the sign out in front, a picture of a cartoon Italian chef perched on a cliff face. I'D CLIMB A MOUNTAIN FOR MIGUEL'S PIZZA! *Might as well go ahead and drop the bomb. It's going to happen eventually, might as well wreck this before it really gets going.*

Instead of meeting his eyes when she turned to him, she fixed on his giant hand, wrapped around the steering wheel. "I bought it with the money that was in my mom's bank account when I was released from Blackfield Psychiatric a few years ago."

Kenway nodded, slowly. "Ahh."

She winced a smile at him in gratitude. "Thank you for the ride home. Oh!" Reaching into her pocket, she pulled out a scant wad of cash and peeled off two twenties, thrusting them in his direction. "Gas money. As thanks."

His eyes landed on the money, his eyebrows jumped, and he twitched as if he were going to take it, but he said, "No, that's—it's all right, I'm good."

"No, really. Take it."

Kenway pointed at the dash dials. "I'm full anyway. I filled up on the way to Movie Night."

Folding the money into a tube, Robin stuck it in the tape deck so that it looked like the stereo was smoking a cigarette. "There." She slid the rest of the way out of the truck and shut the door, walking through the glare of his dingy headlights.

On the driver's side, she stood in the dark hugging herself. "Drive safe," she said, feeling awkward. "Thank you again for the ride home."

He didn't leave. "You're an odd duck, Robin."

Ice trickled into her belly. "Thanks."

"I like odd ducks."

"Quack quack," she replied, perhaps a little too coldly.

The two of them had a short staring contest, the girl standing behind her van, Kenway sitting in his idling truck.

She was about to bid him adieu and climb into her party-wagon when he spoke up. "If you're ashamed about the psychiatric thing, don't be. Lord knows I've spent enough time talking to shrinks that I shouldn't have any room to talk." Drumming a bit on the windowsill, he added, "So...yeah. I don't know what your story is, but you won't find any judgement here."

Robin smiled. "Thanks."

"I don't know how long you're going to be in town, but I'll be around. If you want a real bed to sleep on for a night, you're welcome to crash at my place." He crossed his fingers. "No creep stuff, scout's honor. Just...you know, an offer. I guess. It's there on the table."

"Okay."

She took hold of the rear door handle and started to open the door and climb in, but then had the idea to tell Kenway good night. When she turned to speak, he was already rolling the window up and putting the truck in gear. Robin stood there with one foot on her back bumper and watched the Chevy grumble around the parking area, crunching across the gravel and washing the pizzeria with its headlights. Kenway pulled up to the road, sat still for a moment, then lurched out and disappeared with a roar.

She sighed and climbed into the back of the cold van.

All of a sudden, her mobile candy-van nest didn't look nearly as inviting as it had before. Robin stripped, kicked her fuzzy legs down into the sleeping bag, and lay down with a huff. "Shit," she muttered to herself, regretfully wrenching a beanie down over her eyes.

Five

"CASTLE ONE, THIS IS Castle two. Do you copy?" burped the radio in Delilah's hands. The little girl crouched in the shadows by the corner of the building and gazed out at the night. The playground lights were a dazzling array of suns; white floodlights on the apartment block eaves made the jungle gym into a rib-cage of black shadow-bones.

The day wasn't done yet. Blackfield's sky was a dark, watery indigo, and the sun was a hint of a bruise on the horizon. A giant silver dollar hovered in the dome of blue, the moon a translucent all-seeing face. A huge bunker of darkness loomed in the east, threatening rain.

Delilah put the damp walkie-talkie against her chubby cheek and stage-whispered, "Yes, Castle!"

The girl on the other end of the line sighed in exasperation. "That's not how you say it, Lilah. That's totally wrong. You say *roger, Castle two, over*. That's how they say it in the armies."

Delilah sniffed. The evening dew on the grass was getting her socks wet. She hated wet socks.

The droning of the cicadas made it hard to hear Ginny without having the radio turned all the way up, and didn't that defeat the purpose of being ninjas? You weren't supposed to *hear* ninjas. Though, she supposed, the cicadas made it easy to be sneaky. That monotonous wheeling buzz covered you like a blanket.

"*You* didn't say over," she said into the walkie. She took a deep breath of that sharp cut-grass smell and coughed. "Are you sure ninjas use walkie-talkies?"

"Yes. . . . Over."

"Ninjas don't walk *or* talk. They hide in trees and jump over stuff and throw stars. I *know*. My dad lets me watch ninja movies with him. We have all the best ones."

"Well," said Ginny. "The ninjas in this army use walkie-talkies. I got them for my birthday so the ninjas can use them. Over."

"Over."

"You didn't *say* anything!" squealed Ginny.

"You didn't say *over* again!"

"Over over *over!*"

Delilah shrilled, *"Over over over over over!"* into the mike and it became a battle of who could blast the other off the radio saying "Over" the loudest, then fell apart into the high cackling of little girls.

"I'm sorry I missed your birthday," said Delilah. "I had to go to practice. My mom makes me. How old are you now? Seventy *kabillion?"*

"Noooooo. I turned seven today."

"Good," Delilah said into the radio. "Now we're even. *Oh!* I'm really close to the base."

"How close?"

Delilah looked up at the jungle gym and its birdcage shadow. "I'm like, really close," she said, and then a shape peeled itself away from the darkness under the security lights.

Ginny was making a break for it. The girl ran smack into the metal bars, catching herself with her hands and throwing her chubby legs up into the tangle of piping. She sat down and kicked her feet in satisfaction, peering around the complex like a hawk on the lookout for field mice.

Delilah turned and crept alongside the base of the apartment building, loping around the corner, and then broke into a sprint down the sidewalk, past a row of identical front porches.

Everybody else was holed up in their cookie cutter apartments, living room lamps lighting up windows with a honeyed glow. The detritus of a dozen childhoods lay scattered across the tiny front lawns: tricycles, various pieces of Fisher-Price playsets, plastic ray-guns, action figures.

The parking lot flush with the sidewalk was populated with two-dozen vehicles of various makes, models, and conditions; one of them was her father Billy's rattletrap pickup, a modest brown machine with OY painted on the tailgate, the T and OTA having faded away years ago.

"Where *are* you?" Ginny said.

Delilah keyed her mike. "You'll never know if you don't come looking! You can't sit on the base, I can't get near it. You're cheating!"

"Nuh-*uh!* . . . over."

"Yuh-huh! Over!"

"Okay, okay. I'll come look. But you better be in a *really good* hiding place. I'll give you thirty-five seconds."

A big blue Dumpster loomed at the end of the parking lot. She briefly considered hiding there, but then remembered how bad it smelled the last time she'd been out that way to take out the garbage.

Hmm. She wasn't crawling into one of the culverts by the street frontage, no way. That only left the vehicles.

She tested her father's truck, but the doors were locked. Delilah thought about lying down in the back, but scrapped that as an easily-foiled plan. All Ginny had to do was walk up and look over the tailgate.

She climbed into the back anyway and tried to pry the rear cab window open, but it was latched shut.

Climbing back out again, the girl got on her knees and looked underneath the truck, hoping there was space to crawl under, but there was a patch of oil Delilah didn't want to wallow around in. For a kid, she could be surprisingly meticulous—her stepmother Janele was always saying how proud she was that her baby always picked up after herself. Delilah didn't do it out of some moral rectitude, she just hated being in a dirty house. Hated having crumbs on her bare feet, hated dipping her elbow in ketchup congealing on the kitchen table.

Delilah's biological mother was quite the opposite. In her stale, dark house lived six skinny cats, two big stupid dogs, and a Plexiglas aquarium that allegedly held a hamster that Delilah had never seen.

She hated the cats. They were the worst.

She got down and peeked under the next car. There was considerably less of a mess underneath, but the undercarriage was so low there was no hope of being able to squeeze into it. She stood up and that's when she saw it. On the other side of the strip of parking-spaces, at the end of a row of empty slots, was a pickup truck.

It was a Ford, a big one, old. Comparatively speaking, the red paint job was dull; it reflected the security lights about as well as an eggshell. A camper-shell covered the bed like a turtle, the same brick-red as the body.

But what grabbed Delilah's attention was the bright green snake spray-painted up the side of the bed wall.

This was new. Surely she would have seen such a spectacular work of art around the complex before. This was without a doubt a new neighbor that she hoped her father would befriend in the near future, so she could see who would drive around town with this on his truck. And for certain, that person would have to be a man, because this emerald-skinned jungle dragon could only belong to a man.

An undulating hose of diamond-shaped scales uncoiled from the tail-light to the driver's-side door. Each scale shone with its own sharp shine, reflecting some source of light beyond the ken of the canvas. At the leading end of the dragonesque body was a great gawping mouth full of teeth and writhing bifurcated tongue, dominated by a pair of white fangs the size and shape of bananas.

Honey-amber screwhead eyes gazed out at her, as big as fists and just as menacing. The eye seemed to be three-dimensional. Prying it out, she discovered that underneath was the gasoline receptacle. The gas cap was the snake's eye! How clever.

It was a bit of a ratty truck to have such a gloriously cheesy picture painted on it, but then when you thought about it, the medium fit the subject well. She wondered who it belonged to, and what he was like, as the girl reached up and put her hand on its swollen metal belly, still warm with the day's beating.

She imagined a man with a bushy brown mustache and a bald head, with a band of curly hair that started at one ear and went round the back of his head to the other. He would be wearing a stained white T-shirt and a pair of jeans that never quite managed to hide his butt-crack. He'd be covering his baldness with a ball cap, with some silly saying on it. "I Hunt Because My Wife Can't Climb Trees" maybe, like what her father had hanging from the mounted buck-head in the apartment, along with his *Duck Commander* cap.

She noticed that the snake's tail extended past the tail-light on this side. Delilah went around the back and found that the body stretched across the tailgate, went behind the passenger tail-light, and came out again on the passenger fender.

After that it coiled twice and clinging tightly to the very tip was a barechested woman in Viking gear, her pendulous cone-shaped tits squeezed between her outstretched arms. The barbarian Barbie gripped the last slender inch of the snake's tail as if it were a baseball bat and dug in with both heels. If Delilah were twenty years older, she probably would have read more into the image.

She touched the hand-painted woman; her dusky arms and glowing lightning-god eyes stood out from the truck-body around it, a paint-depth bas relief. The winecork nipples stood out like Braille.

"Time's up!" said the radio.

The sudden voice gave Delilah a jolt and she almost dropped it. Her heart leapt with a shot of adrenaline and she looked around for a place to stash herself. Running around the rear of the snake truck, she noticed that the camper-top's door was open a bit. She cupped her hands against the milky glass and peered through the parentheses of her fingers, but couldn't see inside.

"I'm coming to find you!" Ginny called from somewhere to her distant right, shouting in a singsong voice.

Delilah lifted the sash and climbed into the back of the truck, letting it sigh back down on pneumatic hinges. It closed with a hollow *click*.

Inside the camper shell, it was stifling hot and the air seemed sapped of oxygen; grainy, almost, with the smell of earth and a murk of forest-smells. A dulled tang of pine. The side windows were painted over with the red of the body, coloring the faint light from the streetlamps a boudoir crimson. Crammed against the back of the cab was a fluffy black bale of pine needles. Many of the needles had slipped out and now coated the floor of the truckbed with a thin, crunchy carpet.

To Delilah's right as she climbed in was a burlap sack with *Fertilizer* stenciled across the front, an enormous sack big enough to drape from one end of the bed to the other. It was full of something large, bulbous, as big as the girl herself. Next to that was a Stihl weed-trimmer with a well-gnawed line, encrusted with mulched grass and reeking of gasoline.

A gardener-man, then, Delilah thought, duck-walking over to the bale of pine needles and settling down beside it. *I wonder if he plants tulips?* She loved tulips, loved the light sweet smell of them.

"I'm going to find you," said Ginny from somewhere in front of the truck. It had been parked facing the apartment building, with the rear pointing at the dark street. Delilah could hear her new shoes clopping along the pavement as she skipped from car to car. "Ah-*ha!* . . . no, I guess not."

Delilah froze in place and slowed her breathing; inhaled . . . exhaled . . . inhaled . . . exhaled through her mouth. Her belly rose and fell under her *My Little Pony* t-shirt and she pinched the seams of her jeans, anticipating her discovery in the hot dark camper, studying the rough denim with her fingertips as she listened.

"Are you in here?" Ginny asked. She heard a car door open with a metallic crackle.

A couple of heartbeats passed. "Nope." The door slammed shut, *ker-tunk!*

Silence.

Delilah sat there in the gas-smelling dark, straining at the limit of her hearing, pine needles poking her through her jeans. She could hear the other girl doing something superficial, manipulating something with her hands.

"Over over *over!*" barked the radio.

She gasped and turned it off. Hopefully, Ginny didn't hear that. She slid an inch to her left as quietly as she could manage and pressed her shoulder and hip against the bristly straw bale.

Ginny sounded closer. She gave a surfer-like "Woah," and walked right up to the snake truck. "Check that out."

Delilah listened to her creep around the vehicle, taking in the entirety of the artwork. The girl trailed a hand down the side of the panel, starting at the gas cap and sliding down to the tail-light with susurrant hiss that sounded more snakelike than Delilah wanted to admit. She shifted to get away from a needle that was poking her in the butt and rested her feet against the burlap sack. Whatever was inside was solid but had a strange sort of give. Whatever it was, it wasn't fertilizer.

"Woah," Ginny said again, this time from the passenger side of the truck. She giggled. "Look at those boobies. She looks like Thor. Haha."

Delilah could hear her breathing even over her own. Ginny was a tall, Nordic little blonde girl that never had any trouble clearing her plate at dinner and stayed stocky and moon-faced even though she was an active kid and played kickball. Delilah could see Ginny in her mind's eye, swiping a wispy lock of hair out of her big pink grinning face.

A voice called from the apartment building. Ginny's mother. "Regina! Time to come in!"

Ginny sighed. "Okay, mama," she called back. She walked away. Delilah thought about popping out to surprise her, but realized that she

58

could re-use this spot for next time. Why ruin it now? "Okay, Lilah! You can come out now!" shouted Ginny. "I have to go back in!"

Delilah stayed quiet, took a deep breath and let it out slowly. Then it hit her: she really *was* a ninja! She had gone undetected. She was a stealth master. She was Jackie Chan, Zhang Ziyi, Jet Li, Michelle Yeoh, all rolled into one. She got up off the floor of the bed and crouched there in the womblike red shadow, striking a kung-fu pose. "Kyah," she whispered spirit-shouts to herself. "Wishaw. Eeyah!"

She threw a punch, and then another with the other hand, then tried to kick but the low ceiling didn't give her enough room to maintain her center of balance, so she fell back on her butt. She caught herself with her hands, raking the inside of her forearm down the rock-chipped edge of the weed-trimmer head. "Ouch!"

Her hand was on some angular object inside the burlap bag. It was flat on one side.

She raised her arm into the light and examined it; the trimmer hadn't broken the skin but there was a four-inch red welt that throbbed and smarted. She hugged it to her belly and groaned. Tugging back the rim of the burlap sack, Delilah saw a New Balance tennis shoe.

The great cogs of time ground to a halt. Even the forest full of cicadas silenced themselves, though not all at once—they dwindled to three or four and then one buzzing razz that tapered off into nothing. All thought of kung-fu and ninjas and Michelle Yeoh fled her mind. She was a seven-year-old girl again, bewildered and vulnerable and alone.

Fear didn't quite enter into it, at least not yet. Right then she had rationed off some part of logic that told her the bag was full of old hand-me-down shoes; maybe a load of clothes destined for the Goodwill store. Perhaps the owner of the truck was a good-hearted man that collected old giveaways for the church and took them to the consignment store.

She pressed her fingertips against the burlap sack again and felt another shoe inside. Good. It was a bag of shoes. A big bag of shoes for the church. She relaxed and peeled the bag open a little bit more.

Wrapped in a striped sock, a skinny ankle protruded from the mouth of the shoe. It was slender and hairless, pale. A tiny pink scar at the top of the calf.

Delilah's mouth moved, but nothing came out. If something had come from her mouth, it would have been "Mama. Mama. Mama." over and over again, but for some reason her voice-box didn't want to work, the wind wouldn't catch the guitar strings, her throat wouldn't respond. She just kept mouthing the word over and over again.

Her legs didn't want to work either. She wanted to get out of the truck, to crawl over to the sash and push it open, throw herself out of the camper shell, and run home. But she couldn't quite wrap her mind around the sight of seeing a little boy's legs poking out of a fertilizer bag in the back of a stranger's truck, and it was the confusion that kept her frozen.

Instead of directing her feet to propel her outside, her brain could only spin in place, trying to reconcile one with the other, tires in deep mud.

She touched the leg. It was cold. Dead cold.

This was incorrect. It didn't make sense. People didn't die like this. People died in hospitals at a ripe old age and other people cried over them at Lane Funeral Home in town, people in cheap gray suits and Stan Lee bifocals. They were buried in cemeteries with wreaths of flowers and pretty headstones with carvings of angels and animals, their names and the day they died. *You don't walk on graves. That's rude, Miss Delilah Lee. Go round them.*

She knew it was stupid, knew it was an idiot thing to say, but she pressed her hands into the burlap again. "Are you okay in there?" The words came out wrong; strangled, wet. She touched her own face and realized she was crying. "Boy? Are you oh—are you okay?"

She took the edge of the sack opening in both hands and pulled it up, up, up, past the boy's knees. He was wearing a pair of black gym shorts. She would have kept going but the trailing edge of the opening was caught on the toe of his shoe.

With a reverential respect, Delilah pulled the bag back down, covering the boy's legs. She started sobbing outright. The inside of the camper swam in red chaos, a hot-box full of blood, and she went for the back sash. Halfway there, she snagged her foot in the weed-trimmer's forward handle and went to her hands and knees on the pine straw.

The needles pricked at her palms and legs. "Oooun," she sobbed, and dragged her feet through the straw. She reached up for the sash handle and found nothing but a round hole where the handle once was.

For the second time in as many minutes, the world ceased to color inside the lines. Delilah's damp hand swept back and forth across the middle of the sash, looking for the handle, but it wasn't there. It had been removed, and the only thing marking its prior presence was a round hole in the sash frame.

Inside, she could see the mechanism that operated the latch but there was no handle to turn it. She stuck her finger in and searched the hole, but she couldn't figure out how to move the parts.

In the cab of the snake truck, someone sat up in the passenger seat.

The shadow of a grown man tilted into view through the rear cab window as Delilah watched. She became moveless and silent, unwilling to give herself away, a fawn in the grass. The man fetched a heavy sigh and unlatched the rear window, sliding it open. The pane slid maddeningly slow, catching twice on the way. He shook it and pulled it until it wedged to a stop on the far side.

He twisted in the seat and peered inside, a silhouette crowned with a shock of fiery copper hair. She couldn't quite see his face, but his head was big. He had the affect of a pit viper, with a wide-set jaw and narrow throat.

60

"Hey there," said the man. His voice was dry and high, like sandpaper, like the scraping of sandstone vaults.

Delilah said nothing.

"I know you're back there, your friend woke me up looking for you."

Delilah's burning eyes refused to blink. She was afraid to take her eyes off of the wide-headed shadow in the front seat. Snot crept down her upper lip.

"What's your name?"

Nothing.

"Not talkin, huh? I can dig it. Stranger danger," he said, emphasizing the phrase with a brief jazz-hand. "Smart. Y'know, when I was your age, I was the king of hide-and-seek. Nobody could find me. I knew where all the best hiding places were. That's why my friends used to call me Snake when I was a kid—cause I could wriggle into the littlest places."

"Liah," said the girl. She hunkered against the tailgate, shivering beyond hope of control.

"Hmm?"

"My name is Delilah."

"Delilah," said the man. "That's a pretty name. But yeah, hey. Maybe I can teach you a few things about hiding, huh? You don't want to jump in the back of a crazy-lookin truck like this one. Y'know? This is a bad place."

He put a zip-tie between his lips and let it dangle there, as if it were a wheat-straw in a cowboy's mouth. Delilah thought it looked like a snake's tongue. "I can show you where to hide where no one will ever, *ever* find you."

Deet-deet. The stillness was broken by an electronic alarm.

The snake-man took a phone out of his pocket and studied it, the screen illuminating his face. His nose was pointed, his nostrils wide, his eyes thin and somehow both clever and stupid at once. As he read the message, his cruel slash of a mouth formed silent words.

"Goddammit. Looks like I've got somewhere to be. No rest for the wicked, huh?" His eyes flashed up to Delilah and he got out of the truck.

The back window opened with a thump and a creak, and the Serpent scowled in at the little girl. "Out of the truck, princess," he said, jerking a thumb over his shoulder. "The game's been called on account of rain."

It wasn't raining, but Delilah didn't care. She just wanted out of that truck. She clambered over the tailgate and stumbled onto the pavement.

Leaning over her, the snake-man pointed at her nose with one long, gnarly finger. "Run on home, honey. And if you tell anybody I was here, well…I know where you live. And I promise you, you *don't* want to play the game we'll play if I have to come back."

Delilah stared at his rugged, weaselly face.

"Do you understand me?"

Words bubbled up her throat, but refused to come out, as if they were too big for her mouth, all crowding at the top of her lungs like a rush of people trying to get away from a fire.

He reached out and caressed her cheek, fingertips like rough wood brushing her temple. Then they clamped down on the outer rim of her ear and he shook her with it. Pain streaked down that side of her neck.

"Do-you-under*stand*-me?"

"Oww," Delilah replied, her face twisting up. Tears sprung to her eyes. She nodded, nodded again. "Eeyeahhh!"

The snake-truck man let go. "Good. Now run along."

He didn't have to tell her twice, but at first she had trouble making her legs work, as if they were put on backward and she had to relearn how to walk—and then everything clicked and she turned and bolted over the sidewalk for the safety of her own lawn.

Wet grass crunched under her feet and she slipped and fell with that funny *rrrrt!* wet-rubber croak, landing on her belly with one arm folded underneath.

The shock and indignity was what broke her composure, and she cried in earnest, big quivering tears running down her cheeks. Green skidmarks stained the front of her clothes and the palms of her hands.

Getting back into his truck, the Serpent regarded her with those tiny, venomous eyes.

"Stay outta strangers' cars, kid. You'll live longer."

FRIDAY

Six

SINCE THERE WERE NO curtains or shades in the cupola, the sun pre-empted Wayne's alarm clock. Exhaling faint white vapors, he sat up to discover one of the most beautiful sunrises he'd ever seen in his life. A majesty of royal-purple and orange-gold rippled throughout the eastern sky, an explosion of color and light.

The bedroom was cold, surprisingly so. Wind pressed against the north side of the cupola, making the windowpanes crackle subtly in their frames. Wayne pushed back the covers and ground the heels of his hands into his eyes, stretching like a cat. He was trembling by the time he got his clothes dug out of one of the boxes.

"It's freezing up there," he told his dad as he came down, his shoelaces dragging on the floor. He flinched at the cold chain of his necklace as he kissed his mom's wedding band and slipped it into his shirt.

Leon was brushing his teeth, hugging himself in front of the bathroom mirror. He wore only a pair of sweat-pants. "You're a Chicago kid, and you wanna complain about the cold?" he asked, and spat a mouthful of foam into the sink. "Be glad it ain't snowing. Hell, this is mild compared to what I grew up with."

"I know, I know." Wayne tromped downstairs. "Barefoot in the snow, uphill both ways, blah blah."

"Tie your shoes before you fall and bust your face," said Leon's voice from the top of the staircase. "You don't wanna start your first day in a new school with a broke nose, do you?"

"I thought chicks dig scars."

Breakfast was a bowl of cereal and buttered toast. Wayne was still licking his lips and burping up Lucky Charms as he went out to stand by the mailbox and wait for the school bus.

According to Pete Maynard, the bus ran at seven, but it was six-fifty and he didn't see Pete in the small gaggle of children standing on the other side of the road. Two girls, two boys, all of them but one younger than Wayne. The oldest was a tall teenager in a parachute windbreaker, her straight mousy hair lying curtain-limp down her cheeks.

As he approached them, they stopped chattering at each other and fell quiet.

"Hi," he said to them, kneeling to tie his shoes.

At first they didn't respond, but then the tall girl said "Hi," and rapped a knuckle on one of the boys' chest. "Say hi. It's nice to do that."

"Hi," said the boy.

The others glanced at him and chimed in with their own morose greetings.

Wayne tried to think of something else to say.

"You're the one that moved into the haunted house," said one of the boys.

Wayne twisted around to look at the Victorian, and back to them. His puffy jacket hissed and huffed with every movement in the still morning air. "I *did* come out of it, yeah."

The tall girl backhanded the boy in the chest.

"Ow. Why you do dat?"

"That's rude, Evan," she said. She shrugged in a sulky, downcast way. "I'm sorry. My name's Amanda." She poked the two boys in the temple with her fingertips in turn, pushing their heads. "This is Kasey, and this is Evan. They're my brothers and they're both shit heads. The little girl is Katie Fryhover. She lives in the trailer behind us with her grandmama and their dog Champ."

"My name is Wayne. Wayne Parkin. We just moved here from Chicago."

"Amanda—"

"Hugginkiss," said Evan.

Amanda belted him again. "Shut *up*. My name is not Amanda Hugginkiss. It's Amanda Johnson. *God.*"

"Have you seen any ghostses?" asked little Katie Fryhover. Her upper lip glistened with snot and one of her front teeth was missing.

"I ate breakfast with one," said Wayne, becoming aware of the cold wedding band lying on his chest. The kids' eyes bugged out of their heads in shock. He instinctively reached up to rub the ring through his shirt. "I eat breakfast with a ghost *every* morning."

"Woooaaah," Evan and Kasey Johnson cooed in unison.

Amanda regarded him warily.

"Really?" asked Katie.

"Yup." Wayne smiled. "My dad and me leave a place for her at the kitchen table. Nobody ever sits there except her." The reverent, mild way he said it had a chilling effect on the kids' excitement, and they fell quiet.

A door slapped shut somewhere in the trailer park, and Pete came huffing and puffing up the gravel drive to join them at the road. He was pulling on a jacket as he went, trading a Pop-Tart from hand to hand, and when he reached them he was still fighting with it, one arm hiked up behind his back.

"Goddammit!" he fussed, the Pop-Tart in his mouth. The kids laughed. Pete accidentally bit through the Pop-Tart in frustration and tried to catch it with his free hand, but he slapped it into the culvert. He chewed in anger, the boys laughing even harder. "Are you even *for real* right now?"

Amanda giggled into her hand. "I'm sure it's not the first one you had."

"I just hate to waste food." Pete wrenched the jacket on, popping stitches. His shirt was pulled up, revealing his pale belly and a deep navel smiling under a roll of fat. He hauled it down over his stomach and blew a stream of vapor. "Morning, Bruce Wayne. How was your first night in the House of a Thousand Corpses?"

"It was okay. I only saw a few corpses, though. Nothing special." One corner of Wayne's mouth came up in a smirk. "Nothing like they said it would be in the commercials."

"Not as advertised, huh? That sucks." Pete came across the road to give him a good-natured slap on the back.

The distant snore of the school bus groaned somewhere in the trees, and Amanda and the kids came over to stand on Wayne's side of the road. He knew they were only positioning themselves on the passenger side of the bus to make it easier to climb aboard, but seeing them cross the road and stand beside him felt as if it signified some measure of solidarity, as if they'd accepted him as one of their own, and he let himself believe it was.

A car door clapped shut behind him and they moved out of the way so Wayne's dad could back out of the drive.

The Subaru hooked into the road and Leon paused, rolling his window down. "Have a good day at school," he said, turning the radio off. "If you need me, you know how to get me."

The bulge of Wayne's cellphone lay against his chest inside an inner jacket pocket, next to Mom's wedding ring. "Yep. Have a good day, Dad." The phone was a cheapo crap phone half his own age, didn't have any apps or games other than a measly pinball game and some kind of game where you made a rabbit jump around and eat carrots, but he could make calls on it and text Leon's number.

The school bus came wheezing up the road toward them. Leon pointed at the kids and said, "Stay frosty, compadres," driving away.

Wayne rolled his eyes.

They filed onto the bus, a creaky-drafty thing already teeming with noisy kids. As they sorted themselves into the elephant-skin seats, Wayne gazed out the window. Black wings swooped out of the treeline and a crow landed in the grass by the roadside.

Picking up the remainder of Pete's Pop-Tart with its beak, the bird struggled back into the air and flew away.

After spending his childhood thus far in Chicago, Wayne found King Hill Elementary School almost *too* quiet, funereal in its own country-bumpkin way. The lunchroom burbled with sleepy conversation, puffy-eyed kids mumbling to each other and nuzzling into the crooks of their elbows, trying to catch a few more minutes of shut-eye before the day started.

Most of them were white, he noticed as he and Pete came shuffling in twenty minutes before the bell.

He'd sort of expected that. There were almost no Mexicans at all, not a single Asian, and the handful of black kids he saw were all several years older, a band of gangly teenagers clustered together in a tight group in the corner, slumped against the wall and fighting sleep like a roost full of pigeons. Four of them were wearing King Hill football jerseys.

Lawrence had taught him to stick to the lakes he was used to, as TLC so eloquently put it. The scrawny, bespectacled boy stayed close to Pete.

To his surprise and relief, the morning went smoothly. When he had to stand up in front of homeroom class and introduce himself to everybody, something he'd been dreading since the drive down, everyone chanted, "Hi Wayne," and except for a few half-hearted Batman and cowboy jokes, that was it.

The classwork was easy compared to what he'd been doing back home—almost a year backward in terms of academic progress. It gave him the feeling of having accidentally been enrolled in special education classes, or he'd somehow stepped into a timewarp that forced him to re-live the previous year over again.

Oh well, Wayne thought, *that just puts me a year ahead of the other kids. I can coast through and blast all the tests.*

Another thing he didn't expect was the claustrophobic closeness of the smaller school population—none of the classes exceeded twenty-five children, and a few of them had under fifteen.

Each period had a strangely informal, floaty atmosphere, as if a bunch of people had decided to congregate in one place for an hour and listen to somebody talk. Instead of sulking menacingly at the head of an unruly class, the teachers turned out to be friendly, engaging, and upbeat.

Huge picture windows down the side of each classroom were full of bright sunlight, and instead of being enclosed in the darkness of Chicago's monolithic buildings he could see swishing treetops, but the desks framed him in broad polo-shirted backs and the faint baby-formula body odor of the congenitally rural Caucasian.

Several of the boys showed up in honest-to-God bib overalls and smelled like rotting compost. Wayne felt like he'd moved into an Amish village. Some part of him kept expecting to spot a butter churn in the corner, or for a chicken to wander into a classroom in the middle of a lesson.

He was dismayed to find that no one would really talk to him except for Pete and Pete's friend Johnny Juan. The white kids were cordial but standoffish, as if Wayne were a ghost that was only physically solid and present when someone was forced to interact with him. The rest of the time he was invisible.

"So what do your mom and dad do, Wayne?" asked Johnny at lunch, spooning chili into his mouth one bean at a time.

"Johnny" Juan Ferrera was a skinny Middle American kid that, according to Pete, had moved up from Florida the previous year. Juan and his extended family lived in one of the more urban neighborhoods on the southeast end of town, where several of his relatives worked at the Mount Weynon textile factory and the Mexican restaurant on the south end of town near the college.

Pete had gone to Johnny's place once for a birthday sleepover. According to what Wayne was told, Johnny Juan had the newest Xbox and possessed more Legos than Pete had ever seen in one place in his life, but Johnny and his brother slept on the floor in sleeping bags because his grandparents slept in his bed.

"My dad teaches Literature. He's working at Blackfield High School." Wayne took out the ring hanging in his shirt and stuck his finger through it, rubbing the rough engraving around the inside. The meditative gesture was always soothing. "My mom...she died a few years ago."

Johnny Juan paused for a brief moment to watch Wayne stare into his chili, then scratched his head and went back to eating. A tray clattered onto the table and a girl plopped into a seat between them.

"Howdy, kids," said Amanda Johnson.

Pete looked up from his shredded cinnamon roll. "How's it hangin, dude."

She leveled a glare at him and picked at her food with a spoon, demurely folding and folding her chili if it were expensive lobster bisque. Amanda had wide-set blue eyes and an upturned nose that gave her the affect of a big pink bat. Up close, Wayne could see the shotgun-spatter of acne in the middle of her forehead that she'd covered with makeup.

"What're *you* looking at?" Amanda asked mildly.

Wayne shrugged and went back to eating. His cellphone hummed inside his jacket. A text message from his father. **you wanna ride bus home or me pick u up?**

"So have you kids heard the rumors?" Amanda asked them with the panache of a campfire story. "Apparently there's a killer in town."

Johnny Juan sniffed his milk. "Where'd you hear *that?*"

Tap, tap tap, Wayne sent his father a text in reply: **i guess pick me up**

"Day before yesterday, Jeff Beesler's dog brought home a bone that looked like it came from a human." Amanda's explanation became

68

condescending. "You *know* who Jeff Beesler is, don't you? He's that kid in eighth grade that plays football. I've known him *all* this year. He likes—"

Johnny Juan broke in. "No way."

"Bullshit," said Pete. "What kind of bone was it?"

The girl winced in annoyance at being interrupted. "How should *I* know, do I look like a bone scientist to you? They said it was a piece of a spine. Jeff gave it to the police and they sent it to the GBI Crime Lab in Summerville."

"Man, that's bullshit," reiterated Pete. "Nobody's gonna kill you. It's probably a bone from like a dead deer, or, or something." He gestured with the ice cream sandwich he was eating. "I ain't afraid of no killer. I know how to get home quick and super-ninja, man. Ain't no killer can catch us where I go."

Wayne looked up from his phone. "For real?"

"Yeah. It takes a little bit longer than the bus, but I'm pretty sure I'm the only person that knows about it. Or, at least, the only person that uses it. I know this town like the back of this hand." Pete splayed his thick paw out on the table and played at stabbing between his fingers with his fork. *Thunk...thunk...thunk.* "We should go my way when we go home from school today. You gonna go with me, or are ya chicken?"

"Man, that crap don't work on me." Tap, tap tap.

can i walk home with pete?

Pete tucked his stubby hands into his pudgy armpits and made slow wing-beating gestures with his elbows. His grim face made the Funky Chicken all the more imperative. "Is that so? ...Buckok. ...Buckok."

are u crazy? thats too far.

"If you're scared, I'll even go with you two." Amanda, leaning close. Her spackled-over acne looked like stucco at this range. "As a chaperone, of course. Are you scared? It's okay if you are."

"Cause you're just a wittle guy," said Pete. "Hey, nerd, get off your phone. We're tryin to peer-pressure you."

Pete knows shortcuts. well be home in no time. Johnny leaned into the conversation. "Hey, *I'll* go with you. *I'm* not scared."

No.

"You don't even live out that way," said Amanda. "How are you gonna get home?"

"My uncle can come get me. He works first shift, he gets off at like five." Johnny tossed a shoulder dismissively. "Besides, it's not like they're gonna miss me. They don't even know I'm there half the time. And it's Friday anyway. I don't have anywhere to be until church Sunday morning."

you said to make frends dad. this me makin friends.

There was no answer from the elder Parkin. The lunchroom monitor—a seventh-grade homeroom teacher named Mrs. Janice—started to corral all the children, going by how long they'd been eating, and Wayne shuffled into line with the other kids to leave. He was in the middle of an argument with Pete over the comparative tensile strength of Batman's skyhook and Spider-Man's webbing when the cellphone in his pocket vibrated.

alright. but u go straight home. lock al doors. gota work l8 anyway. b home soon.

"Your dad spells like crap for a Literature teacher," said Pete, peering over his shoulder. "Looks like we're walking home."

Seven

MIGUEL'S PIZZA TEEMED WITH the lunch-time crowd, out-of-towners and locals both trying to get in their climbs before the weather turned. Robin was forced to take her pizza and Macbook out back to the patio, a large conglomeration of trestle tables under an aluminum awning. It was airy and clammy, but she sat at the end of the enclosure where warm sun fell on her and it could have been August again.

She was halfway through a chicken salad when Kenway Griffin appeared and sat across from her with a meatball sandwich and a bottle of local brew. In light of last night's revelation, she was impressed by the ease with which he moved on his false leg—if he hadn't told her, she wouldn't have even guessed.

"Good morning," he said, blowing on his sandwich.

Robin peered at the clock on her Macbook. The sun felt good, but made it a little hard to see fine details on her screen. "It's noon."

"Well, morning for me. I don't sleep well and I tend to get up late." He crammed the end of the sub in his mouth and bit through the crusty bread with a crunch, talking with his mouth full. "I haven't eaten actual breakfast in years. Unless you count lunch as breakfast."

"I'm sure there's a word in German for that."

"Brunch?"

"That's not German. Besides, 'brunch' is what comes between breakfast and lunch."

"*Sprechen ze brunch?*"

She shook her head, smirking. "So what are you doing out here, anyway? Don't you have things to see, pictures to paint?"

"Today's my day off."

"Is that so?"

He washed the sandwich down with a sip of beer. "Yup."

"You're off every Friday?"

"I'm off when I *say* I'm off. That's the nice thing about being a freelance artist."

71

"Artiste."

"No, just an artist. I haven't reached *artiste*-level proficiency yet, I don't think." A floppy pickle-spear wagged in his hand. He took a bite out of it and pointed with the stump. "So what are you up to?"

"Editing yesterday's footage."

"You never did tell me what your YouTube videos are about."

Robin paused, leaning back to brush imaginary crumbs off of her jeans, stalling for time. She took a deep breath and blew it across the keyboard. Finally she said, "If I tell you, do you promise not to laugh or think I'm crazy?"

For a second she thought he was going to say, 'I already think you're crazy,' but all he said was, "I promise."

"I hunt witches," she said, saving the footage progress and opening a browser window. "And I videotape it for the internet." She clicked the bookmark for her channel and hunted through the video thumbnails as if she were rifling through a filing cabinet. "I monetize the videos with ads and sell T-shirts and things like that."

She pulled up a video she'd done and turned the computer around so he could watch it. "Neva Chandler. My first solo witch."

According to the upload date on the page, the Robin in the video was a couple years younger, sitting in the cab of her CONLIN PLUMBING van. In one hand was a baby-food jar full of water. In the other was a dagger, silver and glittering in the rusty glow of the streetlight outside. The camera sat on the dash, recording her half-shadowed face as she spoke. "I've been tracking her for weeks," said the Robin in the video, punctuating *weeks* with the point of the dagger.

Back in those days, she actually had hair, silky black hair in a Russian-burlesque-girl bob. But instead of Uma Thurman from *Pulp Fiction,* she looked more like preteen Natalie Portman in *The Professional,* tiny and delicate.

"Looking for all the signs. Missing pets. Unusually lucky lottery plays. An over-population of cats. Weird accidents. And all that shit I told you about, you know, in that video about runes and witchcraft paraphernalia." Past-Robin tucked the water-jar into a jacket pocket and picked up the camera, aiming it out the window. "I've been hunting down all the runes in Alabama that I can find, and here, in Birmingham, they've started to converge. There are more here than anywhere else in the state.

"Like I told you, they always live in 'the bad part of town'. But I don't think they choose to live there. I think it's shitty *because* they live in it.

"They suck the goodness out of it, they *eat the pride,* they devour the *heart* of the neighborhood until the people don't care about anything anymore. There's just drugs and poverty and garbage. And then when there's nothing left, the witch packs up and moves somewhere else. Like psychic vampires, or something. Tapeworms in the intestines of the world.

"If you've got any doubt about what I'm doing, you've got to get this in your head right now: they're not Wiccans or hippies, they're not those chicks from *The Craft,* they're not Sabrina or the lady from *Bewitched.* These bitches are the real deal. Lieutenants of Hell on a vacation to Earth. Soul-sucking hag-beasts."

Across the street from the van was a board fence. Someone had spraypainted incomprehensible graffiti on it—could have been an ambigram for all she knew, legible upside-down as well as rightside-up. "A lot of times they'll hide the runes in the graffiti. Check out that sideways Jesus-fish in the middle—see how it's a different color than the rest of it?"

Past-Robin's arm thrust into the shot as she pointed at different parts of the graffiti with the dagger. The symbol she indicated appeared to be a simple diamond-shape that crossed at the bottom to make the tailfins of a skyward-facing trout.

"This is what I'm talking about. That's not an English letter, that's a rune. It means *home,* or *homelands.* It's there to let you know you're in a witch's territory. And you see that little crown on top of it? That means there's a witch living somewhere on this block." Past-Robin turned the camera around and put it on the dash again.

Kenway picked up his sandwich and went back to eating it, but his eyes were locked on the Macbook's screen as he chewed.

"The runes, they're there to help them find each other. I mean, there are seven billion people on this planet, even with the internet—which a lot of them don't use—it's not easy. And the taggers don't even know they're doing it, either. The witches, they...I don't know, they *influence* them somehow, it's like they send out a radio signal that the kids can't help but catch. Like queen bees.

"Maybe it's...Hell, I don't know. But whatever it is, it needs to stop." Then-Robin opened the door and got out of the van, slipping the silver dagger into a sheath hidden in the lining of her jacket.

Taking a pull off his beer bottle, Kenway worried at the edge of the table with his thumb. "Intense. You say you do this for a living?"

"Yep." Robin leaned over the table, resting her chin on her folded arms, looking up at him. "For a few years now. I have a little over four million subscribers."

Kenway's eyebrows jumped.

He sipped from the beer again and set it next to her elbow. "Wow. That's a hell of an audience."

Past-Robin was stalking across the night-dark street on the Macbook's screen, clutching the dagger and water-jar inside her jacket. The witch-hunter approached the board fence and rounded the corner, holding the camera up so that it could see into the front yard of a run-down tract house.

Overgrown grass around a lemon tree, shadowy front porch with no porch light. A rocking chair lurked in the gloom.

"It's probably rude to ask, but I'm dyin to know," said Kenway, and he burped into his fist. "What kind of money do you make doing this? YouTube videos, I mean. It *can't* be enough to pay bills, much less car

73

insurance. It's why you're living in the van, right? You know, other than the fact that you travel around to shoot this stuff."

"You wouldn't believe me if I told you."

"Try me."

The Robin in the video crept up the front walk of the tract house. *Hoo, hoo, hu-hu.* Halfway across the yard, she paused and slowly turned to point the camera up into the branches of the lemon tree, the aperture whirring as she zoomed in on it. A snowy owl perched in the hatchmark master-work of shadows some eight feet up, throat pulsing, *hoo, hoo, hu-hu.*

Present-day Robin sitting at the table sighed and mumbled, "A little under three hundred. …A day."

"Three? What—" Kenway's brain seemed to slip gears, and he leaned forward, gripping the table with both hands as he groped for words. "Three hundred dollars a *day?*"

She nodded, blushing.

"Are you *kidding* me? I didn't even see that kind of money in *Iraq.* I don't think *any* enlisted soldier ever has in the *history of modern warfare.*" He did the math in his head, staring up at the ceiling as if God could help him. "Eighty-three-hundred a month. Uhh. …That's about a hundred grand a year."

Robin looked away and coughed, then dug in her salad and pushed a forkful of it into her mouth as if she could chew the math up and swallow it.

She felt about three inches tall. She wished she *was* so she could climb into her salad bowl and hide under the lettuce. Her breakfast turned to bitter grass in her mouth, the Ranch saline and sour.

Kenway's forehead wrinkled and his eyes searched the table. He glanced up at her and paused the video. "You make six figures pretending to kill witches on the internet?" Luckily they were alone on the patio. A brisk wind leapt the fence and ran under the trestle tables, chilling her through her thin sweater.

"Yes," she said, chewing, thoroughly embarrassed.

"Holy god*damn.*" Today he was wearing a blue-plaid sort of Western shirt, with curlicues across the chest. Kenway rolled up his sleeves to reveal the tattoos running up his arms. In the sunlight she could finally make them out: robed Japanese samurai battling each other in a froth of hibiscus flowers and green leaves, katanas raised, screaming silently forever.

Graceful red foxes darted in and out of the scenes on his arms. "I mean, god, *damn.*" He pressed his palms against the edge of the table as if he were going to push away. "Sitting on a secret like *that,* you didn't have anything to worry about, you know," —he drew cursive in the air with his finger at her— "with the shrink thing. I don't think you've…."

She ate her salad quietly, not knowing what else to say.

Kenway seemed to deflate. "I'm sorry, it's just—" A cloud passed across his face. "—a lot to take in, you know?"

74

"I understand."

"Well, hey, at least you know I'm not interested in you for your money," he lilted. "I liked you even *before* I knew."

Robin nodded, staring down into her food.

"What I meant was, what I was saying, with that kind of a nest egg, it's not like you've really got to worry about what anybody thinks of you." Kenway rubbed his face and picked up his sandwich. "I don't know, I mean, you're sort of 'above the fracas', you know what I'm saying? Above reproach." He took a big bite of the sandwich and stared at the wall, chewing, and said, a little quietly, "Hell, out of my *league*, maybe."

A cold shock ran down the middle of her chest.

"*No*, not at all," she told him, not meeting his eyes. "Money doesn't make me better than *anybody*. It doesn't make *anybody* better than anybody else. Besides...I've only just now gotten to that point recently, viewer-wise. It's taken a lot of scrimping and saving to get to this level. I haven't technically made that kind of money yet. And I won't unless I keep swimming." She pointed at the Macbook with her fork. "The videos are passive income, but only so many people can watch them so many times, and if you don't keep producing content you'll start losing subscribers. So it's kinda like being a shark: you have to keep swimming if you want to survive. It's a lot like being an author, I think."

Kenway regarded her thoughtfully for a moment, not saying anything, and then pressed the Play button on the video with his pinky finger. The camera zoomed out as the hoot-owl took flight and left the screen stage-right. Video-Robin turned to watch it dwindle into the night sky.

"Hello, dear," croaked a subtle voice.

Video-Robin whirled around and the world whipped to the left, revealing the front of the white tract house and its shadowy porch, arrayed with boxes of junk, chairs, yellowed and fraying newspaper. A tribunal of cats sat on their haunches all over the porch, fifteen or twenty of them: calico, tortoise-shell tabbies, midnight-blacks, two Siamese, an orange Morris with brilliant green eyes.

Someone stood behind the screen door, a smear of gray a shade lighter than the darkness inside the house.

At the top of the faint figure was the gnarled suggestion of a face. "What brings you round at this time of night, young lady?" asked the old woman, her voice kind but deliberate, with a hint of accent. British? Irish? Whatever it was, it wasn't midwestern or southern.

The motionless cats reflected the streetlight with their lantern-green eyes. Video-Robin threw a thumb over her shoulder. "Ah, my car broke down. I...I was hoping I could use your phone."

"Ah." Neva Chandler paused. Kenway thought he could see her folding her arms, but it was hard to tell. She might have been wearing a pink bathrobe. "I thought *all* you young ladies these days carried those—

75

those cellular phones, they call them. With their tender apps and GPS-voices. Go here, go there, and soforth."

"No ma'am," replied Video-Robin. "I'm kinda old-school that way I guess."

Chandler scoffed. "Old-school."

"Yes, ma'am."

"Well...if you're going to come in, it would behoove you to do so, and get clear of the street," the old woman said in a warning way, even though Robin was fully in her front yard by now. "It's a dangerous place for dangerous people." The short set of stairs leading up to the porch were made of concrete covered in a coat of flaking gray paint, and it turned out the porch itself was as well. Columns of wrought-iron curlicues held up the roof. At Robin's feet was a china bowl with a few pebbles of dry cat-food.

"Yes, ma'am."

Stepping up onto the porch, video-Robin tugged the screen door open with a furtive hand.

The old woman behind the mesh faded into the darkness like a deep-sea creature and Robin stepped in behind her, filling the video window with black.

Click-click. A dingy bulb in an end-table lamp burst to life, brightening a living room positively crowded with antiques. A grandfather clock stood next to an orange-and-brown tweed sofa, its tiny black arms indicating the time was a few minutes to midnight.

No less than three pianos filled one end of the room, two player and one baby grand, all covered in dust.

Four televisions of progressive evolution clustered on top of a wood-cabinet Magnavox, rabbit-ear antennae reaching over them for a signal no longer being broadcast.

The old woman's track-house looked like the 21st century equivalent of the rundown-shack-at-the-edge-of-the-village, the customary domicile of the medieval witch. Gangs of unlighted candles stood atop every surface, halfway melted into the saucers and teacups that held them. Lines of runic script decorated the windowsills and, apparently, the threshold of the front door between her feet.

Another cat sat on top of a piano, running its tongue down the length of one leg. Video-Robin let the screen door ease shut. "I'm so sorry to bother you this time of night."

The old woman shuffled over to a plush wingback chair and dropped herself into it, relaxing. She was indeed wearing a pink bathrobe, with steel-gray hair as dry as haystraw tumbling down the sides of her Yoda face. A whisper of mustache dusted her upper lip. She could have been a thousand years old if a day.

An old pressboard coffee table dominated the space in front of the sofa and armchair. Occupying the center of the table was a wooden bowl, and inside the bowl was a single pristine lemon.

"It's no bother at all, my dear," Chandler said, peering up at Robin with baggy, watery-red eyes. As she spoke, she flashed black gums and the pearlescent-brown teeth of a life-long smoker. "I'm usually up late. No bother at all."

The real Robin sitting behind the Macbook thought about how Chandler's house stank. She remembered the fog of funk like it was yesterday. Boiled cabbage, farts, cigarettes. Dead old things, burnt hair, burnt popcorn. Cat shit.

"The phone," wheezed the old woman in the video, curling a finger over the back of the chair, "is over in there, in the hallway, on the little hutch. Do you see it?"

"Yes," said video-Robin.

As the camera soared past the armchair and toward a doorway in the back of the furniture-crowded room, the Now-Robin sitting at the patio table explained, "Sometimes...when the witches have completely drained a neighborhood down to the bones and they've used it all up, all the— whatcha call it, the 'life', the soul, there's nothing left to move with. They can't migrate to a new town, they get stuck, and slowly wither away. They starve. They die from the inside out."

One shoulder came up as a chill of disgust grated through her guts, made her back tense up. "The deadness slowly makes its way to the outside. After a while they're just a rotten corpse in a living-human costume. Death masquerading as life."

"Jesus," said Kenway. He put down his sandwich and wiped the marinara off his fingers with a napkin.

Neva Chandler's telephone turned out to be a rotary phone. Video-Robin picked up the handset and pressed one of the cups against her ear, listening for a dialtone. She put it against the Go-Pro in her hand.

Nothing came from the earpiece but a muted ticking, as if she could hear the wind tugging at the lines outside.

"So what is a beautiful young lady like you doing in a trackless waste such as this? Can't be the usual. You're not around to buy drugs." The decrepit crone sat up, leaning over to pluck the lemon out of the bowl with one knobbly monkey-paw hand. "No, Robin dear, ohhh, you don't look like the others. You don't look like shit."

"No, ma'am, I don't do drugs." Video-Robin put the handset down and picked it up again, listening. "I'm from out of town, visiting a fr—"

Chandler's breathing came in phlegmy gasps and sighs, tidal and troubled. She sounded like she'd been running a marathon.

"—How did you know my name?"

"Oh, honey, bless your heart," said the crone, "I've been expecting you all day." She pricked the rind of the lemon with a thumbnail and peeled part of it away, revealing not the white-yellow flesh Robin had expected but the vital and fevered red of an internal organ.

Blue veins squirmed across the lemon-heart's surface in time to some eldritch beat. "It took you longer to get here than I expected. But then

Birmingham *is* rather Byzantine, isn't it? I remember when I was a child, when it was all gaslights and horse-drawn carts, the layout was so much simpler then."

The lemon had a *pulse*.

"What the hell," said Kenway, his mouth hanging open.

Lifting the lemon-heart to her widening mouth, Chandler bit into it, spritzing fine droplets of blood into the air.

Video-Robin put down the phone's handset. The chair and the woman sitting in it were facing away from her, so she couldn't actually see what was happening, but ferocious wet devouring-noises were coming from the other side, like wolves tearing into the belly of a dead elk.

More blood sprayed up, dotting the wallpaper, the lampshade.

The remains of the lemon's rind dangled from the crone's hand like a fresh scalp, bloody and pulpy. Red dripped on the filthy carpet.

"That was my last lemon," said Chandler, twisting slowly in the chair.

One twiggish hand slipped over the back, gripping the velvet and cherrywood. "I've been saving it for a special occasion, you know."

Rising, she stared Robin down, eyes that flashed with a red light deep inside. Her teeth were too many for her mouth, tiny canines, peg-like fangs. The wrinkles across the bloody map of her face had smoothed. Her schoolmarm hair had gone from cornsilk to black. She was ten, twenty years younger.

"You think you're the first to seek me?" asked the witch, her lips contorting over the bulge of teeth. "My trees are composted with the rot of a dozen *just like you.*"

She spidered over the chair, her pink bathrobe flagging over her humped back.

Past-Robin said "Shit!" and ran deeper into the house.

Darkness swallowed the camera, shredded by light coming in through the witch's windowblinds. The image went into hysterics as Robin pumped her arms, running through the house. Tripping over something, she went sprawling in a pile of what sounded like books. "God! *Aarrgh!*"

The witch came through the house after the girl, her bare feet thumping the carpet, then bumping against the linoleum, meat drumming against wood. "God won't save you. You'll not have *me*, little lady," gibbered Neva, invisible in the dark. "You'll not have *me*, you'll not have *me.*"

Past-Robin pushed through the back door of a kitchen, bursting out into a moon-lit back yard. Turning, stumbling, she aimed the camera at the house.

Shick, the sound of metal against leather.

The back door slapped open. Something came racing out, a wraith shrouded in stained terrycloth, the lemon-heart blood coursing down her chin and wasted xylophone chest—and then the old woman was gliding across the overgrown yard, reaching for her with those terrible scaly owl-hands.

"Hee hee hee heeeee!" cackled Chandler, instantly on her, shoving her into the weeds. Both went down in a heap and Robin lost the camera.

Whirling around, the video's perspective ended up sideways on the ground, peering through the grass, barely capturing the ensuing melee in one corner of the screen. Neva Chandler landed on top of Robin's belly cowgirl-style and raked at her face with those disgusting yellow nails, so deceptively sharp, and laughing, crowing in her harsh raven-rasp of a voice.

Even though Robin was fighting with everything she had, she couldn't push the old crone away. An astounding strength lingered in those decrepit bones. Tangling her fingers in the girl's hair, Chandler wrenched her head up and down, bouncing it uselessly against the grass.

Behind Miguel's Pizza, two years later, Robin tried to ignore the screaming coming from the video Kenway was watching.

Every sense-memory, every smell and pain, they all drifted in her mind like flotsam, always there, always accessible. Every time she watched one of her own videos, the sensations came rushing back.

In the Georgia sun, the faint scars on her arms gleamed pink.

"Get *off* me!" shrieked the Robin in the video in her tinny video-voice, thrusting the silvery dagger through the pink bathrobe and into the witch's ribs—*SHUK!*

Time seemed to pause as the fight stopped as suddenly as it had started. Chandler's arms were crooked back, her fingers clawed in a grotesque parody of some old Universal movie monster. Her face was twisted and altered by some strange paranormal force, her mouth impossibly open until it was a drooping coil of chin and teeth.

Black liquid like crude oil dribbled out around the blade of the dagger. The witch exhaled deep in her throat, a deathly deflating.

Video-Robin withdrew the dagger, releasing more of the black syrup. Then she plunged it deep into the old woman's chest again, *shuk*, and twice, and thrice, and four times, *shuk shuk shuk.*

With a shrieking snarl, *"Grrraaaaaagh!"* the witch leapt backward—propelled, more like, as if she'd been snatched away by some invisible hand—and scrambled to the safety of her back stoop, cowering like a cornered animal. A stew of red and black ran down her sloped chin and wattled neck.

"*Bitch!* That won't work!" she choked through a mouthful of ichor. Chandler had taken the dagger away, and now it glittered in one warped claw. "It'll take more than that to—"

Hands shaking, Robin produced the Gerber jar full of water and threw a fastball.

The jar went wide, whipping over the old woman's head, and shattered against the eaves, showering her with the contents. The witch flinched, blinking in confusion. "This isn't *The Wizard of Oz*, honey, I'm not going to melt. You were having more luck with the knife." She flourished the dagger as if she were conducting a symphony with it. "You want this Osdathregar back? *Come get it*, whore!"

Video-Robin reached into her jacket and whipped out a Zippo, the lid clinking open.

"Oh *shit*," said Kenway, leaning back. "Wait, I totally thought that was gonna be holy water in that jar or something. That's righteous."

"What have you got there?" demanded the witch. She sniffed the arm of her bathrobe and grimaced. "Oh *hell* no."

Alcohol.

Flick, a tiny flame licked up from the Zippo in Robin's hand, brightening the back yard.

"Get away from me!" the witch shrieked, trading the dagger to the other hand and flinging it overhand like a throwing-knife.

Robin recoiled. The blade skipped off the side of her collar inches from her throat.

Chandler turned and ripped the back door open, scrambling through. Robin snatched up the GoPro and followed, camera in one hand and lighter in the other. She caught the witch just inside the threshold, touching the Zippo's tongue to the edge of her bathrobe. The terrycloth caught instantly, lining the hem with a scribble of white light. It was enough to faintly illuminate the grimy kitchen.

"Oooooh!" screeched Chandler, tumbling to her hands and knees in the kitchen. "You nasty, nasty bitch! You whore! You *tramp!*"

The witch stood, using the counter as a ladder, and fumbled her way over to the sink, smearing black all over the cabinets. Raking dirty dishes out of the way, Chandler disturbed a cloud of fruit-flies and turned on the faucet. "When I get this put out, I'm going to—I'm going to—" She tugged and tugged the sprayer hose, trying to pull it out of the basin. "—Well I daresay don't *know* what I'll do, you naughty shit, but I guarantee you won't like it very much!"

Flames trickled up the tail of Chandler's bloody bathrobe, but they were going much too slowly for Robin's liking. She reached over and touched the fabric with the Zippo again.

This time the alcohol on Chandler's back erupted in a windy *burp* of white fire. "No! Stop!" said the witch, slapping her hand away. The flames billowed toward the ceiling, whispering and muttering.

As Robin went to ignite her sleeve, Chandler reached into the sink with her other hand and came up with a dirty carving knife. She hooked it at the girl, trying to stab her and spray herself with the sink hose at the same time.

Robin jerked away. The plastic nozzle showered the witch's head with cold water, soaking her hair and running down her face, washing away the blood and oil-slime. She maneuvered around, trying to spray the fire on her back, but all she could seem to manage was to half-drown herself and shoot water over her shoulder onto the floor.

"Help me!" cried Chandler, water arcing all over the kitchen. "Why would you do this to an old lady like me? *What have I ever done to yoooouuuuu?*"

Video-Robin flung the refrigerator door open. Condiment bottles and a stick of butter clattered to the floor at her feet. Reaching in, Robin grabbed the neck of a bottle of Grey Goose. The last fifth sloshed around in the bottom.

Chandler shoved the fridge door closed, almost on Robin's head. *"HELP ME!"* roared the slack-faced creature in the bathrobe. Her jaw had come unhinged, and two rows of tiny catlike teeth glistened wetly in the pit of her black maw. Her eyes were two yellow marbles, shining deep in bruise-green eye sockets. "HELP ME OR YOU'LL BURN *WITH* ME!"

Pressing her ragged stinking body against Robin's, Chandler wrapped her arms around the other's chest in a bear-hug.

Prickly, inhuman teeth brushed against the girl's collarbone.

Robin loosed an incoherent shriek and flailed, pushing and slapping at Chandler's shoulders and face. Those horrible teeth scratched at her hands and the witch craned forward, her great moray-eel mouth clapping shut at empty air.

Crash! Robin clubbed the hag across the forehead with the Grey Goose fifth, shattering the bottle. The liquor inside hit the flames and *exploded.*

"EEEEEEE!" the flaming figure keened, fully engulfed now and stumbling blindly around the kitchen, leaving little puddles and clues of fire all over the cabinets and the little dining table with the checkered Italian-cafe tablecloth. Stacks of old books on the table caught, the grimoires going up in a whoosh. Robin fell back, escaping to a hallway which would have been too dark to navigate if it hadn't been for the screaming bonfire.

"KILL HER," Chandler howled. *"KIIILL HERRR!"*

Robin ran down the hallway and came out behind a piano in the living room. She pushed the cat out of the way and slid over the top of the thing on her belly, plowing through a feathery coat of dust and cat hair. Struggling to her feet, she shoved through the screen door and ran out into the front yard.

A crowd of people had assembled in the street, thirty or forty neighbors in various states of undress. They stood stock-still and rigid, their hands dangling at their sides, staring at her, eyes shining green in the dark.

"Mrrrrrr," hummed a man in a hooded sweatshirt. *"Rrrrwww."*

Kenway was entranced by the action taking place on the screen. "What in the balls is even going on right now," he said, leaning over the Macbook, eyes fixed on the video. "Is he—is that guy growling like a house cat?"

"Her familiars," Robin told him, not looking up from her salad.

In the video, she juked left, running underneath the lemon tree and around the side of Chandler's tract house, between the board fence and the clapboard wall.

The pounding of sneakered feet made it clear that the familiars were chasing her. The fence ended near the back corner and Robin jumped the sidewalk, almost losing her footing, sprinting across the street. She opened the driver door of the CONLIN PLUMBING van and threw herself inside, wriggling into the seat.

Through the window she could see half the neighborhood pouring out of the gap behind the fence like hornets from a nest, and just as terrifying.

When she went to shut the door, she slammed it on the meaty arm of a fat man in an old Bulls jersey, the collar frayed around his hoary neck. "*Mrrrr!*" he growled. His eyes were green screwheads.

Her keys were already in the ignition. She twisted it until she thought she would snap it off in the steering column. The van chugged a few times and turned over mightily, *GRRRRUH!*

Crazed, yowling people clustered around the van and started hammering the panels with their fists, clawing at the windows and prying at the hood. Jersey Man's arm flapped into the cab with her, fighting her hands, and he found her throat with the fork of his palm, pressing it against her windpipe.

Her neck was pinned against the headrest. She couldn't breathe.

Thrusting her foot into the floorboard, she found the accelerator and put all her weight on it. The engine snarled, vibrating the van, revving hard, so hard that for a second she thought it would come apart, but nothing else happened.

"Fffffk," she choked out, fumbling for the gearshift.

The passenger window imploded in a tumble of glass and someone reached in at her.

Robin put the van in Drive and stood on the gas again. This time the machine leapt forward, catching hard and plowing low as if she was up to the headlights in water. The engine coughed once, twice, the drive-train rumbled, and then the crowd fell away and she was barreling down the street.

Bodies fell in the headlights and the van clambered over them, *bonk-badunk-clank-bang.*

She twisted the steering wheel this way and that, trying to shake off the two men halfway inside the cab with her, but only the one hanging out the window fell. The van hauled back and forth, teetering with the gravity of a Spanish galleon on the sea.

"Rrrrrowww!" complained Jersey Man, his fingers still clamping Robin's neck to the seat. She could feel her heartbeat in her face.

"Here, kitty-kitty."

She jerked the wheel to the left and sideswiped a telephone pole.

The wooden trunk slammed into the man's shoulder and knocked him off, his fingernails biting into the skin under her ear. Her tires barked and wailed as Robin fought to keep the van under control. The telephone pole scraped down the side of the vehicle, beating on the hollow panels with a noise like thunder.

She glanced at the side mirror. Two dozen men and women were running helter-skelter down the street behind her, looking for all the world like a midnight marathon.

She did not stop. She did not slow down. She drove on.

When the camera cut to a new shot the sun had come up, turning the sky a sickly dawn gray. A firetruck's silent flasher strobed red across the side of Neva Chandler's house, or at least what was left of it. Wet black pikes jutted up from shards of siding and electrical conduits. Robin crept into the back yard and lifted the silver dagger from the weeds, retreating to her van.

"Good work," said a voice from the back.

The video ended and became a grid of links to related videos. Kenway clicked the link at the bottom that took him back to the main *MalusDomestica* page and then clicked through to the list of Robin's video thumbnails.

There were *at least* two hundred videos.

Eight

KENWAY SAT QUIETLY, SCROLLING through page after page of YouTube's MalusDomestica videos. He didn't watch any of them, but he was hunched over the computer like a Hollywood hacker, gazing intently at each thumbnail as if he could divine its contents by osmosis.

Turmoil spun in Robin's head like hot bathwater going down a drain, leaving her cold and empty and apprehensive inside. *What does he think? Is he scared of me now? No, not possible. He's a vet, his leg's been.... Does he think I'm a flake? A fake? A nerd?*

Nerd. I can live with nerd.

Finally, he looked up from the computer and regarded her with a wary, squinty eye. A battle was taking place in his head too, she could tell. She could almost hear the mental gears clanking.

She couldn't take it anymore. "Well? Did I scare you away?"

"*Hell* no," Kenway blurted, talking to the screen with a weird nervous chuckle. "That was bad-*ass*. That was the most badass thing I've ever seen on YouTube. Up til now I thought it was all just—just people falling down and animal videos." His eyes darted back up to her. "Now I know why you make the big bucks. You're a one-woman production company. Do you do all your own special effects and everything?"

Caught off-guard, Robin tilted her head. "Yeeeah, you could say that," she said with a coy wince. Her mouth screwed up to one side. "Sure."

His mouth twitched, his face softened.

"I hate to interrupt you," she asked, reaching out to tug the Macbook in her direction with a finger, "but do you mind if I get back to work editing today's video?"

Kenway's mental gears slipped. "Oh. *Oh!* Yeah. Yeah, here you go." He turned the laptop around and watched her face over the Macbook's lid as if he were waiting for some kind of tell. *Does he think it's an elaborate joke?* She closed the web browser and pulled up the video-editing console.

Noticing the sandwich on the table by his hand, Kenway seemed to remember that he had food and picked it up, eating and staring into the middle distance.

"I want to be on your channel," he said when he finished, startling her. He wiped his mouth with a napkin and wadded it up, shooting at the trash barrel from his seat. The balled-up napkin bounced off the wall and landed on the ground. "I want to fight witches too."

Robin was speechless. "You *what?*"

"I'm tired as shit of hanging around doin what I do. Bein the starving-artist cripple that spends all his time up in his studio painting." Kenway got up and went over to the trash, leaning against the wall to snatch the paper off the ground and toss it.

When he came back to her, he leaned on the table with both hands as if he were about to make a business proposal. "It's okay I guess. I mean, it's better than sittin around with my thumb up my ass. But I do the car stuff because I'm good at it, not because I have a passion for it. And the paintings...eh. I thought I wanted to be a painter a long time ago. I'll be straight with you, it's wearin kinda thin."

Kenway thrust a hand at the Macbook. "Shit! Look at these videos! *That's* passion!" Sitting down, he threw back the last of the beer in the bottle and busied his hands with squeezing the cap into a clamshell shape. "That's different, man. I wanna do something *different* for a change."

"I don't know if that's such a good idea."

He sat there peeling the label off the bottle for a little while, just long enough to give her time to finish the final touches on the video. She went to YouTube and started the transfer. "I didn't tell you the whole truth of why I came here, Robin. And why I stayed."

Cool anticipation trickled through her at recognizing the veiled pain on his face.

"When I lost my leg, it was my buddy Hendry, Chris Hendry, that pulled me out of that vehicle and put a tourniquet on me. Combat medic. He was in the vehicle behind us, he was the first one to get there." Kenway rubbed his nose, pulling on it as if he were about to take a deep breath and dunk himself. He massaged his whole mouth, the beard grinding in his hand like dry grass. "But he couldn't save everybody in there. Just me. It really messed him up, that he couldn't save the others. After we got home, he didn't do so hot. He had a lot of nightmares that year. Hard Christmas."

The YouTube transfer was going rather slow. Way too slow for a twenty-minute video...she was going to have to find an alternative upload point.

"The next summer I came out here to see how he was doing. He was living in Blackfield and working at the mill. Had a Vicodin habit he was trying to kick, said he hurt his back in the, ahh—the incident. He had a job but it was on the rocks. No girlfriend, as far as I know. I got the idea in my head to take him out on the lake for a week, see if I could get him

85

straightened up, right? He wasn't too bad off yet. Not bad enough for rehab, I think. Maybe I caught him in time."

As he spoke, he twirled the beer bottle on its butt, staring down at it. His voice was low, introspective.

"We spent a couple days out on a pontoon boat, fishing, tellin stories, had a good time. He looked good. He was laughing and making jokes. I thought he might be leveling out. Then one morning—that Wednesday—I got up, made coffee, and I was making breakfast when I went in to wake him up, and when I put my hand on him he was fucking *cold.*"

Ice ran down Robin's spine. She didn't know what to do, or what to say, and suddenly this enormous man seemed so vulnerable and dark. He became an emotional hot potato in her hands.

"It was 95 degrees that morning, and it was like, almost noon when I went in there. He was cold, colder than 95 degrees. I remember the temperature because of that giant round thermometer on the cabin porch. How do you get colder than that? He felt like somebody stole him and replaced him with a ham. Right there, in that bedroom, I thought he was playing a prank on me and had put something under his blankets. And he was hiding in the closet, waiting to jump out and laugh at me."

The stupid visual made him smirk darkly, but then he retreated into himself again.

"He brought the Vicodin to the cabin. Nothing left in the bottle." Kenway shrugged slowly. "I reckon he had died during the night. Probably took it all before he laid down." Closed his eyes, pressed the bottle against his mouth and tilted his head back, letting the very last drop of beer trickle down the glass onto his tongue.

Kenway put the bottle down and licked his lips, holding the bottle in both hands and staring down at it as if it were a precious heirloom. "I made breakfast and drank coffee while the man that saved my life was dead in the next room. And I didn't do *shit about it.*"

"Oh my God," said Robin.

Kenway sat up straight and rolled his neck, squeezing his shoulder. "And I've been here ever since. …That was about three years ago." He shot the bottle into the garbage with a bang and a rumble. "I don't know, it just didn't seem right to leave, you know? Felt like I was turnin my back on him. Walkin away from him. I couldn't do it."

Thoughts of hugging him occurred to her, but actually doing it seemed inappropriate. Instead, she reached over and squeezed his hand.

His eyes met hers and he smiled sadly.

"I've been over all my woulda-coulda-shouldas," he said, patting her hand. The palm of his bear-paw was rough, leathery. "You spend a lot of time in your head when you're painting. I think—ahh hell, this…isn't really great lunch conversation, is it?" Kenway's hand slithered out from under her own and he wadded up the sandwich wrapper, pitching it into the garbage too.

He was about to get up and probably say his see-ya-round when she reached out and took hold of his wrist.

"No," she blurted. "—I mean, yes, well, it's *not,* but I—"

He was nibbling the corner of his mouth, studying her face. In the sunlight, his eyes were the pale, dirty blue of a shallow lagoon, almost gray. He blinked and his eyebrows rose expectantly.

"Look, okay," she said, glancing at the progress bar on her video upload. Two percent. The battery in her laptop would die before it ever got to twenty. "Umm. You're already in this video I'm trying to upload. You can be in the next one too. ...You don't have to leave."

Kenway visibly relaxed, settling into his seat. "I don't know why I had to tell you that messed-up story. You... I dunno, you seem like a good listener."

She smiled up at him. "I do a lot of talking to a camera. I like having someone to listen to for a change."

"So what's on the agenda for the rest of the day?" Fetching a deep, deep sigh, Kenway stroked his beard, smoothing it down. "Doing any witch-hunting?"

"Not today. Right now I'm trying to upload this video, but it's taking forever. And I don't have forever."

"I live in the middle of town." He tossed a thumb over his shoulder. "So my internet's great. Fast as hell. You're more than welcome to come over and use mine."

"Smooth," she said, a smile creeping across her face. *An enigma wrapped in pain wrapped in silk.* "But first, I've got something to show you. And if we're telling stories, I should probably tell you mine."

✪

As soon as the back doors of the van came open, Kenway recoiled in surprise, his eyes wide. The swords hanging from the pegboard glittered in the sunlight. "My God, you've got *an arsenal* in here. *Look* at all this."

"Part of being a witch-hunter." Robin gathered her power adapter and— "Actually..." She had planned on riding with him in his truck, but it made more sense to just take the van over there. No sense in leaving it here unattended. "...How about I just follow you to your place?"

"That'll work."

Apparently when he was alone in the truck, Kenway drove like a maniac. She had trouble keeping up with him in her lumbering panel van. The GoPro was mounted on the dash, facing out the windshield, recording the chase. *One of these days I'm going to have to have an actual car chase,* she thought, grumbling up Hwy 9. *The subscribers will love that.*

Traffic was light when they got into town a few minutes later, the lunchtime rush winding down for an afternoon of work.

At the end of his block, Kenway whipped into a parking lot on the corner and she slid into a slot next to him. A sign standing in front of her grille said PARKING FOR STEVEN DREW D.D.S OFFICE ONLY. One just like it was in front of his Chevy.

"What about this?" she asked him as they got out.

"I painted the mural in his waiting room for free. He lets me park here so I don't have to use the parallel parking or the angled parking in front of the shop."

"Oh." Robin gathered her Macbook and charger, put them in her messenger bag, and unhitched the GoPro from its mount.

"Doing some filming?" Kenway asked, leading her up the sidewalk, along the storefronts. His art shop was four buildings down, past two empty shopfronts, a Mexican cafe called El Queso Grande, and a DUI driving course. As she walked, Robin panned the camera around, shooting B-roll of the street and all the buildings that they could see.

"Yep. I like to get as much footage as I can. Makes for a lot of variety and plenty of videos. The more videos you have, the more visible you are on YouTube."

"Makes sense."

I can make today's video a clip episode, like they do on TV shows, she thought. Kenway took out a jingling keyring and unlocked the front door of his studio, pulling the glass door open. *If I'm going to tell him my story, I can illustrate it by splicing in bits of earlier videos.* Silent excerpts would work best, playing under her voiceover.

Kenway flipped a light switch, and a forest of angular shadows turned into a small office, a computer workstation with two monitors, and several enormous machines of mysterious purpose. One of them looked like a giant laminator, or maybe something that pressed trousers for elephants.

A large table stretched to her right, and both the walls and the table were covered in hundreds of vinyl appliques: sports logos, automobile logos, clothing logos, tattoo designs of gryphons, dragons, tigers; mottos like NO FEAR and ROLL TIDE ROLL and ADVENTURE HURTS BUT STAYING HOME KILLS. A huge cutout of a running football player. Big flappy refrigerator magnets and a couple of coffee mugs with promotional artwork for local businesses.

She followed him through a door in the back, coming out into a huge open space with a garage roll-up and a set of steel stairs leading through a hole in the ceiling.

The garage was strewn with all manner of work trash, bits of vinyl, pieces of broken easel, scraps of canvas, a disassembled foosball table, sheets of plywood and pressboard, and four wide boards with holes cut in them.

The boards made her think of skeeball games. Two legs were bolted to their sides so that they stood up at an angle. "What are these?"

"Cornhole."

88

"What?"

"Cornhole," Kenway said again, walking over to a wobbly drafting table and picking up a green beanbag about the size of a baseball. He turned and lobbed it high; she watched it with the camera as it made an arc just under the garage rafters and slapped against the cornhole board, inches from the hole.

"—Oh."

He tossed her a beanbag. "You give it a shot."

Robin caught it and fired it across the room. The beanbag hit the wall and landed on top of an electrical conduit some ten feet up.

"Well, shit."

Kenway laughed, climbing the stairs. "Ten points."

They were impossibly high, climbing twenty feet up the wall and passing between the steel rafters. There were no acoustical tiles, so the ceiling was just gray-green-brown wood that looked like it had been salvaged from a shipwreck.

Emerging from the stairwell, Robin found herself in a space that was somehow majestic and quaint at the same time. The entire second story was one big open space like the garage downstairs, with a naked fifteen-foot ceiling. Taken as a whole it resembled some kind of modernized Viking lodge, all polished dark wood and hard angles. The south wall was plate-glass windows, looking out at the back of the building behind them and a vast blue sky.

Green marble countertops, steel fixtures, and black appliances made a sprawling kitchen to her left. Directly in front of her was a coffee table made out of a front door, with a short pole jutting up through where the knob used to be.

On top of the pole was a flatscreen TV, the wires running down through the door's deadbolt and into an outlet on the floor. Two iron-and-wood park benches made a right angle around the other side of the table.

"Wow," Robin said, still standing at the top of the stairs.

A queen-sized bed pressed against the wall to the right, covered in a cream fleece duvet. *"Who* makes the big bucks, again? This place is amazing."

"Most of it was already here when I moved in, except for the bed and the TV." Kenway went over to the kitchen and stood at the island, pouring a glass of what appeared to be tea. "The apartment was part of the deal when I took over the art shop from John Ward. The VA loan covered most of it; I bought whatever else I needed with my savings. Ranger combat pay makes for a nice nest egg when you're single.

"To save on power, I don't run the heat, which is why it's cool in here. If I get *too* cold, I haul my little fire-pit up here and build a fire in it. Lord knows I have enough crap downstairs to burn. Ward used this place for restoring antique furniture too—sometimes I do—and there's a lot of old wood left over."

Above the bed and above the kitchen, the walls were covered in three or four dozen paintings.

Most of them were without frames, just naked mounted canvas. Impressionistic renderings of forests at strange angles, birds in flight, animalistic women in provocative poses with brilliant lantern eyes and bodies hashmarked with cat-stripes. Men and women running with mysterious machines in their hands that could have been rifles, could have been construction equipment. Bokeh, the circular lights that appear in out-of-focus photos, dominated the pictures, giving them all an element of dreamlike wonder.

A few other paintings depicted pale nude men standing alone in foggy fields. Hands cupping blood. The bokeh made them nightmarish; they were hung off to the side, as if to marginalize them.

Robin put her bag on one of the park benches and opened her Macbook on the door-table, connecting to the wi-fi. Luckily, there was no password, so it only took a minute to get to the channel submissions page. While it uploaded, she walked over to the wall of glass.

Peering down into the alleyway behind the building, she could see a large aqueduct running east to west, water trickling along the bottom. "I guess if we're going to tell stories, I should tell mine."

Kenway's answer was grim but somehow warm. "You don't have to do that."

"I want to. I *need* to."

He joined her at the window. "You haven't told your subscribers on YouTube?"

"Yeah. I did in one of my first few videos. But it's not the same, you know? Talking to a camera. It's impersonal. You don't get the same kind of catharsis. And besides, you'll be the second one I've told face to face, and I need someone that will believe me. Because what I've finally come back here to do is going to require someone to believe me—believe what I have to say."

"The second person?" asked Kenway. "Your therapist?"

"No, I didn't talk about it to my therapist. He wouldn't have believed me. The whole reason I ended up in the psych ward is because I told the cops the truth about what happened." She spoke to the window, looking down into the aqueduct. "No, I had to tell Heinrich everything if I wanted his help, but if I wanted them to let me out of the looney-bin, I had to keep my mouth shut."

"Heinrich?"

"Heinrich Hammer."

"Who is that?" asked Kenway, with a disbelieving chuckle. "Sounds like a fighter in the UFC."

"My mentor. The guy that taught me everything I know about hunting witches." Robin smiled. "He could probably fight in the UFC if he wanted to, but he might be too violent for MMA." She rolled up her sleeves, revealing scars running halfway up the insides of her forearms. "I

90

went to him because I'm going to need everything I know, and all those weapons in my van, if I want to rescue my mother."

Robin's Story

THERE HAVE ALWAYS BEEN witches. According to my research, and what Heinrich told me, the first witch's name was Yidhra. She was a priestess of Ereshkigal, the Mesopotamian goddess of the land of the dead, Irkalla. Yidhra became a witch by sacrificing her own heart in exchange for a piece of Ereshkigal's power.

The goddess replaced Yidhra's heart with what we believe was a *libbu-harrani,* Sumerian for "heart-road", to Irkalla, or more specifically, perhaps a sort of conduit—sort of like how a power-outlet in a house pulls its electricity from the electric company. Her heart had been exchanged for a direct line to the afterlife. From this conduit, Yidhra derived her powers: divination, sorcery, necromancy, speaking with the dead, the familiarization of animals, that kind of shit.

Over time, Yidhra became the Biblical 'Witch of Endor', a minor celebrity in ancient Mesopotamia, a notorious sorceror, oracle, and cult figure that drew in acolytes, followers that also sacrificed their hearts to Ereshkigal.

By the time she was living out her twilight years in the village of Endor, she had convinced hundreds of women to give up their hearts.

One night halfway through my sophomore year of high school, my father murdered my mother right in front of me. Pushed her off the upstairs landing and she broke her neck in the foyer.

He *did* kill my mother, but he *didn't.*

By that I mean it was just something my father never would've done.

I was in the kitchen when it happened, making a pitcher of iced tea. Came running out of the kitchen and basically went into shock. My mother was lying on the floor in a heap of twisted meat, a ragdoll in a dress, her head canted at a weird angle, facing the ceiling. I sat beside her and held her. I didn't know what to do.

A few minutes later, my father snapped out of it. One of us called 911, but I don't remember who.

The tea, I remember…I left the kettle on and almost burned the house down. The kitchen—and part of the living room—was on fire when the police got there, but they managed to put it out, or so I'm told. I don't remember much of that night, or much of that month, for that matter.

No, my father killed my mother Annie because *they* made him do it.

"Cutty. Witch."

My mother's muddled last words, the last thing she ever said to me, as I sat there in the floor holding her useless body.

My father came down the stairs, walking all stiff and slow, not saying a word, one hand sliding down the banister…and when he got to the bottom, he fell on his hands and knees, arching his back, dry-heaving like he was coughing up a hairball. He started throwing up blood.

It was really coming out, I mean *spewing* all over the runner, and then he was choking. He was choking and horking *and then he vomited up a cat.*

His neck bulged out like a cantaloupe, and this gray-striped tabby cat came wriggling up his throat, coming out of his mouth yowling and hissing, with its fur and ears all slicked back with blood so it looked like a waxed weasel. Even lubed up like that, it got stuck. It fought the whole way. Before he could suffocate, my father had to grab that striped tabby cat by the head and pull it out like a…like a birthday-party magician, pulling scarves out of his mouth.

The state of Georgia charged my father with murder. Third-degree, second-degree, premeditated, I don't know, I wasn't at the trial. By then I was a ward of the state—the cops had taken me away. And thanks to my story about witches and puking up cats, the psychiatrist in charge of looking after me pronounced me mentally unfit to serve as a witness.

That's where *he* found me. Heinrich Hammer…this tall, rangy black guy in a three-piece suit, with a face like a pitbull and an attitude to match. I had no idea who he was or how he knew me, but he showed up out of the blue the day I turned eighteen, the day I aged out of the state's care. He offered me a place to stay. Told the hospital he was my new social worker, wanted to take me out of the psych ward and help me rebuild my life.

Not wanting to be homeless, I took him up on it. He drove me back to my old house on Underwood and picked the lock on the front door.

The city still hadn't sold it during my stay in the psych ward, but they had cleaned it up. The blood was gone. The carpets were replaced, and the burns were sanded and painted over. They had changed out all the window treatments and taken out the furniture. Auctioned it off, probably.

"Your mother was murdered," Heinrich said in his customary blunt way. I told him I already knew.

It was tough, but I walked around and broke it down CSI-style for him right there in the foyer, pointing out where she fell, pointing out where Dad had been standing when I came in, up there at the railing. How

93

he'd come down the stairs and horked up a stray cat. I was crying by the time I finished.

"He was their familiar," said Heinrich.

"Familiar?"

He took me to the front door.

"The women that live in that house," he said, and pointed up that gravel driveway at the mission house on the hill. "Marilyn Cutty, Theresa LaQuices, and Karen Weaver. Those women are the oldest and most powerful coven in America. Quite possibly the most powerful witches on the planet. I've been looking for em for years, looking for a way to nail their asses." He eased the front door closed and turned the deadbolt. "And I think you might be the one that can help me do that. ...Come on, help me look for your mother's gear."

"Gear?"

We searched the entire house from top to bottom. My parents' old bedroom, the attic, the kitchen, my childhood bedroom in the cupola on top of the house.

What we were looking for was under the house. The two of us stood shoulder to shoulder in the cramped dirt cellar, in front of the brick well. My mother told me when I was a little girl never to go down there and mess with it, because I could fall in and break my neck.

"See, cats will do anything a witch tells them to," said Heinrich, brandishing a crowbar. "That's not a total stereotype—witches really do have black cats, and white cats, and gray cats, all kinds of cats, but it's a little more complicated than that." Prying off the swollen boards blocking the well, he found the rope tied to the well wall, five feet down. He had to lean over the side and haul the bags up with the crowbar. "Witches can command cats, you know, like the rats in that movie *Willard*, with that skinny motherfucker that was in that *Charlie's Angels* movie."

Now I know why my mother made me promise not to go down there. Old books and incense and crystals and bones and little baggies of weed, each one in a Ziploc freezer bag, all of them tied up in two plastic Walmart bags and lowered down with a nylon calf-rope. There wasn't any water, but it was still damp. The bags were mildewy.

"They can do this because cats belong to, and are minions of, the Mesopotamian goddess Ereshkigal—they're creatures *of* the afterlife, which is why they can see spirits," said Heinrich, glancing at me as we stood down there in the cellar, shining a flashlight on the paraphernalia on the dirt floor. "...Yeah, *ghosts.*"

His voice was hard, but his eyes were compassionate. "I'll get to that in a minute. Right now, you ought to know something: your mother is a witch."

I was stunned. Speechless. All I could do was stand there, trying to compare my sweet, pretty, good-natured mother, that tiny curly-haired housewife with the goofy speech impediment and the deep and abiding love for Christianity, against the sinister image of witches I'd built up in

94

my mind during the months I'd spent in the mental hospital. Months trying to figure out why my mother had accused Cutty in her last moments. Cutty, weird, quaint Marilyn Cutty, who I'd thought of as the equivalent of my grandmother for so many years, whose house I'd played in as a child.

I remembered lying on the floor in her living room, reading the Sunday comics and petting her calico Stanley, a little high from the scented markers I'd been coloring with.

Some days when I toddled over to her house, Marilyn would take me shopping and I'd come home with these complex Lego sets. God, I loved Legos. *You don't have to buy me nothin,* I would tell her, and old Marilyn would say, *I know. That's why I do it.* How could this woman who regularly loved and spent money on a little girl be this kind of evil?

"There are good witches, and there are bad witches," said Heinrich.

Sometimes, it seemed, a witch could be both.

My new friend was carrying a briefcase. He put it on the ground, opened it, and put my mother's things on a bed of foam, one item at a time, delicately and reverently. "Your mother was a good witch, and she was a *new* witch. Cutty probably talked her into giving up her heart only a couple years after you were born." Heinrich aimed those flinty eyes at me, shining the flashlight under his chin, and they turned soft. "You can console yourself with the knowledge that Annie waited until after you were born to give her heart to Ereshkigal. Witches can't have kids, you know…to be a mother, you have to have a heart."

We went back up and stood under the upstairs landing, in the exact spot where my mother had fallen.

"There's this fungus called 'Cordyceps'," Heinrich said quietly and measuredly, as if he were confessing to something. "That's the scientific name for it. It infects ants' brains and it makes them do things they wouldn't normally do, like climb up a tree…where the fungus bursts out of their head and spores out into the air. Reproduces.

"Cats themselves can carry a virus called 'toxoplasma gondii', or some shit like that, in their intestines, and it can infect the brain of its host, influencing its behavior. When it infects a mouse through contact with cat feces, that mouse contracts an illness called 'toxoplasmosis' and behaves erratically.

"Gets real screwed up. Gets real friendly to cats. So you can imagine what happens next: the mouse ends up in the cat's bowels. The only place that particular virus can reproduce. And hakuna matata, the circle of life rolls on."

Heinrich went on to tell me how the witches figured out how to metaphysically 'implant' a cat into a human. You saw them on the video you watched: the people-familiars, they yowl and hiss and claw at you like a cat. It's because they're cats in human bodies. It's a lot like the Cordyceps and toxoplasma—these parasite-cats lie dormant inside their human hosts like hairy tapeworms, sleeping, waiting, until the witches need them.

That's what was wrong with my father the night he pushed my mother off the upstairs landing and broke her neck in the foyer. He'd been familiarized. He 'had a cat in him'.

"You may have a chance to save Annie, you know," Heinrich told me. "She may not be *actually* dead." I scraped the tears off my face with my shirt. My strange benefactor traded hands with the briefcase and put one of those rough, bony hands on my shoulder. "But it ain't going to be easy. You're gonna have to train. Have to learn how to beat em."

"Why did they do it?" I asked.

"Why did they murder Annie?" That three-piece suit of his was slate-gray and pinstriped, made him look like a railroad conductor. But he always wore black combat boots with it, spit-polished half to hell and back. "Robin, baby, they needed her to make a dryad."

As we got in his car and headed out of town, he explained. "A dryad is at its most basic a soul trapped inside of a tree. Or, well, technically it's the name for the tree-prison itself, but it also refers to the tree-and-soul combined. Anyway, dryads don't occur naturally, so you have to make one—provided your ass knows how, of course.

"Now, if you make a dryad out of a normal person...take Joe Schmoe off the street, kill him, siphon his spirit into a tree, all you have is a self-aware tree. Pretty shitty existence for poor Joe, livin out the rest of eternity with squirrels shovin acorns up his ass, but there ain't nothin special about it.

"But if you make a dryad out of a supernaturally-endowed person, for example, another witch, you end up with what's called a *nag shi*. Like the person it was created from, this kind of dryad is an energy-absorber. And with a little coaxing and a bucket of human blood twice a week, it will become a sort of black hole. The tree's roots draw up life for miles around, and if it's in a town like Blackfield, it will tap that town for nourishment.

"Where does all that give-a-shit go, you ask?" We were sitting at a crossroads between two cotton fields, listening to the wind shake a stop sign. "It goes into the dryad's fruit. Flora de vida—the fruit of life."

Heinrich pulled across the intersection, swinging onto the road that would eventually bring us to his house in distant Texas.

"The soul-tree pulls the will-to-live out of the town and converts it to fruit. Peaches, apples, lemons, whatever the dryad happens to flower. The fruit depends on the soul that was used to make the tree.

"I'm sure you can guess why witches cultivate them and eat the fruit." He lit a cigar and rolled the window down a hair to suck the pungent smoke out. "I'll give you a hint: Marilyn Cutty's grandson Leonard Bascombe fought in the American Civil War."

"And that's when I started training with Heinrich," said Robin. By the time she'd finished the tale, they had migrated to the kitchen. She sat on a stool at the island while Kenway cooked burgers on a griddle set in the island next to the stove. Her camera stood on a bendy-legged tripod at the end of the counter, next to a splat of postal envelopes.

"Was it like in the movies?" he asked, flipping a burger. *Ksssss*. "You know, like a montage with a music backing, and you're beating up a kick-bag and throwing wooden stakes at a dummy?"

"That's Buffy the Vampire Slayer." Robin gave him a dark eye. Noticing a glass vase full of coffee beans, she slid it over and took a sniff. "And …well, there were things like that I guess. It was mainly poring over esoteric texts. Library books, microfiche, photocopied newspapers, stolen documents…."

"Stolen?"

"Heinrich was the type, he didn't let a little thing like the law stop him from doing what he needed to do."

"I see." He flipped another patty. *Ksssss*. "I assume you haven't had to do anything like that, since you don't seem to be hiding from the law." Unwrapping a piece of cheese, he added, "You *aren't* running from the law, are you? That living-in-the-van would make a lot more sense if you were."

"Heinrich had already gotten all the stuff he'd needed by the time I met him," said Robin. "Of course there's probably a couple dozen unsolved cases of arson out there." She put a finger to her lips. "But I won't tell if *you* don't."

Kenway sighed thoughtfully and put the cheese on the meat as it sizzled. "You're really something, lady. I don't know what to do with you."

You could kiss me, she thought, but didn't say. "Thank you for giving me a place to hang out for the evening that isn't my van or the pizzeria. And the internet."

He smirked up at her. "And the burger."

"And the burger. I love pizza, but I think I'm overdosing."

"So how did the YouTube thing start?" Kenway asked, putting some buns on plates and scooping up the burgers onto them.

"You know how in football, the team keeps the game recordings and goes over them later? Heinrich used to do that so we could watch them and fine-tune our techniques. I was the one that suggested we could put the tapes on the internet and make money on them." Her stomach growled at the smell rising off the griddle. "At first, he was dead set against it, but after I showed him how much like some of the other YouTube series it was, and how much money we could make on it, he warmed up to the idea."

A noise came from Robin's jeans, startling both of them. She dug in her pocket and took out her phone.

It was an alarm set to go off at six. She put it back in her pocket and slid down off the stool, opening a cabinet. "Where's your glasses?"

"I don't wear glasses."

She grinned awkwardly. "Drinking glasses."

"Oh. Yeah." Kenway opened one of the other doors. Robin took down a glass and filled it at the sink, then went to her laptop on the coffee table and dug a prescription bottle out of her messenger bag. She tipped out a tablet and swallowed it with a gulp of water.

He watched her with curiosity, but didn't say anything.

Putting the bottle away, Robin went back to the island to sit down and drink the rest of the glass. Kenway gave her a curious eye.

"The pills are for, uhh...well, the shrinks say I have schizophrenia, or something like that. I have hallucinations. Nightmares." She picked at a fleck of color in the marble counter. "The medication helps. I did have Zoloft too, but I stopped taking it when I ran out of the bottle they gave me at the psych ward. I don't like it. It makes me a zombie."

Kenway seemed to be uncomfortable. He actually rolled his shoulders and tugged on his shirt as if it didn't fit right.

"I guess that probably put you off me, didn't it?" Robin murmured, folding her arms. "It usually does. The guys. I've...tried to date before, but as soon as I break out the pill bottle, they're out the door."

Pursing his lips, Kenway looked at her—*really* looked at her, a burning, assessing, ant-under-a-magnifying-glass stare—and then he put down the spatula and rolled up one of his pants legs, revealing the prosthetic foot.

He unbuckled it, a laborious process with grunting and pulling and ripping of Velcro, then pulled the foot off, leaving a nub wrapped in a bandage. As big as Kenway was, the false leg looked as if it were three feet tall, with an articulated ankle and silicone cup. It had a shoe on it, of course, the match to his other Doc Marten.

"If *you* don't run away from this—" He stood the leg on the counter in front of her. "—*I* won't run away from *you*."

Nine

HERE'S THE HIGH SCHOOL, where we are," said Pete, his pudgy finger pressed against the paper. Pete, Wayne, Johnny Juan, and Amanda Hugginkiss-neé-Johnson stood in front of the huge map of Blackfield hanging in Mr. Villarubia's fourth-grade classroom. A clock ticked quietly on the wall over their heads: ten minutes after three in the afternoon. They were alone.

The map was as tall as the teacher himself, five feet across, and represented several square miles of the territory of the town, reaching clear out into the surrounding counties. This included Slade, the area north of town where the kids lived.

According to Mr. Villarubia's Social Studies class, Slade was either referred to as a 'unincorporated township', a 'district' or a 'suburb', depending on who you asked. As far as he was concerned, it was basically the northeastern arm of Blackfield, a civilized wilderness reaching up to the interstate freeway that ran between Atlanta and Birmingham, Alabama. Unlike the urban grid of avenues and streets in town, Slade was thick forest and cow pastures, chewed up into a hundred wandering feeder roads. They all branched off of Highway Nine, a two-lane ribbon that dropped like a rock, from the freeway into the heart of Blackfield.

Wayne felt like Lewis and Clark looking at this thing, plotting out tracks and trails. A feeling of adventure swelled in his chest, *safe* adventure, welcoming, inviting adventure, nothing like the streets back home.

They'd find no gibbering crackheads demanding money, or trying to sell them stolen watches, coins, car stereos. There'd be no haggard, barefoot women offering to "make a man" out of him, no Bloods looking to recruit a new pusher. No cops stopping him on the sidewalk to ask him what he was doing, where he was going, what he had in his pocket, *no sir, it's just an action figure, no sir, it's just a piece of candy, see?*

There was only him, a warm sun on a cool fall day, and a bunch of trees. He found a reassurance and confidence in that the other children would never know. *They literally can't see the forest for the trees,* he thought rather suddenly, a realization dawning on him. *They grew up here. They'll never know what this place really is because they've always known it.*

"And here's Chevrolet Trailer Park," Pete said, pointing to a non-descript part of the woods. His fingertip stood an inch to the right of the Nine, and a few inches north of the river that ran across that end of Blackfield.

"That's *Chevalier Village,*" corrected Amanda.

"Whatever," Pete said, grimacing.

He pointed to the school again and traced their route. "Okay, what we're gonna do is cross Gardiner, cross the baseball field, then take Wilmer up to Broad, and then we're gonna follow Broad up to here." He looked over his shoulder. "That's where Fish's Comic Shop is. Have you been there yet, Batman?"

"No," said Wayne.

"It's fuckin awesome. We'll have to stop there on the way. They got a life-size Alien and a Freddy Krueger claw. The guy that owns it does movie nights on Thursdays."

"I love that place," Johnny Juan said to no one in particular.

Amanda rolled her eyes and sighed through her nose. "I wish you would stop swearing so much. It's not right."

Pete winced at her. "*You* ain't right." He went back to his explanation. "Okay, whatever, when we're done there, we'll go up Broad Street for about a block and then there's a bridge that you can go under, into the canal that runs next to the street. It's about eight foot deep. It runs under Highway Nine."

"What about the water?" asked Johnny.

"There ain't no water. Well, not really. There's a little bit. There's not a lot in there unless it rains. Nothin to worry about."

"Oh, okay."

"Anyway, we follow the canal this way." He traced the dotted line east to where it hooked up at a shallow angle, and then he followed it northeast. "Up to the river, and there's a bridge there we'll have to cross. Or we can walk across the big blue pipe that crosses the river next to it. We'll come to the pipe first. The bridge is a little farther down."

"I'll take the bridge," said Amanda. "You guys can fall in and drown without me."

Pete ignored her jibe, tracing a path from the river bridge into what Wayne assumed by the blotchy outline were trees. The blotch was a massive crescent of forest that lined the north side of Blackfield and accompanied another highway going north. "Then we'll cut through these woods here and take this trail going...north." His finger drew an invisible line up into the forest and on up to a trembly, jagged path labeled UNDERWOOD RD. "From there it's a straight shot to Chevrolet."

"*Chevalier.*"

"That's what I said, Chevrolet. Anyway I've got a surprise for you back in those trees."

"A surprise?" Amanda asked, her eyes narrowing. "What *kind* of surprise?"

"Something I found last summer."

"It's not like those old porno magazines you found on top of the ceiling tiles in the boys' bathroom, is it?" asked Johnny. He wiped his hands on his shirt as if the memory alone was enough to soil him. "Those were so gross. So much *hair.*"

Amanda held her stomach and feigned a dry-heave.

The band of explorers headed out the front door, threading a path through the kids outside waiting for the buses and car pickups. When they got to the edge of the parking lot, a police officer in the middle of the road stopped traffic to let them across.

"Y'all be careful goin home," said the cop, a slender man with a weaselly face and *Men in Black* Ray-Bans. His jet-black uniform was impeccable, ironed smooth, and he wore a patrol cap with a badge over the brim that glinted in the sun.

"Yes sir," grinned Wayne.

"I ain't no sir," the officer called to him as he stepped up onto the curb. "Sir's my old man, I'm just Owen."

"Thank you, Owen!"

The officer waved them off and went back to directing pick-up traffic.

King Hill Elementary was three blocks west of the main drag through town, a sprawling complex on a hill at the edge of a wooded suburb. The kids marched resolutely across the school's front lawn toward the baseball field. The only other sound was birdsong and the tidal wheeze of poor Pete's horsey panting.

As Wayne walked alongside the gaggle, the feeling of adventure only grew. It was a real *halleluah* moment. The redneck-ness, the *remoteness* of Blackfield was already starting to grow on him.

There wasn't a cloud in the sky and the sky was a thousand miles wide and twice as high, and if he stared hard enough at the airliner carving a whispering contrail across that blue dome, he thought he could almost make out the faces in the windows. It was as if God had reached down and smoothed the world out like a blanket, leaving only him, his new friends, and the tall blue.

He made a mental note to thank his dad for dragging them out here to 'the middle of nowhere', as he'd been thinking of it all day. With the warm sun on his bare head and healthy green grass under his feet, he found it hard to keep talking trash and playing the pouty transplanted kid.

Children were hanging out in the baseball diamond, chatting in the bleachers and dugouts, and throwing balls to each other out on the dirt. Pete led them around the back of the risers, passing a blue Porta-Potty.

"I heard one of the high-school kids got trapped in this potty by a mountain lion last year," said Johnny Juan.

Amanda watched her feet eat up the grass, her thumbs tucked behind the straps of her *My Little Pony* backpack as if they were suspenders. "There's no mountain lions out here, dummy."

"There's bobcats."

"There's Bigfoots too," said Pete.

Amanda's ponytail flounced back and forth like an actual horse's tail. Wayne found it as hypnotic as a metronome. "No such thing as Bigfoot."

"Sure there is." Pete looked over his shoulder at Wayne. "What do *you* think? Do *you* believe in Bigfoot?"

"I don't know. Maybe. I'd *like* to."

"See? Wayne believes in Bigfoot."

"I think I'd crap my pants if I ever saw Bigfoot," said Johnny Juan. "Have you ever seen him, Pete?"

"No. But I know about a website that tracks sightings. Bigfoot Research Organization or something like that. They had like forty reports right here in Georgia."

Wilmer Street was on the other side of the baseball diamond. They jumped a deep culvert and followed the road's shoulder to where the sidewalk materialized under their feet, assembling itself out of broken slabs where the weeds and mud had started to reclaim it.

That took them up a long valley of nameless brick buildings with wooden house-doors and metal doors without knobs, roll-up garage doors and glass doors with sun-faded signs taped to their insides that said OUT OF BUSINESS and CUSTOMERS ENTER AROUND SIDE and MOVED TO VAUGHAN BLVD. Wayne quit paying attention to where they were going and let his feet carry him along behind the plodding Pete in a sort of auto-pilot.

At one point they passed an open cafe where two men were perched in a large window cut in the side of a twenty-foot shipping container. A hand-painted sign over the dining-area awning said DEVIL-MOON BEER & BURGERS and had a picture of two disembodied red hands cupping a crystal ball.

Despite Johnny Juan's good-natured beggaring, the men wouldn't let them have a beer, but they had cans of something called Firewater, a locally-made cinnamon sarsaparilla, for a dollar. They each bought one and continued up Wilmer drinking them. Amanda bought some fried dill pickles and let Wayne have one. He thought they were the best things he'd ever eaten in his life, and made another mental note to talk Leon into bringing him back to the Devil-Moon.

That means he'll have to go to a bar, though, he thought.

Johnny Juan pulled some berries off of a holly bush in front of a lawyer's office and chucked them one by one at the back of Pete's head.

You keep on and they gon fire your ass, lil brother, Aunt Marcelina had said to Leon.

102

This conversation had taken place back in Chicago, but Wayne could remember it as if it had taken place that morning. She and Leon stood behind the car, almost nose-to-nose, while Wayne sat in the front passenger seat reading the latest Spider-Man comic book.

I know life been tough since you lost your old lady, Aunt Marcelina told Leon, her hands on her ample hips. Her tone was soft but reproachful. *But you can't carry on like this. You keep showin up to work tore up and they gon let you go. And you know what's gonna happen then?*

Leon had said nothing, but his arms were folded. Normally a Leon Parkin with folded arms meant you were about to get an earful about something or other, but this time he was hunched over as though the wind were chilling him, even though it was August and the armpits of his shirt were dark. He looked more like a kicked puppy, sweaty and diminished.

This time he was the one getting an earful. *They ain't nobody else gon hire you.* Marcelina pointed at the school with an open hand. *Ain't nobody gon hire a drunk-ass teacher.*

What you want me to do? Leon had asked.

His neck-tie was loose, his collar open. His hand drifted up to his mouth and he pulled his face in exasperation, wiping his hand on his slacks.

You need to get right with God, Marcelina told him.

God? scoffed Leon. *God needs to get right with me.*

Don't you start, Leonhard Luther Parkin. Marcelina's broad shoulders hulked over him when she handled her pear-shaped hips like that, like she was using them as leverage to make herself even bigger, and she was already built like a linebacker. Her painted lips pursed under flaring nostrils. *I'mma tell you what we gonna do.*

What 'we' gonna do?

I'm gonna give you a little money, and you can get out of town. Get outta your head, get outta that apartment, get away from here and go somewhere you can get clear. Somewhere quiet you can dry up.

Leon jerked with a hiccup, standing a little straighter in his surprise. *Get outta town? What is this, Tombstone? You runnin me outta town now?*

If that's what it takes to fix you.

Marcy, Leon had said, *I can't take your money.*

Yes, you can, she told him, *and you will. Look, you can pay me back whenever.* She pointed at Wayne sitting in the car. The nail on the end of her finger was a bright red claw. *I want you to think of that little boy sittin in there. Do you love him?*

Leon recoiled. *Of course I do.*

Then get outta here, get away from these memories, away from this city, and get right with God. Baby brother, don't make me hafta raise my own nephew. I got three boys of my own. Marcelina hitched up her giant leather purse where it'd slipped down her shoulder and took out a wadded-up tissue. *You know she would want you happy, dammit.*

103

Leon peered through the back window at Wayne, biting his lip in apprehension. His eyes were pink, and his face was twisted like something hurt deep inside. The boy could see the pain sticking out of him like a knife-handle.

I been talkin to Principal Hayes, said Marcelina. *There's a job down south he wanna recommend you for. It's close to Atlanta. Trisha lives in Atlanta. Your cousin, Aunt Nell's daughter, you 'member her? She's all right, you know? You two used to play together before her mama moved them down there to go to school.* She craned her head forward to look up into Leon's face. *Will you think about it?*

"You asshole!" howled Pete, startling Wayne out of his daydream. He looked up from the sidewalk and almost ran into Amanda.

The four of them had come to the intersection of Wilmer and Broad and were approaching the traffic light. To the left and right was a long stretch of two-story buildings: boutiques, offices, shops, storefronts.

A pet shop across the street boasted about its hamsters, kittens, turtles. Next door, a frozen-yogurt shop in pastel colors claimed more flavors than Baskin-Robbins, and after that was a knick-knack shop with bamboo wind chimes and frilly marionettes on tin bicycles.

Broad reminded him of the older parts of Chicago, the streets that led back to the wild-west days, but Blackfield's historical district was cleaner, almost precious in its maintenance. On the other side of the intersection, Wilmer turned into a brick road bisected by a median full of little trees, and lining it was a funnel of fancy bistros and taverns.

Pete held up his sarsaparilla. "You ruined my drink!"

"How did I do that?" asked Johnny Juan.

Pete showed him the can. Johnny leaned in to examine it. "You threw a holly berry in my Firewater!"

Wayne and Amanda clustered around Johnny to see. The girl tugged it in her direction with her long, pencil-slender fingers and he noticed that her nails were green.

"I'll be dang," said Johnny, leaning back to laugh. Wayne looked down into the mouth of the can—which was no bigger than a nickel— and sure enough, a little red berry bobbed at the bottom.

Amanda smirked. "You should try out for basketball!"

"Maybe!"

"Basketball my ass!" fussed Pete. "I can't drink this now."

"Why not?" asked Amanda. "It's just a berry."

"Aren't holly berries poisonous?"

She paused and squinted up at the sky, palming her mouth in thought. "I have no idea."

Johnny shrugged. "You could try it and see. Hey, there were food tasters back in King Arthur's court and stuff. They tasted things to see if they were poisoned before they were served to the king."

"Then *you* taste it, Sir Lancelot," said Pete, thrusting the can in his direction, "and let me know if you die."

Johnny stepped back as if the can were a spider.

104

"You are the biggest wuss," Pete growled, balling up a fist. "That's two for flinching."

"Aww." Johnny hugged himself protectively and Pete punched him twice in the shoulder, hard enough to almost knock him over. He balanced on one foot, rubbing his arm. "Jesus! Do you have to hit so hard? That's like the third time this week."

Pete poked the crosswalk button. "Do you want me to carry you across the street, or do you think you can do it?"

Johnny sulked, his hands jammed into his pockets.

The light changed and Pete trudged across the street, the others in tow. Wayne followed them, looking around at all the shops. He'd have to talk Leon into bringing him back here—especially to the pet shop. He needed a new pet, he thought, walking backward, checking it out. Maybe a dog. *Yeah, that's the ticket. A new dog for a new house. That creaky old house needs a happy dog living in it.* Tappity-tap-tap on his cellphone.

> theres a pet store in town
>
> Oh yea?
>
> Yep. can we go when u get home?
>
> Maybe this weekend. what u wanna go to pet store 4?
>
> can we get a dog?
>
> we'll talk about it.

There was some ineffable quality to his father's texts that Wayne couldn't quite place, something low and dim, or maybe it was an absence of warmth, an uncharacteristic dismissiveness.

In the time since his mother had passed, he had become finely attuned to his father's moods, and he seemed to have developed the ability to glean his father's demeanor from nothing more than a few words on a cellphone screen.

When you've had to wake up your drunk father and make him go to bed a few times, you learn to anticipate his lows. Sort of like an earthquake scientist watching a seismograph for the tell-tale jags and spikes that preceded disaster.

> You doin ok today dad?

The cellphone didn't buzz again for a long minute, long enough for Wayne to look up and sight-see a little more.

They were even with a barber shop, and a man inside was getting his hair cut by a dainty Korean woman. She had already buzzed his head into a brush cut, and was now scraping shaving cream off his neck with a long, curved razor. The blade flashed in dusty sunlight.

> yeah i'm doin alright I guess. as long as I stay busy its all good.

A moment later Leon added,

> I could use a dirnk but if I'm hre @ school I cant get 1. So thats good 4 me.

Wayne answered,

Yeah thats good. U do what u got to. I'll b fine @ home. I can take care of myself.

He put the cellphone in his jacket pocket and took out the ring on the ballchain around his neck. Lifting his mother's wedding band, he peered through it at the world, and at Pete's broad back. *Can you see my new friends?*

Something about doing this lightened him, made him feel like he was sharing his eyes with his mom, as if the ring were a camera, transmitting some ethereal signal that she could see from wherever she was now, if that 'wherever' was Heaven.

"Here we are," said Johnny Juan.

Through the ring, Wayne saw a big storefront picture window with superheroes painted on it: Spider-Man on the left, Batman on the right, both of them in action poses, swinging through the air. Over Spidey's head was FISHER'S HOBBY SHOP, and over Batman's was COMICS, BOOKS, TOYS & GAMES.

Warm sunlight streamed in through the Spidey and Batman paintings, leaking dim and dusty gold beams into the depths of the shop. The door chime tolled like a cathedral bell in the silence; it seemed they were the only customers in at the moment other than a gray cat curled into a ball on the windowsill.

"Hello?" called Amanda.

The place had a generally musty smell of disuse, the action figures nearest the front door sealed in packages bleached green by countless days facing the sun. Most days probably passed without seeing many customers, outside of regulars and the people that came for Movie Night.

Shelves of games occupied the racks alongside the larger graphic novels and action figures: chess, Monopoly, Scattergories, Apples to Apples, esoteric card games he'd never heard of. A council of Halloween masks stared down at them with empty black eyes, perched at the tops of all the shelves—Jason's hockey mask, Michael Myers' white face, a warty pig-man, a grinning devil, Pennywise the clown, Pinhead from the *Hellraiser* movies.

An athletic black guy came out of a doorway stirring what appeared to be a milkshake. "Hey, kids. How's it going?" he asked, walking over to the counter and taking up position behind a laptop.

Directly behind him was a showcase with a glass front, containing a vast array of dazzling knick-knacks and mementos: signed book jackets, DVD cases, and comic covers, a Freddy Krueger claw, and a veritable army of action figures still in their blister packs. The centerpiece was an uruk-hai cuirass, a vest of armor worn by the orcs in the *Lord of the Rings* movies, and if Wayne viewed it at the right angle he could see the silvery writing where someone had signed it with a Sharpie. Peter Jackson, probably. The chainmail underneath seemed older than Blackfield itself.

Pete bellied up to the counter as if he were a cowboy in a saloon, putting his chubby elbows on the glass. Underneath was a carpeted display with rare cards: baseball, *Magic: The Gathering*, *Pokémon*, *Garbage Pail Kids*. "Hey, Fish. It's goin all right, how are you?"

"About as good as good gets. Been a while, Petey boy. What brings you?" Fish chugged half the thick, sludgy milkshake in one go and put it down, waking up the computer.

"We're showing the new guy around."

"His name is Wayne. But we call him Bruce Wayne," said Johnny Juan, clapping his diminutive friend on the shoulder. "Him and his dad just moved here from...?"

"Chicago."

"Welcome to the middle of nowhere, Batman," said the man. He wore a thin blue sweater that hugged every muscle as tightly as a wetsuit. "My name is Fisher. Fisher Ellis." He offered a hand to shake. "Everybody calls me Fish."

Wayne shook it. "Wayne Parkin."

"Sweet name. Well, welcome to my little slice of America," said Fish, gesturing around the shop with a sweeping hand. He leaned over the laptop and started typing furiously. "I've got to do a little work. If you need anything, gimme a holler."

Wandering away, Pete and Johnny took to a table of boxed comic books, cultural geologists flipping through sedimentary layers of superhero history. Amanda simply stood next to the counter, her arms folded, looking uncomfortable. At first Wayne thought about browsing the action figures, but he wanted to know more about Fish and the shop. The fact that it was so empty of people was nagging him.

"So what are you doin?" he asked, pointing at the computer. "For work. On the computer. Do you—" The question felt rude, but he couldn't think of any other way to put it. "Do you *sell* anything? I mean, it doesn't really look like many people come in here."

Fish smiled. "I'm actually a director of IT for a postal company."

Turning the laptop around, he flashed the kids a screen full of cryptic text. Wayne thought it looked like the green code from *The Matrix* turned sideways. "I work from home, doing programming and things like that. 'Home', in this instance, being my hobby shop. It lets me be here at the shop and still do work for these guys." Wagging a finger around the room, he explained, "This stuff is really for sale, but, yeah, I don't do much business. It's more like...like my personal stuff-room, you know? ...You ever heard of George Carlin?"

Wayne couldn't say that he was familiar.

"Well, old Carlin was a comedian, did a lot of stand-up. He had a bit about making money and buying stuff. 'A house is just a place to put stuff,' he'd say. 'Bigger houses are *more room*, to put *more stuff*.' And I don't have any room at my house for it, so here it is. This is my Room of Stuff." He picked up the milkshake and toasted the air with the cup. "If I'm going to have all this Stuff, people might as well see it. What good is Stuff if nobody knows you got it?" He downed the rest of the shake. "Besides, I like the company. The shop keeps me social and out of my apartment."

"Oh!" gasped Amanda, darting over to one of the displays and picking up an action figure package. "I didn't know you had *Adventure Time.*"

The gray cat jumped up on the counter and went to stick its nose in Fish's cup, but he took it away and stroked the cat's back. "No ma'am, that's not for you. You already get enough protein, you don't need anymore."

"I want to have a shop like this one day," said Wayne.

"You look like the kind of man that would take care of a shop like this. Treat it right."

A sheepish pride blossomed in Wayne's chest at being called a man, and a grin crept across his face. "It's really awesome. Maybe when you get tired of running this place and retire, *I* can inherit it."

Fish studied him for a long moment, then tipped the cup at him. "I tell you what. How do you feel about working up here after school a couple days a week? You could stand right here at the counter for an hour or two while I catch up on my code work, and on Thursdays you can help me get set up for Movie Night. Maybe I can start doing em on the weekends, too."

"Are you for real?" asked Wayne, incredulous. "That—that would be so cool!"

"All you gotta do is guess what superhero I'm thinking of." Fish touched a fingertip to his temple. "It's my favorite superhero. You get three guesses."

Wayne eyed the front window. "Spider-Man?"

"No, but you're on the right side. It ain't neither of them guys up there on the windows, though."

"Can I get a hint?"

"Umm. Grass." Fish tapped on the glass counter in thought. "Grass, frogs, and avocados. What do those three things have in common?"

Wayne considered them in turn, picturing them in his mind, chewing on his lip in concentration. "They're all green?"

Fish nodded deferentially.

"Green Lantern?"

"Nope."

"The Hulk?"

Pounding his fist on the edge of the counter in feigned defeat, Fish pointed at him and said, "You got it. Man, I knew I made that too easy. What was I thinking?"

Wayne threw his fists in the air and Pete golf-clapped. "To be fair," he said, "there's only like two green superheroes, and one of em is DC."

"Swamp Thing. Martian Manhunter. Beast Boy. Gamora. You gotta do your research, man."

"Shoot, you know a lot about comic books."

Fish smirked. "Okay. Bonus points if you can tell me what makes the Incredible Hulk so incredible. Why the Hulk is my favorite."

The man behind the counter was chiseled but slim, with a triangular neck and an overhanging shelf of muscle across his chest. *That's an easy one*, thought Wayne, confident in his answer. "Because he's so strong."

"He *is* strong. But that's not why he's incredible."

"Because he's so big?"

"Nope," said Fish, leaning on the counter, his dark eyes pinning Wayne to the spot. "It's because the Hulk *adapts.*"

Flexing his bulging arms, he explained. "The madder Hulk gets, the stronger Hulk gets. It's the stress, y'know, it's what makes him mad. The rage is just a by-product."

Fish spoke with the magnetic didact focus of a self-help guru, his words clear and precise. Between every sentence, he paused for a beat to let his words sink in. His energetic hands did as much speaking as his mouth did, cupping and flinging every third word. "Everybody has to deal with stress. Hulk deals with it by becoming *stronger* than the stress. He soaks up the energy around him and channels it into his strength, uses it to go one step above the problem at hand.

"You hit him with a hundred tons of force?" He punched at the air, slapping his bicep to give the strike a theatrical *oomph*. "Hulk hits you with *two* hundred tons of force. ...He's not my favorite because he's strong. He's my favorite because he never lets a challenge beat him, he's always ready to go that one-step-farther than the other guy."

"Yeah. Yeah!" Wayne nodded, fidgeting as the story soaked in. "I get you. I get you."

His father was pretty much the only adult that Wayne ever had conversations with that felt as intellectually equal as this one, with this well-spoken man and his superhero fixation, and now he felt a bit antsy— almost patronized, except he knew Fish was being earnest. It was a bit awkward, like being drafted into a stage performance in front of all his friends, but he liked it. Made him feel ten years older.

"Absolutely, you dig it?" Fish peered at his computer screen and rattled off a burst of typing. "And that's my motto, man. Adapt and overcome. When life gives you a problem, you gotta adapt and be stronger, you know? Be the Hulk. Be better. Be bigger. Be *badder.*"

Ten

MARILYN FOUND ROY OUT back in the garden beating up the board fence with the weed-eater, his eyes shielded by his cheesy wrap-around redneck sunglasses. *WHEEEER, WHEEEER,* the trimmer-line cut through crabgrass and wild onions, tinting the air with a bitter green scent.

The secluded garden was massive, cutting deep into the encroaching forest. Impeccable landscaping occupied the majority of the space, a field of five one-hundred-yard wire fences, each one tangled in grapevines. Flanking the vineyard were shallow hillocks of purple dahlia and lavender, watched over by trees drooping with Texas mountain laurel.

The girls didn't make their own wine anymore, too much of a hassle; these days with the internet they could very easily purchase much better wine, older stock, and to be honest Roy was a bit of an idiot and couldn't be trusted with the delicate processes of producing a fine red.

The aforementioned idiot was at the very back near the dryad, the bright late-afternoon sun shining on his copper-and-salt hair. He cut the weed-eater off as she approached, pulling plugs out of his ears. "You look like you've had a hard week, dear," she told him, her long hands clasped together over her belly like a gentleman vicar. "Why don't you take the rest of the day off? Get started on the weekend a little early."

"It *was* a pretty long drive down from Virginia. I admit I am a mite run down today." Roy pushed his iridescent NASCAR sunglasses up, revealing his pale, ocean-bleached eyes. Putting down the trimmer, he beat the grass off his jeans with his gloves.

As always, his eyes cut over at the tree. *The* tree, the tallest one on the property.

Marilyn relished the hint of old fear in that anxious glance. She smiled ingratiatingly. "I would like to ask you one favor before you go, though."

"What's that?"

"Mother tells me that there is…well, it seems that our new neighbors have…*disturbed* something in Annie's house. I'd like to go investigate with

110

my own eyes while they are gone to work and school, but I would like a chaperone. Karen and Theresa have gone to the forest to look for wild mushrooms, and I would appreciate the company."

Even if it's you, she thought. Roy rolled his shoulders uncomfortably, his head bobbing as if he could duck the request. He tugged his sweaty T-shirt to air out his chest and Marilyn caught a whiff of him. Pickled asshole.

"...Yeah, sure."

"When you've put away your tools, I'll be in the kitchen, making you something to drink—it's surprisingly warm for October, isn't it?"

"Warmest year on record so far." Roy hefted the weed-eater and headed for the garage. "How about that global warming, huh?" Marilyn watched him track across the back lawn, slipping between two grapevine fences, disappearing.

Standing in the absolute rear of the property, a stone's throw from the back fence, was the apple tree that made Roy so nervous.

Underneath the lush, brilliant green foliage was a sinuous violin trunk, with its suggestion of an hourglass shape, as if it had grown tall constricted by a ring around the middle. Two main branches thrust up from the top of the trunk in a great Y, bristling with smaller boughs and twigs. Apples studded the tree's endmost fingers, gleaming red under the indigo sky.

As if the branches and leaves were an unbearable burden, the trunk seemed almost to kneel like Atlas carrying the globe, as twisted and bent as a bonsai. Marilyn reached up with both hands and took hold of one of the apples—huge, fat, like heirloom tomatoes—and pulled on it.

The bough resisted, bending right down to her waist before the fruit finally ripped free. She buffed the apple on her sleeve and wordlessly toasted the dryad with it in gratitude, heading toward the house.

❂

He had changed into a fresh shirt while he was in the garage, significantly reducing his stench. Marilyn approved of this. She handed Roy a glass of iced tea and they went out the back door and down the driveway.

They said nothing to each other on the way down the hill. Neither of them was much for small talk, and besides, they'd said pretty much everything that needed to be said a long time ago when she and the girls had found him in 2003, living on the streets in rural New York.

She contemplated New York City as she crossed the dirt and gravel on her horn-hard bare feet, her skirt curtaining around her ankles in the breeze.

The city was nice—the buildings, they'd grown so tall since the last time she was there, and it was a sight to see. But all those ugly new cars were so noisy and horrible, and the air stank, and there were so many new witches and their stunted, half-assed dryads. Suckling like piglets at the teat of the Big Apple, sucking it dry until its core was rotten with consumption, apathy, darkness.

She hated it. The poverty and large-scale drain made the people mean, insolent, resistant to influence. Hard to live with. Hard to control. Cows driven mad by flies. Marilyn preferred small covens in small cities like Blackfield, a town with a population under ten thousand.

You only really needed one tree and as long as you had plenty of cats you were always protected. One tree meant you had a sort of bottleneck push, instead of the constant pull of the piglets. It was why Annie's apples were so fat and rich—Blackfield *surged* with life, stupid red-blooded American hillbilly life, and Marilyn and her girls gorged on its underbelly like ticks on a dog, unseen, unnoticed. A bit like having a secret fishing-hole, really.

They were halfway across Chevalier Village when Roy started belting out a country song to himself.

"Shut up," rasped the old woman.

"Yes ma'am."

A slate-gray cat loped out from under one of the mobile homes in Chevalier, and a little dog lying in the yard jumped to his feet and took off after it.

Marilyn held out her hand and the cat ran up to her, clawing its way up her sleeve and perching on her shoulder. As soon as the terrier crossed the Chevalier property line, he stopped short of the man and the old woman, gave a furtive whimper, and ran back to the safety of his territory.

She was sure that deep down Roy knew what they were, even if he couldn't quite put his finger on it. Roy had never been one to ask questions; he was a worker ant, a drone, and they were his queens. But even he wasn't stupid enough to overlook their eccentricities, the creepy tree in the backyard, their too-intimate regard for each other, and then there was the off-limits third floor, of course, where Mother lived.

Are you looking into the disturbance, cookie? The velvet gray cat rubbed his wet nose on her face. His muffled purring oscillated in her ear.

Yes, Mother. That's what I told you I was going to attend to. Marilyn reached up and stroked the cat's back. *What did you see, anyway?*

Something was asleep in there. The nigger woke it up.

Marilyn pursed her lips. *Such language. And you wonder why we don't let you out of the house.*

Oh, fold it into an airplane and fly it up your ass. The cat gave a rusty meow. *Did you take Sling Blade with you? He's a freak. He's full of plans and low thoughts. He's always looking up here at the windows. I don't trust him around the silverware.*

Yes. Oh, you're one to talk about stealing silverware.

Don't forget to water the tree.

I won't.

112

The two of them crossed Underwood Road and started up the driveway toward the old Victorian, the cat still perched on Marilyn's shoulder like a pirate's parrot. Deep in the folds of her burnoose-like sweater, the dryad's apple thrummed and shifted warmly.

"Ain't nobody home," said Roy.

Marilyn bit her tongue. "That was the whole point of coming over here while they were out for the day."

"Right."

She padded up the front walk, her bare feet plopping on each stepping-stone, and climbed up the front stairs onto the porch. Taking a deep breath, she tested the air—nothing but her own lavender, and Roy's briny miasma—and took hold of the doorknob.

Some heady, electric warmth welled from the knob in her hand, like touching an electric fence with an oven mitt.

Marilyn let go. "Mother's right, something is inside." She peered through the parentheses of her hands, face against the glass, trying to see through the window in the door.

The foyer, wreathed in darkness. Nothing else.

It's been here all this time. The cat looked through the window too, its little gray head shifting from side to side, green eyes shining. *Maybe it wasn't the colored folks what woke it up after all. It's been hiding, waiting for something.*

Roy leaned over and rattled the doorknob. Locked. Arching his back, the gray cat hissed. *Oh, cookie, I can feel it from here!*

Marilyn rubbed the cat's scruff, thinking.

She went down to the end of the wraparound porch and down the side, trying to see in through all the windows, but they were all obscured by the brides'-veil curtains, giving her a look only at angles, shapes, glints of reflected sunlight. Stepping down into the grass, she went around back and up the rear stoop, pressing her hands against the window in the door and looking through them into the kitchen.

The same swelling of strength emanated from the doorknob on this side, too. Even the glass hummed against the edges of her hands, so lightly that she almost doubted it, the wingbeats of a trapped butterfly.

Kitchen table. Magazine, salt-shaker, pepper, envelope.

The fridge was new, but it didn't belong to the new occupants. Annie's fridge was an avocado Frigidaire with alphabet magnets all over it; this one was a big black monolith with a water-and-ice dispenser in the door.

Nothing else was in the kitchen.

The hallway on the other side of the kitchen door, however, was another story.

Marilyn couldn't *see* anything back there, technically, but she received a sense of size, of scale. Something *big* was standing in there, something tall and heavy. The floor and walls almost groaned with the strain. The house itself was like a cage, containing some ancient bear just awoken

113

from a decade of slumber, and even though she hadn't been a child since the Louisiana Purchase, Marilyn felt like a little girl peering in at it.

Whatever it was turned and looked right at her, sending a chill down her carrion spine.

This was old power, this was *nasty* power, dirty cheating stinking power, an ace up the sleeve, a blast from the past. She had stolen, killed and eaten, she'd done and wrought terrible things, black unspeakable things, but this beast was ...*deep,* was the best word she could think of. Deep.

Was this Annie's?

The cat licked a paw and combed its ears. *I think it must have been.*

What is—

Before she could complete the thought, the presence in the house moved up the hallway and through the kitchen, rushing the back door. As it passed through a sunbeam, Marilyn got a sensation of deformed, muscular arms.

"Shit!" she gasped, leaning back. The invisible beast slammed against the locked door hard enough to bang it in the frame. *CRASH!*

Roy flinched. *"Jesus!"*

The windowpanes crunched, but stayed intact. A low bass growl came from the other side of the threshold, deep enough to make the glass buzz. Marilyn felt compelled—no, *drawn* toward the door, as if some force were pulling her inside. She braced one hand against the door-frame, and then the other, and her face felt as if she had pressed the end of a vacuum-cleaner hose to it, sucking, pulling her out of whack.

Whatever was in there, it wanted to *eat* her rotten body like a buzzard, pick her worm-dirt bones clean until there was nothing left but a grin and two holes for eyes.

"The hell they got in there?" asked Roy. "A mastiff?"

She came down and stood next to him, her toes clenching the grass in surprise and aggravation. "Did you hear it barking?"

"...No?"

"Then what makes you...oh, forget it." Marilyn threw a hand at him in exasperation and started off back around the house, the cat in tow. *I've never seen anything like this in all my years,* she thought. *What is this? How could Annie, little newborn-witch Annie, just a baby next to us, how could she conjure something like this?*

Catching up, the cat ran ahead of her and trotted through the dry autumn grass. *There are more things in Heaven and Earth, Horatio, than are dreamt of in your philosophy. —That's Shakespeare, you know. I gave him that one.*

"Mother, you are so full of crap," Marilyn told the cat.

Mock me at your peril, lovely daughter. No doubt Annie summoned it to kill you before you could craft the dryad. She knew you had your eye on her. The question is, what woke him up? It weren't Parkin. That thing in there couldn't give less of a shit about some Yankee negro. No, he's responding to someone else. Someone else is here. Someone directly connected to Annie.

114

Marilyn halted so quickly Roy almost ran into her. "I know who's here," she said, staring at the forest in thought.

"What?" he asked. "That thing in the house?"

She scowled at him. "No no, not that, but I know why it's upright and sniffing the air. I know who woke it up."

The gray cat gazed up at her expectantly.

"Annie's *daughter*," said Marilyn, a slow smile creeping under her Big Bird nose. "That's it, that's it...her little girl is back in town. My little-bird. She's come back to the old haunting grounds. Annie's conjuration knows she's here, she's got Annie's blood in her. He can smell it." Her hands found each other and she wrung them together. "We should put together a welcome-home party."

Roy grinned. "I like parties."

✪

After she sent Roy home, Marilyn went back to the Lazenbury House and stepped into the pantry, where a glass decanter with a cork lid stood on a shelf. Inside the jar was a heap of sun-dried tree frogs, all tangled together like electronics cables. She wrestled one of the frogs out, put it into a food processor, and ground it into a coarse powder that quite resembled cilantro. Then she put the powdered frog and two Earl Grey teabags into a kettle with some water and set it on the range.

While she waited for the tea to boil, Marilyn went into her office, retrieved a book of stamps, and went back to the kitchen, where she grabbed a can of Fancy Feast from the pantry.

The gray cat had followed her into the house. As she tore one of the stamps off the book, it sauntered over to the cat-food can and sniffed it. There was no creaky voice darting into Marilyn's skull like a slow-creeping fog; Mother had retreated from the cat. Probably asleep. She slept a lot these days.

"Did I say that was for you? Get your ass down," she said, brushing the cat down onto the floor.

Marilyn put the LSD stamp on her tongue and opened the Fancy Feast with a manual can opener, then sat at the island and ate it out of the can with a silver spoon stolen from Adolph Hitler's tea service. The swastika on the handle glittered in the track lighting over her head, but the spoon's beauty did nothing to lessen the foul meatloaf-in-brine taste of the cat food.

The acid had just kicked in when the tea-kettle began to whistle. She made a cup of it and sat back down to drink it (black, of course—sugar always screwed with the alchemic makeup of the scrying mixture), staring blankly out the window at deepening colors, listening to intensifying sounds.

115

The breathy *hmmmmm* of the refrigerator.

The constant *tick-tock tick-tock* of the smiling Felix clock on the kitchen wall and its swinging tail and tennis-match eyes, off-rhythm with the grandfather clock in the living room (mental note to wind it up).

A pulpwood truck gargled past out on Underwood Road.

Sparse birdsong fluted in the October trees. She took a deep sip of the tea and closed her eyes.

Projected on the silver screen of her eyelids was a house somewhere in Blackfield…not the Lazenbury, but some brighter, cheerier dwelling, closer to the center of town, with pearl-colored wallpaper and cherrywood furniture. Heavy traffic droned back and forth outside this other house. She walked around, inspecting each room until she was satisfied no one was there, and then opened her eyes. Closed them again.

This time she was walking down a street. A side street, one of those that ran perpendicular to the main thoroughfare. A small gaggle of children walked by, three boys and a girl. One of the boys was black, and Marilyn recognized him as the neighbor's son, the new residents of Annie's house.

The children stopped and she went to them. The girl stooped to pet Marilyn. "Aw, what a pretty kitty. Hi there, pretty-kitty," she cooed.

Meow, said the old woman. She sniffed the girl's hand.

"Meow," said Amanda ~~Hugginkiss~~ Johnson.

"Do you speak Cat, now?" asked the thuggish-looking fat boy.

Marilyn knew him from the trailer park down the hill from the Lazenbury. Amanda glared at him over her shoulder and gave Marilyn a few more luxurious strokes. "Pretty kitty," she said, and jogged off to catch up with the others. "Have a nice day, kitty-cat!"

Opening her eyes again, Marilyn took another sip of tea and clamped her eyelids shut.

Now she was in some kind of shop, some weird type of five-and-dime maybe, if those were still around. Funny-books, plastic toys, board games, and Halloween masks were on display all over the room. She was sitting on a glass counter next to a colored man, who was typing on a sleek white laptop computer.

"Not time to feed you yet, Selina," said the man, giving Marilyn a rub around the ears. "I'll give you something when suppertime gets here, I promise." Pleasure reverberated down her spine in spite of the hand on her back. *Prrrrrow,* she said, and opened her eyes again.

Any luck? asked Mother. The gray cat had climbed back up onto the counter and was licking the last few morsels out of the can in her hands.

Not yet. But I'll find her, don't you worry your pretty little head. Marilyn pushed the Fancy Feast away and combed her fingers through her silver hair, reveling in the acid-altered sensation of her nails sweeping across her scalp.

Dropping acid for almost a century and a half had inured Marilyn against its most devious effects; like most practitioners of her brand of

116

legerdemain, she'd had the revelation a long time ago that, like a dream, the LSD's effects could be controlled, harnessed, channeled. In a dream, when you expect something to happen, it will happen. If you dream about a box, expect to find a decapitated head in that box and that's exactly what you'll find. In that way it's a great method for distilling your own subconscious, for defragmenting one's neural pathways. Cleaning house, if you will. Searching out base desires and mental flaws and eradicating them if possible.

The lysergic acid diethylamide functioned in much the same fashion—if you expected to hallucinate something, you would hallucinate it. For a witch of Marilyn's caliber, hallucinations are a bit more...shall we say, *substantial* when the chemistry is altered by certain secondary ingredients. The cat food helped her channel the hallucinations, to 'tune into' the stray cats of Blackfield instead of having a Pink Floyd loopty-doo session. Without the aftertaste on her tongue, she could forget why she was in a fugue state and what she was attempting to do.

Inserting herself into another cat, Marilyn found herself perched in the branches of an oak somewhere downtown, treed by a black Labrador. Cat number five was under a car somewhere, devouring the cold remnants of a discarded styrofoam box of Chinese takeout.

For the umpteenth time, she mused on how much sweet-and-sour chicken looked like battered and fried mice. Another leap put her behind the wheel of a female tabby, in the middle of a frantic mating session behind the Dollar General on 9th and Thompson.

The tom's barbed penis jabbed at her long-barren womb and she almost fell off the bar stool, snapping back to the Lazenbury kitchen. "Aaraaagh!"

Problems? asked Mother.

The gray cat licked its chops and flopped over on its back, studying her face upside-down.

"No...no. Don't worry about me." Shaking, Marilyn caught her breath and took a deep gulp of the bitter toad tea. "While I search for Annie's daughter, I want you to get a good look at that thing down there in Annie's house and figure out which one it is and how we get rid of it."

Who the hell are you ordering around? Reaching up, the cat snagged Marilyn's sleeve with a toenail and unraveled a loop of yarn out of her sweater. *I was one of Rasputin's lovers and pupils, you know! I mixed pigments for Michelangelo! I taught—*

"I'm not in the mood for your sass, Mother. Or your history lessons."

Sass? You ain't seen sass, cookie.

"I have no doubt. Just, please, while I take care of this, do me a favor and take a look at that hairy freako down there in the Victorian. I'll bring you up a bowl of ice cream after dinner."

Do you promise?

"Yes, yes, of course."

117

The tiramisu flavor? It reminds me so much of Giuseppe and his sister back home in Sicily. Oh, how I loved their house, with its rose trellis and the statue of the fisherman pissing into the ocean—

"Yes, the tiramisu. Now leave me be, Mother. I've work to do." The cat got to its feet and jumped down off the counter, trotting away.

Pointing at the stove, Marilyn gestured the tea-kettle into the air. Floating over to her teacup, it poured her another helping and followed her knobbly finger back to the cooling electric eye.

Her head sank forward, she cupped her eyes in her hands, and Marilyn continued scrying.

Eleven

ADAPT AND OVERCOME. AFTER they left the comic shop, Wayne couldn't get it out of his head. *Be the Hulk. Be better than the problem.* He thought this brilliant new proverb, and the eloquent, intelligent, cat-petting, code-breaking, comic-shop-owning man that called himself Fish was the best thing since the invention of the wheel.

He even *felt* stronger, his feet lighter, as he bounced along behind Pete and Johnny Juan, occasionally flexing his chest and biceps. After the warmth of the shop, the crisp wind hurt his nose, but something about the gamma-ray pep rally made it smell sweeter.

"What are you doing?" Amanda asked him as he was crossing his arms in a bodybuilder flex. She had fallen behind, and now tagged along in the rear. "Is your shirt too small?"

"No?" He made an indignant face and put his hands in his pockets.

Pete turned left and trundled down the sidewalk to a short, quaint hump of a bridge with rusted girders and simple steel banisters. Standing beside it, they could see down into the canal. A musky fish-smell coiled up from where water trickled along the bottom some eight, nine, ten feet down.

The channel itself was a square aqueduct with a flat bottom some fifteen feet wide, made of pebbly dark concrete dyed green by algae and moss. Sandbars of dirt and rocks collected along the walls.

Pete scanned the street, reassured himself that no one was watching, and hopped down to a concrete platform with a grunt. The others reluctantly followed suit.

PVC pipes ran along the underside of the bridge, painted with jibber-jabber graffiti. Pete ducked under them and walked beside the thin ribbon of water at their feet. There was barely a current; Wayne could only see it if he bent over to examine the stream, the sky reflecting off of the wobbling quicksilver.

Under the bridge, Amanda's voice reverberated, hollow, intimate. "Are you sure this is safe?"

Corn-fed Pete regarded her with obvious amusement, wheezing through his nose. "Of *course* it's not safe. Fun things hardly ever are." Their excursion definitely qualified as 'fun', though Wayne was getting tired and his feet hurt. This was probably the most exercise he'd gotten in a long time. But then, adventure was *supposed* to hurt, wasn't it? Adapt and overcome.

Soon the novelty was gone and they were marching along the bottom of the channel as placidly as they had the sidewalk. Wayne squinted up at the stark blue sky. The canal cut down the middle of several city blocks, between the buildings to the north and south. This deep in the cut he felt as if he were walking a trail along the lowermost narrows of the Grand Canyon, framed by darkness. The real Grand Canyon, however, wouldn't be this marred by graffiti: RANDY FREEMAN WAS HERE 07/22/2007. YEE-THO-RAH. A cartoonish rendering of a veiny penis and testicles, crude pubic hair corkscrewing from the speedbag scrotum underneath. DIAMOND AND TRAVUS, ♡ 4-EVA.

As Pete led them farther and farther, the water picked up eddies seeping out of the concrete until the floor was rippling glass that clapped under their shoes. Splat, splat, splat.

The canal angled to the left and became deeper, with a dip in the middle, and a gaping black storm drain low in the wall continuously gurgled water into the trough, creating a fast-moving brook. They walked along the side of the ditch then, their ankles turned so they could traverse the incline like billy-goats, and sometimes Amanda would steady herself with a hand on the concrete. Some part of Wayne expected one of them to slip and fall into the water, sliding away and out of sight, screaming and flailing, but it never happened.

The buildings became shorter and shorter until the steel banisters along the top of the channel became a chainlink fence, and the crackerjack *WHZZ, WHZZ* of a power-wrench howled down to them from some mechanic's garage overhead. *PSST, PSSSST,* the pit-viper hiss of a paint-sprayer.

Stands of hickory and ivy and something with broad green leaves sprouted up from the base of the wall, where drifts of sand and trash accumulated. When the children shouldered past them, tiny birds shifted in the foliage, chirping and rustling.

Rumbling water became louder and louder until the children came to the end of the aqueduct and found the river, a wide band of darkness sparkling under the cold afternoon sun. The concrete sloped and the walls flared out like a spout, river-water licking and lapping up onto the stony floor and leaving smears of slimy brown algae.

Pete turned right and clambered up a short grassy hill, pushing past the end of the chainlink fence.

At the top of the rise, Wayne could finally see over the walls of the canal. They had walked east out of the main historical district and they could no longer see it, only the backs of various buildings and groves of hickory and oak.

On the other side of the river, far to the west, an apartment building was half-obscured behind the treeline.

"Where to now, Dora the Explorer?" asked Amanda.

"Down the river to the pipe, and then you cross it to the other side." Their leader set off across the riverbank, stumbling across the uneven grass. Wayne glanced at Amanda, who gave him a noncommittal *whatever* face, coughed into her hands, and fell into step behind Pete.

The pipe turned out to be close enough that they could see it as soon as they went over the hill. In the background to the east, after-work traffic shushed back and forth across a long concrete bridge.

A pile of smashed bricks lay under a froth of dry brown brush. Johnny Juan picked up a piece, flinging it sideways into the river. *K'ploonk.* "I'm kinda getting tired, guys. My feet really hurt."

"You *wanted* to come," said Wayne. "You don't even live out here."

Johnny scratched his face and shrugged. "I know."

Taking off his glasses, Wayne stopped to buff them on his shirt and the world around him turned into a smear of colors. When he put them back on, Pete was already heading for the river.

To Wayne's relief, the pipe was two or three feet across, just big enough that he wouldn't have been able to get his arms around it. Pete and Amanda had no trouble with it at all—the big guy put out his arms and heel-toed across it like a tightrope walker, only stopping once halfway across to bend over at the waist, pinwheeling his arms to keep his balance.

"Watch out!" shrilled Amanda.

Pete sneered at her and straightened, throwing out his belly. "Man I got this. See how a pro does it."

He flipped them all the finger, turned, and wobbled the rest of the way across. When he got to the other side he threw himself on the grass and sat down to watch them make fools of themselves, using the bank as a windbreak.

Amanda stormed down the hill, stepped onto the pipe, and gracefully strolled the entire length of it as easily as if she were on a sidewalk, her long legs scissoring right across.

"Wow," said Wayne.

"It's ballet," explained Johnny Juan. "Her mom takes her every Saturday to the ballet studio over on my side of town, the one in the building that used to be a garage or a hangar or something."

"How did you know *that?*"

Johnny waggled his eyebrows. "It's right next door to my family's restaurant Puesta Del Sol." Turning back to the river, he gave a deep, steeling sigh, and flexed his shoulders. "I guess I'll go across next. See you on the flip side, amigo."

The boy stepped onto the big sky-blue pipe and started off across the narrow water. About one-third of the way across, he lost his balance and bent over at the waist, his ass in the air and one arm thrown out to the side. The other hand was pressed against the top of the pipe.

Johnny quivered there, twitching back and forth trying to find his center of gravity, and then straightened up again and shuffled forward, hunkered down with his hands out like a man trying to catch a mouse. As soon as he reached the opposite side he threw himself onto the grass and clambered away from the water on all fours.

"Your turn, Batman," Amanda shouted through her hands as Wayne climbed down to the bottom of the river-bank.

Up close, the pipe seemed a lot slimmer than it had from the berm, maybe only a foot-and-a-half across, *easily* small enough to wrap his arms around and touch his fingers. Wayne put a foot on the plastic curve and something inside him quailed from the hollow thump.

The others all sat on the far bank, watching him expectantly. *Adapt and overcome.* His reputation hung on this moment, he knew down deep. It wasn't the first time Wayne had been forced to be brave in order to fit in.

Be the Hulk, he thought, standing on the utilities pipe over the Cataloosa River as Blackfield slipped into evening.

Pete, Amanda, and Johnny Juan sat on the grass watching him. *Adapt and overcome.* A band of rushing quicksilver streamed by underneath him, thirty or forty feet across, clear enough that he could see shelves of greasy brown stone under the surface.

"Hell are you doing?" said Pete. The water looked deep. Over his head, at least. "Snap out of it, fool!"

Be bigger. Be badder. Wayne was halfway across, his arms straight out to either side, his hips swaying and twitching to maintain his balance. "I'm comin, I gotta—" he started to say, and then he slipped.

One leg slid into thin air and he sat down hard, the pipe flexing underneath and bouncing him a few inches. Suddenly he was lying on his belly in terror, straddling it, holding on with both hands. The fall had happened so fast that he couldn't remember anything between standing-there and lying-there.

"You okay?" someone called.

Water cackled past the toes of his shoes. Now the burn came, the hot iron belly-ache of blunt force to the testicles.

Wayne sat up, hugging the pipe with his knees. "Yeah," he shouted over the coursing water, wincing up at the sky. He'd hit his chin on the pipe too, banging his teeth together, and now a headache was germinating at the base of his skull.

He slid forward, inching across on his butt. "Uuuggh! I smacked my nuts is all."

Pete gave a Nelson-laugh. *"Ha-ha!"*

Once everybody was safely on the other side, Pete wallowed back to his feet and steamered off across a huge gravel clearing. Now that he'd had a moment to sit and rest for a minute, he seemed to have gotten a second wind, and he was really hustling.

122

Dry grass, like brush you'd see at the edge of the desert, made a crunchy lacework in the chalky white gravel. Clouds had moved in while they were traversing the Broad Avenue canal, and the bright sun was now a smear behind shreds of white, sapping the childrens' shadows of substance.

They passed a big wooden sign that said TRADE DAY. "What is that?" asked Wayne.

Amanda crunched along behind them. "Early every Saturday morning, a bunch of people set up here and sell stuff. A big flea market, I guess."

"Like a garage sale, or a yard sale?"

"Yeah, but lots of them in one place."

"My Paw-Paw used to take me when I was little," said Pete. "There wasn't really ever anything good. They had toys, but they was always old and dirty and sometimes broke."

"My brother got a sword there once." Amanda smirked at the ground, her hair draping down around her face. She'd taken down her ponytail. "But the firefighters stepped on it and broke it when our old house burned down."

"Is that why you're living in Chevalier Village?" asked Wayne.

"Yeah. My dad couldn't afford to rebuild the house."

"Where's your brother at now?" He made a face. "I thought you only had the two little brothers. Kasey and Evan."

"He moved away with his girlfriend a couple years ago. They went to …North Dakota? South Dakota? One of the Dakotas. He went to work on the oilfields, Daddy says. We don't hear from him much. Mama says it's because of 'that controllin bitch' he's livin with. She don't let him talk to nobody."

"Ah." This topic was a bit out of Wayne's league.

"So what were you talkin about this morning?" she asked, her face pinching up in a suspicious way, squinting. "When you said you had breakfast with a ghost."

"My mom died of cancer. This was hers." Wayne took out the ring around his neck. "Dad and me, we always keep a place for her at the kitchen table. We carry her everywhere we go, Aunt Marcelina says, and Dad says she came down from Chicago with us." He put the ring to his eye and ogled Amanda through it.

She smiled wistfully. "That's sweet. I'm sorry about your mom."

"It's okay. It's been a while. …Sometimes I feel like I don't remember as much about her as I did yesterday." He tucked the ring back into his shirt. "I don't like that. I don't want to forget her."

"I don't think you will." The girl reached over and squeezed his shoulder.

She smelled like flowers, pasty acne ointment, the astringent burn of hairspray. Wayne returned the smile and pushed his glasses up on the bridge of his nose.

123

Scraggly pine-trees made a cathedral of the forest around them. The treeline was thick with undergrowth, but Pete picked out a bald spot in the vegetation where rust-colored needles were a carpet under the bushes. Strung across the path was a rusty old barbed-wire fence, presided over by a NO TRESPASSING sign nailed to a tree and shot full of holes.

Pete stepped on the bottom strand of wire and lifted the top, opening a passage for them. Wayne expected Amanda to say something about the sign, but she never did.

As soon as they stepped into the woods, the day faded into a nether-light, streaming weakly through the pine boughs.

The kids moved deeper until they'd left the constant rumble-and-hiss of the highway behind for the forest's cloistered hush. They walked for what must have been a half an hour, traipsing through leafy foliage and across patches of crumbly yellow gravel, climbing over fallen trees mulchy with termite-rot.

At one point they passed a little valley with steep banks, trees standing precariously on the edge with their roots clawing at thin air.

Deep and dark, the pit was full of garbage, old garbage in sun-rotten bags, spilling mush and flaky paper onto the ground. Two new-looking bicycles, their wheels bent and their tires flat. A nude, one-legged Barbie-doll. Beer bottles and cans by the legion, glistening brown and black and white in the straw.

"See?" asked Pete. "Wasn't this better than walking down the street where creepers can pick you up?"

A peculiar feeling of placelessness had come over Wayne—without tall buildings to use as landmarks and reference points, he had lost his sense of direction amidst the endlessly identical trees. He enjoyed being out in nature, but he had developed a creeping sense of panic at not knowing where he was.

"Not really." Amanda's gait had become slow and indolent, and she had crossed her arms, her shoulders scrunched against a creeping chill.

Until then, Wayne hadn't noticed that the afternoon had gotten colder. It was also darker, though they still had plenty of light left. He peered up at the smudge of white sun through the trees and judged that it was probably 6 or 7, on the verge of nightfall.

She tucked her hair behind her ear. "It would have been faster and safer to ride home with our parents. —Or heck, on the school bus, even."

Pete's face fell, his expression going from tired, determined, and content down the other end of the spectrum to hurt and exhausted. "Well, I only wanted to *show* you guys something, you know? And I wanted to show the New Guy here around."

The corner of Wayne's mouth tucked up in a smile. "I appreciate it. I never been hiking before. It's nice." He took a deep breath. "It smells nice. *Pine* smells nice. I like it out here."

Pete shrugged, as if to say, *See?*

"Let's just hurry up and get home before it gets dark, okay?" Amanda shouldered past them and walked down the trail in her stormy, gangly way, her hair swinging from the back of her head. "I think we're close enough now that it doesn't matter."

The trail had widened and was now quite visible, a thinness that meandered across the woods, occasionally meeting a side trail. Pine gave way to white-barked birch and naked dogwood, and little brooks zagged across their path, giving the kids something to jump over, stepping from stone to stone. Tiny silver fish darted through the brackish water.

Wayne had lapsed into a daydream, staring at his feet, when Johnny Juan said, "Woah. That's creepy as hell."

"Oh my God," breathed Amanda.

Deep in the trees was a clown's face the approximate size and shape of a supermarket shopping cart.

Rust-stains streaked down from its eyes and mouth as if it were bleeding from the inside. On closer inspection, he saw that it was a sort of cart, a roller-coaster car or part of a carousel. "Is this your surprise?" asked Amanda.

"No," said Pete, shaking his head and walking away. "That's neat, but it's not what I wanted to show you."

Pine needles and briars choked the passenger seat of the clown-face car. The mess was dark, tangled, ominous. Wayne wanted to get away from it, so he overtook Pete and jogged down the trail.

"Wait up," said Johnny.

Wayne went down a short slope and found a break in the trees where the last dregs of sunlight slanted in from a clearing. He stepped over a half-buried train track and emerged into what might have been one of the coolest things he had ever seen.

The stark umbrella-skeleton of a hulking Spider ride threw stripes of shadow over them, its suspended cars rusting quietly in the white sun. He had come out onto what appeared to be a go-kart track, a paved oval about ten feet wide and painted green. Grass and milkweed thrust up through cracks.

"Ho-lee Moses." The forest stood vigil over the ruins of an abandoned amusement park.

A tree grew up through the middle of a small roller-coaster track, shadowing more rusted-out clown-cars and a broken scaffolding no taller than an adult man.

His friends crunched up out of the woods and stood next to him.

"Now *that's* cool," said Johnny.

Amanda picked a careful path across the buckled road, stumbling over the asphalt and treading on the tall weeds. "I had no idea this was out here. You found this last summer?"

Pete forged ahead, leading them through an aluminum garage at one end of the track. The ground was oily and nothing grew, which made for easy walking. "Yeah. I came out here to, ahh…look for Bigfoot. My mom said this is the old fairgrounds. It's supposed to be one of those travelin amusement park things—you know, how they go from city to city, settin up in mall parking lots and stuff. But she said this one, the people set it up, and then they disappeared."

"Disappeared?" Wayne's neck prickled. A go-kart was overturned against the wall, its axle bent, its guts pulled out. Parts lay strewn around it.

Leading them through the heart of the overgrown carnival, Pete goosestepped and lurched over the dead weeds, trampling briars, sticks cracking under his shoes. "Yeah. She said it happened back in the 80s. Before any of us were born."

Gradually the brush gave away to open gravel and dirt. "Mom said the city tried to open it anyway, and it ran for like a year, but they couldn't make any money on it and it was too expensive to clear it out. So they left it here."

A long arcade leaned over a bushy promenade, its game-booths frothing with hickory and blackberry bushes. HIT THE PINS! POP THE BALLOONS! THROW A DART! WIN A PRIZE!

"Y'all don't tell her we were out here. She said not to come back. It's dangerous here." Pete gazed up at a ten-foot board standing at the end of the concourse, with a round bell at the top. "...Is this what I think it is?"

Wayne came closer. "Hey, yeah. It's one of those strong-man tester things. Where you hit the thing with the hammer and the slider hits the bell." He grinned up at his big friend. "Man, I bet you could knock the crap out of this thing."

"Let's find the hammer," said Amanda.

Wandering in separate directions, the children searched through the dry grass and weeds. Johnny and Amanda went to root around under the Spider, while Pete went behind the north side of the arcade. Wayne kept going west, and found himself in an intersection between a funhouse and a caved-in concession stand. The funhouse was sooty black, heavily damaged by fire and overgrown with creepy ivy, so he didn't bother going in.

The marquee over the concession stand read FUNNEL CAKES, SNO-CONES, CANDY APPLES. The sign underneath the sales counter told him he was in WEAVER'S WONDERLAND, and that it was FUN FOR ALL AGES!

That must be the person that built and abandoned this place, he thought, cupping his face against the cloudy windows.

The concession stand was empty except for a chest freezer with the lid open. It was nasty with black gunk. *I wonder what happened to him.* Wayne couldn't imagine anybody willingly walking away from owning their very own amusement park.

When he looked away, his eyes were caught by a giant contraption down the right-hand street.

Like a flying saucer crashed to Earth, a huge purple Gravitron rested in a bed of brush, its door wide open to reveal a dark mouth. Strips of dead bulbs marched in ribcage rows down its sides and down the frames supporting it from above. Wayne ventured up the bulkmetal ramp into the gawping machine. The curved black walls were lined with padded seats that, in the rundown darkness, could have been gurneys rather than seats meant for park patrons.

A Formica coffee-table stood near the back of the Gravitron chamber, the woodgrain skin rubbed away at the corners. Several half-melted red and white candles stood in brass candelabras around a white bowl.

Wayne crept closer. The bowl was full of some black substance...or perhaps it was the shadows playing a trick on him, he couldn't tell; the cavernous dark of the machine's interior made it hard to see.

Picking up the bowl, he tilted it toward the light. Whatever it was, the black stuff in the bowl smelled foul: pennies, cigarettes, burnt hair.

The inside of the bowl was black but dry—burned out, the contents had been cooked. He turned it upside-down to look at the bottom (MADE IN CHINA, maybe?) and saw the jagged rim of a pair of nostrils, and the two guileless eye-sockets of a human skull. The teeth had been sawed away under the nose.

"Uhh!" he exclaimed, snatching his hands away. The skull hit the carpeted floor with a thump.

He felt like he ought to scream. That seemed like the logical thing to do, to draw a great big breath, open his mouth, and belt out the loudest shriek he could muster, but his lungs were too small and he couldn't get purchase on the air. As if the Gravitron's door had closed and Martians were sucking out all the oxygen.

"Uhh," he said again, backing away.

KSSS! A blast of air came out of the floor behind him and he leapt away in fright, shouting, almost falling over the coffee table.

Finding his feet, Wayne saw that it wasn't air—it was a *snake*, dear God it was a long fat snake, a firehose the olive-brown of poop, draped across the black carpet in swoopy cursive. Darker markings like Hershey's Kisses ran down its smooth, flabby sides.

The snake had reared up and now watched him warily, its fat jowls puffing inside its pink mouth, fangs bared. *Damn*, thought the boy, *what do I do what do I do what do I do?*

"HELP!" he screamed, or that's what he tried to do, but it came out a whispery squeak, flitting through the constricted tin whistle of his throat. Coiling protectively in the center of the Gravitron, the snake kept hissing at Wayne in that low nail-in-the-tire way, barely audible. It lay between him and the front door of the carnival ride, between the boy and any chance of escape.

"Get out of here!" Wayne snatched up a candelabra and hurled it at the snake.

The candle and candelabra hit the floor and broke into two pieces, whipping over the snake's head. *Fsssk!* The reptile struck at it as it went by, punching out and withdrawing again.

Wayne stumbled up on top of the creaking-cracking table and pressed himself against the Gravitron wall. The padded gurney-seat behind him was wet and stank of mold.

"Go aw—" he began to scream, but the snake slithered after him, climbing up. Before he could get away, it jabbed in and bit him on the left leg just below his knee, *fsst!*, fangs stapling through his jeans into the soft meat of his calf.

Startled and confused, Wayne softshoed backwards off the table in a tumble of candles, skidding, collapsing into the floor. His knees and shoulder reverberated against the wooden platform with a kettle-drum *boom-boom*.

Coiling on the table, the snake peered up out of the bowl of its chubby chocolate-kisses body, puffy pink yawning, the tip of its tail wriggling as if it had rattles to shake.

Wayne's leg felt broken. Knife-blades from the sun swarmed and clashed under his skin, fighting each other in the flesh behind the bite, cutting him to ribbons from the inside. The pain was unlike anything he had ever experienced in his life—*burning, pinching, stabbing, angry,* it was hot coals and hornets and rusty nails all mixed together, scraping the bone clean with rending red teeth.

He wrenched back the leg of his jeans expecting to find a white bone protruding from his brown skin, but there were only two puncture-wounds, beading raspberry blood.

Cold numbness and needles took over his left foot, prickling his toes, his heel. His calf was beginning to swell.

His tongue was too big for his mouth. His throat was closing up. He turned over on his back and goldfish-gawped at dry air, tears in his eyes. The boxing-glove pressing against the roof of his mouth tasted like batteries.

"Hep!" he wheezed as loud as he could manage, his lips tingling, and fought for air. His shirt was ten sizes too small, constricting his lungs in belts of cotton. "Huuuk—huuuuuk—"

BOOM, BOOM, BOOM, somebody came running up the ramp into the Gravitron. A barbarian giant plastered the far wall in shadow, filling the doorway with his body, and in his thick hands was a mallet with a striker-head as big as a mailbox.

Pete lingered for about two seconds, taking in the scene, and then he charged across the Gravitron and brought the strength-test hammer down on the snake, smashing it so hard the table trampolined the reptile into the air. Someone—*a girl?*—screamed, but to Wayne it was the muffled keening of a kitten.

The ceiling fell slowly away piece by piece, unmasking an abyss of shimmering red stars.

128

Big old Pete, good old Pete, Petey-boy, the Incredible Pete, he demolished both table and snake, swearing at top volume, unleashing every swear and curse he knew, even as the blood-galaxy uncovered itself above his head. The huge hammer came down on the snake again and again, *fump!...fump!...fump!*

The night sky glittered with rubies. Wayne couldn't understand any of Pete's shouting through the cotton in his ears, like an AM broadcast on a bad signal. His stomach churned, but he didn't have the strength to turn over.

Silky foam seethed out between Wayne's lips and ran across his cheeks. A force lifted the boy up—*Aliens,* he thought, as he rose toward that malevolent universe, *they're taking me away into their purple spaceship, they're gonna cut me up and do tests on me*—and then he was gone.

Twelve

B1GR3D: hey

Received at 9:42pm
pizzam4n_1982: what u want stepchild
B1GR3D: nice pictures. U look good
pizzam4n_1982: thanks
pizzam4n_1982: you don't look so bad yourself, ol man. I am diggin that red hair. Always wanted me a wild irish rose
B1GR3D: old man? haha
B1GR3D: what you doin
pizzam4n_1982: gettin off work, u?
B1GR3D: bored
B1GR3D: i want sum of that goodlookin body
pizzam4n_1982: boy you wouldnt know what to do with it
B1GR3D: I bet I can figure it out. Why dont u swing by on the way home an let me hit it
pizzam4n_1982: let u hit it? Lol
pizzam4n_1982: oh ho ho you aint even gonna buy me dinner first. I see how it is
B1GR3D: if you want dinner I got plenty of food here. hell I'll cook u a steak if you want. damn good steak. Bake potato, whole 9 yards
pizzam4n_1982: you know the way to a mans heart, don't you?
B1GR3D: I sure do.

✪

Black Velvet grumbled into the parking lot of Riverview Terrace Apartments, Joel Ellis behind the wheel, his cellphone clutched in one hand. The iPhone's screen illuminated his face with B1GR3D's address. *This redneck better be a good cook*, he thought, peering through the windshield at the apartment numbers, looking for Apt 427. *I ain't fitna put myself in some stranger-danger for no cheap-ass meat.*

Building Four was in the back of the complex, a brownstone bulwark against the dark woodline. The Monte Carlo eased into a slot, washing 424's windows with bright yellow headlight, and the engine cut off. Joel got out and scanned the row of doorways.

Eyes peered through the blinds in 427's window.

There you is. He slipped his phone into his pocket, locked his car, and sauntered up the sidewalk. 427's door opened and a man stepped out, considerably taller than he expected, with a slender neck and a jawline that could cut glass.

"Hey there," said the man. He was dressed conservatively, in a flannel button-up with the sleeves rolled, and well-fit jeans.

"Sup, stepchild. You must be Big Red."

B1GR3D smiled and gave a bashful chuckle. "That I am."

This was always the hardest part, the awkward introductory phase, where they were still feeling out each other's body language and weighing their own regrets and needs, trying to get comfortable and break the ice or find a reason to leave and forget it ever happened.

"Well, come on in."

"Thank-yuh." Joel stepped inside.

The tiny apartment was meticulously clean. Hanging on the walls were impressionistic paintings of wildlife posing dramatically in the forest—deer, foxes, mice, wolves. Large prints, from the look of it, no brushstrokes. Joel touched one of them. Thin cardboard. A ten-dollar Walmart poster, still shrinkwrapped. Other than a black sofa, there was only a desk with a bulky gray laptop on it and a flatscreen TV on a squat, altar-like entertainment center.

Joel sat on the sofa as Red went into the kitchen, and it crackled under his body. A slipcover encased the futon in clear protective plastic. The aluminum shafts that served as its legs stood on wooden medallions, like coasters.

To protect the carpet, he supposed.

"This remind me of my grandmama," he said, brushing his fingertips over it. He could see himself in the TV screen as clearly as if it were a mirror. "Every piece of furniture in her house was covered in plastic. The couch, the mattresses, there was even a floormat in the living room on top of the carpet."

"I like a clean, healthy house," said Red's voice. "I grew up with filthy people, neatness suits me."

Machinery whirred to life in another room. As Red returned with two glasses, a robot hockey-puck came humming out of a dark hallway and vacuumed the carpet in front of the couch. "Roomba," said Joel, as Red handed him a drink. His new friend had the craggy hands of a workin' man. "I always wanted one of those."

"It's handy."

Joel sniffed the water-glass and took an exploratory sip. Whiskey, and it went down smoother than soda. Hardly any burn at all, with a vague maple undertone, so faint he wondered if the honey-color was playing tricks on his tongue. "Damn, that's nice," he said, holding the glass up so he could see through it.

"I got the steaks on out back." Red walked away. Joel swirled the whiskey, washed it all down his throat, and followed him through the kitchen, pouring himself another couple of fingers on the way.

'Out back' was a concrete patio about the size of a walk-in closet, with two plastic lawn chairs and a huge grill. A lone lantern-style porch light brightened the scene, and a damp phantom of October breathed across the wet grass.

At the edge of Red's tiny yard was a wilderness of pines, quiet and still and impenetrable in its darkness.

The grill was obviously where most of Red's money went—a top-of-the-line charcoal-fired beast with wood-slat leaf tables on both sides. He opened the top and smoke billowed out, two levels of grills scissoring open like the trays in a tackle box.

On the bottom grill two porterhouse steaks, charred black and Satanic-red, sizzled angrily over a bed of glowing coals. Nestled between them were a pair of potatoes wrapped in tin foil.

Joel settled into one of the lawn chairs while Red used a pair of tongs to place spears of asparagus around the steaks, and four medallions of buttered Italian bread on the upper shelf. The aroma streaming out of the cooker was immense, an enveloping sauna of rich salt. Joel wanted to take off his shirt and bathe in the savory steam, absorb it like a sponge.

"That is outstanding."

Red smiled over his shoulder and flipped the steaks. *Ksss.* "I used to be a cook, on a boat."

"Yeah?"

"Yep. I used to live in Maine. Near the ocean. My father worked on fishin boats all my life and when I graduated high school, he wanted me to follow in his footsteps. But I wasn't into that. Dangerous work. Boring. You lose fingers. Fall overboard. Break your legs."

He tapped his head with the hinge of the tongs. "Not enough of a challenge up here. *But,* it was what my father wanted, and there wasn't any convincing him otherwise. After I looked and looked for work at home, I finally had to admit to myself that I was going to have to take up the family business and catch fish for a living."

Joel sipped his whiskey, listening raptly—or, at least, the best approximation he could manage.

"So, I hooked up with this crew goin out that season and went out to sea." Red flipped the bread, piece by piece. "Unfortunately, I wasn't cut out for it after all. Those guys really shit on me. But, here's the funny part, I turned out to be a pretty good cook. So they stashed me in the galley and put me to work makin dinner. That was actually where I shined."

"Ah." *Sniff*. "So what you doing now?"

Red wagged the tongs at him reproachfully. "I can't tell you that. I'm sorry."

"If you told me, you'd have to kill me?"

It was a joke, but Joel's face went cold anyway.

Red smirked, snorted through his nose. "Let's just say I'm kind of a big shot around town, and if word got out that I'm, uhh—"

"Gay as a three-dollar football bat?"

"Well, heh. I actually swing both ways, but yeah. And you know how it is in these small-minded little quarterback-hero southern towns. My name wouldn't make a very valuable currency anymore, put it that way."

"*Hmmph*, yeah. I catch what you pitchin."

"*Do* you?" Red went past him into the kitchen, squeezing his knee on the way by. "You're a catcher, hmm?"

"Why, you tryin to score? Cause I'm lookin for a batter, baby. With a big ol bat."

The former mess cook came back with plates and tonged the food onto them, then closed the grill lid and went back into the kitchen for a bottle of steak sauce and the rest of the whiskey.

Glorious, the steaks were absolutely glorious, worthy of being remembered in song, they didn't even *need* the A-1. Joel and Red sat on the porch eating quietly, staring out at the twilight forest behind the building.

"So what do you do?" asked Red.

"I cook and run the register at Miguel's Pizza up in the mountains. Up there at the bottom of the ridge from Rocktown." Joel bit the end off of an asparagus spear. "You ever go rock climbin?"

"Nah. Never saw the appeal."

"Yeh," said Joel. The moon was an orange-wedge behind the trees. "Me neither."

Taking out his phone, he checked to see what time it was. A quarter to eleven. Man, he never got sleepy this early, after work he was usually up until two, three in the morning. Joel put down his fork and screwed a fist into one eye.

"Tired?" asked Red.

"A little bit."

"Maybe you should take a vacation day. Play hookey." Red grinned. "You can play hookey here with me."

"Hookey? You think I'm a hooker, hooker?"

Red laughed and sawed off a piece of steak. "You tell me."

Joel's good-natured snort turned into a yawn. He slumped in his chair, feeling more and more comfortable by the minute, until his plate was on top of his crotch and he was squinting at it, slowly cutting off bites and putting them into his mouth.

"Oh," he said, dropping his fork with a clatter.

He tried to sit up, pushing with a heel, but his foot slid. Bracing himself with his elbows, he wriggled up a few inches and twisted to collect his fork up off the ground.

It was like trying to pick up a stuffed bear with a claw machine: loose, weak, fumbly. The fork seemed immaterial until he managed to put a finger on it. "Whassup here." Tines scraped across the concrete.

"Having trouble, pizza-man?" asked Red.

"Yeah, shit, somethin wrong with me."

The whiskey must have been a little more powerful than I gave it credit for, Joel mused, wrapping a fist around the fork and picking it up.

Goddamn, but he was so exhausted. The kind of bone-tired exhausted when you got up early but you ain't done nothin all day and you want to lay down at three in the afternoon and take a nap and sleep all day and not really eat anything and when you wake up you're like *what year is it*—

He deposited the fork on the plate in his lap and rubbed his eyes. His fingers felt like they belonged to someone else and his head was half-full of water, spinning and swaying as he tried to get a fix on Red's face.

"I think...I think I drank too much."

"Maybe. This stuff is smooth. It sneaks up on you. Hey, why were you calling me 'stepchild' earlier?"

Joel waggled a handful of fingers at his own head, then at Red's, then at his own again. "Cause the hair. Red hair. You know—what they say, whip you like a red-headed stepchild."

"I see. You want to whip me?"

"Kinda. Maybe. Maybe *you* can whip *me.*" Joel lifted his plate in both hands and shimmied upward in his chair, trying to sit up straight. The remains of his dinner slid off into the floor, his fork ringing across the concrete again in a mess of potato-mush and bits of asparagus. "Shit."

"I'll get it," said Red, putting his plate on the grill and rising from his chair.

"I got it, I got it." Leaning forward, Joel reached for the food to pick it up with his hand and put it back on the plate, but to his surprise the back yard, grass, rocks, and all, pivoted up and hit him in the face.

✸

"Ugh." Joel opened his grainy eyes to find himself in some kind of...basement, or a garage or something, a grungy space full of junk.

For some reason, the room was upside down. Water dripped somewhere.

Drip. Drip. Drip.

Everything was cloaked in shadow, except for a piss-yellow fluorescent bulb inside the upper half of a workbench. Tools and engine parts lined the walls and scattered across the floor, and at the far end of the room was a giant wooden cutout, a spray-painted portrait of that old Creature from the Black Lagoon.

A long plastic marquee leaned sideways against the wall, a dingy white antique. ARE YOU TOO COOL FOR SCHOOL?, it asked cheerfully, next to a cartoon coyote holding a glass with flames licking up out of it. DRINK FIREWATER SARSAPARILLA!

"Whhfffk."

Joel's head was pounding and drool ran up his cheeks, collecting on his forehead. When he tried to rub his face, he found that his hands were cuffed together, and the cuffs were chained to the floor.

Drip. Drip. Drip.

"Mmmmff."

Cotton pressed against his tongue, and something tight was bound around his face and the back of his neck. He was wearing a gag.

Looking down (or up, as the case may be) he saw that he was hanging from the ceiling by chains around his ankles. All his clothes were gone except for his underwear, a blue cotton banana-hammock. Subterranean chill raised goosebumps on his naked thighs.

Jesus Christ, his worst sensationalist fears had come true—somebody he met on the internet for sex had abducted him.

Was Red a cannibal?

Oh God that's it, ain't it? Your cheap bitch ass gonna get ate up, just cause you don't wanna buy your own steak.

He twisted and jerked, trying to see more of the room, trying to ignore the dripping water. Revolving slowly to the left, he saw that he wasn't the only person hanging out, so to speak. A white guy, also dressed only in his Hanes, ankles chained to the ceiling. He was facing the wall, bruises all over his shoulders as if he'd been beaten unconscious.

"Hey," said Joel through the gag, *hhnnngh.* Swaying his head from side to side, he swung his center of gravity back and forth, pulling on the chain around his cuffs. He managed to bump the guy with his shoulder, causing him to wobble and turn slowly on his chain.

When his fellow abductee-in-arms turned all the way around, Joel pissed his hammock.

The man was dead—*very* dead, his throat cut, his neck a slack grin stringy with red-black fibers, the white of his larynx glinting in the worktable's light. A sheet of dried blood ran up his purple face, collecting on the top of his head, where it was dripping on the dark floor.

He'd been bled dry like a pig.

Drip. Drip. Drip.

SATURDAY

Thirteen

WAYNE PARKIN WOKE UP in a cold, dark room under a too-thin blanket. After a moment of disoriented, delirious eyerolling, he concluded that he was in a hospital room. The only light came from the bathroom, seeping in around the hinge, giving shape to dark angles.

Someone was asleep in the chair next to the bed. Wayne shifted to that side and discovered Leon, sound asleep, his rumpled army-jacket folded up under his cheek.

As soon as he saw his father, something inside Wayne broke, a brittle eggshell crumpling deep inside of him, and tears sprang to his eyes. His throat burned with shame and embarrassment. *I bet I scared you so bad,* he thought, grimacing. *I am so sorry. I am so sorry I asked you to let me walk home.*

"Daddy," he said to the dim figure, but all that came out was a breathy squeal.

Leon snored.

Discouraged, Wayne lifted the covers and examined his left foot, the soft cotton sliding across his sensitive knee like the roughest burlap. There had been at least a tiny part of his mind that'd expected it to simply be gone—hacked off with a bonesaw and stapled shut, wound about with a bloodstained bandage. But other than tenderness and mild swelling, the extremity was present and accounted for. The bandage around his calf was tight but clean.

Too many horror movies.

He lay back down and again considered trying to rouse his father, but in the end he decided that it would be better to let him sleep. The ol' man probably had a hard night, and without his patent-pending liquid courage, it must have been twice as hard.

Sitting up, he winced as his bladder ached. He had to pee so bad he was about to wet the bed.

Wayne grabbed his crotch (not quite the way Lawrence always did when he did his 'pimp walk', but close) and kneaded it in frustration as if he could keep himself from peeing by squeezing it shut.

A clamp on his finger radiated a feverish red light, and a wire ran from it to an outlet in the wall over his head. A pair of flatscreens mounted to the wall next to the bed displayed a whole litany of inscrutable numbers and the ever-familiar heartbeat line of an ECG.

The lightning-bolt of his heart booped slow and stately.

At first he was afraid that taking it off would set off some kind of chirping alarm, waking up the whole hospital and summoning a nurse…but when he screwed up his courage and pulled it from his finger, nothing happened except the glowing blue seismograph turned to a flat line and all the numbers disappeared.

He glanced at his sleeping father again and slid out of the bed. The floor was like ice under his left foot, searingly cold. Limping across the room, the boy went into the bathroom, closed the door, and pulled up his gown, pinning it with his neck.

If the suite floor had been cold, the tile in the bathroom was blistering-Arctic, and the light was the heart of a nuclear explosion.

Dark yellow urine arced out, directed quietly around the side of the bowl. Wayne flushed and opted to use the sanitizer foam from the dispenser on the wall instead of washing his hands. As he rubbed them together, his stomach gnarled up and growled, and he wondered how long it had been since he'd eaten lunch the day before. He was starving.

Back in the room, he found the trip to see a man about a dog hadn't woken up his father. Luckily, the flush had been quiet: one ragged gulp and the water was clean again.

In a chair underneath the TV were his clothes and his shoes, and in one of his shoes was his mother's wedding band. He slipped the cold chain around his neck. To his dismay, he saw that his jeans had been cut off, and now they were only denim rags.

Underneath the chair was a black gym bag. Wayne opened it and rooted around in it. Clothes. Probably his own.

He thought about putting something on, but the idea that he might need to stay in his gown for some reason or another made him reluctant, so he left it alone. He stood at the foot of his bed and watched his father sleep, still racked with shame.

I just know you been scared as hell all night. I'm so sorry. I had no idea there would be a snake in there.

Really, though, he was lying to himself.

Of course he'd been afraid of stumbling across a snake. It was why he'd hustled to get away from the weedy clown car, wasn't it, all full of snaky-looking brush and sticks. But he'd just walked right on into that Gravitron, hadn't he, without a care in the world.

And God in heaven! The bills would be astronomical, he just knew it.

On top of everything else, his dad was going to have to pay the hospital a kajillion dollars because Wayne was so stupid. He remembered reading about antivenin in Science class. The exotic names of the drugs had sounded so expensive.

This was my fault. His hand instinctively went to the ring dangling against his chest. He felt puny, unworthy. Raising the ring to his eye, he studied his father through the golden hoop. *I knew it was dangerous and I did it anyway. I am so stupid. I'm a stupid kid. A stupid baby. I deserve to be grounded. I deserve to be locked up in my cupola and never let out.*

"I'm sorry, Daddy," he squeaked.

Leon just snored. A wooden door, like the kind you'd see in an old house, stood behind Leon's chair, leading out of the room. Paint flaked from its surface.

Wayne blinked.

The ring dropped from his eye and the rusty door vanished.

Astonished, he shuffled over to where he'd seen it and put his hand against the wall. Cold cinderblock, painted gray, nothing else. Gently feeling the wall with both hands, Wayne searched for the door he'd seen, but there was no indication it'd been there at all—no doorframe, no knob, no nothin'.

He stepped back a pace and looked through the gold wedding-band monocle again.

There it was again, big as shit, and solid.

The doorframe was the green of grass, of frogs and avocados.

He stepped close and put his hand against it. Instead of the cold block wall, he pressed his palm to wood, rough and jagged with paint, as warm as if the sun were hitting it from the other side. The doorknob throbbed in his hand, hot but not painfully so, invitingly, radiating from within like the hood of a car on a sunny day.

He turned the knob. The latch disengaged with a click.

Wayne threw a glance over his shoulder. Leon was still asleep. Probably a sleeping pill—his father was given to using medication like Benadryl and Tylenol PM to knock himself out when he was having a bad night. And this definitely qualified as a 'bad night'.

Opening the door, he wasn't sure what he would find on the other side...but it sure wasn't his own house.

Dark and deep, the Victorian at 1168 Underwood Road gaped before him. All he could see was a blotch of the floor and a bit of the wall, illuminated by a weak, aquatic light from above...but he'd seen this sight, at this angle, often enough in the last couple of days to recognize it. He was looking at the second-floor landing, from the perspective of the doorway that led up to the cupola.

Hunger still gnawed at his insides. Maybe...

Wayne glanced at his father again. He didn't know what was going on, but if he'd been given some strange extra-dimensional superpower by being bitten by a snake, he ought to take advantage of it and duck into the house for a bowl of Fruity Pebbles. And with great power comes great responsibility, you know, so he'd grab Leon a couple of his energy bars while he was in there.

The snake. Was the snake radioactive? Gamma-ray snake? *Hmm. No,* he mused, peering through the wedding band.

Light coming in under the hospital suite door glinted on its gold surface. The ring was the power, not him. It had nothing to do with the snake. He let it drop to his chest, hanging from the necklace.

The door remained, still open, still revealing the interior of the Victorian. Steeling himself, Wayne stepped into the darkened house.

It eased shut behind him. *Click.*

❂

Wayne's heart leapt and he spun around, but the door was still there. He tried the doorknob. It wasn't locked.

Relieved, he looked around the landing. Something was subtly off about the house, but he couldn't quite put his finger on it. He reached behind his back to pinch his gown shut and made his way down the stairs.

The foyer was quiet. A little table stood against the banister at the bottom, and on it was a black rotary telephone, something Wayne had only seen in old Hitchcock movies. *Why did Dad buy an old telephone?*

As he thought about it, he realized what was different about the house.

The walls were supposed to be blue, dusky raincloud-blue…instead, they were green, the pale Fifties-green of spearmint gum and the floors at his old school in Chicago, the green that belonged with salmon-pink on the flank of a Cadillac convertible parked at a drive-in movie.

Wayne picked up the receiver and put it against his ear. No dialtone.

He stuck his finger in the rotary dial and turned it. The earpiece made a subtle *tikkatikkatikkatik* sound, but nothing else happened. Listening to the faint tappling, his eyes wandered over to the left and he noticed that the front door was a different color. Wayne hung up the phone and went over to check it out, his bare feet padding on the soft, intricate runner carpet.

The front door was white, the bottom chewed up by time and neglect, the paint coming off to uncover rusty metal. A placard in the middle said WOMEN.

A restroom door? Wayne's hand found his face and he rubbed his forehead in confusion.

This was too strange. Time to get to the kitchen, get what he came for, and get back to the hospital. He would talk to Leon when he woke up later, and see what was going on, but for right now he just wanted to get something to eat and get off of his increasingly tender foot.

Wayne limped down the dark hallway and hooked right into the kitchen, stopping short.

A pale, dirty light filtered in through the window over the sink, like sunbeams coming through the scummy surface of a pond. This sickly glow drew the contours and corners of a black kitchen—black walls, black ceiling, the stove was black, the paint bubbling and peeling. He touched the stove, and his fingertip came away with a paste of damp soot.

One winter when he was in...second grade(?), Wayne caught chicken pox and had to stay with his Aunt Marcelina. She'd turned on the stove to boil water for a cup of hot chocolate, but it had been the wrong eye, searing the painted tin eye-cover on top of it.

The foul smell of burnt paint had hung in the air for weeks, like a curse on Marcelina's apartment. This same acrid stink now lingered in the black kitchen.

Wayne opened a few cabinets, searching for his cereal, but there was nothing in them except for canned food with old-looking labels and brand names he didn't recognize, many of them with dented sides. The cabinet where they kept the drinking glasses had a box of cherry Pop-Tarts and a box of Life, but he didn't like cherry and had never tried Life, so he left them alone.

"What is goin *on*, man?" he asked the strange kitchen.

The floor creaked in the living room, the slow tectonic croak of a ship's deck.

Wayne's head snapped up and he fled to the other side of the table, which was not their small round wooden table, but a large Formica oval with metal trim, like something out of a diner. It was thick, and bulky, and felt protective.

"Who's there?"

No answer. His heart fluttered in his chest.

"Pete?" he asked the darkness. "Is that you?"

Wayne stood behind the table for a long minute, waiting for a voice. None came.

He opened the silverware drawer, found hand-towels, opened another drawer, found a jumble of random utensils. One of them was a big serrated bread knife, which he snatched up and brandished at the dark doorway next to the fridge.

Weak ocean-floor sunlight whispered into the living room as well, bandaged by the sheer white curtains. The suggestion of a brown sofa lurked next to the rumor of a coffee table that resembled a pirate's chest.

Wayne chewed his cheek, eyeing a weird wooden TV with a rabbit-ear antenna and a bulging gray screen, accompanied by a panel of numbered dials. Creepy wood-framed pictures lined the walls: praying children with bulbous Casper heads and shiny blond hair, painted on black velvet.

He leaned over and was reaching for the television's power button when something inhaled behind him, a ragged wet *grarararararuhh* that made him think of engines and dragons.

Ice raced down his legs and arms into his feet and hands, his mouth falling open in terror.

141

Behind him, a mass of greasy, rumpled hair was wedged into the back corner where the watery sunlight faded into shadow. Green owl-eyes opened in a massive head that brushed the ceiling like a grown man in a child's playhouse.

Rarararararuhhh....

The beast leaned away from the wall, reaching for Wayne with orangutan arms and too many fingers, smelling of filth, of old blood, of death.

The boy ran.

Leading out of the kitchen and out of the house, the back door was metallic gray, patchy with rust.

A sign near the top said NO ADMITTANCE—EMPLOYEES ONLY! He shoved it open, running through it into what should have been the back yard, but was a dark indoor space swampy with the stink of old motor oil.

Turning to face the monster, Wayne found a blank wall of corrugated aluminum.

Tears made cold tracks down his cheeks. He ground them away with a wrist and sank to his hands and knees, shaking and nauseous. The constricting bandage around his swelling leg was killing him and his left foot buzzed with pins and needles. "What...in the *world*," he asked the silence.

Chains rattled on the other side of the wall.

Wayne stood up. The back door of the strange green version of his house had brought him to what appeared to be some kind of mechanic's garage, the cement floor dark and greasy under his bare feet.

Sun-bleached kart bodies rusted quietly in the shadows, strewn with broken engine parts. Signs made out of plywood and sheet-metal leaned against the wall in piles. The first one was a menacing cartoon of a clown. VISIT HOOT'S FUNHOUSE! GET LOST IN OUR HALL OF MIRRORS!

Another sign, this one as big as a barn door, welcomed him to Weaver's Wonderland, and beside that was painted a picture of a mom and a dad walking into an amusement park, a little girl sitting on her father's shoulders.

The clanking of chains and muffled growling echoed from a black doorway.

A huge roll-up garage door dominated one wall. Moonlight slipped underneath the bottom panel as Wayne hooked his fingers into the gap and heaved upward with everything he had.

Clack! The door moved about an inch and ran into latches on each side. Hasps were pushed through slots in the doorframe, and padlocks were attached to the strips of metal, preventing them from being pulled out. He jerked and wrenched them, but they were brand-new and he had no chance of getting them off.

"Grrnngh!" growled something from the other room. "Hhhngh—*thp thp thp puh, puh*—HELP!" Goosebumps prickled Wayne's skin. He sidled over to the doorway and peeked inside.

Planter hooks had been screwed into the wall by the door, stuck through the links of three chains. One of them lay useless underneath, but the other two ran across the room to ceiling pulleys.

Men hung upside-down from them, a black guy and a white guy, both of them naked except for their skivvies.

The one in the thong was squirming and undulating furiously, jerking on the chains binding his hands to the floor. A cloth gag dangled around his neck. "Jesus Lord help me, get me the hell out of here," he pleaded, and noticed Wayne peering through the doorway. "Oh God, oh God, get me *down*, get me *outta here*, you gotta get me out of here, *please.*"

Wayne ventured into the room. ARE YOU TOO COOL FOR SCHOOL? asked the coyote on the sign. "What's goin on?"

"I been kidnapped, this man has kidnapped me, I don't know if he put something in my drink, or put something in my steak, but he knocked my ass out and when I woke up I was chained up in here and right now I need you to go over there and unhook me so I can get down and I need you to do it *right now. Right now right now right now.*"

Taking hold of the chain, Wayne tried to pull the man up to give himself enough slack to pull the hook out of the link, but he was just too heavy. The gritty floor bit into the sensitive sole of his left foot.

"I can't do it." Panic overtook him and he started weeping again, his throat burning. "I got bit by a snake on my foot and I'm so tired. I been in the hospital—"

"Honey, what's your name?" asked the man.

"Wayne."

"Mine is *Jo-elle*. Okay, Wayne baby, Wayne, take the chain in both your hands. See how the hook curves up?" The chain had been lowered down onto the point of the hook. "I want you to take the chain in both hands and push it toward the point. Can you do that?"

Bracing himself, Wayne got under the chain and pushed. Jo-elle's weight made it seem impossible at first, but when he put his hands close to the hook and hauled upward as hard as he could, throwing his whole body into a series of shoves, the link began to scrape free.

The sleepy growl of a four-stroke motor grew outside the building, reminding Wayne of the golf carts the security guys drove at the mall up north.

Jo-elle shook with fear. "Oh Jesus, hurry up, he's back, God almighty, he's back."

Shove, shove, shove. *Almost there.* He renewed his grip on the chain and ignored the tingling-prickling in his swollen leg. The filthy floor caked dried motor-oil between his toes.

Tink! The chain slipped free and whipped through the pulley like slurping spaghetti, making a loud clatter. Jo-elle fell on his head, swearing in pain.

Outside, the golf cart engine shut off.

Jo-elle scrambled to his feet, freeing his cuffs from the hook screwed into the cement and wriggling out of the chain wrapped around his ankles. "We got to go, we got to go."

"What about the other guy?" Wayne asked, pointing at the man still chained to the ceiling. His bruised back was to them.

"He's dead, baby, there ain't nothin we can do." Jo-elle took off into the other room, staggering in circles and looking around wildly. "How did you get *in* here? Where did you come from?"

Wayne held up his mother's wedding band. "You're gonna laugh at me, but I think I made a door. Or maybe I found one."

"You made—*what?*" Jo-elle winced in confusion. "You *made* a door? How do you 'make' a door?" He waved off the coming explanation. "Just show me the way out so we can get—"

"But there's a monster—"

"What?"

Keys jingling in the workshop. Door unlocking.

"A monster in my house—" Wayne began to say, and recoiled as Jo-elle lunged for him, grabbed him by the head, and gazed into his face.

"We got to *go*. We got to go *now.*"

The door in the workshop opened, and someone thumped across the oily floor in boots, tossing a keychain full of keys on the worktable. Hollow *thunk* of some sort of plastic container. Gas can? The rattle of chains.

A raspy voice. "Hey, how'd you get down?"

Jo-elle ran over and slammed the door, swearing under his breath, bracing himself against it.

The handle rattled.

"There ain't no way out of there, pizza-man," said the killer's muffled voice. "You might as well come on out. I'd lock you in there and let you starve, but I kinda need to bleed you like your buddy in here." He coughed, cleared his throat. "Nothin personal, you know. It's my job. Well, part of it. Blood-collecting. The people I work for, they need it for the garden. Always blood for the garden."

Boots scuffing on cement: the man walked away. The bump and clatter of tools being rummaged through, assembled. "It never ends, it never ends."

"You ain't got to do this, Red," said Jo-elle.

"Sure I do." The killer paused. "You know what? Call me the Serpent. That's what the papers back in New York used to call me. I like it. My friends called me Snake when I was little, but 'Serpent' sounds so...I dunno, *Biblical,* doesn't it? Man, it just rolls off the tongue."

Everything went quiet.

A burst of noise came out of the door-crack as the Serpent spat a hiss through, his lips against the jamb.

Jo-elle twitched, almost losing his leverage on the door. "You let me out, and I ain't tell nobody, man," he said. "I swear. You let me go and it'll be like this never happened. We both go our own way and it's all good."

The Serpent laughed. "Fat chance, homo. You've seen my face. Not gonna happen."

"Homo—?" Jo-elle's face darkened. "You mean...?"

"Oh hell naw. I don't swing that way, pizza-man. You kidding me? I mean, yeah, I done some things I ain't proud of to put food on the table, but deep down I'm as straight as a..." The killer drummed fingers on the door. "Help me out here, what's something really straight? You know, other than 'not you'."

"An arrow? I don't—"

"Be original!"

Something pistoned hard against the door, *BANG!*, and Jo-elle jumped away. "Ow!"

A nail protruded from the door's surface, dripping blood. Taking advantage of the moment, the Serpent kicked the door so hard one of the plywood signs fell over. The sign behind it was a painting of a sweating glass of lemonade.

WHEN LIFE HANDS YOU LEMONS, GIVE EM BACK—OURS IS BETTER!

Wayne pressed the gold ring to his eye.

Adapt and overcome.

Nothing about Jo-elle's end of the room was special, but when he turned to the back wall, there it was again, the doorway back to the green house with the burned kitchen. *Be bigger. Be stronger.* He was going to have to brave that strange dark place with its giant hairy creature.

It's got to be better than this Serpent person. I know he's going to kill me, but I don't know what the monster wants. It came down to 'the evil you know' versus 'the evil you don't'. Adapt and overcome. *Think. Think.*

Summoning up all the courage he could find, his body cold and trembling in deepest terror, Wayne opened the strange door. Beyond, the hollow Victorian promised nothing but darkness and silence.

"The hell—?" Jo-elle was staring at him.

BANG! Another nail shot through the door, appearing between his fingers as if by magic. He snatched his hand away, cursing. The Serpent gave the door another kick and it flew open squealing.

Scooping up the boy, Jo-elle fled through the door into the Victorian. Wayne got a quick glimpse of a shock of the killer's red hair, beady eyes, a scrawny throat, and then the door slammed shut behind them, plunging them into blue-green twilight.

The afterimage of the killer's face resonated in Wayne's mental eye. Seemed so familiar...where had he seen that face before?

Jo-elle breathed, "Where are we...?"

They were back in the burned kitchen. Wayne pressed against the man's clammy side, ignoring his sweatiness and the fact that all he wore was a pair of bikini underwear. Jo-elle was solidly built—if a little soft around the midsection—and that was all that mattered.

"It's supposed to be my house," he explained in a pained whisper, "but for some reason it's painted green instead of blue. And...and there's some kind of monster in here."

Peeling him off, Jo-elle squinted at Wayne in flippant disbelief. "A monster?"

"It's big and hairy. It's like...I guess it's like a Bigfoot."

"You got a Sasquatch. In y'house."

"I'm not sure this is my house." Wayne pressed a finger to his lips. "Shhh, or it's going to hear us and come after us."

"It is, or it isn't. How can it *be* your house *and not be* your house?" Jo-elle blinked in recognition. "Wait. *Wait*. I *know* this house. I've sat at this table before. This is Annie Martine's house. She used to babysit me and my brother when I was a little boy like you." Now that he was out of danger, Jo-elle seemed to favor his right foot, using the kitchen counter as a crutch as he left the room.

Out in the hallway, he supported himself on the armrest of a chair. "Yeah, this mos' definitely Annie's house. You mean you livin here? I didn't even know it was still for sale. I figured it would be fallin apart by now."

"Is Annie Martine the witch that died here?"

Jo-elle eyed him. "Where you hear that?"

"My friend Pete told me." Wayne stopped to rub his leg. The gauze wound around his left knee was so tight he couldn't stand it, and his ankle felt plump, tender, like a big warm sausage. "He lives over in the trailer park. He said her husband pushed her down the stairs."

"...I don't know if I believe in witches, but I don't speak ill of the dead. Annie was a good woman."

He sat down in the chair. Wayne grabbed his arm and tried to pull him back up. "No, we can't stay here. It's not safe. I told you, there's a monster here."

"Just let me rest f'minute. I been upside-down for like, two hours. My head is spinnin."

"No!"

"Little man, just cause I'm sittin here in a clearance-rack thong don't mean I ain't gonna slap you. I hurt myself fallin on the floor, and you makin it worse." Jo-elle took his hand away, rubbing his wrist.

Wayne scowled and headed for the stairs. "Okay, then. ...I'll leave you here. You should—"

Deep, gutteral breathing rumbled along the hallway like an engine underwater, *grararararararauuuh*, and the floorboards groaned.

"You on *y'own!*" said Wayne, running for the foyer.

As soon as he got there, the hulking green-eyed shadow reached out of the living room doorway with those long, hairy arms. *"Oh!"* shrieked Jo-elle. *"What the Christ!"*

Halfway up the switchback staircase, Wayne paused to make sure he wasn't alone, and he wasn't, because the lamp-eyed creature was crawling up the wall and across the ceiling at him like some kind of huge horrible spider-bear. Wayne screamed and fought to get up to the second floor, slipping, clawing at the steps, banging his knees.

Inhaling, the creature made a deep crooning foghorn noise—*"Hhhrrroooohh!"*—and crabbed over the edge of the landing. When Wayne reached the top of the stairs, it was already there waiting, crawling over the banister.

"Oh!" he just had time to shout, and then the creature was on him, mumbling, wet, reeking of mold and garbage.

The thing's mouth widened, a pit cracking open a long head like a watermelon, and rows of slimy teeth glistened in that eerie sea-light from above. It leaned forward and took Wayne's entire head in its jaws.

A leathery tongue pressed against his eyebrow, hot breath washing his face.

Clang!

The monster straightened, growling at Jo-elle, who stood over it with the rotary-phone in one hand. "It's for *you*, bitch!" He brought the phone cradle down on that shaggy head again. *Clang!*

Grateful for the distraction, Wayne clambered on his hands and knees across the landing.

Since the monster had cut him off before he could reach the cupola door that led back to the hospital and Leon, he fled down the hallway to the upstairs bathroom. Flinging the door open, Wayne was surprised and dismayed to find only a bathtub and a toilet.

He looked back just in time to see the deformed Sasquatch pin Jo-elle to the floor and rake fingernails across his bare chest. Blood pattered up the wall.

Gathering his feet, Jo-elle leg-pressed the creature's chest, almost lifting it into the air, and pried himself free, loping after Wayne on all fours. They crowded into the bathroom and Jo-elle shut the door, locking the knob, as if that would help.

BANG! The thing outside threw itself against the door. A cup of toothbrushes toppled into the sink.

The window over the tub was painted shut. Mysterious night lay opaque against the windowpane like black felt. "Now what?" asked Wayne, on the verge of hysterics. He ripped open the mirror.

Instead of a medicine cabinet, a dark living room gaped inside, viewed from a high angle some ten feet in the air. Huge plate-glass windows to the left showered the room in soft gray moonbeams.

Wayne climbed up on the sink and through the medicine cabinet. "Come on!"

147

On the other side, he stood on top of a refrigerator. Wayne climbed down onto the counter, stumbling over a panini press, and jumped down to linoleum. His new thong-bedecked friend leapt down after him and fell, swearing about his ankle.

The crawlspace they'd escaped through slammed shut, becoming a painting.

Bleeding on the floor, poor Jo-elle had a mini-breakdown, his hands flapping. "Mother of God and home of the brave, what in *the* hell *was* that?"

The kitchen lights came on, dazzling them both.

A blond man with a crutch under one arm and a pistol in the other trained his muzzle on them. A pretty woman with a shaved head stood next to him, and they were both in T-shirts and underwear.

"Joel?" asked the man.

Joel squinted. "Kenway?"

"The hell you doing in my kitchen at—" Kenway glanced at the microwave, ejecting the magazine from the pistol and racking the slide. A bullet flipped out and he caught it in his other hand. "—Two in the morning? ...Butt-ass naked in hand-cuffs. With a little boy."

Wayne's eyes trickled down until they came to rest on the blond's left leg, which ended in a nub just below the knee.

"What's it look like, Cap'n Hooker?" demanded Joel, panting and grimacing, his hand over the lacerations on his chest. "I needed to borrow a cup of sugar."

Fourteen

AND THAT'S HOW WE ended up here," said the kid. They were all clustered around the island in the kitchen, wide awake. Robin's camera still stood at the end of the counter, recording his tale. Kenway made them all omelets and coffee while Joel and Wayne told their stories. His eyebrows stayed high and his forehead furrowed through most of it, but to his credit he never challenged them or made any disbelieving noises.

Wayne had traded his hospital gown for a sweater and a pair of cargo pants from Robin. They were feminine and a couple sizes too big, but it was a good look with his glasses. A ten-year-old hipster.

Joel was wearing a pair of Kenway's jeans. With some alcohol, Neosporin, a bandage, and a bottle of breakfast stout, he was sore and bitchy but otherwise good as new. He'd only been nicked by the nail through the door, and his cuts weren't as bad as they looked—more scratches than anything else, not quite bad enough to need stitches.

Robin walked around the apartment, looking through the boy's ring like Sherlock Holmes with his magnifying glass, trying to detect anomalies. No such luck. It seemed that whatever the ring was capable of, only its owner was able to take advantage of it.

An engraving inside the ring said, *Together We'll Always Find a Way*.

This was significant. Words hold power, and Robin knew from experience that text—whether engraved or printed—could absorb and retain or channel that power.

"I need to call my dad and let him know I'm all right," said Wayne. "If he's awake now, he's probably really worried. Probably wondering where I am." He sighed. "I don't have my cellphone or I'd text him."

Pouring herself a cup of coffee, Robin joined them at the island. She gave him her cellphone and the ring, and he typed in his dad's number, pressing the phone to his ear.

"What troubles me the most," she said to Kenway, "is that the Sasquatch-monster they said was hiding in my old house is...well, I've

149

been seeing it for a long time. I've always thought it was a hallucination. A part of my schizophrenia."

"Really?" He sprinkled cheddar on an omelet, dropped a scoop of sour cream on it, and pushed it in front of her.

"Yeah. I don't know what to think about knowing someone else saw it too." Robin drizzled the omelet in sriracha sauce and sat there picking at it, carving off little bites and eating them in a daze of deep thought.

"I'm with friends, Dad," Wayne was saying, trying to lay down some damage control. They could hear the mosquito-buzz of Leon Parkin shouting through the phone. "Yes, friends. No, not Pete. I'm fine, I'm fine. Something happened in the room and I ended up somewhere else. I mean, I don't know. It was weird. Yes."

His face scrunched up on one side and he screwed the heel of his hand into his eye sleepily.

"Dad, I can explain it better when you're chilled out, okay?" A tear rolled down his face. "Hey. ...I'm sorry. For making you worry." The boy turned away from them, hugging himself, trying not to sob outright. "Do you forgive me?" Several quiet seconds passed. "I love you too, Dad."

"Hey," said Joel. "Tell him we're gonna take you back to the hospital as soon as we get done eating."

Wayne did so. "I'm sorry for making you worry," he reiterated, his voice breaking. "Are you doin okay? Dad, you ain't drinkin nothin, are you? ...Don't worry about me if that makes it harder. Yeah. I just don't want...y'know?"

He hung up and gave the phone back to Robin. She took a sip of coffee and asked them, "So you said that the walls were green when you went into the old Underwood house?"

"The kitchen was burnt slap up," said Joel. "And your mama's old diner table was in there, too."

"My mom painted the walls green when I was a kid. When they prosecuted my dad and I became a ward of the state, the city fixed it up and painted it blue."

"Other than it bein burnt, it looked like it did when we was kids." Joel gingerly explored the bandage taped to his chest. It was an adhesive combat bandage from Kenway's old Army supplies, like a big square Band-Aid. "Man, this makes me glad I shave."

Wayne made a face. "You shave your chest? ...Do you shave your legs and *everything?*"

"I don't really consider this an appropriate topic of breakfast conversation." Joel winced in mock offense and he tossed one leg over a knee, sitting back with his beer. "Is you always this rude?"

"That's so *weird.*"

"Little man, don't be sassing your elders."

Kenway scoffed. "You just got away from a serial killer and fought off Bigfoot, and you think a guy that shaves his balls is weird?"

150

They all burst out laughing, Wayne hunkering sheepishly over his food.

After gulping down breakfast, they loaded into Kenway's truck and headed to the hospital. Robin rode in the back, wearing a thick jacket with the hood pulled over her head to protect her from the wind. It was still dark out—a little after three in the morning, according to her phone—and the autumn air bit her face. She squinted in the gale, holding the GoPro out. This would make good transitional footage. She wanted to monologue, but the snapping of the wind would make it impossible to hear.

As they pulled into the parking lot of Blackfield Medical, Leon Parkin came striding out the front door, followed by an old woman in a raggedy petticoat that seemed to be made out of swatches from the fabric section of Walmart.

Kenway was barely out of the driver's seat when Leon marched up and started raining blows on him, cornering him inside the truck door.

Everyone exploded into movement, shouting, running to stop him. Joel and Robin got them separated and Leon threw his elbows, trying to shake them off. "Y'all motherfuckers take my son?" he raved, seething in the middle of their circle. White vapor coiled from his mouth. "Who *are* you? What *is* this?"

"Now wait—" Kenway began, putting up his hands. Blood trickled from his nose. Leon charged him again and Joel and Robin wrestled him away.

Wayne got out and ran to his dad. Leon clutched him against his side. "Get inside, son."

"But Dad—"

"Get your ass inside and I'll be in there in a minute."

The boy looked up with a stern face that belonged on a grown man and pushed away. "Dad, I left on my own. It was an accident."

"*What* did I tell you?"

"No!" said Wayne, clenching his fists and shivering. He was limping again, his left foot a faint shade of purple. "I been helpin—I been, I been dealin with you, and things, you know, for long enough, Dad, and you owe me. I've always been there. *Always*. Even when you weren't. So right now, I need you to listen."

Stunned, Leon's face softened as he seemed to see his son, really *see* him, his eyes wandering up and down Wayne's strangely effeminate outfit.

"We *both* lost her, Dad. I hurt too. You know that?"

Leon nodded. "...Yeah. Yeah...man...yeah," as if he were coming out of a trance, and he stooped to gather Wayne up in a huge hug. The old woman clutched the collar of her heavy wool coat, her stringy hair whipping around. Her face was pinched into a vapid smile until she caught Robin's stare.

Recognition flashed in her eyes. "Why don't we all go inside and sort this out somewhere warm, yes?"

"My name is Karen. Karen Weaver," she said to Wayne, leading them to a back corner of an isolated waiting room. "Believe it or not, I actually live right across the street from you, in the big Mexican church-house. Me and my friend Theresa were out hunting mushrooms by the old fairgrounds when I heard your friends screaming that you'd been bitten by a mean old snake."

Robin followed them, her GoPro clipped to a jacket pocket, recording the conversation. Children's books and old magazines littered an end table, and behind them an aquarium burbled peacefully.

"What kind of snake?" asked Joel.

Weaver smiled. "Well, that big kid—Peter, was it? He did a real number on it with that mallet, but from what I saw it looked like a copperhead. Anyway, I put a...a special salve on you, a poultice, I suppose, that worked to nullify and draw out most of that venom, and then Theresa carried you out to the road."

With a giggle, she added, "For an old lady, she's stronger than she looks." She bent to watch the fish darting back and forth in the aquarium, talking to the glass. "One of your friends got your cellphone and called 911 for you—Johnny, I suppose his name was."

Weaver wagged a finger at Wayne. "A very dear little boy, you ought to thank him, and Peter, for their heroics. They're quite exceptional for children these days."

Turning to Kenway, Leon rubbed his head. "Hey, look, man...I'm sorry about the—"

The vet had produced a paint-smeared handkerchief from somewhere, and was holding it to his nose. "Unnerstandable," he said, checking the fabric. His nose had stopped leaking. "Enh, I been through worse, trust me."

Kneeling to get eye-to-eye with his son, Leon said, "Now...tell me what happened. You said you would explain everything. I want to know the truth."

Wayne's eyebrows scrunched. "When have I lied to you—"

Leon smirked dryly.

"—in the last week?" Before his dad could answer, Wayne took out the ring and showed it to him. "It was this."

Leon took it in his thumb and forefinger, at the end of the chain still around the boy's neck. "Your mother's wedding band?" His features softened, his eyes wistful. "I didn't know you were wearing this."

"I been wearin it for...well, ever since." Wayne held it up to his eye. "I woke up in my hospital room, got up and peed, and when I came back

152

to my bed I looked through Mom's ring and saw a door in the wall where there wasn't one before."

He went on to describe the strange past-version of the Underwood house, and the bizarre owl-headed Sasquatch, and rescuing Joel from the Serpent.

"A killer?" Leon stiffened. "You saw a *dead guy?*"

Joel spoke up. "I was chained up in a garage somewhere next to a dude with a cut throat. This red-headed guy had knocked me out and I guess he was drainin people for their blood. Said something about 'blood for the garden'. He was about to stick me like a pig too, until Bruce Wayne here showed up outta nowhere like Batman hisself and saved my sexy ass."

"And you saw this weird dark version of our house too?"

"Yes sir, I did." Joel peeled back the lapel of the jacket he'd borrowed from Kenway, exposing his bandaged chest. "And that monster damn near opened me up."

The old woman coughed…once, twice, then started hacking into a lacy cloth and struggling to breathe.

"You okay?" asked Kenway.

"Oh, yes, yes. It's getting that time of year when it gets dry outside," choked Weaver, waving him off. "And I've got a bit of congestion. Nothing, really. I'm going to get a glass of water, if that's all right with you-all."

Robin got up and excused herself as well, following the old woman out into the hallway. Weaver glided around the corner and into the restroom, still crouping and wheezing into her napkin.

The restroom turned out to be empty. Five stalls occupied the back of the room, and a bank of three sinks were set in a marble countertop under a huge mirror.

Carefully prodding each door open, Robin checked the stalls until she was satisfied no one was in them. "Dammit."

She went to the sink and cupped herself a handful of water, washed the sleep out of her eyes, and when she straightened back up, she toweled her face dry.

When she opened her eyes again, Weaver's reflection stood behind her own.

Robin gasped and spun to face her.

"I know who you are," said the crone, backing her against the sink.

"You do?"

"Oh, yes, of course. You're huge on the internet, you know." Weaver grinned, flashing peanut-colored teeth and blue-green gums. Her breath smelled like skunky weed. "You're the witch-hunter on that Malus Domestica channel, aren't you? Oh, I've been subscribed to you for ages. I even have a few of your T-shirts." She threw her hands up in mock exasperation, her gaudy rings glittering in the fluorescent lights. "My

153

friends, they don't think much of you, but I think you're a very brave young lady to do what you do."

"You believe in witches, then."

"*Believe* in them?" Weaver laughed. "My dear, I *am* one."

Robin had already suspected as much. "You're one of the coven that lives in Lazenbury House."

"Ah, it looks like you've done your homework." The witch wrung her knobbly hands. "Are you here to, ahh, *slay* us too, then?"

Swallowing, Robin put a little steel in her spine and stepped into Weaver's personal space. "You murdered my mother and turned her into a dryad. ...If you've been watching my videos, you know I've been doing this for a couple of years now—"

She ripped the collar of her shirt open, popping a button. Tattooed on her sternum, just below the pit of her throat, was an algiz rune, a symbol like a Y with an extra limb in the middle:

"—So I've learned a few things...from Heinrich—"

Weaver was unimpressed. "Honey, Heinrich is a fool," she said sweetly, encouragingly. "The only reason he isn't dead yet is because he quit hunting us years ago. He's made a puppet of you, a henchman, a bloodhound to hide behind and exact his mad, mean crusade against us without having to risk his own life. ...You know, you should be proud of yourself. You've done more than *he* ever did."

The witch traced the symbol with a painted claw. "Now, this is very pretty, dear, quite a lovely tattoo, but it won't save you. You may be protected against being made a familiar, but it won't protect you from the rest of our bag of tricks."

Weaver laid a cold palm on her cleavage, and Robin sidled away, sliding her butt along the edge of the sink.

Following her, the witch migrated her hand from her left breast and then to her belly. Her fingertips were cold as December, even through the cloth. "Oh, dove, I think I feel something kicking. Don't you?"

Robin pushed her away. "Get off me."

"Wait a minute," said Weaver, snatching her hand away. "Did you say *dryad? Mother?*"

Her rheumy eyes widened and she swept in, taking off her bifocals and staring into Robin's face. "Are you...? Could you be? Annie Martine's daughter? Oh how you've grown, my dear. How lovely you are now! Who could have guessed that such a beautiful girl could have come from such a homely woman?"

"*Don't talk about my mother,*" growled Robin, and she let out a mild cough.

There was a bit of a tickle in her chest...maybe she was coming down with a cold too. "She may have been a witch, but she was a good person, and better than any of you. You had no—*cough*—no right—"

"Who knows rights better than you, eh Malus? Malus Domestica, YouTube star, traveling the roads, living the American dream, killing innocent witches by the fourscore. You wouldn't know your right from your left." Weaver emphasized *right* and *left* with palsied fists, then marched off in that sweeping, handsy Gargamel way of hers, reaching for the door handle.

Before she could leave, Robin had a fistful of her coat. "Tell Marilyn I'll be—*cough, cough*—making a house call." She pulled the witch close and said through gritted teeth, "You three can prepare all you want, but—*coooough, cough*—I've gotten a lot of practice doing what I'm gonna do to the three of you."

The threat devolved into a coughing fit, and she gasped for air. Her lungs felt like they were full of down feathers, itching and wispy.

"You don't know your mother as well as you think you do." Weaver opened the restroom door and wrenched her sleeve out of the girl's hand, her expression one of genuine concern. "And you don't know what you're getting yourself into. Stay away from the Lazenbury house, and we'll leave you be. Get out of Blackfield and I'll...I'll convince Marilyn not to come after you, yes, that's what I'll do."

With that, the witch had the last word and slipped out the door. Robin wanted to retort, but she couldn't stop coughing and catch her breath long enough to speak. The cavity of her chest was alive with fluttering-itching-whispering.

A lump in her throat. She made long, drawn-out *huuuckkkk* sounds as if she were trying to muster up a loogie, and some wet little wad popped up into her mouth, lying on her tongue like a swallowed cigarette butt.

Robin staggered over to the sink, coughing as she went, and spat it into the basin.

A dead moth.

"Ugh," she said, and coughed again.

This time the tickling sensation intensified, rushing up her windpipe, and when she coughed again a cloud of fat fluttery moths burst from the depths of her lungs.

Their tiny legs fought for purchase on the roof of her mouth, filling her throat. The ones that managed to escape fell into the sink and battered the mirror, dragging their saliva-wet bodies across the glass, leaving smears of bitter wing-powder.

Bits of insect were caught in her teeth. Her stomach rumbled and gnarled, and her mouth flooded with salty spit. She was going to puke.

Wheezing, sucking wind, fighting to breathe, Robin pushed open a toilet stall and braced her hands on the seat. Tears clung to the rims of her eyelids. The convulsion came without preamble, as it always does, and she unleashed a torrent of sour vomit.

"Guh," she gasped, staring down into a brown slurry of coffee and eggs. She flushed the toilet.

Pulling down her jeans and sitting on the john, she spooled out a handful of toilet paper and scrubbed her tongue with it in disgust. The sensation of having moths in her mouth was unbearable—after chasing the supernatural for several years there wasn't much on this planet that Robin was still afraid of, but insects never failed to make her skin crawl.

Urine trickled into the water as she relaxed, covering her face with her hands.

Shivers danced down her back, turning into a pins-and-needles prickly feeling, goosebumps running across her shoulder-blades and down her arms. The hair stood up on her wrists and the backs of her hands. She hugged herself against the chill, wringing her hands.

Itchy, *so itchy,* suddenly she was scratching her hands, and then her arms, the goosebumps had become this helpless, crazy-making itchiness...it wouldn't go away but it felt so good, it was so satisfying, Jesus, she was digging miniature orgasms out of her skin like a paleontologist unearthing fossils. Her fingernails left burning streaks down her forearms.

Opening her eyes, she looked down and saw that her arms were covered in pimples. Dozens—no, *hundreds*—of whiteheads. Not only were they on her arms, but they'd spread to her thighs, too.

"What the hell?" If she didn't know any better, she'd have thought she had chicken pox, or perhaps impetigo.

She'd caught impetigo once, back in the mental hospital. She dropped her soap on the shower floor and picked it up again, shaving her legs with it. Washing it off apparently hadn't rid it of bacteria, though, because the next day her legs were covered in whiteheads like this. A month of rubbing them down with antibacterial cream had cleared it up, but she'd been a religious user of bottled shower gel and body wash ever since.

The crawling sensation came back. *This is wrong,* she thought, slowly turning her arms this way and that, inspecting the surprise acne. *Something is wrong. Something is really wrong here.* She dug at one of the largest whiteheads, picking at it until it came loose in a tiny plug of wax.

Two little red-green eyes stared up at her.

She watched in horror as a housefly wriggled up out of the pore and struggled to its feet. The fly rubbed its forelegs all over its head as its wet, glassy wings unraveled, drying and hardening.

Robin slapped it away. "No. No no no *no.*" Her boots clomped a jig of panic on the tile floor.

This dislodged several other whiteheads on her thighs, and she leaned back on the toilet as if she could possibly get away from the spectacle. More flies pushed and floundered up out of her skin. "No, no, no, *no, no.*" As the flies emerged they left holes, stretched and hollow like toothmarks.

Within seconds, her arms were covered in a honeycomb of gaping pores. Her thighs resembled the surface of a sponge, freckled with holes. Some of them were still packed with tiny black bodies.

Dead flies littered the floor around her boots, rolled into wet bits by her frantic slapping and rubbing. Hundreds of them buzzed and droned around her head, crawling up the sides of the lavatory stall. She pressed her palms to her face again and tried to will it all away.

That's it—maybe it's an illusion. Maybe I can think it away. Acne littered her cheeks with lumps. The pimples on her forehead squirmed restlessly under her fingers. *I think I can, I think I can, I think I can, I think I can. The little engine that could, goddammit, let it be an illusion and not an actual conjuration. Let it just be a visual suggestion, don't let these flies be real—*

Robin opened her eyes to silence.

No flies. She checked out her arms, expecting the holes to linger, but they were gone.

Relief crashed into her system, such blessed relief that she actually peed again. Her skin was smooth once more, the fine hairs ruffling under her hands as she rubbed the heebie-jeebies away. Pulling up her jeans, she stumbled backward out of the toilet stall and spat several times into the sink, washing her mouth out, washing dead moths down the drain.

Some of them still flapped and fluttered around the ceiling, trying to find a way out.

As she noticed them, the moths winked out of existence.

"Oh, that *bitch*," she said to her subscribers, checking for acne in the mirror. She shuddered, pulling the camera off of her jacket and pointing it at her own face. "I am so going to kick *her* ass first."

When she was finally convinced the illusion was out of her system, she washed her hands, washed her mouth out again, and went back to the waiting room. Karen Weaver was gone, and so were Wayne and his father.

Kenway looked up from an issue of *National Geographic*. "Everything come out okay?"

❂

The ride back to the apartment was much warmer inside the cab of the truck. She stared out the window as she rode, her mind sorting through options, the GoPro aimed out the window collecting B-roll footage. Joel rode in the middle, the gearshift protruding suggestively between his knees.

The protective *algiz* rune on her chest had been mostly sufficient until now, defending her from all manner of energy, ricocheting it back into its source. It still worked on familiarization, but Weaver's moths-and-flics illusion...well, it had been a bit of a shock.

But why shouldn't she have been surprised? After all, according to Heinrich, the Cutty coven was the most powerful in America.

And now it was one of the last. Under his tutelage, she had roamed the continent, hunting down every witch she could find in the Lower Forty-Eight, and a couple in Canada. Nineteen of them, from Neva Chandler, the self-proclaimed Witchlord of Alabama, to Gail Symes of Arizona, who called herself the Oracle of the Sands. There were still hundreds of minor witches out there—newbies, idiots, little girls who had no idea their hearts had been sacrificed to Ereshkigal, and like Neva, vapor-locked mummies too run-down to migrate out of their own ghetto—but most of them were too embedded, too well-hidden, or so weak that they might as well have been your normal every-day palm reader.

The witches had no real hierarchy. They had no structured government. Most of them had divvied up the country as the first Presidents were buying it piece by piece from the Mexicans and the Spanish, and ripping it from the hands of the Native Americans.

Ever since, they moved from town to town every couple of decades, eradicating the weak ones or dueling each other like Highlanders.

Robin had never witnessed a witch-duel, but it must have been a sight to see. She turned the camera inward at the truck's cab and spoke to Joel. "I think you should stay a couple nights at—" (dear God, she almost said *our place*) "—Kenway's place, with us. Y'know, in case the killer knows where you live."

The pause earned her a coy side-eye from the driver. Did he catch that?

Joel wore one of Kenway's old gray exercise shirts, ARMY across the chest. "I'll be aight, I got my mama's old shotgun at the house. I don't think he knows where I live anyway." Pointing at the camera, he added, "How you gonna put me on YouTube, and I ain't fixed up at all? I look like I been through a wood chipper."

"You look fine."

"At least give me a ride back there and let me take a shower and pack a little bag." Joel tugged the chest of the huge T-shirt out. "This thing like a tent on me. And, no offense, hero, but your clothes are all beat to Hell."

Kenway smirked. "None taken."

Joel pointed at the symbol tattooed on her chest. "What's with the plunging neckline all of a sudden? And what's this? You all up in that magic too?"

"It's called *algiz*."

"*Owl jizz?*" asked Kenway.

"*Nooo,*" Robin said, rubbing her face. "I said 'all-geez'. It's a protective rune from the Elder Futhark alphabet, one of a number of sigils witches use to channel and catalyze their Gift."

"Gift?"

"...Their power. That's what they call it. They don't like calling it magic, and I don't either."

"Why not?"

Kenway stopped for a red-light. At four in the morning, the roads were nearly dead except for a few people going to work. Without the radio on, the atmosphere inside the truck was quiet and contemplative.

"Magic is...something wizards and magicians do in fantasy movies and on stages in Vegas, you know? Magic is David Copperfield and David Blaine. Card tricks, cutting women in half, pulling rabbits out of hats, kids' birthday parties." Robin retreated into jargon and esoterica, not telling him the reason she didn't like calling it magic was because her mother Annie called it magic. And after seeing how evil and dark it was, she didn't like associating it with her mother, even if it took pedantry to separate the darkness from her memory of Annie.

Everything she could do to distance that addle-tongued lady from the sinister craft of the witches, she did. Yes, Annie was a witch...but that didn't mean she had to be lumped into the same gang. Annie was Glinda; she was Sabrina; she was Hermione. She was good and she did Magic, because Magic was what good witches did.

On the other side of the intersection was a Starbucks. Kenway crossed the road and pulled into the parking lot.

Robin continued. "What the acolytes of Ereshkigal—*true* witches—do is far less whimsical, and goes a lot deeper. They channel the essence of the spirit world itself, guiding it with language, and intensifying it with sheer will." She pointed at the rune on her chest. "Using language to guide it works both ways, fortunately. We can't draw it like they can, but we can manipulate their energy. Think of their power as a laser, and words and symbols as mirrors and lenses."

Joel nodded in understanding as Kenway pulled up to the drive-thru menu.

Robin offered him her debit card, but his face conveyed reluctance. "Go ahead," she said, urging him on with the card in her hand. "You know I'm good for it. I'm staying in your apartment, after all. I owe you anyway."

While Kenway ordered them coffee, Robin took out her cellphone and dialed a number. It rang several times, but no one picked up. A recorded voice told her that the owner of the number hadn't set up his voicemail yet, so she couldn't even leave him a message.

"Dammit," she told the mechanical voice. "Heinrich, when will you ever get with the times?"

This hadn't been the first time that Robin had made plans to go after a formidable witch alone. She peeled back the lapel of her shirt, looking not only at the *algiz* on her chest but the stab-wound scar at the top of her right breast.

The Oracle of the Sands had been a hell of a fight—Symes had been hiding out in one of the smaller, dinkier, rundown casinos on the outskirts of Vegas. Robin had gone in masquerading as one of the customers, but as soon as the Oracle realized she was there (thanks to a particularly eagle-eyed pit boss and an armada of surveillance cameras), every customer in sight lost their minds. Suddenly the casino was full of crazed cat-people out for her blood, and Robin barely made it out with her life.

She found out after the fact that Symes had gassed a cage full of house-cats in a specialized panic room in her penthouse suite. A familiar-bomb, basically.

Joel borrowed Robin's cellphone and tapped a number into it. "Hello? Blackfield Police Department?" he said, pressing it to his ear. "I need to be talkin to y'all about something, and you gonna want to hear this. I think I just got rescued from a serial killer."

He paused. "Yeah, I'll wait."

Accepting the steaming cup in Kenway's hand, Robin cradled her coffee. He put Joel's coffee in the cup holder next to his own, and pulled back into traffic.

"Hello there, Mr. Officer," Joel said, folding his arms. "I almost got killed by some maniac, and I thought y'all would like to know about it. Yeah, he drugged me and when I woke up I was chained to the ceiling next to a dead guy. Yeah. No, he said he was going to bleed me dry, because he needed 'blood for the garden'. No, I have no idea what that means. No, the only enemies I got live in glass bottles. Yeah, glass bottles. As in alcohol. ...It was a joke."

He sipped coffee. "You want me to come up there and take a statement? Aight. I'll be up there in a little bit. I got to go get my car and some clean clothes."

"So what you gonna do now, Malus?" asked Kenway.

"After we take Joel to his apartment, I want to try to edit and upload today's video," said Robin, glaring smouldering daggers out the window. "And then head out to my old house and formally introduce myself to Mr. Parkin. If there's really a monster in there, I'm sure my mother had something to do with it. And I'm sure there was a good reason."

"Point of order," said Joel, holding up a finger.

"Hmm?"

"I need to get my car. Black Velvet is not at my house."

"Where is it?" asked Kenway.

"I drove Velvet to my date with the mysterious Mr. Big Red last night." Joel massaged his face with both hands, talking through his fingers. "I left it parked in front of the serial killer's apartment."

Fifteen

THE STETHOSCOPE WAS COLD on Wayne's back. A latex-gloved hand cupped the curve of his ribs as he breathed in, out, in, out. "Do me a favor and breathe *real* deep," said the doctor, in his soft Australian accent. Morning sunlight streamed in through the window, throwing bars of gold over Leon. He stood at the end of the bed, his arms folded imperiously, his eyes red and squinty.

Wayne filled his lungs with the hospital's minty-sweet air and expelled it slowly.

"Hrrm. This is weird."

"What's weird?" asked Leon.

"Well…" Dr. Kossmann took a Dum-Dum sucker out of his labcoat pocket. He was an athletic, fresh-faced young man that looked like he could be the Blackfield High football captain. As he spoke, he emphasized his words with the sucker. "…We gave your son a dose of antivenin last night when he got here, but I've got to say, this is the fastest I've ever seen anybody recover from a snake-bite."

He gave the sucker to Wayne, then lifted the boy's left leg with gentle hands and placed it on the bed. "The swelling's gone down precipitously."

The bandage had been removed so the bite could be examined. "There's very little discoloration, there's no necrosis or infection at all in or around the punctures. I don't know what this lady Mrs… Mrs. Weaver put on you before they brought you here, but whatever it was, it must have been some kind of miracle salve."

Wayne unwrapped the cream soda Dum-Dum and stuck it in his mouth, staring at his leg and marveling at his own luck.

"Obviously I've never been one for homeopathic hoo-doo," said Dr. Kossmann, picking up a clipboard and clicking an inkpen. "But judging by the effect this had on your son, Mr. Parkin, maybe it's time to start believing."

"Maybe she's one of those crazy religious snake-handlers you hear about in this neck of the woods."

The doctor grunted.

They hadn't told the hospital about Wayne's strange absence in the middle of the night. As far as the ward's nurses were concerned, Leon had fallen asleep and his son had inadvisedly wandered out to the parking lot for some fresh air. This explained why the soles of Wayne's feet were dirty, and Kossman didn't seem to even be aware that anything had happened, so they didn't trouble him with it. Which was good, because he really didn't want to have to tell the story again.

"So he's gonna be fine?" asked Leon.

Dr. Kossmann nodded. "*Oh* yeah," he said to the clipboard, writing. "He's more than okay—all things considered, he's fantastic. A week or two of taking it easy, maybe stay off that foot as much as possible, and he'll be good as new. And that's a liberal estimate. Honestly, I think he ought to stay here another night for observation, but in truth he's not really gonna get any better day-to-day care here than he would at home." He winked. "And there's no Xbox here either."

"Point taken."

"Is there any pain?" asked Dr. Kossmann, gently feeling the flesh around the bite. "On a scale from one to ten, ten being the worst pain you ever felt?"

"One?" said Wayne. "I mean, I guess it just feels like a bruise."

That seemed to satisfy the doctor. "Like I said, he can stay here another night if you're on pins and needles about his condition, but if you want to take him home…I'm not going to put my foot down. To the best of my knowledge, he's through the worst of it.

"Usually a bite from a copperhead isn't much to an adult man—most of the time it doesn't even warrant antivenin—but to a child his size and frame, it can be serious. Your son actually had an allergic reaction, which is why he'd initially gone into anaphylactic shock and gone unconscious. But whatever Mrs. Weaver did eliminated that factor. She saved your son's life."

Leon picked up his jacket. "My insurance is probably turnin over in its grave. I guess we'll head on home. Maybe give you guys a call or run him up here if anything happens."

Dr. Kossmann peeled off his glove and dropped it into a wastebasket. "I'll have someone bring you a wheelchair. …And then I guess I'm going to go turn in my resignation and take up faith-healing."

✪

As the elevator door eased shut, Wayne reached out and tugged his father's sleeve. Puzzlement came over Leon's face.

"You know I'm not lyin, right?" Wayne looked up from the wheelchair. "About the door in the wall...and the monster. Jo-elle was there. He saw it all."

He had changed into the fresh clothes from the bag he'd seen under the chair the night before. Wayne wondered if he'd see the pretty girl with the shaved head again, so he could give her her clothes back. It'd felt supremely strange wearing them...but admittedly he had liked it, because they smelled like her.

Leon leaned against the wall. The lights in the elevator were stark but dim, turning his skin from its usual healthy umber to a greenish beetle-black. "I don't know what to believe, son. You ain't got a very good track record."

Wayne glumly sucked his upper lip.

"I thought we were gonna—I thought this was gonna be a fresh start, Wayne. For both of us. I thought we were done with Lawrence-level shit. I got you away from his little proto-gang, and...you got me away from Johnnie Walker."

"I'm tellin the truth."

Leon watched his face. "Yeah."

Reaching into Wayne's shirt-collar, he pulled out the ring. It lay on the pale of his fingers, twinkling dull in the elevator lights. "I didn't even know you *had* this. How long you been walkin around with it? Did I even say you could have it?"

"I got it that night I tucked you in the bed after you sat and watched the ball game and finished off that bottle you had hid in that basket Mom put on top of the bookshelf." Wayne made no move to take the ring away or even lean back, only stared up at his father.

Adrenaline thrummed in his veins. *Be stronger. Adapt and overcome.* "After you passed out, I got it off your nightstand and put it on my chain. I call it your stupid tax."

"Stupid tax," said Leon, slowly, gently, suspensefully tucking the ring back into his son's shirt, shaking his head as if in disbelief.

It kinda says something that you didn't even realize I had it.

The bizarre notion occurred to Wayne that he was about to get hit in the face, which had blessedly never happened before. Leon might have had a drinking problem, but even in his worst moments, he never struck his son. He may have put a couple holes in the walls, but that was the extent of his furor.

Leon winced, rubbing his chest as if he were having a heart attack. He leaned against the wall and pressed the Lobby button.

"...You okay?"

"Yeah." He gasped and gave a slow sigh. "Pulled a muscle clockin that dude in the snoot."

"He's all right, you know," said Wayne.

"Maybe."

"Was that the first time you ever punched a guy?"

Leon cracked a crooked grin. "Heh, yeah."

"You hit him hard as hell."

"Man, watch y'mouth," said Leon, getting behind the wheelchair as the door clunked open.

He pushed Wayne down the hall and into the waiting room, leaving him in front of a television while he went to the receptionist to process out. The TV was playing the local sports scores, which were Greek to Wayne. He took the opportunity to polish his glasses, feeling like a gigantic nerd.

Luckily, it was still early in the morning, so the lobby was relatively quiet except for the gurgle of the aquarium. A man and two women sat in the waiting area, reading magazines.

The sports scores returned to the local news, and the anchorwoman talked about two Jehovah's Witnesses that had gone missing earlier that week in the middle of their mission ride. At this point in their investigation, authorities believed David Hansford and Greg Tell had used their absence to slip away from the church.

She handed it off to an on-the-street interview with the boys' pastor in front of the local Witness chapter. "They'd never do such a thang," said Jackson Reilly, a beet-faced old white man in a navy blazer. "I know their families, and John Hansford, for one, wouldn't put up with that kind of nonsense."

Leon asked incredulously, "What do you mean, it's taken care of?"

Wayne turned the wheelchair to look. His father scratched his head in confusion, rotating an upside-down clipboard so he could read it. "Karen?" he asked, pressing a fingertip to the paper. "That old lady?"

The receptionist smiled. "Yes sir. She paid you up in full."

"Just the co-pay, right?"

"No sir, Mrs. Weaver paid everything in full. She was the one that brought him in, and she took responsibility for his care, so your insurance is totally irrelevant."

Leon's hand crept up to his mouth and he rubbed his mustache, either contemplating or trying to put his brain back together. "How...how much was the bill?" He flipped through paperwork and actually ducked in surprise as if he'd been shot at. *"Thirty thousand dollars?"* His eyes were bowling balls. "How was *that* thirty thousand dollars? All they did was give him a shot and keep him overnight!"

The receptionist helped him look through the papers. "Right here... the CroFab antivenin, twenty thousand a vial, plus the medical procedure, the room, workups, all—see this?"

"I see it, I don't believe it."

"Well, it's not *quite* thirty thousand."

"Close enough, twenty and some change." Leon signed where signatures were needed, but he shook his head as he did so. "A *hell* of a lot of change. How is an ambulance ride worth several thousand dollars?"

The receptionist smiled. "It's a bit of a sticker shock, but look at it this way, Mr. Parkin: thanks to your new friend, it's totally out of your hands, and out of your wallet." Taking back the clipboard, she went to work typing up the information. "Sounds like you've got the biggest thank-you card of your life to write."

✪

Leon was quiet crossing town in the morning rush-hour chaos. It wasn't exactly Chicago-busy, but everybody drove like they were in a funeral procession. He chewed his lip, so deep in thought that the glacial flow didn't even elicit his usual fussing and complaints. Wayne was glad. At the moment, he was savoring the relative peace and quiet of the car after sitting in the hospital all morning.

"That Weaver lady said she lives in the hacienda across the highway," said Leon. "I think we ought to go over there and say thanks. Maybe invite her over for dinner. What do you think?"

"Sure." Wayne fidgeted with the crutch in his lap.

"The doc says you should be fine in, like, a week. You won't be on that crutch long."

They rode on, neither of them saying much of anything. The Subaru was gliding up Hwy 9 into the hills when Wayne happened to glance at his father and saw a tear slip down his cheek.

Leon swiped it away and saw that he'd been caught. "I thought I was gonna lose you yesterday, man."

Wayne smiled. "Adapt and overcome."

"Where'd you hear that?"

"The guy at the comic store in town." He remembered the job offer from Fisher. "Oh! He gave me a job helping him run his comic shop after school!"

Leon grinned. "That's pretty cool. Gonna have you runnin the register, or…?"

"Yeah, I think so. And helping him do his Thursday Movie Nights or something."

"All right, my son's a work-a-day man now."

"I can walk there from school in the afternoons. It's only a few blocks down."

"As long as you don't go back in those woods."

"Nope." Wayne drew it out long and deep: *"Noooooooope. Nooooope."* Leon joined in and they made a frog-chorus of Nopes.

As the Victorian sidled into sight, Leon thumped the steering wheel. The U-Haul truck still sat in their driveway. "Shit—! With all the drama I forgot to take the truck back yesterday." He pulled in next to it.

165

"Hopefully they're open on Saturdays. Do you think you can chill here at the house while I take care of that?"

"Sure."

Wayne got out of the car and put his weight on the crutch, shoving the door shut with his snakebit foot. He was at the bottom of the stoop when he realized he was about to go back into the house where he saw the owlhead Sasquatch thing, and a cold wet blanket of oppressive fear fell over him.

Leon unlocked the front door and looked over his shoulder as it eased open. "Hey, you all right?"

Some dark part of Wayne expected to see the monster standing in the foyer behind his father, peering over his shoulder. The steps in front of him exuded some repellent force, as if they were magnets and his shoe-soles were made of metal.

"Remember how I told you I saw that monster in our house when I went through the door in the wall?"

Annoyed concern flashed across Leon's face. "Yeah. I get it, man." He came back down to the front walk and gave his keys to his son. "Tell you what. I'm gonna leave my keys with you. You can be my wheelman. I'll go check the house and if I come running out, you start the car."

Wayne felt a bit patronized, but he accepted the keys. Taking the tire iron out of the Subaru, Leon crept into the house.

Out in the middle of the expansive front lawn, the boy stared up at the windows, looking for shadows, glowing eyes, twitching curtains, the vaguest hint that something other than his father was lurking inside. The siding was raincloud-blue again, which mitigated some of his fear.

Shoes scuffed on the pavement behind him. Wayne twitched.

Pete and Amanda were coming across the highway from the trailer park, followed by little Katie Fryhover, who was carrying a plastic kite with a picture of Sully from the movie *Monsters, Inc.* on it.

"Hey, man," said Pete. "You're out of the hospital already?"

Amanda broke into a run and wordlessly gathered Wayne up in a hug, pressing his face against the cool vinyl of her windbreaker. She was wearing some kind of perfume that reminded him of pancakes.

"We've been worried as hell, Batman," said Pete, his hands crammed in his jacket pockets. "I figured you were gonna be up there for at least another week."

"The doctor said I was doing really good. Said the main reason I was even there was because I had an allergic reaction."

Pete stared at his feet. "That's good."

"Hey," said Wayne, pointing at him with his crutch. "I saw what you did before I passed out. I saw you hit that snake with that hammer." The smile spreading across his face belied the burn flowering in his throat. "Man, you got balls." He let out a hoarse laugh. "Thank you. For smacking that snake."

Pete looked up, one corner of his mouth quirked up in a half-smile. "I wish I could have gotten there before it bit you."

Wayne spread his arms, putting his weight on his good leg. "Hey," he said, holding up the crutch. "I'm fine. I'm fine, you know? Everything aight." He tucked it under his arm and leaned on it. "I just gotta take it easy and stay off it for like, a week."

"Sounds like time to bone up on your PlayStation skills."

"Heh heh, you said bone."

Amanda was meticulously wiping tears out of her eyelashes with her fingertips, trying not to ruin her mascara. "You kids are a bunch of nerds."

"What did you do with the hammer, anyway?"

"I took it home." Pete jerked a thumb back at the trailer park. "When my mom saw the blood on it, she didn't want it in the house, but when she heard what I did with it, she let me do whatever I wanted with it." He laughed. "Actually, when she saw me coming with it, she thought I hit somebody with it. I got in trouble for going to the fairgrounds again, but—"

The front door of the Victorian scraped shut and Leon came down to join them, his phone to his ear. "And I wanted to know if you could give me a ride home from the U-Haul place," he was saying. "I'll give you gas money. Yeah. Yeah, the one on Quincy. Okay, thanks."

Leon hung up the cell and stuck it in his pocket. "I checked every room in the house, including the cupola. One-one-six-eight is officially monster-free," he said, taking his keys off of Wayne, the tire iron dangling by his thigh. "Hey, y'all. What's up?"

Pete pointed at the tire iron. "What's that for?"

Leon held it up and regarded it as if it had magically appeared in his hand. "Oh, this? I'll let Master Wayne tell y'all about this. I got to go run an errand. I'll be back in a little bit. You guys hang out in the house or something, I'll bring back pizza for lunch." He left the tire iron in his car and climbed into the truck. Starting the engine, he rolled the window down and pointed at the kids. "And by 'something' I don't mean go out in the woods and get bit by a snake again."

"You got nothin to worry about there," said Pete, saluting. "Bruce Wayne is safe with us."

"That's what I'm afraid of. Y'all be good." Leon saluted them and backed the cumbersome truck out of the driveway. After grinding a few gears, he managed to get it into first and trundle down the road and out of sight.

Katie Fryhover looked like a windsurfer, trying to control the kite in her hands. "You got bitted by a nake?"

"I'm babysitting her until her grandmother gets home," said Amanda. "Is it okay if she comes in too? She's a good kid, real quiet. She don't get into anything."

167

"Yeah, of course," said Wayne, but he didn't lead them into the house. Instead, he lingered there on the lawn, absentmindedly rubbing the aluminum shaft of his crutch, staring at Katie as she fought the wind.

"Sooo…" Pete stared at Wayne's shoes, then met his eyes. "What was up with the tire tool? Your dad said something about a monster?"

"Y'all gonna laugh at me," said Wayne, crutching over to the front porch. The October breeze was brisk, chilling the toes of his left foot (which was only wrapped in a tight elastic bandage) but it was nothing compared to the chill he got when he looked at the house's sheer white curtains.

The others followed and sat down on the stoop alongside him. Katie tucked her kite into the corner between the porch and the stoop, behind a bush.

"I'm not." Amanda still stood on the stepping-stones in front of them, trying to keep her balance on the edge of one stone.

"Me neither," said Pete.

"Me needer!" said Katie.

Wayne turned sideways and sat back against the stoop banister. He didn't like having his back to the house. "I think my mom's ring might be magic," he said, taking the wedding band out of his shirt and off his neck.

"*Magic?*" Katie shouted. Her mouth fell open, her eyes wide. "Like a *widzerd?*"

"Not really like a wizard. …I don't know. It started when I woke up in the hospital." He launched into yet another rendition of the story, going on through the garage rescue straight on to falling through the painting into Kenway Griffin's kitchen.

"Dude that's crazy," said Pete. "I mean, that's—*that's* crazy, what you *said,* I'm not saying *you're* crazy, just that, y'know, what you *said* was crazy."

Wayne nodded, looking down at the ring in the palm of his hand. "I know what you're sayin. It does sound crazy."

"So you said a Sasquatch? In your house?"

"I don't think it was a Sasquatch." The crutch rested on Wayne's shoulder, feeling like a rifle. He lifted it up and pretended so, pressing the armpit pad against his shoulder as if it were a stock and aiming down the side of it. "But it kinda looked like one. Except it didn't look like a gorilla. It had a big head like a hoot-owl and glowin green eyes, and fingers kinda like Freddy Krueger."

"Wow," said Amanda. She was hopscotching from stone to stone, counting numbers under her breath. "No wonder you don't want to go in the house. I wouldn't want to either."

Pete got up and fetched Leon Parkin's tire tool from the Subaru, then marched up the steps and opened the front door. "Let's get it over with," he said in mock exasperation.

"Didn't Wayne's dad already say the house was clear?"

"He didn't go in with the ring." Pete swung the tire tool like a Vaudevillian twirling his cane.

"Good point."

Putting his necklace back on and tucking the aforementioned ring into his shirt, Wayne was reluctant. "Are you sure this is a good idea?"

Pete made a face and walked away into the Victorian. "You can't stay on the front porch forever. Your dad's not gonna let you sleep out here." He leaned back, peeking out. "You comin, or not?"

Wayne sighed and followed him inside.

The house was quiet and dark, but at least the walls were still blue. Wayne crutched into the kitchen to make sure the table was their round wooden one, as opposed to the faux-diner table with the metal trim. The room was unburnt, as well.

"Shh," he said, flashing his palms at the others. The floor creaked and popped as they crept from room to room. "Stop movin for a second and listen."

They all froze, even little Katie Fryhover.

Click. Click. Click. Click. The clock on the kitchen wall ticked. Wind rushed against the side of the house, breaking like a tide. A few birds sang outside, distant and muffled through the walls.

Katie sniffed wetly.

Taking out the ring, Wayne put it to his eye and peered through it. To his relief, the kitchen and the table in it remained the same.

"I don't—"

Hhhhrrrrrrooooooo! An eerie howling sound came from the living room, pouring ice down his spine.

Two heartbeats later, the front door slammed shut. *BLAM!*

Katie and Amanda both screamed, running for the front door and wrenching it open. Wayne limped along right behind them, toting his crutch like a briefcase, and all three children sprinted out onto the grass. They were halfway across the front lawn when Pete yelled after them.

"It was the wind, you idiots!" He stood on the porch, waving the tire iron. "The wind blew the door shut!"

✦

Once Pete had talked them back in, they went about their search for Owlhead (as they'd taken to calling it) with a little more levity, sweeping each room. Wayne would throw open a door and Pete would step in, the tire iron up in both fists like a Jedi with a lightsaber. By the time they had canvassed the entire house, they were up in the cupola and in pretty calm spirits.

"You can see everything up here," said Amanda, her nose almost touching the north window. "I can even see my house, and Pete's. They're both in the back of Chevalier Village." *Sha-vall-yay*, she said it, as if it were some kind of fine wine.

169

"Where's *my* house?" asked Katie, climbing up onto the wide sill.

"Right behind that one." Amanda braced her with a hand, pointing through the glass at a little white terrier sitting by the drive to the Alamo house. "Be careful, don't lean against the window. See Champ down there, layin in the grass?"

"Yep!"

Pete was staring out the opposite window. He climbed up and crouched on the sill, the top of his head against the arch of the windowframe. "Hey, I didn't realize you could see the fairgrounds from here."

"Really?" Wayne joined him.

Rising over the forest far to the south were the tallest buildings of Blackfield, tiny windowed spikes jutting up from the trees. The huge thirteen-floor Blackfield University Library scraping sky way in the back. The sand-colored cathedral spires of Walker Memorial. The nameless twelve-story office building with the fire-damaged penthouse floor. Much closer, off to his left, Wayne could see the suggestion of shapes just visible over the leaves and scraggly black trees—the highest hump of a roller-coaster, the peak of a free-fall tower. A smear of color that might be the front of the funhouse.

"We were that close?" he asked, marveling. They had certainly walked a long way home...and they'd almost made it.

"Yep." Pete climbed down and sat on the bed. "Man, those women that found us were creepy as hell. I've never seen them up close like that. That Theresa lady was strong."

He flexed an arm and squeezed his bicep, speaking in a bad Russian accent. "Strong like bull."

Amanda said over her shoulder, "*Yeah* she was. Super-strong for an old lady. She carried Wayne all the way down the fairground road out to the highway where the ambulance could find him."

"Like a quarter of a mile."

Turning on his TV and Playstation, Wayne sat next to him. A videogame started up and he went into a virtual garage, absent-mindedly cycling through customization options on the muscle car he'd been grooming all month. Anonymous rap-rock whispered from the speakers.

"That's a badass Mustang," said Pete.

"Thanks." Wayne fiddled with the car some more, and then his curiosity finally nibbled at him a little too hard. "So that one lady...I think she said her name was Karen. She said she lives in the big house across the street."

"All three of them do." Getting down from the windowsill, Amanda sat in the floor in front of the TV with Katie and the two of them leafed through one of his comic books. It was a newer *Batman*, one of the New 52 and he'd read it a hundred times, so Wayne didn't jump to its defense. "They all live in the same house together. They're not sisters, though, I don't think." She cupped her hands over Katie's ears and said, "People in Chevalier say they're lesbians."

Wayne's forehead scrunched up and he looked to Pete for confirmation. The other boy shrugged as if to say, *It is what it is.*

"She paid my whole hospital bill."

Amanda looked up. "That was nice of her."

"I think my dad said it was like thirty thousand dollars."

Pete said in a dramatic movie-trailer voice, "Sweeeet Jesus."

"Sweeeet Jeedzus," echoed Katie. "Can I draw? Do you got any paper and crayons?"

"I think there's some paper in my dad's printer." Wayne stared at the TV screen as he talked. The videogame was a balm to his nerves. "I don't have any crayons, but my dad's got some markers, if he didn't leave em at school." He handed the controller off to Pete and clomped downstairs. He was on the landing before he discovered two things: (1) he'd forgotten his crutch, and (2) he was by himself. Suddenly he felt very small and alone.

Luckily he didn't have to go all the way to the first floor. Making his way down the hall, Wayne pushed the door to his father's bedroom and watched it swing slowly open, revealing the room and everything it contained a couple inches at a time.

A tall wooden dresser from Aunt Marcelina...a window...Dad's pressboard desk from Walmart...several liquor-store boxes still full of their stuff...a window...Dad's bed....

No Owlhead looming in the corner.

Muscles slowly relaxed that he didn't realize were locked solid. He remembered to breathe again.

It was going to be a long night.

Sixteen

LUNCHTIME TRAFFIC SHUSHED PAST as Robin and Kenway ushered Joel onto the front porch of a Bungalow-style house, perched on a hill overlooking downtown Blackfield. Through the screen of trees below the house, Robin could see an ocean of rooftops.

Instead of dropping him off, they stopped by to pick up some clean clothes. Kenway didn't seem to mind playing chauffeur all day; he didn't have anything better to do, especially since it was a Saturday.

"Hey, you wouldn't mind checkin the place out for me, would you, hero?" asked Joel, unlocking the door.

The veteran looked like a barbarian as he climbed the front steps behind the line cook, six feet of blond hair and muscle crammed into a black T-shirt. He moved into the house and stood motionless in the foyer, listening, his fists clenched, his eyes wandering slowly over the old-fashioned decor and flowery wallpaper.

"So is—" began Robin, but Kenway held up a hand.

He checked behind the front door and pulled a baseball bat out of the umbrella stand, but paused in surprise when it sparkled in the sunlight. The striking end was covered in five-pointed stars made out of fake diamonds. "You Bedazzled a baseball bat?"

Joel shrugged sheepishly.

Shaking his head, Kenway stalked into the living room with the twinkling Slugger, and on into the kitchen. Joel went to his dish drain and pulled out a bread knife. Put the bread knife back, pulled out a silvery hammer. A meat tenderizer.

"You two stay here," said Kenway, and he left through a doorway.

Robin scowled. "I can take care of myself, Major Dad. I'm probably more dangerous at hand-to-hand than you are. Did you forget the video I showed you so soon?"

"Nobody could forget *that*," he replied from the hallway.

"What video?" asked Joel. "I ain't seen no video."

"I showed him the video of my first kill—the Witchlord of Alabama."

"Huh. How many witches you done killed, anyway?"

"About twenty."

"You killed twen-ty witches. Twennnnnty! Ah-ah-ah-ah-ah."

She smirked at his impression of the Count. *"About* twenty. Nineteen. I've kicked the shit out of a lot more people than that, though."

"You stone-cold, hooker." Joel opened the fridge and took out a beer, opening it sabre-style with a single swipe of the meat tenderizer. He handed the bottle to Robin and opened another one for himself.

"Where'd you learn a trick like that?"

He smiled slyly. "I ain't *always* been a pizza-boy."

"Anyway," Robin said, sitting down, "As I was going to say earlier, is this your mother's house?"

"Yep. My brother Fish don't like livin here, though. That's why he moved into the back of his comic shop. He says this house reminds him too much of Mama."

With its speckly-green Formica countertops and avocado appliances, the kitchen was a picture-perfect representation of what it must have looked like when Joel and Fish were boys. "She went a little crazy at the end. Lost her mind. She lived here for about a year, me here takin care of her, and then I eventually had to put her in the home. I couldn't do it no more. She died there a year and four months later. Massive stroke."

"I'm sorry to hear that."

"I think it must have been the witches that did it." He took a swig of liquid lunch. "I don't mean they put a spell on her or nothin, but it was...you know, her knowin they killed your mama Annie, she got real paranoid. She turned into a real basketcase. Used to say she saw demons in her closet. I'm so glad she didn't do that when I was *little* little—can you imagine how much that would have jacked up a little boy?"

Kenway came back, the Bedazzled ball bat resting on his shoulder. He and Robin sat at the kitchen table as Joel put on fresh clothes—skinny jeans, black boots, and a spaghetti-strap top. He was tying a silk do-rag around his head when he came back, dragging a cloud of tart perfume.

"You should polish your boots," said Kenway. "I used to wear some like that. I can show you how to spit-polish them so shiny you can see yourself in em."

Joel looked down. "I'll skip the spit, but I do appreciates ye."

"So are we gonna go pick up his car by ourselves, or do we want to get a cop to follow us down there?" asked Robin.

"I fear for my car," said Joel. "There ain't no tellin what he's done with it. But I fear for myself a little bit more. I think if I'm gonna go knockin on a serial killer's door, I want a trigger-happy cop there with me."

The officer on duty at the police station took them into the break room and made a cup of coffee while Joel gave him a statement. Kenway and Robin sat at a hand-me-down trestle table from the local school that folded up in the middle and had attached stools.

"So you say he had you tied upside down by your feet," the cop echoed for clarification.

Lieutenant Bowker was a tall, corn-fed man. The back of his neck cradled his shaved skull in a fat roll. Stirring his coffee, he came over to the table and sat down with a clipboard. "And he had another man tied up there? You say this killer was…collecting blood for a 'garden'?"

"Yeah." Joel sat with his fingers templed under his nose. The studs in his ears twinkled in the fluorescents.

"Now, are you *sure*—" Bowker lifted a sheet of paper to peek underneath, let it fall, "—that this wasn't just some kind of sexual fetish game gone wrong? Maybe things got a little out of hand and maybe you misconstrued the, ahh, the situation, so to speak. I mean, people get roofied all the time, and stuff like this happens. Not to diminish that kind of thing, you know, but, ahh…murder is kind of in a whole nother ballpark."

Joel had already detailed the series of events that had led to waking up in the garage—talking to B1GR3D online about dinner and sex, meeting him at his apartment, getting halfway through a steak and passing out.

He closed his eyes as if in restraint, and a few seconds later, opened them. "Yes. I'm more than sure it wasn't a sex game."

"Now, he, ahh…" Bowker wrote some more. "You said you escaped. How did you 'escape'? Seems like it would be hard to get out of a hogtie like that. Especially in fuzzy cuffs."

"I didn't say the cuffs were fuzzy."

"Ah, right." Bowker crossed out some text.

"I squeezed one of my hands out the cuffs—they weren't put on tight enough—and I got myself down while he was gone." The cuffs themselves had, in reality, been removed with Kenway's bolt cutters and were now rusting quietly at the bottom of the dumpster behind his studio. "I ran through the woods until I got to the road, where Mr. Kenway here found me."

"What about the other man?" asked Bowker. "The other one that was tied up. You just left him there?"

"He was dead. There was nothing I could do."

"How d'you know?"

"I knew because his throat was cut." Joel drew a finger across his neck, and his voice became urgent, exasperated. "Blood was runnin up to the top of the motherfucker's head *and drippin on the motherfuckin floor.*"

174

Bowker leaned back warily. "Well now there ain't no need to get excited, Mr. Ellis."

"*There ain't*—" Joel stopped himself before he could become fully livid, and spoke in measured tones, bracketing each point with his hands. "I almost got *killed*, and you want to make a *joke* out of it because I'm gay. Ain't you s'posed to protect and serve?" He sat up straight and boggled at some spot on the wall with a dazed look. "Oh, hell. I must've forgot where I was at. I'm black in a *got*-damn police station." His eyes focused lasers of sarcasm on Bowker's pink face. "What was *I* thinkin? Maybe I shoulda kept the cuffs on."

The officer pursed his lips, flustered, his face darkening. He glanced over at Kenway and the American flag shirt taut across his broad chest.

"We ain't got to go *there*, Mr. Ellis," grunted Bowker. "I'm honestly tryin to help you in good faith. Now I don't much care one way or the other what your proclivities are, and I'm real sorry that you must have got the wrong idea here." He twiddled the inkpen between his stubby fingers and went back to writing, his tone hardening, losing that good-ol-boy apathy. "Can you tell me what this man looked like?"

"He had red hair."

"Anything else?"

"Yeah, he was real skinny, had a skinny throat and skinny arms, but he was—he was *sinewy*, you know? The strong kind of skinny. Big hands." Joel traced the edge of his jawbone. "Had a real sharp jaw. Nose like a beak, big nostrils. Itty-bitty beady eyes, dark eyes."

Bowker wrote for a long time, pausing every so often.

"Is there anything you can tell me about where this man was holding you?" He fidgeted, rubbing his nose, scratching his cheek. "Do you remember any details about where you were detained?"

"Yeah. Yeah... there was a lot of signs and pictures and stuff leanin against the walls. Like, advertisin signage. Stuff about Firewater sarsaparilla, a big picture of the Loch Ness—no, I mean, the Creature from the Black Lagoon. I think there was something with a clown. I saw something about Wonderland. Welcome to Wonderland?"

"Weaver's Wonderland?"

"That's it."

Bowker sighed in a way that seemed like dejection to Robin. Or perhaps disappointment. "That sounds like the old fairgrounds out in the woods off the highway." The pen tapped the clipboard. Reaching up to the radio on his shoulder, he keyed the mike. "Hey, Mike. This is Eric. Can I get a ten-twenty?" They all sat staring at each other expectantly for an awkward moment.

"I just got done with lunch and now me and Opie are uptown goin south down Hickman," said a static-chewed voice. "Ten-eight."

"I want you to do me a favor." Bowker examined the clipboard. "We ain't got a key to the gate out there at the fairgrounds, do we?"

175

"...Naaah...the city probably does, somewhere, God knows where," said the radio. "But that don't stop me from getting out of my cruiser and walking around it. What's goin on?"

"I'm taking a statement from a fella that says he escaped from involuntary confinement in that location. He was put there by someone he describes as a 'serial killer'." Bowker coughed into his fist and keyed his mike again. "I want you to head up there and see if you can find anything shady."

"Ten-four."

Bowker sat there, breathing through his teeth and staring at the clipboard. Robin could almost hear his gears grinding. "Okay," he said, rising up out of his seat and adjusting his patrol belt. "I'm gonna go get this keyed into the system. I'll be right back."

As soon as he left, Joel leaned over to Robin and Kenway. "These redneck-ass small-town cowboys..." he growled under his breath.

Robin hugged herself. The break room was cold, it seemed, colder than the actual October day outside. *Must be the slab floor,* she thought. "He's going to send those two cops out there by themselves? To look for a serial killer?" She smirked. "Isn't this the part of the movie where the hapless cop wanders into the killer's lair and gets offed?"

"He prolly don't even believe there *is* a killer. He prolly still just thinks it was a—" Joel made air-quotes with his fingers, "—sex game."

The conversation dwindled into silence, and Robin finished off the last of her coffee, putting the empty cup into a trash can that was already full of garbage. Digging some quarters out of her pocket, she went to the snack machine and browsed the junk food inside.

"How long does it take?" asked Joel.

"You know these Barney Fife guys," said Kenway, poking at the table with his index fingers. "Hunt and peck typists."

Bowker stepped into the break room and Kenway looked up from his derpy impersonation of the man's keyboarding skills, casually leaning back and folding his arms, nothing to see here.

The officer paused awkwardly, then sat down and shuffled a stack of papers against the table.

"Okay." He folded his arms and leaned on his elbows, speaking confidentially. "I've got the report filed. You're on the books." He twiddled the pen between his forefingers again. "How come it took you so long to come down here and talk to somebody?"

"I don't know." Joel sat back and anxiously picked at his fingernails. "I guess I was so freaked out and glad to be away from it that goin to the cops didn't really occur to me." Of course, he glossed over the necessity of getting Wayne back to his father at the hospital, the explanation of which would have thrown a real wrench into the situation.

"Fair enough."

"Besides." Joel pointed at his face. "I'm black *and* gay. Goin to the cops ain't gon' be my first instinct."

176

Bowker gave it some thought and tapped the pen on the table. "Mr. Ellis, we here don't discriminate, okay?" He pointed at his own face, to the *Jarhead* high-and-tight haircut. "Now, I may *look* like Cletus T. Asshole, but I want to assure you that you're as important to me and everybody else here as the next guy."

He glanced at Robin. "...Or gal."

Joel nodded quietly. "Okay." He bit down on a tight smile. "All right. Aight, we're cool."

"Now, you said you met him at *his* apartment. I'm assuming your vehicle is still over there on the property, if this 'Big Red' hasn't moved it to another location." Bowker fetched a huge sigh. "What I'm gonna do is, I'm going to follow you-all over there to his apartment and we're gonna kill two birds with one stone—get your car and see if this fella is at home."

✸

The closer they got to Riverview Terrace Apartments, the antsier Joel became until he cracked the window and bummed a cigarette off of Kenway. Robin sat in the middle, the twenty-sided die gearshift between her knees. He had power-smoked the Camel down to the filter by the time they pulled into the parking lot fifteen minutes later. As soon as they came around the corner of the building and started seeing the 400 block, Joel threw his head back and swore in anguish.

Black Velvet was gone.

"I'm not surprised," said Kenway. "It's probably at the bottom of Lake Weiss."

"You better hush your mouth. I'd sooner you take the Lord's name in vain than insinuate somebody's hurt my baby," Joel told him, and slipped into a loud and vehement string of curses, his fists clenched. "Hell to the naw—I just *had* that sound system put in there. This is some grade-A bullshit." The truck curved to a stop in front of 427 and Bowker's cruiser slid into a space across the way.

They all got out, except for Joel, who stayed in the Chevy. As soon as Robin shut the door, he locked her out.

The bitter, clean smell of cut grass lingered in the air, even though the lawn was brown. Bowker knocked on Red's door. "Police." No answer. He knocked again, this time more insistently. After there was again no answer, he went to the front office to fetch the property manager and get a key.

Robin pressed the rims of her hands to the apartment's window and peered through them, trying to see past the blinds, but they were turned so that the cracks between the vinyl slats afforded no visibility at all.

177

Even though she knew full well that the front door was locked, she took hold of the knob and tried to turn it.

(gotta go gotta get out pack it up go go go)

She snatched her hand back. That was strange. She stepped away, cautiously, as if she'd encountered a beehive. Disembodied smells filled her nostrils: expended gunpowder, sizzling steak.

The green scent of cut grass became stronger. She was overcome by the sudden and intense need to flee, mixed with a cold cloak of guilt. Not remorseful guilt, but only the clear recognition of culpability; she felt chastised for something she'd never done. Abstract words flickered in her head, Polaroids of excited fear.

(stupid let your guard down shoulda done em both)

"What was *that* about?" asked Kenway. "You jerked like you touched a live wire."

"I don't know." She looked at the palm of her hand. *Residual paranormal power? Am I picking up on it?* If so, it was the first time anything like that had ever happened. She wasn't even sure if it was a thing that *could* happen—the witches were the only ones with any paranormal ability, weren't they? The sigils and runes decorating her body deflected paranormal energy like a sort of metaphysical armor, but other than the hallucinations of the owlheaded Sasquatch, Robin had never been privy to any kind of paranormal sensitivity. The sigils were an umbrella, but she had never felt the rain itself before. It was a bit like discovering a new sense.

Maybe her sigils being overpowered by Weaver at the hospital had left her sensitive, like sunlight on a burn. Maybe...maybe it was the proximity to Cutty. The creases in Robin's palm shined in the sun as she flexed her hand. Was Cutty so powerful that her power overflowed into the streets?

Could simply being the daughter of a witch mean Robin could siphon off surplus power like some kind of psychic vampire? She had certainly wondered over the years whether she had inherited some modest fraction of whatever paranormal talent lay within her mother Annie. As far as Robin knew, witchcraft began with a singular ritual, and had nothing biologically to do with the witch herself—it was all on the paranormal side of the equation, spiritual, exterior to genetics, initiated by the sacrifice of the heart to Ereshkigal.

She checked her cellphone. *Call me back, Heinrich, damn you.* Robin crammed it back into her jacket pocket.

Lieutenant Bowker came back with the property manager, a limping stump of a man with a Boston terrier's googly eyes and a salt-and-pepper beard. His golden bouffant was parted in the center like a monkey's ass. The name embroidered on his shirt was ROGER.

The manager unlocked the door and stepped aside for Bowker, who strode in with his hand on the butt of his pistol.

"Well, damn," said the officer.

178

The living room was completely devoid of furniture—of anything, really, that said a human had been living here until last night. The walls were bare, and the spotlessly clean carpet wasn't even marred by the footprints of a sofa's legs.

Robin searched the kitchen with her GoPro. No appliances stood on the counters. No food in the cabinets, no food in the fridge except for a single Arby's sauce packet in the crisper.

Bowker came out of the bedroom. "Can you tell me who the apartment is leased to?"

"Yeah, sure." Roger stared at the clipboard in his hand. "Says here it's a fella by the name of Richard Sutterman." He looked up and shrugged. "I don't get back here much other than to check on old Mr. Brand in 432. Always havin to snake his toilet out, sewage backin up into his bathtub and whatnot. I don't recall what this Sutterman looks like."

Joel leaned against the front door's frame. "That name mean anything to you?" Bowker asked him.

"Never heard it before in my life."

Bowker rubbed his face in exasperation and tossed a hand. "I can head back to the station and look through the database, or maybe go talk to the county clerk and see if he can find any info more concrete on this Sutterman fella, but…." His offer tapered off, the unspoken admission hanging in the air: it ain't much to go on.

Psychic whispers still lingered in the air, tracing cobweb fingers along the rims of Robin's ears.

She got a faint mental flash of a vial, and a hand using a hypodermic needle to draw out a tiny bit of the contents. Then she flashed on an image of that same needle being injected into a grilled steak. She also got a flash of three words—*Yee Tho Rah*—but had no idea what they meant.

"Come on, the trail's cold for now," she said, sidling past Joel. "I've got some editing to do while I think, and then I want to go have a look at my old house."

Seventeen

THE SHOPS AND OFFICES of Blackfield wheeled past the windows of Mike DePalatis's police cruiser. "The old fairgrounds?" asked Opie from the passenger seat. "I ain't been out there in a long-ass time. Not since I was a kid."

"I never been there." Mike's eyes darted up and down the street as he sucked on the last of his milkshake. "I moved to Blackfield in 2006. When did they shut that place down, the 80s?"

"1987, I believe."

Mike closed in on Broad Avenue and headed east toward the highway, passing the city limits sign.

It took him longer than he expected to find the turn-off for the fairgrounds. Lined with trees the whole eight miles out to the interstate, the highway was littered with weedy side-roads, all of them twin dirt ruts with mohawks of grass. A few of them went out to abandoned properties with overgrown houses, some to improvised dumps with rusty mattress-frames, ragged recliners, weatherbeaten sofas. One even went to a rumored pet cemetery, and you weren't going to get Mike out that way if you offered him a million damn dollars.

Ultimately what tipped him off that he'd found the right track was the NO TRESPASSING sign nailed to a tree, thirty years old if a day and speckled with .22 holes. On the other side of the highway was a small gravel clearing, presided over by a dilapidated aluminum gas-station awning.

Some forty yards back, a steel pole as big around as Mike's arm stretched across the grassy path. He angled the police car into the ruts and drove into the woods, the undergrowth brushing and clattering against the Charger's undercarriage.

Pulling up to the gate, Mike opened the door and started to get out. "I got it," Owen said helpfully, throwing himself out of the car. He checked the gate and found that there was, indeed, a chain confining the gate to its mount, and a padlock secured it. Two of them, in fact.

Hypothetically they could go around it, if not for the impenetrable forest on either side.

"Shit." Mike put on his hat and got out of the car anyway. "Looks like we're walking." He hopped over the gate, his keys jingling.

"Maybe we could try our keys on them padlocks," said Owen, glancing over his shoulder as they set off into the tall grass. "I locked my keys in my truck once, one of them GMC crew cabs? And my neighbor? I don't know what got into his head but he tried his minivan key and I'll be damned if it didn't unlock my truck."

"Weird. I don't think a car key will work on a padlock, though." The grass beat against Mike's shins, and hidden briars plucked at his socks. "When we get out of here, you might want to check yourself for ticks. Few years ago I was part of a search effort out in woods like this, and when I got home I found one on my dick." He made a fist and held it up, demonsrating the tick's exact placement by pressing his other thumb to his wrist. "It was snuggled up right behind the head."

"Oh, that's horrible," said Owen. "I would've lost my mind."

"I had to go get my wife to pull it off. We tried to suffocate it with nail polish, we tried heating it up, we tried alcohol. No fun. You ever held a lighter to your dong?"

Owen laughed like a kookaburra.

Conversation slipped into silence again. The two men walked for what felt like a half an hour, forging through tall wheatgrass and the occasional clump of blackberry brambles. This time of year there weren't any berries, and what there was, had rotted into pulpy purple tumors that oozed at the slightest brush.

Mike glanced at his partner as they walked. Officer Owen Patrick Euchiss was a scarecrow with an angular Van Gogh face. The black police uniform looked like a Halloween costume on him. They called him Opie after the sheriff's son on *The Andy Griffith Show* because of his first two initials, which he signed on all of his traffic citations. It looks classier, he'd said one day. Like one of those 'fancy-pants authors'.

His constant sly grin reminded Mike of kids he'd gone to school with, the little white-trash hobgoblins that would snort chalk dust on a dare and brag about tying bottle-rockets to cats' tails. Middle-age had refined him a little, but the Scut Farkus was still visible under Opie's mask of dignified wrinkles. Rumor around the station was that Owen had never passed the Georgia civil service test, but had gotten the job through nepotism. Apparently someone was good friends with the chief, and a late-night phone call was all it took to make Chief Lowry look the other way.

And somehow, in the end, DePalatis had gotten stuck with Opie.

It never paid to be the nice guy, did it?

"Ferris wheel," said Owen, snapping Mike out of his reverie. He straightened, peering into the trees.

The track they were walking down began to widen, grass giving way to gravel, and skeletal machines materialized through the pine boughs. They emerged into a huge clearing that was once a parking lot, and on the other side of that was an arcade lined with tumbledown amusement park rides, the frames and tracks choked with foliage.

Had to admit, the place had a sort of post-apocalyptic *Logan's Run* grandeur about it. A carnival lost in time.

Not any better than the pet cemetery.

The two policemen walked aimlessly down the central avenue, heels crunching in the flaky gravel, their eyes searching the remnants of Wonderland. "What are we supposed to be looking for?" asked Owen. "Demon clowns? 'Uh heh heh! We all float down here, Georgie!'"

"You heard the same thing I heard."

"'Something shady'."

"Ayup." Mike made a face. "That's really not a very funny joke, by the way."

Owen grinned.

They came to a split, facing a concession stand. Owen took out his heavy skullcracker flashlight and broke off to the left, heading toward a funhouse. "I'll check over here."

Mike went right. A purple-and-gray Gravitron bulged from the woodline like an ancient UFO. Across the way from that was a tall umbrella-framed ride, chains dangling from the ends of each spoke like fishing poles.

He contemplated this towering contraption and decided it had been a swing for kids, but without the seats it could have been a centrifuge where you hung slabs of beef from the chains and spun the cow blood out of them. Or maybe it was some kind of giant flogging-machine that just turned and turned and whipped and whipped.

When the rides had been damaged enough and lost so much of what identified them, they became alien and ominous.

Deeper into the park, Mike found a gypsy village of third-wheel mobile homes, giant holes punched in their roofs by the elements. Bushes cloaked their flanks and bristled from inside.

Something whiny bit him on the face and he slapped a mosquito. Blood on his fingers. He wiped it on his uniform pants.

After wandering in and out of the nine caravans of the carnie village, Mike decided that none of them were in good enough shape to sustain life. Every one of them was beat to hell and falling apart, scrap metal and flat tires. He headed back into the main arcade.

At this point he had developed an idea of what Wonderland looked like from above: an elongated I like a cartoon dog-bone, with a Y on each end, the arcade forming the long straight part down the middle.

Mike stood at the west end of the dog-bone, staring at the concession stand, and took his hat off to scratch his head.

182

He took the left-hand path, walking toward the funhouse. Behind the concession stand to his right was a series of roach-coaches: food trucks with busted, cloudy windows, wreathed in tall grass. After the funhouse he found a Tilt-a-Whirl, an honest-to-God Tilt-a-Whirl. Bushes and a tree thrust up through the ride, dislodging plates of textured metal and upending the seashell-shaped cars.

"What a shame," he told the wilderness.

A wooden shed with two doors stood behind the Tilt-a-Whirl, quite obviously an improvised latrine. He wondered if Porta-Potties had even been invented in 1987. He opened a door and found it full of hickory bush, leafy switches bursting up out of the shit-hole.

"Hey Owen!" Mike shouted into the trees. "Where'd you go?"

A behemoth of a generator trailer lurked in the tall grass, an olive-gray box the size of a minivan with cables snaking out of it every which way. Here, the treeline marked the end of Wonderland. A chain-link fence tried to separate fun from forest, but sagged over, trampled by some long-gone woodland animal.

Mike went around the generator to the woodline and looked both ways. Tucked behind the back wall of the Tilt-a-Whirl, a pair of gray-green military Quonset huts nestled against the trees. One of them opened at the end in a door with no window in it, secured with a padlock.

NO ADMITTANCE—EMPLOYEES ONLY!

"The hell?" He lifted the padlock. It was a new Schlage, no more than a couple of years old.

The door itself wasn't quite up to snuff. As Mike tried the doorknob, the entire wall flexed subtly with the muffled creak of leather. Old plywood? He pressed his palms against the door and pushed. The striker plate crackled and the wall bowed inward several inches.

"Geronimo," he grunted, and stomp-kicked the door. The entire wall shook and dirt fell out of the hut's roof.

Another kick set the door crooked in the frame. The third kick ripped the striker out and the whole door twisted to the inside, the hinge breaking loose. Inside was pure jet-black car-full-of-assholes darkness. Mike took out his flashlight and turned it on, holding it by his temple.

Dust made soup of the air. He stepped into the hut.

A workbench stood against the wall to his right, and a dozen buckets and empty milk jugs were piled in the corner, all of them stained pink. Wooden signs and pictures were stacked against the walls:

VISIT HOOT'S FUNHOUSE!

ARE YOU TOO COOL FOR SCHOOL? DRINK FIREWATER SARSAPARILLA!

GET LOST IN OUR HALL OF MIRRORS!

Three hooks jutted up from the bare cement floor in the middle of the room. Chains were attached to them, and the chains led up to three pulleys, which angled them down to hooks on the back wall.

Old blood stained the floor around the hooks.

"Ah, no," said Mike, drawing his pistol.

On the other side of the workbench was a door. He gave the stains a wide berth, sidling along the wall.

The door was already cracked open. Flashlight in one hand and pistol in the other, he crossed his wrists Hollywood-style and pushed the door open with his toe. Behind the door, the polished black body of a Monte Carlo reflected his Maglite beam.

POW! A Taser cartridge exploded in the eerie stillness. A bolt of lightning hit Mike in the ass and he barked like a seal, his knees buckling.

Staccato electricity pulsed down the Taser's flimsy wires, *tak-tak-tak-tak,* racing down the backs of his thighs. Streaks of prickling pain shot up his spine. He hit the floor bleating in a weird tremolo. His hands balled into fists and his toes scrunched inside his shoes.

The pistol fired into the wall between his jitterbugging feet, blinding him with a white flashbulb.

He couldn't open his hands. He couldn't point the Glock. All he could do was lie there and vibrate. "You *had* to come in here, didn't you?" asked the silhouette in the doorway, tossing the Taser aside and plucking the pistol out of Mike's hands.

Chains rattled through a pulley and coiled around his ankles. Someone hauled him up by the feet and suspended him above the floor. One of those white five-gallon buckets slid into view underneath his forehead, knocking his useless arms out of the way, and then his hands were jerked up behind his back and he was locked up in his own cuffs, dangling like Houdini about to be lowered into a glass booth full of water.

"This is what I should have done to that faggot, instead of lettin him hang around," said a man's voice, reminiscent of Opie but growlier, deeper, more articulate.

Mike's heart lunged at the *snick* of a blade being flicked out of a box-cutter.

"No, *please!*" he managed to grunt.

"You live, you learn, I guess." The man cut a deep fish-gill V in Mike's neck, two quick slashes from his collarbone to his chin.

The pain came a full second later, a searing cattle-brand pincering his throat. Both his carotid and his jugular squirted up his cheeks and over his eyes, beading in his thinning hair. He gurgled, sputtered, trying to ask 'Why?' and 'Why me?' and 'What did I do?' and shout 'Please don't leave!' and 'Help me!,' but there was nobody in the garage to hear him.

The door slammed shut, leaving Mike in musty darkness.

Blood dribbled steadily into the bucket as he slowly regained control of his body.

Being upside-down invested what blood he had left in his brain, giving him a clarity he wouldn't have been able to achieve standing up. He tried to twist his tingling arms around, but the cuffs were so tight his hands were falling asleep. Or maybe it was from the blood loss? He wasn't sure anymore.

184

A sit-up was out of the question, at least from this angle. Mike flexed his abs, but only got high enough for the blood to run into his ears before the front plate in his Second Chance vest made it impossible to bend any further.

He relaxed, setting himself to swinging. "Gob-dab," he said, blowing blood from his lips. Some of it pattered on the floor.

I guess this is the end of the line, then.

A strange sort of samurai tranquility came over him as Mike hung there, listening to the drum solo of his life ebbing away. Tap-tap-thump-tap. There was no denying it. This was it, and to his surprise some part of his psyche relaxed, serenity unfolding inside him like a paper flower.

Nasty way to go, but shit, it was a great ride, wasn't it? He thought about his wife; thought about his dog; thought about his car. This became a taking of stock. He had accomplished quite a lot in his life, he decided. Not everybody had their own house, not everybody found their soulmate. He was comfortable. He had nine hundred and sixty-two TV channels and a Keurig. His dad was proud of him, as far as he could tell.

God, how morose!

After what felt like an eternity he tried to tell himself a joke, but he couldn't quite grasp any good ones. Any other time he would have had a great joke ready to go, a real bawdy knee-slapper, but none came to him just then.

As he began to slide into death, Mike DePalatis opened his heavy eyes.

In the corner of the Quonset hut, a figure stooped under the curve of the roof, as if it had slipped in under the wall. The woman gleamed as if she were made of light *(photons,* he thought, a random interjection of 5th grade Science class, *she's made of photons),* and even though she didn't seem to be wearing any clothes, a reassuring vibe told him it didn't matter. Nothing mattered anymore, least of all modesty.

Gliding into the room, she came to his side and leaned over, her hands on her knees, regarding his upside-down face as one does a puppy in a pen.

I'm so sorry this happened to you, she said but didn't say.

Up close, he was surprised to see that she was Asian, with fine features and smiling, merry eyes. *Me too.* The room spun. Mike licked his dry lips. *This sucks.*

You already know there's not enough time to save you, the woman said but didn't say. *But rest knowing that there is a plan in place.*

That's good. He allowed himself to smile.

She reminded him of the Blue Fairy, graceful but melancholy, welling with a spectral blue light. *Hey, am I a real boy now?* he thought hopefully.

The woman chuckled, her laughter the tinkle of a wind chime. She straightened and stepped away, fading until the only evidence of her presence was like the faint warmth of heat left in stones, after the sun has gone behind a cloud.

185

A dark stillness overtook the room as Mike relaxed, sighing deep in his throat.

Eighteen

LEON HAD RENTED A couple of movies from the Redbox—the new *Teenage Mutant Ninja Turtles*, some Alex Cross movie with Tyler Perry, and whatever the latest Nicolas Cage flick was. Except for Wayne, they all sat in the living room eating pizza and watching the movies, Katie lying on the floor drawing her pictures.

The sun settled on the purple-gold horizon, fleeing from a speckle of stars, and the summer's last serenade of frogs and crickets trilled in the trees.

The kids had gone home to get permission from their parents to spend the evening at 1168. Katie's grandmother had been more than happy to have the night off, and started filling a hot bath before Amanda even left. Pete's mother and Amanda's dad, on the other hand, came over to get the lay of the land.

Pete's mom Linda sat on the stoop, hunkered over a cigarette. She was tiny and mousy with a husky radio-DJ voice and a twitchy, good-natured personality.

"Yeah, that's fine," she was saying to Leon. "Pete needs good friends. I'm proud of that guy, what he did with that big ol hammer. He can be kinda moody sometimes, and he swears a lot, but he'll surprise you. He takes care of people he likes, he really does. He's a good kid." She had apologized profusely for Pete taking the kids to the fairgrounds, and she did it again for good measure. "I told him not to go back up there, but, you know, he does what he wants. Not that he's a rebel, he... he's an independent kid, yeah?"

"I understand, totally," said Leon. "Wayne's got a bit of a wild streak himself sometimes. He used to run with a couple of bad kids back in Chicago. I had to tell him what's what a couple of times."

Amanda's dad Warren hulked over the slim, spindly Leon. Blond curls tumbled out from under his do-rag like an extra from *Sons of Anarchy*. His neat beard was laced with white. "Really?" he asked, leaning against the wall with his fingertips in his jeans pockets. *"That* little guy?"

Leon chuckled. "Yeah, believe it or not. When his mom died, I didn't take it so well. Got to drinkin a lot. Wayne got a little rebellious—or maybe just lonely—tried to make friends, fell in with the wrong crowd. Little bastard named Lawrence, him and a couple of his hard-head buddies. They talked him into one too many things and he got picked up skipping school. Luckily it happened to be a cop that worked with my dad, so he knew us. Brought him to me at work because it was so late there wasn't no point takin him to class."

✿

This was last year, give or take a few months; at Wayne's age, time was a stretchy, malleable thing, distorted by the sagging weight of boredom. Every day was a week, every minute was an hour. The years were all a thousand days, but the sun was never up long enough.

"If you wanna be friends with *us,*" Lawrence, the tallest of them, had said. "You gotta get past Sam." He and three other boys were standing outside a Quik-Trip, surrounded by the gray-and-brown galleon hulks of Chicago's dour architecture.

"Get past him?" asked Wayne. "What does that—"

"*Steal* somethin, dumbass."

All three of them had several inches and a dozen pounds on him, Lawrence in a giant basketball jersey that looked like a flashy nightgown on him, the other two in huge white shirts. They had all started wearing their pants low, but Wayne never caught on. In fact, he had been wearing a T-shirt that day with *Pokémon* on it, and a pair of chinos Aunt Marcelina had given him for Christmas.

"*Tch,* I don't even know why we doin this," said one of the other boys. Wayne never caught his name, but Lawrence had called him Casper 'cause the shape of his head', so that's what Wayne used. In his own mind only, of course.

"Look at this four-eyed kid," Casper said, pointing at him. "Got on a *Pokémon* shirt like he tryna catch monsters and shit. Hey. Imma give you one of them Pokey-balls and you go in there and throw it at Sam. Suck 'im up, *SSSSLLLURP!*"

"*SSSSSLURP!*" The third boy's name was Quennell. He wore a black and gold ball cap with some sports team's logo on the front, the brim as flat as a dinner plate. He burst out laughing, almost collapsing on the sidewalk.

"That shit is so funny," said Lawrence, grinning.

As if he'd flipped a switch, his face fell slack. Wayne found the effect terrifying, and ice-termites scurried up his arms. "Aight, nerd-boy. Time to bleed. You one of us?"

At this point, Wayne couldn't believe he was still being tested. Lawrence and his cronies had milked him for schoolwork and test answers all year, pushing him around, teasing him with friendship—circling him socially like wolves, getting closer and closer, ingratiating themselves with smiles and backslaps, only to harry at his nerves with mean-spirited comments and shoving. Their cruelty inflicted, they would fade away again, leaving him alone and frustrated.

It was maddening torture, like some kind of idiot Good Cop/Bad Cop routine, and he was beginning to feel like they only drew him close to get him into biting range.

"Yeah," rasped Wayne. His throat and mouth were dry, and his tongue clicked when he spoke.

"Aight then."

Lawrence turned without further ado and pulled the Quik-Trip door open, stalking into the store. *Bing-bong.* They followed him inside in a flying-V formation and went straight to the front counter, where a middle-aged Indian stood behind a bulletproof window, packing boxes of Marlboros into the overhead display bin.

"Ay, lemme get a box em Swisher," said Lawrence, carrying his crotch in one hand. The register area was raised up a step above the sales floor, so his chin only came up to the countertop.

Sam shook his head, making a face. "What are you, nine?"

"Eleven." Lawrence threw his hands at Sam to emphasize his point. "Old *enough.*"

Sam had the gall to laugh at him. The old man was rough, thick-faced, pox-scarred, looked like he'd been dragged through life by his ankles. "That is so cute," he said in his dancing accent. "Get out of here with that. You ain't hard."

Taking this as his cue to leave, Wayne stepped away from the argument and padded deeper into the convenience store. Two aisles in were racks and racks of candy. He weaved back and forth anxiously, as if he were doing the mating dance of some tropical bird, combing the shelves with his eyes.

3 Musketeers, M&Ms (peanut, pretzel, and plain), Juicy Fruit—

"Come on," Lawrence was saying. "My mama let me smoke em."

"I am not your mudder."

—Reese's Cups, Nerds (tropical, kiwi-strawberry, and cherry-grape), Chunky Bar—

"*Tch,* that's for sure. My mama look good. You look like you been shot with a shotgun. In the face. All em holes."

Sam sounded more proud than hurt. "These are acne scars."

"Ugly as hell."

—FastBreak, Whatchamacallit, Sour Ropes—

"What are you doing?" Sam asked. Wayne could hear the jingle of his keys as he fumbled for his keyring.

"Nah don't worry bout it," said Quennell.

189

"Put that down!"

Wayne picked up a pack of Skittles. At the same time, a burst of squeaking sneakers told him that someone had taken off running, and the door-chime went off. *Bing-bong.*

He crept to the end of the aisle right in time to see Casper and Quennell run out the front door with boxes of canned Budweiser. Lawrence was already gone.

Unlocking the sales-counter partition, Sam came out from behind the glass window and ran for it, but stopped short on the doormat. Lawrence and Quennell were lightning-fast, even with their pants low, and there was no doubt that they were already out of the parking lot.

Sam slumped, defeated. "Goddammit." He punched the doorframe and turned to schlep back to his place behind the counter, but noticed Wayne standing there in the candy aisle.

"YOU!"

He stormed toward Wayne, taking his *Pokémon* shirt in both hands and shaking the boy so hard he dropped the Skittles.

Wayne's glasses slid, coming to rest on his upper lip, where they fogged under his nose. "I dint have nothin to do with that!" cried Wayne, trying to get away. His heart was a rabbit in a cage, banging hard and frantic.

"You're one of them!" Sam told him, that beefy, scarred-up face inches from his own. "Tell me where did they go? Where are they going?"

Adrenaline surged through Wayne's body and his eyes teared over, spilling down his face. "I don't know, man, I swear, please—I don't even *like* them." Sam's breath was noxious, like farts and pickles, and he couldn't get away from it. "They told me I had to steal somethin if I wanted to be friends with em, but I didn't want to. I didn't want—"

"Steal something?" demanded Sam. "Who do you think you are being? Do you think you are hard? Is that who you want to be?"

"No. ...No sir." Wayne shook his head ferociously, so hard he thought his neck would break. His glasses fell off, swinging from his ear into a display of potato chips.

Sam let go of his shirt and walked away, pacing slowly in front of the sales counter, flexing his hands and wheezing through his nose. Remembering the candy, Wayne bent over and picked it up, and fished his glasses out of the potato chips. He didn't know what else to do, and leaving seemed like the dead wrong choice, so he stood there and watched the man fume.

"Always with the tricks and the bullshit," said Sam. "Stealing of beer." He pointed out the window with both hands, on the verge of a tantrum. "Is that who you want to associate with, young man? Is that the kind of friends you want? The kind that steal and crap on people?"

"No. *No!*"

Wayne put on his glasses and dug in his pocket to see what kind of money he had. A rumpled dollar bill and two dimes. When he looked up, he noticed that Sam had stopped pacing.

"What are you still doing here?" asked the man. "Are you not going to run after them?"

The boy looked down at the Skittles in his hand and he armed the tears off his face with one wrist. His breath hitched as he spoke. "If you don't run—*hup-hup-hup-hup*—you won't have anything to run from." Sam's face softened as he saw the money in Wayne's other hand. "That's what my mama said," he added. "'A grown-ass man don't run.'"

"I will tell you what." Sam pointed at the Skittles. "If you make me a promise, you can have those for free. On the house. And you can walk out of here—when I call the cops to report the theft, I'll say there were three children, not four." Pointing at the camera mounted on the ceiling, he appended, "I will delete the footage also. It will be like you did not even exist."

Wayne studied the Skittles, not really comprehending the shapes and colors through the mottle of tears in his eyes. His brain was having trouble gaining traction on reality.

"Yeah, okay."

"Promise me," said Sam, cupping his hands at Wayne as if he were begging for alms, "that you will not hang around with those boys anymore. Leave them alone. They are the bad news. Do you know what I say?"

Wayne nodded, staring into the saddle-leather basin of Sam's hands.

The proprietor folded his arms and studied Wayne's tear-streaked face for a moment. *"Do* you?"

"Y—yes. I do. Yeah."

Sam stuck his hands in his pockets and jingled coins, and then he tossed a hand at the door. "Get out of here."

Opening the glass partition, he was about to step back behind the counter when he paused, standing in the archway. "Remember," Sam said, tapping his temple. "Stay away from them. They are on the wrong road. Be a good person. For your father, be a good boy."

❂

Leon glanced at Wayne, who sat in the porch swing behind him. "That was the day my sister Marcy talked me into moving down here. Neither one of us was handling it. We had to get out of there."

"Welp," said Amanda's dad, checking his watch. "I got work at four in the morning, so I'm gonna pack it in for the night. Y'all take it easy, brother."

His heavy black biker boots clomped down the front steps. Pausing on the lawn, Warren chuckled. "I'd tell you to look after my little girl, but to be honest she's the one that takes care of us." Leon saluted him as he sauntered off into the velvet purple twilight.

Linda stayed behind, finishing her cigarette. "Why ain'tcha in there watchin the movie with the other kids?" she asked Wayne.

He shrugged. "I don't know. I just wanted to see the sunset." He didn't want to admit that he was still afraid to spend time in the house.

Royal colors made a masterpiece of the western sky. Linda took it all in. "Yeah, I see what you mean. They are nice down here in the south, ain't they? The sunrises are even better." She smiled at him. "I still remember the very first sunrise I ever saw when I got clean. My husband come and carried me home from the hospital. I sat in the parking lot of a gas station and cried my eyes out over it."

"I did the same thing on Wayne's birthday last month," said Leon, yawning. "Well, I didn't really sob, but...you know, I went through like half a box of Kleenex."

"How long's it been?"

"...How long's what been?"

"Since you quit drinking."

Leon tilted his head. "How did you know I was drinking?"

"You said so a minute ago."

His look of surprised confusion broke into a grin. "I guess I did. Man, it's been a long day. I need some sleep." He sighed. "I figure a couple of months."

"You figure?"

"I didn't drink long enough that I feel like I need to do the anniversary thing. The coins, all that." Leon took out his cellphone and fiddled with it. "I never did go to AA. I gave my debit card to my aunt and let her buy my groceries, so if I felt like I needed a drink I wouldn't have the money to run out and get something."

He stared into the sunset. "It was tough, and I still get that hook pullin my insides every now and then, but...you know what they say. One day at a time. That's what my dad always said. He was a cop. He didn't take no flak from nobody. I guess that's where I get it. He did whatever he put his mind to, and damn the help."

"Tommy's daddy, he drank *real* hard. Drank like a fish."

Linda took a long drag off her cigarette and ashed it into the grass.

"He got so bad he was hallucinating. A couple of years ago it got about as bad as it was gonna get. He was seein Vietnamese soldiers out in the woods and he said he was gonna shoot me so the 'gooks' couldn't rape me. And he didn't even know who *I* was. So Tommy got it into his head to save his daddy's life. Took him to the hospital to get him clean. Stewart broke down so bad he ended up in a wheelchair and almost lost a leg from a staph infection."

Leon winced.

"Bout gave him brain damage. He was in a coma for near two months. It's crazy how dependent you can get on the booze...after so long, you literally can't survive without it. Going clean will kill you. So it's a good thing you got out of there while the gettin was good." Linda put out her cigarette. "So is your dad still around?"

"No." Leon shook his head. "He died when I was seventeen."

"What happened? —If you don't mind me askin."

"He pulled over the wrong car. He saw the passenger throw something out the window into the woods, and when he went to go ask about it, the passenger shot him."

Horror and sympathy warred on Linda's face.

The conversation was dragging Wayne down, so he got up and went inside to face his fears, letting the screen door slap shut behind him.

Thump, thump, thump, he crutched into the living room and plopped down on the couch next to Pete. They were watching the Alex Cross movie, or at least Pete was. The girls lay on the floor making pictures; Amanda was drawing them and Katie was coloring them.

Standing next to the TV was the blood-smeared strength-test hammer. Wayne leaned up and took a piece of tepid pizza from the box on the table, sitting back to nibble on it. He couldn't pay attention to the movies because his eyes were fixed on the far corner, opposite the TV, where he'd first seen Owlhead.

The monster had been tall enough that the top of its broad head brushed the ceiling, its back to the nearly empty bookshelves on that side of the room. It reached for him with long arms, as long as he was tall, covered in copper-wire hair, streaked with the swampy green of old filth.

"I owe you, man," he said, when he'd gotten down to the crust.

Pete tore his eyes away from the screen. "What?"

"I said I owe you."

"For what?"

Wayne looked at him as if he'd grown a third eye. "Savin my life?"

Pete shrugged, squishing his chubby face with his shoulder. "It was the w— the woman, I told you. The old woman. *She* saved you, alls I did was smack the snake."

"Was you about to call that old woman a witch?"

"So what if I was?" Pete chewed his cheek. "I mean, I guess? People say they are. My mom says they used to be friends with the lady that lived in this house." He grinned. "Lesbian Satanists. Sounds like a rock band."

Wayne peered at his leg. "Do you think she did magic on me?"

"I don't know what magic looks like, but I don't— I, I feel like that's not it."

A faint disappointment settled over Wayne. "Oh."

Settling into the couch, he pulled his knees up to his chest and tried to lose himself in the movie. His eyes were growing heavy when he heard his father shout outside.

"Ay! *The hell* you think you doin?"

All the kids scrambled up and went to the windows, Wayne looking through the screen door. Apparently Linda had gone home while they were watching the movie, because she was no longer on the stoop. Instead, two people had come marching out of the night, approaching the house. He recognized them as the big blond guy and the lady with the mohawk.

"We don't want any trouble, Mr. Parkin," the woman was saying. "We just wanted to check on your son and talk to him about what he saw in his hospital room."

Without her bulky jacket, Robin turned out to be slender and small, with narrow hips and a graceful neck, but Wayne had the feeling surprising strength lurked in her wiry body. Veins stood out on her forearms. She was wearing a nylon chest harness, and a small camera was mounted between her breasts.

"I appreciate you finding him after he wandered off, but I don't know you from Adam," said Leon. "And frankly I'm not sure I'm comfortable with any of this. What he saw was a hallucination brought on by his episode, and that's the end of the story."

"You know that's not true."

The blond man shrugged. "He's got another witness that says he was there for the whole thing."

"I know that guy even less." Leon paced slowly, talking with animated hands. "How do I know *he* didn't lure Wayne out of the hospital room while I was asleep and run off with him?"

Wayne's father had apparently been thinking about the circumstances of his son's disappearance, and to his dismay had come up with the worst-case scenario. "That's not how it went, Dad," Wayne said, pushing the door open and stepping outside without his crutch. "Joel is all right. And you know it."

Leon simply pointed at him with a *shut your mouth* finger, daggers in his eyes. Wayne recoiled at first, his eyebrows rising, but he stood his ground.

"Your son is a good kid," said Robin. "And smart. I feel like he deserves the benefit of the doubt. He wouldn't be defending a kidnapper, would he?"

Folding his arms, Leon seethed at the two interlopers for a long moment.

Then his eyes drifted over to Wayne, who was trying his hardest to project a vibe of honesty. "I'm a teacher, man," he finally said, a look of defeat coming over his face. He leaned over and rested his hands on his knees as if he were about to vomit, then straightened up, his hands meeting.

He slowly cracked each of his knuckles as he talked. "I'm a teacher, and what if I just can't get on board with this story, of-of-of doors that aren't supposed to be there, and monsters in shadow-houses? I need empirical proof, goddammit. I believe in the scientific method, you know?

194

Theories, hypotheses, experimentation. Like the doctor at the hospital said, this is hoo-doo. And I don't go to church because I don't believe in hoo-doo."

"This has nothing to do with a lack of religious faith," said Kenway. Realization dawned in his eyes and he spoke to Robin. "Wait, if these witches take their powers from the goddess of the underworld, does that mean God is real? And Heaven, and Hell, and all that?"

Robin shook her head. "Ereshkigal is the goddess of the afterlife, the spiritual realm, not the 'underworld', because there *is* no underworld. Heaven and Hell are states of mind in the void of the afterlife, not physical locations. The classical Hell and its nine Circles that Dante Aligheri described in *The Divine Comedy* doesn't exist. Heaven is sublime contentment. Hell is sublime regret."

This was all gibberish to Wayne. Comedy? This didn't sound funny at all. Limbo? Like the party game where you bend over backwards and walk under a bamboo pole? His head spun with strange names.

Kenway waved away all that poetic mumbo-jumbo, pressing the point. "What about God, though?"

"There *is* a force, but it's not the belligerent all-knowing Old Testament sky-wizard so many people think it is. God—or Allah, or Ahura Mazda, or Jehovah, all different names for the same thing—isn't an old bearded man in a toga and sandals, it's a word for the attracting force of unconditional love itself. It can be the strongest force in the universe if you let it."

His laugh echoed off the side of the house. "That was uncharacteristically sentimental of you, lady."

Leon took a deep breath and blew out a long, exasperated sigh. "Maybe I should talk to you the next time I feel like I need a shot of Jack. When I lost my wife, I lost my belief in bullshit."

Robin grinned crookedly. "I sound like a TV evangelist. But it's true. At least, that's the conclusion I've gathered in the couple of years I've been doing this. You kinda get a feel for the supernatural when you deal with it on a regular basis. But I don't really traffic in churchy matters, Mr. Parkin. My job is a little darker than all that."

"...Darker?" Leon went over and sat on the stoop, and Wayne joined him. His father slipped an arm around his shoulders. "What, you mean like an exorcist or something?"

"Of a sort. I hunt witches."

"I didn't think you looked like the convent type. A witch-hunter? I thought that went out of style with bonnets and butter churns."

"Those were delusional Puritans in Salem times, Mr. Parkin. Using superstition and dogma to eliminate anybody they didn't like. I'm sure you've heard that refrain many times, being a teacher."

"I'm a Literature teacher, not History. And you can call me Leon." He pointed at the camera on Robin's chest. "Are you filming this?"

She nodded, detaching it from her harness and handing it to Kenway. He aimed it at her and she gave him the finger. "I run a YouTube channel about my travels. Do you mind that I'm filming?"

Leon hesitated. "…I guess not."

"So how are you feeling, Wayne?" asked Robin, her tone clinical.

"A lot better. Whatever Miss Weaver put on me was—" He almost said *was magic,* and amended himself, "—like, a miracle. The doctor said so. And she even paid my hospital bill. Twenty thousand dollars."

Kenway whistled.

"I am forever in her debt," said Leon. "The hospital would have been chasing me for that money until the day I died. She saved both our lives."

"I've got a little secret for you, that I never got to tell you back at Kenway's apartment—" Robin began, but Wayne guessed at what she was about to tell him.

"I remember you sayin something about your mama and your kitchen table in our kitchen." His mouth tucked to one side in a coy, assessing way. "This used to be your house, didn't it? Was your mama the one that died here?"

"Yes. Yes, she was."

"My mama died too." He took out the gold ring around his neck and showed it to her, the inscription sparkling in the dull yellow light of the wall sconce. *Together We'll Always Find a Way.* He was glad Dad let him keep it; he felt naked without it. "This was hers."

"I'm sorry," said Robin.

"Me too."

She paused, an uncomfortable warmth on her face, as if consolations were unusual for her.

"It was cancer," said Leon. "Throat cancer. She was getting better, but then they let her get an infection and it spread to her lungs. She went downhill fast. Like the song, it's been *Just The Two of Us* ever since." He hugged Wayne tight. "So you used to live here. What you talkin about, your mom dying here?"

"My father murdered her," said Robin, pointing back at the Lazenbury. The huge house loomed over them in the background, a black square jutting into the night sky. "And it's them, those women up there in the mission-house, that made him do it."

Wayne stared. "Are they really witches?"

"Yes. Very dangerous and very old witches."

"Does this mean you're here to…what?" asked Leon. "Kill em?"

She stared at the stepping stone under her foot.

Leon rubbed his forehead, his eyes darting around at the grass as if he were trying to read it. He tossed a hand up for emphasis. "I don't know if I can condone that, Miss, ahh—"

"Robin Martine."

"—Miss Martine. They saved my son's life. They paid for his hospital visit. They've barely said one word to us, much less brought over a basket of poisoned apples. Surely they can't be *all* bad, can they? Three little old ladies, for Christ's sake."

Robin pulled her lips into her mouth, staring at the stoop in thought. When she looked up again, her face was dark, her eyes piercing. She licked her lips and said, "They're pitting you against me. This whole thing—the snakebite, Weaver paying your bill, all of it—they're using you as a human shield. They know I'll hesitate because of you."

"That sounds like crap," said Leon. "How could they orchestrate my son getting bitten by a snake?"

Robin regarded Wayne. "How did you kids end up at the fairgrounds, anyway? Whose idea was it to go out there?"

He didn't say anything at first, for fear of incriminating Pete. But then he got the idea to pull a Spartacus and said, "It was me. It was my idea. Somebody told me about—"

"Oh, bull," said Pete, pushing the door open and coming outside. "It was *my* idea, ma'am. I wanted to show em my secret way home that nobody knows about. I take the Broad Avenue canal down to the river and then there's deer trails that go up to the fairgrounds. They come out behind this house, back there in the trees."

"Hmmm." Robin took out a Sharpie. "Take off your shirt."

"Take off my shirt?"

"Yes," she said, coming up onto the porch and uncapping the marker. Pete wriggled out of his shirt and stood there with it bunched up in one hand. Robin zeroed in on his chest and drew a meticulous symbol in the middle. "What's your name, by the way?"

"Pete."

"Nice to meet you, Pete."

He looked down at the marker, scrunching his second chin. "Why?"

"It's not a Y, it's an *algiz*. A prot—"

"No, I was asking you *why* you drew on me."

Robin looked up at him; she was still hunched over with the heel of her hand on his right boob.

"Do you feel funny?"

"Other than the fact that I took off my shirt and you're drawing pictures on me? Not really."

She stood back. "The symbol I drew is an *algiz* rune."

"Owl jizz?"

Robin massaged the bridge of her nose, closing her eyes. "No, 'all-jeez'. It's an ancient Druidic protective symbol that blocks or dampens supernatural influence."

Pete tried to angle his head for a better look at the symbol, making a scrunched-up face that gave Wayne the giggles. "Is something supposed to be happening?"

"Yes."

She seemed disappointed at first, but then a new zeal took over and she capped the Sharpie. "But it doesn't look like what I expected is going

197

to happen. So you can put your shirt back on. I guess you taking the kids to the fairgrounds was just a coincidence."

"Or maybe Karen Weaver really *did* do what she did out of the goodness of her heart," said Leon. "I'm thinkin of goin up there in the morning and inviting her to Sunday dinner as thanks." He watched his hands worry at each other. "It's not exactly twenty thousand dollars worth of thanks, but it's the best I got."

"What did you expect to happen?" asked Pete.

"You don't want to know," Robin told him, and turned to Wayne's father. "I would steer clear of them from now on, honestly. They're bad juju. In fact, everybody needs an *algiz* while I'm here and I've got a Sharpie in my hand."

"You're not drawing voo-doo bullshit on my son."

Wayne pushed himself to his feet. "I don't mind. You can draw on me," he said, beginning to unbutton his shirt. "What is this symbol supposed to do? I know you said it's 'protective', but what does that mean?"

Leon took his wrist and tried to pull him back down, his eyes steely. "No. You're not getting mixed up in this."

"I'm *already* mixed up in it."

Wayne tugged back the leg of his jeans to expose the snakebite. The only visible evidence that he'd ever been bitten were two tiny scars halfway between his knee and his ankle. If he compared both legs side by side he could see the difference. The bitten one was almost imperceptibly larger because of the swelling. But at a glance, it was as if he'd never been bitten at all.

Robin stared at the living room window, where Amanda ~~Hugginkiss~~ Johnson and Katie Fryhover were peering over the back of the sofa. "Mr. Parkin, if I can prove your son saw a monster in your house, will you trust me?"

All of the children's eyes were suddenly as big as cantaloupes.

Leon took out his cellphone, turned it right-side up, and examined it. "It's eight-thirty on a Saturday night, I ain't got a date, there ain't anything to drink in the house, and I ain't slept worth a damn in three days."

He threw his hands up in resignation. "Why the hell not?"

Nineteen

JOEL DIDN'T FEEL LIKE he would ever get clean, would ever get the smell of that filthy garage out of his skin, the penny-smell of blood and the mungy stink of old engine grease. He took another shower after Kenway dropped him off, standing in the hot water for the better part of an hour, scrubbing and sipping Alizé Bleu out of the bottle until his skin was raw.

He'd taken off Kenway's combat bandage to clean his scratches, and the body wash stung as it ran down his chest. Joel winced, squeezing lather all over himself and gingerly patting his wounds with a washcloth.

Blood pooled around his feet, streaks of pink. He sang the same Beyoncé songs over and over, the words reedy and hesitant. Every time he stopped singing, he saw the dead man with the cut throat again, that severed larynx glistening in the workbench light.

"All the single ladies...all the...single...."

Reaching out of the spray, Joel turned off the water, *squeak squeak squeak*, listening intently.

Coulda sworn he'd heard something outside the bathroom.

"Hello?" he called, straining to hear over the sound of dripping water. The clock on the bathroom wall counted down the seconds. *Click. Click. Click.*

His mama's shotgun was propped up between the toilet and the vanity, a pump-action Weatherby Upland with a walnut stock. Joel whipped aside the curtain (relieved to find no one standing on the other side), wrapped a towel around his waist, and traded the cognac for the shotgun.

"Yo!" He racked the action loudly, ejecting a good shell into the toilet. "Shit."

A plastic Dr. Pepper bottle full of rocks had been balanced upside-down on the doorknob. He took it down and left it on the sink. Snatching the door open, he leveled the shotgun at the hallway, his finger tensing on the trigger.

199

Nobody out there.

He relaxed, but only a bit.

Someone banged on the front door, making him jump. Joel padded down the hallway to the front door, looking through the peephole. A man in a black uniform was standing out on the porch. Lieutenant Bowker saluted as if touching the brim of an invisible cowboy hat. "Bitch better found my Velvet," Joel muttered under his breath, standing the shotgun behind the sofa. He opened the door.

The autumn breeze that wafted in around the officer's considerable bulk made Joel's nipples hard. "Hi there," said Bowker, saluting again. "Thought I'd stop by on the way home and check up on you. You doin all right, buddy?"

Joel shivered uncontrollably. "Y-yeah, I'm aight."

"The hell happened to your chest?"

He glanced down as if he'd forgotten about the scratches.

"I fell."

"Christ Chex Mix, what'd you trip over, a freakin mountain lion?" The officer looked down at Joel's towel. "Mind if I come in? Looks like this draft is cuttin you in half."

"Oh Lord yeah. Come in."

He stepped into the foyer and Joel closed the door behind him. When he turned around again, Bowker had pulled out what looked like a phaser from *Star Trek* and was pointing it at him.

After Joel's brain eventually settled on what it was an awkward three seconds later (a Taser), he recoiled, showing the man his palms. "I'm sorry," Bowker said, stepping forward, pressing Joel backward into the living room. "This wasn't supposed to happen. And I really hate to do this to ya. It's probably the first time we've ever really had a problem like this. Normally he's tidy enough that we can keep our hands clean."

"What you mean? Who's tidy?"

The edge of the coffee table bumped into Joel's calves. His hands hovered at waist height, held open as if he were about to catch something. Bowker had walked him far enough that the cop now stood between him and the sofa, where the shotgun was hidden.

The cop's eyes wandered around the room, assessing the curtains. They were all drawn, the venetian blinds air-tight. Whatever happened to Joel would be between them and them alone. "You wasn't supposed to live." The beats of his speech stretched luxuriantly, like Foghorn Leghorn. "Blood for the garden, son, it's the Serpent's job to thin the herd. And it's *our* job to keep people out of his business."

"The Serpent?" Joel let his hands drift downward to his sides.

"Their man. He does what they need him to do, we keep them safe from prying eyes. In return they let us live."

"Who is 'they'?"

"Don't be coy with me, boy. You know who I'm talkin about."

200

"The witches?" Joel gaped at him. He surreptitiously tucked his thumbs into the towel around his waist like a ranchhand. "You in cahoots with them witches that killed Annie Martine? Marilyn Cutty?"

"I don't know about any 'witches', but they run this here town. They run *everything*. They always have and always will." Bowker flicked the safety on the Taser. "And like I said, I hate to do this, but it's got to be done. No loose ends, boy. Can't have you runnin around tellin stories, you know."

"Cletus, you call me *boy* one mo goddamn time and I'm gonna break your leg off and beat you with the tender end."

"I doubt it," said Bowker, firing the Taser.

At the same time, Joel ripped off the towel, holding it out like a matador teasing a bull with a cape. The electric barbs tangled up in the terrycloth, *tak-tak-tak-tak,* and he charged forward, shoving with both fists. His knuckles slapped into Bowker's Second Chance vest as if Joel were hitting him with shock paddles. The cop's feet cycled, trying to find traction, and he stumbled backward into the foyer, slipping on a rug.

Joel reached behind the sofa, scooped up the shotgun, and pirouetted away. *BOOM!* Bowker fired his Glock into the living room, shattering a window.

Darting through the living room, Joel burst through the door at the other end and came out down the hallway from Bowker.

BOOM! A mirror hanging on the wall shattered, spraying glass all over him. He yelped and kept running all the way down to the end of the hall. *BOOM!* The glass in the back door imploded all over his hands as he wrenched it open. "Ohh! Jesus!"

The Glock barked again, flashing in the shadows. Joel shoved the storm-door open and something punched him in the right thigh, blood spattering the screen.

Throwing himself out onto the back stoop, Joel's knee gave out and he stumbled down the back stairs, dropping the shotgun in the dewy grass. Luckily, it didn't go off.

Cold air shrouded his wet, naked body, raising goosebumps and wracking him with shivers. The back yard was only a narrow strip of grass running alongside a paved alley, and another house loomed behind a board fence.

Joel staggered out into the alleyway, dragging the Weatherby by the barrel, the gravel digging into his bare feet.

BOOM! Splinters exploded from the fence. He threw up an arm to protect his face, running naked into the night. Dogs barked in the distance.

"Police!" spat Bowker. "Stop!"

The lights came on in the house across the alley, cutting the shadows and washing away the hiding spots. Joel kept sprinting, his bare feet slapping on the alley's buckled asphalt.

A gate in the fence. Joel hauled it open and *BOOM!*, a bullet thumped into the wood slats, almost tearing it out of his hand. He forged through

201

into darkness again, this time watched over by squares of light on either side.

An air conditioner grumbled in the shadows. Joel ran full-tilt across the gravel and grass, hurdling the AC unit. When he landed, he paused, turned, aimed at the gate he'd just ran through.

As soon as Bowker pulled it open, Joel fired a shell at him. Buckshot roared through the gap. Bowker swore out loud, flinching. Joel racked the shotgun, *cha-chak!,* ejecting the empty casing against the side of the house.

The gate came open again. He turned and ran, exploding from between two porches into the sickly blue glow of a streetlight, almost slipping in dewy grass. He ran catty-corner left, throwing himself across the hood of a car.

Skrrrrrt! Naked ass won't slide like Luke Duke. "Ow!" Joel flailed onto the street.

BOOM-CRASH!, the windshield behind him collapsed.

He half-ran half-crawled toward a house, the shotgun clattering across the road, the night wind curling around his shoulders and legs. Bowker's pistol went off again, the bullet sparking off the driveway, close enough to bounce chips of tarmac off Joel's ankles.

Between the garage and the house was a wooden gate. He slammed into it at full-speed, throwing it open.

In the last second before he turned and shut it, he could see Bowker hustling across the road in that shuffling middle-aged-cop way, mincing and huffing with his elbows up.

Behind the fence was a below-ground swimming pool. All the lone security light in the back did was silver the surface of the water. Frantic and bleeding, Joel sidestepped into the corner between the fence and the wall.

As soon as his back hit the fence, Bowker tore his way in and lumbered to a stop next to the pool.

The gate flapped open in front of Joel's hiding spot, covering him in shadow. "The hell you go?" demanded the cop, panting like a plowhorse. Cradling the Weatherby against his cheek like a bouquet, Joel tried to stop breathing so hard and stay as still as possible. The cognac in his system had all but burned off with the adrenaline, leaving him trembly but clear-headed. Cold blood trickled down his smooth shaved leg like a crawling spider.

He was steeling himself up to shove the gate out of the way and ambush Bowker when the officer turned and closed it himself.

"*Ooo!*" Joel screamed in terror, hipfiring buckshot into Bowker's chest with a burst of light and a noise like a grenade going off. The black uniform shirt disintegrated in a blizzard of fabric and the force toppled the cop backwards into the pool. *Splash!*

Blinking away the muzzle-flash, his ears ringing, Joel stood over the water with the shotgun pressed to his shoulder. The ironsight lined up on the man splashing and gargling in the water. Fish in a barrel.

Click. Empty.

Shit.

The lack of recoil he'd braced for never came, making him wobble. He scowled at the shotgun in surprise as if it had offended him and flung the gate open. "That's all, folks!" he said, running back the way he'd come.

"I'm—gonna—get—" Bowker ranted with a mouth full of water, kicking and thrashing like a beached whale.

Running across the street and ducking back down into the shortcut between the houses, Joel saw a lot more windows shining in the dark. The impromptu gunfight had disturbed half the town.

He didn't bother locking the doors when he got back to Mama's house, Bowker would just kick the doors down and ruin the locks anyway. He ran into his bedroom, wriggled his way into the first outfit he laid hands on and a pair of boat shoes. Grabbed his cellphone, wallet, and keys.

A sudden dilemma presented itself: shotgun or cognac? Shotgun or cognac?

He left the Weatherby Upland lying on his bed and rescued the Alizé from the bathroom—no point in keeping the shotty, he didn't have time to forage in his sock drawer for the rest of the shells or load them. But the cognac was fifty bucks a bottle and he'd be damned if he was going to let it sit around open until he came back. Besides, he needed the liquid courage. In the foyer, he noticed the handle of the Bedazzled baseball bat sticking out of the urn by the front door where Kenway had left it, and snatched it up.

"Bubba, you gotta come get me," he said when Fish answered the phone. Joel shut the front door, almost stopped to lock it, thought better, jumped down the front steps, vaulting the fence with the cellphone in one hand and the blue cognac and ball bat in the other. The officer's gray-brown police Charger was parallel-parked on the street, one tire on the sidewalk.

"What are—" Fish started to say.

A splotch of blood was seeping through Joel's jeans where the Glock had clipped him. His voice jiggled with every footfall. "I been shot. A cop came to Mama's house and tried to murder my black ass. I'm runnin down the hill right now."

"I'm on my way," Fish told him. "Why is—"

"Because I was supposed to *die*," Joel said breathlessly. The slope turned precipitous and he ran down the sidewalk past a row of townhouses, moonlight showering through the mimosa trees. "I got hemmed up by a mufuckin serial killer last night, and—"

"A *what?*"

"Dude drugged me, strung me up in a garage with another dude but the other dude was dead. Little boy saved me. I got out."

Fish was incredulous. "The hell? *Why didn't you call me?*"

Joel winced at the shock in his brother's voice. "Didn't wanna bother you. You got y'own thing goin on—"

"Didn't wanna *bother* me? Are you insane?"

Thank God for cardio. He glanced over his shoulder, expecting the flashing lights of Bowker's police cruiser at any moment. "Insane—that shit is debatable. Anyway, this killer is apparently on police payroll and a boy in blue came to my house to finish the job."

At the end of the block Joel cut right, running down the street. "I'm gonna hide in the park. The one down the hill where they do the farmers' market. Come get me."

"What on Earth have you got yourself into, big brother?"

"I'll tell you more when you get here. Peace be on ya." He slowed enough to slip the iPhone into his pocket and took off again, trading the Batdazzle to his free hand. As he ran, he tried to figure out how he was going to climb a tree with the bottle of Alizé without breaking it.

Twenty

TO ROBIN'S DISAPPOINTMENT, THERE was no psychic blowback as she walked into her childhood home. The house had no aura of paranormal energy. To her eyes, it was what it had always been: a lonely, drafty gingerbread with memories hanging in the corners like cobwebs. Not that she had anticipated it. This strange extra-sensory perception she'd picked up since coming back to Blackfield was thoroughly new, and in fact she couldn't be sure it wasn't a delusion. Regardless of what Kenway had insinuated, she had been dealing with schizophrenia for the majority of a decade. At this point she knew what was a hallucination and what wasn't.

In fact, in many cases the Abilify had helped overwhelm illusions induced by witches. The colony of newbie heartless that she'd encountered in Oregon last August—a backwoods death-cult commune led by a 110-year-old woman calling herself Susie-Q—had tried to trick her into believing she was in the middle of a roaring forest fire, but an emergency thirty milligrams of anti-psychotics had sufficiently untied her brain. Night-night for the newbies.

Checking her own phone, she silently cursed herself for missing her medication deadline. She'd been so focused on getting the videos edited and put up and so anxious about going back to Underwood Road that she'd forgotten all about it. She asked Leon for a glass of water and Wayne led her to the kitchen sink, pouring some tap water into a Mason jar.

TAKE 2 5MG TABLETS BY MOUTH EVERY DAY, the directions on the side of the bottle said. Her pill bottle only had a handful of doses left in it. She would have to pursue another prescription soon. She had been titrating down, rationing them at one five-milligram tablet a day, trying to make them last. The prescription was always hard to get, because she was so outwardly high-functioning, and to be honest, other than hallucinating the tall hairy thing again and the occasional voice,

(the ring ring the ring i need the ring)

205

she felt okay.

What was that? she thought, reeling, the glass in her hands.

The last doctor, the asshole in Memphis four months ago, he'd been an uphill battle. "I'm sorry, ma'am, the medication's side-effects—ischemic stroke, seizures, the risk of anaphylactic shock…. I mean, two hundred and forty pills? I can't advocate prescribing this much on a whim."

"Attention whore," the nurse at the mental hospital had called her. "You just want the pills because they make you feel special. There's nothing wrong with you. You're faking it; mental illness ain't even a disability to you, is it? It's a badge of honor. To you, it's an excuse to be a shit."

Attention whore. And now she had a YouTube channel with five million subscribers. Pushing one tablet between her lips, she gulped it down with some metallic-tasting water.

Wayne stared at her, his jaw set. "Are you okay?"

When he went around to the other side of the kitchen it seemed like a preemptive gesture, as if he wanted to put the table between them. "I'm fine," she said, pouring out the rest of the water and leaving the jar in the sink. "Have a headache, is all. Thank you for the water."

They regarded each other from across the room.

(t h e   r i i i i n g)

"You're welcome," said the boy, and he stumbled back into the living room, giving her the side-eye as he went.

Robin hugged herself, letting her eyes wander around the familiar-but-not-familiar kitchen. What she remembered as green was now blue, and next to the replaced appliances it gave her an odd sensation of Capgras delusion, as if she were talking to an old friend wearing a mask. Holding up her GoPro, she stared into the lens and sighed, giving it a meaningful look. The show wasn't just about the things she faced, it was about her…that's what the viewers were there for. Come for the demons, stay for the girl. But this time, she couldn't find the words to encapsulate the way she felt in this alien home.

So she capped off those bottled-up feelings with her ringmaster top-hat. "You guys out there in Internet Land ready for a show?"

When she came back to the living room, the children sat on the sofa watching her raptly, as if Robin were a magician about to put on a show. Leon was propped against the bookshelves next to the television, his arms folded impatiently, and Kenway leaned in the foyer doorway.

"The creature you saw in that shadow-version of your house," Robin said, wringing her hands as she paced in front of the TV, "I've been seeing it off and on for a couple of years now." She debated telling them about the schizophrenia, but the look on Leon's face told her that it would erode his trust. "…I *think* it's the same thing, anyway. Whatever it is, I've been seeing it more since I came back to Blackfield. Since this is my old house, I think it has something to do with me."

206

"What do you think it is?" asked Wayne.

"I don't know. But I'd like to try to find it and get a better look at it."

He shook his head emphatically. The expression of terror on his face was genuine. "Oh, no, you *don't* want to see it. Owlhead is scary as hell."

Pete spoke up. "Your mother was a witch, wasn't she, ma'am?"

"Yes."

"Maybe it's here because of her."

Robin was quiet for almost a full minute. She thought about asking the boy *Why would my mother call down something like that?*, but she knew he would have no answer. She wanted to be offended at the thought of sweet, demure Annie being responsible for the monster they were calling Owlhead, but it was pointless. "I don't know," she said again, and sighed deep. "Well, if we're going to get on with it, there's no time like now. Wayne, do you have your mother's ring with you?"

He took the wedding band out of his shirt and handed it to her. Robin held it up to the ceiling fan light. "The inscription on the inside of the ring says *Together We'll Always Find a Way*. Words and symbols can bend or break the witches' power, and what the inscription says is important. 'Together we'll always find a way.' Think about it. The connotations of words are what have an effect on their hexes, curses, and spells, and what is this saying?"

(t h e r i n g r i n g t h e r i n g g i v e i t)

The slow gutteral voice crept in around the edges of the conversation, under their words, like a television in another room. Robin took a deep breath and tried to ignore it.

Pete raised a hand. "What does 'connotation' mean?"

"The way a word makes you feel. How does the word 'videogame' make you feel?"

"It makes me feel happy? I guess?"

"But it's just a word for a box of circuits and wires."

He shrugged sheepishly. "I really like videogames. They make me happy."

"A videogame is only a box of circuits and wires, but the word makes you happy because you have fun with them—and that happiness is the connotation. It's the deeper meaning of the word. If I said, 'Let's go play videogames,' in your mind you're gonna be gearing up to go have fun, right?"

He nodded, rapt.

"So what does the phrase 'find a way' mean to you?"

"To literally find a way," said Amanda. "Wayne accidentally found a way with the ring—an actual way, a doorway."

"Yes. And that's how it works. The meanings of words, whether it's runes, English, or Japanese pictographs, affect Ereshkigal's power." Robin went back to pacing. "I've been thinking about this. When Wayne's father mortgaged the house, he also bought—"

"Renting," said Leon.

207

"Hmm?"

"I'm just renting the house. From the realty company. They're renting it out."

"Oh." A pang of dismay, or perhaps inferiority, flickered through her, as if merely renting the house instead of buying it outright devalued it, and by proxy, Robin and her family as well.

Leon sat on an ottoman, templing his fingers. "You were saying something about buying a house?"

"Well, my analogy is sort of shot now, but what I was going to say is that now that you and Wayne live here, you're part of the residual energy of the house." She held the ring up to her eye and looked through it, turning in a slow circle, searching the faces throughout the room. "And that includes your belongings, like this ring. From what I can tell, the engraving is channeling my mother's latent energy."

Kenway squinted. "What if I gave them a blender with 'Let Nothing Stop You' engraved on it? Would that mean they'd have a blender that could blend anything? Even steel?"

Robin scowled at him over the ring, a wry smirk playing at her lips. "It doesn't work that way...as far as I know. The symbols have to have emotional or cultural meaning. The older languages, like the Elder Futhark rune on Pete's chest, naturally have more power than modern-day English. But you can augment English by lending the words importance, or gravity. Like this ring. The engraving lends the ring weight. Makes it an artifact."

"It meant a lot to me and Haruko," said Leon.

He held up his left hand, flashing the mate to the wedding band.

Robin's eyes lost their edge and she smiled softly. "Was that your wife's name? Haruko?"

"Yep. Haruko Nakasone."

"It's very pretty."

"I met her at the Lunar New Year party in the Chicago Chinatown when I first started going for my bachelor's degree at UIC. I was teaching English classes in Chinatown at the time." His face lightened with a wistful grin. "I knew she was the one when she started showing up for classes as an excuse to come talk to me."

"How—" Amanda started to say, and hesitated. Leon watched her expectantly, his face impassive but warm. "How come you don't have any pictures of her?"

Leon twisted to look at the bookshelves behind the TV. There were books, of course; a scattering of knickknacks, a trophy with a little man on top swinging a bat at a teeball post, a small crystal award with the word *Poetry* etched front and center on the plaque. Framed photos of Leon accepting certificates, shaking hands. Wayne with other children, candid scenes of Wayne and Leon, class photos.

"I dunno. It's just easier that way." He picked at his eyebrow as if he wanted to hide his eyes behind his hand. "I guess they're still packed up in my room with the other boxes."

Robin sighed in irritation, inspecting the room with the ring up to her eye again. Nothing special leapt out at her, no doorways made themselves apparent in the walls of the living room. She wandered out into the foyer hallway, and the children scrambled off the sofa to follow her. She ended up in the kitchen, turning in a slow circle again.

"This is where I found the door that led to the garage," said Wayne, pointing at the back wall.

Robin faced the wall, but saw nothing out of the ordinary.

"What about the rest of the engraving?" asked Amanda. "It says *Together* We'll Always Find a Way'. What if it's only Wayne that can do it?"

"Worth a shot." She handed the ring back to its owner.

Wayne put it up to his eye, and for a long second she almost convinced herself he could see the door. But then he relaxed, his hands sinking to his sides, and he frowned at her. "Nope. I don't see nothin."

"Maybe it don't work when you're actually *in* the house," offered Pete. "Maybe it only works when you're somewhere else and you want to come *here.*"

Robin had to admit, that made sense.

With a sigh, Leon took off his wedding band.

"What about this one?" It took a bit of twisting and pulling to get it loose. "Maybe if—"

As soon as it came off, a shine emanated from inside, a faint javelin of white light jutting out of the hoop of the ring. Leon blinked, speechless. Tiny motes of brighter light sparked out of the epicenter of the glow, slow-motion welding slag drifting outward like dust in a sunbeam. Katie Fryhover grinned a snaggle-toothed grin. "Preeeetty."

"*That's* different," said Robin. "How come you haven't seen that before?"

"This is the first time I've taken this ring off in months." Leon put his ring on the kitchen table as if he were afraid to touch it, standing it on edge. The ring turned by itself and the light-javelin flared. Now it was two feet long and hard to look directly at, a never-ending camera flash compressed to a smear the width of a human finger.

"It's a compass," breathed Amanda.

Leon picked up the ring and the javelin faded to a mere whisper. "I can feel it tugging," he said, holding it up. "Like a magnetized compass needle." He rotated on the spot and the javelin faded down to a vague blur hovering in the C of his thumb and forefinger. He turned the other way and the javelin grew again, spearing over his shoulder and out in front of him.

Acrid ozone-stink floated in the air. Robin put her palm in front of the light. It wasn't hot at all. The back of her hand glowed orange, the finger-bones dark shadows in veiny flesh, sprouting from her wrist.

"Nothin to it but to do it, I guess," said Leon, and he marched out of the kitchen. Out in the hallway, the javelin faded, even though he was still facing the same direction. Leon turned to his left and the ring flared again.

209

He walked toward the foyer. The ring led them to the second floor, the kids clomping up the stairs behind him as if he were the Pied Piper.

"Here," Leon told them, opening the door to the cupola.

The only thing on the other side was the stairway hooking up into the shaft's spiral. Wayne held Haruko's ring up to his eye. This must not have had an effect, because he closed the door and opened it again. Closed it, opened it. "I don't know, there's nothing."

Leon's ring was still pointing at the door. He went upstairs, Robin, Pete, and Wayne following.

With four people standing in it, the cupola was unusually crowded. Examining the room with his ring, Wayne turned every which way, looking up at the ceiling, looking out all the windows, even squeezing between Robin and Pete to check under the bed.

Now the javelin of light pointed down the stairs. "Come on," said Robin, herding Wayne down them. At the bottom, she closed the door leading out to the landing (wincing apologetically to Kenway and the girls as she did so) and braced the boy with a hand on his shoulder. "Now yours. Open the door."

Wayne eyed the door through the monocle of Haruko's ring and turned the doorknob. It scraped and creaked as if it were a thousand years old. He pushed the door open, revealing an archway full of deepest darkness.

A breath of frigid air wafted out, curling around their knees, chilling their hands. Groaning from the depths of the shadow-house was the immense galleon-creak of shifting timbers, as if the earth below that strange foundation was constantly moving.

Robin sat down and Leon settled behind her, putting his ring back on. "I'm not going in there," said Wayne, staying on his feet, as if he would bolt at any moment.

She adjusted the GoPro on her chest rig. This was going to require a Spielberg-worthy framing.

"Hopefully you won't have to." She drummed her fingernails on the doorframe, lightly at first, then a little more insistently. "Here it is, buddy," she said, her voice soft, as if perhaps she were speaking to herself more than anything on the other side. "Here we are. Come show your face. I know you're in there." The dark doorway yawned apathetically for a long several seconds, as if it had nothing to prove to her. She leaned forward, trying to get a better look at the faint light down the hallway.

Bursting out of the shadows, a shaggy arm reached through the door, claws flexed a hair's-breadth from her face.

"Oh!" Robin threw herself backward against Leon's shins, and Wayne screamed, running up the stairs into the cupola. Pete let out a shrill shout.

Before she could properly react, the coppery hair all over the arm burst into flames, *WHOOSH*, as readily as if it were drenched in gasoline. The arm withdrew and the fire diminished in the watery darkness, a single flame licking one last time.

A pair of bright green eyes blinked sluggishly, each one the size of a softball.

Grrrrururururuhuhuh, rumbled Owlhead.

His wet, ragged respiration reminded Robin of a tiger, or perhaps a dragon in a movie, but muffled, heavy, languid.

(g i v e   m e)

"No," she said, and realized that she was still cowering against Leon's feet, halfway up the stairs. She sat down, but didn't lean forward. "I got some questions."

No voice reverberated in the corner of her mind.

"You there?"

Grrrrururururuhuhuh.

She checked over her shoulder. Wayne was still upstairs—he wanted no part of this, and she didn't blame him. Leon's face would have been as white as virgin snow if he could go pale, but his open mouth and wide eyes were more than enough evidence of his terror.

He didn't leave, though, she had to give him that. Neither did Pete, though he had moved halfway up the stairs, watching around the corner.

"What *are* you?" Robin asked the empty doorway.

Grrrrururururuhuhuh.

(t h e   r i n g   t h e   r i n g   f r e e   m e)

Robin had never addressed anything like this before. She tried to remain assertive.

"No. You answer my questions."

Well...there *was* that one witch in New Orleans, the one the priest had claimed was possessed by a demon. Taking the same tack with this thing seemed like the right course of action.

I wonder if Owlhead is a demon, she thought, looking down at the protective runes tattooed in the palms of her hands. *Is this what demons actually look like?* After dealing with the paranormal as long as she had, the visual of pitchforks and goat-horns certainly seemed whimsical. She'd never actually *seen* a demon, but it stood to reason that they looked nothing like colonial woodcuts or monastic illustrations.

In retrospect, so many layman artists knowing what a real demon looked like seemed unlikely...artistic hubris, even.

(s o   h u n g r y)

"Hungry?" Owlhead's eyes were like green Christmas baubles with lights inside them. "What do you eat?"

An image squirted into Robin's mind, indistinct, piecemeal, like a half-finished jigsaw puzzle. Her subconscious fluttered around the edges, trying to make sense of the shards, and she caught glimpses

liver-spotted hands, wielding a knife, coming around a boy's throat, slash of various things, faces,

a curtain of blood

places...no names, but

tiny graves in the woods

a distinct motif she thought she could sort through...

broomstick leaning in the corner, flickering firelight, bubble and gurgle of boiling water

Marilyn Cutty's birdlike smirk swam in the gloom. Robin leaned forward, disregarding the fact that she was within arms' reach of the creature again. *"Cutty?* You eat witches?"

No answer.

The stairway creaked slowly. Robin looked up and saw Wayne creeping down, his eyes curious. She threw out a hand. "No! Stay upstairs! Keep the ring up there, away from the door."

Grrrrurururuhuhuh.

(t h e   r i n g   t h e   r i n g   s h e   i s   c o m i n g)

"Why do you want the ring? Does it protect you? Does it allow you get out of that house?"

Grrrrurururuhuhuh. Owlhead blinked slowly.

"If it eats witches," Wayne said from the cupola, "ask it why it tried to bite my damn head off."

A hand slipped over Robin's shoulder. Leon in the corner of her eye. "Are you psychic or somethin? How is that thing talkin to you? I don't hear nothin but the breathin."

"I don't know," she admitted. "I don't know! Until I came back to Blackfield, I hadn't ever heard voices like this—"

But she had, hadn't she? The schizophrenia.

Maybe Kenway was right...maybe it hadn't been schizophrenia at all, all this time. Maybe she had inherited something from her mother. If not her witch-ness, but perhaps some obscure level of paranormal sensitivity. She frowned. *Am I a witch and I don't know it?* What if her mother had sacrificed her when she was a child, without her knowledge, and she's grown up without a heart all this time? *Nonsense. Bullshit. Heinrich would know, I'm sure. Besides, you'd know if you were dead inside, right?*

Heinrich. She really needed to talk to him, but he wasn't answering his phone. He had a bad habit of that.

"Why are you here?" she asked the eyes.

Grrrrurururuhuhuh, breathed Owlhead. Sensory echoes welled out of the darkness, like heat distorting the air over a fire. When the ripples broke over her mind's eye, she saw her mother's face.

"Mom?" Robin stared. "Mom brought you here?"

Another ripple issued from the doorway, but this time when it touched her, she went blind.

✸

Light flares in the ink-black void, resolving into a face. Annie Martine materializes, illuminated by candles, as if fading in from black. Gradually, the scene makes itself

212

clear: her mother is kneeling in a dirt-floored, stone-walled room, surrounded by thousands of stumpy white candles—on the floor, arrayed along the walls, standing in floor brackets.

Annie mutters to herself, her eyes closed. The incantations she's saying are too low for Robin to make out. She is nude, nubile, her late-teens body sleek and glittering, her breasts high and firm. Sweat beads on a bunny-tail of brown pubic hair. Occult symbols have been painted in key positions on her body with some dark paste like melted chocolate. Not blood. Some kind of mixture. They look like kanji, but…wrong, somehow. Upside-down, maybe. Too many dots.

A round diagram six feet across has been drawn on the floor with chalk, a ring of incomprehensible symbols. A man lies in the center of the runic circle, stripped naked, his paunch sweaty, his balding scalp glistening in the candlelight. His arms and legs are outstretched like the Vitruvian Man, his wrists and ankles tied to steel tent-stakes, driven into the earth. He is waking up, blinking, looking around worriedly.

A folded dishtowel lies across his groin, obscuring his genitals, for which Robin is grateful. "Where am I?"

Annie finishes muttering and looks up at him from under her brows. She is indebatably angry, but it is a long-simmering rage, ripe, reptile-cold. "You're in my cellar, Edgar."

"Why am I naked? What is this?"

"This is a ritual. I've chosen you as my sacrifice." Annie stands up, presenting the full glory of her lithe, petite body. Her dark hair is feathered and parted in the middle, in that iconic Eighties way, and it makes everything feel like a scene excerpted from a horror movie from the Me Decade. The only thing missing is a synth score from John Carpenter.

"Sacrifice?" He angles his head up, peering over his belly. "What the hell are you going on about?"

"Shut your mouth." Annie walks slowly around the runic circle, pacing like a predator. He watches her, his eyes trickling up and down her sweat-slick body, and the lust hiding behind the terror in his eyes is disgusting.

"Listen, I'm willing—"

"I know about the children," says Annie.

Edgar immediately stops talking. The girl-woman makes a complete revolution around the circle before he speaks again. "The children."

"The amusement park you built in the woods with your wife's money."

"Weaver's Wonderland."

"Whatever you want to call it."

"Those kids are trash," Edgar says at first, then seems to realize he's spoken harshly, frowning, biting back his words. "They come from broken homes, poor homes, dead homes. No one's going to miss them. Nobody's even going to look for em, we got the county in our pocket."

"Someone will miss them." Annie picks up a kitchen knife from the floor and points at him with it. Liquid fire dances on the blade. "I found out what you and Cutty are up to. The tree. You know the trees are unnatural. Disallowed—"

Edgar laughs nervously. "The dryads? Everyone has them."

"No. Only the ones willing to kill for them. That's—"

213

"They're the only way you can live on, you idiot bitch. You want to die like one of us?"

She scowls. "That's fell magic. You know that—"

"Falling apart at eighty years old?"

"And I know that. Cutty knows that."

"Cutty doesn't care." His chuckling grows in confidence. "Marilyn is just over three hundred years old. She was around when they signed the Declaration of Inde-fuckin-pendence! Can you grasp that? Can you even wrap your pretty little head around it? Cutty's been crafting nag-shi since long before you were born. She does what she wants. That's the consequence of self-government, isn't it? It's no different from anarchy. 'The honor system'. Ha! There's no honor among thieves, and even less among witches."

"What would you know about witches...man?" She says 'man' as if it is a derogatory term, like 'imbecile' or 'outsider'. It doesn't affect him, because he's heard it a hundred times.

"I know Cutty and my wife are going to kill you if you hurt me."

"Not if I kill you." Annie gestures to the runic circle, drawing a broad oval in the air with the tip of the knife. "Do you know what this is, Edgar? My new friend knows a lot about us. And about—"

"It's bullshit. You don't know anything." He spits at her, but most of it only speckles his own legs. "You and your so-called friend, Annie, you don't know shit. And I don't know what you're planning, but when you're done, the coven is going to kill you. No—they're going to flatten you. Squash you like a bug. Fledgling. You're a baby witch."

"The nag-shi came from the Dream-Witch, she's the first one to have made them—she was the Prometheus that showed them how it was done. And they'll kill you to protect it."

"Not if I kill them." Annie smiles.

"And how, pray tell, do you intend on doing that? Cutty's too powerful. They all are. Even my wife's got forty years on you."

"I found a way."

"The only thing capable of killing a witch as old as Cutty is a demon. And nobody's brought a demon into the material world in centuries."

She stands over him, smiling knowingly. A drop of sweat trickles down her belly, zagging through the fine hairs like a bolt of lightning.

Edgar's angry expression sours and his eyes dart around the room, widening in revelation. "Wait—that's what this is?" He flexes his arms, straining against the ropes, kicking. "You think you're going to summon a demon?" Now he's flailing, pulling at the ropes as hard as he can. The anger melts away, replaced by crazed, fearful giggling. "Who the hell do you think you are?"

Annie steps over Edgar's thrashing legs and takes a knee between his thighs, crouching over his pelvis. She hovers over him in a three-point stance, her black hair spilling around her face, burying her eyes in shadow.

"What good is immortality with a price like this?" she asks him, tracing curlicues in his chest hair with the tip of the knife. "A blood price? Innocent blood? Come on, Eddie. Even if I condoned the crafting of nag shi, they've been watered with

214

the blood of criminals before. Murderers, thieves, rapists. Not children. Not that it's any—"

"Plenty of children." Edgar smiled. "What do you think the Countess Bathory did with all those virgins?" He shook his head sadly. "The virgins are best, y'know. They're like Miracle-Gro."

Straightening, Annie leans back, tilts her face to the hidden heavens. She's obviously heard enough. Words in a dead language Robin doesn't recognize stream out of her mouth in a muttering tone. She lifts the knife toward the ceiling, the incantation rising, becoming faster, louder, a rapid-fire litany of gibberish. Robin realizes what she's speaking, even though she can't understand it—Japanese. Annie is shrieking in Japanese. Where would her mother learn a Japanese ritual?

Edgar looks as if he's trying to press himself against the dirt hard enough to sink into it, trying to will himself away from this lunatic woman-child. Annie's eyes roll back, her eyelids parting to show only the white sclera.

"What the hell?" the man under her pleads. "Stop! Please! Stop this crazy shit! We can talk about this! I swear to God, I'll—"

Her head sinks forward and her irises roll down out of her eye-sockets again. But she's not looking at him, she's looking at a point somewhere far behind him, somewhere deep in the soil. Annie brings the knife down, but not into his chest like he expects, not yet, no, not yet, she opens her mouth and slips the tip of the blade into her mouth like a spoon. The steel scrapes against her teeth as she opens her mouth wide.

Annie presses the blade-point against the floor of her mouth, turns it up so that she's holding it like a bridal bouquet, and flicks it up and out. The knife penetrates her tongue and rips it open up the middle, splattering Edgar's face and chest with blood.

He flinches, squinching one eye. "Jesus Christ. You're insane."

Crimson wells in her mouth and spills over her teeth, down her chest and between her breasts. Annie leans forward, trying to speak, trying to continue the incantation, choking on the blood. It collects on his chest in a hot puddle. "Uckkkk, ffnnnggkk, uurkk."

Her eyes: they're almost all white, except for pinprick black pupils.

Now she raises the knife and drives it through his ribcage into his heart. Edgar seizes up, hissing through his teeth. Veins rise in his neck as he pulls at the ropes again, fists clenched, knuckles white.

One final breath huffs out of his lungs and he goes limp, the light draining from his eyes. Annie leans on the knife, the strength going out of her, and it sinks up to the hilt in his flesh, more blood pulsing from the wound. She stays that way for half a minute, her eyes closed, willing the dizziness to go away. Blood continues to trickle out of her mouth. It is everywhere, now a pool collecting under Edgar.

What snaps her out of her reverie is the sick bbbrraaaap of Edgar's corpse as it relaxes and lets go of the gas still in his system. The fart reverberates in the dirt chamber.

"Jevuf, Eg," Annie complains, getting up.

The cellar spins. The girl spits a stream of blood through her teeth like a farmer. She slides the knife out of the body's chest and stands back, nausea churning cold in her guts. She collapses to her knees, sitting down, the dirt cold against her naked *buttocks. Nothing seems to be happening. Self-pity blooms in her chest. The ritual doesn't seem to have had an effect...did she kill someone for no reason? She scowls at the dead man and tears roll down her face. No, there was a reason: Edgar was a horrible person who did horrible things, and he deserves this. And if she hadn't done it, someone else would have.*

Wait.

Something's going on. The corpse is different.

She gets up on her hands and knees and crawls over to Edgar's side. The wound she made with the knife—it's turning black, rotting, withering like a bad apple. It's larger, too, easily three inches long, where the knife-blade had only been an inch wide, if that.

The darker it gets, the worse the wound smells. The odor of anise, of licorice and absinthe, and the smell of sulphur too, rotten eggs, rises out of it. The flesh around the hole withers and turns black, radiating outward in black veins, as if infected with darkness. It's caving in, a depression falling through like burning paper into a hollow cavity in Edgar's chest. Annie slinks away, her eyes locked on the spreading, sinking blackness. The body is eroding through the middle, deteriorating from the inside out, not so much hollowed but becoming the growing hole itself.

Fear streaks through the girl at this bizarre, terrible turn of events. Was this what she expected? Was this even what she wanted?

Underneath her, the ground shudders. Annie's hands instinctively snatch away and she crabwalks backward until her shoulders smack into the stone wall. The dirt stirs slowly, like a blanket over the tossing and turning of a sleeping giant. Dust clouds down from the ceiling. A dozen lit candles topple over, rolling around on the floor. Some of them put themselves out in the blood with a crisp, venomous hiss.

"Oh, my God, what did I do?" Annie asks herself, her voice a strained whisper.

Edgar's remains (if one can call it that at this point) seem to be sinking into the dirt floor, as if his blood is acid and it's eating a crater in the soil, a crater that's confined by the shape of the symbols chalked around him. His torso is now a black hole demarcated by four disembodied limbs and a head.

The hole grows in depth and diameter until whatever's left of him slides or tumbles down into the darkness, leaving a pit six feet wide in the middle of the room.

Everything falls dead silent.

Dank, cold air layers over the rim of the pit, licking boldly, invitingly at Annie's hands. Hesitant at first, she crawls toward it and peers over the edge. The blood pooling in her mouth still runs down her chin, and now it strings syrup-thick straight down into the new abyss. Down it goes, where it stops, nobody knows. The darkness appears to be infinite.

"What in the name of God," she says, but the words are addled by her ripped tongue and come out garbled.

Something is moving down there. Annie stares.

Without warning, the darkness rushes up and she bowls over backward, scrambling to get away. It rushes against the floorboard ceiling, pooling between the joists, falling upward like water. It doesn't seem to have any real mass, and makes no sound at all as it fills the room—it's more of a gas, a billowing fog that turns the wood as black as ebony and leeches the color from the Georgia-red dirt.

This was a bad idea. Annie flops over and runs for the cellar stairs, scrambling up the board risers toward the door, catching a splinter in the palm of her right hand, but there is something crawling out of the pit, something ponderously heavy and seething, and when she looks over her shoulder she sees two green eyes: Chinese lanterns the color of grass, of frogs and avocados, glowing dully in the dark.

Grrrrururuuruhuhuh.

A clawed hand with too many fingers grips her ankle.

SUNDAY

Twenty-One

ROBIN AWOKE WITH A reflexive gasp, scuttling backward, her heart stomping against her ribs. The top of her head bounced off a wood headboard with a noise like a bowsprit hitting a rock and she bawled a stream of profanities, clutching her skull with both hands.

She lay on a duvet in a chilly room where gray-blue morning light limped through the curtains. The master bedroom, her parents' bedroom—no, now the man's room, the boy's father. Leon? Yeah, that was his name.

Mr. Parkin himself stood over her. "Good morning."

The digital clock on the nightstand said it was a quarter to eight. Robin turned over and held her aching head, curling into the fetal position. Leon rubbed his face with his hands and folded his arms. "You scared the hell out of me, lady."

"She scared *you?*" Kenway sat on the mattress next to her and put a hand on her leg. It was the first time he'd touched her; a pleasant if skittish warmth spread across her chest.

"What happened?" Her back, her head, and her elbows felt like she'd seen the business end of a Cadillac. For a weird second, the rough blanket underneath her felt like a dirt floor, and she could still smell the dank, musty, dungeony forgotten-ness of the cellar.

"You had a seizure," said Leon.

"A big one." Kenway squeezed. "You were freakin out, man, you fell down and started doin the jitterbug on the stairs." He did an impression of it, his back stiffening, his arms locked against his sides and his eyes rolled back.

Looked like Frankenstein being electrocuted. Must have been a *grand mal.* First she could remember ever having. There had been a few *petit mal* the last couple of years—a few minutes of lost time here and there as she'd zoned out. One of them she'd actually caught on videotape. A spooky twenty minutes of watching herself stare into space. But she'd never had a shivering, tap-dancing, knock-you-on-your-ass episode before.

219

"Scary," she noted.

"No *shit.*"

A bolt of pain next to her right ear made Robin wince. "Down there. In the cellar, my mother called that thing here with some kind of a ritual, a spell, I don't know what. And it summoned that monster, that demon thing."

Leon frowned. *"That's* what that was? —A demon. For sure. There's a demon. In my house."

She dragged herself up and sat against the headboard. "I saw it…in my mind. Was like a letter from the past, you know? Like I was watching an old videotape, except the VCR…was in my head, and the tape was shitty and dirty but I could still see. She was trying to stop them, to kill them, the other witches. She was trying to summon a demon, but instead of making it manifest here, she accidentally created another—I don't know, it's like she cleaved off a second copy of the house. This dark copy. Or maybe she didn't, maybe it was the demon that created it."

The bedroom fell silent as the three of them sat there trying to process this new information.

A cup of coffee on the nightstand next to the clock was pushing a rich aroma into the air, and Robin couldn't stand it any longer. She rubbed her temples, her eyes cutting sidelong at the cup like a jonesing junkie. "I need a cup of that and I need it ASAP."

Kenway pushed himself to his feet. "How do you like it?"

A tall, long-limbed man sauntered through the bedroom door and pushed his fingers into the pockets of his coat like Vampire Columbo. The Kangol fedora on his bald head, along with the black overcoat, even made him look like a pulp-fiction detective.

Heinrich's eyes were inscrutable behind silver aviator shades. "She likes it black."

✲

"I watched your video Friday and saw you were in town. I caught the first plane outta Houston and hauled ass out here." They all sat around the kitchen table nursing cups of Folger's and listening to Heinrich. Robin's GoPro camera lay on the counter next to the coffee-maker, recording their impromptu pow-wow. The kids were all still asleep on the living room floor, lying on pallets, except for little Katie Fryhover, who woke up with the sun and was wrapped in a blanket in Leon's recliner, reading one of Wayne's comic books and eating a Nutrigrain bar.

To Robin's eternal surprise, Heinrich took his coffee as sweet as a granny. She studied his face as he took off his sunglasses and folded them neatly, hanging them from the collar of his shirt. The old man's eyes were limpid but yellowed. He'd grown a goatee at some point, and it was as gray as brushed steel.

"Did you come out here to help me, or stop me?"

Heinrich regarded her with his characteristically flat stare, Kenway and Leon sitting quietly to either side. Taking off his fedora, he placed it in the center of the table, revealing his glossy brown head.

He finally said, "Do you *need* help?"

"Do you think I need help?"

"None that I'm qualified to give."

Robin smirked. "Har-de-har. Speaking of which, I'm almost out of Abilify. The doc in Memphis wouldn't prescribe more than a month's worth. He says I'm overdoing it."

"What are the side effects?"

"Ischemic stroke. Anaphylactic shock." She looked out the window at a slate-gray sky. "...Seizures."

He rolled his head in astonished agreement. "Well. Where there's smoke, there's fire. You had a seizure last night, according to these two men. Sounds like Mr. Doctor knew what he was talking about. Maybe you *do* need to ease off."

"I have been cutting back." Robin frowned. "But I need them to make the voices go—" She interrupted herself. Leon seemed unsettled, his brow knitted together in ...not quite fear, but at least a considerable amount of unease. He was staring at her as if he expected her head to fall off.

Might as well drop the bomb. "...To make the voices go away."

Leon glanced toward the hallway door, as if Wayne were standing there. She could see the protectiveness written all over his face.

"Voices?" he asked. "What do you mean, voices?"

"I'm schizophrenic," she explained, her voice low, her face pinched.

An embarrassment she hadn't experienced in a long time made her face burn. She probably wouldn't have felt this way if Wayne weren't involved; she could almost hear Leon thinking of ways to keep him away from her.

"We'll see what we can do." Heinrich took out a cigar and leaned forward with his elbows on the table, examining it at length as if it was the bullet destined to end his life. "I'm sure there's some other anti-psychotic that won't fuck you up so much." He didn't offer one to anybody else, even though he knew Robin was a smoker. "Anyway. I sure as hell ain't here to stop you. I ain't never been able to stop you before."

"I talked to Karen Weaver yesterday."

"Oh yeah? What about?" He stuck the slender cigar between his lips and dug a matchbook out of his shirt pocket, the Royal Hawaiian wagging as he spoke. Robin knew what it would be before she even saw the label: Vanilla Coconut. "You two catch up on life n' shit? Quiche recipes, grandkids, who's fuckin who on *The Young and the Restless?*"

Robin cut in while he cupped the cigar with a hand and lit it, shook the match out, and dropped it into the dregs of his coffee. "She put an illusion on me and left me in a hospital restroom, hallucinating that bugs were crawling out of my skin."

Leon leaned away from her. His brow knitted together in an almost angry disgust, but the tilt of his frown telegraphed sympathy.

Heinrich took a deep draw, the cherry flaring, and blew it at the ceiling. The rich smell of coconuts floated in a dragon of blue smoke, turning the kitchen into a dingy cabana. "The *algiz* didn't protect you?"

"No. Just from being familiared—she's too powerful." Robin started to take a sip and put the mug back down. "She told me that I'm a puppet. Your henchman, your human shield." *Your personal Jesus,* interjected some weird neuron in her brain. "That you groomed me to be a witchhunter so you could quit the game and keep yourself safe."

She leaned over her coffee. "You didn't teach me how to fight so I could avenge my mother, did you? You did it so you could hide in your fortress in Texas, and let *me* do all your dirty work."

"As George Washington was wont to say, I cannot tell a lie. It was, indeed, me that chopped down the cherry tree." Heinrich ashed the cigar into his coffee mug. It was white and had a picture of Snoopy on it, fast asleep on the roof of his doghouse. "I'm turnin sixty-six this year. I can't fight the good fight forever. Somebody's gotta take over, and you were ready to be sculpted, a block of marble ready for Michelangelo's chisel." He shrugged a shoulder. "Or whoever it is that carves statues of naked-ass men. I ain't no damn art historian."

Robin's face darkened as she overcame the urge to throw her coffee in his face. "I'm not your bitch." She took a deep shaky breath and let it out in a sigh.

"You were never meant to be."

Heinrich ashed his cigar again and leaned back, clasping his elbows. "They're turnin you against me, Robin. Fragmenting the opposition. If you're gonna make the decision to come back here and fight, you're gonna have to keep your head together. Don't let Weaver tie you up in knots. That's what she's good at. They've all three of them got specialties, and hers is getting inside that thing you call a head."

"Maybe."

Heinrich stared at the table, woolgathering.

"I saw a little girl with a lot of hurt and hate in her heart." His voice was torn between defensiveness, compassion, and anger. "I seen good people turn to shit tryin to burn it all out with drugs. When I found out that Annie had a daughter and she was in the mental hospital, I knew I had to get to you before the streets did. Or worse, you tried to fight Cutty with no preparation." He took another draw and talked the smoke out. "Bein homeless ain't no joke. The hell you think you'd be if I hadn't taken you in?"

Reaching across the table as quick as a cobra, he grabbed Robin's wrist and held it up to the dim morning light. The pink rope of scar tissue running down the inside of her wrist shimmered with a faint opalescence. "You were already cuttin yourself when I got to you. You just got out of Blackfield Psychiatric and you were already lookin for the fire exit of life."

She wrenched her arm out of his hand, his fingertips slipping shut on empty air.

"You'd be dead in a gutter," said Heinrich, pointing at her with the two fingers pincering the cigar, *"that's* where your skinny white-girl ass would be. Listen to your heart and use your head, Robin Hood." The term of affection he'd been using since the day he'd first driven her to Texas and put her up in his guest room. It was not lost on her. "Ain't nobody against you but them. Don't let em talk you in circles. That's their first trick. You know that."

Robin stared into her coffee. "I saw her."

"Her who?"

"My mother. In a dream, when I had my seizure."

She recounted the contact with Owlhead and the demon's vision from start to finish. Leon choked on his coffee, dribbling it on the table. He got up to fetch a paper towel to mop it up off his shirt. "There's a gateway to Hell in my goddamn basement?"

"I don't know what it is, specifically, but—"

"No, that's exactly what it is," said Heinrich. "In a way. Sounds like what happened was, Annie thought she had sacrificed Edgar Weaver to draw a demon into our world to kill Cutty, but what she did was sign a blood contract that allowed Hell to annex the house."

"In plain English, please," said Kenway.

Heinrich swept a hand down his face, pulling at his cheeks. His lower eyelids were rimmed in red; he obviously hadn't slept since he got off the plane. As he talked, he stroked his mustache. "Basically, like Puerto Rico is a territory of the United States, this house is now a territory of Hell. It has been for about two decades. I imagine it's why ain't nobody lived in it since Annie died."

He pointed toward the living room. "The dark version of it that little boy in there found with his mama's ring? That's the Hell-side of this house."

Both Kenway and Leon stared at Robin. "I thought you said there wasn't a Hell," said the vet, folding his arms.

The old witch-hunter grimaced, tossing a hand. Ashes dusted the tabletop. "Of *course* there's a Hell." He swept them off onto the floor. "Is she filling y'all's heads with her Dalai Lama God-is-love-and-Hell-is-regret bullshit?"

They smirked at him. Robin gave him the finger.

"There for a while last year she got real deep into Nichiren Buddhism," said Heinrich. "She even had me chanting *Nam Myoho Renge Kyo* over and over again, doin yoga and shit and eatin rabbit-food. *Me—!*

The last time *I* did the Downward Dog, I got crabs and a ticket for public indecency."

Their laughter was interrupted by a knock at the front door. Heinrich's grim smile disappeared and he eased out of his chair, his head hunched down.

"You expectin visitors?" he asked, glancing at the window over the sink.

Leon got up, shaking his head. "No." He started toward the hallway leading to the foyer, but Katie Fryhover stepped into the doorway.

The little girl knuckled one eye sleepily. "Witch-lady is outside."

Heinrich pointed at Robin, jerking a thumb over his shoulder. The universal sign for *You. Come with me.*

"Why is she wearing a bunch of rags?" asked Katie, watching them cross the hallway and slip into the downstairs bathroom, a cramped half-bath with a toilet and a sink. The walls were tiled in a dizzying motif of hornet-yellow sunflowers.

"Go see what she wants, Mr. Parkin," Heinrich said through the half-open door, flicking his cigar into the toilet. "Don't let her know we're here."

Kenway sidled inside, squeezing between them. Robin stood in the corner behind the sink, pushing a wastebasket out of the way. "If she sees me, she's gonna know you're here," he said to her, closing the toilet's lid and sitting on it. Heinrich tried to close the door, but there was a soft knock.

He opened it a crack. "I need to use the bathroom," Katie whispered through the gap.

The grizzled old witch-hunter palmed the top of her head and tugged her inside, closing the door for good. Robin clutched the little girl against her knees. "Shh," she murmured, looking down at Katie's inverted face with her finger across her lips. "Gotta be quiet, okay, honey? We can't let the witch-lady know we're in here, or she'll turn us into bugs."

"I don't wanda be a bug," Katie murmured back, shaking her head slowly.

"Then be as quiet as you possibly can."

In perfect unison, Heinrich turned off the light and Leon opened the front door.

"Good morning."

"Good morning from the Welcome Wagon!" hooted Karen Weaver. "I was out and about, and I wanted to stop by and see how your boy was doing."

"Actually, I'm glad you came by. I was going to come up and see you today."

"Is that so, is that so."

"Come on in, ma'am…feels a little clammy out there. I'd hate for you to catch your death of cold."

224

"Too true, too true." Weaver's boots thumped on the entryway rug and knocked on the hardwood floor.

The front door closed with a soft *click* and the two of them went into the living room, which made them a little harder to hear. In the bathroom, Robin was dead silent and motionless, straining to listen. The smell of ointments and cigar smoke wafted out of Heinrich's coat, making a murk of the air. Robin tried not to cough.

"Well, hello there, children! Ah, oh, a sleep-over! How wonderful!"

"What's this?" asked Leon.

"Oh, it's an icebox cake. I thought the boy would appreciate a sweet treat while he convalesces." The rustle of paper. "Look through the glass dish—see how the cake is marbled underneath? You bake the cake and pour Jello mix into it, and let it soak in the fridge. The Jello sets inside the cake."

Some strange sensation of hunger echoed in Robin's bones, reverberating from deep in the center of the house as if the creaky Victorian itself were tired of nails and mice and wanted something fresh. A half-presence lurked out there with them, the same eerie weight you sense when you know someone's home with you but you haven't seen them yet.

Owlhead, she thought. *You can smell the witch, can't you?* When she closed her eyes, she could almost hear his ragged, leonine breathing.

"Wow, that's really nice of you. That sounds great."

"This particular cake is lemon, and the Jello inside is lime. A lemon-lime cake! Quite clever, huh? And the icing is just Cool-Whip, dusted with lemon zest and graham-cracker crumbs. Oh, it's very lovely, quite tangy and delicious, you really must try it."

"After breakfast, maybe, I'd love some."

"Yes, yes, after breakfast, of course, of course. Here, I'll stash it in your Frigidaire."

The brittle rapping of Weaver's boots clattered down the hallway toward the kitchen and the bathroom. Robin realized she was scrunching up the little girl's shirt and let go.

Weaver kept going and hung a right into the kitchen, opening the fridge. "Oh, boy, oh boy oh boy oh *boy.* I can tell you're a bachelor, sir. Heavens. Nothing but takeaway leftovers and condiments! Cold pizza indeed! Looks like I'm going to have to treat you two more often." The heavy Pyrex dish thumped onto the metal rack inside and she closed it up.

"That's sort of what I wanted to talk to you about, actually," said Leon, right on the other side of the bathroom door.

"Oh, we've got all the time in the world for small talk." Weaver came back out into the hallway and paused. Her breezy bulk was almost palpable through the door, like a winter wind through an autumn window. *Here it comes,* thought Robin.

A faint ratcheting noise was followed by a gush of warm air from the vent next to her toes.

225

"It's so drafty in this old house, isn't it?" asked Weaver. Come on, let's turn up the heat a bit. Don't want the boy to catch a cold on top of everything else, hmm?"

The witch thumped back into the living room and clapped once, rasping her dry old hands together. Robin's mind produced a mental image of a house-fly furiously rubbing its forelegs against each other. She shuddered.

"How are you feeling, dear boy? How is your leg?"

Wayne mumbled something not quite audible.

"Very good, very good. Sounds like the poultice did the trick, hmm? Drew the poison right out of you as easy as...well, dirt out of a carpet! It's the salt, you know, that does the trick. You toss in a few secret ingredients and it'll draw the venom right out of the bite."

(bite you, *want to bite you*)

The feeling of starvation surged in Robin's chest, dropping into the pit of her belly, and for a terrifying second she thought her stomach was going to growl out loud.

"People have lots of mean things to say about our country remedies and old wives' tricks," Weaver was saying, "but when they work—and they always do—oh, those folks shut their traps, they shut em right up."

Leon took the opportunity to jump in. "Mrs. Weaver—"

"Oh, do call me Karen."

"Karen, then...I just—"

"Or, you can call me Grandma if you like. Granny, Gramama, Mee-Maw, I come a-runnin to bout any of those."

"Mee-Maw? I wanted to thank you for what you did at the hospital. For...for footing Wayne's hospital bill. I don't—I don't even know *how* to voice my gratitude enough. You have no idea how much you helped me out. I mean, twenty-thousand dollars? As a high school teacher, that's like a year's pay for me."

The witch tittered. "It was no trouble, lovebird, no trouble at all. You save up a lot of money living with two other old biddies in a crumblin pile in the ass-end of nowhere. Chicken coops're cheap, and we're all hens down that way."

"I see."

"You know, speakin of teachin, it's a shame those hokey old boys on Capitol Hill don't put more into education. They keep on rolling the way they're headed, and soon enough this grand old country of ours is gonna be nothing but a nation of imbeciles. Not to say it ain't halfway there already."

Leon scoffed politely. "Well, there's not much I can do to repay you, at least for the time being, but I, uhh...I wanted to invite you over for dinner. My treat. It's the least I can do for the lady that saved my son's life and me a ton of heartache."

"How lovely of you. I would be delighted. But your kitchen is awfully small...and not exactly geared to the quills, is it? Now, *our* kitchen, on the other hand, *well*. You could roast a buffalo in that sucker, hooves and all, and dress it up no worse than Wolfgang Puck himself! And it's been quite a long time since we've had any company up there."

Silence lingered for a few seconds, and then Weaver went on talking.

"I'll make a deal with you, Mr. Parkin. You put together what you want for dinner—steaks, chicken, lamb, whatever you fancy. Bring it on up to the house. We'll sizzle it up fine and dandy with some veggies and baked tubers and yeast rolls, hmm?"

"Yeah, okay. That sounds good to me."

The uncertainty in Leon's voice made that a bald-faced lie Weaver would have to be an idiot to miss.

"You seem reluctant, love. What's the matter?"

"I hate to impose."

"It's the stories, innit? The tall tales about us being a bunch of witches. Bubble-bubble-toil-and-trouble and all that. I expect the folks over there in the trailer park ha'been tellin you tales out of school." Weaver chuckled dismissively, airily. "Take a gander at my face, hon. What color is my skin? Green? ...No? And where's the wart on my nose? My pilgrim hat and buckled shoes? My bristly dustbroom and black pussy-cat?"

Another stretch of quiet, and then Leon said with a soft laugh, "Okay, yeah. I get the point. Sometimes I'm bad about letting what people say get to me. Not quite gullible, but—"

"Too trusting?"

"I guess? I guess you could say that."

"Trust is a good thing, Mr. Parkin. A good thing. I think this world could use a bit more of it. Without it, where would we be? Kids don't hardly get to play outside these days, do they? They just sit in the house with their internet and videogames because the world out there scares the hell out of them. We don't trust them around strangers anymore. We don't trust *Halloween candy* anymore, for Pete's sake, and as an alleged witch I can tell you without a doubt that that's a cryin shame."

Robin could only think of her mother pinning Weaver's husband to the floor two decades ago. Edgar, the real-life boogeyman, making children disappear out of his homegrown Six Flags. She had no doubt that Weaver was complicit in the racket. *Hypocrite bitch,* she thought, squeezing little Katie's shoulders.

The girl squirmed. She pressed her hand over Katie's mouth before she could complain. *Sorry, sorry—don't squeal! We'll all be shitting bumblebees if she finds us in here!*

"Anyway," said Weaver, "I need to get back to the ranch. I've got a dress I've been working on for a month or so now and I'm starting to get down to the wire on my deadline. These young ladies these days, they don't have any patience for craftsmanship."

"A dress?"

"Oh, yes, yes. I design and make wedding dresses and sell em on the internet. A real cottage industry, all by myself. Can you believe it? I talk down at the internet like it's some kind of lark, but really, it's been a Godsend for an old lady like me. Why, I can visit the Great Wall of China from the comfort of my kitchen!"

The two of them headed to the front door, Leon with his slow cowboy stride, Weaver bustling along in a constant swish of fabric and a bootheel drum solo.

"How does steak sound?" Leon asked, opening the front door.

"Like this: *MOO.*"

The kids in the living room giggled. Katie snorted against Robin's fingers, reminding her she was covering the girl's mouth.

She took her hand away and softly petted the top of Katie's head. It was supposed to be an apologetic gesture, simple casual affection, but out of nowhere she registered the feel of the child's silky brown hair spilling through her fingers. She was savoring it. *Urk. There goes that biological clock. Ring-a-ding-ding, rock star.*

"Steaks sound just fine, Mr. Parkin," said Weaver.

"Please, call me Leon."

"Ah, the lion! I like that quite a lot. You strike me as a man with a lion's courageous heart, Leon. That boy's quite lucky to have such a father."

"Thank you."

"Seven o'clock? Six? I don't want to keep the lion-cub up too late. It is a school night, after all."

"Six is fine. I'll be there."

"It's settled." Weaver's voice became a little clearer, a little louder. She must have leaned into the doorway to shout. "Have a good sabbath, everybody! Dig that cake! There's more where that came from!"

An awkward silence followed this as the children hesitated, unsure of how to respond.

"Thank you, Miss Weaver," called Amanda.

Pete and Wayne echoed her. "Thank you, Miss Weaver."

Meanwhile, Robin could feel the witch's laser gaze through the wall, as if she had Superman's eyes. *She knows we're here. She knows, dammit.* Even though they'd parked in Chevalier Village so the plumbing van wouldn't be sitting in Leon's driveway for Cutty to see. She hoped Heinrich had the presence of mind to have done the same.

"You're very welcome," grinned Weaver. "Au revoir!"

The front door closed. The whole house seemed to hold its breath for a full minute as everybody stayed locked in position, listening. Almost as if they were waiting for something.

Katie stirred. "I have to *peeeeeee.*"

"All right, all *right.*" Heinrich cracked the door open. Wayne's father was standing by the front door, peeking through the side-light windows. "Is she gone?"

228

Leon spoke over his shoulder. "Yeah. She's gone."

"*Gone* gone? She's off the property?"

"Yeah, she's crossing the highway right now." Leon gave them a pointed look as they came out of hiding. "Man, for a bunch of big-shot witch-hunters, you guys sure are hot to stay outta sight."

Robin was the last out of the bathroom, closing it behind her to give Katie some privacy. "You remember that green-eyed thing in the darkhouse?" She said 'dark house' as one word, *darkhouse,* as one would say 'big-house' or 'outhouse'. Seemed to be evolving into her name for it. "Well, that thing is the only thing that can kill those witches. That's how powerful they are. They'd tear through us like wet toilet paper."

"Then what made you think you'd be able to take em on by yourself?" asked Leon, going into the kitchen. The water ran as he washed out the coffee carafe, staring out the window over the sink.

She put her fists on her hips and stared darkly at the foyer rug as if she could find wisdom in the intricate red-and-blue curlicues.

"The demon," said Heinrich. "The hallucinations. Owlhead was drawing you here." He shook out another Royal Hawaiian and stuck it in his mouth, but didn't light it. Instead, he paced slowly up and down the foyer hallway, one hand in his pocket, the other holding the cigar to his mouth. "He wants you here for some reason."

"But why *now?*" asked Robin. "I've always seen him, but it's only been every now and then. The first nineteen years of my life, I saw him four times. Once when I was as young as that little girl in there, once in middle school, and twice in the mental hospital. The last two years, I've seen him at least fifteen times. What's special about now?"

"It *is* close to your mother's birthday."

"Would that be numerologically important, though? Would that have any kind of occult relevance?"

He shook his head. "No...none that I can imagine. If it were *your* birthday, maybe." Heinrich gestured with the cigar. She could tell he didn't think much of it anyway. Numerology is bullshit, astrology for math nerds. They were grasping at straws. "Maybe he thinks you've passed some kind of threshold that would make it possible for you to let him manifest in our world? You are Annie's daughter, after all. Maybe there's a link somewhere."

"You know as well as I do that demons have never manifested in the material plane." Heinrich had been a demonologist in a previous life and had a library of reference works, including a stash of material stolen out of the Vatican's archives in 1976. As part of her training, Robin had studied them all, and she knew that he'd forgotten more than she'd even learned. "They can't. That's why they possess people."

"What *are* demons, anyway?" asked Leon. "That didn't look like any demon *I've* ever seen. I would have expected, y'know, the usual—cloven hooves, pitchfork, horns, the whole nine yards."

Heinrich sat on the stairs. "Demons are viruses."

"I ain't pickin up what you're throwin down."

"Goddammit, I knew you was gonna make me explain it. All right, look. A virus is basically a piece of DNA wrapped in protein. You could say it's dead, but it would have to have lived to be dead, and it's never been alive. And the only way a virus can assume some semblance of life is by infecting a living being."

"...Stillborn."

"Yeah, kinda. I like to think of it as a Terminator—a facsimile of life that's never been alive itself, wrapped in meat."

He sighed and took the cigar out of his mouth, staring at it as he rolled it in his fingers.

"The way it's been explained to me is, there are two kinds of souls. The souls that come out of Creation's oven well-formed and functioning find their way into a living body at some point. The souls that come out deformed don't get a body. They just sorta float around out there in the dark, in the primordial ghost-soup of Limbo. Demons are those two-faced, waterheaded, heart-on-the-outside, too-fucked-up-to-live souls. And the only way they can reach the same level of life that *we* enjoy is to possess a living body, the same way a virus possesses a living cell."

"You say 'Creation's oven'," said Leon, wiping his hands dry with a towel as he came back to the foyer. "So you're tellin me there's an actual God up there, cranking out souls in His spiritual bakery?"

Heinrich guffawed, leaning back to laugh at the ceiling. "That's the million-dollar question, ain't it?" He put the coconut cigar back in his pocket. "Welcome to the clergy. Nice to meet you, hope you guessed my name."

Robin went into the kitchen to fetch her cup. Sitting on the counter was her camera, the RECORD light burning red, in full view of anyone putting an icebox cake in the Frigidaire.

230

Twenty-Two

YOU *WILL* TELL US how it went, won't you?" asked Amanda, as the kids headed home after breakfast. "You know, dinner with the witches?"

The Parkins didn't have any of the ingredients for breakfast, but Leon needed to make a trip to the grocery store anyway to get the steaks, leaving them with Kenway and Robin. To the boys' surprise, the veteran was quite a gamer, and the boys geeked out with him over Wayne's PlayStation. The tall black guy, Heinrich, spent most of the morning sitting on the back stoop smoking his cigars and staring at the forest out back. Wayne kinda liked that dude—he was standoffish and creepy, but in a cool, self-aware way, as if it were a facade he'd developed over the years.

"Why don't you go with us?" Wayne offered, and both Pete and Amanda blanched at the thought. "What, are you scared?"

"Hell yeah," said Pete. The carnival hammer rested on his shoulder.

"They're super-creepy." Amanda folded her arms. The three of them were standing on the front porch of the Victorian. The day had grown cool, and the overcast sky was the blank, featureless white of an unwritten story. "I don't think you understand, Wayne."

"Understand what?"

"We've been living down the hill from those women our entire lives," said Amanda. "Our parents...I don't know if they're *afraid* of them, but...nobody in Chevalier Village goes outside much after dark unless it's an emergency, you know? The women don't talk to *us;* we don't talk to *them.*" Her eyes found their way up to the hacienda. "This morning was the first time I've ever heard Karen Weaver speak. Or really, the first time I've ever been close enough to *hear* her speak."

"They're kinda like you guys' Dracula, huh?" asked Wayne.

Pete's head tilted. "What do you mean?"

"The mysterious Count Dracula, livin up on the hill overlookin the town. Nobody goes up there, and the village warns away anybody that comes snooping. Chevalier is kind of a mini-Transylvania, ain't it? They got you spooked like a vampire."

231

Amanda nodded, but didn't say anything.

"Astute observation," said Robin, startling Wayne. She was sitting in the swing at the end of the porch.

"We'd better get out of here, I guess," said Amanda, bouncing down the front steps. As she stepped into the grass, she turned back to him. "Be careful. If they really *are* witches, they're dangerous. Take care of your dad, okay?"

"I'll try. I don't think they're gonna do anything. We're just eatin steak, right? We're going to dinner there. They can't violate guest right."

"Real life isn't *Game of Thrones*, Wayne."

Wayne swallowed anxiously and sat down on the steps to watch them trudge back to the trailer park.

Robin came down to his end of the porch. She wasn't wearing her chest harness, but she was toting the little camera she carried everywhere. Her messenger bag was slung around her shoulder. She put the camera on top of the newel post at the end of the porch railing, facing them, and the red light on it told him it was recording.

"So you got a YouTube channel?" he asked her.

"Yup. It's got all my detective work and encounters on it. All my fights this far. Well, almost all of them. I've been ambushed a couple of times." She sat down next to him, leaning over with her elbows on her knees. "You and your dad should watch a couple of them. So you can—I don't know, maybe it'll help you trust me."

"I think after showing him the monster in the doorway, he believes," said Wayne. The woman's eyes sparkled even in the dim light of the overcast day. She was intensely pretty, he thought, fine-featured and pale, but her eyes were old. Or maybe tired. There was a sharp, almost unsettling intelligence in them, like a hawk. "I know *I* believe."

"I have a plan," she told him.

"A plan for what?"

"I want to use your ring to get into their house without having to walk through the front door. Take em by surprise."

"Why would you want to do that?"

"There's a fourth witch, somewhere on the property," she said, looking up at the Lazenbury. "I'm pretty sure she lives upstairs. She's much older than the other three. Heinrich believes that fourth witch is the one augmenting the power of the rest of the coven. Witches can band together and draw on each others' power—that's the whole point of a coven."

"What good is *that* going to do?" he asked, studying his mother Haruko's ring.

She delved into her messenger bag and took out a beautiful, ornate dagger. A few emeralds were laid into the hilt. "Except for the core, it's made of silver. The entire thing, from point to pommel."

"I thought silver was for werewolves."

"This silver is…." She turned it so that the stiletto caught the white sky, and ivory shimmered down the mirrored metal blade. "To use a comic book analogy, it's spiritual adamantine. Witches can't change it or defend against it. It's magically inert. Energy-neutral. If you had enough of these, you could pin a whole coven of witches to the floor and there's nothing they could do about it. Only lay there cussing at you."

"*Do* you?" He lifted the dagger out of her hands and examined it. "Do you have enough?"

"Heinrich says there are two others in the world, but this is the only one of these I've ever seen."

"Can't you make more?"

"According to him, they were made using the nails that the Romans pinned Jesus Christ to the cross on Golgotha with. The nail is the core of the blade. Whether that's total bullshit or not, I have no idea. For all I know, they're made with Elvis Presley's melted-down fillings. But I'll tell you right now, this one works. It's helped me kill a lot of witches."

"What do you do, stab em in the heart?"

"Witches don't have hearts to stab." Robin explained the ritual of Ereshkigal's sacrifice. "You pin her down with it and set her on fire while she's immobilized. Fire is the only thing that can stop a witch. You can't kill them, you can only destroy them."

"I thought it was water you had to kill em with."

"Nope."

Wayne screwed up his face. "Why can't you tie her to a stake like the old witch-hunters used to do?"

"Because those weren't witches," said Robin. "They were just your normal every-day humans. A rope isn't going to hold a real witch, and that's assuming you can even keep her still long enough to tie her up." She put the dagger away. "Anyway, if I can get to the fourth witch and pin her down with this, I can burn her. With her out of the picture, the other three will be a lot easier to handle. Hopefully, if I play my cards right, I can take them out one at a time."

"Why don't you go do it right now?" he asked, showing her the ring.

"I need the diversion to make it work. I can't match them all three at once. You and your dad are gonna go to dinner and keep them busy. Meanwhile, me and Heinrich will go into the Darkhouse and look for a door that'll take us into the second floor of the Lazenbury."

Twenty-Three

WHEN JOEL AWOKE, THERE was a silhouette standing in the doorway. Officer Bowker, aiming a pistol at his face.

"Jesus God!" he shrieked, scrambling backward and off the end of the futon, tumbling to the floor. A rusty sawband of hot pain raked across his thigh. "Don't shoot me! Don't—"

"Hey-hey-*hey*. Hey."

Bowker turned a switch—*click click*—and a lamp filled the room with a soft glow. It wasn't Bowker at all, it was his brother Fisher, and he was holding out a cup of coffee, not a Glock. "It's all right, man! You're all right! It's me."

Joel's mouth tasted like he'd been helping himself to a litter box. Hangover pain ran laps around the inside of his head, the scratches on his chest were still sore, and his entire body was stiff and achey, but none of it could hope to compete with the gunshot wound in his leg.

He was wearing nothing but a pair of Fisher's boxers and gauze had been wrapped around his thigh in a thick band, affixed with a pair of tiny aluminum clips. The gauze was clean, but he didn't know if that was because it was fresh or because he wasn't bleeding that heavily. The stinging agony went bone-deep, as if he'd been shot with a nailgun and the nail was still in embedded in the muscle. He got a mental flash of the Serpent shooting nails through the garage door and squinched his eyes until it went away.

His hands were shaking too bad to hold a cup of coffee. "Just put it over here," he said, his nervous fingers pattering on the end-table. "I'll get to it."

The walls of the cramped room were lined with bookshelves, and the shelves were full of hundreds of VHS tapes: all the best and most obscure horror and fantasy movies of the last forty or fifty years. Nestled into a space between the shelves was an old Magnavox television/VCR. A bundle of clothes lay on the end table (a shirt and a pair of jeans, both folded as meticulously as a display in an Abercrombie and Fitch) and the Bedazzled baseball bat leaned against the end of the futon.

Fish left the coffee next to the clothes and sat next to his brother. "How's your leg feel?" he asked, handing Joel a couple of pills.

"Hurts."

Extra strength Tylenol. It wasn't much, but it would have to do until he could get back to the stash at Mama's house. He dry-swallowed the Tylenol one at a time.

"I bet. Luckily it was just a graze. Cut a hole in the outside of your leg about the size of a quarter, but that's all. Coulda been worse. At least he didn't hit an artery or clip the bone."

Underneath the gauze was about ten or twenty stitches. Joel didn't know the exact amount and he really didn't care, to be honest—the night before was a haze of alcohol and pain, only broken up by memories of running from the police lieutenant and hiding in a bush in the park like a wino, finishing off a blood-slick bottle of cognac. Fisher had picked him up on the back of his motorcycle, one of those sleek Japanese deals in cranberry red and black, and spirited him away.

He vaguely remembered refusing to be taken to the hospital. "Who stitched me up?"

"Ashe."

A huge shadow stepped into the doorway. "I hear voices. Sounds like the patient is awake."

Ashe Armstrong was a local veterinarian and the comic shop's equivalent of Norm from the TV show *Cheers*—a regular and Fish's most loyal customer. If he wasn't at work, he was here, sitting on a stool at the end of the counter and talking comics with Fish. They'd called him around nine the previous evening with a breathless plea to make a house call, and to his credit he'd showed up with bells on.

He was also a little over six feet tall and nearly sturdy enough to arm-wrestle a grizzly bear. Plenty of muscle to hold down a struggling drunk.

"How you feeling?"

"Like I been shot in the leg and like I *need* to be shot in the head," Joel said testily. The god-rays of morning sunlight shifting through the doorway around Ashe's frame were sending shards of glass into his brain. After his initial snap was met with silence, he added, "...Sorry. I'm jus a little beat-up. Thank you for patchin me up."

"No biggie. Anything for my friends."

"'Beat up' is putting it lightly," said Fish.

Stepping into the room, Ashe sat on a milk crate with a creak of plastic. "You said a *cop* shot you? I take it that's why you didn't want to go to the hospital."

"Yeah. He said somebody he called 'the Serpent' was supposed to have finished me off. The cop said they're all workin together...said Marilyn Cutty owns this town." Joel tilted his head back and slumped down, pressing a palm against his eyes. A kaleidoscope of geometric shapes flashed behind his eyelids. "I'm guessin this 'Serpent' guy is the dude I met on the internet Friday night."

"A booty call?" Fish sighed. "Brother, you got to quit cattin around like this. You gonna end up with something they don't make vaccines for."

"I got rubbers."

"That's always what you say, ain't it? A raincoat ain't gonna keep you dry forever. Besides, you came within a hair of getting yourself killed by some looney-tune cracker with a knife."

"Livin on bacon and cauliflower ain't gonna make *you* immortal, either. You can't jog your Jamaican ass away from Death, and he don't care how much you can dead-lift." Joel picked up his coffee and cradled it under his chin. "Complex carbohydrates ain't what drove Mama crazy and pushed her into the grave, you know. They ain't gon kill you either."

Fish turned and walked out, shaking his head. A radio in the shop came on, obnoxiously loud, tuned to some local station in the middle of their drive-to-work morning chit-chat. It snarled through a dozen stations before landing on classic rock. Guns N' Roses wasn't Fish's forte, but this was how his brother dealt with turbulent conversations between the two of them: blocking it out with music. Any kind, it didn't matter, as long as it was loud.

This is probably why we ain't never fixed nothing, thought Joel. *He storms off into his bedroom and plays The Roots at three hundred decibels, and I go find something to smoke.* Ashe quietly watched him drink his coffee, his hulking body hunched over with his elbows on his knees and his hands slowly wringing each other. The veterinarian's dark hair and heavy features made him look like a young Penn Gillette.

"You gonna give me the After-School Special too?"

Ashe briefly opened his hands in a sort of awkward, blameless shrug. "I'm just glad to see you doing okay."

"You off today?"

"Yep. I get weekends off."

Joel nodded in that *cool, daddy-o* way and sipped his coffee. Black, only sweet enough to take the bitter edge off. Hot enough to fog up his eyeballs. Oily. Vaguely salty. He sighed. "He put butter in my damn coffee."

"Gross."

"Yeah."

The vet shrugged his hands again. "I hear it's good for you. I don't have the stomach to subject myself to it, though."

Joel stared at his coffee, grinding his incisors together. "The cop came to my house. He knows where I live. I can't go back there to lock up. They're gonna leave my doors wide-ass-open and I ain't gonna have nothin left…if I can ever even go back."

"I'm sure it'll be okay. I don't imagine the cops would leave your front door unlocked."

"I didn't imagine they'd show up out of the blue and try to shoot me, either." Setting his coffee aside, Joel wallowed his butt out to the edge of the futon and braced himself on the armrest, trying to stand up. He hissed as the imaginary nail in his leg drove a little deeper.

"Take it easy," said Ashe.

"Take it easy and give it hard, that's how I roll."

He unfolded the clothes, feeling an unsolicited pang of regret at ruining Fish's folding job, and put them on, starting with the shirt. The jeans were a little harder. Every inch of denim drove the rusty nail in his thigh a centimeter deeper. "Damn. He said this hole in my leg was the size of a quarter. Right, the French Quarter, maybe."

"Okay, so he was downplaying it." Ashe made that weeble-wobble seesaw motion with his hand. "I'd say it was more the size of a…silver dollar?"

Joel blew through pursed lips and opened the door at the end of the couch, limping through. On the other side was a narrow stairway leading up to Fisher's apartment over the comic shop. He put his good foot on the first riser and steeled himself for the climb. Taking a deep breath, he picked up his right foot and put it on the second riser. His thigh flexed, pulling at his stitches, grinding the denim against the bandage.

Sharp hot pain swelled in the muscle as if there were a lit cigarette trapped under the gauze. Twelve steps to go. "God help me."

Halfway up, he had developed a system; he leaned to his left, bracing himself against the banister screwed to the wall, and lifted himself with his left leg, holding his right out stiff to the side. Instead of stepping up with it, he humped it up on the left like Bugs Bunny's flute-playing Revolutionary War soldier. By the time he had reached the top, his left thigh was on fire and sweat was running down his temples.

He stood at the top of the stairs to survey Fish's apartment. He hadn't been up here since his brother had bought the place, he realized with shame. He really ought to visit more often, and not under duress like this.

The walls were alive with artwork. Superhero posters were hung at tasteful intervals—*Avengers, Hulk,* and *Spider-Man* movie promotionals, artsy minimalist pieces, and comic-book panels so big the individual colors pointillized into sprays of red-and-yellow dots and bold fronds of sharp white lettering. *BOOM! BANG! POW!* There was a television, a large flatscreen standing on a low-slung entertainment center with a small collection of videogame consoles.

No sofa. Nowhere to sit, really, except for a beanbag chair right in front of the TV. The only other piece of furniture in the room was a treadmill on the opposite side of the room, but it faced the wall, running up under a computer desk with a Macbook on it. It was a standing desk; the woodgrain surface came up to Joel's chest, standing on a sturdy telescoping frame.

A small pile of unopened mail lay next to the laptop. Joel briefly thought about checking his email, and then decided it was going to be a while before he wanted to look at a computer screen again.

The kitchen was a Spartan nook on the other side of a Formica breakfast bar, everything done up in 1960s greens and whites. A window over the sink overlooked Broad Avenue, the daylight shooting razorblades into his eyes. He went to the fridge, drank several pulls straight out of a carton of orange juice to wash the taste of sleep out of his mouth, then went into the bathroom to piss.

Something darted into the bathroom while he was standing in front of the toilet. Fisher's cat Selina meowed, curling around his ankle.

"What up, cat."

He flushed, washed his hands, took another few swigs from the orange juice in the fridge, and flopped down in the beanbag chair to rest. A long, groaning sigh rolled out of his mouth and he wiggled himself deeper into the styrofoam peanuts.

A remote control lay on the floor next to the beanbag. He aimed it at the TV and pressed the Power button, but the TV didn't come on. Instead, the treadmill behind him growled to life and slowly climbed to jogging speed. Nonplussed, he got up and found the TV remote on the stand-up desk. A control panel that looked like something from a Houston space terminal was mounted to the back of the desktop. He stopped the treadmill, but to his annoyance, the power button wouldn't turn it off.

Selina jumped up onto the entertainment center as he turned the TV on. The eight o' clock morning news filled the screen with the pitty high-def face of an anchorman and the cat sat in front of it, stretching luxuriously and throwing out one leg so she could sit and run her tongue down her haunch.

Joel scowled. "Well. I didn't wanna see the screen anyway, bitch."

A shiver passed through the cat, some weird shudder rolling up her back. Selina hunkered down, her eyes darting around the room as if she'd heard a mouse behind the baseboards, but she didn't get down and start hunting...she spaced out for a second. Then she stiffened, sitting pretty as if she'd suddenly remembered where she was, and proceeded to glare daggers at Joel's face.

The anchorman talked into the cat's back, her tail curling back and forth under his nose. "Sources say that the driver was not intoxicated, but a police investigation is still ongoing in this case. We'll return to this to give you details as they emerge."

Joel sat back down in the beanbag and stared right back at the cat. "The hell *you* looking at?"

Selina meowed.

"Get down. Boo. Giddown. Hiss."

The cat scowled at him, if such a thing was possible.

238

He was still holding both the remote for the TV and the one for the treadmill, and since the cat had decided to park her hairy ass in front of the TV, Joel occupied himself by looking at the buttons on the treadmill remote. There were a hell of a lot of buttons for a machine that did precisely one thing. It was almost as intricate as the TV remote, with buttons for speed and incline, as well as a tiny LCD screen with a line graph for peaks and valleys and a menu for running different types of cardio sessions. *I'll have to come back up here and see if Fish'll let me use his treadmill. It'd be cheaper than the gym, that's for sure.*

He turned the treadmill back on and revved it up as high as it would go. The sheet of texturized rubber scrolled across the platform with a high, whining burr. *Damn. You fall on that and it's all over for yo ass.* He stopped the belt, but the power button still wouldn't turn it off.

Selina padded into the kitchen and leapt up onto the counter. "Eww, hey, get down," Joel called from the living room.

He hated when cats got on kitchen counters. They kicked around in their litter boxes, shoveling up sand and shit with their paws, and the thought of preparing food on Fish's counters where the cat was walking around with her shitty feet sent a chill down Joel's spine.

The cat found a light switch on the wall by the microwave and pawed at it.

"What you doin, cat?"

She managed to flip the light switch and the sink growled loudly. She'd activated the garbage disposal.

Joel stretched to look over the bar. "Hey, what are you up to? Get down and leave things alone." He struggled up out of the beanbag chair and stood up in time to see the cat slink under the faucet and shove her face into the sink drain.

GGRRRRRRROOOOWWNT! Blood sprayed up out of the sink, spattering a fine mist across the kitchen ceiling.

A shock of amazed adrenaline whipped through Joel's body.

The grinder inside the garbage disposal bogged down like a truck in deep mud, snarling low as it chewed Selina's skull into pulp. The cat went apeshit, flailing around, beating herself against the inside of the basin, making that scribbly-fussy Donald Duck quacking sound.

Snapping out of his startled trance, Joel ran into the kitchen nook (almost slipping on a pool of blood) and turned off the disposal.

He stood there in a stunned silence, his hands laced on top of his head. Eventually, he found the power of speech again. "What the actual fuck. Jesus Christ, what the hell just happened," and then the logical conclusion was, "Fish is going to *kill* me."

Joel pushed the treadmill remote into his pocket, opened the cabinet under the sink, found a box of trash bags, then picked up Selina's limp, headless body by the tail. He scanned the nook, looking for the garbage. It was in a tall cabinet in the corner. He put the dead cat in the bin and tied it shut, then pulled the bag out and put a new one in it.

"Why did you do that, cat?" Joel asked the garbage bag in an accusing, astonished hiss, shaking it. "Why did you *do* that?"

Clenching and unclenching his fists, he stood at the sink shaking in excited fright, his eyes alternating between the window in front of him and the sink full of blood. He ran the water and used the sprayer hose to knock most of it down into the drain, but there were clumps of hair and … *gristle* stuck in the toothed rubber gasket that kept silverware out of the grinder.

Silverware, but not cats.

A drop of blood fell off the ceiling and tapped the top of his head. Joel hobbled into the bathroom to vomit.

It was a good one, a projectile gush hard enough to make his thigh throb. The puke was Easter-egg green and stank of Alizé and orange juice. *Blue and yellow make green Ziploc seal.* He spat and flushed the toilet, lingering over the bowl, hunched forward with his hands on his knees. *Why in the name of God did I just see a house-cat commit suicide?* He took a dirty towel out of the hamper and wiped the blood off his head and shaking hands with it. A crazy idea came out of left field: *she coulda come to me, I would've talked her down, come on, cat, you got so much to live for,* and he barked out crazed laughter.

Bloody footprints led into the bathroom, ground into the carpet and plastered on the linoleum.

"Ah, damn." Joel wet the towel and lowered himself onto his hands and knees with a grunt of pain, using the towel to scrub at the red prints. "Jesus, Jesus, I don't know what I done, but I need you to give me a break now. I'ma need you to give me the wheel back and let me drive fa minute."

When the toilet finally finished refilling itself with a noisy sigh, Joel heard voices through the vent under the sink. The radio in the shop had stopped.

Fish. "No, I haven't seen him all day."

Joel sat on his haunches, shooting straight up like a meerkat. A flashing light on the ceiling caught his attention and his head tilted back.

"Are you sure?"

The frenetic blue flashers of a police car were strobing through the bathroom window. He got up and stood on the edge of the bathtub, looking through the casement window behind the shower, his heart thumping. For three insane seconds, he was convinced the law had come to arrest him for killing Fish's cat, and then the reality of the night before came crashing down around him.

A Blackfield City Police cruiser was parked in the diagonal slot-parking in front of the comic shop.

Bowker had found him.

Fish's voice wafted up from the heat register. "Yeah, not a peep. I talked to him last night on the phone…sounded like he'd been drinking. He's probably still passed out at his mama's house. What did he do?"

Joel very nearly pissed his pants. He briefly thought about going back to scrubbing the blood off the floor, but decided to close the door and hide in the bathroom. He threw the bloody towel in the hamper and pressed his back against the wall. "You got to be kidding me," he murmured to himself, looking at the ceiling for guidance. "How did this Roscoe P. Coltrane lookalike find me?"

"We been to his house," said the other voice. It was familiar, but it didn't sound like Bowker. *Where have I heard that voice before?* "He ain't there, sir. This is the next logical place to look."

How did they know he and Fish were brothers? *I mean, there's the fact that we both got the same last name, but come on, lots of people have the same last name.* It was quite a jump of logic, even for Joel's paranoid state of mind. *Maybe they talked to Miguel. That's it. Oh, that son of a bitch. I gotta have a talk with him … if I get out of here in one piece.* Or maybe it was that open container stop when he was seventeen. He vaguely remembered putting Fish on his paperwork.

Yeah, that was probably it.

"I hate to have to tell ya, but you're wasting your time. He and me, we're kinda on the outs these days. You know…family stuff. He hasn't been here in months. Are you going to answer my question? What did my brother do?"

The police officer grunted, "Family stuff. Yeah, I can understand that. Well, last night your brother assaulted a police officer. Put a load of buckshot in his vest, almost killed him. *Tried* to kill him."

"That doesn't sound like the Joel I know."

"Maybe you don't know your brother as well as you think you do." The officer paused for a beat and said, "…So what are *you* doing here? According to the hours-of-business up there on the door, it don't look like the shop's open yet. But here *you* are."

"I come down here to hang out every weekend and most evenings," said Ashe. "It gets awful quiet at my place when it's nobody but me."

"Today's Sunday. You don't go to church?"

"I'm not really a church-going man, Mr. Euchiss."

Euchiss…Euchiss…. Joel tried to place the name. It wasn't one he'd heard before. "That's a surprise, down here in the South," said the cop. "You don't believe in God?"

"That's…honestly a can of worms I'd rather not open this early in the morning."

"So what d'you do?"

"I'm a veterinarian."

"Ah…. Well! Mr. Ellis. D'you mind if I take a look around?"

"Don't you need a search warrant for that?" asked Fisher.

"Not if I have probable cause. Do I *have* probable cause?"

Fish hesitated a little too long. "…No."

"Your lips are saying *no*, but your eyes are saying *yes.*" Euchiss started toward the back of the comic shop. "Other officers may not appreciate

241

pushback, but you know what? I *like* a challenge. Victory is so much sweeter if you've had to fight for it."

"Adapt and overcome," said Fish, repeating his life mantra.

"I like that. Mind if I borrow it?"

"Go right ahead."

"This shouldn't take long. I'm sure I don't need an escort...you two can hang out here. I'll be right back."

A half-minute later, Euchiss's voice came from the bottom of the stairs. Before his arduous climb, Joel had forgotten to close the stairwell door. *Dammit.* "Looks like somebody's been sitting in here sippin on a cup of coffee. There's a blanket in here too...whoever it was, they was sleepin on the futon."

'Somebody ate my porridge,' said the baby bear.

Fish said, "The heat works best in that little back room, so I like to sit in there with my blanket and watch the news when I get up."

"I hope you don't mind if I don't take your word on that, Mr. Ellis." Euchiss chuckled. "Hey, anybody ever told you, you look like that guy from that old show *Reading Rainbow?*"

"Levar Burton?"

"Yeah."

"No, not really. You used to watch *Reading Rainbow?*"

"Us cops ain't *all* Neanderthals, you know. Some of us can even read. Yeah, I know—shocker, huh?"

The thumping of shoes on the stairs told Joel that the cop was coming up. He got back down on his hands and knees and looked under the door as a head and shoulders rose up from behind the banister. What he saw trailed fingers of ice down his spine. That same shock of red hair...that narrow, corded neck and arrowhead jawline...those beady black eyes.

It was B1GR3D. Red was a cop.

"Oh lord, oh heavenly God," Joel whispered under his breath, his face pressed against the blood-smeared tiles. "You got to be shitting me."

Euchiss paused at the top of the stairs. "What in *all* the hell happened up here?"

"What?" called Fish.

"Is this *your* mess, Mr. Ellis?"

"Mess? What are you talking about?"

The cop stepped cautiously into the kitchen nook. "There's blood and hair all over the kitchen, man! It looks like somebody tried to mulch a raccoon in the garbage disposal."

Fish charged into the apartment, thundering up the stairs and into the living room.

"What the hell?"

"That's what *I'm* sayin, Mr. Ellis. You might want to work on your taxidermy skills if you're gonna—"

242

Euchiss went silent. Joel's heart was thumping slow and hard like the 1912 Overture, throbbing in his temples. Cautiously, the cop crossed the room, and Joel heard the soft plastic slurp of vinyl against gunmetal. *The footprints on the carpet. The footprints leading into the bathroom.*

"I know you're in there, buddy," said the cop. He was standing directly across from the bathroom door. "You might as well come on out. There ain't nowhere for you to go."

"Joel!" squawked Fish. He sounded like he was on the verge of tears. "Why you kill my cat? *The hell is wrong with you?*"

Reluctant at first to let Red/Euchiss hear his voice, Joel hesitated, his hands floating up alongside his face out of pure instinct. "—*I didn't*, I didn't do that! The cat did it! I was sittin in the beanbag watchin TV when—"

"You tryin to tell me Selina turned the garbage disposal on all by herself? And stuck her own head in it?"

"Y-yeah!"

"Do you understand how crazy that sounds?"

Joel's throat burned with fear and guilt. "Yeah." Everything seemed unreal, glossy and false, like the bathroom's tiles were going to break off and go spinning into a black void, leaving him adrift in a cosmos of lies.

"You need to come on out of there," said Euchiss. "Don't make me open that door myself. You ain't gonna like it when I do."

Joel knelt prostrate again, looking under the door. The stitches in his leg pulled painfully, the agony blunted by the Tylenol.

The treadmill was directly in front of the bathroom, some six or seven feet away. Euchiss had stepped up onto it—to provide better footing than the carpet, to give Joel room to come out of the bathroom, to give himself distance to fire his pistol, Joel didn't know...but it gave him an idea. He took the treadmill remote out of his pocket and got up on one knee, grasping the doorknob.

Aiming the remote under the door, he screwed up his nerve and pressed the START button.

Zerp! The treadmill belt, already turned up as high as it would go, whipped the cop's feet out from under him. Joel flung open the bathroom door to see the side of Euchiss's head smack against the edge of the desk.

The machine log-rolled the policeman and carried him away on his back. Bursting out of the bathroom, Joel leapt the treadmill, vaulted the banister and landed halfway down the stairs, popping a couple of stitches. Hellfire raced up his leg, but he ignored it, jumping again straight down to the bottom and darting through the open door.

He juked to the right to get out of the videotape room and shot across the comic shop toward daylight. Ashe was standing behind the counter, leaning on the glass. The vet started to say something, but Joel shoved the door open and threw himself outside.

Lieutenant Bowker turned around in surprise, reaching up to pinch the cigarette in his mouth.

243

Joel froze, his heart dropping into his stomach.

"Good morning!" the officer said cheerfully, throwing down the butt and shoving him in one fluid motion, bouncing his head off the doorframe.

Lightning flashed behind Joel's eyes and then he was facedown on the sidewalk, rough grit sandpapering his naked chest. The sun cut the brisk October air like a hot knife, turning the cement into a griddle. Objectively he knew that the monster's scratches were burning, but the pain in his thigh was extravagant, bright as a cattle-brand, and it eclipsed the world.

Bowker wrenched his arms up behind his back, zip-tying his wrists together. "Nice to see you again, boy." The officer turned him on his side and allowed him to get his feet underneath him. "You thought you was gonna get away?"

Looking up and down the street, Joel saw a few people on the sidewalk stop to rubberneck. Of course, they were all white. *Go ahead and look, assholes. Look at me. You like it, don't you?* Salt tainted his mouth and he licked at it, found blood from a busted lip. Twisting, he tried to stomp Bowker's knee, but the cop threw his ass out like a cabaret dancer, scooting out of range.

"Help!" Joel shouted into the morning stillness, trying to wrest his arm away. "They're gonna kill me! *Help me!*"

"Ain't nobody gonna kill you, y'idiot," growled Bowker, hauling the back door of the police cruiser open and bundling Joel inside. To his relief, the lieutenant didn't bang his head on the roof on the way in.

"*Help!*" Joel shrieked, and Bowker slammed the door in his face.

He was on his side. He wallowed and kicked to a sitting position and pressed his forehead to the window, wedging his bare feet into the cramped footwell. Fisher and Ashe came out of the comic shop, the tall veterinarian supporting Euchiss.

Next to Ashe, the policeman looked like a little boy. Euchiss sat down on the exterior windowsill, hunched over and cradling his head in the bowl of his hands.

Cool wind breathed through the mesh partition. The front windows were rolled down, so Joel could hear what they were saying. "Opie! What the hell happened to *you?*" asked Bowker, hovering over the other cop.

Euchiss looked up, squinting into the sun. "I fell."

"You fell," sneered the lieutenant. Euchiss gave him a glare that could melt steel. Joel was abruptly all too aware of who wore the pants in this partnership, even though the physically imposing Bowker technically outranked the redheaded patrolman. "Assaulting and evading a police officer," said LT Bowker, turning his attention to Fisher. "Attempted murder with a freakin shotgun. Your brother's got his plate full, ain't he? Would you like to explain why you were hidin him?"

Instead of taking the bait, Fish leaned into the passenger-side window of the cruiser. "I don't know what the hell happened to my cat, but I'm gonna follow you to the police station and bail you out."

"Ain't no bailin me out. They ain't gonna put me in jail," Joel said, pleading with his eyes. "They're gonna take me somewhere and put a bullet in my head." He thrust his knee up for emphasis, wincing at the stab of pain. "They already tried to shoot me once. They're gonna—"

A look of irritation dawning on his face, Bowker pulled another zip-tie out of his patrol belt and came up behind Fish. "Hey, no! *No!*" cried Joel. Fisher started to turn, but the lieutenant had snatched one wrist and twisted him back around, pressing him against the side of the car.

"You're fit as a fiddle, huh?" the cop asked, zip-tying his wrists together.

"What are you doing? Let me go—"

"Arresting you for harboring a fugitive and resisting arrest." Joel leaned back as Bowker opened the door and crammed Fisher inside, piling them on top of each other. He wriggled backward, trying to get out from under his brother.

Fisher was livid. "When I get out of these cuffs," he said, baring his teeth, his breath redolent of the protein shake he'd had for breakfast, "I'm going to kick your ass."

Joel pressed himself against the opposite door; Fisher looked like he wanted to rear back in the seat and kick him to death. The situation was almost funny, if it weren't so dire—reminding him of sultry summer evenings in their parent's car as children, Mama and Daddy in the front seat, Joel and Fisher in the back. *Stop touching your brother! Don't make me turn this car around!*

His head tilted back and he licked dry lips. "My leg is killin me. Look, man, I didn't kill your cat. I swear to God it turned the garbage disposal on by itself. I don't know why, but it did." He looked up and nodded toward Euchiss sitting on the windowsill holding his head. "And that guy," he said, in a confidential mutter, "is the serial killer I got away from. The one Bowker called 'the Serpent'."

Fish stared. "*That* guy? But he's—"

"Yeah, a cop. Like I told you, they're all in it together. They're workin for those witch-bitches out in Slade. The ones that lived across—"

"I'm fully aware of who they are. Mama died thinkin they were coming after her like they did that Martina lady."

"Maybe Mama wasn't so crazy after all." Joel shifted in the seat, inching his fingers up to the waistband of the jeans he was wearing. He pulled it down, revealing the right cheek of his ass and the scar on his skin. "I'll be damned. It all makes sense now."

"What does?"

Bowker's cellphone rang, cutting into their conversation with the theme to *Bonanza!*. "Y'ello."

Glancing pointedly down at the ass-cheek he was displaying, Joel said, "Look. The brands Mama burned into our asses when we were kids. They weren't a chicken-foot at all. They were 'protective runes' like what that Robin girl's got tattooed on her chest." A four-lobed Y about an inch long had been scarred into the flesh of his rump.

The middle lobe of the rune was longer than the other two, making it look like a rooster's footprint. "Robin Martine called it Al-Jazeera."

"The Arabic news network?" Fish winced in confusion. "What have *they* got to do with this? That woman's daughter is in town? You been talkin to her?"

"Yeah. I don't know, maybe your cat committin suicide was those witches tryin to do something to me, and this thing on my ass saved me. Maybe I was supposed to kill myself and Selina got it instead."

Fish pursed his lips, giving him a wry look.

"Yes ma'am," said Bowker on the phone. "You want me to do *what?* …No, I wasn't questionin you, not at all, ma'am. A little taken back, I reckon. Struck me as a funny request. …No, I don't think it's funny at all. Nothin's funny. Yes, I do have a sense of humor. No, I don't bring it to work."

"This ain't a joke, man," Joel was saying to Fish. "I promise. We in real trouble here."

Bowker hung up the phone. "Change of plans," he told Euchiss, who seemed to be shaking off the blow to the head. The redheaded scarecrow got up and put on a pair of sunglasses. "Boss called and gave us a job to do. Come on."

"What about these two?"

"We got bigger chickens to pluck."

The pear-shaped lieutenant lumbered around the back of the cruiser and got into the driver's seat, and Euchiss plopped down on the passenger side.

"What about that guy?" asked Euchiss, jerking a thumb at the veterinarian as he put on his seatbelt.

Joel glanced out the back window and saw Ashe Armstrong standing in front of the comic shop, a keyring full of keys in one hand, looking confused and dour.

"We'll take care of him later. We ain't got the room in the car for his big ass anyhow." Bowker put the car in gear and backed out into traffic. "He'll be all right until we get back, he thinks we're goin to the station. When we get done with this, we'll grab somethin quick to eat and come back here, have a word with him."

Euchiss turned and glared at Joel through the partition screen. Joel stared back, wary. "I bet you thought that was funny, huh? Runnin that treadmill with me standing on it?" Euchiss asked, venom in his voice. "I almost got a concussion."

"What, you expect me to be sorry about it? Bitch, you had me chained up in a garage. You were gonna cut my throat."

Euchiss pointed a jittery finger at him. His lips stuck together as he spoke. "Blood for the garden, asshole. Forget cutting your throat—I'm gonna string you right back up and cut your head clean off with a hacksaw like one'em raghead terrorists. Won't *that* be—"

"Hey, enough of that," warned Bowker, backhanding him across the chest and jamming a finger at his face. "We ain't no damn Taliban."

Discomfited, Euchiss turned around and folded his arms, sitting back like a little boy throwing a tantrum.

The lieutenant shook his head. "You can pitch a fit if you want, son—I don't give a rat's ass who y'know. But I got lines, and you steppin on em. My mama raised me to be a God-fearin man, not no heathern savage."

"God-fearin men don't do what you do," said Joel.

"Did I ask you for your opinion?" Bowker snarled over his shoulder. "I ought to shoot you right now for what you did last night with that scattergun. But we got things we got to go take care of, and you can help us."

"What kind of things is that?" asked Fisher.

The policemen didn't respond. Bowker drove them west along Broad and south onto Main, cutting through the heart of the downtown commercial district. Restaurants and gas stations scrolled past the windows in a parade of colorful logos. Lunchtime traffic surrounded them in a scrimmage of lights and steel.

Fisher pressed them. "Where we going?"

No answer.

Joel leaned forward. "Why you call yourself the Serpent, anyway?"

Euchiss cut a deadly glance over his shoulder and went back to burning a hole in the windshield with his eyes. The wind buffeting through his open window smelled like French fries.

"Stupid-ass name. Who gives theirself a nickname? That's lame as all hell. Nobody does that."

Euchiss's upper lip twitched and he smoothed back his hair, putting his patrol cap on. "You better shut your mouth, fag, or we're gonna be shorthanded one Negro."

Lieutenant Bowker regarded him for an instant and went back to driving.

"What?" spat Euchiss.

"Nothin, man."

The redhead fired another pair of eye-daggers at Joel and slid the panel in the vinyl partition shut, rattling the steel mesh.

"What are you trying to accomplish, there?" asked Fish.

Joel just stared out the window, trying to come up with a plan but able to think of nothing but Mexican food.

Burritos would have been a good last meal.

The police Charger slithered through downtown Blackfield, passing the university and its thirteen-story library, leaving the surface streets for more and more obscure neighborhoods.

Bowker's convoluted path cut through subdivisions Joel had been to a number of times, mostly to buy weed. Dealers and hookers milled up and down the sidewalk in front of rundown tract houses with boarded windows, and weeds sprouted from the walls of abandoned, broken-eyed factories. They drove past several convenience stores with iron bars on the windows. Grimy, slat-sided cottages on overgrown lawns strewn with dirty toys.

A googly-eyed old woman in a nightgown stood at the roadside with an oxygen tank, screaming gibberish at passing motorists.

The lieutenant finally slowed and pulled into a side street that wound into a wooded area, and the houses became fewer until there were none at all, only dead brown trees reaching for the sky and leaf-litter on rolling hills. Exposed hips of granite jutted from hillsides. Joel was beginning to think they were leaving the city altogether when the car grumbled into a gravel parking lot. A metal sign zip-tied to a chainlink fence told him that they had arrived at Blackfield Animal Shelter.

The only other vehicle was an unmarked box truck. Bowker pulled in to the side and the two cops got out, letting themselves into a large brick building. Euchiss came back and opened the cruiser's trunk, taking out a hunting rifle. Joel wasn't sure what caliber, but it had a bolt-action and a scope.

Euchiss took out a box of cartridges, slammed the trunk shut, and disappeared into the shelter.

Once they were gone, silence fell over the car, broken up by indecipherable garbage honking out of the police-band radio. A legion of dogs barked behind the fence.

Fish's eyes were full of fear and confusion. "What are we doin at the animal shelter?"

"Beats me."

"What were you saying about protective runes and witches and Robin Martine?"

Joel pressed his forehead to the window at an angle, trying to see through the windows of the shelter's main building. Inside the fence enclosure was a labyrinth of chainlink panels: smaller pens for individual dogs. From where he sat, he could see dozens of large-breed canines: Rottweilers, German Shepherds, a small army of pitbulls.

"Well, according to what Robin Martine told me, the witches' magic is guided by words and symbols." Joel went on to explain to his little

248

brother what Robin had told him and Kenway in the truck after leaving the hospital. "The symbol on our hips is the same one that's tattooed on Robin's chest. It protects you from their magic…like bug spray protects you from mosquitoes, I guess. Hell, I don't know."

The two of them sat in frustrated, anxious silence. After what felt like half an hour, Bowker and Euchiss finally came out. The lieutenant went to the far side of the building, opening a large swing-gate in the fence. Euchiss carried the hunting rifle out to the box truck and reversed the lumbering short-hauler into the enclosure.

Bowker came toward the cruiser, pulling his pistol. As he walked, he pulled the slide, loaded a magazine, and let the slide drop forward, *ch-clack!* Joel's heart jumped into his mouth, but the cop stood next to the car, staring out into the woods and rubbing his goatee.

A few minutes later, the self-styled Serpent strode out of the enclosure and Bowker opened Fisher's door, while Euchiss opened Joel's. "Get out," growled the killer, pulling him up by his armpit. Joel staggered, the gravel bruising the soles of his bare feet. "You try anything and my buddy blows your brains out." He dug in his pocket and came up with a utility knife, whipping it open.

Joel flinched, but Euchiss held him fast, cutting the zip-tie cuffs. Then he twisted Joel around by the shoulder and shoved him toward the animal shelter. "Walk."

Joel rubbed his wrists where the plastic had chafed. "What are we doing?"

"Did I say talk?" Euchiss cut Fish's cuffs, then pulled out his Taser and loaded a fresh cartridge. "We're going to perform a little manual labor. Miss Cutty wants us to load a bunch of cages onto this truck and carry em out to the quarry."

"Cages?" asked Fish. The four of them went into the chainlink enclosure and around the back of the building, down a gravel path to where the box truck had been backed up to an open door. As they approached, Joel could hear the yowling of cats from inside the shelter. Inside, they were met with a pitiful sight. Maybe a hundred, two-hundred wire kennels were stacked in a spacious concrete room, six to a column. The raunchy smell of cat feces made an eye-watering murk of the air, and an army of tiny paws reached through the gleaming bars like prisoners-of-war in a medieval dungeon.

The cages were small, more like raccoon-traps than kennels. "Jesus," said Fish.

"Start loading these cages onto the truck," said Euchiss.

"What are you gonna do with em?"

"That's for me to know and you to find out." The redheaded killer urged him on with the Taser. "Zap zap. Get to work."

The polished cement floor was as cold as a well-digger's ass under Joel's bare feet. He went to the nearest stack of kennels—this one only three cages high—and laced his fingers into the bars, lifting it up. The fluffy cat inside reached out and pinned his hand with a paw, pleading in a smoky voice. "*Yowwwww. Yowwwww.*"

Joel glanced at Bowker. The LT tucked the corners of his mouth back in a mean, imperative smile. *Go on now, do what you're told.*

Twenty-Four

KENWAY MADE BURRITOS FOR lunch while the two witch-hunters talked shop at the kitchen table. The GoPro sat on the table, dark and deactivated, staring straight up at the ceiling as everybody talked over it.

Leon wanted to save room for the steak, so he passed on lunch. "No point spending that much money on something and not be starving when you dig into it." So he sat in the living room getting ready for the coming week, going over lesson plans and grading a pop test he'd given Friday. He hadn't gotten around to it with Wayne's emergency hospital visit. "Witches and monsters can't make your job disappear," he said, and dived into his homework.

There was something else eating at Dad, that much Wayne could tell, at least, and it wasn't the sauce. Leon didn't seem amenable to talking about it, though. Wayne left him to his own devices and sat in the kitchen, eavesdropping on the conversation.

The table was piled with a dozen old books, bound in choppy chunks of thick, yellowed pages. Titles in obscure Latin and insignia that looked like geometry diagrams were etched on their covers in faded gold. The ones in English had pretentious or boring titles like *Chronology of Cabbalistic Philosophy*, *Essential Demonic Taxonomy*, *Invisible Science*, *Western Applied Invocation*. If he didn't know any better, he'd think they were college textbooks. They certainly sounded like the ones Dad had stacks of, boxed away in his bedroom.

Robin told Heinrich about her plan to use Wayne's ring to get upstairs to the fourth witch without Cutty seeing her.

"Dangerous," he said. "But I guess it's our only choice."

She'd put on a heavy-looking hoodie and now sat slumped back in a chair, one hand bundled into a pocket and the other flipping aimlessly through the contents of her cellphone. It struck Wayne that this was the first time he'd seen her behave so much like your average young woman, and to be honest it looked rather strange on her. He had grown accustomed to seeing her pacing around with restless energy, explaining things to the GoPro.

"You look like you're only really alive when you're on camera talkin about paranormal stuff," Wayne told her in a conversational lull.

She regarded him with those tired, ancient eyes. "What do you mean?"

"When you're not on camera, you're quiet. Shy, I guess. Like, when your internet camera is rolling, that's when you come alive."

"Yeah?"

The corner of Heinrich's mouth twitched. "You do, actually. As soon as that red light comes on, you start talkin your ass off and gettin yourself into trouble. The rest of the time your head is in the clouds. You're in your own little world."

"One of the nurses at the hospital used to call me an attention whore." She shucked up one of her sleeves to show Heinrich the cut on her wrist. "She said that's why I did this. And why I was faking schizophrenia and asking for medication."

"Sounds like you're not so much an 'attention whore' as you got acting in your blood. Maybe you missed your calling in Hollywood."

Robin laughed. "I couldn't act my way out of a wet paper bag."

"That's true. You don't even act like you give a shit half the time." Heinrich drummed a jaunty rimshot on the table.

She snorted.

"At least you know it's not schizophrenia." He squinted in annoyed disbelief. "Besides, who the hell joneses for anti-psychotics?"

"I don't know *what* it is, schizophrenia or not. Or how it involves the demon my mother summoned." Opening one of the books on the table, she flipped through page after page of demonic drawings and handwritten text. "I've been researching this thing. Wayne here calls it Owlhead."

The left-hand page had a detailed but primitive drawing of a man with a bird-head and huge staring eyes. His right hand clenched a broadsword, and his left hand was up in the air as if trying to get someone's attention. It didn't quite look like the thing in the Darkhouse, but Wayne could see how somebody could extrapolate this drawing from what he'd seen in there.

"This guy right here is the closest I can find to what we're dealing with," she said, holding up the book so they could all see it. "He's a killer spirit, a chaos-maker."

"A cacodemon," said Heinrich.

On the right-hand side was a long passage, preceded by a circle full of lines and symbols. "'The sixty-third spirit is Andras,'" she said, reading from the book. "'He is a great Marquis of Hell, appearing in the form of an angel with a head like a wood-owl, riding upon a strong black wolf, and having a sharp and bright sword flourished aloft in his hand.'" She paused, her lip curled in disgust. "If that was the body of an angel, angels are freakin hairy. 'His office is to sow discord. If the exorcist have not a care, he will slay both him and his fellows. He governeth thirty legions of spirits, and this is his seal.'"

Heinrich was meticulously folding a piece of paper into some elaborate shape. "The Ars Goetia."

"What's that?" asked Wayne.

"One part of a very old spellbook called *The Lesser Key of Solomon*. Basically a demonic encyclopedia."

The boy's face flashed cold. "Ah."

"Not the original, of course. This one is four transcriptions removed from that one." The old man put the paper on top of the pile of books. He had folded it into the rough shape of a dog, or perhaps it was a horse.

"So Owlhead's real name is Andras?"

"I don't know," said Robin. "Maybe."

She stared meaningfully at the corner of the kitchen next to the back door. Heinrich shifted in his seat to look, and a thrill of adrenaline buzzed through Wayne's system. "Is he there?" asked the boy, his voice barely above a whisper. "Can you see him?"

"No, but I can feel him. You know when we were in the bathroom? I could *feel* him in the house. Like a sort of mental radar. Like heat coming off an oven."

"I have a theory," said Heinrich.

"Lay it on me."

"It explains why Cutty used a familiar to murder your mother, and why they haven't preemptively attacked you." As if to illustrate his point, he thumped the paper dog across the room. It landed in the sink. "They're afraid of the demon."

"Weaver came into the house, though. She wasn't afraid of him. And I could feel him here, looking at her like she was a cheap piece of meat."

He gathered up a fist with an elaborate gesture. "Demons eat their energy. They're psychic vampires. Like a poltergeist feeds on emotional energy, demons feed on paranormal will."

"They don't eat the witch herself?"

"Not that I can tell. I would have to see what Andras would do if he and the witches were in the same space, but he can't get to her from where he is." Heinrich picked up a book and studied the cover. "Which I'm calling the Dreamlands, by the way. From the old H. P. Lovecraft books."

"You're finally getting into something even *I'm* familiar with," said Kenway, pointing a spatula. He was stirring a pan of ground beef, filling the kitchen with the smell of taco meat. "When I was in high school, I read a lot of Lovecraft stuff. 'Colour Out of Space', Cthulhu, 'Cold Air', all that jazz."

"Cthulhu." Wayne smiled.

That he had heard of, being a horror fan—the giant green octopus-faced monster from the ocean.

"Anyway," continued Heinrich, "the demon is accidentally keepin us safe. I don't think Andras can see us on this side—he can only find you if you're expending spectral energy, like some kinda magic-seeking bloodhound. I think if any of them bitches up there try to use their power here in the house, Andras will tear into em. And they know it."

"If only we could get Andras out of there." Kenway tore open a bag of tortillas and laid them out on a plate. "Maybe we could lead him up to their house and let him go to town on em. Sic him on em like a dog."

Robin smirked. "You want to let a 'Marquis of Hell' loose in the material world?"

He paused. "...Yeah, now that you put it that way, maybe it's not such a good idea after all." Opening the fridge, he took out sour cream and pico de gallo, then opened a can of refried beans and put them in the microwave to heat up. "Maybe we could trick the witch into going into one of Wayne's doorways."

She eyed Heinrich. "There's a thought."

"Maybe." An absent look came over his eyes, and then he nodded. "That'd be a better plan than trying to nail her down with the Osdathregar."

"What's the Oz—thad—garerer?" asked Wayne.

"The dagger I showed you." Robin made a fist and thrust it forward as if stabbing something. "It's called the 'Osdathregar' after the ancient Zoroastrian priests that used to wield similar daggers in purification ceremonies. People at the Vatican call it the Godsdagger."

"Is it really made with the nails from Jesus's cross?"

Heinrich sat back and laughed. "It's made outta the shoenails from John Wayne's horse. Who the hell knows what's in it? All *I* know is that it does what it's supposed to, and that's all that matters to me."

Letting out a frustrated sigh, Robin got out of her chair and paced around the table, her hands in her pockets. "I'm thinking of contacting Andras again."

"That's not a good idea."

"I need to know what happened to my mother. In the vision from Andras, I saw him climb out of the well she opened with the ritual and drag her back into the cellar."

"She must have escaped like Wayne did."

"Maybe. I doubt it. I think the demon let her go for some reason. I want to find out what that reason was."

Heinrich shook his head, his voice hardening. "I still don't think it's a good idea. The last time you had a seizure. A bad one. Exposing yourself to the demon that way again might give you more brain damage than you already have."

She huffed in derision.

"I agree." Kenway turned off the stove and ran hot water over the steaks to speed up their thawing. His eyes were furtive, bashful, as he told her he'd rather not see her that way again. "That scared the hell out of me, Robin." The look on his face said *if not for you, then do it for me,* so obvious that even Wayne could see it.

Robin stood at the door and stared out into the hallway. "Why am I so sensitive to this thing? Why can I feel it when you guys can't? Why is it sending *me* visions?" She looked over her shoulder. "Am *I* a witch? Did my mom sacrifice *my* heart when I was a baby?"

"That would be the ultimate irony," said Heinrich. "A witch hunting witches. And economical, to boot—a two-for-one ceremony. But no...that's not how it works. For starters, if you'd been initiated when you were a baby, you'd still be a baby. Witches grow old, but they don't grow up. They die inside, remember? The power of Ereshkigal is what keeps them alive. Besides, you have a heartbeat. A pulse. You have a heart. And I assume you have monthlies, something witches don't."

Robin barked nervous laughter. "Yeah, that's true." She ruffled a hand through her wavy mohawk and leaned against the doorframe. "Boy, that's a load off *my* mind."

"Andras has haunted this house your entire life." Heinrich got up from the table, tapping out one of his coconut cigars and sauntering toward the back door. He took out his lighter. "I can't imagine you would grow up with that ugly bastard and not acclimate to his presence to some degree," he said, lighting the cigar and heading out to the back stoop to sit and smoke.

While he was gone, Robin put together Wayne's burrito and the three of them sat down to eat. "I really like you guys," Wayne told them. "I'm glad we moved in here and met you."

"Yeah?" Robin smiled. "I like you too."

There was a faint bruise in the corner of Kenway's mouth, as if he'd wiped at it with dirty hands. "Your dad's got a hell of a haymaker, too. Can't hate a guy that can throw a punch worth a damn at a guy with fifty or sixty pounds on him."

✪

Robin spent the afternoon editing footage, sitting in the cupola with Kenway and Wayne while they riddled each other with bullets in *Halo*. Heinrich had convinced her not to upload any more video since they were aware that Karen Weaver watched them, and he didn't want to advertise their plans. "That's how a lot of units got their asses kicked in the Civil War," he told them. "Their tactics and plans got published in the newspapers. *114ᵗʰ So-and-so Regiment Marching to Antietam Monday*. Stuff like that. Loose lips sink ships."

"I'll save it up and make a feature-length entry out of it next weekend, then," she said.

"Assuming we make it to next weekend."

"Ye of little faith."

Around four, Kenway went down to prepare the steaks. He covered both sides in a layer of sea-salt and seasonings, then lay them on plates in the fridge to rest. "The salt breaks down the proteins and draws out the water. The seasonings take the water's place in the meat. You let it sit for an hour or two, then take it out, rinse off the salt, pat it dry, and there you go—dry-aged steak, just like you'd get in a fancy restaurant."

"How'd you get so good at cooking?" asked Leon. "I thought you were in the Army. Were you a cook?"

"No. I was stationed with an Italian unit. Every weekend, or every other weekend, we would buy some cheap steaks off the civilian dining-facility contractors in Camp Stone and grill them on this big piece of wire mesh laid across stacks of cinder blocks. This Italian fella Sergeant Querini showed me how to salt a steak to dry-age it."

As six o'clock drew nearer and nearer, the house seemed to tighten around them. Wayne could feel the clock ticking like a man on the morning of his execution, a slow dreadful stretching of time. Nothing on TV could hold his attention for long, and a book was out of the question. All he could focus on was the mission-house at the top of the hill.

"I want to go with you," he finally told Robin, tearing his gaze away. The two of them were playing *Halo* against Kenway, and they were losing because Wayne kept staring out the window.

"Go where?" She jumped into a jeep and tore across a virtual landscape. "With me and Heinrich?"

"Yeah."

"*Nooooo.* Even if the witches didn't expect you at dinner, your dad would never agree to that."

Kenway came out of nowhere on a flying purple jet-thing, slamming into Robin's jeep and flipping it over. She fell out of it and lobbed plasma grenades at him, but he was already too high, corkscrewing through the sky. "What do you mean, 'me and Heinrich'?" he asked, firing blasts of energy. "I'm going too. We agreed: I'm your sidekick now."

She sighed, running into a cave, dirt pluming up behind her from his volley of gunfire. A rocket-launcher lay on the cave floor. "That I did. But I need you outside, watching the house. You're my lookout."

"Lookout?" He crammed the Banshee jet into the cave opening and ejected from the back, trapping her inside.

"Yeah. We'll plug hands-free earbuds into our cellphones and use them as tactical radios. I bought a couple of em this morning." She blew the jet to pieces with a rocket, loaded another, and came charging out, firing at Kenway. He sprayed her with a hail of rifle bullets, but the rocket hit the ground at his feet and blasted him into the air. "You take up position outside the garden wall where you can see through the dining room windows."

Kenway's soldier tumbled against a boulder and collapsed in a lifeless heap. He materialized on the other side of the area behind a massive stone monolith, standing next to another jeep. He snatched up a nearby rifle and took off, driving through a grove of trees.

"I'm assuming all three of them are going to be at dinner, and the fourth will stay upstairs as usual," said Robin, trading the empty rocket launcher for the rifle off of Kenway's body. "As far as I know, she's bedridden. Or disfigured."

"Or maybe they keep her up there to keep her safe." Wayne came trundling over the hill in a tank, driving down into a valley as Robin came along.

"Or that."

Pride lifted the corner of Wayne's lips in a crooked smile.

"If you see any of the other three behave strangely, as if they're aware I'm in there, or if you see them head upstairs, I want you to alert me." The jeep burst out of the foliage at the top of the river bed, heading straight for Robin's face.

Wayne fired a tank shell into the jeep's passenger side, exploding it in midair, and the flaming vehicle sailed over her head. Kenway's armored corpse flopped into the brook at Robin's feet in a shower of discarded weapons and grenades.

He elbowed Wayne in the ribs, grinning for the first time since they'd met. "All right now, kid...you're gonna make me go into Beast Mode here." Kenway leaned forward in concentration, sitting on the edge of the bed.

Climbing out of the tank, Wayne switched to his sniper rifle and ran away, throwing a grenade underneath. He was already crouching at the top of the river bed looking through his scope at Kenway when the tank exploded.

"Bring it, old man."

Twenty-Five

A COUPLE OF HOURS later (without his cell Joel couldn't tell, as though constant access to his iPhone had damaged his perception of time), the two brothers wedged the final kennel into place.

Surprisingly, all but three of the cages fit in the back of the truck. Euchiss took two of them and put them in the cab up front. Bowker urged Joel and Fisher into the cargo hold with the cats and pulled the rolldown shut on them.

The air stank of cat piss and the space they were confined to was only the last couple of feet of the compartment, a gap two feet wide, nine feet tall, and seven feet across. Joel sat down and listened to the officer put a padlock through the handle...which was a feat in itself, because the darkness was a near-unbearable chaos of agonized groaning and keening.

He leaned back against the wall and rubbed his face in exasperation and fear. The cats were too loud to talk to Fisher, so he just closed his eyes and tried to think of a way out of this mess.

Prayers seemed trite and useless. Joel thought of himself peripherally as a Christian, but he hadn't been to church since he was a teenager and was always at a loss for words when someone asked him to say Grace over dinner.

It was no different today as he rode blind and disoriented back into the hustle and bustle of urban Blackfield, but the irony was not lost on him that if he'd gone to church that morning, he probably wouldn't be in this mess. Who thinks to look for a fugitive in church?

Once he'd exhausted his reserve of plans and mental preparations— daydreaming about leaping out at Euchiss when he opened the back of the truck, usually getting shot or Tasered for his troubles—he played around with the reasons for why Fisher's cat had killed itself, turning the scene over and over in his mind like a Rubik's Cube. The way the cat had hunkered down and stared at Joel as if he were a piece of string or a laser-dot...the fixed stare of a predator watching for movement, sizing up a target.

The truck drove a shorter route than the one they'd taken in the police cruiser, but more circuitous. He counted at least seven stops, four of which were at traffic lights (this was determined by the fact that the driver only made a cursory effort to stop at stop-signs). The animals never stopped yowling; if anything, it only got worse and worse, increasing whenever the truck paused and the engine quieted.

The Tylenol was wearing off, and his leg radiated heat through the bandage, throbbing and aching like a live wire under fabric.

He had actually started to doze off when the truck's horn blared. An engine somewhere off to their port side revved, rising in volume, and then, *WHAM!*, an incredible force slammed into them, throwing Joel onto his hands and knees at Fisher's feet.

Someone had side-swiped them. The tires barked a squealing tremolo, *EEEEE-E-E-E-E!* Dozens of wire kennels toppled over in a riot of metal and screaming animals.

"Who the hell!" shouted Bowker, his voice almost obscured by the cats. The offending vehicle crashed into them again, partially caving in the wall and knocking down cages. A dozen lasers of daylight streamed in through pinholes bashed into the side of the cargo compartment. Joel scrambled into Fisher's reach and the man dragged his brother into his lap, clutching his head in powerful arms.

For a few seconds, Fish's cologne overpowered the cat-stink. *If I live through this I'll never bitch about keto again.*

A shadow loomed at them from the fast lane, blocking out the light, and beat against the truck—*BAM.* This time their mystery assailant pressed against the truck's flank, trying to fishtail them. The sound of their engine reverberated through the wall, bogging down, straining.

Bowker managed to keep it more or less on the straight and narrow, but some sort of structure collided with the right side and scraped endlessly down the fender like rolling thunder, drumming at regular intervals, a giant metal heart, *boom-boom, boom-boom.*

A guard-rail.

As soon as Joel placed the sound, a tremendous noise—a great shuddering *BOOM* like the world tearing in half—told him that the truck had broken through, and the entire cargo compartment capsized to the right. Joel and Fisher and a hundred and forty-two cats slammed into the starboard wall and free-floated for about two and a half seconds.

Instead of crashing into water like he'd anticipated, the truck piledrived itself into solid ground.

Forward momentum threw every cage into the front of the compartment and tore the brothers away from each other. Joel cartwheeled backward into the pile of kennels, bounced and fell on top of Fisher. The ceiling sheared open with the furious, ear-destroying roar of a hundred thousand dragons.

Blood dripped on the back of his head, an insistent *tap, tap, tap*. Joel opened his eyes to find himself lying on top of his brother, his face pressed against Fisher's chest, listening to a chorus of tuneless, defeated howling. He was pinned under a tangle of cages. Dead, dying, and injured house-cats lay in slumped piles of hair all around him, suspended in a masterwork of bent wires.

Fish groaned. "What happened?"

"We crashed."

A familiar chemical smell tainted the air, overpowering the cat urine. Gasoline. Diesel. The fuel tank had ruptured. "We gotta get out of here," said Fish, and he tried to stir. Sharp pain needled Joel's left shoulder.

"Oww, fuck. *Quit movin.*"

Fish relaxed. Joel tried to push himself up, but the cages were too heavy. A cat's paw groped at his face.

He shivered as a surge of adrenaline ripped through his core, his heart flaring, and he tried to push again. This time the cage against his back snapped, and a wire bar twanged like a broken guitar string, scratching his side.

"Hold on!" someone shouted from up the bank, feet thumping through dry leaves. "I'm comin! Hold on!"

Joel gazed through a galaxy of aluminum wires. The back door was smashed open, and he could see the bridge they'd fallen from, and the guardrail they'd smashed through.

A Frontier pickup was parked on the shoulder. Ashe Armstrong ran sideways down the slope in an awkward loping gallop. The big veterinarian took hold of the roof where it'd been peeled away and hauled on it, tearing it open further. "Hey," he called over the howling of the cats, spotting Joel through the twisted bars. "I'll get you guys out. Hold on."

He worked his way down the side, wrenching it down, filling the box with sunlight. Joel called out, "I'm holdin, man, I'm holdin."

Reaching into the cargo compartment, Ashe started grabbing at kennels and dragging them out onto the bank. The cats inside them complained, but right now his first priority was freeing Joel and Fish.

Fisher coughed in Joel's ear. "You all right?"

"Yeah." Joel winced. "Got a wire jabbin me in my back and I got one foot in Hell, but otherwise, I'm aight. You?"

"You had your tetanus shot, right?"

"No, but it looks like I'm gonna need one."

"How did you find us?" Fish asked Ashe. "Was that you that made the cop crash?"

"Followed you guys all the way to Glen Addie, but I lost you at a red light." Pulling on a cage, Ashe lifted it over his head and flung it into the weeds. The cat inside was already dead, flopping around limp and shapeless. "I was driving around the 1800 block, thinking of checking the animal shelter—since it was the only thing out that way that made any sense—when I saw those two cops and followed em."

The next cage was stuck fast and the cat inside, a black shorthair with white patches, yowled pitifully. Ashe pulled and pulled until it let go with a *twang* and he set it aside. "I don't know why I rammed the truck," he said, grabbing another one. "It seemed like the thing to do. Those guys are shady as hell and I figured you were in the back."

"It's a good thing you did," said Joel.

"Figured they were gonna try to finish the job they started last night. Take you somewhere and kill you. Guess it seemed safer to run the truck off the road and pull you out than try to stop em and get myself shot like they shot you."

"I'm glad you believed me."

"It's hard to disbelieve a gunshot wound to the leg."

Fisher coughed again. "Come on, man, hurry up. We need to get out of here." The smell of diesel fuel was growing stronger. "Those two cops. Are they out? Are they out there?"

Ashe shook his head. "I ain't seen em. Looks like they're still in the front."

Bracing himself against the wall of the compartment, Joel did a pushup and found that the load on his back was considerably lighter, affording him a few inches of wiggle-room.

"Almost there," said Ashe. He laced his fingers through another kennel and paused.

"What is it?"

Joel blinked. The vet was staring into space, hunched over with his shoulders squeezed into the roof opening.

"Why'd you stop?"

"Nnnrrrrrrrr." Ashe was growling, a weird nasal growl like an impression of an airplane. Choking and snuffling, he shrank away from the opening, disappearing, and daylight poured through in his place.

Joel met Fisher's eyes and the two of them struggled with the cages. Ashe had taken enough of them out that they had room to push them out of the way. Fish reached up over his head, shoving the last couple of kennels toward the gap. The cages on top of them shifted precariously.

Dragging himself underneath them, Fisher pulled his body through the hole and out into the grass.

Orange light flickered from the back of the compartment. Through the chaos of wires, Joel could see a fire guttering somewhere deep in the pile of kennels. The diesel had leaked into the cargo hold and something had set it ablaze. The smoke was foul, thick and pungent. He shoved at the cages, crawling forward, and Fisher pulled them out from the other side, throwing them away.

Finally, he was free. Joel dragged his legs out and lay exhausted in the churned-up dirt. The truck had come to rest on its right side at the bottom of a slope, next to a river.

"*Rrrrooowwwwwrrrrll,*" said Ashe.

Joel turned over. The vet was doubled over in a crazy Spider-Man pose on his hands and feet, crawling along the riverbank and staring at them.

"The hell are you doing?" asked Fisher, and Ashe lunged at him, slamming him against the back of the cargo box.

Fish bounced off the aluminum sheet and the two men went down with Ashe on top, hissing and growling like a man insane. The vet's ponytail had come undone and his hair was a wild brown Tarzan mane. Ashe tried to bite Fish and the smaller man pushed at him, fending him off with a bloody forearm.

One of the cages lay next to Joel, bars twisted in every direction, the cat gone. He grabbed a bar and bent it until it broke free, then scrambled over to Ashe and jammed it deep through his shirt, feeling skin give way.

"*ROOOOWL!*"

Flinching and screaming, the vet rolled off of Fish and spidered backwards. One of his shoes pried free of his foot, stuck in gluey mud, the sock still inside. Joel stared, kneeling in a three-point stance, the wire jutting from his fingers like a knife fighter. That feeling of unreality came back. *The man is acting like a cat.*

His brother snatched up a rock and threw it—"*Bitch-ass bitch!*"—and Ashe blinked just as the rock hit him in the forehead. *TOCK!* He fell over and writhed like a crushed bug, holding his eyes, his heels grinding furrows in the dirt.

In the fight, Fisher had been pushed backward on the ground, and his pants were shucked down off his hips, revealing one butt cheek. Joel caught a glimpse of the *algiz* brand on his ass and got an idea.

"Hold the man down," he told Fish, scooping his hand through the mud.

"What?"

"*Just do it!*"

Fish clambered up and clapped his hands to Ashe's biceps, pinning him down and uncovering his face. Ashe snarled at the sky and twisted back and forth trying to free himself, a livid purple bruise rising over his right eyebrow.

Grinding up the mud in his hands, Joel ripped Ashe's shirt open. A white belly glowed underneath. Joel painted Robin's *algiz* on him with the mud—one long smear and two little arms on top—and then Ashe overpowered them, throwing Fish aside. Joel crawled away, using the side of the box-truck to climb to his feet.

Flames crackled inside the cargo compartment, and when he looked inside he saw the beginnings of a roaring bonfire. He swore out loud and pulled out a cage with a howling cat inside, and another and another.

God, there are so many, he thought, pitching the kennels into the weeds like a baggage-handler.

"What's *wrong* with him?" shouted Fisher.

Ashe Armstrong lay on his back, thick spittle-foam collecting between his lips, convulsing violently and thrashing his arms and legs like a man electrocuted. His eyes rolled back in his head.

Struck by indecision and driven by the smell of burning cat-hair, Joel couldn't figure out what to do—help Ashe? Save the cats? Yell at Fish to help him get the cages out of the fire? The dilemma was rendered moot when Ashe opened his mouth and the face of a cat pressed itself out between his teeth, eyes squinting, fur matted.

The vet's face had become a livid lavender. He grabbed his neck with both hands as if he was trying to pull off his own head and rolled over on his hands and knees. He convulsed again—this time slowly, methodically, his stomach tensing the way a dog sicks. His whole torso inchwormed back to front, his shoulders bunched up to his ears.

A cat's head protruded from his mouth like a big hairy tongue. Ashe reached up with one hand and took hold of the cat's neck with an A-OK gesture, and pulled.

The cat let out a strangled duck-squawk.

Standing half-naked in the mud under a cooling overcast sky, black smoke billowing past, Joel lost his handle on the present. Somehow the threads of reality had unraveled to the point that his mind refused to put two and two together anymore, and all of a sudden he forgot what his hands were for. The only thing he could do was watch helplessly as Armstrong struggled.

Fisher snatched him back with a slap to the face. "Stop screamin and go check on those two cops."

He had been screaming? Joel shook his head and a pang of dizziness almost sprawled him in the weeds. The birds were singing in the trees. Why were the birds singing? *Look at this shit! What is there to sing about?*

"I said *go!*" growled Fisher, pushing him out of the way. Fish went back into the cargo compartment and pitched a kennel outside. Smoke was roiling out. A few seconds later, he came out, coughing hard and wet. He didn't go back in.

Staggering through the mud, Joel went around to the driver's side of the truck and was amazed to see a wall of black, dirty machinery. Then he remembered that the truck had fallen over on its side; the door was now on top. He climbed the underside of the cab and pulled himself up and over the running-board.

Through the window, he could see the two men inside. Euchiss was unconscious behind a deflated airbag, slumped against the passenger side door with blood trickling down the side of his face, but Bowker was dead. He was *extremely* dead. The steering column had been driven backward, but the Second Chance vest he'd been wearing had prevented it from impaling him. Instead, it had caused the armor plates to squish his torso like a

263

s'more, breaking his ribs and pinning him against the seat. His eyes and throat bulged like a toad and his face was grape-purple, gray viscera flowering from his mouth.

Luckily, the window-glass was smashed out. Joel reached into the cab and plucked the Glock out of Bowker's hip holster, jamming it into the back of his jeans.

Movement on the other side caught his eye. Euchiss's eyes were open, and he was staring straight at Joel. Without a word, the cop drew his own Glock and pointed it up at him.

Joel recoiled away from the window and jumped down into the mud, heading back to the rear of the cargo compartment. When he got there, Ashe Armstrong was lying on his back in the undergrowth where he'd fallen, cradling a blood-wet cat in his arms like a new mother and looking thoroughly wrung-out. "Uuuunnggh," the big man grunted hoarsely, and closed his eyes, exhausted.

By now, the fire was licking up out of the hole in the roof. Cats screamed inside in a great siren-chorus of panic and agony, consumed by the flames. Fish was on his knees in the mud, his eyes red and streaming down his face, though Joel couldn't tell if it was because of the smoke or because of the cats.

"I can't save them," Fish sobbed. "I can't get in."

"We got to go."

Fish got up, still weeping. Ashe lay in Roman repose, his head lolling back, his eyes closed. The newly reborn cat wriggled out of his arms and shook itself, crawling weakly into the treeline.

Ashe opened his eyes. "My throat. Killing me."

"Come on," said Joel, grabbing his hands. "We got to go. Get up. We got to go." The brothers helped the vet up off the ground and they headed up the slope toward the highway. Ashe's pickup truck waited for them at the gap in the guardrail, the right quarter smashed in a way that gave Joel pause.

A sluggish, raspy voice echoed off the trees. *"Where you goin'?"*

They all looked up. Euchiss had climbed over his partner and was now standing up in the sidelong driver window as if it were a tank hatch. He pulled the rifle out of the cab hand-over-hand and cycled the bolt, *chik-a-chik!*

Joel reached behind his back and came up with Bowker's pistol, pointing it at the Serpent. It went off as soon as he tugged the trigger, firing with a paper-bag *POP!*, and the bullet kicked sparks off the side of the truck.

Euchiss slithered down into the window for cover.

Reaching the roadside first, Joel went around to the driver's side of Ashe's truck. The highway was a lonely country two-lane out in the middle of nowhere, stretching toward the horizon in both directions. Soldier pines made an impenetrable wall on either side of the highway under a sky like stirred milk. There were no power lines or poles, which made the road look naked, unfinished.

The Frontier's door was open and the keys were still in it, but the right front of the truck was smashed in and smoke was snaking out from under the hood. Joel twisted the keys and the engine grunted—*grrr-unh-unh-unh, grrr-unh-unh-unh.*

It wouldn't start. "Damn!"

The windshield imploded with a delicate smash, raining glass all over the dash, and Joel dove out onto the highway. Lying on his belly, it occurred to him that Euchiss could still see him underneath the truck, but when he peered through the gap he saw that the shoulder of the road concealed him well enough.

Fisher and Ashe came bounding around the back of the truck and hunkered down behind the Frontier's bed. "Wouldn't start?" croaked the vet, wincing.

"No."

"Now what?" asked Fish.

Ashe's fingers curled over the bed wall and he rose up to peer over the edge. A bolt from the blue exploded on the other side, whispering across the forest, and a bullet fanned his hair back in a mist of blood.

Both brothers swore out loud as Ashe toppled over and slapped against the asphalt.

"No!" shrieked Fisher. *"No!"*

Joel looked away, squeezing his eyes shut and covering his face, trying to collect himself.

Staring into the abyss behind his eyelids, listening to Fish curse over the dead man, he knew they had no other recourse but to run or be shot. He could hit a man point-blank with a shotgun, but with a pistol and a handful of bullets, Joel knew he had no chance against Euchiss's scoped hunting rifle and a whole box of rounds.

He tangled a hand in Fisher's shirt and pulled him to his feet. "Let's get out of here."

Twenty-Six

AT LEAST THE FIRE had taken care of the cats, which was what they'd come out here to get rid of anyway.

When Euchiss finally managed to get out of the overturned truck, he twisted his ankle jumping down. He sat in the back of the Frontier for a few minutes, massaging his ankle and waiting for someone to happen by with a vehicle he could commandeer, but the road to the quarry was a long and lonely one. Nobody came out this way except for the pulpwood trucks going to the clear-cut out on the ridge, and that had dried up three weeks ago. There would be no more traffic.

They had only been six miles from the quarry when the big guy with the ponytail ran them off the road.

He kicked the lanky vet for good measure before he left.

Two hours into the pursuit, the pain had drained out of his ankle and it'd become stiff and swollen. Euchiss paused to examine it and found a portwine bruise the size of a baseball across the outside of his heel. Sprained. Damn.

The forest crowded around him in an infinity of tall pine trees, and the ground was a carpet of rusty red needles. The sky behind the treetops was an endless wind-blasted white. Four-fifths of a box of 6.5mm rustled softly in his pocket.

He took his phone out and woke it up. No signal. His LMR was also out of the picture—too far away from town for the walkie. "Son of a bitch," he fussed to himself in his New England drawl. He carried the rifle, a scoped Nosler M48 Patriot, underhand like a briefcase. *Oh well. Cutty would just be pissed I messed up.* Better he get this tied off by himself, ASAP.

He wriggled back into his shoe and picked his way over a brook. On the other side was the decades-old remains of a barbed-wire fence, and several yards to the south was a NO TRESPASSING sign. *We've been curving in a northeasterly direction,* he thought, slinking through the rusty wires like a wrestler getting into a ring. *Must be getting close to the mines.*

The aforementioned quarry that Bowker had been heading to lay at the far end of a network of mine shafts snaking through the belly of Red Hill Mountain. The locals called it the Mushroom Mines because the damp conditions inside the cave caused white fungus to grow on the wooden tables and scaffolding. The air inside was thick with mold spores. He wasn't sure if it was poisonous, but he and Bowker never took any chances and usually went in with gas masks.

They were in the foothills of Red Hill Mountain now, crossing increasingly steep and stony terrain. Up ahead, the trees thinned out, and Euchiss found himself on a bare shelf of limestone overlooking a large gorge some two or three hundred yards across—the sort of gap that would have warranted a bridge were it more traveled. Briars and heather choked the bottom, but the sides were steep and clear.

The two black guys were scrambling up the opposite bank, picking their way through the boulders and briars. They were almost to the top, no more than a stone's-throw from the treeline. Euchiss threw himself down and shouldered the rifle, a frisson of glee coursing through his body. A quick adjustment to get an optimal angle, cocking one knee up, and he thrust the gun forward, resting his elbows on the cliff and looking through the scope.

In the sharp magnification, he could have reached out and plucked the two men off the valley wall with his fingers. Euchiss licked his lips and steadied himself, the crosshair settling over the athletic one with the buzz-cut. Breathe in, breathe out, relax. He tugged the trigger back until the firing pin hammered the cartridge.

The sharp, hollow *CRACK!* surprised him and sent a pulse of pleasure through his testicles. The two men flinched and dirt spewed up inches to the right of Fisher Ellis's head. He looked over his shoulder, scanning the gorge wall.

"I'm up here, you dumb shit." Euchiss cycled the Nosler's bolt, ejected the empty casing, and chambered a fresh round.

Something went off with a *pop* like an M-80 and a bullet whirred into the trees behind him. He peered through the scope and remembered that the faggot with the shaved head had stolen Bowker's Glock. Joel fired several more rounds, all but one whizzing into the trees behind Euchiss. "You can't hit me from there with that. Who are *you* foolin?"

He took aim on Joel, who seemed to realize the futility of shooting back and threw the empty pistol into the gorge. As Euchiss was getting ready to pull the rifle's trigger, his trousers vibrated and a jangly melody came from his pocket.

Being this high up, he must have gotten a signal. He dug out his phone—yup, four bars. Euchiss grunted in irritation at a text message.

Cutty having steaks w neibrs @ 6. U in?

Steaks? Who gives a rat's ass about steaks? He sighed and looked through the scope. Joel had made it to the treeline, and the Billy Blanks wannabe was almost over the gorge bank. Euchiss put the crosshairs on his back, center mass, and fired another round. That warm ache hummed in his balls again at the sound of the blast.

This one plugged Fisher in the upper left arm, blowing a chunk of meat all over his brother.

By the time he'd cycled the empty casing out and sighted on them again, the fag had pulled him out of the ravine and they were running into the trees. The pine trunks flickered across their fading bodies like a picket fence.

Euchiss snatched up his phone and typed a text.

Had accidnt on way 2 quarry. LT dead. Chasing 2 guys @ Red Hill on foot. Come get me. Take E acc road, bring gun. Ill B there in abt 45 min

The reply was immediate:

On my way.

Euchiss jumped up and shouldered the rifle, skirting the limestone and billygoating his way down a trail into the wash. The brambles plucked at his thin uniform pants, scratching his legs, and he ignored them. The scars on his back and across his thighs were evidence that his father had done worse than anything Mother Nature could inflict with thorns and claws.

Twenty-Seven

A HALF AN HOUR to six, Robin took Wayne into the cupola to have him open the way to the Darkhouse again. But before she could close the stairwell door, Leon put his hand against it, holding it open. "For the record, I want to vote against this."

"Vote against what?" Robin and Wayne sat on the stairs, and her camera was attached to her chest harness, ready to record her foray into the strange other-version of the house. "Opening this door?"

"That too, but I'm talking about attacking those women. I haven't seen any hard proof that they're..." Wayne could tell Leon hated even saying the word. "...Witches. Hell, even if they are, what's to say they aren't *good* witches?"

"There's no such thing as good witches, Mr. Parkin."

"What about your mother?"

Robin bit back any further words. She had a toothpick in her mouth in that Sly Stallone *takin' care of business* way, and as she let Leon's admonishment slide, the toothpick rolled around in her teeth.

"They paid my son's medical bills. Paid em off, every red cent. Even if they *were* bad people—and I haven't seen a bit of evidence to support that claim—I don't know if I can condone this." Leon gestured to Wayne, beckoning him down off the steps.

With a heavy heart, the boy stood next to his father, pushing his glasses up his nose. He tried to apologize to Robin with his eyes. *I'm sorry, lady. I got to do what my dad says.*

Leon rubbed his scruffy chin and folded his arms. "I'm sorry...but if you do this, you're gonna have to do it without me or Wayne."

She was crestfallen, but only briefly. her face hardened and she stared at the steps between her knees. "I understand." Getting up, Robin sidled past them and went downstairs.

Wayne traded a glance with his father, put his ring-necklace back on, and followed her. They found her in the living room with Heinrich and

Kenway. "Change of plans," she told them, standing in the doorway. "I'm going to dinner with Parkin and his son."

Heinrich put down the book he was reading. "What? Why?"

"Because I want to talk to Marilyn Cutty face to face. I used to consider her a grandmother, and I want to see the evil in her eyes before I go through with what I came here to do. And..." She took the toothpick out of her mouth and glanced at Leon. "Mr. Parkin has reservations about what we're planning on doing. He's not going to let me use Wayne's ring to traverse into the Lazenbury."

The old witch-hunter got up off the couch and came in close, talking in a low, venomous tone everybody could hear. "What Parkin thinks don't matter. They been killing children for years. You *know.* Andras showed you. That run-down park out there wunt no fun-joy-happy-happy place—it was a goddamn slaughterhouse. Those women are singlehandedly responsible for nearly every missing-persons poster and cold-case in the Blackfield Police Department. And when your mother tried to stop them, they killed her and put her soul into a fucking tree."

"You seem awfully ready to put boots on the ground when this morning you were ready to call the game on account of rain."

"I didn't think you were ready. In light of what you just said, I don't think you'll *ever* be."

"Parkin deserves to see proof before I enlist his son into being basically my secret weapon. I want to show him the dryad. They've been through a lot, and I owe them that much. They deserve to see the truth. And *I* deserve—"

"You're lettin them use him against you. You think Weaver bein out there in them woods was an accident? I wouldn't be surprised if she's the one that planted that snake out there for the boy to find in the first place." He threw a hand toward the window, toward the mission-house. "You know what this tells me? This tells me that they're *afraid* of you."

"Why on Earth would *they* be afraid of *me?*" Then something occurred to her, something so staggering that she actually recoiled. All her fervor faded. "You *know,* don't you?"

"Know what?"

Heinrich's question was still as angry as his speech, but he stepped away and went to the window to stare out at the early evening. Wayne thought he looked like he was running away from the interrogation.

"What happened to my mother after she summoned Andras," Robin said in a leading tone.

"I don't know what you're talking about."

"I told you what happened in the vision the demon gave me. She opened the house to possession and invoked Andras into it, but he caught her before she could escape. You know what happened down there, don't you?"

Heinrich said nothing, his hands clasped behind his back, turned away from them.

"What did the demon do to my mother?"

"I think you know already." The old man sighed, his shoulders rolling. Leather creaked as he did so, even though his jacket was wool. Robin's accusatory finger sank to her side and she stared at his back. Her face gradually twisted into a mixture of disgust, horror, and...relief? She went to the couch and sat down, staring at the TV as if it were on.

"I am completely lost," said Kenway.

Leon put his hands in his pockets. "You ain't the only one."

Clearing his throat, Heinrich spoke to the window. "'He is a great Marquis of Hell, appearing in the form of an angel with a head like a wood-owl. His office is to sow discord, and if the exorcist have not a care, he will slay both him and his fellows.'" He glanced over his shoulder.

"I know that much from what Robin told us." Kenway got up out of the recliner and stood next to Heinrich, staring at the side of the hunter's face, his arms folded, his eyes challenging.

Heinrich didn't return the glare. "What the Ars Goetia doesn't include is that in addition to being a cacodemon, Andras is known to some demonologists to also be an incubus. He doesn't always slay the exorcists tasked to remove him, or the individuals complicit in his invocation."

"What's an incubus?"

Robin was staring at her hands as if she were on a bad acid trip. "The demon took advantage of my mother." Realizing she had the GoPro attached to her chest, she turned it off. She drew her legs up under her, boots and all.

"I know at least this much, being a Literature teacher," said Leon.

Kenway rounded on him. "You know what?"

"A succubus is a female demon that ambushes sleeping men and has sex with them." Leon's face darkened and his chest heaved as if thinking about it winded him. "An incubus is a male demon that preys on women the same way."

Sympathy and dismay gave Kenway the expression of a man visiting someone in the cancer ward. "You mean that owl-headed monster *raped* Annie Martine?"

Heinrich finally met Kenway's eyes. "Yes."

"It must have happened when I was a baby," said Robin. "She's had that scarred-up tongue as long as I can remember." She turned to look at them. Tears stood in her eyes. "Now I know why my mama turned her back on—on magic, and went to religion the way she did."

"Yeah," said Heinrich. "When you were a baby."

She scowled at him, and a tear raced down one cheek. "Are *you* the one that gave her the Japanese invocation?"

His head bowed and he spoke to the windowsill. "Yes."

"Why?"

"Because I thought it would be the only way to finally destroy Cutty."

Taking out one of his coconut cigars, Heinrich studied it in the last light of the day. "*She's* the one that came to *me*, you know. I mean, when I found Cutty's coven here in Blackfield, your mother was the one I approached because she was the youngest, and I knew she would be the easiest to influence. —To turn against them.

"But back then, I didn't know about Edgar Weaver and his carnival. She came to me to tell me about them, to ask me for help making Edgar pay for killing those kids. She didn't want anything to do with the coven. That's when I knew I had the sacrifice I needed to complete the ritual." He sighed. "I had no idea the house itself would be possessed, and that she would get trapped in it with Andras. I only found out after the fact that he's an incubus."

Robin sneered. "And you call *me* impetuous. You almost got my mother killed."

Heinrich gave her a look that might have said, *still didn't stop that from happening, did it?* and stashed the cigar in his jacket pocket again.

After a contemplative pause, he looked at his watch.

"It's almost six. If you're goin to dinner, you'd best get going. You can chew me up when you get back."

Twenty-Eight

ASHE ARMSTRONG OPENED HIS eyes and rolled over onto his hands and knees, upchucking that morning's Grand Slam breakfast on the asphalt. The puke burned like magma in his stretched and abraded throat.

Blood dribbled on the puddle of vomit. He touched his hairline. Electric pain shot across his scalp and he snatched it away.

Dragging himself to his feet, he staggered across a highway that swung like a hammock and he examined his head in the wing mirror. His hair was sopping wet and his whole face was coated in streams of crimson—he looked like Sissy Spacek in *Carrie*.

As far as he could tell, the rifle bullet had skipped off the crown of his skull, cutting his scalp open and knocking him unconscious.

Dad always said I was hard-headed.

His eyeballs throbbed in dull agony. He climbed into his Frontier and tried to will the nausea away. Several minutes passed before he realized the windshield was shot out.

The truck full of kennels was now a roaring bonfire, black smoke rising in a column to the white sky. Cats yowled helplessly from their cages out in the grass, safe but abandoned. *Those poor babies. When I get back to town, I have to get Dave and Susan to come down here and pick them up.*

The cat.

He vaguely recalled a cat. *What the hell happened with the cat?* He remembered reaching into the cargo compartment of the overturned truck, and then nothing until a few minutes later, on his hands and knees in the mud, choking. He'd vomited then too, but it wasn't food, it was *hair*. A huge wad of hair that scratched his gullet coming out.

Ashe swallowed. Felt like strep throat, needles in his esophagus.

The hair had claws. He remembered holding a cat in his arms. Had he saved the cat from the fire? He couldn't be sure. It had been wet, he knew that much. Maybe it'd fallen in the river? He casually leaned over and vomited again, this time nothing coming up but sour bile. Tears ran down his face from the pain, cutting streaks in the blood. Did he have a concussion? He didn't think so, but it was possible.

God, he felt drunk. He grabbed a wad of Arby's napkins out of the door pocket and mopped at the blood on his face with trembling hands, scraping it out of his eyelids and the creases beside his nose, wiping his face in the sunvisor mirror as if he were removing makeup. Before he knew it, he was crying quietly, his shoulders shaking. *Lucky, so goddamn lucky,* he thought, wadding the napkins up and tossing them into the floorboard. If he made it out of here he was going to have to go skydiving or swimming with dolphins or ride a bull named Fu Manchu or something.

His cellphone lay on the floor mat. It must have fallen there when he was ramming the truck. Ashe brushed the bloody napkin out of the way and picked it up, fighting a wave of dizziness.

No signal. Shit.

He pushed it into his pocket and closed the door, his head tilting back in exhaustion. The Frontier slowly maneuvered into a series of barrel rolls and he sat up straight again, saliva pooling in his mouth.

The smoke roiling out from under the hood had stopped. *Might as well give it a try while I'm in here.*

He took the ignition in one bear-paw hand and twisted it. The engine gave a sick grunt and chugged a few times, but refused to turn over. He tried it again. Still nothing. He sat back and rested. Thought about puking again, but he didn't have anything left. He rolled down the window and spat, and in the side mirror he caught a glimpse of a vehicle coming down the road. Ashe squished himself down, his knees pressed against the dash, his balls at six o'clock on the steering wheel.

The driver drew even with the Frontier and slowed, rubbernecking at the crash. Whoever it was honked the horn, two quick Morse-code toots, and then put it in park and let the engine idle.

Ashe thought about getting out, asking for help, but something about it seemed wrong—why would they simply honk their horn and sit there instead of getting out to go look for survivors? His forehead throbbed and his skull felt like it'd been cracked down the middle like a walnut. Drowsiness crept in around the edges and he clenched his fists, trying to will himself awake. *Come on, man, keep it together.*

The slam of a car door. Someone walked around to the Frontier. Ashe kept his eyes closed, held his breath, and pretended to be dead, which was easy, as he already had the disguise down, with the gash running along the part in his bloody hair.

"Nice shootin, Tex," said a hoarse voice right next to the open window. The man coughed and got back into his vehicle, pulling away.

Ashe peered over the windowsill, catching a glimpse of a red pickup and what appeared to be an airbrush painting of a Valkyrie with big boobs, catching a giant snake by the tail. He watched through the arch of the steering wheel as the pickup dwindled down the lonely highway.

Grrrrowl, chugga-chugga-chug. He tried the key again. Grrrrowl, chugga-chugga-chug. He coughed, spat blood out the window, and turned up the radio. Lynyrd Skynyrd told him to be a simple kind of man.

Twenty-Nine

FOR A CHILD TO whom every experience under the sun is new, time is a long and stately thing, passing with a gargantuan battleship slowness. An hour in a doctor's waiting room, restlessly leafing through magazines and studying the walls, becomes a hobby in itself. Every school day is a lifetime.

Wayne thought the walk up the Lazenbury's chalky dirt driveway felt like a death march, like a convict's trip to the gallows. He carried a bottle of steak sauce in one hand and a bottle of Ranch dressing in the other. The iron sky roiled slowly like a dying snake, threatening rain. Thunder mumbled to itself somewhere in the east, disconsolate, testy, as if the storm had gotten lost on the way.

Robin walked alongside him, staring up at the sky. "I should've brought umbrellas."

The bottles felt like offerings. Something about the way his sneakers scuffed across the packed dirt made Wayne think of a western, of outlaws and high-noon duels. "Be on your best behavior," said his father. Leon carried the steaks in a glass casserole dish.

When am I not? Wayne wanted to ask, feeling vaguely offended. What he said was, "Are they going to turn us into frogs?"

"No." Robin had turned the GoPro back on, but instead of wearing it herself, she'd made Wayne the designated cameraman, and he wore it on his chest with the nylon harness. The camera's red eye burned like a cigarette cherry in the darkening daylight. "Witches don't do that," she said, "it's a fairytale. Love potions, flying on brooms, talking mirrors, that's all Disney stuff." Her lips twitched as if she were about to say more, but she didn't. He wondered what it was.

The hacienda seemed to grow as they approached it, beyond the aspects of perspective, as if it were swelling, lengthening, rising, and suddenly he realized how very *tall* it was, and how much of the property was bound by the adobe privacy wall. The facade towered over them at

276

three stories (*when had it become three?* he thought), and then another six or seven feet for the bell's arch.

Gothic wrought-iron spikes rimmed the top of the wall, and weeping willows on the other side of the wall obscured most of the front porch. "It looks so out of place this far north, doesn't it?" asked Leon. "Like a Mexican fort. Bigger than I thought it was. It's less of a house and more of...of a compound, I guess you could say."

They walked the rest of the way in silence. As they approached the house, Wayne spotted an expensive gas grill standing out on the patio, and flames licked inside, visible through a gap in the lid.

A heavy-set woman stepped outside to greet them. "Well, hello there!" Her olive skin contrasted richly against the starch-white of her festive peasant dress, which was trimmed in a sort of lace and edged in red and blue. Gold jewelry lay across her dark cleavage. "My name is Theresa," she said in a Louisiana drawl. "Theresa LaQuices. And you must be Mr. Parkin." *Mistah Paaaahkin.* "It's so nice to meet you."

"Likewise," said Leon. "This is my son, Wayne."

Theresa pressed a hand to her pendulous bosom, flashing a fistful of gaudy rings. "Oh, I know who *this* little gentleman is. Why, *I'm* the one that carried him from the fairgrounds out to the road where the ambulance could get to him. We are already well-acquainted, even though he don't rightly know it."

That's the one...? Wayne couldn't imagine being carried by this country-fried behemoth, but he could very easily see the strength in her thick arms. *She looks like a Mexican Paula Deen.* Her fists were small and clubby like dolls' hands, but her forearms were dark hamhocks, her shoulders sloping like mountainsides. She seemed implacable and constant, a fixture in the earth.

Gesturing toward Robin with the steak dish, Leon began, "And this is my new friend—"

"Oh, I'm well aware of who *this* young lady is." *Well awaya*, she was. "I didn't expect to see you here, I'll admit. Little Miss Martine. I ain't seen you in a dog's age. You ain't here to start no shenanigans today, is you?" Theresa put her fists on her considerable hips and peered from under her thick black Esmerelda eyebrows. "It won't come to nothin, mind you, but all the same I'd really rather not have to put up with it. This ain't nothin but a friendly Sunday dinner between neighbors."

Robin shook her head. "No. I'm just here to eat and talk to Marilyn. I feel like we've got too much history for me to bust in guns blazing."

"A dinner truce, eh?" The old woman squinted, assessing her, then turned and trundled across the driveway toward the house. "Be sure you keep it that way. I been puttin together a mighty nice repast, and I'd hate to see it ruined by a jackass."

Jack-ayass. Leon wheezed Muttley-like laughter.

Wayne marveled at how easily the old woman seemed to walk across the jagged gravel as if it wasn't even there. Theresa had on a pair of slippers like nothing more than dainty satin bags on her feet, and the stones she trod on seemed no more consequential than cotton batting. *Tough tootsies,* his Aunt Marcy would have said. *Sorry, kiddo,* she said in her Chicago accent, *No ice cream without dinnah. Tough tootsies.*

Crowding into the kitchen, Wayne was overcome by extravagance. Every surface, stone or steel, was polished to a high gleam. If he didn't know any better, he'd think he'd stepped into a showroom at a home improvement store.

His dad whistled, leaving the casserole dish on the counter. "Nice place you got here."

"Thank you much," said Theresa. She cracked the oven door open to check on something and closed it up again. She headed back outside to the grill with the steaks and opened it. Gray charcoal glowed subtly in the evening light. "Marilyn's in the garden if you want to visit while I knock the hooves off this beef."

Robin hesitated, taking Leon and Wayne aside. "You two drew your *algiz* like I told you to do, right?"

"Yep."

"Yeah," said Leon.

Theresa snorted, smirking as she laid the steaks over the coals with her bare hands. *Do what thou wilt,* she seemed to be thinking, *for all the good it's gonna do ya.*

The patio occupied the top of the driveway, a large area about the size of a basketball court that separated the back of the house from the two-car garage. The garage was a big adobe knot in the side of an adobe privacy wall like the one that ran around the front garden, but this one ran clear out to one side all the way to the treeline some eighty or ninety yards out. A tall wooden gate allowed them into the back garden. Inside the wall, they were greeted by rows and rows of trellis fences crawling with sickly ivy.

Grapes withered in clusters. "A vineyard," said Leon. "Man, I could go for some wine."

Marilyn Cutty and Karen Weaver sat at a table to the east, a large one with a white linen tablecloth thrown over it. Marilyn slouched down in a chair with one elbow on the table, nursing a glass of what looked like iced tea and staring out into the pinewoods.

As they came shushing across the close-cropped grass, Weaver stood. "Hi there!" Then she noticed Robin. "*Oooooh,* it's *you.* I told you to vamoose."

"I'm hard to vamoose."

Wild-haired Weaver had on a rather witchy petticoat that looked as if it were made out of a hundred silk scarves of as many dark colors, all tied together. It might have been ragged were it not so artfully arranged. She pushed up her sleeves. "Was the illusion not enough? I can conjure up some *real* flies, you know."

"Excuse me?" said Leon.

"I assume our self-proclaimed witch-hunter here has taken it upon herself to unload all her knowledge on you, including her ghastly internet videos."

"A man once said in one of my favorite books, 'First comes smiles, then come lies, then comes gunfire,'" said Robin. She put up her hands to demonstrate that they were empty. "For the sake of transparency and trust, I think it behooves all of us to skip the polite make-believe. I'm not here to fight. Just to talk."

"A palaver, eh? The hunter comes to parley?" Cutty folded her arms. "Yes. Well, the truth will out, I've always heard, so there's no reason to tell lies when we can keep it at smiles, and I think we could all do without the gunfire."

"I've been told what you are, yes," said Leon. "I'm still not sure I believe it one hundred percent, but I am informed. And after what happened Friday night and yesterday morning, I'm also not convinced that violence is necessary, so consider me the dove of peace in this here scenario, yeah? I really appreciate what Miss Weaver here did for us, and I'd like to avoid bloodshed."

Her hands still raised like Madam Mim, Weaver looked back and forth between them. "Truce, then?"

"Truce," said Cutty.

"Truce," said Robin. "For today."

"For today."

The witch in the ragged petticoat lowered her hands dejectedly. Wayne remembered to breathe.

"I guess I knew you were going to come eventually." Weaver sighed, shaking down her sleeves. The bracelets and beads around her wrists rattled. "I'd hoped you'd ha'been smart enough not to." The three of them took a seat at the table, and Weaver sat back down with what was probably a mojito, judging by the lime wedge.

Thunder mumbled again to the east. The evening was darker than it ought to be for six o'clock, although a hard blue luminescence lingered on the western horizon. Humid air made soft halos around the candle-flames, like lamps in London fog.

"I'm surprised you guys want to eat outside," Leon said, studying the sky. "Looks like rain."

"Nah," said Weaver.

"How do you know?" He fidgeted, a coy smile on his lips that betrayed the anxious look in his eye. "Did you see it in the knuckle bones, or tea leaves, or something?"

"Nope. The Channel Six Action News five-day forecast."

She smiled.

Thirty

AFTER A COUPLE HOURS of running on pine needles and rocks, Joel's feet felt like hamburger, but he had nothing on Fisher. His brother's shoulder looked like someone had taken a bite out of it, and blood ran down his elbow. His face had gone from a dark brown to a sort of charcoal-purple, and his lips were almost lipstick violet.

The stitched-up bullet gash in Joel's thigh hurt like hell—the Tylenol had definitely worn off by now—so he could only imagine how Fish was faring. He'd never been in so much pain in his life.

They emerged from the woods into a huge gravel clearing furrowed with dry ruts. To the far right was a small collection of unfinished buildings, all naked studs and skeleton roofs. Building supplies lay rotting in the elements. A low stone bluff lay on the other side of the gravel, topped with a crown of longleaf pine, and a cave some twenty feet tall led into the depths of the bluff.

At first, he wanted to hide in the unfinished building, but he realized it would only be a matter of time before Euchiss found them there. "Come on," he urged Fish, mincing across the gravel. "We'll hide in the cave."

The cave floor was smooth dirt, burning his feet with cold, but it was much better than pine needles and gravel. Anemic white sunlight filtered in through a dozen holes in the wall, revealing enormous rooms with flat, cracked ceilings. Graffiti spraypainted on the jagged stone declared long-dead relationships and cryptic utterances. BRAVERY IS NOT THE ABSENCE OF FEAR. ED BRIGHAM WAS HERE (AND SO WAS ARDY) 1976. FRODO LIVES!

"I dunno," said Fish.

Thunder broke outside, and a bullet whip-cracked against the lip of the cave, flicking chips of rock at him. Fish ducked and ran for the cover of the mine.

The main shaft drove straight into the heart of the mountain, side-tunnels branching off at constant intervals into side rooms. The air was thick and close, wet, musty. Moisture speckled Joel's face. It didn't take long to lose nearly all light, stranding them in a void of darkness traced only by the distant star of the cave opening behind them. He could cover it with one hand.

Euchiss stepped into the void's only sun, a tiny silhouette. He slipped a flashlight out of his patrol belt and turned it on, shadows capering at his feet. "I know you're in here," he called, his voice a flat, raspy echo. "There ain't no other end to this mine. You're trapped; might as well save us all a headache and give up now."

Go to Hell. Joel stepped out of the faint light into a side room and into abject and total darkness. Fish followed, clutching his shoulder.

"You go to the other side," Fish whispered.

"Why?"

"You get a rock or something. Hide in the dark. I'm gonna come out with my hands up and distract him. You come up behind him, hit him with the rock."

"That sounds like crap. That's a crap plan. He's going to shoot you."

"Do you have a better one?"

He didn't. Joel crossed the river of light again and into the dark, shuffling around, his hands fluttering across the floor. No rocks, but there was a metal bucket with a rope attached to the handle, a heavy coal bucket with a thick bottom. The rope was spongy and wet, but intact. He carried the bucket to the edge of the shadow and held it aloft like a flail. As he waited for the cop to get close, something occurred to him. *What if Euchiss happened to point the flashlight this way before he could spot Fish? What if he shot Fish on sight?*

His lungs itched. He needed to cough; every breath he took seemed more and more congested until he was shuddering. *What's wrong with the air in here? It's like suckin in sawdust.*

The flashlight came closer, the floor swimming with blue-white light, throwing stones and ripples into sharp relief. Euchiss's Oxfords scuffed across the hard-packed dirt. *Come on, come on.* Joel extended his arm back, bracing for action, getting ready to swing the bucket at the cop's face. Euchiss came around the corner into view, his Maglite a cone of hard white. He'd slung the rifle over his shoulder by a strap and drawn his own service Glock.

No! The flashlight was wobbling in Joel's direction! The circle of light swept back and forth, and brushed his toes.

"Hey," said Euchiss almost casually, and flashed him in the eyes. Joel flexed, started to step forward, but Fisher coughed. The beam of light swung in the other direction and revealed Fish standing in front of a long wooden table, his hands up, squinting. *"There* you—" Euchiss began to say, the pistol in his hand following the flashlight.

Joel lunged blind, swinging from the side with a right cross. The bucket cut an arc through the air and missed completely.

281

Euchiss flinched and snorted laughter, but Joel followed through, swinging the bucket around his head, and hit him on the second go-round. The bucket whipped the redheaded killer square in the face, burying him in a cloud of black soot.

The Glock flashed, *BANG!,* and the flashlight's beam danced across the ceiling. The bucket hit the floor and left Joel holding a rotten rope.

"Run!" shouted Fish.

He considered grabbing the light, but the pistol made him think twice. He ran after his brother's fading footsteps and they fled headlong into the silk shadows of the cave.

Thirty-One

DINNER WAS AMAZING. KENWAY'S trick with dry-aging the steaks had worked perfectly, and to her chagrin, Robin found the witches' side dishes more than adequate: potato salad with tender little chunks of boiled egg, dusted with paprika; garlic-buttered corn on the cob; bundles of asparagus spears, each wrapped in a piece of bacon and fried; French bread smeared with bruschetta; and to cut the savory, sweet-potato casserole topped with toasted marshmallows and crushed pecans.

They ate at the table in the garden, the lowering dusk kept at bay by citronella tiki-torches that smelled like grapefruit. It occurred to Robin that Kenway probably couldn't see them inside the garden because of the wall.

That felt like bad news, even though she was probably more capable of defending herself against the coven than he was. *I wonder if he's even observing. When I decided to go to dinner I didn't fill him in on an alternate plan.* She couldn't communicate with the earpieces like she'd planned. Hers was still in her pocket. *No doubt Heinrich is out there, though. Probably in a tree with a directional microphone, knowing him.* Her eyes scanned the dark forest, raking the pines for a glowing cigar-tip.

She missed Kenway, wanted him here, should have brought him in. Needed his warm Viking closeness.

It made her realize that he made her feel safe and normal, two things she hadn't experienced in a very long time. Him and his broad back and Thor hair and quietly dark demeanor, constantly coiled and coolly hungry, like a one-legged James Bond. He made her feel like someone stood beside her against the world for a change.

Maybe that's why I like him so much, she understood, watching the old women eat. Not that she was weak without him, but it was nice to be able to rely on someone other than yourself for a change.

"So you really *are* witches?" asked Wayne.

"We are, mon garçon," said Theresa.

"You don't *look* like witches."

Cutty smiled graciously. Robin knew enough about her to see under the mask and knew that it was an act. "Pray tell, young man—what is a witch *supposed* to look like?"

Wayne's eyes danced from his father to Robin, and then he murmured to Cutty, shrinking a little bit, "I don't know." A piece of bread touched his lips, clutched in his hands like a squirrel. He spoke into it bashfully. "Green? With all black clothes and a big floppy hat?"

"And a wart on my nose and a broom and a cauldron full of bubbling brew?"

He pushed his glasses up on his nose.

"Well, you can thank artistic license for that depiction. Pure fiction." She cut into her steak, talking as she did so. "...It's sort of like Santa Claus. You know what the real Santa Claus looks like, yes?"

"Santa Claus?" Wayne sat up, putting down the bread and pantomiming a beard. They had obviously strayed into something a ten-year-old could be enthusiastic about. "Yeah! He's all dressed up in red, with white bits around his wrists and the edge of his hat, and he's got rosy cheeks and a big red nose, and a big white beard. He carries a giant sack full of toys and rides in a sleigh pulled by reindeer."

Cutty forked the bite of steak into her mouth and waved this away as if to dispel it. "A fiction, concocted by a newspaper cartoonist and perpetuated by the Coca-Cola company to sell soda. The real man looked *much* different, and didn't live on the North Pole."

"Really?"

"Really. The name 'Santa Claus' comes from *Sinterklaas,* which is the Dutch name for Saint Nicholas, also known as the bishop Nikolaos of the ancient Greek city of Myra. People left their shoes out on the stoop at night, and Nikolaos would leave coins in them."

Leon paused, corn cob halfway to his mouth. "Santa Claus was a Greek priest?"

"Yes. He was a very generous man, and he was also one of the most powerful magicians and alchemists that ever lived. He was tall, with a long beard, and not thick about the middle or rosy-cheeked as pictures would make you think. Nicholas died in the year 343 and his remains were buried in Italy." Cutty swirled her tea, the ice clinking musically against the glass. She eyed Robin. "The point of my history lesson is, most things are not as others would have you believe. There is always a long story behind an old face."

"So witches aren't the only ones that can do magic?"

Weaver stifled a burp, speaking dismissively. "Heavens, no. Well, it depends on what you call 'magic'. ...We don't really like to call it 'magic', by the way. That's reserved for busking, card tricks, that kind of thing. Pulling rabbits out of hats."

"Witches are the most prominent users of paranormal energy these days," said Cutty. "Always have been, really. Men can do it as well, like Nikolaos of Myra, but it requires artificial means. They can't do it

284

naturally like we can. They require conduits, such as crystal balls, alchemy, staves. As a Christian, Nicholas used a shepherd's-crook…which is where candy canes came from, if you can believe that.

"Whole secret societies have risen and fallen over the centuries, seeking to channel the Gift. Thaumaturgy, which is the name we use for it, is threaded into our very being. Men—wizards, warlocks, magi, magicians, whatever they choose to call themselves, can only borrow this force. We are *filled* with it. Thanks be to the goddess of the afterlife, Ereshkigal, we *are* magic."

Robin smiled. "You make it sound so noble."

"Is it not?"

"Not when you bleed people dry of their lives with the nag shi. Drain them of their happiness, their spirit—"

Cutty held up a hand. Her fingers were slender and pale, young-looking. Robin realized that underneath the warm, diffuse glow of the citronella candles, the old woman's face was softer, less creased than it ought to be. *She's been partaking of the nag shi's fruit,* she thought. *She geared up for a tussle.*

Mom's heart-tree fruit. The witch said earnestly, "You promised you weren't going to bring us any drama, littlebird."

Littlebird.

That term of endearment brought back old, old memories. Robin's mind flickered with images of herself as a tiny child, sitting in the Lazenbury's kitchen, eating Chips Ahoy cookies and drinking apple juice, reading the comics out of the Sunday paper or watching *ReBoot, Pirates of Dark Water,* or *Darkwing Duck* on the wood-cabinet Magnavox.

Grandmother Marilyn had a dog back then, a miniature Pinscher named Penny, for the coins of copper fur over his eyes. She loved that dog almost as much as Mr. Nosy.

Littlebird. She cast a glance at Wayne. "I did."

"You're an honest soul," said Cutty. "I remember when you used to call me Grandmother. Hell, two days out of every week you'd be up here knocking on my kitchen door, crying about your mummy and daddy fighting about this or that. Do you remember that?"

"I do." And she did, vaguely. There was a mental image of the Lazenbury's back patio, and a sense-memory of knocking on the door. Cutty had a station wagon back then, gray, and she kept a tarp strapped over it to fend off the pollen. When she was little, Robin always wanted to open the car door and climb in under that tarp, the windows covered, and hide away from the world where no one could see her.

"Why didn't you get another dog when Penny died?"

Cutty stumbled. "Oh…well, I don't know. I suppose it just hurt too much to lose him. And besides, there was no little girl to come around and play with a dog anymore. Once you found makeup and boys and such, my little tomboy stopped visiting."

285

She cut a spear of asparagus into several bites. "I came to visit you in the hospital after...after your mother, you know."

Robin blinked. "You did?"

"Oh, yes. They wouldn't let me see you, though. The shrinks told me you weren't stable enough for visitors, especially none so close to you and your mother." Cutty punctured the asparagus with her fork and slipped it into her mouth. "They said it could possibly sabotage your progress."

"Maybe," said Robin. She pushed food around on her plate for half a minute. "I knew it was you back then." Her words were grim but gentle. "Your name was the last word on my mother's lips."

Leon and Wayne had stopped what they were doing and were sitting there with their forks and knives on their plates frozen mid-cut, watching expectantly.

Cutty chewed, staring at Robin without expression. "I wanted to bring you home with me, littlebird," she said, sighing. "I would have raised you as my own. There would have been no...whatever *this* is." Cutty made an inclusive gesture at Robin with her fork, as if pointing out her bad taste in shirts. "Blood feud, vengeance, vigilantism, I don't know."

"How?" Something burned deep in Robin's chest—not quite rage, but it was headed that way. "Lies? Keeping my mother from me?"

"Your mother is dead, love. There would have been nothing to hide."

"Because of you."

Karen Weaver cleared her throat, butting in. "Your mother murdered my husband. I couldn't stand there and—and—take that lying down," the witch said indignantly. "Edgar may have been a shit, but I loved him, you know."

"So you turned my mother into a tree?"

"Eye for an eye."

Cutty interjected, "Besides, we had to replace the nag shi Annie burned down." She shrugged and took a sip of her iced tea. "She brought it on herself, Robin. Annie thought she could punish her own coven and renounce her vows. Out of—out of disgust, I guess, she called it *sins*, transgressions against nature and decency, as if we had any choice. She thought of herself as a sort of whistleblower, thought she was better than us, better than her vows.

"In retrospect, she discovered she wasn't prepared to make the moral sacrifices required to live this life. It was darker, uglier than Annie expected. But that's not the way it works. Once you promise your heart to the Goddess, it's Hers for life, for good or for ill. It's like the Mafia, like Hotel California, once you're in, you don't get to leave. And you do what you can to stay alive."

"Killing innocent people?" Robin screwed up her face.

"You think rabbits are evil creatures? Flies? Mice? Where is your righteousness when the owl plucks the mouse from the fields? When the bear catches the fish in the river?" Cutty pointed at her with her fork again. "Subsistence. That's what it is. That's all it's ever been. You don't understand."

"You're predators, but you're not eagles. That's too noble. You're spiders, if anything. You're unnatural. You're rotten inside. You've been alive too long."

"Who are you to tell me when I should die? Where is your cloak, Death? Where is your scythe and hourglass?" Cutty bit her lips and looked at the table, and back up at Robin. "These are laws you haven't bothered to know anything about, littlebird. There is an old way, sacred traditions, that you ignore in your crusade to avenge your mother, who was not blameless. You haven't given any consideration to that, you murder and murder and you think it's okay because of what we are. And you videotape their anguish and put it on the internet, like it's some kind of goddamned circus!"

"Forty-six," said Weaver.

Robin and Cutty faced her. "What?"

"Forty-six. That's how many people you've killed." Her eyes wandered the table and her plate as if she were looking through them at her computer screen, and then rose to meet Robin's. "The commune in Oregon, the Sand Oracle's coven...."

Leon licked his lips. "I thought you said you'd only killed, like, twenty."

"I have," said Robin, feeling defensive. "Like nineteen. About that many. *Witches!*"

The situation was slipping out of control, if it ever had been to begin with. Again, Weaver was trying to turn the Parkins against her. Cutty was trying to talk her over to the dark side, so to speak, with her *littlebird* and pouty wistful woe-is-Granny faces.

Weaver's head shook slowly and she said, *"People.* Witches *and* familiars. Robin, dear, I've watched your videos. I told you I was subscribed to your YouTube channel. I've also been following you."

"What? Following me?"

"My specialty is the thaumaturgy of illusions and conjurations, remember?" Weaver reached out a hand and snapped her fingers, once, dramatically, *click!,* and the citronella torches turned from white to a deep oceanic blue. All of a sudden the grove looked like some kind of rave out of 1993.

Click! Back to white. "I'm the best there ever was, devil, you can't win *this* golden fiddle. And once you decide what people can see, you can decide what people *can't* see." Weaver pointed to herself, her smile a mixture of pride and idiocy. *"Me,* in case you were wondering."

"You think I'm a fool?" Cutty asked, her voice wry, her face disbelieving, one eye scrunched. Robin's heart had begun to pound in her chest. Leon had turned his knife around in his fist like he was getting ready to stab somebody. "I already told you I knew you were in Blackfield Psychiatric. What kind of an idiot would I be if I didn't keep tabs on you when Hammer came and took you back to Texas? If I'd known he was at the hospital the day you were released by the state, I would have killed him and took you myself. But you two were driving across the state line into Alabama by the time I got there."

I honestly hadn't even considered that, Robin thought. Back then she had been nothing but a confused, angry, small-minded girl with a prescription for anti-psychotics and anti-depression medication, psycho-analyzed half to death and more than ready for the wide-open skies of Texas after spending so much time in the stark, sterilized hallways of the psych ward.

All this time she'd considered Cutty's coven passive, oblivious, just sitting here in Blackfield unknowingly waiting to be killed...but it was now evident that she was still that angry, ignorant girl. She hadn't been the cat, she'd been the mouse the whole time. Running the maze, looking for the cheese, completely in the dark.

But Cutty put it even more aptly. "You were so focused on building the gallows you didn't realize it was your own neck in the noose," she said with a soft finality, her eyes sinking from Robin's face, across the tablecloth, and onto her own plate. She went back to eating quietly, gazing into her food.

"Dinner truce, y'all," said Leon. "Don't forget about that."

Robin's eyes were pinned to Cutty's face. "Why didn't you kill me? You had so many chances."

The witch ate as if she hadn't said anything.

Eventually Cutty said, "I thought of you as my grand-daughter, Robin Littlebird. That tiny girl that spent so much time in my big house, lying on the floor coloring with her stinky markers and playing with my dog...how could I stand to hurt you? I may be heartless, but not that way."

Theresa made a droll face. "You got more willpower than me. I'da done killed her. She's dangerous."

"Yes, well, *hyenas* have more willpower than you do, dear Reese."

The elephantine witch huffed and dug into her food with renewed enthusiasm, as if in spite. She ate her steak with her fingers, ripping it into pieces and pushing them into her gob like jerky.

"At any rate, I didn't consider the daughter responsible for the mother," continued Cutty. "I still don't. Annie did what she did and you had nothing to do with it. I saw no reason to go after you." Her lips pursed, the corners drawn into a frown, and her next words were made hoarse by emotion. "I *loved* you, Littlebird."

Pouring it on thick now, thought Robin. "That's why you let me go? You let me train to kill your kind, and you let me rampage across the countryside doing it, because you loved me?"

Cutty bit her lip, and then nodded.

Silence fell as the garden party ate and sat processing the conversation. After a while, Wayne told Theresa, "This orange stuff with the nuts is really good, ma'am."

"Thank you, mon garçon."

"You're welcome."

"That's sweet-potato casserole." She smirked, wiping her saucy hands on her napkin. Theresa's face was smeared with Heinz 57. "I'll give you a piece of advice: never trust a skinny cook."

"Yes, ma'am."

"You got such good manners. I like you. Y'all all right for colored folk."

Leon choked, pounded on his chest, took a drink of tea.

✪

"What is that spectral beast living in Annie's house?" Cutty asked out of the blue, when they had all finished eating and were dabbing their lips and sipping the last dregs of their tea. The crickets were in full swing, and the black forest breathed music all around them.

She asked it of all three of them, the witch-hunter and the Parkins, her eyes dancing between Robin and Leon. "What did Annie do? Is that thing—"

"A demon," answered Robin.

"A demon." The witch spoke with a disbelieving curiosity. "What kind of demon? Where did she get her hands on such a ritual?"

"A cacodemon named Andras. A Discordian and an incubus."

"I expect Heinrich Hammer provided her the necessary texts. A meddler, that one. Probably using her to get to us, since he's a *man,* and *men* have no power over the likes of us. I'll bet he got the ritual's material from the little…group that he used to be a part of."

"Group?" Robin's head bobbed back in bewilderment.

"He never told you? He was expelled from a secret society of magicians called the Order of the Dog Star. They're conceptual descendants of the Thelemic Society founded by that charlatan Aleister Crowley."

Leaning over her empty plate, Karen Weaver growled, "So *that's* why that bitch killed my husband? To summon a 'demon'?" Her fists were clenched against the white tablecloth, and had none of the palsied shaking that a woman her age would normally display. All the witches, really, moved like teenagers, which never failed to unsettle Robin. "No one's ever brought a Discordian into the real world. This reality was sanctified against them when the Christ's blood was spilled—that was the whole point of his sacrifice."

She sought validation in Cutty's stoic face. "Wasn't it? Or am I thinking of an episode of *Petticoat Junction* again?"

"You are right, for a change," said Cutty. "In the Old Testament days, demons walked this world with impunity. The only way to seal them outside of the material plane was with a carefully ritualized self-sacrifice."

I have to admit, that makes sense, Robin considered. You didn't see much mention (if any at all) of fully-materialized demons on Earth in the Bible after Jesus was crucified. "I want to know more about this Dog Star order, Marilyn."

Something soft wrapped itself around Robin's leg. She looked underneath the tablecloth and found a spotty gray cat rubbing himself against her ankle.

"Ask your friend about the Dog Star when you see him again." Cutty smiled. "I'm sure he'd be glad to tell you all about it. Besides, I'm afraid I don't know a lot about them myself, other than the fact that they hunt witches. They're quite elusive." Robin shooed the cat away and it popped up on the other side, climbing up onto the table next to Cutty, where it hunkered down and busied itself chewing on the witch's table scraps.

Cutty stroked the cat. "I'm sure they're where Hammer stole the Osdathregar that you've been killing witches with. I wouldn't be surprised if they've been looking for him."

The ominous stormfront had faded while they were eating, revealing a deep violet sky hidden behind shreds of blue-jean clouds. The sun was setting somewhere to the west, throwing a warmth on the heavens like a great bonfire at the edge of the world.

Kenway was probably worried about her, Robin decided, and she didn't want to be here any later at night than she could manage. Not that daylight made the witches any less dangerous, but she preferred it to the darkness. "Before I go," she said, finishing her drink, "I want to see my mother. I think I deserve it."

"I'm impressed," said Cutty.

"At what?"

"At how civil you're being." Marilyn Cutty narrowed her eyes. "I've watched some of your videos. There is a determination to you…this past couple of years has made you *ferocious,* for lack of a better word. Damn near feral. Is it the memories holding you back, littlebird?"

Robin wasn't sure. What she said was, "No." That hate was still back there somewhere, but in the intervening time between Then and Now, it had grown cold and smooth and dark, like polished obsidian.

The reply to that was wry and reflective. "You're such a bad liar. It's a good thing you got into killing witches and not professional poker." Cutty rose from her chair, unfolding herself. "Welp, come on. Who am I to begrudge a daughter a visit with her mother?" The cat leapt down and followed her as she walked toward the darkness at the edge of the torchlight, pulling up one of the torches as she went.

The last of the sun was enough to paint the vineyard in a muted haze of red and purple shadows. Robin followed the silhouette of the robed witch through the trellis rows and the citronella torch in her hand. Were it not for the sickly-sweet aroma of rotting grapes, the soft darkness would have made it hard to tell that the vineyard wasn't some labyrinth of *Shining* hedges.

Footsteps in the grass behind her. Theresa and the Parkins had joined them. The bayou witch walked like a man, her pudgy fists driving back and forth with each stride.

Leon was closest, walking in Robin's shadow. "You ain't leavin us alone."

This entire experience must have been a shock for the man and his son, even after the past couple of days. They'd showed up for a peaceful steak dinner and ended up in the middle of a slow-motion battle of will. Robin hated to see them embroiled in it, but it had been inevitable from the moment Parkin had signed the lease on the house, regardless of how careful she could have been to exclude them.

"I won't," she muttered to him. "Stick close, okay?"

His jaw was set in stone, his eyes a combination of fear and strength. She could see the man in him that had socked Kenway Griffin in the face.

291

Thirty-Two

THE CONSTANT FEAR OF stepping off into a vertical drop made Joel reluctant to run full speed. He was one-hundred-percent blind back here in the depths of the mine shaft, and had no idea what he was running toward. Fish, on the other hand, seemed to have no such reservations, and Joel could only track him by the sound of his sneakers clapping against the sooty stone ahead.

Behind them, Euchiss was swearing at the top of his lungs, cycling through a thesaurus of every curse and epithet he could come up with, and threatening every conceivable form of death and torture. *"I'm gonna rip your dick off and feed it to birds! You broke my goddamn nose!"*

Deeper and deeper they went, the air thickening to a warm soup. Joel didn't have any kind of cloth to cover his nose and mouth with, so he settled for breathing through his teeth and spitting every so often. After twenty minutes of running, he slowed to a jog. The cop's shouting had dwindled away, leaving them in a bone-chilling silence.

His mouth tasted like he'd been eating cheese and his jeans were wet where his stitches had come loose. "Wait up, Mr. Goodbody!" he pleaded with the invisible Fish.

"I ain't waitin up for shit. Come on."

"You need to slow down before you run off in a hole. I ain't carrying your carbless ass out of here with two broke legs."

"He's done shot me once, I ain't about to sit still and give him another try. This ain't Chuck E. Cheese, Joel, he ain't here to win tickets." He pronounced it *Johl* instead of *Jo-elle*, which he only did when he was pissed off. Joel figured it was his version of calling him by all three of his names. "Now how about you shut up before he hears us?"

"We ain't exactly church mice."

"Well, you ain't helpin!"

The tunnel extended on and on, some three or four hundred yards, he guessed, or maybe a quarter mile. Who knew?

His sight returned some ten or twenty minutes later and the darkness became a faint, dreamlike hint of gray rock as light bounced in from some distant nook. A colorless square loomed ahead of them, only a shade lighter than the black around it. Rough surfaces led them into a tunnel that ran perpendicular to the first one, and as Fish stepped into reflected daylight, Joel understood that they'd reached a branching path.

The right-hand shaft led toward the source of the sunlight. He came out into the intersection and squinted at a point of fierce white. Wind whispered and the sound of the cicadas drifted down to his ears.

Fish took off running and a gun thundered behind them. A bullet ricocheted off the cave wall in front of Joel with a flower of sparks.

"I see you down there!" shouted Euchiss.

The two brothers burst out into fresh air and found themselves in an enormous rock valley, occupied by a handful of dilapidated wooden structures—a tall coal elevator and several small cabins. Beyond the buildings was a pond full of orange water, milky and placid. From here, it resembled tomato soup.

To his surprised horror, Fish stopped and put up his hands. "The hell you doin?" Joel asked, rounding on him in shock. "We gonna—"

"You'd be smart to join in, buddy," said a man standing next to a red pickup truck, pointing a revolver at them. He wasn't *dressed* like Euchiss—he had on a pair of Wranglers, snakeskin boots, and a blue chambray shirt—but he had Euchiss's *head,* he had the man's beady eyes and Irish-red hair.

Exhausted confusion hit Joel so hard it was like a physical blow to the skull. "What…?"

"I'd like you to meet somebody," said a voice from the darkness behind them. Owen Euchiss came out of the cave with his rifle tucked under his arm like an English fox-hunter, pale cave-dirt smeared all over his black uniform shirt and trousers. His nose was a starburst of blood in the middle of his sooty face.

'Opie' Owen smiled, joining his Marlboro Man doppelgänger by the truck. "This is my brother Roy," said the cop, clapping his brother on the shoulder. He spat blood. "Say hi, Roy."

"Hi, Roy," said Roy.

Twins.

"This here's who you were talkin about when you were jabberin about the Serpent in the car earlier. I take it our dearly departed Lieutenant Bowker said something about him when he came out to your house yesterday."

Roy smiled.

"It's okay, people have been confusing us for each other since we were kids. It's nice to see you again, by the way, Pizza Man."

"You're Big Red?" Something inside of Joel crumbled. He wasn't sure if it was his heart, but it left him full of shards of disappointment and shocked anger.

293

"I should shoot you right now for breakin my nose." Owen lowered the rifle in a sharp, disengaging way and leaned it against the side of the snake truck. "But before we kill you, I want to show you something I think you're gonna find high-larious." He opened the snake-truck's camper shell and pulled out a steel pole as tall as himself, and then another, and screwed them together.

On the end of the two-piece pike was an L-shaped hook. "We use these to catch snakes," he said, putting on a pair of rubber gloves. He cut across behind his brother and sauntered toward the pond. "Come on."

Roy urged them along with his own rifle. "You try anything, I'll shoot your balls off and watch you bleed to death."

A boardwalk led from the base of one of the cabins and ran down the hill, becoming a narrow dock. Owen led them down it onto the rust-orange water, the polehook thumping along like a walking stick.

Monster-movie fog hovered around them, and the water was cloudy with some blotchy substance that resembled vomit. "Them women we work for, Cutty and them, they must think we're stupid or something. They like to be secret-squirrel about it, but we know they get up to weird shit. Devil-worshippin and black magic and whatnot." Owen spat blood in the water. "They do what they do and we do what we do, and they do it when we ain't there. That's fine with me: I don't want to see it. Roy here works for em part-time, so I don't go up there much. I'm okay with that."

At the end of the pier were two cinder blocks, and on top of them was a plank with two beer cans and a bottle. Somebody's shooting range. Owen turned the polehook over and dipped it into the water. "This little pond didn't always look like this," he said, lowering it hand by hand. "I understand it's here because the shaft flooded when the miners hit a big vein of iron-sulfite and pyrite back in... 66? 76?"

"65," said Roy.

"Thanks." Owen manipulated the pole like a gondolier. "Anyway, mines below the water table usually flood if you don't pump em out regular, but this baby is fed by a gee-oh-thermic source. That's a hot spring."

"I know what geothermic means," said Fisher.

Owen scowled, but continued. "From what I've been told, the iron sulfite dissolves in the water to create sulfuric acid. The county clerk calls it 'acid mine drainage'. That's why it smells like the devil's farts." He gestured around the pond, coughing once, softly. "As you've probably guessed by now, sulfuric acid makes this little spot a fantastic place to get rid of things. Everything you throw in here sort of drifts toward the shaft in the middle and disappears into the mines underneath, never to be seen again. It can't be dredged by divers because of the acid and the heat, and it can't be drained because of the spring. It's *perfect.*"

The water stank in a caustic, chalky way, burning Joel's eyes with the smell of rotten eggs.

"Still want me to whip you?" asked Roy.

Joel glared at him, pointing at the rifle. "If you'll let me stick that gun up your ass."

"Kinky." Roy laughed. "So how was that steak?"

"I've had better."

"Sorry, it must have been the carfentanyl I injected into it after I cooked it. How the hell did you get out of that garage? That roll-up was still locked when I got the door open. I didn't see a damn thing back there in the dark."

"Magic, bitch. I'm a witch too, you know?"

Roy's smirk was a suspicious one. Joel coughed, breathing through his mouth again. The rotten-egg sulphur smell was getting to be too much.

What came out of the water wasn't a cat kennel full of bones like Joel expected, but something that looked like a piece of tinsel. They stepped aside so Owen could lay the pole down on the dock and he picked up the metal with his glove.

"It's braces," he said, holding it up.

Roy nodded. "Neither of them two Witness boys last month had braces. Must have been the girl from Thursday. *Cough*, I don't remember her having dental work, though." He coughed again, into his sleeve. The fumes from the pond were irritating their lungs.

"Who gives a shit?" Owen tossed it back into the acid water.

Fisher's fists tightened, his biceps flexing. He was covered in sweat, and he was so pale from pain he'd gone the gray-purple of a California Raisin. "This is where you assholes were takin the cats?"

"Yup." The cop twin made an inclusive gesture, waving his gloved hand. He seemed to relish talking about the pond, like a proud fisherman demonstrating his secret spot. "We been dumping cats in here for ages. Shelter fills up four or five times a year. Only reason there were so many in there today was—*cough, cough*—we been up north with the girls all summer. I'd say there's probably a good two or three thousand dead cats down there."

Jesus Christ, thought Joel.

He fought the urge to kick one of them into the red-orange-brown water. *I wonder how fast it burns. I wonder if they'd scream.* "Why are you showin us this? Why the science lesson?"

"Because I want you to go down knowin ain't nobody ever gonna find you. Nobody will *ever* go lookin for two dumb niggers, especially not at the bottom of a eighty-foot sulphur spring." Owen smiled. His teeth were stained with blood. *"That's* for the treadmill."

"Man, let's do em and get out of here, I'm chokin to damn death," said Roy, slinging the rifle over his back and drawing his revolver.

"Sounds like a plan. My nose is killin me anyway. I got to get to the hospital or somethin." Owen stepped on each of his gloves, pulling them off, and pulled his Glock out of his service holster.

Joel's heart surged. "Wait—"

Pointing the pistol, Owen flicked the safety and shot Fisher in the head.

Gray and red billowed across the air in a fine spray and the whip-crack of the shot whispered through the trees. Breathless and surprised, Joel watched Fisher topple over (he would dream of this very moment, forever and ever amen, on the eternal DVR of his mind, backward, forward, and in slow-motion) and crash into the rust-colored water, flat on his back.

The two redheads turned away as the splash flecked their skin and clothes with acid-water. Joel squinted against the droplets, letting them dot his naked chest, arms, face.

The acid should have hurt, he assumed, but he couldn't feel anything because he'd gone numb from the inside out. His heart tumbled into the pit of his stomach; his legs gave way and he fell on his hands and knees, staring down at the shadow that had once been his brother.

Joel slumped forward, his forehead on his fists, his fists on the deck. All those times they'd fought, it would all now go unresolved. All those years they'd drifted apart, Joel taking care of their demented mother while Fisher steered clear of the blast radius, afraid and stricken at seeing her deteriorate, they'd never get to fix that.

It was gone, forever and ever.

Desolation shattered his thoughts into a million pieces. All he could do was stare bleakly. The wound in his leg burst its stitches as he'd knelt, but it was a thousand miles away. His lungs were squeezed empty and he couldn't fill them again, like the hand of God was around his chest. His eyes swam with dangling tears, turning the planks under his hands into a dark kaleidoscope.

"I figured I'd do him first, in front of you," Owen said, coughing politely. He spat into the water again. "That was for the bucket. Hah, comedians always get it worst."

"Cruel, brother." Roy pulled the revolver's hammer back and coughed. The grumble of an engine reverberated from somewhere far away, sounding for all the world like a bumblebee in a tin can. "Sometimes I think you've got a mean streak in you."

Joel turned his head and growled at the muzzle of the Magnum, as venomously as he could manage.

Roy smirked. "Little late for gettin pissy, don't you—"

A voice echoed from the cave at the top of the slope. Freddie Mercury howled, *"Who waaaants to liiiiive foreverrrrr?"*

"The hell is that?" asked Owen, looking up.

A pickup truck barreled out of the mine shaft, bearing down on them with one headlight. Ashe Armstrong stared through the Frontier's smashed windshield, blood streaming down his face.

Even as the truck swerved toward the pond and the boardwalk, Owen fired three shots from the Glock, *POP, POP-POP.* The first sank into the smashed quarter-panel, the second and third punching through the hood and knocking the rear window out.

Ashe slammed up onto the dock, his engine squealing, and drove toward them. The boards crackled and popped under the weight of two tons of metal, threatening to collapse, leaning forward.

Three things happened at once then:

1. Roy flung himself into the water,
2. Joel rolled over like a dog and lay flat on his back,
3. and Owen fired one last panicked shot into the Frontier's crooked grin, screaming *"Police—!"* as if that would work.

The Frontier slammed into Owen, the murderer's body clattering against the front like a bag of bowling balls, and its undercarriage roared over Joel's face with barely an inch of clearance. He rolled over onto his belly just in time to watch the truck drive off the end of the dock into the acid pond.

In a daze of adrenaline and fumes, he stood up and his eyes wandered giddily around the scene. The truck must have carried Owen away, because he wasn't anywhere in sight. Roy thrashed around in the red water to his right, screaming incoherently, his green shirt turning black. Joel stumbled down to where the home-made shooting range used to stand. The Frontier's ass end stuck up out of the water like the Titanic, air-bubbles gurgling out from under the body.

It was sinking. "Aaugh!" shouted Ashe, as he ripped the frames and broken glass out of the cab's rear window, wedging himself into the gap. "Jesus! *Jesus Christ!* What is up with this water?"

"It's sulphur acid."

The tailgate was a few feet away, and the bed only had a few inches of water in it toward the front. Joel stretched out and stepped on the bumper, one foot on the dock and one foot on the Georgia license plate. "Climb back here, man, come on, I'll get you out."

Ashe hauled himself through the back window and out, flopping like a newborn rhino into six inches of acid runoff. "Oh, ahh, shit," he hissed, scrambling onto his hands and knees.

Soupy water gushed through the gap between the bed and the frame, soaking his shirt and pants in foul rusty patches. Taking the vet's hands, Joel pulled backward with every bit of strength he could muster, and Ashe clambered up and over the tailgate, throwing his weight over onto the dock. He sat up and gave Joel a hand back across, and the two of them sat there coughing, watching the truck sink into the pond.

Queen's operatic howling slowly become a gargling chant until the radio shorted out with a crackle.

Ripping off his ruined shirt, Ashe threw it in. His back and belly were mottled with patches of pink, raw skin. "D'you think my insurance will cover acts of heroism?"

Joel went to his hands and knees again over the side of the dock, looking for his brother. "God, oh God," he wept, shuffling back and forth on his hands like a fearful dog, but Fisher had already submerged, fading away into the corrosive depths. "Where *is* he? I can't see my brother no more, Jesus, he's dead, fuckin *dead*, he's dead."

"Where is he?" asked Ashe. "Did he fall in?"

"They shot him. That son of a bitch shot him in the head. God help me, I saw his brains. He fell in and now he's gone."

CLACK! The entire wooden platform shuddered and shifted, one of the boards coming loose and falling in. Ashe helped Joel to his feet. "Let's get off this thing—*cough*—and away from this water before we end up in there too."

They hobbled up to the rocky shore and rested, coughing, trying to catch their breath.

The Serpent Roy Euchiss lay motionless at the edge of the water. Most of his hair had burned off, leaving him as straggly-bald as a baby, and his clothes were waterlogged tatters, everything stained vomit brown. He was covered in angry red welts and it looked like he was sweating droplets of blood, but what struck Joel, and startled him so badly, was that Roy's ears and nose and fingers had turned as gray and dry as ash.

Blisters were forming across the back of the man's neck and around his eye sockets, big pillowy blisters that were butter-yellow and translucent, like Dial soap.

The rotten dock finally collapsed, crashing into the water with a flat noise and a harsh clatter of nails and bits of wood. Concrete pylons jutted up from underneath it, as pitted as golf balls, and stained red.

"I need to get to a hospital," said Ashe.

Joel looked over at the veterinarian's blood-slimed face and the pink patches across his elbows and love-handles—which had begun to turn an angry red—and his pants, which were smoking and had become like threadbare linen, fine and screenlike.

His scalp was split in the middle, and Joel could see a glint of bone inside the gash. "Okay."

He climbed into the snake-truck and sat in the driver's seat and listened to his heart continue to break, feeling that, now, maybe, it was imperative to be worthwhile—to make something of himself, and he understood in his exhaustion and sorrow that up until now, he hadn't made much of an effort to do so. He thought about the sight of his brother toppling backward into the water and decided that perhaps it had finally come time to stop caring for a crazy old woman that was three years dead, and take care of himself.

The door opened; the door closed. Ashe sat sprawled on the passenger side, his head back and his mouth tilted open like a man already dead.

The keys were still in the ignition. Cranking it, Joel grabbed the windshield-wiper lever in a fist and wrenched it down, almost breaking it off. "Oh hell…this ain't my Velvet." He grabbed the gearshift jutting up out of the center console, then paused and swore again.

"I can't drive a stick."

"I think I might have a concussion," said Ashe. His voice thrummed at the lowest register, muttering from the back of his throat. "You better fake it, buddy."

Joel sighed, depressing the clutch and twisting the shifter into first. The Serpent's truck jerked forward.

Thirty-Three

THE HOLE IN THE clouds made it feel as if the vineyard were at the bottom of a vast dark canyon, and the trellis rows seemed to go on forever, dwindling to a vanishing point in the distance.

Deeper and deeper into the garden, Robin began to feel as though they had gradually stepped out of the world and penetrated a quiet savage unnamed wilderness where no civilized man had been in quite some time, if ever. Her imagination painted grotesque Lovecraftian coyotes lurking the trellises, tendril-eyed hounds that ate rotten grapes and anyone stupid enough to wander into their territories.

Territories, that's what it felt like. Robin expected to see a signpost at some point, with arrows directing her toward points unknown: WONDERLAND, 88 MILES. THIS WAY TO NARNIA. MID-WORLD, NEXT EXIT.

The phrase 'back forty' kept popping into her head. *Back forty. Back forty. Forty what? Miles? Leagues?*

She was about to ask Marilyn how far it was to the Tennessee border when the grapevines came to an abrupt end and they emerged into a neatly-mowed clearing.

Lavender made a sweet game of the evening air. Impeccable landscaping flung out skirts of purple wildflowers to either side, lorded over by several trees that drooped with dark fuchsia blossoms. Underneath the trees were pools of cotton shadow.

In the very center stood the tallest tree, an apple tree, *Malus domestica,* the reason for her being and the catalyst of her fate. Robin approached the nag shi, hugging herself against a damp breeze sweeping across from east to west.

The apple tree was tremendous, larger than any apple tree had a right to be, carrying a globe of green foliage as big as a house. The twisted trunk underneath was a stout and heavy ten or fifteen feet in diameter, stooped in burdened anguish. In the front of the tree, the bark had grown around a collection of knotholes and contour grains. What might have been the motionless shape of a face peered out at them, a pareidolia face like the Virgin Mary on a piece of toast, smeared sideways in a half-grimace half-smirk.

Robin put her hand on the dryad's rough bark. Warmth radiated from underneath, as if the wood were a door leading to a room full of fire.

"I told you I would be back one day, Mama."

She'd hoped there would be an echo of thought, a ripple of sentience like she'd received from the demon Andras, but there was only a warm apple tree.

"That's your mama?" asked Wayne.

She nodded. "She died when I was only a little older than you. Now she's resting in this tree."

"You put her there?" he asked Marilyn Cutty.

The witch only stood there silently, but then said, "Yes. For killing her coven-sister's husband, and for burning the previous tree."

He came up and put his hand on Annie's bark. A swell of emotion exploded in Robin's chest at the sight of it and she thought she would burst into tears. "She looks like she's in pain," he said, the citronella torch glinting off his glasses. Cutty's long-staffed tiki torch gave the scene a strangely cultist vibe. "That's a long time to be like this."

"Little different than prison," said Cutty. "If not better. She has no idea where she is, or what's happened to her. There's no thought, no regret, no spiritual agony."

Robin savored the dryad's maternal warmth. She leaned in on both hands and pressed her face to the trunk, rough against her cheek. She wanted to build a treehouse in its branches and live there always. She wondered if the plank swing was still hanging from the tree behind their old house...she would go get it and tie it up here, and swing on it every day.

Wayne pressed his face against the tree as well. "She loved you very much."

Her throat burned and tears spilled down her face, threatening to turn into sobs. "Yes she did. She loved everybody. Everybody that was good. And even some that were bad."

"Go home, littlebird," Cutty said quietly.

Turning, Robin looked over her shoulder. "What?"

"Go home," the witch repeated, "the Victorian across the street, Hammer's hidey-hole in Texas, I don't even care if you drive around in your van and do what you do, as long as it doesn't involve this coven." Her face softened, as did her tone, and she gazed up into the tree's branches. "Annie is mine and here she'll stay. This *town* is mine. Take my advice and forget about her, and Blackfield, and me. Leave. She is paying penance for her foolishness and there is nothing here for you but heartache. And if you persist, death."

The GoPro on Wayne's chest cast a red glow on Annie's bark, firelight through a keyhole. Robin straightened and stepped back from the dryad. "What if I said I—" she started to say, but then Marilyn Cutty's face twisted into the most frightening expression of rage she'd ever seen.

"*You bitch—!*" snarled the witch.

The spotty gray cat had followed them out here, and was sitting on Cutty's shoulder. Cutty reached up and snatched the animal down, holding it by the throat. "*You tricksy trollop whore!*" Taking the cat's neck in both hands, she wrenched it violently in opposite directions with a sickening celery-like *crunch.*

"Holy *shit,*" blurted Leon.

As if his brain had been unplugged, he bonelessly sank to his knees and fell over.

Foam spittle bubbled between his lips. He writhed and thrashed on the grass like an earthworm, his eyes rolled back and his fists curled tight by his ears. Wayne ran to his father's side and tangled his fists in the man's shirt, screaming in confused horror. *He didn't put an algiz on himself,* thought Robin, as Marilyn Cutty flung the dead cat into the flower bed and stormed away, hitching up her skirts. *That skeptical idiot—!*

"You," shouted Cutty, pointing at Theresa LaQuices as she left, "kill the girl and come to the house. Hammer is in the Lazenbury, and he's trying to kill Mother with the Osdathregar."

Theresa turned and grinned at Robin. Her gums were jet-black, and now too were her eyes.

Throwing Wayne off, Leon scrambled up and hurtled into the vineyard after his new master, loping and capering, using his hands as much as his feet. The boy shouted after him and started to follow, but the frothing darkness in the spaces between the trellises cowed him and he hesitated, glancing at Robin for guidance.

"My covvy-sister Karen is good at illusions, you know," said the cumbersome crone.

Theresa's breasts and thighs bulged and rolled under her peasant dress like a sack of potatoes as she paced around in front of Robin in a languid, confident way. "But do you know what *I'm* good at, girl?" Her head tilted as she said this, and at first it looked as if she were cracking her neck, but it was immediately obvious that the muscles around her throat were thickening, tightening.

"Alteration," she said, her voice going bell-deep and sonorous, threaded with pain. "Transfiguration." Her elbows rose as if she were about to dance the funky chicken, but then her shoulders broadened, and her hands began to enlarge, and she stumbled and fell on her hands and knees. "Transformation."

Bones crackled thickly inside Theresa as if her skeleton were rearranging itself. Her dress split up the back with a brittle *pop!* of white linen, revealing her shoulder blades and flabby, age-spotted flanks, and then her bra strap broke in half. Vertebrae surfaced from the flesh behind her head, widening, standing up, becoming spines.

The witch's head turned and bobbypins slipped out, her coal-black hair spilling free. Her jaw was lengthening, and she growled through a maniacal jackal grin. Her face was the pink, hairless bastard of a dozen beasts.

Robin ran.

"Go!" she bellowed, sprinting at Wayne, paralyzed in terror at the edge of the torch's light. "*RUN!*"

His eyes widened behind his torch-glared glasses, and he sprinted into the vineyard.

The darkness enclosed them, and silent heat lightning flickered across the clouds, affording her the occasional glimpse of the trellises blazing past. Wayne was running at full speed and she was pleasantly surprised to find that he was not the asthmatic nerd of a thousand after-school specials, regardless of the nerdy eyeglasses. That kid was *hauling ass.*

"Don't stop," she panted, clawing handfuls of air with each step. "She'll kill you when she's done with me."

"My dad. What?"

"Familiar. Witch put a cat in him."

"A cat?" He glanced over his shoulder, losing a bit of ground.

"Tell you if we get out. Focus!" She jabbed a finger at the night ahead like a Civil War general. "Don't slow down!"

The ground shook, the grapevines rustled, and Robin could hear a growing rumble—the three-note gallop of the William Tell Overture: *boom-boom-boom, boom-boom-boom.* Something big was chasing them. She ran backwards for a few steps, checking her six, but if there was anything back there in the dark, she couldn't see it.

Echoing from the vineyard to their left was a great noise of grinding and snuffling like an engine made of meat, and it was only after it had faded away that she understood it as beastly, inhuman laughter. Wayne shouted, "What is—" and the arbor trellises to Robin's left exploded in a fury of wood and wire as the thing that was Theresa LaQuices smashed through them.

Ivy whipped across the air and she smelled the sick syrup of mashed rotten grapes. Theresa kept going, crossing the row and crashing through the other side.

We're never going to outrun this monster, she thought, and poured on a little more speed, snagging the hood on the kid's shirt. He yelped at first and she said, "Hold up," and Wayne skidded in the wet grass, wheezing.

Robin pulled him through a gap between two of the vine lattices and shoved him down in the grass, lying down next to him. "We can't outrun it," she told him. His breath came over her face in waves, redolent of steak. "We'll hide—*pant*—and sneak out when—"

Boom-boom-boom, boom-boom, CRASH! The trellis some thirty yards to the south went down in a tangle.

Whatever the witch had transformed into trampled across the grape arbor until it was halfway to merlot and crossed several rows, smashing

303

sidelong through the vineyard. Apparently the coven didn't care about wine or grapes anymore, because she was giving it hell, tearing down fences left and right.

"YOU CAN'T HIIIIDE" roared the Theresa-beast, snorting a blast of air and aerosolized mucus. "I CAN SMELL YOUUU"

Lifting her head a bit, Robin peered up the row. The sky's last light traced blue sweat across the shoulders of some mammoth creature. Heat lightning whispered across the sky and she caught a flicker of pink, a glimpse of scimitars of bone jutting from the lips of a snot-slick muzzle. Theresa's black hair had become a mane of coarse wool bristles, and fat nipples jutted from a swinging bitch-dog belly.

It turned and scooped up air with the glistening nostrils of a boar. Theresa had become a giant amalgamation of boar and old woman, an abomination of varicose veins and stretched tattoos.

Striations of cottage cheese skin sagged down her naked ass like jagged granite. A picture of a crescent moon on her shoulder had been taffy-pulled into something like a yellow scythe-blade.

Robin swore and pushupped to her feet, pulling Wayne up with a pop of shirt-stitches and shoving him through a gap in the ivy into another row.

The three-beat gallop came at them and Theresa plowed up the trellis where they'd been hiding with her tusks. Her stony hooves pounded the grass flat in a thunderous jig. The witch-hunter and the boy zig-zagged across the vineyard, coursing down rows and cutting through gaps, wending and weaving back and forth.

Suddenly the trellises fell away and she found herself in an open space where a white gazebo waited in a grotto garden. Pergolas made a cage of the arbors, grapevines hanging from their rafters in sweet stinking curtains.

"Hide here," she gasped to Wayne, pointing him into the gazebo.

"Robin!" shouted a man's voice from the shadows.

She almost yelled in fright before she recognized the voice's owner. Leaping the gazebo's banister, she ducked through a scrim of ivy and found Kenway. "The hell are you doing here?" she growled. "Shut up before it hear—"

He grabbed her shoulders and brushed her sweaty mohawk out of her face, cupping her jaw in his big warm hands. "Heinrich went into their house looking for the fourth witch, but I heard you hollering out here, so I came to—"

"I don't *need* saving!" Robin growled. "You shouldn't be out here!"

The trellis next to them erupted in a chaos of leaves and wires and squealing hog-beast, throwing them both out from under the pergola. Robin hit the ground on her shoulders and skidded backwards through the grass, her feet pedalling the sky. She rocked forward to her hands and knees, and the heat-lightning flashed on an image buried in the foliage: a broad pink-brown face the size of a car.

Tiny black eyes glittered in leathery flab and darkness fell over them again.

"You want me?" Robin bellowed. Blood ran down her neck from a cut on her temple. *"Come get me!"*

"No!" shouted Kenway.

The admonishment came from somewhere to her left, on the other side of the gazebo. The razorback's enormous head swiveled in that direction, splintering one of the few posts still standing.

Inside Robin's jacket was a baby-food jar full of rubbing alcohol. She pulled it out and clutched it like a grenade. It wouldn't be much, but hopefully it would keep Theresa off of Kenway and Wayne long enough for her to figure out what to do.

"I'm over here!" She ran back into the vines and into the velvet night.

Thump-thump-thump,

Thump-thump-thump,

The beast plunged through the trellis behind her and Robin hightailed it down the vineyard row, back toward the north, toward Annie's sacred grove. Theresa was so close she could smell the boar's breath, feel the blasting breath pushing at her hair.

As she ran, Robin reached behind her back, underneath her jacket, and pulled out the road flare jammed into her jeans. (Dinner had been rather uncomfortable with what felt and looked like a stick of dynamite wedged into the crack of her ass, but she was nothing if not prepared.) She turned to throw the jar, but Theresa was already on her.

A fleshy nose as big as a watermelon slammed into her belly and scooped her up. The world plummeted and then Robin was upside-down some fifteen feet in the air, gazing at a dark maze. Grass flew up and the horizon wheeled over her head, and the breath was driven out of her lungs as she hit the ground on her back.

Jar and flare both were knocked out of her hands and she lay there, stunned, gasping for air. A callous moon laughed down at her through the curtains of the sky. *This is it,* she thought in broken fragments, *I've met my match.*

"I got you, baby," said Kenway, coming out of nowhere.

"Way," she grunted. *Go away! Not your fight, stupid! This is my battle, goddammit! This is what I was born and bred for, don't you see? This is what I'm here for, don't take this away from me!*

Theresa had pulled a U-turn somewhere out in the sticks and came back, bearing down on them, shouldering through the vineworks. Kenway snatched up the jar, wound up like a Major League pitcher (his fake leg kicked up, say it ain't so kipper), and fastballed it at the hog-witch's face.

Glass shattered across Theresa's snout, splashing her with alcohol. Robin smacked the end of the flare on the ground and it ignited with a flash, *SKSSSSSH!*, and a shower of red sparks.

She didn't have anything clever to say, so she just threw it. The flare bounced off Theresa's monstrous face and the alcohol went up in an arc of dim blue light, sweeping up the bridge of her nose and into her hairline. She shook her great face and tried to back away from the flames like a cat with a bag on its head.

Lifting her tusked snout to the sky, Theresa gave a trumpeting scream and galloped toward them.

Pop! Pop! Pop! Kenway had brought his pistol, he was firing at the flaming thing as it charged like a shrieking meat meteorite, *it's not working,* Robin thought, *nothing is working oh God,* and she crabbed away, still on her ass, but she couldn't get away in time. The meaty snout came down on top of her and drove her into the dirt, and now she was flattened against a seething-working mouth full of teeth, foul carrion breath washing over her.

Robin's hands pushed at snot-slimed lips. "Get off me!" she cried, punching the Theresa-thing's cheeks.

More gunshots. *Click click click.*

Wind gusted from nostrils big enough to jam her hands into, so she did. Reaching up Theresa's nose with both hands, Robin grabbed fistfuls of greasy hair and yanked it out by the roots.

"AAAAAWK" howled the witch, recoiling in pain. It moved back enough to relieve Robin and she took a deep breath.

Kenway grasped the rims of the boar's nostrils and pushed, throwing all of his weight like a man pushing a minecart up a hill, trying to keep it off of her, but Theresa was too strong. She shrugged, shaking her boar-head, and he slipped loose, falling over the hoop of a tusk and stumbling by the wayside.

Robin thrust out her hands as the beast dove at her again, opening its mouth, trying to bite her.

She managed to catch Theresa's nose, but her left hand skidded on mucus and slid into the boar's cold mouth. Theresa bit down and grinding-chopping incisors pierced Robin's forearm, tweezing the two ulna and radius bones together.

Pain unlike anything she'd ever known whipped through her system, ten thousand amps of agony along her elbow and up her arm, and she screamed in wordless horror. Hot blood squirted between those jagged yellow teeth as they rasped through the vessels in her wrist. Theresa let go, but only to gulp forward for higher purchase, biting down on Robin's upper arm, right below her shoulder.

She's eating me.

Tastebuds bubbled under Robin's fingers at the back of the witch's throat.

She's eating me. She's eating me. She's eating me.

Reaching toward the witch's beady black marble of an eye with her free right hand, she tried to claw at it, but it was too far away, three feet at least. She punched and punched and punched at the nose pressed against her chest, but it was like boxing a mattress.

"Let go a' her!" snarled Kenway, and then he was working Theresa's fat warty cheek with both fists like Rocky Balboa, *whump-whump, whump-whump.* It simply snorted and stepped back, dragging Robin helplessly through the grass. The joint of her shoulder was a knot of torture, but it was nothing compared to her bicep. Muscle shredded and a vessel ripped open, pumping into Theresa's mouth.

When the witch laughed, she misted Robin with her own blood.

The behemoth warthog tossed its flaming head, lifting her to her feet, and the humerus bone in her upper arm broke with a hollow, singular, drumstick *SNAP!* over the fulcrum of its teeth. There was no pain at this point; her system was amped to hell and back by adrenaline, just a dull sense of *cutting, dividing.*

Again the thing that had been Theresa raised its head, rooting her into the air by her arm, and the skin and muscle ripped apart in fleshy strands of red and yellow curds. Cartwheeling over two trellises, Robin landed upside-down in a third as if she were a fly in a web. The arbor collapsed and she sank to the ground in a net of wire and grapevines.

As soon as she settled, she reached out to pull herself back up, but she couldn't get a grip on the wire. The instant she managed to struggle to a sitting position, her head swimming, it became abundantly clear why she couldn't grab anything.

Her left arm was completely gone.

She stared in disbelief at the ragged stump of her shoulder. Blood trickled out of the pulped gore.

There were no words she could call to mind, looking at this lie of reality, so her mind was simply a whirlpool of abstract perceptions. The remains of her left arm were something out of a horror movie, like a rubber special-effects prosthetic, leaking red-dyed Karo syrup, but it was all too real.

The blood soaked her shirt. Her stomach heaved, on the brink of vomiting. Her face felt ice-cold. This was *real,* it was really happening.

Firelight flickered through the trellis in front of her, and the gigantic witch-hog stepped into view. Theresa's mouth hung open, and Robin could see her arm lying inside on a yellow-purple tongue. A dagger of bone protruded from the sloppy stump. The hog tossed its head several times, swallowing the arm inch by inch like a crocodile will swallow a fish, until one last gobbet of skin slipped through a gap in its teeth. Then it rumbled with surety and self-satisfaction, thumping toward her on stout, rippling legs.

Snot crept from the warthog's nostrils in cheesy black strands. A few alcohol flames still licked around her eye sockets and the crown of her sweaty black mane.

Dark pulsed at the edges of Robin's eyes, and she couldn't seem to catch her breath. Her body was as numb as a waxwork statue. She raised her right hand to fend off the encroaching monster, though of course she had no delusions that she could prevent another catastrophe.

307

This is it. I have officially messed up, Mom.

The behemoth overwhelmed her with bloody lips. Wind tugged at Robin's hair, whistling into those cavernous nostrils.

She reached out and grasped the rim of Theresa's snout as its mouth came open, revealing that bilious tongue and those disgusting teeth. Her own blood still stained the pebbled tastebuds, still dripped from the boar's upper lip.

The wind that tousled her mohawk hair wasn't coming from Theresa's nostrils—it came from nowhere and everywhere at once. Restless air churned around the two of them. Her right hand had fallen asleep somehow, still clutching the edge of the flabby pig-snout. Pins and needles swirled along her skin and deep inside, prickling up her arm in a helix of bright pain.

No—wait—this wasn't what it felt like, it was *something else,* something strange. Swamp-light radiated from her fingers, tracing green radiation along her wrist, following the veins along the back of her hand toward her elbow. The bones were visible inside as murky shadows.

Something was coming out of Theresa and coursing up Robin's right arm, some kind of essence.

Care Bear Stare, she thought drunkenly.

The boar's flanks quivered and the beast trembled, trying to pull away, but Robin's fingers held it fast. She was a live wire, grounding the witch, but instead of electricity flowing out of her, it was flowing *into* her, draining the Stygian source where the witch's heart used to be. She could feel something withering inside of Theresa, healing over, closing up.

The libbu-harrani, Theresa's heart-road to Ereshkigal.

The beast shook like a dog with a rope in its mouth, trying to break free, but Robin's right arm was an iron chain.

I'm sucking it out of her. I'm closing the door. She's diminishing.

The hulking Grendel-hog was not so hulking anymore, now only as big as a horse. Heavy sheets of collagen drooped from Theresa's sides and thighs like raw dough, and her brown areola dragged in the grass. She pulled and jerked, her cloven hooves shoveling humps of churned dirt, but to no avail.

I've lost too much blood.

Her fingers were locked, a perfectly relentless clamp. The pergolas behind the boar were on fire, orange flames licking at a night sky, but she could feel unconsciousness lurking behind her temples.

Whatever this is, I don't know how much longer I can keep it up.

An old woman knelt on her hands and knees between the witch-hunter's feet, as naked as the day is long, heaving and porcine and dark. She slavered like a winded horse. The tip of Robin's thumb was still up Theresa's nose, as she still had the witch's nostril pinched in her fingers.

"My God," breathed the witch, her voice muffled. It was probably an epithet she hadn't uttered in a very, very long time. "You're his daughter."

Robin bared her teeth with effort, on the brink of passing out, going deaf from blood loss.

"What—"

"You're the demon's daughter," said Theresa, and then Kenway was by her side. He pressed the muzzle of the pistol to the witch's skull and pulled the trigger, barking silent fire.

Robin slept.

we got to hurry

fifty cc, stat

come on come on

i need that hemostat

we're losing her

Thirty-Four

SHE OPENED HER EYES and found a hospital room. The windows were dark, but a soft fluorescent light above her head picked out the foot of the bed, a chair to her left, a flatscreen TV hanging from the ceiling.

Even though Robin felt like a mashed insect, the bed and duvet were astonishingly comfortable—other than the post-seizure snooze on Leon Parkin's bed, she couldn't remember the last time she'd slept on something that wasn't a couch or the floor of her van, and she'd forgotten how nice it was. The mattress felt like something she could sink into, warm and deep. Her legs were more or less pain-free except for a dull ache in her right knee, but she was sensitive, and the rough linen felt pleasurably like burlap.

Rain tappled restlessly on the window.

It told her the world outside was still going, it had moved on without her for the evening. From time to time, the wind would rake a gust of water against the glass, like a pearl necklace with a cut string.

A blond head was buried in a pair of folded arms, nestled into the duvet. She reached over and stroked his hair, and her abdomen howled in tormented chorus with the stump of her left arm.

Kenway sat up and took her hand. "You're awake."

"I'm awake."

"How do you feel?"

"You know how they say hot dogs are made out of ground-up lips, foreheads, and assholes?"

"Yeah?"

"I feel like a hot dog."

Kenway smiled in sympathy.

Robin sat back, her head flouncing into the pillow. The angry burn in her abs faded. "Take me out to the pasture and shoot me. I'm no good to you anymore. I'm glue." Her stomach gave a gnarly growl. "I'm also starving."

"I'll get you something." He stood up and dug in his pocket for change. "I'll have to get you something from the vending machine. It's too late for dinner. Is that okay?"

A lap tray on a floor-stand stood next to the bed, on the other side from Kenway, and there was a cafeteria tray on it, covered with a lid. She didn't have to open it to know that the food inside would be cold.

"Yeah. That's fine. What time is it?" She thought. "What *day* is it?"

"Monday night, about nine."

"I slept all Sunday night and all Monday?" She frowned and glanced at the ceiling. "Where's Wayne? Did he make it out okay?"

"He's fine. We put down that hog-monster and he called 911 for me while I carried you out to the road. The ambulance was taking forever so I drove you here myself."

"What about his dad?"

"I haven't seen him. Wayne came to the hospital with me last night. He hasn't been to school—he's afraid to go home. He couldn't sleep in these chairs, so he's in the waiting room down the hall."

"Leon will be fine. He's been familiared and there's no reason to kill him, so they'll let him stick around. We can un-familiar him with an *algiz.* "

"That's good. I've been worried about that. So has Wayne."

"What about Heinrich? Have you seen him?"

Kenway shook his head. "Not since he went into their hacienda."

She sighed. Whatever mess he'd gotten himself into, she decided he deserved it. "He messed everything up. This is *his* fault. If he hadn't gone in there like that, Marilyn would have let us walk out of there and I'd still—" Robin looked down at where her left arm had been, at a thick bandaging and gauze, and saw that there wasn't even a stump; everything was gone right up to the shoulder.

Peeling back the adhesive gauze and padding, she could just see it out of the corner of her eye: a swollen hump, bristling with hairy black stitches, stained with orange Betadine. A hot bomb of loss and dismay dropped into her chest and tears sprang to her eyes.

She pressed the padding back down, less out of a desire to protect it than to hide it.

"What happened?"

"The bone was too damaged," he told her. "Lots of splinters. They had to take everything up to the joint."

It couldn't be helped. She cried, big wet pitiful boo-hoo sobs, salt-water streaming down her face. Kenway came over and bent to kiss her forehead, which only broke her heart and made it worse, and squeezed her remaining hand.

"What am I going to do?" she asked. "What kind of a witch-hunter am I going to be with one hand?"

Kenway bit back a sad smile. "I do okay with one leg."

Shame burned her face.

312

"I don't know how I'm going to keep doing this with one hand. This is all I know. It's all I've ever done. I can't even open jars now."

"We'll figure something out." His smile became earnest and she reached up to feel his face, combing her slender fingers through his gingery beard. "I can be your camera-man," he said, his mustache brushing the pad of her thumb. "We'll figure out the rest as we go."

Giving her hand one last squeeze, he stepped away and left the room. Robin stared at the dark television. It was still raining. She listened to the rain clatter softly against the window-pane.

Her cellphone lay on the bedside table. She picked it up and logged into Facebook, and then YouTube, and finally her Gmail account. All three were full of posts, emails, and comments from strangers emotionally hooked into her video series:

"Where are you?"

"What's going on?"

"Are you okay?"

"You haven't posted any new videos. What's happening?"

"Did you kill the witches?"

It was true that she marketed and produced the video series as if it were a fictional affair: scripted, staged, cinematic. Where the public-facing front of her 'business' was concerned, it was common knowledge that the videos were fake. Seriously, witches that turn into monsters and people possessed by cats don't exist, right? (Right about now, she wished they didn't.)

But the people that watched her videos treated them as if they were real, they commented on each upload with words of encouragement and asked after her well-being, remarked on how attractive she was (even though she didn't believe that, not for a second), begged her for a chance to fight alongside her. Ex-military, male and female both, asked to join her personal crusade, sometimes dozens a week. Cops offered their protection on the downlow and insinuated that they'd turn a blind eye to the legal vagaries of her adventures. A national spectrum of neckbeards professed their love for her.

Searching the nooks and crannies of her mind, she couldn't think of anything to tell them. Seemed like all those four million or so people that'd followed her shenanigans thus far deserved a well-thought-out, optimistic, detailed answer, and right now she didn't know if she had one in her.

Besides, it was damn hard to type with one hand.

She tested the voice-to-text function on her phone, but the pain meds had slurred her speech and the results were less than satisfactory. "The rain in Spain falls mainly on the plain." *The brain in Spain follows mainly on the plane.* "The rain in Spain falls mainly on the plain." *The rain in Spain hauls manly only praying.*

"Come on, you asshole. I know how to speak English."

Come on your asshole, uno how do speakeasy?

313

Kenway came back a little while later with cheese crackers, candy bars, chips, M&Ms. It looked like he'd bought half the machine. She cried again at the sight of it all.

"Okay, okay," he said, piling red bags into her lap, "you can have the Cheez-Its."

Her sobs broke up into pained giggles.

Since it was October, there were several cable channels showing marathons of horror movies. They sat up for several hours, eating vending-machine snacks, drinking vending-machine coffee, and watching masked maniacs slay their way through half a thousand promiscuous teenagers.

At some point Robin slithered out of the bed and took a shower, but she had to do it with the lights off, going through her ablutions by the night-light over the sink. Every time she caught a glimpse of that stitch-haired vacancy on her left side, it was everything she could do not to burst into tears again. The effort it took to avoid this, and the constant pain and itching, felt as if it were slowly driving her mad.

Crawling back into bed, she fixated on the TV screen so she didn't have to see the expression of pity and sympathy almost gushing from Kenway's face. Every time she noticed his hurt puppy-dog look she wanted to throw Cheez-Its at him, throw the TV remote at him, anything to make him stop.

I asked for this, she thought.

I didn't ask for this, she thought.

She was still somewhat upset by his decision to jump into the fight in her defense last night. *You could have gotten killed.* She stared at his big dumb face. *If anyone's to be killed doing this, it's me. Not you. I'm the one that chose—no,* accepted *this life. Not you.* Kenway noticed her watching him and his face softened into a tired-eyed smile. Robin locked onto the TV screen again.

Don't feel sorry for me, she thought.

Please feel sorry for me, she thought.

The longer the movies droned on, the heavier her eyes got. She finally fell asleep again about the time dawn-light turned the windowshades blue.

314

TUESDAY

Thirty-Five

SHE WOKE UP AGAIN around lunchtime. Kenway showed up with a sampler platter of sushi and two blueberry parfaits from the hospital cafeteria, and revealed that he'd retrieved her camera and Macbook when he'd taken Wayne to school that morning.

"Did you tell him his dad would be okay?" she asked.

"Yeah. I don't know how we're going to get him back, though, without you and Heinrich. I don't know shit about witches."

"As soon as I'm back on my feet, I'm going up there myself to end this." She flexed her right hand. "Theresa told me something right before you put a bullet in her head. She said that Andras is my father."

"Is that how you made the transformation go away?"

"Yeah. Demons eat their magic, their…essence. I don't know how or why."

He talked with a mouthful of sushi, which he'd never really eaten before and had now developed a serious hankering for. For hospital sushi, it was pretty damn good. "When you and Heinrich were talking about demons, he said that they're deformed souls, adrift in the afterlife."

"Right. Ambulatory crystallized egos, deprived of physical form except in—"

Kenway's eyes were glazed.

She left off. "—Uhh, as you were saying."

He continued. "Maybe demons are like unborn babies, in that they need the sustenance of that energy from the afterlife to maintain their existence. When they devour a witch's magic, since it's one of those— what'd you call it, a 'heart-road'?—they're usin that heart-road as an umbilical cord back to that space-womb that they came from."

Robin blinked. "The *libbu-harrani*. The demons suckle on that source like plugging a lamp into a wall-outlet. …That makes perfect sense."

A proud grin spread across Kenway's face. "See? You need me. I'd be a perfect witch-hunting sidekick. I totally think outside the box." Robin's heart thumped once, hard, a sweet drumbeat. "So you think you're gonna

316

go back up there and do it again? Suck the magic out of them like you did Theresa?"

"If I can."

He stared at her, his eyes searching her face. "So what does this mean? You're half-demon?" She shrugged. It was a novel concept for her too. "I thought you said witches couldn't *have* children."

The nub of her left shoulder itched like ants were crawling around in it. She was about due for her pain meds again. She rubbed the padding gently as she spoke, careful not to pull the stitches. "I didn't think so."

"I wish Heinrich was here," he said, staring at the window. "We could ask him. Maybe he knows."

Robin scowled at the TV, clenching her remaining fist. "If Heinrich was here, I'd punch him in the goddamn nose for lying to me. And for ruining my life."

❂

After lunch, she transferred all the footage from the camera to her laptop, and spent the afternoon editing and uploading it, while watching more horror movies with Kenway. They made it through *Sleepaway Camp* (which lost a lot of its nostalgic effect with all the censoring) and *Day of the Dead* before Kenway got up and put on his jacket.

"I'm gonna go pick up Wayne from school and bring him up here," he said, jingling his keys.

She smiled. "Thank you for taking care of him. —Thank you for *everything*, really. You don't have to, but you are...and that's really good of you. You know? You don't even know these people. Hell, *I* barely do. I only know them because they're living in my old house."

Kenway tossed a shoulder. "What else am I going to do? Besides, I like doin things for people like this. I like having a purpose. Sitting around my apartment feeling sorry for myself and for Chris Hendry, painting depressin-ass pictures...what kind of life is that?"

Feeling sorry for myself. Robin nodded. "Yeah, okay. Well, be careful out there. It's been raining."

He saluted, letting himself out.

She sat in the bed, editing footage until her bladder felt as if it was about to burst. She'd been to the bathroom once that morning already, as soon as she got up, and twice last night—a laborious, pain-wracked trek on cold tile—but the coffee she'd had with lunch was going right through her.

Leaving the Macbook on the duvet, she swung her legs down onto the floor, slipped her feet into a pair of gift-shop slippers, and shuffled into the bathroom.

The itching in her shoulder was getting worse. She massaged the bandage, which wrapped around her boobs like a banding and held a thick wad of absorbent material against the surgery area. "Damn, I'm glad I can afford insurance," she told the cold desolate bathroom, releasing a stream of urine into the toilet.

She peeked between her thighs at the honey-colored water. *Getting dehydrated. Maybe I should pop down to the cafeteria and get something to drink.*

When she came out, a man sat in Kenway's chair, a handsome, clean-shaven fellow in a neat suit of rich navy-blue. Everything else about him was pale: his wolfish alabaster face, his sea-water eyes, his bone-blond hair. His angular stick-figure frame—along with the creepy black cane in his hand—made him look like a European fashion model.

"Hello," she said, surprised. "Can I help you?"

"You don't know me, but I know you." He spoke eloquently enough, with a hint of an accent she couldn't quite place. Robin regarded him warily. "My name is Anders Gendreau. We've been watching you, Ms. Martine. You're one of the most prolific witch-hunters that's ever operated in the United States."

"There are others?"

"Only my people. And Heinrich. I don't suppose Heinrich ever told you about the group he used to be a part of."

"No," she replied. "But Marilyn Cutty said something about it last night, right before she ordered her coven-mate to tear my arm off. Which, you know, wouldn't have fucking happened if you'd been there to help me. *Where the hell* have you guys *been* all this time?"

The corner of Gendreau's right eye twitched. "If you'll sit and listen, I'll explain everything."

"How about you explain my foot in your skinny ass?"

He cleared his throat, looking bemused. Robin sat on the bed in a huff.

"Heinrich Hammer, whose real name—or I should say, his previous legal name—is Henry Atterberry, was once a member of our organization, the Order of the Dog Star. We're a society of practicing magicians, and proudly count a great number of famous, influential, and affluent individuals among our members."

"She said as much," said Robin. "So, your basic secret world-governing cult, right? You're the Illuminati, aren't you?"

"Not so much. We're more like...the Avengers."

She snorted grimly.

"Too precious?" smirked Gendreau. "The U.N. of magic, then."

"A tribunal."

"Nothing so barbaric." He produced a folded piece of paper from his jacket pocket and handed it to her. She unfolded it and found a black-and-white sketch of the Osdathregar, in high resolution. "I'm here because you and he have something that belongs to us."

She'd been carrying the dagger for the better part of two years, but until she'd seen this flat, super-contrast rendition of it, she'd never noticed how very Nordic and austere the dagger was.

Hollywood had conditioned her to expect the eldritch and the ornate: a wavy flambergé silhouette with a pewter skull hilt, cord-wrapped handle, and a spike for a pommel, a Gil Hibben monstrosity from a catalog. But the real Osdathregar was a simple main-gauche with a gently tapering blade a little wider than a stiletto. The hilt was a sideways diamond, the handle was wrapped in leather, and the pommel was only a brass onion-bulb. The diamond of the hilt contained a small hollow, and engraved inside the hollow was a scribble that, according to Heinrich, meant "purifier" in the Avestan language.

Sitting here in this hospital bed, staring at this drawing, Robin felt as if she had drifted out of the shallow end of the pool and now a deep darkness had materialized underneath her.

"We've been trying to find his place in Texas for several years now, and searching for you for about a year, ever since you started posting videos of your exploits to YouTube." Gendreau's grin displayed the toothy canines of a meat-eating man. "You're a hard woman to track down, living on the road like that. We knew where you'd been, thanks to your videos, on about a week delay, but we never knew where you were heading."

The toothy grin faded. "But that's no matter now, is it? Here you sit in front of me, and here I sit, and this is the end of the line."

"How did you finally, *finally* find me?"

"Your videos indicated that you were in Blackfield. From there it was a simple matter of going to your childhood home in Slade township. But when I got there last night, you were being carried away." Gendreau sat back and leveled the black cane across his knees. "All that blood...I decided it wasn't in either of our best interests to interrupt your trip to the hospital."

"Why didn't you try to contact me through my YouTube channel? Or my Facebook? Or my Twitter?"

Gendreau glanced at the TV, sighed, and said to her, "We've emailed you several times, to no avail. I figured Heinrich had poisoned you against us."

The shaft of his cane was made out of a twisting dark shape that seemed organic, but not very wooden at all. The head was a pearl the approximate size of a billiard ball.

He smiled. "Admiring my cane?"

"It's...different."

"It's made out of the penis of an Indian bull." He raised it until it pointed straight up in the air, and Robin couldn't help but draw the obvious parallel. "Which makes it an apt magical conduit. The pearl contains a heartstone, a *libbu-harrani* drawn from the breast of a witch in Philadelphia, 1796. The pearl was formed around it, in the mouth of a giant clam."

319

Robin wondered if she could close Gendreau's heart-road if she touched the cane. She probably could. But in this state, the man would make short work of her if she tried.

She folded the paper and gave it back. "I assume you're here for the Osdathregar."

"Among other things."

"I don't have it."

"That much is obvious. I assume Heinrich has it, wherever he's hiding."

A pack of cheese crackers lay on the bedside table; she picked it up and tore it open with her teeth, taking out one of the crackers and gingerly breaking it in half.

"He's not hiding, as far as I know." She bit the half-cracker into a quarter, which satisfied a deep neurotic need for order she didn't know she'd been craving until she did it. Then she ate the third quarter. "He's still with the witches. He could be dead, for all I know, and good riddance. Lying bastard." It felt good to have new hate for someone inside of her, a freshly-stoked fire in her chest. The cold, desultory determination she'd felt for Marilyn had dwindled over the last five years to a dull ache.

But now she had a new face to want to punch. It was a driving, satisfying need that gave her an edge. "That's too bad." Gendreau stood the cane on the floor. "That means Marilyn Cutty's coven is now in possession of the Osdathregar. It may very well be beyond our grasp now."

"*You* can't go get it?"

The magician's sleek, vulpine smile reappeared, but this time it was tinged with regret. "Cutty is quite powerful, even by herself, nevermind the fact that she's got two coven-mates and a Matron. With the Osdathregar the danger would only be moderately lessened. Assaulting her property would be like attacking the White House with a salad fork."

"What if I told you I killed her middling coven-mate last night with my bare hands?"

"I'd call you a liar. Not only that, but a *damn* liar."

She corrected herself. "Well, with *this* hand." She held up her right fist. "As you can see, I seem to have misplaced my other one."

The magician wheezed a chuckle. "So you have. At any rate, beside the fact that you can only kill a witch by pinning her down with the Osdathregar and burning her to ashes, the youngest member of her coven has almost a century on you."

"Theresa LaQuices had transformed into a huge boar-monster and attacked me and the people I was with, and bit off my arm. Before I passed out, I grabbed the witch's nose like this," Robin said, and pinched the rim of her nostril, "and somehow I managed to draw the power out of her and close the *libbu-harrani* inside her. I didn't let go until she was back to normal again, and then my friend Kenway blew her brains out."

"Bullets don't work on them—" began Gendreau.

320

"This time it did." Robin bit the other cracker-half and chewed. "I think closing the heart-road turned her human again for a few min—"

She stared.

She had. She really *had* turned Theresa human again, there at the end, hadn't she? She'd closed the witch's heart-road and reverted her. *Holy shit.* "So that's how he…"

Gendreau openly boggled at her. "The ritual Heinrich gave to your mother all those years ago," he said, his words coming out in a breathless murmur, "your mother was…*taken* by Andras, wasn't she?"

"Yes." Robin's lips were numb with epiphany, and so was her hand. "And I'm the offspring of that encounter."

"The demon closed your mother's *libbu-harrani* and made her human again, and that's when he got her with child. *You're* that child. And you've got that, that…*way*, that talent of devouring their power, don't you?" The man shifted uneasily, his eyes wide and staring. "So *that's* why Heinrich gave the ritual to your mother. He wasn't trying to bring Andras into the material world, he knew he couldn't do that. By God, he was trying to bring *you* into it."

"He *engineered* my entire existence?" she demanded. "Why? Why would he do that?"

Anger flared in her chest. Absentmindedly, Robin reached up to rub at the padding over her stitches again, trying to quell the constant itching that had flowered there since last night. The pain underneath was monumental (especially here on the back-end of a dose of Percocet), but it was nothing compared to the phantom-limb itching.

"To buy his way back into the Order." Gendreau leaned forward. "We assumed that he was trying to replicate what got him drummed out of the Order to begin with: summoning a demon and using it against the witches." He cleared his throat politely, pointedly, *ahem.* "We have rules about trying to conjure demons, as you can imagine. Fully summoning a demon into the material plane for that specific purpose would be like wiping all of Europe off the face of the planet with nuclear bombs…just to get rid of Italy."

"But he figured out how to use a demon to craft a secret weapon that would make it through the barrier." Robin gave a shallow, petulant sigh. "Me. Annie was his Trojan horse, his drug mule, to get *me* into the material plane."

"Exactly. He knew the—"

"No." She glared at him. Robin knew what he was about to say, and she knew better. She knew *Heinrich* better. "He *hoped.* He didn't know for sure. My mother was his guinea pig. The demon could have just killed her, and he would have found someone else to manipulate."

Gendreau went quiet. He swallowed, smoothing his tie down his chest. As she watched him fidget (so unlike her first impression of him), she realized that he was anxious. Afraid of her?

"You are ... a cambion," he said, finally, with a grim, revelatory wonder.

"What's that?"

"It's a very old word for a being that's half human and half demon."

He cleared his throat and leaned forward, his head sinking and his eyes closing as if reaching back in time. Then he looked up at the ceiling, and at Robin. "Enfans des demons. 'Cambion' is a word, I hear, for the term 'changeling'; it was first published in the 1818 Dictionnaire Infernal, and stems from the Celtic root *kamb*, meaning 'crooked'."

Robin frowned. Crooked? As if she didn't have it bad enough this week. As if she weren't crooked enough already, with her candy-van and her YouTube channel.

She didn't think she would ever stop thinking of that word. 'Crooked'. Time passed while she stared at her duvet and Gendreau simply sat there, quietly, doing nothing but staring at her. She supposed he was allowing her to absorb and internalize what he'd told her. The academic, self-satisfied expression on his face—like some haughty tenured professor that's successfully gotten his idiot students to work through some moderately difficult equation—made her want to whop him in the chin.

She sighed. "So now what?"

"It appears that the ball is now in your court, cambion. Perhaps you can go after Cutty yourself, and retrieve the dagger."

She already knew she would be going back to the Lazenbury to rescue Leon Parkin, free her mother from the apple tree, and satisfy her curiosity as to whether Heinrich Hammer was still alive (and if so, make him pay for what he did to her).

But something told her that the Order's imperative against demons might extend to her.

"I meant with *you.*" She ate the last quarter of the cracker for no other reason than that she had grown tired of looking at it. "You said your people have a thing against summoning demons. I thought secret occultist societies were into that kind of thing.

"For that matter, why *do* you hunt witches, anyway? Aren't you guys like this?" she asked, twining her index and middle fingers together.

Gendreau shook his head. "The Order of the Dog Star has come a long way since Aleister Crowley's death. His Thelemic Society splintered into a dozen disparate factions, some following the path of White, some following the paths of Black and Red magic. The Dog Star is one of White and light."

"Ah." Something told her that his occult Justice League wasn't as virtuous as he made it out to be, but she didn't interrupt.

"It was once a dark collective called the Aster Argos after Crowley's Castle of the Silver Star, until my grandfather Francis Gendreau ascended to a leadership position in 1964. The Aster Argos became a White organization called the Order of the Dog Star and dedicated itself to the dissolution and eradication of fell magic."

Folding the cellophane over the rest of the cheese crackers, Robin put them back on the bedside table. "But what does that mean for me?" she asked, picking crumbs off the duvet and folding them up into the napkin from lunch.

"What does that mean for you as far as being part demon, you mean."

She nodded, not looking up.

Gendreau sighed. "I expect I'll need to consult with the others and see what they say." He studied her at length. "As for what *I* think...if it were entirely up to me, as soon as the Osdathregar is back in our hands, I would leave you alone and let you go back to what you were doing. You seem to be getting on pretty well to me. *Damn* well, honestly.

"In hindsight, I suspect it's because of your demon heritage. You've probably been sipping at their essences without knowing it these past two years, growing stronger with every kill, the demon side of you unconsciously nibbling at their heart-roads. It's probably why you're sitting up and cracking jokes two days after your arm was bitten off by a monster." The corner of his mouth rose in a half-smile. "Didn't that seem strange to you?"

After the last few days, it was hard to pick out what was the strangest, and sitting up watching cheesy horror movies on AMC the day after amputation surgery seemed like the least strange of all.

Robin stared at the Macbook sitting open in front of her, trying to process all this new information. She'd been keeping her mind busy with video-editing all afternoon, but now there was no way to block it out of her head. The pieces of the last two years—hell, her entire *life*—were coming together and creating a great jagged-edged puzzle picture.

So this is who I am, she thought.

That was a liberating revelation to be sure, to finally find her identity buried at the bottom of the toybox of life. She rubbed the padding on her shoulder again. It felt like she had ants under her skin, which did not bode well under these circumstances. She hoped Karen Weaver wasn't screwing with her in some long-distance bid to drive her out of town.

"I'll do my best to convince the Order to leave you alone," said Gendreau. "It may help to introduce you to them, and allow them to see how—*ahem*—relatively harmless you are. You're no rampaging monster, I can see that as plain as the nose on my face."

The sleek magician got up from the chair and went to the door. Before he pulled it open, he turned and tucked one hand behind his back. "When you're ready to go after Cutty, come get me. I'm staying at the Lake Craddock cabins down by the interstate." He smiled and hitched the cane into the air, catching it in the middle. "The little café at the top of the mountain has the *best* view."

Thirty-Six

AFTER GENDREAU LEFT, ROBIN put on a pair of sweatpants and went to the cafeteria for something to drink, wishing the hospital served whiskey. Sitting at a table in the back were Joel Ellis and a tall guy in scrubs, with bandages around his head. Joel was fully dressed in a sweater and jeans, though his skin was livid with tiny cuts and scrapes. The do-rag on his head matched his undershirt.

"Hey, man. What are you doing here?" she asked, sitting down at their table.

Joel and the tall man looked at each other as if conversing by eye contact. "What are *you* doing here—" he started to say, and then he sat up in shock. "What the hell happened to your arm?"

Robin glanced at the padding. "Oh this?"

"Yeah, *this*, hooker. Y'dadgum *arm* is gone." He got up and sat closer, on her left side.

She rubbed the cotton again. *If only my arm was still there so I could scratch the damn thing.* "Sounds like we've both got a story to tell." She took a deep drink of her soda to wet her whistle. "I guess I'll start, since you seem to be so up in arms about my...arm." She told him about going back into the Darkhouse and receiving the demon's vision, right on up to the doomed dinner party and the Hogwitch biting her arm off.

"Sweet baby Jesus," said Joel. "You're that thing's *daughter?*"

(crooked)

She nodded sadly. "Looks like it."

(crooked cambion)

The tall man pulled out a labeled sandwich baggie with yellow pills in it and swallowed one with his drink.

"Sorry." He belched. "I'm not high enough for this shit."

"This is Ashe," said Joel, "Ashe Armstrong. He's a veterinarian, he used to hang out with my brother." This introduction segued into *his* story about getting jumped at his house by Bowker, getting shot in the leg, the

324

truck crash, the cat fire, Fisher's execution, and the Queen ambush at the sulfite drainage pond in the quarry.

"I thought the cop guy gave me a concussion, but he actually cracked my skull, so I had to stay a couple nights for observation," said Ashe.

Robin's remaining hand clasped Joel's. "I'm so sorry about your brother." His eyes sank to their hands and he stared at their knuckles. When he'd given the moment a little room to settle, and he could talk without choking up, Joel told her about yesterday.

"The cops came to talk to us after we told the nurses how we got hurt...I guess the hospital called the law. I rode out to the Mushroom Mines with a couple officers to show em the cat truck and Bowker's body, and told them what happened up at the quarry. They're investigatin everything, I guess. We're not being charged with anything—nothin *yet*, anyway—but neither one of us can leave town until it's finished. They said something about dredging the pond, but with all that acid...I don't know if it's possible.

"Anyway, it turns out that Bowker and Euchiss were the only two cops on the take. None of the others knew anything about it." Joel took his hand back and studied it grimly. "They don't believe me when I told em who was behind it, though."

"Heh." Robin's mouth turned up in a dry smile. "Yeah, they do that."

Joel darkened. "They may come and talk to you."

"That's fine." She opened her styrofoam cup and crunched some ice. "So they said they'd been dumping stray cats in that drainage pond for years?"

"Euchiss said there was two or three thousand down there."

Robin studied the people around them—nurses, doctors, patients. She wondered how many of them were carrying around a secret cat. *God that sounds crazy as hell,* she thought, not for the first time. "They've been familiarizing the city. At two or three thousand, they've probably got their claws into a third of Blackfield's population."

A man in a white labcoat standing in line for hamburgers stared at her. Even from here, she could see his honey-colored eyes and the vertical slits of his pupils.

Maybe not so crazy after all.

"Familiarizing?" asked Joel. "What is that?"

"The witches can sacrifice cats to the goddess of the afterlife. As soon as the cat dies, its essence jumps into either the human that the witch was thinking of, or the closest alternative."

Ashe blinked. "Is that what happened to me?"

"I guess it was," said Joel. "Now I know what it's called." He showed Robin the *algiz* branded into his hip. "My mama burned these into me and my brother when we were little. That must have been what kept me and Fish from being taken over."

"Attack of the Body Snatchers," said Ashe. "That's *awesome.* I've always wanted to be in a pod-people movie."

325

He held up a hand for a high-five, but Joel only scowled at him.

"You gonna leave me hanging?"

"Hero, you need to ease up on them pills." Joel leaned an elbow on the table, supporting his head with a hand. He looked exhausted. "So what happened with Fish's cat? That crazy animal put her head in the garbage disposal and killed herself."

"That must have been Cutty." Robin stole one of his French fries. "She took over the cat and tried to familiarize one of you with it kamikaze-style. I've seen it before. It didn't work, though, because you had the *algiz* on you. I can't really speculate where it went after that, unless it jumped into Ashe here and didn't manifest until later, at the truck crash."

"There you are," said Kenway, sitting down at the table. Wayne Parkin was with him, wearing a bookbag.

The boy was downcast, staring down at the table and eating a granola bar in tiny, disconsolate bites. Robin reached over and squeezed his shoulder. "Don't worry, kiddo," she told him, staring into his eyes. "We are absolutely going to save your dad." Speaking to the whole table, she announced, "Tonight. I'm going to go up there and end this. Tonight."

Kenway frowned. "Are you sure you're up to that?"

Their eyes were all locked on her. *Ah, damn—they're all relying on me. They know I've got the hammer for this particular nail. This is* my *show now.*

A feeling of angry misery passed briefly over her *(thanks, Heinrich, you asshole)*, followed by a sensation of anxious responsibility. It was surprising to realize that she actually sort of liked it, liked this feeling of purpose, and of being held to a task. It shouldn't have been; she had grown accustomed to being relied on by the subscribers to her YouTube channel.

But this was different. These people, they were *real*, physical, close enough to touch, and they had real stakes in the game she was going up to bat in. Robin took a deep breath and sighed through her nose, feeling burdened.

"My Aunt Marcy calls me that," said Wayne, bringing out a sad-eyed smile.

"Calls you what? Kiddo?"

"Yeah."

Joel tapped the table as if he were putting down a poker hand. "I'm goin with you."

Cool resolve had materialized in his eyes, a steely effect Robin wouldn't have thought him capable of. Pride swelled in her chest. "They killed my brother. I'll be damned if I'm gonna let em get away with it without puttin in *my* two cents' worth."

"Of course, you know I'm goin too." Kenway folded his arms, his elbows on the table. "Bein your cameraman sidekick, and all."

The ball was really rolling now. Robin regarded them all with respect and anxiety and only hoped she could keep them all alive to the end. "I'm used to working alone," she said, giving them the Batman spiel. "I can't protect you all."

"We can protect ourselves." Joel's head bobbed from side to side in coy indignation, and his hoop earrings danced. "I think we've proven *that* to be true. *I* ain't afraid to smack a bitch with the phone. Ring-*ring!*"

✪

"You said you quit taking your schizophrenia medication over the weekend," Kenway said when they got back to the hospital room. "How long have you been taking that stuff? What did you say it was?"

"Abilify." Robin climbed into the bed and sat on the duvet. The TV was still on, and it was still turned to a horror movie, this one being *Psycho*. Anthony Perkins' black-and-white face filled the screen as they talked.

"What does it do?"

Wayne came in behind them and sat in the chair next to the bed, rummaging through his bookbag, which looked quite full. *Kids these days have a lot of homework*, Robin thought, watching him. He still seemed despondent, always watching the floor with a frown, and she couldn't help but feel for him. *He's still broken up over his dad. Man, I have got to pull through for this kid.*

"Umm…" She rubbed her face in thought. "It's a dopamine agonist."

Kenway shrugged in confusion. "Mickey Mouse-style, please."

"Okay: dopamine is the pleasure chemical. Your body releases it when you do pleasurable things, like cocaine, sex, when you get chills from listening to orchestral music. An agonist makes you more receptive. It's used to treat low-dopamine conditions."

"You really know a lot about this stuff," said Kenway.

Robin shrugged. "A couple of years living with taking them every day, you eventually learn a few things about them."

He paced back and forth between the bed and the TV. "Since we found out that you don't actually *have* schizophrenia—that the voices and hallucinations have been Andras trying to draw you here, back to your childhood home—then I imagine the Abilify's been, what, double-dipping your dopamine? If that's even possible?"

"I guess it has. Maybe? I don't know." She laughed. "I guess that makes me double-dopey, dude."

Kenway leaned his elbows on the footboard, putting his weight on one foot. He did that from time to time, presumably to give his prosthetic foot a rest. "So maybe it's what's been suppressing your demon side all this time. Maybe having a high load of dopamine in your system keeps a lid on that side of you."

Another tingle of itchiness. Robin rubbed the dressing again, wincing at the deep ache. "When you lost your leg—" She hesitated. "Did it itch all the damn time like this does?"

327

"Yeah," said Kenway, tugging at his jeans leg so that the prosthetic foot glistened in the sunbeam coming through the window. "It still does, sometimes. I can tell you a trick they taught me at the VA for dealing with that kind of thing if you want."

"Please. It's driving me nuts."

"What I do is, I take a hand-mirror and put it next to my foot so the reflection of my good foot overlaps my fake foot, so it looks like I still have two real feet. And then I scratch the real foot."

Robin angled her head so she could see her shoulder out of the corner of her eye. "Where would I put the mirror? Between my boobs?"

"Uhh. Good point."

Someone knocked at the door and a doctor let himself in, checking his watch. "Good afternoon, folks," he said amiably, taking note of Kenway and Wayne. Despite the authoritarian white labcoat and clipboard, the visitor's shock of dark hair and youthful face made Robin think of Doogie Howser, but his Australian accent was the strong and surprisingly sonorous tone of a much older man. She was glad to see that his eyes were normal and not the gimlet screwheads of a familiar. "I'm Dr. Kossmann. I'm just going to take a look at you right quick. How ya doin?" His very human eyes rose from the clipboard and widened, magnified by his glasses. "Wow, you're already up and moving around?"

"I come from hearty Irish stock," said Robin, closing her Macbook.

"I see. Your paperwork says you were...in a car accident?"

"Yep."

"Jesus." The doctor hung the clipboard on the end of the bed. "How fast were you driving?"

"Not fast enough, apparently."

He shot her a look of grim concern and glanced down at the scars running up her wrists. "It pains me to ask and I know you probably don't want to hear it, but...you're not having suicidal ideations, are you, ma'am?"

"Not these days." Robin sucked her upper lip, noticing him noticing the scars. "So sue me. I took it really hard when they discontinued Crystal Pepsi."

Dr. Kossmann shook his head and stuck his hands in his coat pockets, eyeing Kenway and Wayne. "You're going to have to take your gown off for me to examine you. Are you all right with your friends being in here for that?"

Wallowing around in his chair, Wayne faced the wall.

"I can turn around like this." He opened the textbook he'd been reading again, tossing his legs over the arm of the chair. "Is that okay?"

"That's fine," said Robin.

She met Kenway's eyes and he stood there obliviously for a second. "Oh, right." He turned to face the TV and watched an Arby's commercial.

While Robin shrugged out of her hospital gown, Dr. Kossman's brow went up in recognition as he glanced over his glasses at Wayne. "Ah!

328

I thought you looked familiar. I didn't expect to see you back so soon, Mr. Parkin. How's the leg? I trust you've been staying away from the snakes this weekend."

"It's a lot better," Wayne said over his shoulder, pushing his glasses up with his knuckles. "Thank you."

The doctor's eyes focused on Robin. "You aren't into country cures too, are you?" She wadded up the gown and tossed it onto the bed, sitting up straight and dangling her feet off the edge of the mattress.

Kossmann went to work peeling off the adhesive gauze and removing the dressing. Orange Betadine and dried brown blood made a pit in the center of the absorbent padding. "I swear, it's been one hell of a weekend," he was saying in that clipped, sporty Aussie brogue, "I'm starting to wonder if my medical license is becoming obsolete. First some lady brings in a kid with a snakebite that she's put a witch-doctor poultice on and he's walking around that night and even sneaking out of the hospital. I mean, really? And now I've got a girl that lost her arm in a high-speed car accident and she's up two days later joking about oh fuck me dead! *What the hell is that!*"

An iceberg dropped into the pit of Robin's stomach.

Even though her boyish breasts were still on stage, Wayne and Kenway immediately turned to look. Dr. Kossmann had completely removed the dressing, revealing the angry, gnarled flap of skin where the wound had been sealed over in a huge U of whiskery stitches and glinting steel staples.

A thin black tendril four or five inches long was tonguing its way out of the surgery scar, reaching out like a time-lapse video of a tree-sprout germinating from an acorn.

"Unnnh!" grunted Kenway. *"What the hell."*

The tendril writhed and explored like an earthworm seeking moisture, groping around Robin's armpit.

Wayne stared. "Woah."

On closer inspection, it was the red-black of raw liver, or a dry kidney bean. The worm-thing didn't stink—didn't even have a smell outside the fact that her armpit was right there—but the sight of it was enough to turn her stomach. Robin covered her eyes and faced away like a little girl getting a vaccine, but she could still feel it licking insidiously at her ribs and the swell of her left breast, the faint tickles of a ghost-finger.

She stared in terror at the insides of her eyelids, shaking. "What in the world *is* that? Why is it *inside* me?"

"Hell, I don't know!" Kossmann said, his voice breaking.

Panic set in and then she couldn't seem to get enough air, there wasn't enough oxygen in the room no matter how hard she gasped for it. "For the love of God, get it *out* of me. Get it out get it out get it *out.*"

Digging in his pocket, Dr. Kossmann took out a pair of purple nitrile gloves, wriggling his hands into them, *snap, snap.* He licked his lips in thought and his head darted this way and that, searching the room.

"Dammit," he said, patting himself down. "I don't have anything to grab it with."

"Just use your fingers!" cried Kenway.

"Yes, well, too right," said the doctor, and he put his left hand on Robin's ribs, gingerly taking hold of the tendril with his right in a sort of pen-grip, as if he were going to sign his name on the surgery scar. It snaked back and forth, curling around his finger, and he tucked his face into the pit of his own shoulder to gather himself.

"So help me God," the doctor said with a muffled cough, and he pulled the tendril.

A few months after she'd been released from Blackfield Psychiatric Hospital and she'd discovered her mother's savings account through the debit card that she'd found slipped into one of Annie's grimoires, Robin had purchased the CONLIN PLUMBING candy-van for nine hundred dollars.

After the van she'd had a little more than three grand left over, so to celebrate her newfound freedom (against Heinrich's better judgement, it must be said), she went to purchase the barbell piercing that was currently resting in a hole punched through her tongue. Pulling on that fresh tongue piercing was a bit like what Robin was experiencing right now as Dr. Kossmann tugged on the worm-thing sticking out of the amputation scar.

"Owwww!" she shouted into the quiet hospital room as tears flooded her eyes. *"Rrrrhhaaaah!"* Even under the Percocet, it hurt like it was stapled to her very heart.

The doctor let go and stepped back with his hands up in surrender. Robin uncovered her eyes. Kossmann was shaking like he'd been shot at. "Wait right here," he said, ripping off his gloves as he strode at the door (*at*, not *to*, he pretty much walked *at* the door in his haste to get out). "I'll be back in two shakes." He snatched the door open and stepped outside, pulling it shut.

On the other side, they heard him say, "Bugger me through a hula-hoop," as he left.

She slid out of the bed and crammed her feet into her combat boots, digging through the overnight bag Kenway had packed from the clothes in her van. "Come on," she said, forcing herself into a T-shirt and zipping the bag shut, picking it up. "We need to get out of here."

"What? Why?" asked Kenway.

"Because I don't know what this thing in my shoulder is, but I feel like they're not going to be able to get it out without really hurting me." Robin went to the door and pulled it open a crack, pressing one eye to the gap even though she didn't know who she expected, if anyone at all. Other than a few nurses bustling up and down the hall and a man sitting in a wheelchair at the end, there was no one on the wing.

She looked back at the man that had followed her this far and told him with her eyes that she needed him to go a little farther. "Also...I think it's got something to do with Andras, and I really don't want hhh— ...I don't want doctors messing around with it."

Good God. Skin crawled down her spine. She'd almost said "human doctors".

Kenway's face tumbled through concern and confusion, settling on grim acceptance. He put all of Wayne's stuff back in his bookbag and grabbed the baggie of pain meds off the nightstand.

"Okay," he said, shoving the pills into his pocket, "let's go, lady."

The nonchalant scurry down the hall and past the nurses' station was a lot less intense than Robin anticipated, though she couldn't have told you who she thought would show up to stop them. Riding four floors down in the elevator was an exercise in restraint, because the tendril was nosing around inside the sleeve of her T-shirt like a cat lost in a bedsheet. Looking at it made her want to throw up. Wayne happened to see it out of the corner of his eye and he sidled away against the wall, folding his arms.

"Did that really hurt as much as it sounded?" asked Kenway. "Is it attached to something?"

"I think so. It felt like it."

The elevator door clunked open and the three of them hustled through the lobby at a walking pace. "Ma'am?" said a woman sitting behind the help desk. She called again, a little more insistently this time. "Ma'am?" Robin pushed the front door open, feeling totally nonconformist and about as punk as you can get in the capitalist 21st century. She didn't check out or *anything*.

To her surprise, the sun made her sneeze, and with the Percocet in her system it jarred her like a blow to the head and she had to steady herself against one of the protective pylons in front of the crosswalk. As soon as she was sober, she took off running into the crowded parking lot, her combat boots clopping across the tarmac. It didn't help that the missing arm threw off her balance; she usually ran as much with her fists as with her feet, in a sort of driving, heavy-footed lope, so it felt as if she were running with one hand in her pants pocket.

She half-expected to see her candy-van, but Kenway's land yacht of a pickup was parked out there instead. The top of scrawny Wayne's head appeared from the labyrinth of cars, and then Kenway came jogging awkwardly along on his fake leg like a bicycle with square wheels. He unlocked the doors and the three of them piled in.

"Are we going to save my dad now?" asked Wayne.

Robin's heart plunged a bit at the excited hope in his voice. "Not yet, kiddo. I gotta see a man about something first."

He bit back a frown. "Where we going?"

"To the cabins up by Lake Craddock," Robin said, pulling on her seatbelt. The gruesome worm-thing sticking out of her stitches was seven or eight inches now, long enough to curl lasciviously around the vinyl strap. She craned her neck, trying to get her face as far away from it as

331

possible. "I know somebody that can help us save your dad...and who might know what the hell *this* thing is."

Thirty-Seven

THE OLD BLUE CHEVY coursed down the highway into the hills north of Blackfield, passing through the township of Slade, or at least the primordial wilderness people referred to by that name. Other than the turnoff for Underwood Road (which gave her a shiver as it whipped past the truck) and a few other roads, there was little else out this way for almost ten miles besides a large brick garage with three rollups and aluminum letters across the eaves: SLADE VOLUNTEER FIRE DEPARTMENT.

On the way out of town, she'd noticed attentive men and women standing stockstill in parking lots, like scarecrows over fields of steel and paint, turning to watch them pass with glittering feline eyes of jade and venomous honey. Meerkat strangers frozen in storefront windows and gas stations with pump nozzles and shopping bags in their hands.

Cutty was watching them through Blackfield's eyes. Robin didn't say anything; she didn't want to upset Wayne any more than he already was.

Soon they came around a wide curve and down a hill into a little valley with a neatly-mowed rest stop and a visitors' center, presided over by a stately four-lane freeway running west to east. Traffic shushed overhead at breakneck speeds as Kenway slipped underneath the overpass.

On the other side was a tiny hamlet consisting of a dark-eyed Texaco gas station that had seen better decades, a log cabin hiding in the treeline, and a Kangaroo convenience store, lit up like an airport. Tucked back a few hundred yards behind that was a clean, oddly mediterranean Subway sandwich shop that seemed embarrassed by its own cozy grandeur in the middle of all this hillbilly austerity. On a better day, Robin would have wanted to swing by and grab a sandwich, but they'd left her appetite back at the hospital.

A paved two-lane climbed a slope choked with pine trees, skirting a log cabin with LAKE CRADDOCK tool-burned into a wooden sign over the road. Kenway crossed the access road, rumbling up the hill.

A sign next to the cabin announced it as the rental office-slash-tackle shop. They didn't bother stopping, heading deeper into the pines.

The road eventually hooked to the right and followed a ledge along the south side of the mountain, rising higher and higher until Robin began to see the distant buildings of Blackfield as specks of gray and light twinkling in a bear-fur landscape of dead trees. Gravel driveways tunneled away from the burro-trail now and again, leading to quaint little hunter-lodges. The road bent back on itself at the edge of a several-hundred-foot drop and continued to climb until the trees thinned out and the road became a parking lot. At the other side of six rows of empty slots was a sprawling Brady Bunch split-level with splintery gray walls.

A sign out front called it TOP O' THE MOUNTAIN CAFÉ & RESTAURANT. Kenway parked at the sidewalk and they marched up the hill toward the restaurant, climbing three flights of cross-tie steps in a broad zig-zag.

At the top he paused and leaned against the aluminum handrail, sucking in a great big breath of air that had rolled in off the lake and brushed up the mountain. To the north, the mountain crumbled away into a treeless granite headland, revealing a sparkling seagull-gray lake and a distant horizon of naked trees. In this dim white end-of-the-world sun, she saw a much older man hiding behind that long blond surfer-hair and copper beard. His neck had an almost reptilian texture, leathered by a desert sun in a savage world thousands of miles away from here, and his forehead was creased with lines.

His eyes were closed, and in any other circumstance, Robin supposed his grim face would have been serene. The wind teased his cottony scruff. "When this is over," she told him quietly, "we'll get a boat and go out there for a while."

"That sounds nice."

Wayne pulled the front door open and let them in.

The Top O' The Mountain Café and Restaurant was quiet for lunchtime. Deathly quiet, in fact, and there wasn't an employee in sight. This made sense, it being a Tuesday in the off-season. The three of them slipped through a shadowy foyer, passing racks of tourism pamphlets and a cash register, down a short corridor past restroom and kitchen doors, and into a cavernous great-hall. To the right was an open dining area with a dozen white-draped tables, chairs neatly turned on top of them.

The walls were floor-to-ceiling plate windows, affording a beautiful view of a dismal October lake to the north and miles of woodland to the south, the white sky hemmed by the jagged jawline of Blackfield.

Tucked into a dark recess to their left was a rustic bar. Anders Gendreau leaned behind it like an old-timey soda jerk dressed way above his station, peering at them from underneath a rack of glass goblets. "It's about time you got here, cambion," he said, tossing a bar towel over his shoulder. Against the dark blue suit, it almost resembled a sort of holy vestment. "I can only drink so much gin before I'm useless."

He poured Robin and Kenway each a finger of bourbon, then poured Wayne something that looked like gin or vodka out of a bottle with an orange on the label.

She frowned. *Cambion. Crooked.* "Please don't call me that."

The magician nodded deferentially.

Wayne sniffed the drink, sipped it, and coughed. "Man. I don't know how my dad goes crazy for this stuff. Tastes like straight gasoline."

Gendreau smirked. "Don't worry, little man. One day you'll develop a taste for the finer things." He looked over his shoulder at the choir of multicolored bottles. Against the mirrored back wall, the collection seemed infinite, and on the other side their doppelgängers stared back with haunted eyes. "You won't find any of those finer things here at the Hayseed Café," he chuckled, "but you mark my words. Every good man knows the virtue of a smooth libation."

"I'll take your word for it, mister."

"So what are we doing here?" asked Kenway, wincing appreciatively at the taste of the liquor.

"This is Anders Gendreau," said Robin. "He's from an organization called the Order of the Dog Star. Anders, these are my friends Kenway Griffin and Wayne Parkin." She indicated them with the bourbon glass as she introduced them. "Wayne is the owner of the ring that opened a way into where the demon's trapped."

"Aaaaa*aaaa*ah." Gendreau held out a hand. Wayne shook it. "Pleased to make your acquaintance. I bet it would enchant you to know that we are magicians."

"Magicians. Of course there are magicians." Sitting on a stool, Kenway poured himself another finger of bourbon and threw it back. "Witches, demons, giant pig-monsters, and rings that open doors to Hell—why didn't I think there would be magicians?"

"I have an issue, Anders," said Robin.

By now the Percocet was wearing off again and the pain had returned in earnest...but there were three distinct sources of agony now: the papercut screaming of the stitched-and-stapled scar itself, a deep, knotty kinking that she supposed must have been the muscles or ligaments that were once attached to her tricep, and then there was an ache in her rib reminiscent of the side-stitches you get when you're running.

She grabbed the left hem of her shirt and hiked it over her shoulder. This revealed her left breast, but at this point she didn't care. It also uncovered the writhing foot-long earthworm-thing hanging out of the nadir of the U-shaped surgery scar.

Gendreau flinched. "*What* the dickens!"

"*You* don't know what it is?"

"Dear *shit!* No, I do not," said the magician, leaning over the bar to get a closer look, a disgusted grimace spreading across his pale vulpine face.

The bloodworm, as Robin had come to think of it, had grown longer on the way over here (or perhaps more of it had emerged, and perhaps there was a whole *coil* of the thing inside the cage of her chest, and that horrible thought made Robin want to pitch herself through the closest window) but it seemed to have calmed, and now dangled from the stitches, the end twitching every so often in the come-hither motion of a cat's tail.

Coming around the end of the bar, Gendreau came out and walked past, his bull-dick cane thumping insistently on the carpet. "C'mere into the light and let me take a look at it."

She followed him over to the massive south window and her entourage joined them. The wan sunlight picked out a blue vein wandering across the cream-white dome of her left breast, and her skin prickled at the visual of that repulsive subtle tendril sliding through the warrens of her arteries. This thought made the areola of the nipple on that side pucker up, but something about the magician's effete mannerisms told her that she might as well be a goose.

"I feel as though I should know," said Gendreau, hitching up his cane in that jaunty way again. "It seems supernatural in nature."

"You think?"

His glacial eyes flashed up at her in faint indignation and narrowed on the tendril again. This close to his face, she noticed how intense they were: gasflames in porcelain. The magician reached for it, hesitated, then drew up his courage and took the worm in his bare hand. It curled warmly, twining around his knuckles. His fingernails were clipped to a microscopic uniformity and reflected the windowlight as if carved from soapstone.

"It hurt me when the doctor pulled on it," she told him. "I think it's connected to something." She swallowed terror and added, "Something inside."

A peculiar heat radiated from Gendreau's hands, as if her hip was too close to a stovetop, and she angled her head to see that it was the pearly head of his cane. He held the simmering orb close to the tendril, and let his eyes slip closed.

"What are you doing?"

"Testing it," he murmured.

Did he say *tasting* it? She couldn't be sure. The heat emanating from his cane flared brightly for a brief moment, and then faded away, leaving a cool emptiness. He rubbed the tendril between his thumb and forefinger, rolling it softly, squeezing it, and then he released it and stood straight.

The cane-tip rested on the floor by his foot. "It's not a separate creature," he said with an authoritative finality. Robin studied his haughty, borderline-impassive face.

"What do you mean? You mean it's become *part* of me now?"

"No, I mean it never was. It *is* you." Gendreau's thumb worried at the smooth surface of the cane's iridescent white head. "There's only one life, one individual source of vitality occupying the space you're standing in—

other than your intestinal flora and mitochondria, of course—and that is *you*. There's nothing else. That…*spaghetti noodle*…is your flesh and blood."

"What does that mean?" Kenway stooped with his hands on his knees, his eyes wide and brow severe. "Is—is she growing a squid-leg to replace her missing arm? Can demons even *do* that? Grow back limbs?"

Gendreau's face twisted as if he had a lemon-wedge in his mouth. "If she were going to grow something, I must say, what a horrendous thing to substitute a perfectly good arm with."

Robin scowled. "You're not helping."

His face softened. "Ahh. Well…who knows, really? We do know that you absorbed Theresa LaQuices' heart-road at the point of her death, yes?"

She nodded knowingly, but said nothing, urging him on with her pointed silence.

Gendreau spread his hands as if it were obvious. "Her particular Gift is the talent of transfiguration, alteration—if I were a betting man, I'd say that when you absorbed the witch's *libbu-harrani*, you also inherited her Gift. In this case, you've inherited the ability to reconfigure matter."

Kenway scratched his beard. "If Theresa could do *that*, why was she so heavy? Couldn't she have just shaved herself down and made herself svelte?"

"Maybe she simply preferred herself that way." Gendreau shrugged, twirling his cane under his armpit like a swizzle stick, and spoke with a campy dismissiveness. "Who are we to speculate on an immortal death-hag's body image issues?" He scooped up Robin's arm-worm in his gentle palm as if it were a diamond bracelet. "Anyway, it looks like your unconscious mind is trying to grow something to replace the arm that Theresa took."

Robin rubbed her face with the hand that wasn't an octopus tentacle. "Jesus freakin Christ. Could my unconscious mind come up with something that doesn't look like carp bait?"

"Oh, hello," Gendreau interrupted. "What's this?"

She glanced at his face, then at the object of his focus: her shoulder. "What?" Her eyes ached as she stretched her neck to look.

"There are *two* now," said Kenway.

Wayne adjusted his glasses, gazing through the bottom, his nose wrinkling like an old man reading the newspaper. "There's another one coming out next to the first one."

"Oh God, give me my meds," Robin pleaded, jamming her fingers into Kenway's jeans pocket and fishing out the baggie of Percocet.

The sharp pain of the U-scar was getting worse and worse, dulling into a coarse, grinding torment, fibrous and woody like chewing popsicle sticks. A headache bloomed at the base of her skull. Going over to the bar, she grabbed the club soda tap, hauled the sprayer hose out, and put a Percocet in her mouth. She thought it over and gave herself another dose, then sprayed them down her throat with club soda.

"Errruuhuhuh," she shuddered at the bitter taste.

A chilling thought passed over her: the sound she'd produced reminded her of the dragon-gargle that Andras made when he exhaled.

(crooked)

Robin pushed it out of her mind and let the soda hose reel back into its socket.

"Are you—" Kenway started to say, then thought better of it.

"No, I'm really not okay," she observed with a gentle scoff. "I am *miles* from okay."

"Perhaps you should take it easy for a couple of days and let, ahh, nature take its course," said Gendreau. "Cutty's group is weakened by the loss of its eastern corner, and it will take some time to find and recruit a fresh member. In the meantime, I can prepare myself."

"No. It's got to go down today."

Robin came back into the light, tugging her T-shirt back down. The tendril snaked back and forth under her shirt-tail. "They've got Wayne's father. I've got to get him out of there, for Wayne. And the longer we wait, the more pod-people they'll be able to make, and the more prepared Cutty, Weaver and their Matron will be when we actually come. We're wasting time."

Gendreau stared at her, his face gradually darkening. "All right; all right. We'll have to make do with what we've got. But we're going to have to storm the hacienda like the flippin Blitzkrieg, yeah?" He breezed past her, carrying his cane by the literal shaft. "We can't give em any time to react."

They followed him back toward the front of the restaurant. The magician led them outside to the narrow patio that served as the front porch. Feathery flakes of snow sparrowed down from the washrag sky, melting on the cement.

Wayne stopped short. "Woah, it's snowing!"

"That's weird," said Kenway. "Isn't it a little early in the year for it?"

Robin held up a hand to catch snowflakes. "It's a little early in the *decade* for it. It hardly *ever* snows here."

Gendreau shrugged with a knowing smile.

Instead of taking the zigzag of stairs back down to the parking lot, he cut left and went down a sloping sidewalk that led along the restaurant's north side. An access road curled around the back of the building for deliveries.

Gendreau crossed this and made his way to a balcony that had been erected at the edge of the lakeview bluff.

Coin-op binoculars punctuated the balcony's parapet, and two people stood at the edge watching the wind kick skirls of sunlight across the water's surface hundreds of feet below. Sitting at their feet was a Boston terrier, a piebald dog with bulging eyes and sharp, pert ears.

Down feathers of ice danced around them like a scene out of a snow globe. "Friends, Romans, countrymen," said Gendreau as they approached.

"Do you think *Deliverance* is based on true events?" the woman asked him, turning away from the lake. Elvira's spooky face stared out from the front of her T-shirt, and her arms were livid with tattoo sleeves of Día De Los Muertos skeletons and curlicues.

"God, I hope not," said Gendreau. "Friends, these are my colleagues Sara Amundson, Lucas Tiedeman, and Eduardo Pendergast."

"I'm using these binoculars to look for sexually ravenous troglodytes, but all I can find are birds." Sara's lipstick was blood-red, her fingernails were as black as murder, and her hair was silver-white, shot through with streaks of pink. Jutting from the prow of her skull was a spiraling bone point about seven inches long.

Robin liked her immediately.

The man standing next to her was dressed like an FBI spook, in a black suit and tie. Even though the sky was a pool of dirty cotton, his eyes were inscrutable behind a pair of shades. What Robin could see of his face was young and handsome, with a princely profile. *Too* young, maybe—she could see him getting carded a lot. "It's too bad Gaiman couldn't come," he said, leaning on the parapet. "This lake is positively dismal in the fall with all these dead trees and cloud cover. He would love it."

"Gaiman?" asked Kenway. "As in, *Neil* Gaiman? The guy that wrote *Anansi Boys* and *Neverwhere?* That guy's a magician?"

"*Oh,* yeah, sure."

Gendreau smiled widely. "Mr. Gaiman is one of the Order's foremost magicians. We were going to bring him along as well—he voiced a desire to sample authentic Georgia 'bulled peanuts', and see The World's Largest Chair, but unfortunately he's got a book tour."

"Bulled peanuts," said the spook, in a deeply-affected twang.

"Buuuuullllled peanuuuuuuuts," said Sara, drawing it out, and the in-joke dissolved into polite laughter. She rapped knuckles on the spook's shoulder. "This is Lucas, by the way, if you were wondering. Eduardo Pendergast is the ankle-biter."

While they were talking, Wayne was petting the bug-eyed terrier. He squinted under his generous head massage, his tongue lolling happily.

"Eduardo. Odd name for a dog," noted Kenway.

"That's because he hasn't always been like this," explained Sara. "He was transfigured by a witch in Germany a few years ago and he liked being a dog so much he refused to let us change him back."

Eduardo's mouth slapped shut and he seemed to come to attention, listening to the discussion about him, but then he relaxed and went back to panting. There was a disconcerting intelligence in his face, Robin thought, so like a real dog, but with the weary self-awareness of a man.

She pushed the urge to rub his head out of her mind, discouraged by the idea of petting a stranger.

"So, what…he's a magician too?"

Sara grinned. "That he is."

"This is the assault team I've assembled to help us storm Cutty's stronghold," said Gendreau, turning serious. "Each one has in his or her possession a *libbu-harrani*, a heart-road artifact imbued with a Gift, confiscated from a defeated witch. Mr. Tiedeman here has the unusual talent of 'channeling'. I'm sure you're familiar with this, Robin," he offered. "Amelia Burke could do it."

Robin had fought and killed Amelia Burke in a condemned mall in Iowa and then spent two weeks in the hospital with a concussion suffered from, of all things, a teddy bear. "Yeah." She asided to Kenway and Wayne, "Channeling is the ability to shift and focus energy."

"Like Gambit from the X-Men?" asked the boy, his eyes lighting up.

Robin smiled. "Yeah, sort of. I've done a little research on it, and from what I can understand, the energy is derived from the adenosine-triphosphate of the body's mitochondria." Also known as ATP, the respiratory cell-energy produced by ancient foreign organelles living inside the cells of the majority of living beings.

Molecular biology, started in high school and continued in Heinrich's training. Robin had spent dark, lonely nights during that monastic first year, locked up in his Texas compound, learning about her new enemies and studying the techniques that would help her exact the vengeance she thought she needed.

But apparently like everything else Heinrich told her, his theory on channeling was bullshit too. "If only it were that simple," said Gendreau. "That would make for a temporarily accelerated metabolism, wouldn't it though, every time the individual used his or her Gift? But that isn't the case." The magician's marble-pale hand clapped on Lucas's shoulder. "We've done our own research, since we can capture and contain the witches' *libbu-harrani* and we can observe their properties at our leisure. No, we believe that the Gift of channeling stores and redirects bosons."

"Bosons?" Robin was at a loss.

"Bosons are what gives matter mass," said Wayne. "People call it the God Particle because it's part of the glue that holds the universe together."

Gendreau pointed at him, *you win the kewpie doll,* a grin breaking across his face. "Yes! What a clever little boy you are. Yes, among other properties, bosons are what give matter its mass, which is why channeled objects exhibit disproportionately concussive force. We only managed to come up with this theory after years of experimentation with CERN's Large Hadron Collider."

Wayne blinked. *"That's* what the LHC is for? You guys are researching *magic?"*

340

"We're given access to their results in exchange for funding. The LHC was constructed for legitimate scientific research, but during the construction our leadership was made to understand its potential in the world of supernatural sciences, and we've …diverted funds in their direction. It's a mutually beneficial arrangement." Turning, Gendreau marched out several paces away from Lucas and the edge of the parapet, doing an about-face with a swirl of jacket. Sara moved away as well. "Now, if you'll all take a few steps back, Mr. Tiedeman here can demonstrate the power of channeling."

Lucas knelt down and picked through the dead leaves until he found something suitable, which turned out to be an acorn, new and green at the tip. He held it up to them as if it were a card trick

(if the audience will please examine the ace of spades and ensure that it has not been altered in any way)

and made an OK with his fingers, the acorn pincered between his thumb and forefinger. This Lucas held for five, ten, fifteen long seconds, his arm beginning to tremble like a weightlifter at the end of his reps. Robin thought he was trying to squeeze it to pieces, but then he spun on his heel and whipped his hand toward one of the coin-op binoculars mounted on the parapet, his tie flapping.

His hand opened up like a pantomimed pistol, his index finger pointed out—*bang bang, my baby shot me down*—and the acorn razored across the air into the teardrop-shaped machine, embedding itself, *ptank!*, in the steel housing. Both eyepieces exploded in unison with sharp crystalline snaps and the whole machine came loose from its pedestal, plummeting over the side. Broken screws tapped across the cement.

The binocular pod smashed open halfway down the bluff, cartwheeling along the rocks through a glitter of quarters.

Gendreau looked up from the gorge even as it continued to tumble down the mountain, scattering change. "I can't say I approve of unsolicited vandalism, but … impressive as always, gunslinger."

Kenway whistled.

"Lady Amundson, on the other hand," the magician said, gesturing to her with his pearl-headed cane, "possesses the Gift of illusions and conjurations. She is the one responsible for this rather anomalous weather."

"I normally make people hallucinate monsters, but I figured making you see a physical manifestation of your worst phobia might've made a bad first impression." Sara emphasized each point with a sinuous gesture. Illusory snow danced around her hands, transforming into monarch butterflies, which then burst into flames and burned into flakes of ash. "Bedbug monsters, rainbow LSD monsters, monsters made out of tax paperwork (ugh), all kinds of monsters. That's kinda my thing. Why sublimate when you can intimidate?"

341

Gendreau cracked a genteel grin. "Your only limit is your imagination, dear." He gestured at the dog. "Eduardo here, on the other hand, is our resident manipulations expert."

"Manipulations?" Robin stared. "The dog is psychokinetic?"

"As well as clairvoyant." Gendreau dug in his jacket pocket and produced a dog treat, wafting the smell of fake bacon up Robin's nose. He leaned his cane against the parapet and briefly turned away from them. Kneeling in front of the dog, Gendreau held out both fists. "Okay, Eddie, which hand is the dog treat in?"

Eduardo reached up and brushed his left hand with a paw. Gendreau opened it. It was empty.

The dog touched his other hand. It was empty as well.

"Not so clairvoyant after all," said Wayne.

The pale magician rose into the air, kicking and flailing. "Hey, all right now, Eddie." Then he was upside-down, pinwheeling his arms like a newbie astronaut on his first day in the Space Station. The tail of Gendreau's bespoke jacket flapped over the back of his head and several Beggin' Strips fell out onto the asphalt. "Put me down, or you'll be sleeping in the car!"

Eduardo ducked underneath Gendreau and snagged one.

"Nice," laughed Kenway, turning him right-side-up and standing him back on his feet. Gendreau jerked his lapels, straightening his jacket.

Lucas Tiedeman grinned over his shoulder. "Welcome to the A-Team."

Thirty-Eight

THE MAGICIANS WERE STAYING in one of the larger lodges down the hill, a rustic frontier shack full of fragrant cedar furniture, dizzying quilts, and deer heads mounted on the walls. Robin and Wayne watched Kenway help them load the last of their belongings into their vehicle. "We've still got the cabin for the week," Gendreau told her as they crammed luggage into the back of a Chevy Suburban. "But if we don't survive Cutty's wrath, it wouldn't do at all to leave our things here where the normals can find them."

Robin elbowed Wayne. "I'm so glad they don't call us Muggles. That would just be too much." The boy grinned, the white windows flashing on his glasses. "We're gonna go get your dad, okay?"

He traded the grin for a sad but confident smile. "I know."

Sara Amundson joined the two of them as Lucas and Kenway hauled the last couple of bags. Robin eyed the horn sticking out of the part in her hair. "What's with the, uhh..." Robin made an A-OK with her hand, pretending to loop an imaginary unicorn horn on her own head.

"It's a wig," said Sara, tugging the horn. Her entire head of hair lifted up to reveal fiery red underneath. She readjusted the pink-white wig, twisting it back down onto her skull. "Last Halloween I went as what I like to call a 'Murdercorn' and everybody liked it so much I thought I would do it again this year."

"Don't let her lie to you." Lucas shut the back of the Suburban. "She's been wearing it ever since."

Sara lowered her head and jabbed him in the arm with the horn.

He backed away, making the sign of the cross with his fingers. "The Murdercorn is murderous."

The seven of them piled into the SUV. Gendreau was driving, Lucas sat up front in the passenger seat, and Sara sat in the back with Kenway and Eduardo. A farty funk hung inside the car, the smell of the Taco Bell the magicians had eaten for lunch.

343

The minute she was nestled in next to them, Robin felt fraudulent by association. She reflected on the past couple of years and the battles and hardships she'd had to endure alone at the hands of America's witches, and she couldn't help but feel like the one hardass in a car full of untested rookies. Suddenly the Suburban had the silly yet claustrophobic feel of a clown car. *They're not taking this seriously enough, including Gendreau,* she thought, looking around at them. Sara gave her a pinched, disaffected smile that didn't touch her eyes. *It's a field trip for them. A woman in a unicorn wig, a cock-eyed dog, and a Quentin Tarantino character.*

I've got half a mind to tell them to stay in the cabin and let me *handle Cutty. This is my fight anyway.*

A sensation of impending doom came over her, as if she'd bought a ticket on the Titanic. Robin faced front and buckled her seatbelt. *Isn't the dog supposed to be the clairvoyant one? What good is a clairvoyant that can't talk?*

Eduardo barked. A pocket watch dangled from his collar, the cover gone, the protective glass cracked.

Pain throbbed in her shoulder, taking her mind off the dog. She caught a glimpse of herself in the rearview mirror and marveled at how sallow her face looked. Her eyes were dark pits in her face, glassy in the watery Tim Burton daylight.

I look like I'm dying of exposure. Donner, party of six!

Gendreau drove them down the mountain, winding back and forth through the switchback and the hairpin curves running across the south slope. The woozy snaking of the top-heavy vehicle turned her medication-and-booze-marinated guts into a churning lava lamp.

When he got to the bottom and passed the office lodge, Gendreau paused at the frontage.

The Subway's sign glowed yellow in the failing afternoon light. "Last chance. Smoke em if you got em," he said, looking back and forth down the access road. "Anybody for a last meal?"

Lucas grunted. "Your confidence inspires me."

"Let's just get this over with," grouched Robin. The bourbon was dancing with her Percocet and every reel and sway of the Suburban made her want to throw up. The feeling of her worm-arm-thing curling and flexing gently by her side wasn't helping.

They crossed the road and headed under the interstate toward Blackfield. Robin peeled back her shirt to uncover the red-black tendril and saw Wayne surreptitiously cower away from it. The sight of him leaning against the window dug deep and left embarrassment.

"Oh my God," said Sara. "What is *that?*"

"According to Gendreau, it's my new arm."

Robin picked it up the same way he had, the coil of sausage-flesh draped over her palm like fine jewelry. Not only had it grown another several inches while they were getting ready to leave, but now it was as thick as a finger. "Evidently I absorbed Theresa's gift for transfiguration when I closed her heart-road, and it's causing...*something* to grow in its

344

place." She hoped it wouldn't turn out to be a tendril forever. A six-foot squid tentacle would definitely strain things between her and Kenway for sure.

"There's *two more of em*," said Wayne.

Sara leaned forward to see better. "Jeez, they're braiding together."

Out of the corner of her eye, Robin thought the intwining tendrils resembled a sort of ponytail made out of Slim Jims. Nausea flopped her stomach back and forth and salty saliva leaked into her mouth.

"Stop the car," she almost shouted, unbuckling her seatbelt.

Gendreau pulled to the side of the highway and Robin wrenched the side door open, staggering out into the weeds and chalky gravel. She went to her knees on the shoulder of the highway, audienced by a wall of pines and a sun-faded Mike's Hard Lemonade can. The tentacle under her shirt coiled and flexed. Robin gargled hot vomit into the dry brown grass and then convulsed again, heaving the rest of her stomach's contents with a splatter.

Exhaustion settled over her and she rested, trying to catch her breath, sucking and blowing wind through a rawhide throat.

Someone got out and before she knew it—or could say otherwise—Kenway was crouching beside her. "You don't have enough hair to hold out of the way when you puke," he said, the dull glint of his prosthetic leg peeking out from under his jeans, "but I can at least be there to help you get back up."

Robin spat and straightened, sitting on her haunches like a samurai at a shrine. Tears tumbled down her face (when had she started to cry?) and she spat again and started to wipe her slimy mouth on the collar of her T-shirt—a thing that people do when they're not used to being in the polite company of living breathing humanity—but Kenway was there with a wadded-up napkin.

She wiped her face down with all the ceremony of scrubbing bugs off a car fender.

"Other than Heinrich—and I'm not even sure about him—the last person I can remember ever giving half a shit about me died years ago," she told him, her voice distant and reflective. "Mom was all I ever had. Even in high school." The wind plucked and pushed at the gaudy paper in her hand. "I don't know what to do with you, dude. You're like...a riddle, you know? I feel like you're a mystery I need to solve. What do you even *see* in me?"

"All those YouTube subscribers," said Kenway. "What, four, five million people? I've never even *met* five million people. There aren't even that many people living in this town. And you walk around thinking you're alone in this life." He shook his head. "You're a princess that thinks she's a frog."

A breathy, sarcastic laugh huffed out of her. "I am *such* a frog. My life is so jacked up, Kenway." She looked up at him. "Are you sure you want to be a part of it?"

345

"Am I a part of it?"

"I'd like you to be. Is that okay?"

His beard separated like stage curtains, uncovering a grin as warm as sunshine. "Yeah. I think I'd like that very much."

Eduardo came trotting up and sat on the gravel beside her, resting a paw on her thigh. The boggle-eyed dog commiserated with a whine, though coming out of a Boston terrier, it was more of a shrill, hiccupy scrape.

A laugh forced itself through Robin's lips and she combed a hand through her unruly brown mohawk. The I.D. bracelet the hospital had put around her wrist scuffed across her forehead. She'd forgotten about it. Biting the paper, Robin pulled until it broke, and she held it into the wind, watching it twitch and dance. Her fingers let it fall away and the hoop curled into the afternoon, rolling along the roadside like a tumbleweed.

"I forgot to thank you for coming to my rescue back there in the vineyard." She squinted into the wind, regarding Kenway's face. "I didn't need it—"

"Obviously."

"—Obviously, but nobody else has ever helped me before."

He looked at the Suburban, and so did she. The misfit Dog Star magicians (how much that sounded like some dirty-southern-rock band from the Seventies, don't tell me no lies and keep your hands to yourself) looked back from the front window and the open door, empathy written on their faces.

"You've got lots of help now." Kenway reached out with his big hands and framed her jaw, wiping the tears off her cheeks with hard leather thumbs. "Whether you need it or not."

Relief tightened her throat and chest, the solace of a long-mourned castaway being picked up by a passing ship.

She put her hand on Kenway's shoulder and got back to her feet. His hands stayed right where he'd put them, clamped to his own thighs, and she was grateful that he seemed to know the difference between helping her up and being the rock she could lift herself up with.

✪

The road sign moved in the breeze, nodding and jiggering like the palsy of an old woman.

Underwood Road. It stood at the edge of a clearcut shoulder stubbly with juts of broken hickory, a weathervane pointing in uncivilized directions. The Suburban was still parked by the side of the road where she'd gotten out to blow chunks. Robin leaned against the car with the door open, her forehead on her arm and her arm on the frame, trying to let the fresh air settle her stomach.

"You okay?" asked Wayne. He had taken off his glasses and was buffing the lenses with his shirt.

"Yeah, it was…the Percocet, the bourbon, being cooped up in the car, *this* thing—" She shrugged the shoulder with the bloodworm hanging out of it. "Got to be a little much for me. Needed some fresh air."

Kenway was beside her. He followed the line of her eyes to the road sign and put his hand on her back. The tendril curled as he did so and she felt him tense up, but he didn't snatch his hand away. God, but she loved him for that. She really did.

"Are you *sure* you want to do this today?" he asked.

For sure, she was having second thoughts; her mother had been locked inside that tree for half a decade now, and a few days wouldn't make much of a difference.

But—

"—They've got Leon," she said. "I can't leave him there."

Gratitude loosened Wayne's features. She could tell he wanted to say something like, *My dad's tough, he would understand if you wanted to psyche yourself up before you jump into Hell,* but the relief, and the eagerness to rescue his father, kept him from opening his mouth.

She hoisted herself into the seat and pulled the belt across her lap. "Let's go. Make hay while the sun shines. Strike while the iron's hot."

Kenway lingered in the door, assessing her.

Finally he slithered into the back of the Suburban next to the dog and she pulled the door shut, *clunk.* Gendreau put on his blinker, waited for a Camaro to go shushing past, and pulled back out onto the highway.

The Suburban crossed both lanes and eased into a crotch of asphalt slicing through the grass median, nose pointed across the northbound lanes. He paused in what could have been propriety—there were no other cars coming; the highway was clear in both directions—and pulled into Underwood Road.

The magician drove like a car commercial. His pale, slender fingers handled the steering wheel in a delicate but businesslike way, a conductor-motorist that poured the Suburban down Underwood's sinuous length. The constant trees enclosed them on both sides with wet, skeletal trunks still stained a raw strawberry-blonde by the weekend's rains.

NO TRESPASSING. The sign was still nailed to a tree, speckled with bullet-holes.

It occurred to Robin that the South had a lot of these signs distributed throughout the wilderness, as if the great landgrabs of the colonial days had never truly ended, the countryside still scissored into a patchwork of a thousand discrete estates protected with musket and handaxe. She had seen a lot of these signs in the past few years, less of them up north until you got into Canada, and almost none in New England except for Maine and swaths of upstate New York. The commune in Oregon had them, but only because the hunters that used to

347

own the property had put them up; the witches didn't need them, didn't *want* them

(welcome, sir, welcome, have a seat, have a beer, welcome to hotel california)

because they *liked* it when trespassers showed up uninvited. The things she'd seen in her travails criscrossing the country, following Heinrich's leads, following Heinrich's orders...the human finger-bones hanging from porch eaves in gruesome wind-chimes, the skulls full of burnt blood, the decaying figures sitting in iron cages,

(so much like mummies, shriveled ash-brown skin glued to thin rods of bone, hands clawed around their knobby knees, stiff lips stretched across yellowed piano-key teeth)

the cries of children locked in cellars, their minds wiped bare by the Gift of illusion, yes, it worked both ways you know, the crones can make you see things and they can make you *not* see things as well.

But those horrible sights are still buried down there deep beneath the surface, memory-sharks that only breach and flash their cuttlebone teeth in the dead of night. Those children, all grown up, will sit straight up in the bed next to their wife or husband as the last foaming tide of a nightmare ebbs into the darkness of sleep. Nightmares of things they saw as children but have forgotten as adults, their recognition stolen by smiling hags with chips of ice in their eyes, hobgoblins who would have stolen their hearts for an ageless star-beast if not for hungry Robin and the gleaming silver dagger in her hand.

The mouldering orange recliner flickered into view through the picket-fence trees.

Like she'd done a hundred times growing up, Robin tried to imagine what that ancient tweed chair smelled like. She wondered what, if anything, lived in it. Maybe it was full of spiders, an arachnid apartment building—or maybe it was full of paper, rinds of pulp machined by the clockwork jaws of a hundred chewing wasps.

She was still lost in thought when Gendreau stopped at a stop sign. Another highway interceded, running perpendicular to Underwood Road, and as soon as Robin's eyes drifted north, she knew that it ran all the way out to Miguel's Pizzeria in the mountains. They had met the road on the other end of her childhood home, the 'shortcut' Kenway had driven when he had first taken her back to her skeezy candy van to lie in the dark and cold, miserably horny and staring at the ceiling. (Plumbing indeed.)

Robin twisted in her seat and looked through the rear window. Kenway did as well, and then Sara. Eduardo panted obliviously, eyes cocked to either side.

"Did we pass it?" she asked.

Kenway faced front again. "I think? I guess we did?"

"I don't even remember going through the neighborhood and seeing the trailer park on the left." Maybe she wasn't paying attention. She was pretty deep in her own head there for a few minutes.

348

Gendreau said over his shoulder, "Shall I turn around and go back? Or are we on the wrong road?"

"It's the right road," said Lucas, still wearing his slick wasp-eye shades. "Underwood." He reached under the front seat and brought out a folder, opening it and displaying the contents to the driver. "That's what the file says."

"It's right." Robin scanned the road behind them. "It's the right road, but something's wrong."

The Suburban dipped into the southbound lane, doing a U-turn back onto Underwood, and Gendreau piloted them into the woods again. This time Robin clutched the passenger headrest in front of her, her head on a swivel as she watched the road for landmarks.

Power poles kept a steady cadence on the left side of the car, and the familiarity of almost twenty years tinged every leaf and sign they passed. Robin stared at the mile markers cruising past the window, but they were useless, numberless reflective discs. The familiar swoop and sway of the road's subtle waveform settled over them once more, but this time Gendreau slowed until they were at a funereal pace, the asphalt grumbling under their tires, trees parallaxing past at walking speed.

"Wait a minute," said Robin.

She stared through the right-hand windows of the Suburban, where a power pole loomed by the road's shoulder.

Kenway shifted. "What is it?"

"The power lines are on the right side now." Robin looked through the left window, then over Kenway's shoulder through the rear window. "They cross the road at the Lazenbury. I know because the line comes down from the pole in front of my old house, then the lines cross the street to the transformer in front of the Lazenbury, where lines go up to the hacienda and over to the trailer park, and from there the lines stay on that side until it gets to the highway."

Making a three-point turn, Gendreau maneuvered the Suburban east again, putting the lines on their left.

A few minutes later, Lucas said, "Now the lines are on the other side."

"Karen Weaver is hiding the house." Sara Amundson peered up at an angle through her gray window. The tint layered a sullen darkness over the world outside. "I know it. She has cropped that *whole quarter-mile* out of the road. Like cutting the middle out of a string and tying the ends back together."

Gendreau put the Suburban in reverse and they whined backward— slow at first, and then faster, until they were racing west ass-first, the engine whining with an inhaling burr like an electric track-car.

"Stop," said Sara. "Let me out."

They drew up short, catty-cornered in the eastbound lane. Robin threw open the door and got out, followed by Kenway and then Sara. The illusionist clawed the Murdercorn wig off her head and tossed it into the back seat, letting the wind comb fingers through her brilliant red hair.

"Look. You can see it there." Sara pointed east, at the south side of the road.

A splintery power-pole towered over them sixty feet away, topped with gray beehive electricity components. Rubber-coated wires emerged from the couplings, protruding into the air some twenty or thirty feet, where they just...*faded away,* as if God had stooped down with a giant Pink Pig drafting eraser and rubbed it out of existence.

"What the hell?" asked Kenway, shading his eyes against the drab white sky. "What is this, the Bermuda Triangle?"

Robin turned. The power-line coalesced into being on the north side of the road and hooked into the couplings at the top of another power-pole. "They pick back up over there."

Taken as a whole, the arrangement over their heads seemed to refract like a pencil inserted into a glass of water, the black cables diverting diagonally and invisibly across the sky. There was no visible difference in the unending army of trees all around them, but when you paid attention to the power-cables you could see where Weaver had excised the Lazenbury and everything around it.

To the west, she could see the faint speck of orange where the old tweed chair stood abandoned. To the east, a barbed wire fence marked the beginning of the old horse-farm on the far end of Underwood.

Gendreau got out and went to Sara. His cane rapped on the road twice as he walked, and then he directed the tip at the strange refraction. "Can you nullify it?"

She shook her head and her face darkened with irritation. "I can't even find the edges. Except for that weird lensing with the power-lines, it's almost seamless. It's like trying to open a fire exit from the outside, except there's not even a door. It's a blank wall that I know has a door on the other side of it."

A desolate satisfaction came over Robin. "Now d'you see how powerful they are?" she asked, trying not to sound smug.

"I was *always* aware." Indignity and sheepishness swirled in Gendreau's aristocratic face. "I've seen this sort of thing before, Miss Martine...but not this well-done. The others, they've—you could get your fingers under the illusion, to so speak, and pry it up like a rock so you can find the worms underneath. But this... I can't find where in the fabric of space and time that the illusion begins and ends. It's completely flush with reality."

Robin didn't fail to notice the irritated way the magician referred to her by her surname.

A bird came sailing across the trees, a big black raven. As it drew near the place where the cable refracted out of view, she almost expected it to disappear, slipping into oblivion as soon as it crossed that invisible

350

boundary and possibly re-appearing a few minutes later, but it passed by without so much as a flicker.

Robin watched it glide away and the visual image of the bird vanishing pushed an idea into her head.

She rounded on Gendreau. "Can you *un*-conjure something?"

He grimaced in baffled contempt, but then lightened. "I've never heard of it before, but yes, I suppose you could. I mean, you can conjure things—"

"—So why can't you *un*-conjure them?"

"That would explain why the illusion is so finely grained." Gendreau stared at the smearing end of the powerline, rubbing the corners of his mouth. "Yes...yes, perhaps what she's done is, instead of...yes...." The bull-pizzle cane came to rest on the pavement and he tucked a hand into the breast of his suit blazer. "...It's not an illusion at all, is it? Weaver has un-conjured the area around the house. She's pinched a pouch out of the fabric of reality and sewn the gap shut, isolated it, like a pocket hidden in the lining of a jacket."

He brought out his hand, holding a steel flip lighter, and he stood there absently flipping it open and shut, staring with unfocused eyes, his mind idling high and out of gear.

Sara folded her arms. "Riddle me this, riddle me that: how do you get into a house with no door?"

Wayne suggested from the Suburban, "You make one."

Goosebumps of excitement tingled across Robin's scalp. "Yes! Your ring!" She strode straight to him as he was climbing out of the car and clutched the boy against her chest in a one-armed hug. "Your ring! We can use it to get into the isolation!"

He grinned, tugging the ballchain necklace out of his shirt, revealing Haruko's ring. Gendreau and Sara came over and the thin magician stooped to level his face with Wayne's, his hands on his knees. A piquant warmth came over him that reminded Robin of Gene Wilder in *Charlie and the Chocolate Factory*. "Is this it, then? The ring that opens magic doors?"

It sounded about as silly as it possibly could coming out of Gendreau's girlish cupid's-bow mouth, but there wasn't really any way of getting around it. Life is stranger than fiction, as they say. Wayne explained how it worked. "And from inside the dark scary version of my house, all the doors lead to other places in town."

"Like a hub," said Robin.

She pushed her fingertips into her jeans pocket and shrugged a shoulder, slowly, deferentially. It was her left shoulder, which sank a shock of blunt pain through her side. "The only problem is, the demon is in that Darkhouse, trapped, waiting for prey to come into his cage. And I'd bet money that magic isn't *all* he eats."

✸

A few minutes later, they were back in town. As soon as the Suburban slipped over a hill and they were greeted by the first thrust of civilization, Gendreau slipped into a Sonic Drive-In to grab something to drink while they planned their next move. Robin ordered a Sprite to help calm her stomach and sat back, sipping the soda, relaxing as the coolness funneled down her chest into her belly, unlocking a tight band of anxiety around her lungs.

Her heart galumphed rhythmically and feverishly inside the birdcage of her chest, throbbing down her arms and into her feet. Gendreau started the Suburban and backed out of the Sonic stall, pulling into traffic. She didn't know where he was going, and he didn't seem to either; he seemed to be driving aimlessly through Blackfield, stalling for time.

"You're bleeding," said Sara, behind her.

Robin opened her eyes and examined her shirt. "Shit." A slick of red ran from the top of her shoulder all the way down her flank, and when she peeled back her shirt-tail she saw that it was spreading into the waist of her jeans. The nausea returned, but it was tempered by the chill of the Sprite.

A hand appeared from the front seat, clutching a fistful of Sonic napkins: Lucas, his eyes still unknowable behind those black sunglasses.

She took them and pressed the wad against the surgery scar, dabbing at the blood, gasping at the fresh pain that erupted underneath. The tendril-braid thrashed under her shirt, painting red hoops and commas across her belly.

"I'm sorry about the mess I'm making in your car, Andy," she told Gendreau, hissing through her teeth.

"It's a rental," he said quietly, without turning around.

Silence fell over the car as Robin hiked up her shirt and dabbed at the blood seeping out around the thing in her shoulder.

It was as big around as a garden hose now, pushing the staples out and loosening the stitches, stretching the wound open. The flap of skin that had been inside the U-scar was now a shriveled epaulet lying on top of the tendrils. There were five of them now, closely intertwined into a hard but yielding cable that felt like warm, wet rubber.

Lucas's hand appeared again, this time holding a spool of Scotch tape.

Robin accepted, confused. "What's this for?"

He handed her another cache of napkins. "Tape it over the, umm—" He traced a circle on his own shoulder with his fingertips, *wax on wax off.*

Robin tucked her shirt under her chin to keep it out of the way and sat there for a baffled moment trying to figure out how she was going to do dress her shoulder with one hand.

"Here, I'll help you," said Sara, reaching for the tape and napkin.

"...Thank you."

352

Sara pressed the napkins to her amputation scar. "Here, hold this down."

She held the napkins in place, glancing back at the woman. Sara Amundson could have been an Old Hollywood lounge singer, buxom and pretty, her red hair an Aphrodite tumble. She must have read Robin's eyes because she said dryly, "It's okay. I've seen worse."

As they spoke, Wayne fed French fries to Eduardo, the dog gnoshing and slurping noisily.

"I didn't tell you where I came from, did I?" asked Sara.

"No."

The magician jerked out a second strip of tape and laid it across the top of the napkins, along the first. "The Order rescued me from a coven commune in Ireland."

"Really? You don't have an accent."

"I was a baby. Abducted. The coven was going to sacrifice my heart and make me one of their own, but the Order attacked the commune and rescued me, and several others." She laid a third strip of tape down, and continued to put three strips on the bottom, and then a fourth. "The boys, they were on borrowed time. Witches already killed one of em that day."

"What were they—" Robin started to ask, but she already knew.

"Yeah."

The witches were eating the boys. Robin had seen the tiny bits and pieces in their brick ovens. That, at least, the fairytales had gotten right. Sara gave her a knowing look. *And that's why you'll never see a witch-hunter eating bone chicken, fried or otherwise. Once you've seen what an hour at 350 degrees can do to a baby, you'll never touch rotisserie again.* "The Dog Star brought me to America and I've been here ever since." Sara leaned over and stage-whispered, "So I know what monsters look like."

Eduardo polished off the fries and heaved a deep, oinking sigh.

"So now that we've reconned, regrouped, and refreshed," said Anders Gendreau, "what's our current plan of attack, Miss Martine?"

Robin thought about it, sipping at her drink. She asked Wayne, "How did you get into the Darkhouse the first time? Are there specific ways or methods you have to get there from here? You said you got there from your room at the hospital."

"Yeah," Wayne said through a mouthful of hamburger.

A speck of lettuce was stuck to the corner of his mouth. He knuckled it in. "But you can't go back there cause that Australian doctor guy's gonna want to keep you, ain't he?"

"Yes, I can't go back there. Not right now."

"Well me and that Joe-elle guy in the banana-hammock came out through a painting in Kenny's apartment." He chewed the hamburger up and swallowed. "Maybe we can go in the same way."

Gendreau pulled into a parking lot and did a U-turn, easing back into traffic. An old man selling home-grown produce out of a raggedy-ass *Sanford and Sons* pickup stood up out of his lawn chair to watch them pass.

353

His hands gnarled into stiff claws, a slow, angry grimace crawling across his face.

His eyes were not his own; they were hollow cat's-eye marbles, full of the swamp-light of tapetum lucidum.

"Hi-ho Silver, away," Gendreau sang, heading back north.

"Keep going straight." Kenway gave the blond magician directions to his art shop in the historical district. He startled Robin with a reassuring hand on her good shoulder. "When you get to the Bojangles, keep to the right and turn on Broad. My place is a couple blocks down that. It'll say 'Griffin's Arts and Signs' on the window with a big red gryphon."

Robin's face flushed and she flashed a smile back at him. He didn't withdraw his hand right away. His eyes were deeply warm and locked on her face, darting from eye to eye to nose to mouth.

You make me hope I survive this, she thought.

"Ark," barked Eduardo. He almost sounded as if he were sobbing. *"Snort-snort-*karoooo! *Snort*…karoooooo!"

"What are you yelling about?" Sara picked the dog up and put him in her lap, holding his haunches. Eduardo trembled. "He's not going to hurt her," she said in his ear. "He likes her, you goofy dog."

*"Snort-*barooooo! Ark! Barooooo!"

Kenway sat back. "Okay," he said, putting up his hands. "I'll stop touching her! Does that make you happy, ya flea-bitten mongrel?"

The Boston terrier licked his lips and climbed down out of Sara's lap, dancing up into Kenway's, and he jammed his wet pug-nose into the crook of the veteran's elbow, wriggling between his arm and his side as if to hide his face.

"What's your deal?" Kenway asked. "You act like you're afraid of something."

Lucas Tiedeman turned in his seat to glare back at them, finally taking off his sunglasses. Robin was relieved that he did, indeed, still have eyes, and they looked perfectly normal. "Whassamatter, boy? What's wrong? Did Timmy fall in the well?"

Eduardo howled again into Kenway's shirt.

Thirty-Nine

JOEL ELLIS MARCHED MINDLESSLY down the sidewalk through Blackfield, his hood up and his hands jammed into his pockets. The sky threatened rain, and part of him hoped it would come again. It suited him today.

It had been a pretty good thumper last night, and something about torrential downpours made him feel safe, made him feel buffered against the slings and arrows of the world. Caveman remnants nestled in the nooks of his brain told him that creatures afraid of getting soaked didn't go out in the rain to hunt, didn't brave the elements; if he stayed in his cave with his fire and his spear and his fingerpainted self-expressions, he would be okay.

Nobody goes out in the rain. Nobody will get you while it's raining.

Mama's house had a tin roof (and did he ever love the sound of rain hitting those warbling red sheets), but that's not where he was headed this evening; he was headed for the comic shop. It was close enough to the hospital to walk to, and when he got there he could decide where to go from there. All that mattered now was finding shelter, and it had nothing to do with rain. If he decided to go back to Mama's house (never *his* house, always *Mama's* house), he'd take the 6:15 from the bus stop by Broad Plaza.

Fisher had given him a key to the shop

(just in case you ever wanna get out of that house, you know)

but he hadn't had it on him and didn't even know where it was, now, honestly, so he had the one from Ashe Armstrong's keyring, the keyring that also held the key for the Frontier pickup that was now resting at the bottom of the acid mine drainage in Lipton Quarry, Owen "Opie" Euchiss's corroded corpse plastered to the front.

As he walked, Joel studied the key in his hand. It had a Captain America cover on it—the back end was coated in rubber like a car key, blue-and-white-striped, with a red circle and a white star inside. It was a commercial key for a commercial lock, and it felt like an alien artifact in his hand, a lightsaber, Excalibur, a tool meant for someone vastly more important than himself.

He mourned to himself as he walked, and as he was crossing the Martin Dupree Bridge over the river that cut through the center of town, traffic hissing and crashing obliviously past behind his back, Joel found himself racked by sobs and unable to see where he was going. He clutched the guardrail of the bridge and stared through a quivering screen of tears at the dark quicksilver cackling some thirty or forty feet below. A python of heartache coiled hotly around his chest, twisting the breath out of him until black spots, cigarette burns on a film reel, bloomed in his eyes.

The wind blustering up the channel boxed him with wet, cold fists. Another part, darker and less vestigial, shoved in meanly next to the caveman neurons in his brain, told him to jump.

Rationality told him that the fall wouldn't kill him; the water wouldn't even hurt him at this height. He'd just be going for an impromptu swim.

"Goddammit," Joel told the river in a pinched growl, wishing he could rip the guardrail out of the cement with his bare hands. There was something *missing* now, wasn't there? An out, a back door—under it all, there had been an emergency exit, and now that it wasn't there anymore he recognized it for what it was. Fisher had always been his golden parachute, he knew, for when living in the house their mother had died in would become less of an inability to move on and more masochism, maybe a self-flagellation. Punishment for not being able to repair the woman that had raised them. He knew in the back of his mind that he would one day tell the difference and step back, and Fish would be there waiting to help him back up.

What happened ain't your fault, big brother, Fish had said one day.

Serendipitously, they had run into each other at Kroger. Joel was so drunk he was sweating, and Fish was trying to talk him into staying at the shop and sleeping it off. *You couldn't stop it and you couldn't fix it, and it ain't even your place to. Sometimes people just lose their minds and all you can do is watch it happen and make it easier on em and move on.*

Fuck you. Joel had stumbled away, getting the last word (as he always did, as he always had to). *You didn't even try.*

"Why didn't he shoot *me* first?"

Dry birdshit ground under his right thumb like flour.

"Why didn't that son of a bitch shoot the one that *didn't* have everything in the world goin for him? Why not *me?*" Joel lingered there until he'd collected himself, and went back to walking, watching his feet eat up the sidewalk.

What was he going to do with the comic shop? He didn't have any idea how to run it. All he knew was making pizza and makin himself purty and drankin and color-coordinating his clothes. Maybe he could sell it. *No, you asshole, you can't sell it. That's all you got left of him.* Then what? He could move into the loft apartment, maybe. No, that wouldn't work. Mama's house was paid for, and Fish was still leasing. Unless he could turn a profit on a store that hadn't seen black ink since the first six months it'd been open, he'd be out on his ass.

He couldn't even count on his savings—he had, maybe, eight hundred in the bank and another three hundred stashed at Mama's house, in a Folger's House can buried in the back yard, and *that* was only because all he had to worry about was utilities (Mama's bungalow was a 110-year-old protected historical structure, a train depot built in 1904 and decommissioned in 1962 when the trainyard in Glen Addie was built).

That money'd be gone in a flash if he had to throw it at a commercial property.

Didn't that kid with the magic ring say something about Fish givin him a part-time job at the shop? That was one nerdy-ass kid. Maybe he could get ahold of him and bend his ear. What was his name? Wayne Newton? No, that's that white dude in Las Vegas that sang "Everyone's Gotta Be Beautiful Sometime", or "It's Not Unusual To Be Loved". Some cheesy hot mess like that. *Wayne Parker? Parkin? Yeah, that's it. Ashe would know a few things too, I'm sure.*

"Unh!" he grunted, knocked out of his thoughts as a woman shoved past, running full tilt.

She wore a red wool peacoat and black leggings, gold hoops in her ears, Ugg moonboots. Her crinkly dark hair streamered out behind her as she ran. "Watch where you goin, bitch!" Joel called after her, dimly aware that she was dressed way too nice to be running down the sidewalk.

Another hand slammed into his back and he caught himself over the guardrail. A man in a Members Only jacket sprinted by and Joel surged after him in a rage, snagging his coat. *"Who do you—"*

The man rounded on him and whipped fingernails across Joel's face. Blood dotted his sweater. Instead of the angry warning he expected to come out of the man's mouth, it was the vehement yet ridiculous puff-adder hiss of a movie-of-the-week vampire. Members Only's eyes were the split jade of a cat's.

Joel recoiled, baffled, putting up his dukes.

The man turned and ran. Another woman came along behind him as well, and that's when Joel scanned the parking lots and sidewalks around him and realized that while he'd been walking with his head down, feeling sorry for himself, the world had come alive with running people. In every direction, men, women, and children sprinted north at top speed, some of them loping along like chimpanzees.

They were heading the same direction he'd been walking: Broad Avenue.

With an expression of deepest confusion still on his face, Joel jammed the Captain America shop key into his pocket and started jogging in that direction. Whatever was going down, it couldn't be good, and he wanted to get behind a locked door ASAP.

Forty

THE DOG STARS' SUBURBAN approached the four-lane intersection of Broad and Main, and Gendreau maneuvered them into the right-hand lane, the turn signal metronoming.

His gasflame eyes burned at them in the rearview mirror. "The dog is clairvoyant," he said imperiously, easing past the traffic light, turning right on red. "Did you forg—"

A trumpeting rumble like a charging elephant shook the Suburban, drowning out whatever Gendreau was saying.

Brilliant headlights turned the inside of the vehicle into a blinding lightbox. Robin spun to see where it was coming from and found herself face to face with the front-end of a garbage truck. The truck's grille and MACK logo swelled across the left-hand window.

BOOM! An angry god tackled the rental Suburban broadside, the side caving in under an onslaught of steel.

Windows imploded, showering them in sea-glass diamonds. Gendreau's airbag deployed, pounding him against the seat with a giant white boxing glove. Wayne was thrown rudely against Robin, and Robin's head bounced off the grille of the garbage truck with a guitar-like *spronk!*

The street reeled out from under their juddering tires, *skrrrrrt-rt-rt-rrrrrt*. Everybody leaned hard to the left for about a half-second as the Suburban capsized to the right and hit the curb, the tires still screaming. Gendreau's hair hovered without gravity in a flaxen halo.

Darkening sidewalk raced past Wayne's silhouette and something like a wrecking ball punched against the roof. A singular blast of water rushed at their faces and fell away. The droplets transformed into beads of light as cement ground against the body, flinging firework sparks with a deafening roar.

The chaos and noise disappeared abruptly, as if she'd gone deaf. Robin found herself hanging from her seatbelt over Wayne.

The window under his cheek was nothing but a yawning mouth full of glass teeth. Water welled across dirt and grass. An overwhelming maternal pang came over her at the sight of the unmoving boy, and she reached out and shook him.

"Hey, Wayne, *baby*, wake up."

At first he didn't move, and Robin's heart thudded painfully in her chest. *God help me, he's dead.*

But then he opened his eyes and his head rotated slowly, creakingly, to regard her with stunned eyes, looking up into a shaft of light coming down from Robin's window, which was now pointed straight up at the steel-wool sky. "What happened?" he asked, and groped at his face for glasses that weren't there.

"We got hit."

Blood, paint-thick on her fingers. A cut on her forehead was leaking down her cheek. She shimmied around, trying to get away from the seatbelt. The tendril-braid-thing under her shirt squirmed angrily, the tape around her dressing pulling loose.

"Hit?" He said it like the word had lost all meaning for him.

Gendreau stirred as if waking from hibernation, his mental gears grinding to life, glass falling out of his china-doll hair and the wrinkles of his jacket. Then they all were, Sara and Kenway and Lucas, coming out of their individual daze, docile turtles from shells.

"Did we just get hit?" asked Sara, in stunned outrage. No one answered, except for Kenway coughing.

Then: a strange, rising wail outside the car, distant, a faraway siren. But it was high, too high, nonsensical, small and multiformed like a fleet of tiny police cars. Their tiny tin wheels crackled along the sidewalk as they rushed to her aid from some tiny police station, their rollercoaster howl shrilling into the evening.

No, she thought, as Wayne found his glasses and put them on. The left lens was knocked out, giving him one goofy Sherlock Holmes magnified eye. *I've heard that before.* Those tin wheels were the faint clatter of shoe soles on asphalt.

The city of Blackfield was coming for them.

"We've got to get out of here," she told them all, panic filling her up. Loose glass rattled, settling like Pachinko pieces through broken gaps as they undid their seatbelts. "We've got to get out *now.*"

"What is that noise?" asked Kenway. His seatbelt uncinched with a sneezy *sz-chik!* and he fell against the starboard window, crunching more glass.

Sara groaned. "Where's the dog?"

Robin braced one foot against Lucas's seat, her forehead against Wayne's headrest, and undid her own seatbelt. The buckle came loose but the pulley in the doorpost was damaged, so the belt only dangled pointlessly in her hand. She threw it aside and lowered herself, sliding on her face across the vinyl seat, until she was resting beside Wayne on her knees.

359

Water soaked into her jeans. "The city is full of cat-people, and they're comin," Robin grunted. "They're on their way here to tear us limb from limb. Cutty's playing her trump card."

Leaning against the passenger door, Lucas upended a tire tool and crunched it into the webbed windshield, turning the sheet into a blue craquelure and ripping a hole in it. As soon as he did so, a shadow passed over the oceanic shimmer and an arm exploded through the hole he'd made, grabbing his wrist.

Lucas was hauled through with a hoot of surprise, safety-glass crashing down his shoulders.

Through the ragged gap of glass, Robin could see people shuffling back and forth in a dark parody of a mosh-pit, shadows criscrossing over white. More arms reached in for Gendreau, and he jabbed at them with his cane. "Back! *Back!*"

The rear cargo door fell open, scraping on the sidewalk. Kenway tangled his fist in Robin's T-shirt, trying to scrabble for purchase on her armpits.

"I'm okay," she told him. "Don't worry about me. I'll follow you."

Out in the failing daylight, Robin rested against the Suburban's rear bumper, a busted tail light throwing hot red across her face. The garbage truck had knocked them through a fire hydrant, and water blasted out of a hole in the sidewalk, raining a torrent of cold water.

All three of them were bleeding from cuts on their faces; Kenway's shirt had a ragged rock-punk slash over one shoulder and glass glittered in Sara's cardinal-red hair. She was on her hands and knees, blood streaming down her face, looking around in a daze.

"Get off me!" Lucas shouted on the other side.

Robin staggered around the car to help him and someone tackled her against the roof-rack, a fat woman in a brown spring parka, a shopping bag from The Gap still looped around one elbow.

The woman hissed madly, trying to claw her throat open, and Kenway wrenched her away, throwing her to the asphalt.

Robin's demon tendril was going crazy, writhing, pushing out her shirt at an angle. She jerked her bloody shirt-tail up to her shoulder to uncover it and discovered a grotesque braid of fibers in the rough shape of an arm, bent at the middle in a macabre imitation of a human elbow. Fine red peach-fuzz grew from the backhand side of this new appendage.

Bristling from the end were five dark roots as smooth and steely as meathooks. She willed them to flex like fingers and they did, crimping and creasing in all the right places.

This was her inheritance from the shaggy, monstrous stranger that had attacked her mother, she understood now, suddenly faced with the new normal, this inner darkness, this insidious evidence of her mother's violation made physical.

Forced to confront it, Robin couldn't look away; she hated it but was fascinated by it at the same time.

360

She made a fist. "Well, I'll be damned."

A clamorous gang of familiared people had gathered around them. Dozens and dozens of brainwashed people inched closer, green and yellow cat-eyes shining at her, their fingers bent into rigid claws, their stupid, blunt human teeth bared in distorted grins.

The intersection seemed to have frozen in time, idling cars littered all over the road, their doors thrown open, exhaust guttering from their tailpipes. The traffic light turned red for cars that weren't going anywhere anyway. *"Come on!"* Robin told them, slamming her new fist against the Suburban's roof. *"Come get me."*

One of them peeled off and ran at her with a choked snarl, and her sinuous new arm lifted him by the throat and flung him back. Another one, a tall woman with a stupid expression and a Carhartt jacket, ran at her and Robin rounded on the woman, slapping her across the face hard enough to cartwheel her against the Suburban.

Incensed, they ran at her as one, a surging mass of people. Stepping from between Robin's feet, Eduardo barked and the water gushing out of the broken fire hydrant turned downward at a right angle, becoming a high-pressure crowd-control blast. The first rank of people gusted backward in a stumbling, screaming phalanx, revealing more familiars, who clambered over them into the gush like sewer rats.

The little dog barked again and the water swept from side to side, breaking against the bulk of humanity teeming in front of them, sea crashing on a headland of human beings.

Behind the teeming crowd, the dark shape of the garbage truck loomed, a glass-eyed green monolith.

The driver door opened and a man leaned out, or at least she thought it was a man; he was as bald as Mr. Clean and his skin was an angry, welted red. His ears were black holes and deranged eyes stared from deep in his knothole eye sockets. Teeth glistened in the pit of his withered mouth.

To Robin he was the angel of Pestilence.

The disfigured man shouted something—*screamed,* actually, the shrill, mad whoop of a baboon—but she couldn't understand him over the noise of the crowd. Then he drew a rifle out of the cab of the garbage truck and settled it into the valley between the open door and the doorpost, hunkering down, staring through the ironsights at her. Robin ducked and made for the back of the van, intending to hide behind it.

Thunder cracked down the valley of the street and a hole appeared in the Suburban's roof, *ptunk!*

Kenway was wrestling with two people now, both of them trying to bite his face. The pestilence-man fired the rifle again and one of the familiars, a tall thick redneck in Wranglers, jerked as if he'd been goosed. A hole blew open in his neck and sprayed Kenway with red gristle.

The veteran shouted and threw the man aside, shoved the Gap woman away. Robin grabbed Sara's shirt, popping stitches. "We gotta go!" she shouted over the roar of the fire hydrant. "Man with a gun!"

One of the familiars shoved his way through the crowd and at first Robin couldn't believe what she was seeing—Joel Ellis? How could he be a pod-person if he had an *algiz* tattooed on his ass?—but then Joel shouted, "Y'all follow me! Come on!" and took off running east up Broad.

The deluge of hydrant water eased upward, relinquishing its force on the crowd, and Eduardo blasted the garbage truck. The gunman hid behind the door and let it wash over the windows, forcing the door shut.

Robin shoved Sara and Kenway after Joel, "Follow him!" and turned back to the crowd to catch an elbow to the face.

A man in a puffy jacket lifted her and slammed her against the inside of the SUV's back door, breaking the hinge, and lunged at her throat with his teeth. She shrugged, scrunching her shoulders, and his bristly mustachioed face wedged against her cheek.

"No!" shouted Kenway, pausing in his escape.

The man in the marshmallow jacket floated away bodily as if repelled by a broad force.

Lucas Tiedeman had snatched him up by his neck and the waist of his jeans. He flung the snarling man into the crowd as if he were nothing but a suitcase and turned back to Robin, pointing after the others. "Run, we got this." His spook suit was sopping wet and he was deathly pale— milk-white, even, his skin almost translucent like marble. He had channeled the man's mass into *himself,* making his body heavier, his skin more resistant, and his blood was having trouble pumping through it.

Lucas was a Greek statue, clothed in black.

Regret burned inside her chest. "This wasn't how it was supposed to—"

"We knew the risks." A legion of cat-eyed people burst through Eduardo's fusillade of water. *"Go!"* Lucas lumbered into the fray, fists and feet bouncing off of his stony body, familiars hanging from his arms. *"DISTRACTION!"*

A hand snatched at her T-shirt, at her arm. "Let him work." Gendreau, his eyes severe, his hair a nest of milkweed fluff. Deep gouges ran across one cheek, blood dripping into his white button-down. "Come on, let's go."

Reluctantly leaving Lucas to the fight, she fled with Gendreau down a Broad Avenue choked with running people.

If she'd seen photographs of it, Robin would have been hard-pressed to tell if the photos were of a European football riot or the final mile of the Boston Marathon: wild-eyed civilians poured from the restaurants and shops lining the historical district, funneling out of doorways and storming into the road. Some of them galloped sideways in a simian fashion, pawing across the pavement on their hands; most of them ran like velociraptors, their shoulders bunched up by their ears and their hands bent under into obsequious pianists' hands, banging imaginary Steinways.

Kenway led the escape with his fists, forging through the seething crowd toward some point. Robin fought the men and women off with the little martial arts Heinrich had been able to teach her. Augmented by the demon arm, she was a force of nature, throwing leaping haymakers and hammering knees and elbows into chests and faces.

A blood-tingling Godzilla roar echoed off the buildings around them. The throng of familiars parted and a bear, an honest-to-God *grizzly bear,* eight feet of primordial tooth and claw, came loping out of nowhere.

Familiars scattered in every direction, braying and hollering. Even Robin stopped short, but when she caught a glimpse of Sara Amundson with her temples in her hands and her fingers sunk into her red hair, the spitting image of an actor in an Excedrin commercial feigning a migraine, she knew that the grizzly belonged to the magician.

"I thought you could make monsters," Robin told her, the bear following them, driving a wedge through the crowd.

"So sue me, it was the best I could do on short notice."

Joel stared at the bear, stumbling over the curb and onto the sidewalk. The trip seemed to bring him back into the moment and surrender flashed across his face as if he were thinking, *hell, that ain't the craziest thing I've seen, and it's only gonna get worse.*

"We'll hide in the comic shop," Joel told them, his arms up. He pointed to something colorful in his other hand. "I got the key!"

The grizzly bear shambled along behind them, roaring and challenging the familiars as they got close. Spider-Man and Batman appeared ahead of them, Fisher's window mural flickering into view through the mob. Joel ran for the front door and jammed the key home, his hands shaking.

Skittering out of the chaos, Eduardo leapt into Sara's arms. "Oh thank *God,*" she muttered, clutching the dog.

The front door of Fisher's comic shop stood in a shallow alcove on a short ramp. There were two locks—one was a latch in the center of the door, and the one above it, a larger deadbolt, commanded a pair of sliding bars that secured the top and bottom of the door. "What have y'all crazy-ass white people done got me into now?" demanded Joel, the lock disengaging with a double-barreled *clank.* "I got people actin like cats, car accidents, people shootin at me, and now we got freakin *bears* in the middle of town?"

"The bear isn't real," Gendreau told him as they all ran past into the darkened shop.

Joel tossed a hand and rolled his eyes. "Of *course* it ain't."

As soon as they were inside, he pushed the door shut on its hydraulic hinge and locked it again. Robin counted them...Kenway, Gendreau, Sara, Joel, and herself.

Her heart lunged painfully. *"Where's Wayne?"* she shrieked, surprising herself. *"Where's—"*

"I'm back here!" a voice called from the feeble darkness.

Such intense relief settled over her that she could have collapsed. Robin lurched past her friends and into the depths of the comic shop, where Wayne stepped out of the shadows. He'd found a Batman cowl somewhere and was shrugging into it.

She snatched it off his head, eliciting an indignant yelp of pain, and squeezed him against her chest.

"I thought we left you out there, kiddo."

"Nope." He rubbed his ear. "I'm right here."

Standing by the window, they watched the imaginary bear distract and fend off the crowd.

As the familiars tested the giant creature, dancing in to bat at its non-corporeal body and leap back, Sara released her grip on the hallucination and it faded with all the ceremony of turning off a television. The sudden disappearance left the cat-people stupefied and they boggled at the space where it'd been with vacuous screwhead eyes.

"Get away from the window before they see us," warned Gendreau.

Heeding his advice, they retreated deeper into the shop, gathering in the clear space at the back where Fisher had once held Movie Nights. Someone tripped over a chair with a clatter. Kenway's face was a smear in the darkness, the windowlight sparkling in his eyes. "Where'd that kid in the Blues Brothers suit go?"

"Lucas?" Gendreau sat in a chair, wheezing. "He'll be all right, I think."

"Why didn't *you* magic those people?" Kenway asked. "You look like you could handle yourself more than the other two." He caught his breath, his face drawn into the grimace of a side stitch. "You look like the third member of Siegfried and Roy went off and started a menswear line."

"What witty commentary, coming from the lead vocalist of a Nickelback cover band."

Kenway snorted. "Them's fightin words, Snagglepuss!"

The atmosphere in the dark room chilled as everybody paused for a long, pregnant moment. Then Kenway chuckled, shaking his head dismissively, breaking the tension.

"I didn't participate in the combat," said Gendreau, "because I am not, ahh, versed in combative magic."

Sara put the dog on the floor and sat down to rest as well. "Anders is a sensitive. He's our ... supernatural GPS. He's how we found you Sunday night, and he's how we knew which hospital they took you to."

He sat back and tugged at his jacket, straightening it. "I am also a superlative alchemist, and I am quite useful at curative properties— removing poisons and illnesses, knitting small wounds, that sort of thing. I was made an official *curandero* in Chile six years ago and some call me Don Gendreau, the Healer of Caddo Parish."

"Some, as in like, twelve people," rasped Sara. She had found a roll of paper towels with the party supplies on a table in the corner and was mopping at the now-tacky blood on her forehead.

Gendreau got up and went to her, his hands gravitating to her face. "Here, love, let me take a look at that for you." He *tsk-tsk*ed, combing through her hair. "You poor dear; banged your head pretty badly, didn't you, Murdercorn?"

"Oh, stop petting me and fix it, please."

"Sensitive." Kenway watched Gendreau dress Sara's head wound. "Hey, does that mean you can see ghosts?"

The magician glimpsed something in the veteran's eyes and went back to work. His delicate hands probed a gash at her hairline, his fingers sweeping and flourishing in graceful, encompassing gestures.

"No," Gendreau said quietly, "I'm afraid it doesn't."

"Okay, enough banter. We need to figure out what we're going to do now," said Robin. "We barely made it just now, and I don't think we'll survive another round with the Thundercats out there."

There were at least a hundred people shambling back and forth in the street now, picking fights with each other and sniffing the air. Many of them had taken off their clothes, their breasts swinging, and three of them rutted madly in the middle of the street. "Man, I've never seen this many familiars in one place before. Most I've ever seen was at Gail Symes's casino in Nevada, and the only way I got away from them was by cutting the power and sneaking out."

One of the familiars peered through the gap created by Spider-Man's thighs and his retinas flashed white-green in the black silhouette of his head. Robin stooped instinctively, watching over the edge of a shelf. "And even then, darkness doesn't always save you."

"Where is your sign shop, Ken?" asked Wayne. "Maybe we can make a break for it."

Kenway thought about it, rubbing his nose with his forearm. His hands came to rest naturally on his hips, and with not a small amount of humor and attraction, Robin thought it made him look like a superhero.

"Umm." He pointed one way and then the other, turned around, then jerked a thumb over his shoulder. "About a half block that way. On the other side of the street."

"Isn't the canal behind us?"

Kenway nodded. "...No, it's behind my shop. But I think I might know where you're goin with this. There's a storm drain in the alley behind *this* shop. It probably runs past the drainage grate in my garage and empties in the canal out back. You figure we could use it to sneak over there?"

"Yeah." Wayne got up and went through the door in the back, shouldering past the movie screen hanging from the ceiling.

Joel followed him. "Hold up. Make sure there ain't no fire alarm."

The adrenaline in Robin's system began to fade, her shoulder singing Halleluah. She sat down in a booth and pulled her shirt back down, ferreting her new left arm out of the sleeve; blood still leaked freely from the surgery scar and now all of the stitches had been broken, the staples pried loose and jutting out haphazardly, so that they caught on the fabric.

"When you finish with Sara," she asked, "will you do something about my stitches and stuff? It's killing me."

Gendreau nodded. "Almost done."

In the grey light seeping through from the front of the shop, she could study the arm's fibrous surface, a thick plait of hard but yielding cables. It was as if she'd never lost her arm at all and now it was sheathed in a tight gauntlet of vulcanized tire-rubber. Her hand was as tough, the fingers pliant yet hard. Taking her demon hand in her human hand, the silky copper hairs brushing her palm, Robin felt an awed chill and wondered if this was what Andras felt like.

Does he know? Does he know who I am? What I am? The next question was *Will he recognize me?* but she realized that she didn't care.

Or perhaps she did; she wanted Andras to see her face and know her as she killed him. A compelling, irrepressible anger billowed up inside of her and Robin wanted to smash things, she wanted to destroy and pulverize. *No, It. That thing is an It and It is going to die. That thing is going to die for what it did to my mother, and what it's done to me. For the life it's forced me to live.*

"Wow," said Kenway, leaning on the booth table. "So your arm grew back. That's pretty damn sweet, yeah?"

Robin nodded, forcing a smile.

When he spoke again, she could tell his smile had drained away and left him cool, his voice low. "I know it's weird. And it's hard to deal with. I don't know what to tell you."

His own hand curled around hers and it registered that she could feel it with the Andras-arm, she could *feel* things with it, and compared to the leathery skin his fingers were as soft and warm and fragile as a very old man's.

Instinctively, Robin shrank away. She didn't want her strange demon hand to touch him.

"If my leg grew back I wouldn't care *what* it looked like," he said. "You know? I'd be happy just to have it back."

A sick thought occurred to her. *Is he jealous that this happened, that it grew back? Was there a part of him that felt...that felt a kinship, or a satisfaction when he'd found out she'd lost her arm to Theresa?* Robin brushed it aside. *Of course not. What kind of a person would he be to think that way?*

Her fears were vanquished handily when he leaned over and kissed her on the forehead. "I like you anyway, the way you are," he said, and kissed her on the forehead again, "hell, I think it looks badass—you're, like, a superhero now," and then he kissed her on the mouth and a flashbang tumbled pleasantly down her chest, her heart thumping.

Robin reached up with her human hand and clung to him, mashing their lips together, and kissed him back. His beard clouded against her face like candy-floss made of silk.

"Thank you," she said, finally.

Her cheeks were wet. She scraped them dry with the demon-hand and winced at the hard crag of her thumb.

"For what?"

She didn't know what to say to that, so she kissed him again.

Forty-One

THE BEDAZZLED BASEBALL BAT glittered in Joel's hands like a disco ball, flinging arrows of light all over Fisher's videotape room. He'd found it where his brother had left it Sunday morning, propped against the futon. Along with the half-cup of cold coffee he'd never finished.

Joel stared at the coffee, thinking about Fish.

"Mister."

He snapped out of it. The boy, Wayne, was a collection of shapes in the darkness. "Do you have a key for this back door?"

The movie room—Fisher's personal home theater, at least as theatrical as a futon in a closet and a thirty-year-old TV and VCR could be—had three doors: the one leading back to the shop, the one on the right that opened on the stairway to Fisher's loft apartment, and one on the left at the end of a short hallway. That one went out back.

"I don't know." He fished the shop key out of his pocket. "I hope so. The rest of the keys are with Fish."

They stood there in the shadows, regarding each other. For the millionth time, the pistol in Owen Euchiss's hand barked fire into Fisher's face and Joel watched his brother's body capsize languidly into water the color of time. Joel had closed his eyes but he didn't flinch, weak acid spattering his face and chest in a mist.

"I'm sorry aboutcher brother, mister Joe-elle." Wayne's glasses reflected the light from the shop in two bulging squares of white. "He was cool. A real nice guy."

"Me too."

Joel sighed and followed Wayne down the little hallway to the fire exit, choosing action over thought.

The more he did, the less he could think, and the less he thought the less he could watch those brains spray on the Movie Night screen of his mind.

Feeling around the surface of the door, he found a handle with a keyhole in it and a deadbolt. The deadbolt didn't behave like the front door, it was a simple house door. He unlocked both of them and pushed the door, a heavy wooden solid-core.

Silver daylight rushed down the inside as it came open and stuck, scraping on the concrete. Joel shoved it the rest of the way with a dull scuff. Outside, a narrow alleyway ran to their vanishing points in both directions. Boxes were piled in one corner by a steel utility door that led into the water heater closet, and two wheel bins leaned against the far wall.

A chain-link fence framed the area on both sides. Joel was peering into the storm drain when a dark figure came out of nowhere, crashing into the fence and scaring the hell out of him. He flinched, raising the Batdazzler.

Blood ran down the man's temples in heavy blotches and made glossy sealskin of his black suit. His shirt was ripped open.

"It's Lucas," said Wayne, opening the gate.

The magician staggered in, arming blood and sweat from his forehead with a trembling hand. "Goddamn, damn, *damn,* I thought that was the end of me." He leaned against the wall. "Everybody make it okay?"

"Yeah."

Lucas thumped his chest with pride. "Then my glorious sacrifice was not in vain."

They brought him into the comic shop, where Sara gave him a hug and Gendreau shook his hand. "Good work back there, soldier," said the self-proclaimed curandero. "How did you get away from the mob?"

Lucas collapsed into the booth, wiping his face with Miguel's Pizzeria napkins.

"Well, I lasted about ten seconds and then they had me on my back, kickin the shit outta me." He fished a cigarette out of his shirt pocket and shakily stuck it in his mouth, patted himself down for a lighter, didn't find one. "But then I heard a roar—I guess Sara did something?—and then everybody ran away. I don't know where the burnt-lookin guy with the rifle went; he ran off while I was gettin worked over."

He scanned the dark shop. "Did the dog make it?"

A little black shadow came out from under the booth table. Lucas picked Eduardo up and hugged him.

"My leedle Dog Star mascot," he said in a bad moose-und-squirrel accent, making air kisses. The terrier slavered all over his face, knocking the cigarette out of his mouth. He crooned at the dog, tousling and rubbing him all over as if he were fluffing a pillow. Eduardo did the shimmy-shimmy-shake, an expression of dumb pleasure on his face. "You knocked em all down with water from your magic mind-powers, yes you did, yeah! Yes you did! What a *good boy.*"

Sara shook her head. "Sometimes I think Ed forgets he's supposed to be human. And maybe you do too."

"Now you're making it weird."

"*I'm* making it—?"

369

"We've got things to do," said Robin, getting up and heading for the back door. "We don't have time to sit around petting dogs and chit-chatting."

Kenway stopped her by the movie screen, his shadow sharp on the giant white-silver sheet. His hand lightly cupped her elbow. "Slow down," he told her. "Take a minute. You just got out of the hospital and lived through a roll-over *and* a mob. I thought you wanted dude over here to take a look at your, uhh ... your arm?"

She hesitated, her face grim.

His look of concern became one of reproach.

Sighing, she came back and unfolded one of the Movie Night chairs, plopping down into it. Gendreau took off his jacket and pushed up his shirt-sleeves.

His shirt was tailored, but without the Willy Wonka blazer his sleeves belled at the elbows and narrowed at the cuffs. With his platinum-blond hair, Arctic eyes, and Nordic face, it made him look a bit like a cover model for a romance novel. "All right," he said, as Robin wrenched up her shirt impatiently. "This may hurt a bit at first—I'm going to have to pull the rest of these staples out, because I can't quite achieve the effect I need with them in the way. And then I'll need to press the wound together manually."

"Whatever you need to do, doc," Robin said noncommittally. She took off the helmet and let her head tilt back. "I took another couple of pain pills a minute ago. I figured I might as well, since I threw up." A hard, workmanlike sort of temper had come over her since Joel had seen her last.

This must be her Go Mode, he decided. This was what it looked like when the going got tough and Robin Martine shifted into Four Wheel Drive.

"You're pushing yourself too hard," said Kenway.

She pointed at him. "You have no idea what—"

Joel thought he could tell what she was about to say, and that would have been the wrong thing. *Was* the wrong thing, he knew, because he could tell by the hurt look on the veteran's face that he had read between the lines too.

"Don't even go there," Kenway said, grimly.

"I'm sorry." Robin winced as Gendreau picked the bent staples out of her.

Her eyes were rimmed in red. "I didn't mean it that way. I'm just saying ... I've pushed myself harder than this." She stretched the neck of her shirt open and pointed at a scar on the left side of her chest, high, directly under her collarbone. "This came from a girl in Connecticut last spring. She stabbed me with a pair of kitchen shears. Missed my heart by two inches."

She pointed to the tiny pink commas peppered up her arms and the blade of her jawline. The pea-sized pit by her ear. "Scratches. From Neva

Chandler, and others. God, those bitches always scratch." She hiked up her left jeans leg and pointed at her shin, even though it was too dark to really see. "Got whacked with a shovel in Florida, ended up with a minor fracture.

"I've broken three toes and two fingers." She waggled the fingers of her right hand. "I'd show you one of those broken fingers, but Theresa took it. Along with the rest of my arm."

The more scars she explained, the angrier and more harried she seemed to get. Ferociously unbuckling her belt, she ripped her fly open and thrust out her pelvis, shucking her jeans with one hand, flashing utilitarian white panties. Her voice took on a choked, raw quality. "I got burnt all over my legs tryin to light up this witch in St. Louis—"

Both of her thighs rippled with pink, gnarly patches of long-healed burns.

"I been doin this for a long time now." The tears on her cheeks silvered in the light coming back from the shopfront windows. "I can *handle myself*, goddammit."

"I need you to quit moving," Gendreau said blandly.

Robin looked at him, irritation clouding her face. Her eyes briefly danced between the curandero's, and then she pulled her jeans back over her hips.

The noise of the crowd outside gradually began to diminish to an occasional shout. Joel thought he heard police sirens, but it was so far away it could have been more cat-yowling from the familiars.

Robin buried her face in her hand and sat quietly.

Kenway's arms were folded. He stood at the edge of the generous Movie Night space, leaning against a rackful of action figures, his ankles crossed so that his prosthetic leg lay on top.

"I love you," he said, after a not-inconsiderable amount of time.

"No, you don't," said Robin.

He thought about it a minute and said, "Yep. Maybe I do."

She shook her head. Her voice was still rusty. "Look at me. Look at this thing I have for an arm now. You just *think* you do. Why would anybody love me?" The demon-hand flexed with a stony rasp. "Look at it. It's a… it's a piece of *him*. He ruined my mother and now I have to carry a goddamn piece of him. I belong in Hell with the rest of the devils."

The edges of her front incisors met in a disgusted grimace as she balled a dragonish fist. She growled through her teeth, "What even *is* this?"

Gendreau had no answer. Neither did anyone else. Sara pretended to be absorbed in picking her fingernails, while Lucas babied the man-dog in low muttering tones. Kenway stared at the floor as if chastised, his brow dark.

Joel got up and knelt by her. "It's *you*, is what it is."

Robin looked down at him and he felt a thin ripple of fear. There was a terrible, angry thing in her spooked-horse eyes, a sweaty sort of madness come to the surface, and suddenly it was as if he were a vassal supplicating to a medieval lord drunk on both power and liquor.

The baseball bat even completed the analogy, because as he took a knee in front of her the business end of it rested on the floor and leaned against his knee like a knight's sword. The fake diamonds glued to the wood even mirrored the faint light much the same way.

He thought to hold her hand, but had the idea to take the strange dark hand; he held it and was struck by how alien it was, like a sculpture of a human hand made of driftwood and sooted in a fire—a human hand but larger, the fingers hooking in blunt claws. Fleecy red hair grew all down the back of it in a singular finlike shag and ended in a final punctuating tuft over her knuckles. Up close, he could see veins of dark green tracing between her jagged knuckles.

It was the most foreign, outlandish thing he'd ever seen.

"I love you too, girl," Joel said, gazing up at her half-mad face. "We're almost brother and sister, you and me. We grew up together, remember?"

She said nothing, but the corner of her mouth twitched and her eyes lost a bit of that fearsomeness.

"You think of me as a sister?" she asked.

"Y— Yeah, I do." He was still wearing his silk do-rag. He took it off and bunched it in a ball in his fist against his chest.

"I never had a brother before."

Joel smiled. He had put on eyeshadow and eyeliner that morning before he'd gone back to the hospital to check on Armstrong, and even though it was dark and he was slick with sweat, he knew he still looked good. "I ain't *got* to be your brother. I can be your sister." The smile widened into a grin. "Either or, you know, it's okay. Whichever one you want, baby."

"It's okay," she echoed, a bit dreamily.

"You're the same Robin I grew up with, all right?" He put his other hand on top of the dark hand, and it was as if he clasped the horny, splintered base of a broken branch jutting out of a tree. He wondered if it hurt, the hand, as dry and hard as it felt. "You're that same little girl me and my brother ate breakfast with in that big ol house. You remember what I said at Miguel's?"

"Ain't nothin in this world that good bacon can't make better." Robin's eyes focused on his.

"That's right. That same little girl that me and him played with in your big ol back yard. We used to take turns swingin on that swing back there, you and your mosquito. What was his name?"

"Mr. Nosy." A faint smile. "I still have him. He's in my van."

"He must be old as hell now."

"Falling apart. I've had him fixed so many times I can't even remember." The smile spread a bit more. "I love that stupid mosquito so much." A fresh tear re-wet the track on her face. "I remember playing dress-up with you and Fish in my room in the cupola. Oh my God, you used to love puttin on my mom's old dresses and pearls. I remember that."

Joel stroked the strange hand.

"You're still here. You're that same little girl with that same stuffed mosquito. Only you growed up now, and there's a *little* different but not much. I've changed too—there's been a few dirty things in my system and my lungs are prolly as black as my outsides by now—but under it all I'm still that little boy in your mama's old dresses and high-heel shoes too big for my feet."

All the hardness had drained from Robin's face, though her tone was still a bit lost, as though she were speaking from the far side of another world. But with each word she seemed to get a better handle on herself.

"Yeah. We're still the same. Okay."

He let go of her demon-hand and she balled her fist again. The sound of it flexing was simultaneously like the creak of oiled leather and the thin, fibrous crackle of wicker.

"This ain't *him*," Joel told her, taking her woody fingers in his. "It ain't. This is *you*, lil girl. It's just a little more badass than the rest of you."

She nodded and wiped her cheeks with the heel and then the back of her human right hand.

"You can't go through this life and not pick up a little shit here and there. We are all the sum of our lives, hon… and we all gotta carry a piece of crazy to the end."

Joel got up off the floor, using the Batdazzler as a cane. The bullet-graze across his thigh had been re-closed at the hospital and now it only hurt when he bent his knee. Of course, the pain meds they'd given him were helping with that. "Yeah, you got a *big* piece. But Imma help you carry it, aight?"

She nodded again, and a hardness came back to her, but it wasn't the Crazy-Eyed-Lord-on-His-Throne, Off-With-Your-Head look again; it was a positive and steely resolve. The *lost*-ness was gone. Joel sensed that he had dragged his childhood friend back from the edge of some dark, destructive, self-loathing promontory.

"I love you, yeah?" His tone said this was not optional. "And this boy over here—" Joel pointed at Kenway with the end of the bat, "—he love you too. Dig on *that.*"

Robin wiped her face again. "I can dig it. Yeah."

"I *know* he does," Joel said, eyeing Kenway. "It's written all over him. This boy wanna marry yo mohawk ass."

Kenway put his hands up in a guarded way, his beard parting in an embarrassed grin. "All right now."

Joel paced in the other direction, twirling the bat. "Just sayin."

The sound of someone knocking on the front door echoed back to them. Kenway turned and peered through a gap between the shelves. "Who the hell…?"

"I thought I heard a police siren earlier," said Sara. "Maybe the cops are trying to disperse the familiars. —Hell, maybe the familiars have even come back to their senses."

"No. I don't think—"

Joel looked as well. A man stood on the other side of the glass, his hands cupped around his eyes so he could see through into the shadows.

Roy Euchiss.

"Hey, anybody in there?" called the Serpent, wispy strands of colorless hair haloing from his acid-burned head. "I know you're in there. I saw somebody movin. You open yet? You got this month's *Iron Man?* I'm a fan, you know." He raised the rifle, shouldering it. "Don't get up. I have a key."

The first shot thundered in the comic shop like a judge's gavel. A hole appeared in the Plexiglas door.

"Shit, we got to get out of here." Joel pushed away from the rack and held the bat in front of his face, a Jedi with his lightsaber. "Y'all go on out the back. This the bastard that killed my brother. Imma have words with *his* ass."

BOOM! Euchiss fired another bullet through the glass.

Everybody paused except for Robin. *Fish would be chewin her tail if he could see this,* he thought.

But then Kenway fist-bumped him. "Beast mode, man."

"Beast mode."

"Speaking of beasts," said Sara Amundson, as Wayne led the others out the back, "I'll stay here and give you a hand, if that's okay. I'll make a monster."

Joel shrugged. "If you—"

CRASH! The front door imploded. Joel and Sara ducked down behind the shelves.

The rich, buttery stink of gunpowder mixed with the feeble vanilla funk of old comic books. Euchiss stooped underneath the mullion that ran through the middle of the door, passing through the gap where the pane of glass had been. Glittering grit crunched under his bootsoles.

When he stood up, Joel grimaced. Up close, Roy Euchiss looked horrendous.

His ears had deteriorated, leaving ragged stumps of raw skin, edged in black. Two gaping Boris Karloff *Phantom of the Opera* nostrils marked where his nose had melted, and one of his eyes was a milky cataract. The skin all over him was red and peeling like an all-day sunburn. He looked like a bratwurst that'd been on the grill too long.

Euchiss racked the bolt on his rifle, so pissed he was shaking. An empty brass casing flipped out and tinkled across the glass sales counter. *"Where the fuck are you, ya brother-killin' porch monkey son of a bitch!"* he bellowed, the words leaving him in a wrathful shiver.

374

"Y'all killed my brother first, motherf—" Joel yelled, anger stripping him of self-control, and he knew it was a mistake as soon as *brother* passed through his lips.

Euchiss's head jerked in his direction and he shouldered the rifle. Joel snatched himself away; a box exploded above his head, peppering him with bits of plastic and paper.

Stomp, stomp, stomp. Here comes the gunman, racking the bolt. Euchiss stormed down to where Joel had been hiding, looked up, saw him crouch-running around the other end, and fired at him.

BOOM! A *Walking Dead* coffee mug shattered.

Joel scrambled across the aisles of toys and games. The rifle coughed fire again, *BOOM!*, and a hole appeared in a MONOPOLY! box behind him. He turtle-crawled as quietly as he could, trying to put as much space between him and that gun as possible.

His shoulder bumped into a knee and he found himself looking up into the telescoping jaws of an alien. Joel almost screamed until he realized it was Fisher's replica Xenomorph statue.

Outside, someone shouted through a loudspeaker. *"Attention! This is the Blackfield Police! You are ordered to disperse!"*

The cops? Joel crept behind the Alien statue. Had the cops come to put the hurt on the mob out there? The crowd became chaotic, screaming and angry. Footsteps raced past the broken front door, and he could hear the familiars snarling ferally.

"Get your asses outta here!" continued the bullhorn warning. *"Right—"*

It was cut off by the hollow slap of gunfire.

"You might as well stop running," warned Euchiss, turning and striding back the way he came, following the sound of Joel scuffling against the carpet. He racked the bolt, loading a fresh round.

Boxes throughout the comic shop began to blow open by themselves in shreds of cardstock, one or two at first, like the first kernels of popcorn in the bag.

Euchiss stopped to look around in confused surprise.

They were all cracking open in a percussive symphony, *POP-POP-POP!* Action figures tumbled to the floor in a rain of plastic arms and legs.

"What kind of trick is *this* shit?" Euchiss asked the shadows. "Let me guess, here's the twist: you're some kind of Negro hoo-doo magician descended from Haitians or Jamaicans or somethin, right? Ain't that how these things always go? I watch movies when I ain't cuttin throats, you know. I ain't *completely* uncivilized yet."

Something brushed Joel's ankle. A tiny plastic superhero scuttled under a shelf.

Another miniature man slid past, and another. The floor was suddenly an ant-like armada of action figures, all tumbling and rolling toward the other end of the sales floor.

Euchiss opened his bolt, checked it, slammed it home again. "Well listen here, Afro-cadabra: you ain't got *nothin* on Miss Cutty, I can tell you that. She got more magic in her pinkie finger than in *all* your queer little body."

"You'll never win, Red Skull," said a tinny voice.

As if by instinct, Euchiss spun and fired at it. *BOOM!*

Captain America flipped ass over teakettle into the shadows. "I am vengeance!" said another voice, behind him. "I am the night!" Others chimed in, growing into a cacophony of chirping battle cries:

"This is where it ends, Skeletor!"

"Thundercats, Thundercats, Thundercats, *hooooo!*"

"Transformers! More than meets the eye!"

Soon the voice-chip recordings of dozens, *hundreds* of action figures swelled into a singular angry robot chorus, a dissonant and anticipating pitchfork mob. Vibrations welled in the floor, radiating from some ponderous epicenter in the middle of the shop, a rumble that rose and opened into a slow roar.

Euchiss recoiled, wheeling on the source of the noise.

Rising from between the racks was a great hillock of jack-shapes, a head and shoulders and then a towering manycolored gestalt, five feet, six feet, seven feet tall, a Grendel made of action figures.

It lurched down the aisle toward him on two swimmy elephant feet as if it were wading in deep mud, the soft light glistening on shins and biceps. Sightless electric eyes winked all over, red and green laser-dots flashing and flickering like Christmas lights. The synthetic bravado of battery-operated ray-guns and lightsabers hissed and whizzed from deep inside: *pew pew pew! Bzzzz-bkow! Boom! Bling-bling-bling!* The dwindling electronic *eeeeewwwww…BKSSHH* of a blockbuster bomb.

"SURRENDER," chorused the toy-monster, "OR DIE."

Euchiss made a face, wincing almost in embarrassment. "Is this supposta *scare* me, pizza-man?"

Joel stepped from behind a shelf and swung the Batdazzler up into the front of the rifle, shattering every finger-bone in Euchiss's left hand. Fake diamonds broke loose, glittering across the carpet.

The Serpent's right hand impulsively pulled the trigger, *POW!*, tearing through boxes of toys, and he screamed in pain and rage. The rifle's muzzle dropped to the carpet.

Joel raised the glorious baseball bat.

"Nope. *Distract* you," he said, and brought it down in the middle of the gunman's forehead.

Euchiss's skull cracked and his head snapped back; the impact jolted Joel's forearms, numbing his hands. Euchiss backpedaled, collapsing against a shelf, and the whole thing toppled over in a spill of sleeved comics.

Joel lunged in and hammered him across the chest before he could get up. Ribs gave way underneath with a muffled, delicate crunch.

"UUNGH!" Euchiss corkscrewed out of the way and *BANG!* like a drum, Joel knocked a splintery hole in the back of the wooden shelf.

Diamonds pattered across the wood. Euchiss spun off onto the floor, hugging the rifle, and as soon as he fell on his back he came up with it, the barrel pointed at the man with the ball bat.

Blood trickled from a dent in the crest of Euchiss's skull. Joel paused in terror, the Batdazzler raised.

A surge of hot madness roiled up inside of him, becoming a strained, kamikaze sort of bravery. *"Shoot me, son!"* Joel bellowed in challenge at the supine killer.

Euchiss pulled the trigger. *Click.*

"Shit!" he hissed, and started to rack the bolt.

Joel clubbed the rifle out of the way, striding across the back of the fallen shelf, and stomped his chest as if he were killing a particularly foul insect. The bones flexed protestingly under Joel's foot.

"URRRFUNNNNCK!" spat Euchiss, saliva misting.

He flipped over, abandoning the rifle, and beetled away across the carpet, drooling.

Having jarred so many of the diamonds off, the Batdazzler was little more than your average baseball bat. Joel stepped down from the overturned shelf and walked almost pleasantly alongside the belly-crawling Euchiss. He twirled the bat in a jaunty, careless way, but his face was the essence of grim, hard-bitten rage.

"This for all em cats you burnt," said Joel, and whipped the bat hard across the killer's spine. Vertebrae snapped with a soft, brittle crack.

Euchiss screamed into the darkness of the comic shop.

He turned over and put up his hands, trembling, his eyes wide and pleading. Only his upper body did so, his waist helixing, his legs sprawled uselessly where he'd left them, heels pointed upward.

Joel nosed the bat sharply back and forth, knocking his hands out of the way.

"No!" Euchiss cried, and then he started shrieking.

"This for my brother," Joel grunted.

The bat slammed into Euchiss's face on the diagonal, caving it in with a thick, wet *sputch* and cutting him off mid-scream.

The bat's business end stayed in the ruins of Euchiss's face. Cracks had appeared in the haft where it fractured on impact, and one eyeball bulged from underneath the wood, staring at the floor.

Joel stood up slowly, warily, as if he were afraid the floor were about to fall in. Sara stood next to him; he hadn't even heard her come out of hiding. She didn't say anything, but her face was pinched in disgust.

"Adapt and overcome," Joel told the corpse.

Forty-Two

ROBIN LED THEM THROUGH the grate behind the shop into a storm drain the approximate height and width of a fireplace. The drain was filthy, strewn with old trash and dried mud, and smelled musty; it was all she could do to keep from dry-heaving. Kenway struggled along behind her, his prosthetic leg scraping on the concrete. Gendreau duck-walked, his jacket rolled up under his arm so it wouldn't get wet.

She checked over her shoulder. Her new friends were only moving shapes in the shadows. Wayne's glasses flashed white.

Sixty or seventy feet in, the ceiling opened up to the dim ink-blue clouds of the afternoon sky, and through a grate that ran the width of Broad Avenue they could see the familiars shambling around above. Shoes clomped across the steel as the crowd capered back and forth, shrieking and fighting each other.

"I forget," said Lucas, bringing up the rear, "how long does the feral stage last after a dormant familiar is activated?"

Gendreau grunted, "Several hours. It really depends on the witch. But Cutty? Who knows?" A little girl on her hands and knees over the grille searched the darkness for them, her fingers laced through the steel slats. Her eyes were softly luminous moon-dimes.

Robin shushed them. "Shut up before they hear us."

"Attention!" shouted an augmented voice above, echoing through the valley of the street. *"This is Blackfield Police! You are ordered to disperse!"*

Lucas blinked. "Police? Do they think it's a riot?"

"Get your asses outta here! Right—"

The amplified voice was interrupted by the high crack of a grenade launcher, followed by chemical hissing and the *rakka-tak* of non-lethal rounds and the chest-thumping *boom* of beanbag shotguns.

The acidic reek of tear gas wafted down through the grille, making Robin's eyes water. "It's happened before. There was a pretty bad incident with familiars in California last year. The state claimed it was a riot over that court case. You know, the officer shooting?"

Familiars ran past, their shoes clattering across the grille in a cascade. "That was you?"

"Yeah. I was trying to kill Adeline Stidman and she had the whole damn neighborhood after me. Chased me into a college campus, had the campus police involved. Biggest cock-up ever. Anyway…I guess when people don't have any other explanation, people make shit up to fill in the blanks, you know?"

Gendreau chuffed humorlessly. "Connect the dots."

"Here we go," said Kenway.

Robin had been so focused on moving that she hadn't noticed that they'd crossed both lanes of Broad, gone under the opposite sidewalk, and were underneath his sign shop. A grille showered the drain floor with warm yellow light. The two of them positioned themselves under it. The floor was sooty with black engine grease.

"This is gross."

"Sorry," he said. "This is where I park cars for vinyl wraps." Kenway gripped the drain grille with both hands and braced himself, pushing. "Damn." He stood up, bent over at the waist, and raised himself until his shoulders and the back of his head were against the metal, and he pushed with his legs. After only a few seconds he was straining so hard he was vibrating. "Unnngh, *damn*. It won't move. It's glued in by all the muck. It might even be bolted down."

Robin pressed her human hand to his chest, gently shooing him out of the way. "Here, let me try."

"I don't know how—" he started to say.

She cleared her throat. "Trust me."

Taking his place, Robin looked up through the grate. She could see the ceiling of the garage. Kneeling on one knee, she reared back with the demon-hand and struck the grille with her open palm as hard as she could. Her freakish left hand, twice the size of her right hand and as hard as wire, clanged noisily against the steel.

Bits of grease and dirt rained down onto them and Robin shielded her face, scraping her lips with her shirt. She'd expected it to hurt to some degree, even though it was tough, but there was nothing—only the reverberations of the impact traveling up to her shoulder.

It was sort of liberating, to be honest; what else could she do with this? How sturdy *was* this thing?

The self-proclaimed curandero had worked his strange shamanic healing-magic on her arm (she still hated calling it magic, and now she began to feel this was because that the word *cheapened* something she'd come to know and fear as a powerful force), and somehow without the bent staples embedded in it, the scars of the surgery had dissipated. The fibers were almost as big around as her original arm; they had stretched out the U-shaped scar like a yawning mouth, the edges strained and ripping until the hole had been five, six inches across. Skin pulled taut over the scabrous blackwood bone that was now her new arm.

379

Now the pain had abated to a constant arthritic ache. Whatever Gendreau did, had blended her skin with the demon-skin; the cells combined in a jagged, organic fashion, interlocking and growing together, like splinters embedded painlessly in her flesh. It was as if she'd been born this way, and in light of Joel's pep talk, she supposed she had been.

She slammed the demon-hand against the grille again, producing a slap-bass thrum of steel. More foul dirt crumbled onto them.

Kenway spat and coughed. "Man, that is heinous."

"Can we hurry this up, please?" complained Gendreau from the darkness behind them. "My knees are killing me."

Robin steeled herself and took a deep breath of cold fouled air, then whacked her demon-hand against the grille, *CLANG*, and again, *CLANG*, and again, again, again, *CLANG CLANG CLANG*. Each strike was accompanied by a grunt of effort.

Finally the grille began to come loose, scraping and shifting upwards. "There, I loosened it for you."

Kenway stood up in the drain, shoving the metal free. "Hardy-har," he said, and let it fall to the side, the hinge chiseling up more of the loamy grease-dirt. He lifted himself out and then gave Robin a hand up, and the two of them helped Wayne, Gendreau, and Lucas out.

The pitter-patter of little feet made Robin look into the pit. Eduardo Pendergast whimpered, only visible by the patch of white on his face.

"Sometimes the abyss looks back." She reached in and hauled him out by his collar.

The dog gave a great big shiver, jitterbugging across the garage floor, shaking off the muck. Robin stood straight and appraised them all, and found a bunch of dirty-faced street urchins. They all looked like coal-miners from 1920 West Virginia. "You guys are gonna need a shower."

"And a trip to the mall, no doubt," said Gendreau, smelling his shirt.

Robin followed Kenway upstairs to his apartment, careful to wipe her feet on the doormat at the foot of the stairs. Wayne and the magicians pursued her like a brood of ducklings.

At the top, Lucas whistled. "Nice digs, dude."

"Thanks."

"These are the paintings I was talking about," Wayne said, heading into the open kitchen area.

All Kenway's works of art hung on the wall over the fridge and cabinets, intricately arranged so that each made room for the other and left little of the wall itself uncovered. Robin noticed that the darker, more introspective paintings were down at the ends, framing the brighter, lusher ones in the middle, which made the presentation feel like a mosaic of a sun in outer space, as if viewed through a mail slot.

Gendreau spooled off some paper towels to wipe at the grease on his plush-looking jeans, even though his shirt was a fingerpainting. "Very nice work, I must say, Mr Griffin. Do you ever sell any?"

"I've had some offers…."

Wayne put his ring to his eye, looking up at them. Then he let it dangle from its chain and climbed up onto the kitchen counter, pushing aside a bag of chips, and very carefully slid up onto the top of the fridge. He put the ring to his eye again and pressed on a tall portrait depicting a horse's white foreleg, each muscle and vein rendered in exquisite, almost nightmarish detail.

"...But considering why I painted em," said Kenway, "where the inspiration came from—it seemed a bit morbid. Or maybe like I was tryin to capitalize on my friend."

The canvas billowed a little bit like sailcloth, but otherwise didn't move. No dice.

"Morbid—?" Gendreau tilted his head as he pulled his jacket back on, tugging the lapels. "What happened, Mr Griffin, if you'll pardon my curiosity?"

Wayne turned on his butt, kicking a fridge magnet off onto the floor, and splayed his hand on the surface of a painting of a shirtless woman as viewed from the back. Like the horse leg, this one was also in bright, washed-out colors and sharp photographic detail.

"Ask me later, Mr G."

With a faint *click*, the painting swung inward on darkness. They all paused to regard it in awed, stony silence.

Gendreau pontificated with his arms wide. "I've seen a lot of things in my time—boson redistribution, tactile mass hallucinations, even psychokinesis—but this is remarkable, simply remarkable: an inter-dimensional crawlspace."

Wayne smiled proudly.

"You understand, of course, that my theory of Karen Weaver's de-conjuration on Underwood was just that: a theory. I've never seen anything like this in my life, you know."

I thought it was my *theory.* Robin shook her head.

Wayne was wearing the GoPro chest harness; he must have put it on by himself. The fluorescent lights over the kitchen reflected in its soulless black eye. She blinked. How long had he been wearing it? She supposed she'd grown so used to seeing it that her eye had danced right over it. "I'm gonna go in first," Robin told them, lifting herself up onto the island in the middle. She crouched next to the stove. "If that thing is waiting to amb—"

A huge orangutan arm slithered out of the hole in the wall, black, covered in matted red hair. It was so big it was unreal, a Halloween-spider decoration, with long knuckly fingers and too many of them.

Gendreau shrieked like a horror-film ingénue.

The cacodemon's hand folded around Wayne's throat and pulled him against the wall with a *thump*, the bicep flexing, dragging him inside the hole.

It happened so quickly, and had taken Robin so much by surprise, that at first she found her body unwilling to move. But as the boy began to slide through into that deep velvet darkness, he shouted her name, *"Robiiiiin!"*, and that was enough to animate her. Reaching up with both hands, she grabbed his ankle, and for a brief instant they were playing Tug-of-War with him, and then his foot slid out of his sneaker.

Wayne slipped into the dark.

"No!" She dropped the shoe and scrambled on top of the fridge, thrusting her left arm into the hole before Andras could close it.

The painting slapped shut on her wrist and bounced open again. Before she could second-guess herself or the others could follow, Robin grabbed the edges of the crawlspace and hauled herself through into the upstairs bathroom of 1168 Underwood Road.

❂

She vaulted the sink headfirst and hit the opposite wall, crashing into a towel rack and punching a hole in the sheetrock. Robin bounced off the radiator underneath and onto the floor, where the rotten terrycloth flag that had been hanging from the rack covered her face like a death shroud. The medicine cabinet clicked shut and the mirror shattered, shards of silvered glass crashing into the sink.

"Robiiiiin—!" screamed Wayne from deeper in the house. The adjuration was pure terror.

She staggered through the bathroom door, which had been torn from its hinges and lay flat, propped up by its own doorknob. The Hell-annexed otherhouse was waiting to blind her with its utter lack of light.

As she made her way down the hall, pinballing back and forth with her hands out, her eyes became used to the dark and a faint glow gave shape to the furniture. It hung in mid-air as a formless fog, a fungal subterranean light. Robin reached the end of the hall just in time to see the cacodemon break for the stairs, Wayne under his arm like a football.

Goddamn but that thing was *huge*. No wonder the children had been so afraid of it. A thrill of terror racked her system.

It was all head and lanky frame, a giant toddler with the jagged, distended jacklegs of a praying mantis. Andras's oversized skull was as wide as his already ample shoulders, a punchbowl dome feathery with filth. Before he slipped over the banister, he flicked those tennis-ball eyes back at her, those Edison-bulb eyes throbbing sea-green filaments, and then he crashed to the switchback landing below.

Robin hurled herself over the banister. The fingers of her left hand penetrated the drywall on the landing below. She turned and launched herself onto the demon's broad back.

It was like leaping onto a wicker sofa with a rug thrown over it, with the same dirty-woody smell of neglect and musty filth. Andras's skin actually *creaked*, and his hair was long and shaggy and crusty. Robin sank the fingers of her black left hand into his hairy-splintery flesh and found that he was, indeed, hollow on the inside as if he *were* made of wicker. He was a wicker sculpture made of a hundred thousand cords all wound together.

Unlife jostled and rustled inside, as if his heart were a trapped bird.

Andras shrugged his free arm, twisting back and forth with a sound like breaking branches, and the scissor-blades of her fingers drew loose from his dry meat. Robin whipped free of him and tumbled to the floor in the foyer a half-flight below, sliding on a threadbare runner damp with dust.

The demon tossed Wayne away and leapt down to the foot of the switchback stairs. The boy collapsed next to the baseboards; his glasses fell off and skittered across the hardwood.

(w h o   a r e   y o u)

the monster asked, regarding her. The words flickered in Robin's head like a pilot-light, a secret match-flame. They were less words than abstract concept-shapes, Rorschach blots.

She growled, pivoting about to face him on the fulcrum of her human hand, pinwheeling the rotten carpet into a pile against the wall.

She would not give this violating devil the dignity of an answer. Robin flourished the strange left claw and ran at him, fury compounding inside of her. She meant to sink those coal-daggers into him again and tear him apart, rend him by pieces and see what was inside.

(t h e   r i n g)

he said, flinging one hand across his chest in a capeless parody of Bela Lugosi's Dracula,

(i   w i l l   f i n a l l y   b e   f r e e)

the demon told her, and as Robin came at him he backhanded her. That long insectoid arm battered her out of the way, a beam of hard bone piling against her right flank, and she flew aside.

She hit the wall with an *OOF* and crashed through a curio arranged with dusty pictures, sprawling on top of jagged things that hurt her side.

(w h o   a r e   y o u)

repeated the demon the children called Owlhead.

"I'm Annie's daughter, you son of a bitch," Robin told Andras, even though it had no mother of its own, she was sure. Her heart thundered in her chest and she was flushed with an incredible heat, almost embarrassing in its fury. "This is all *your* fault." The knot in her throat burned. *"You* are why I'm here, and why I am the way I am, and why my mother is dead."

Cambion. Crooked woman, half-monster. She wanted to cry, to sob in defiance and rage at this monstrous creature, this avatar of corrosive lust, but she refused to give him the satisfaction.

Andras grinned with a rack of teeth like jags of broken wood, serrated prongs long enough to bite clean through her neck.

383

Closing her eyes against those darning needles, she plunged the hand he had given her into his belly, breaking skin too hard for her human hand to damage, and pulled it open like Christmas wrapping.

Fluttering sensations whickered up her arm and touched her face. She opened her eyes and pure disgusted fear shot an iron bolt through her core.

Spiders.

He was full of spiders,

fucking *spiders,*

THOUSANDS OF THEM.

They crawled out of the empty darkness inside his body and up her arm, a legion of bristling marbles marching toward her face.

Each one was a nightmare unto itself, she sensed, each one an embodiment of some base desire, each one a walking prejudice or an evil thought; in the three seconds that passed as they scuttled out of hiding, Robin caught intrusive snippets—flashes of murder, physical violation, undiluted hatred or lust.

Andras picked her up by the scruff of her neck as if she were a kitten. He held her against the wall.

(y o u   a r e   m e)

he said, and she could hear the grin in his mind-voice

(y o u   a r e   m e   a n d   i   a m   y o u)

and to her shock and terrified surprise the swarthy skin of her draconic left arm began to *spread,* leeching across her collarbone and into her shirt, filling her in with its wicked black hardness.

—Crooked, more crooked than ever—

The black widows poured out of him and enveloped her from left to right, carrying a payload of licorice-smelling ink, engulfing her breast until it was a round bulb of wicked thatch. The soft pink-brown smear of her nipple transformed into a rusty bolthead.

Spiders crawled into her mouth, tangled in her hair. Andras was spreading the darkness, infecting her, infesting her, *changing* her.

Robin looked down, her neck crackling like cellophane, and saw her heart behind her chest; she could actually *see* it like the sun in a picnic basket, burning and blazing inside of her with a warm amber light. Rays sifted through layers of pigiron twine, sending blades of gold shimmering across the ceiling.

My God, is that me? Is that mine? she thought, her lips stiffening, her eyes burning, her hair turning to crimson jackstraw. Her tongue began to harden into a pitted black blade.

A framed photo hung on the other side of the hallway.

Her own reflection swam in the cloudy glass. Her face was blackening and warping; her eyes bulged and shined from deep within, dirty green foglamps. Her pupils were sharp electric pinpricks.

(I   A M   Y O U)

Andras laughed. It was the sound of a whetstone coughing down the length of a sword-blade.

—*Cambion, crooked cambion*—

"*No!*" she cried.

Her voice was a watery scrape. She inhaled and the breath shook dirty cords in her chest. *Grrrahuhuh.*

"*NO!*" she cried again, and hammered Andras with her black fist.

The demon's sternum cracked and he let go of her, stumbling away, clutching his chest like he'd had a heart attack.

"I am *not* you!"

Robin found her feet and fell against the wall, the plaster crumbling under her corded shoulders. Both her hands rose up and she stared at them. They were spun from smoky iron thread and dry vine, and hair the color of merlot grew down her wrists in woolly shags like the sleeves of a wizard gown.

Her heart gleamed from inside, a imprisoned pulsar, an orrery of light, flashing tiger-stripes of white throughout the Darkhouse.

"You can claim me all you want," Robin snarled up at the owl-headed wicker man. The words were oily and metallic, syllables chiseled out of the workings of the earth. She pounded a fist against her chest, *CLACK*, "but you'll never get that last five percent. I am *not* you! *My heart is my own!*"

Fear, real fear, and bewilderment guttered in the demon's dull lamp eyes. She ran at him and plunged both fists through the mesh of his chest, ripping him open.

Piles of spiders spilled out in a whispering rush, recluses and orb-weavers, tarantulas and fat scuttling hobos. Wayne shrieked somewhere, but Robin did not falter or relent. Clutching the demon's bear-trap lips, she gripped the rim of his lower jaw, her fingers settling between his teeth, and tore his face in half as if he were made of papier mâché.

Inside his head was the biggest spider of all. Eight finger-bones as long as umbrella-tines unfolded from the ruins of his wicker skull, revealing a pale hard growth in the middle.

Eight onyx eyes glistened at her from a clump of stony yellow bone. Miserable disgust skirled through her at the idea that this abomination could be her father. Robin gripped the creature and hauled it out of its shattered shell, wrestling it over to the nearest window.

It tried to bite her face, lunging between her arms with clicking-grinding mandibles.

(S H E   C O M E S .   I   M U S T   H A V E   H E R .   L E T   M E   G O ,   L I T T L E   O N E)

A shiver of revulsion shot home like a deadbolt. He had recognized her for what she was. Andras knew that she was his daughter. She had nothing to say to that "little one" at the end, no wise-ass retort. A term of endearment from this monster? Intolerable.

She jammed one of her spun-iron elbows against the window and the glass shattered, shards sucking violently away into the deepest darkness Robin had ever seen.

On the other side of the frame was nothing. Not just a space with nothing in it, there wasn't even a space—a lightless vacuum. And yet...a silvery malevolence breathed and watched back there, an invisible entity that she could only feel as a pulsing idiot wrath.

Faintly, distantly, she heard the tuneless trilling of flutes.

Thrusting the bone-spider through the broken window, Robin shoved it out into the void. Andras disappeared, its flailing legs swallowed up and away.

She searched for the fingery creature in the dark, and when she was satisfied that it was gone, she inhaled—*grrrrahuhuhuh*—and roared into the nothing, *"Fuuuuck! Yooouuu!"*

It felt impotent, a wretched scream into an unfeeling abyss, but it had a certain gratification.

No echo came back.

Forty-Three

ROBIN FOUND WAYNE IN the upstairs bathroom, lying in the clawfoot bathtub. Red rust stains dragoned down the porcelain from under the faucet, licking at a drain clotted with dried paint. Dirty tiles marched across the walls in broken, snaggletoothed rows.

The medicine cabinet door was still shattered. Wayne had pulled it open, trying to find the way back, but behind it was nothing but glass shelves arrayed with ancient orange prescription bottles. She could see all this because her heart continued to shine through the tines of her chest, illuminating the house around her.

"No!" shouted the boy, curled into the fetal position. "Please don't kill me!" He turned and threw something at her. "Just take it! Please don't hurt me!"

Crooked, she thought sadly.

She picked up whatever he'd thrown and found Haruko's ring. "I'm not going to hurt you," she said. Her voice seethed, deep and hot like a Ferrari engine.

Wayne didn't turn, and only shivered harder.

"We've got work to do." She knelt by the side of the tub. "Look at me, Wayne."

Finally, his head swiveled slowly, and Robin handed him his eyeglasses. He took them and slid them over his awed, terrified eyes.

"Oh my God," Wayne said, one lens still broken out. Blood trickled from a cut in his hair. "You really *are* a demon."

She smiled. Her lips ground against each other. "Only ninety-five percent." She tapped her chest, where the shining evidence of that last five percent rested. A loud but muted kickdrum thumped in time with her nuclear heart, sending subtle ripples across the bathroom. *Lub-dub. Lub-dub. Lub-dub.*

"I can't get the crawlspace open." Wayne pointed at the broken mirror. He spoke in the petulant, tired tone of a boy that can't get to sleep.

Robin stood at the sink, her dark fingers curling around the basin's edge.

"I can fix this, I think."

She picked up a shard of glass and slipped it into the door of the medicine cabinet.

Then she took another and slid it into place next to the first. It should have taken her a long time, but the mirror was dirty and had broken in large pewter daggers held together by filth, shattering outward from a point in the center.

Placing the final shard, Robin pressed her fingertip to the starburst of silver cracks and concentrated.

While Gendreau had been healing her surgery scar in the back of Fisher Ellis's comic shop, she had been subtly tapping the *libbu-harrani* buried in the pearl at the end of his cane, drawing off some of his curandero power for herself. At the time she'd figured she would need it to keep herself together in the battle to come, but now she found she could use it to put the mirror back together.

Sliding the pad of her demonic finger across the refractive edges, Robin traced each crack out to the frame of the mirror. Each time she did so, it faded, the glass smooth and unmarked underneath, as if she were erasing them.

"There we go," she said, thumbing the final crack away. She stepped back to admire her handiwork.

Wayne was speechless. Taking his mother's ring out of his shirt-collar, he lifted it so that he could look through it and focus its magic, and opened the cabinet door. The stark glow of the fluorescent lights in Kenway's kitchen tumbled through as if they'd been waiting all along.

To Robin, the light fell brisk and sharp, like the chill of a winter door left open. She diminished into the shadows, stepping away until nothing was visible but her eyes and the pulsar-heart still throbbing in her chest.

"Go," she told Wayne.

"No."

"Go." Robin took his shoulder. "Go to Kenway's apartment and wait there for me."

"I want to go with you," said Wayne, backing against the tub. "I want to save my dad. I want to help you."

She sighed, making that disturbing underwater-engine noise again. Her voice was an impossibly deep rumble. "You can help me one last way before you go back. You can help me find the door that leads to the Lazenbury."

"Okay."

"Robin?" called someone from the other side of the mirror-hole. Sara Amundson. "Wayne? Are you...you okay in there?"

Kenway said, his voice shaking, "Is that you?"

"Tell them not to be afraid of me."

Wayne climbed into the sink and leaned through the portrait-mirror-hole. He glanced back at her. "You can't go out there anymore, can you?"

"I don't know." She really didn't. "It's … cold out there. Cold like… fire." It was counterintuitive, but she knew deep inside that if she went through that hole, if she tested the sanctification, she would burn in that katabatic superfreeze, as if the thermometer had gone all the way past zero and come back around to the top.

He turned back to the kitchen. "She can't come to the window," Wayne told them. "But she—"

"Is she okay?" asked Joel.

Kenway sat on top of the fridge next to the painting. Now he leaned over to look through the hole. "Babe? You there? Are you okay?"

"I'm fine," Robin told him, even though she wasn't, not really. In her present condition, she felt no pain; she felt godlike, perhaps, indestructible, aware only of the press of the floor against the soles of her feet and the constant draft of supernatural cold seeping through the hole.

He stared at her. The sensation of invincibility melted away under his warm eyes, leaving her feeling naked and vulnerable.

"I'm coming in," he said, climbing into the hole.

Wayne scrambled out of the way and Kenway clambered over the sink, lowering himself to the bathroom floor.

He stood in front of her, abject wonder and terror in his eyes. "Is that really you?" he asked, reaching for her. At first she wanted to move away, or maybe push his hand back, but she let him touch her, rake his fingertips softly down the coiling slope of her chest and feel the rough wasp-nest swell of her left breast. The starshine of her heart filtered through his fingers.

His hand found its way up to her cheek and stayed there. She closed her luminescent eyes and pressed against the cooling cup of his palm.

"You're still beautiful to me," Kenway said. "If not even more than before."

A rusty laugh bubbled up out of her. "You think a demon is prettier than me?"

"Uhh…" His hand twitched.

"…I'm kidding."

"Your skin kinda reminds me of a shredded mini-wheat."

"You're really pressing your luck, sir."

The others were coming through now, all except for Joel. Sara came through first, and then Lucas, who helped Gendreau down from the step of the sink. "Simply remarkable," the curandero said again, eyes wandering the decrepit bathroom.

A dog barked on the other side.

"Sounds like Eduardo wants to go too," chuckled Lucas. Joel handed the terrier through the hole. Safely on the Darkhouse side, Eduardo shook himself and panted up at them, his tail waving back and forth.

Robin got as close to the hole as she could tolerate, looking out at the pizza man. He sat on the fridge with his elbow in the dimensional hole, as pretty as you please. It could have been the windowsill of his Black Velvet.

"Are you staying here, then?"

He gawped openly at her. "Yep. I'll keep the light on for ya, and the way open. I think I been through enough today, and you look like you can handle yourself. I'll leave you to it." The moment lingered between them for a second, and then he added, "You gonna be like that forever, Girl Wonder? It's a nice look, but … it'll be hard gettin a table at IHOP lookin like modern art."

"It doesn't feel sustainable. I don't know." Robin looked at her hands. "I'll figure something out."

"We'll get you a hat and a nice pair of sunglasses."

Robin laughed again. "Yeah."

The others were already filing out of the room. "We'll be back soon," she told him, backing out, and he saluted.

"I'll be here."

✺

After trying every door in the house—including the back door, which led into the go-kart garage in Weaver's Wonderland, where they found Joel's car and the body of Michael DePalatis—the one they needed turned out to be the front door, and Robin couldn't overlook the irony. Apparently the front entrance of both 1168 and its Hell-annexed alter ego were linked in some deep way.

She stood way back while Wayne opened it, but no rush of wintery cold came in, even though she could plainly see the front porch of her childhood home outside. It was night-time out there, but she wasn't sure if that was because it was getting close to six, or because it was *always* night in this strange new aberration of a timezone.

"I don't feel the sanctification out there," Robin told them.

"Perhaps it doesn't apply to a piece of reality when someone has tied it off like a puppy-dog's tail," said Gendreau.

Eduardo whined.

"—Err, sorry."

Robin stepped toward the door and, with a brief pause, put her hand outside. There was a bad moment where she felt the creep of ice—as if there were a holy residue—but then it passed.

"It's safe." She stepped out onto the porch and they followed her.

Someone sitting in the swing down at the end loosed a shriek worthy of a Sioux warrior and vaulted the railing into the bushes.

"Pete?" called Wayne, squinting into the darkness. "Amanda?"

390

"Batman? Is that you?"

"Yeah, it's me." Wayne walked down to the swing where Amanda, her brothers, and little Katie Fryhover cowered in the dark. Evan and Kasey Johnson stood in front of their sister, wielding heavy-looking sticks and shields devised from garbage can lids.

Leaning on the banister, Robin gazed out into a dark sky strewn with unfamiliar constellations that hung low in the night like electric bulbs screwed into the clouds. The trailer park's mobile homes were pale, dark-eyed hulks run aground on a black shore. There were no lights. The de-conjuration must have interrupted the electricity in the power lines.

"Looks like when Weaver tied off the neighborhood," said Kenway, "she took Chevalier Village and 1168 with it."

Evan Johnson coughed, wiping his face with his sleeve. "It's been dark out for like two days straight. The power went out and all of a sudden the sun went away at like three in the afternoon yesterday."

"Ever since," said his brother, "we can't get out. The night makes a wall."

"The night makes a wall," echoed little Katie.

"Me and Evan tried to get out." Kasey pointed west with his stick, down the road. "But it's like…it's like the air gets *hard.*"

Evan giggled in spite of himself.

"I ain't jokin, turd-vert."

"It's like we're in a giant aquarium, you know?" said Amanda, standing up. Katie Fryhover clung to her leg with the desperation of a castaway on a life-preserver. "We don't know what's going on. Our parents don't either."

"It's the witches," Wayne told them. "They did this. And we're here to fix it."

Pete came swishing through the grass, dusting off his shorts, and climbed the front steps. When he saw Robin, he stopped short, his hand on the banister. The other hand held the strength-test hammer, resting on his shoulder.

"It's okay," she told him. "It's me. It's Robin, the crazy chick with the camera."

"Miss Martine?"

"The one and only."

"What the hell *happened* to you?" he asked in the bravely rude way that is the kingdom of children.

"I did the drugs. All of them." Robin pointed at him with one wire-coil finger. "Be smart, kids, stay in school."

Lucas Tiedeman burst out laughing.

"We came over here to Wayne's cause it's the farthest away from the witches' house," said Amanda. "It seemed safe. Well, the safest place, anyway. The witches never come over here. I think they're afraid of it." Her eyes wandered out to the trailer park. "My dad seems like he is, too. He won't leave the house."

"He's been drinking since the sun went away," said Evan. "He sits in the dark and drinks and stares out the window."

"Maw-Maw sleeps." Katie Fryhover peeked at Robin and hid her face again.

Kasey Johnson's stick slowly sank until the end of it was resting on the porch. "None of em will go outside," he said, his tone flat and demoralized. "Not even our neighbors, like Mr Weisser and Mrs Schumacher. They won't even answer the door when we knock."

"I think you should take your friends to the hole that goes to my apartment," said Kenway, his hand resting on Wayne's shoulder. "Make yourself at home. There's some stuff in the fridge if you get hungry. I don't know how long this is going to take."

The boy peered through his one spectacle eye at him. "Okay." Wayne waved the other children into the house. "Come on, guys."

They followed him willingly enough, but Pete stopped at the front door and turned back to Kenway. "Hey, mister?" he said, hefting the carnival mallet.

"Hmm?"

Pete grinned. "Take this with you," he said, offering the mallet to the tall Nordic vet. Kenway's big mitt closed over the wooden handle and he lifted it over his head like a barbarian straight out of a Boris Vallejo painting.

"Mjolnir," Wayne said in awe from the foyer.

Kenway flourished it. The big hammer-head made a swooshing noise through the air. "Thanks, kid."

"Kick their asses, man," said Pete.

"Oh, I almost forgot—" Taking off the GoPro harness, Wayne handed it off to Robin. "Here's your camera, ma'am." He smiled and pushed his broken glasses up on his nose. "Thank you for lettin me be your cameraman for a little while."

"Thank *you.*"

She adjusted the straps and put it on Kenway.

"And now your watch begins, Mr Cameraman." The GoPro's evil red on-air light burned in the dark, a solemn, watchful eye.

With a soft and concluding *click,* the front door eased shut behind them, leaving the magicians, the veteran, and the demon-girl alone on the front porch.

Sprawling in front of them was a twilight zone of shadows, only interrupted by the sight of the pale mobile homes marching darkly into the distance, a cemetery for giants. The night was windless and heavy, a smothering summer twilight three months too late. No crickets sang. The silence was absolute.

✪

The dirt road leading to the Lazenbury was a dark and lonely one, winding for what felt like a quarter of a mile through suboceanic darkness. With no wind and no nightlife, the trees around them were nothing but a silent wall of black paranoia, beat back only by the crunching of their heels on the gravelly dirt. Above them, the sky remained a chintzy model-town facsimile of the real thing, the stars almost low enough to reach up and touch.

Robin's glowing heart illuminated the path around them, but did nothing to assuage the feeling coming from that lightless storybook forest of being watched.

"Is that Heinrich?" asked Sara.

A wooden crucifix stood by the road some nine feet tall, overlooking them like a warning from an old pulp western. Heinrich Hammer was pinned to it with long roofing-nail spikes through his wrists and wire around his elbows.

In the green-yellow light of Robin's pulsar heart, the blood running in blotchy ribbons down his chin and chest was a glassy obsidian. He'd been worked over good; his legs were obviously broken by the crazy bandy way they angled, and his chest was a litany of gills, a dozen fleshy pink stab wounds. The witches stripped him of everything except for his slacks, but his black duster caped from the back of the cross like Christ's tomb shroud, the sleeves tossed over his shoulders as though he were being embraced by the Grim Reaper himself.

She thought he was dead, but as they approached, Robin was surprised to see his eyes crack open.

He coughed weakly. "Hi, folks."

"Good evening, Heinie," said Robin.

Heinrich spat blood into the weeds. "You know I hate when you call me that." He stared at her with one glassy, jaundiced eye. The other was swollen shut. "See you found your daddy. I bet you got some questions, hu—" His gentle prodding was cut off by a wet, productive cough.

"Is this why you trained me to kill?" she asked.

"Yeah."

"You weren't helping a bereaved girl find closure. You were sharpening a sword. *Your* sword." Robin got up close, close enough to smell the sweet, coppery smell of blood, and…something else, something both ammoniac and sugary. "Your golden ticket back into the Order." Ah, he'd pissed himself. That's what it was. They'd either really scared him or really hurt him, and at this point she hoped it was the latter.

"You tried to break one of our cardinal rules, Mr Atterberry," said Gendreau, taking off his jacket and stepping closer to place a hand on Heinrich's shirt. "Bringing a demon through the sanctification. Did you think we'd let you back in if you actually managed to *break* it?"

Robin felt ectoplasmic energy skirl up and out of the curandero's slender arm. She could see it, as well, a throbbing aura the dusky sapphire blue of the sky over a Dustbowl farm.

"I thought I could tame the demon," said Heinrich. "Filter it, *extrude it,* through the girl."

Robin made a face. "I'm not the best part of waking up, you dick."

"You thought you could *smuggle* it," Gendreau noted in droll disbelief.

Heinrich sighed. "I messed up. I did; I freely admit it. I made an ambitious mistake. But hey, look at it this way—you didn't turn out so bad, did you? Right?" A fat tear cut through the blood on his face. "My God, look at you, Robin—*cough*—you're—"

"A monster."

"—Beautiful! You're *beyond* extraordinary." He chuckled, and the chuckles turned into full-fledged (if exhausted) laughter.

"What's so funny?"

The crucified man shook his head slowly, dejectedly, and his grin drooped into a desolate grimace. She thought he'd started laughing again, but the convulsions turned out to be silent sobs. Drool slipped down his chin in a spider-silk strand.

"You have no idea what Cutty is up to in there," he told them, his breath hitching. "I found their Matron upstairs."

"You did?" Gendreau twitched. "Who is it?"

"She *claims* to be Morgan le Fay."

"The sorceress fairy-queen from Arthurian legend?"

Sara folded her arms. "You are so full of shit. That's impossible. Morgan le Fay wasn't even real. Those were stories."

"Hey, don't shoot the messenger," said Heinrich.

"Even if that *is* le Fay up there, she'd have to be *hundreds* of years old."

"Almost two thousand years old," said Gendreau. "According to Arthurian legend, Arthur Pendragon defended Britain against Saxon invaders in 510, 520 AD. He *was* real, if embellished. If Morgan was real, she was contemporary to that time."

He stared at the dirt under their feet in thought, drawing curative runes with the tip of his cane. "She first appeared in an 1170 book by Chrétien de Troyes. I can't remember the name, though. For some reason I want to say it's *Enid Blythe,* but that's not right. Oh no, wait, it wasn't de Troyes, it was *The Life of Merlin* by Geoffrey of Monmouth."

"You can remember all that," asked Sara, "but you can't remember your order between the radio and the window at freakin' Chik-Fil-A? Some savant *you* turned out to be."

Robin's eyes rolled up to the temple-like silhouette of the Lazenbury. The lights were still on in there, hollow orange eyes in the black, but it might have been candles. Probably was. "If their Matron is really Morgan, she's...."

"Old as hell?" asked Lucas.

"To put it bluntly," interjected Gendreau. "And more powerful than any witch alive."

The unspoken insinuation was obvious to Robin. *We may have bitten off more than we can chew.* She hoped she was the secret weapon Heinrich had intended her to be.

"I didn't see much of her." The old witch-hunter flexed one arm as if getting comfortable and jerked in sudden sharp pain, crying out, his legs twitching and curling like back-broken snakes. His cries were desperate, pitiful, and nothing at all like the commanding, brooding presence he'd been.

Fresh blood dribbled from the nails through his wrists. Every fifth or sixth word was interrupted by a panting breath. "They're tryin to bring someone—some*thing* back. Tryin to resurrect something. They been tryin for a long time. It's why Annie's apples are so fat. They been nibblin' on em, savin em up for the resurrection."

Heinrich hung his head. "They've always been here, Robin. I was too big for my britches. We *all* was. Cutty and her Matron have been here since the inception of this town." He grunted and cried out in pain again. "I'm sorry I dragged you into this, babygirl."

"If you'll open your eyes again, you'll see that I'm neither baby nor girl. Or even human."

He did so, and looked at her for a long time with drowsy eyes.

"Get out of here," he said. "While you still can." Heinrich coughed, spattering Robin's wirecoil chest with blood. "However you got here, use it to get back, and stay away. This some Plan 9 top-level Pentagram Pentagon black magic. They gonna jump up and down on you til you die, then wake you up and beat you some more."

"We're here, and I can't leave until this is done." She pointed north, toward the black mission-house. "My mother is in that nag shi. I'm not going to abandon her again. I can't have her back, but I can set her free."

Even in his state, Heinrich still managed to give her that under-the-eyebrows *you better do what I say girl* look. She knew it well; she'd seen it enough over the last few years.

When he couldn't elicit a change in her, he turned to Gendreau. "What's the verdict, Doc?"

"Hypothetically, I could pull you back from the brink." The curandero left off, shaking a handkerchief out of his pocket and wiping his bloody hand on it. "But you're so far gone that you're going to die before I can make much of a difference. I would need a lot more time. To be honest I'm surprised you've lasted this long."

"The human body is a miracle thing, Doc," said Heinrich with a scoff. "It can take a good whoopin before it gives up. And I ain't never gave up." He coughed and choked, grimaced, spat to the side. "Before you go, will you take me out a Hawaiian and light it for me? They're in my coat pocket behind me."

Robin dug in one pocket, then another, found the box and the Zippo. Tapping out a cigar, she paused to drag it under her nose, savoring the rich coconut smell.

"S'good shit, baby," said Heinrich.

She stuck the cigar in his mouth, and if she'd told you she didn't do it to shut him up, she would have been by all rights a liar.

He walked it in with his lips. She flicked open the lighter, ignited it, and lit the cigar with it. He took a deep draw and a cloud of smoke billowed out of his face. He winced, his hands flexing against the nails and fence-wire.

"I can't fuckin reach it."

She dropped the lighter in his shirt pocket and patted it neatly in place. "You'll figure it out."

He grinned, squinting in the smoke, the Hawaiian caught in his teeth. "You a cold-ass cambion, Robin Martine. Colder n' a welldigger's ass."

"It's the season of the witch."

He took another draw and let it go, coughing with a pained wince. "Give em hell, babe."

Forty-Four

THE DIRT ROAD SEEMED interminable, a ribbon of dust and gravel snaking into the false night. She didn't remember it being this long, or the upslope being this dramatic.

As they got closer to the Lazenbury, they got quiet, rolling their steps and abandoning conversation, assumedly trying to preserve some element of surprise. Robin had put on Gendreau's jacket, buttoning it closed to mitigate the shine of her heart inside her chest.

She looked back at the others. Gendreau's face was the picture of dark focus, but Lucas and Sara were scared as hell.

"How many have you killed?" she asked them.

Lucas spoke to the ground. "Three."

"What about you, Sara?"

Sara didn't speak at first. Eventually she said, "My Gift isn't meant for combat."

"So...none."

Irritation simmered in the back of Robin's mind, but what Gendreau said next fizzled it. "She's not here for fighting," mumbled the curandero. "She's the most talented conjurer and illusionist in the Order outside of my father. Sara is here to dispel Weaver's illusions for us."

"Ah."

The ground leveled out and the west face of Lazenbury House hulked at them from the darkness like a ghost ship. Faintly to the north, past the end of the driveway, they could see the rollups of the garage. Except... the longer she looked at it, the less it resembled a garage and the more it appeared to be a stable. The doors shimmered and wavered, and she could see the cars inside—an RV and a Plymouth Fury—resting on a layer of scattered straw and rushes.

And then they were horses. Two chestnut quarterhorses and a painted mare. Tails swished against the night.

Robin glanced at Sara. Her fists were clenched at her sides and she leaned forward as if pressing her forehead against some invisible surface, a look of immense concentration on her face.

The Lazenbury itself came alive with raucous noise and movement. The playful fey laughter of young women, tinkling piano music, shuffling boots, the heady *thunk* of glass mugs on hardwood tables. Windows that had been clear and modern, doublepaned to retain heat, became warped and cloudy leaded glass.

Through them Robin could see shapes moving back and forth, as if there were some kind of party going on inside.

An electric wall-sconce next to the exterior-opening kitchen door jiggered like a film-reel and suddenly it was a gas lantern, dull and hissing with a sick green-orange light. The door itself transformed, melting with LSD fluidity from an aluminum screen door into a heavy wooden one with a head-sized password hatch cut in the middle. Iron pencil bars were bolted over the hole.

Lucas asided to Gendreau, "Why didn't you *tell* me you were taking me to a whorehouse?"

"Because it hasn't been a whorehouse for almost a century." The curandero asked Sara, "This is, I'm assuming, an illusion. Can you dispel it?"

"I'm trying. It's pretty well stapled down." She raked her fingers through her hair, tousling it, and her hands went back to her temples, clutching the sides of her forehead. "I'll keep working on it."

"You do that," said Robin, opening the kitchen door, releasing a burst of fragrant steam and a wave of incredible heat. "I'm going in."

"Not by yourself you ain't." Lucas followed her.

Gendreau grumped. "Oh, piss and potatoes. Wait for me, then."

The forge-hot kitchen was a bustle of movement, lit only by gas lamps on the walls to either side. Three women and a man in greasy white smocks shuffled in a coordinated dance between two bubbling stock pots, a brick oven full of Halloween-orange light, and the gruesome cadaver of a wild boar

(stab it with their steely knives)

suspended on a spit over glowing coals in the middle of the room. Both left haunches, the flank, and half the face were gone, leaving clinical cross-sections open to the heat of the air. Robin saw an empty skull, a crabbish cluster of teeth, the pallid stripes of rib-bone, and looked away, queasy.

A preoccupied, dreamlike ignorance hung over the scene like Scrooge being shown his own memories by the Spirit of Christmas Past, and the cookies took no notice of their new visitors—or if they did, paid them no mind.

Robin pushed through a swinging door and went into the saloon.

Filthy workmen in chambray shirts and dungarees played cards, told jokes, and drank at five round tables in what should have been Marilyn

Cutty's living room. A thin cirrus haze of cigarette smoke hovered around an iron chandelier arrayed with hurricane lamps. A passel of whores in bustiers and striped hose leaned against an upstairs railing.

Below, a bar ran across the room on their left, staffed by a ginger in arm-garters and a villainous mustache. At the far end was a player piano, where a slope-shouldered minstrel in a ratty hide coat and hat sat on a stool tickling ivories.

The barman poured liquid honey into a glass and pushed it toward a grungy hobo in a Stetson and a leather duster. Twinkling beneath the flap of the hobo's coat was a mint-condition breaktop Colt revolver.

Kenway stared. "Did we wander into the holodeck from *Star Trek,* or what?"

Gendreau's face was grim. "This is quite possibly the most realistic illusion I've ever seen. Hell, I'm not one hundred percent sure it's not a conjuration...or even, God help me, a temporal anomaly."

"It's not a time-warp," said Sara, snapping her fingers in front of a man's face. He sifted through his poker cards, oblivious to her attempts to distract him.

"Do they know we're here?" Robin asked. "Do Weaver and Cutty know we're here?"

The piano stopped abruptly, mid-melody.

Eyes burned at them from every direction as the miners and cowboys looked up from their liquor and card games and fixed on Robin and the Dog Star magicians.

"Ah," said Lucas.

The pianist wheeled about on her stool and clutched her bony knees, standing up.

"Yes, we're quite aware you're here, love," said Karen Weaver. Her dark-rimmed eyes blazed underneath the floppy brim of her hat, a loose hatcord under her chin. She looked like an elderly Annie Oakley in her tweed vest and paisley cravat. She appraised Robin from where she stood by the piano. One hand softly closed the piano's key cover and rested there.

"How did you get in here?" Weaver's other hand went to the hatcord and worried at it. "How did you get into my poke?"

"Your poke?"

"My tesseract," Weaver said sharply, impatiently, as if talking to an idiot. "My tesseract, *my tesseract!* You know what that *is,* yes?"

Gendreau nodded. "A simple enough astrophysics concept: the folding of space to make a distance shorter. Folding point A to point C to eliminate point B."

Weaver stepped away from the piano, her age-spotted hands clutched over her heart, and retreated to touch it again as if it could lend her some degree of protection, or comfort. "Well of course, of course. But ay; what happens to point B, then? Ah, you're standing in it, you are, you are. This is the land between: my ...poke." The witch continued to stare at Robin. "Who are *you*? ...*What* are you?"

"Annie's daughter." Robin took off the plush navy jacket and handed it back to Gendreau, revealing the lighthouse pulse of her heart. "It turns out the ritual my mother used Edgar for—"

"Killed!" spat Weaver. *"My husband, killed!"*

"—*killed* Edgar for wasn't entirely wasted. She *did* manage to summon a demon. But it was an incubus. And it... took her."

Weaver's face soured. "A half-breed, then. You've got the blood of a demon in you. I should have expected as much. It was always a mystery to us how your mother could have given birth to you after her sacrifice to the Goddess...we always assumed she'd been with child since before. Children carried through the ritual usually come out stillborn...but not always. There are exceptions...."

"This time, I wasn't the exception."

"No, no, I suppose not..." The witch remained by the piano. "Oh, but you're such a deadly-beautiful snake, aren't you? A regular prize. I've never seen a demon before. Marilyn says, she says they're dangerous; they *eat* magic, you know, they feed on the energies out there—" She swept a pensive hand at the ceiling, as if the afterlife rested just outside the atmosphere.

"But when we're here among the living," said Robin, "we prefer to suckle on the heart-roads of witches."

All the desperados' eyes tracked her as she took a step across the saloon.

Weaver recoiled, shaking.

She shouted, "Don't you take another step, you snide hobgoblin, you worthless cur-dog—! You stay away from me, you hear? I *told* you not to come here, didn't I? But you didn't listen. You *never* listened." The witch bit back a grimace, flashing her buckish front teeth. "Always knocking on the door, *let me in, Gramma, let me in,* little whelp making a mess, screwing up my seamstress work."

She pinched at the air to emphasize. "I thought maybe if I left a few of my needles in the carpet, you'd stay out of my sewing room, maybe a few pricks in your pink little feet and you'd stay the hell *out*, but nope! I'd get up to go piss and when I came back you'd be right back in there again, pulling out my pins and knocking my dummy over!

"And Mary didn't care, oh *no*, she'd laugh and laugh, and tell me, *She's just a little girl, Karen, you had a little girl once, you know they're a handful,* and yes, I had a little girl once, but did she have to rub it in? Did she always have to rub it in?"

Robin took another step.

Weaver pointed at her. "Go back where you came from, goddamn you!" she said in a rapid, poisonous hiss, "I'm not going to tell you again!"

"Enough of this—" Robin lunged at her, clutching her jacket.

It came away in her hands as if the witch had slipped right out of it. When she looked up she saw that the witch had evaporated, leaving Robin holding empty clothes…if she'd ever really been there at all.

Robin turned to say something, and saw that *all* the cowboys now had Weaver's face.

Two, three dozen Karen Weaver clones played cards at the tables. The man drinking at the bar was Weaver. The ginger behind the bar was Weaver, mustache and all. Even the whores upstairs were Weaver, her eight mushy old hippie tits wobbling in their bust-cups like tapioca.

"Time to take you all out to the woodshed and give yuns a whoopin," said one of the gambling Weavers, tossing back a glass of whiskey.

The Weaver bartender rolled up her sleeves, flourishing handfuls of gleaming black claws. "Yessssss," she snarled, her face lengthening, her mouth drooping open. Wolven teeth dripped saliva on the bar.

Weaver-doubles all over the saloon rose from their chairs, stripping off their hats, faces and fingers stretching, becoming swarthy and hideous. Their eyes deepened, darkened, red marbles glittering in black pits.

Kenway let the carnival hammer drop into his other hand and rolled his neck with a sick crackle.

"Ah, well, you see—" Gendreau started to say.

The lights went out, leaving them in a moonlit tangle of shadows.

"—Piss and potatoes!"

The saloon exploded into movement as every witch in sight descended on the magicians like a murder of screeching ravens.

Snatching up a deck of poker cards, Lucas started whipping them overhand into the crowd. One of the witches fell away, a Jack of Diamonds sticking out of her chest, and collapsed on the floor, melting into smoke.

The *thwock! thwock! thwack!* of Kenway's hammer echoed off the high plaster ceiling, swinging in great overhead arcs. The vet staggered from one encounter to another, smacking their foreheads in a frenzied game of Whack-a-Mole.

Witches' skulls whiplashed, bouncing off Kenway's bloody mallet head. "Little Bunny Foo-Foo!" he was singing with maniacal glee, "a-runnin through the forest!" The hammer struck at the end of every line. "Pickin up the field mice, and boppin em on the head!"

Gendreau and Sara backpedaled, the curandero leading her out of the way and defending her with his pizzle cane, twirling and striking with some clever sort of martial art. The fist-sized pearl at the end made for an outstanding bludgeon. The illusionist made obscure symbols in the air with her fingers, trying to dispel the imagery.

Robin waded into the melee, attempting to grab a Weaver and suck the juice out of her, but it was like herding cats—the clones would flinch or duck, fending her off with chairs and bar stools, juking out of the way. The two she managed to lay hands on vanished into egg-smelling smoke.

401

"One of them's got to be the real witch!" she told the magicians, "grab one and hold her and let me—"

Something hard slammed into her shoulder, almost knocking her down. Kenway winced, lifting the carnival hammer. "Woop, sorry!"

"Watch where you're swingin that thing!"

"Yes ma'am!"

He turned and smashed it through a chair and into a clone's head, evaporating her. Then he missed a swing at another one and upended a table with it, raining beer, broken glass, and 19th century dollar-coins across the ceiling.

A witch leapt on his back and sank her yellow fangs into his shoulder. *"Aaaaah!"*

Robin took her by the hair of the head, marching her over to the bar to slam her facefirst into the polished counter, breaking her nose with a thick *bang*.

This one didn't disappear.

"Got you now, chick," said Robin, and grasped her by the throat. Oily blood streamed out of Weaver's nose, dripping from her hellacious gargoyle teeth.

Concentrating, Robin pushed her consciousness into the witch, a sort of mental pseudopod, and found the heart-road deep inside. Then she withdrew, pulling the energy with it like a fish-hook. It came thin and watery into the center of her being, and a dank salty taste welled in her mouth.

The light of her heart flashed brightly through her fibrous chest, casting disco-ball flares around the room.

Weaver gasped. The skin of her face became sallow and shrank taut against the bone, every curve and socket suddenly reliefed in sharp detail.

"Nooo!" cawed the witch, wresting herself out of Robin's grip.

The other shadow-Weavers converged on Robin as the real one shrank away, and she found herself battling a flock of shrieking harpies. They shoved her down on the floor and raked and wrenched at her with their claws, tearing away strips of skin that bent and ripped like chicken-wire.

"I'll kill you, you demon whore!" screamed one of them, wedging her nails under Robin's right breast and tearing it away. Another one scrabbled at her ear, breaking it off. *"You and your mother took my Edgar away! I'll swallow your soul!"*

Robin punched her with a wire-coil fist, shattering the witch's teeth. "Not if I swallow yours first."

The head of Kenway's mallet came down on a clone's head, snapping her neck. Weaver's double collapsed like a house of cards, mushrooming across the floor in a carpet of smoke. Lucas hauled one away and threw her down on the floor, stomping her face; she, too, went *poof.*

Kenway growled, hooking the handle of the mallet under a witch's chin, pulling her out of the fight. The two of them were locked in a staggering dance, the big veteran strangling her with the hammer.

Robin watched out of the corner of her eye as the witch in Kenway's arms finally gave up, going limp—

—and turned into Sara Amundson.

He let go with a stifled scream, and Sara's slack body crumpled at his feet. The hammer fell out of Kenway's shocked hand. "Oh God!" screamed Lucas, shoving a path through the last of the witches. "No! *Sara!*"

If that's Sara, thought Robin, *then who is—*

Gendreau stood paralyzed with horror and confusion at the edge of the room, watching this tragedy play out.

"Watch out!" screamed Robin.

But the Sara behind him was already stepping forward. She hooked an arm around the curandero's neck.

At the last instant, he spotted the blade, and squeezed his eyes closed. That was probably the worst part—he saw it coming. The knife in her hand flashed, and she zipped open his throat as easy as you please.

A sheet of arterial blood poured into the collar of Gendreau's effete white shirt, dyeing it a rich watercolor red.

Weaver shoved him and he stumbled over a broken chair, faceplanting onto the dusty boards.

The witch cackled, flaunting the knife.

Black blood from her broken nose made an inky bib down her face and chest. "You thought you were gonna beat the greatest illusionist that ever lived, did you? You thought you could see through my tricks, eh? Well, Ole Miss Tricksy got the best of *you*, didn't she?"

"*Eeeerraaaaaahh!*" roared Lucas, hurling the remainder of his poker cards. It looked like almost a whole deck.

A dazzle of cards arrowed across the saloon, passing through an open gauntlet formed by the crowd of clones, and the spinning squares tore through the true Weaver like a volley of flechettes fired from a rail gun.

Each card struck and lodged in the wall behind her in a rapid *tunk-tunk-tunk-tunk-tunk!* and a spray of black.

Some of them were intercepted by her ribs and face. A card protruded from the divot between the witch's eye and nose.

Every shadow-clone in sight disappeared as one, extinguishing en masse, and the saloon itself flickered like a bad television signal. One second there were overturned tables and poker chips and smashed pint glasses all over the floor, then reality seemed to hiccup and suddenly they were standing in Marilyn Cutty's living room.

The flatscreen TV had been knocked over and smashed, the chairs were against the walls, and the sofa had been shoved into the entertainment center, but otherwise they were back in the twenty-first century.

Weaver slumped onto her knees, *thump-thump*, and fell over.

"Somebody help, goddammit!" bellowed Lucas. He sat on the floor, with Gendreau dragged up into his lap.

The curandero was holding his neck, trying to magic it back together, blood squirting through his fingers. His face was a drawn gray and his eyes were huge and terrified.

"Must—" he choked, blood gurgling out of his mouth.

"Don't speak." Robin took his cane away from him and clutched the cueball pearl in her strange hands, gazing into its smooth, iridescent white surface as if it were a crystal ball. She pushed her mind against the pearl and felt the heart-road inside, but it was muffled, weak, a whisper through a pillow, the thoughts of a chick in an egg.

She could take it, take it all, but it would require time. Twenty, thirty minutes, at least.

Time she didn't have. She whacked the pearl against the floor.

Lucas gritted his teeth. "What are you doing?"

CRACK! She banged it against the glossy hardwood again. "I'm trying to get at the *libbu-harrani* inside," she told him. "I can absorb it and use it to fix him—" *CRACK!* "—but I can't get it out fast enough with this hard matter around it."

Finally, the pearl exploded into three heavy chunks with a puff of white dust. Robin picked up the largest piece.

In the middle was a tooth.

A human tooth: a pristine white molar.

Surreal alarm briefly scrambled her thoughts, a bewildered panic with wild, terrified wings, beating against the inside of her skull. *A human tooth—?*

"Come on!" shouted Lucas.

"Yeah, okay." Squeezing the ancient tooth in her fist, Robin tapped the ethereal energy inside, reeling it out like fishing line.

Visions from the 18th century clouded her mind, hitchhiking on the power pouring from the tooth. Images of a petticoated woman tied to a maypole; men in buckled shoes. She ignored them and put her other hand on Gendreau's throat

(Lucretia Melcher: we of the town of Philadelphia,)

and proceeded to channel the ectoplasm from his borrowed heart-road up her left arm and down her right and into Gendreau. The pulsar in her chest became

(hereby sentence you to be burned at the stake)

a stuttering supernova strobe. The bleeding stopped as Gendreau's cells mingled, reattaching to each other, intertwining, reforming the pipettes of

(for the crime of being a witch.)

404

his severed carotid and jugular. His larynx, nicked by the blade, smoothed over and was whole. Bandy red muscles that had been split reached for each other and braided. The ragged smile stretching across his skin pursed together and resealed from ear to ear like the lips of a Ziploc bag.

Robin felt for a pulse. There wasn't one. She tried his wrist; none there either.

No, wait—there it was. A bare sliver of movement, a fleeting squirm under the skin. The relief overwhelmed her and she sat back with a near-delirious moan.

"Oh my God," said Lucas, looking over her shoulder. "You're alive!"

Kenway hauled Sara up to a sitting position. The illusionist coughed and gasped for air, holding her throat, pain written on her face. "What happened?" she croaked.

"Uhh…" Kenway glanced at them. "The witch tricked me, and I choked you out on accident."

Sara coughed again, wincing, glancing daggers of ice at the poor man. Then her eyes fell on the blood-soaked curandero in Lucas's lap. "Oh! *Ohhhh! Doc!*" She struggled to her knees and hovered over Gendreau. "Is he gonna be okay? Is he *alive?*"

"He's still alive, but…I don't know." Robin fixated on the tooth in her palm. "I don't know."

✦

Karen Weaver dragged herself across the living room floor through a slimy, gritty, steak-sauce puddle of her own rotten blood. Dozens of Bicycle playing cards bristled from the wall above.

The Queen of Hearts was buried in her face up to the number, leaving only a tab of paper showing, as if her brain had been bookmarked.

She'd been shot full of holes by thirty-eight of them, six of them lodged in her ribs and spine. She was half carrion, her supernaturally-altered cells half a century old, extended by the life-force stored in Annie Martine's apples…but a severed spinal cord is a severed spinal cord, and Karen no longer had the use of her legs.

Robin stood over her.

The witch rolled over and put up her shaking hands. The eye on the card side of her face was lax and dead, refusing to move. "I'm d-done for, you wuh-wearisome harlot." Her mouth pooled with black. "Leave me buh-be."

Robin knelt and took hold of the lapels of Weaver's riotous rag-coat, lifting her. *"You* may be done," she said, her voice without fire or ice, "but *I'm* not." Her mind dived for the source of that dark power again.

This time she found a thread of warmth, and recognized it as stolen life-force, the give-a-shit from what Heinrich would have called Annie's *flora de vida*.

She drew them both out and internalized them.

Weaver's face emptied, a jaundiced canvas pulling tight across her skull. Her nose caved in like melting wax and her eyes retreated, shriveling. Her lips thinned and shrank, sliding back to reveal horsey yellow teeth, giving her the silently screaming face of a peat-buried corpse.

"I'll be waiting," the witch wheezed in an arid whisper, and died for the second time.

❂

Marilyn Cutty's clairvoyance proved to be to her advantage, as neither she or her Matron were anywhere to be found in the Lazenbury. Robin explored the house, moving purposefully from room to room like a SWAT cop. The second floor was occupied by the witches' three spacious and palatial bedrooms, each one containing a four-poster bed and resplendent with each woman's tastes.

Karen Weaver's looked like the inside of a homestead lodge, with framed paintings on the walls depicting wildlife and mountain ranges, and there were bolts and scraps of cloth and half-finished projects all over the room.

The bedroom belonging to Theresa LaQuices held the austerity of a nun's cell but it was messy, the bedquilt and wood floor strewn with clothes and dirty dishes.

Cutty's was probably the cleanest and most ostentatious of the three, well appointed with baroque cherry furniture and silk fleur-de-lis wallpaper the oceanic green of seawater at the shore. The curtains were spiderwebs of white, lacy gossamer.

A descending-ladder hatch led up to the attic.

Robin pulled the hatch down and climbed into darkness, her shining heart cutting the soft shade like a torch.

The attic was enormous, running the length and width of the house. Dusty furniture and assorted bric-a-brac made a dark, cluttered forest of antiques, but there was a labyrinthine path cut through the middle; this she trickled carefully through, constantly on the lookout for an ambush, but when she found the Matron's Anne Frank hideyhole in the very back she knew they were gone.

The door was half-hidden behind an armoire. She pushed it aside and behind it was a small room with a simple bed, a television, and a window overlooking the vineyard grove.

A chair sat abandoned in the middle of the room, arrayed with cushions and a warm blanket.

406

Robin went back downstairs, wondering if the Matron really *was* the Morgan le Fay from the Arthurian legends. No matter. If she *was* that old, she was dangerous regardless of what she called herself.

Leon Parkin was nowhere in the house either. A hot pang of shame drilled through her when she thought of the talk she would have to have with Wayne. What would he say? What would he *do*? What would *she* have to do?

Of course, she would have to hunt down Cutty and her Matron wherever they went. That was a given…this blood feud didn't stop just because Robin eliminated her coven. The two of them had probably jumped ship to settle down somewhere else, God knew where. But that was their way, wasn't it? The witches were most often nomadic. They roamed like rats from town to town, country to country, looking for a place to chew a hole and make a nest.

Wayne would undoubtedly want to go with Robin when she went after Cutty.

Could she allow that?

Did she have a choice?

He couldn't stay here by himself. He needed to have a real life, a *normal* life, go to school and live in a house, not in the back of a van, running from maniacs and starting fires.

On the way through the living room, she checked on Gendreau. The blood-soaked curandero was breathing shallowly, his eyes slit open just enough to see her. They closed and his face darkened in pain.

The kitchen was abandoned and dark, no boar, no oblivious chefs. She fetched a glass of water from the tap.

On the way out, she heard a scuffling noise at the driveway door, and when she opened it Eduardo the dog came trotting out of the night. They must have accidentally shut the door on him.

"We really could have used your help back there, Eddie," she told him.

Eduardo whined.

She brought the water back and gave it to Gendreau, who was sitting on Cutty's sofa recuperating from having his throat cut. It felt a bit strange to see real people get really hurt—and almost *die*—and realize how long it takes for fully human people to get over their injuries. "Now I know why I've always been so strong," she mused to herself, looking at her strange wire-and-vine hands. "So resilient."

Gendreau winced, whispering, "We'll figure out how to fix you. Come to the Order." The slash across his throat was now a jagged pink lightning bolt.

"Fix me, or kill me?" She folded her arms. "Or do experiments on me?"

He smiled. "Can't promise the alchemists won't want a urine sample." Wincing again, he swallowed. The knot of his adam's-apple curtseyed under his new scar. "We're not the Pentagon. Nobody will be dissecting you, promise."

Sara combed his hair out of his face, petting his head. "Shut up, old man. Rest yourself. Are we going to have to get Thor here to knock you out with his hammer?"

He gave a weak grin, flashing one pointy canine.

"So now what?" asked Lucas. "I'm guessing that since you're here talking to us, Cutty wasn't upstairs."

"No, she's flown the coop. Took Wayne's dad with her, too."

"She left her dryad here?"

There was no way Cutty could have dug up Annie by herself in two days, much less transport a tree half the size of the Christmas pine in Rockefeller Square. "I guess she considers herself and her Matron more important than the nag shi tree." Robin sighed. "She can always make another one, after all."

"That's true. Man, that kid's gonna be bummed his dad wasn't here."

A few minutes passed as Robin considered her options and let them comfort Gendreau.

"Kenway," she said, finally.

"Hmm?"

"Will you come with me into the vineyard?" she asked, pointing toward the rear of the house. "I don't want to go by myself. I want you with me." Her hand rested on Lucas's shoulder. "You guys stay here and take care of Doc."

Kenway got up out of the chair he'd been sitting in, with the hammer across his knees. Now he stood and wordlessly slung it over his shoulder.

❂

Night rested in the vineyard clotted and cold, an ocean floor that rustled with dead grapevines instead of kelp. Robin's heart was a depth charge of light, sifting through the trellises in soft tines of gold.

Kenway walked silently alongside her, flint in his expression.

His furrowed brow and downcast face almost made him seem as if he were a pouty little boy, and suddenly she wanted to be far from this grave place, somewhere warm and far away from the world where she could be alone with him.

He noticed her watching and smiled, though his eyes were still hard. She wondered what he was thinking. She stared up at the stars as they walked. The "poke", as the witch had called it, had straightened itself out on her death, and now the galaxy no longer seemed to be twenty feet above them.

Without Weaver around to alter the lay of the land back here, the vineyard turned out to be a lot smaller than she'd thought. The first time

408

she'd been through it felt like they'd walked for miles, passing out of the world and into the leagues of some alien wilderness of vines and fences. Now it only took them a few minutes to reach the end of the property, and even the landscaping seemed smaller than she remembered it: four scant patches of purple flowers and stunted trees barely twice as tall as the fence, all of it scattered with lavender that drooped and shook in the wind.

The nag shi, the dryad, the Malus Domestica, her mother Annie Martine stood in the center of the clearing at the end of the path.

All the apples were gone. The tree had been picked clean.

That, at least, Cutty had been able to undertake in the last two days. A mixture of solace and irritation passed through her. To Robin, the apples themselves represented the witches' repulsive influence, their fell intent, and to see her mother rid of them was like seeing a loved one come out of rehab, free of heroin and ready to live again.

Robin went to the tree and looked up into its branches.

"I'm back, Mom. Marilyn is gone and I'm here." The wind sighed in the tree's leaves, a sound that Robin would swear until the day she died carried a certain relief.

"I'm here to … to fix what … what they did to you."

She placed a hand on Annie's rugged hip, and then the other one, and closed her eyes. She let her mind relax and flow in a rivulet downhill through the slopes of her arms, into the apple tree.

It was dark and quiet behind her eyelids.

She had the feeling that she was standing at the bottom of a dry well; she could even smell the dank fossilized memory of water.

Mom?

A lambent spirit lustered softly in the narrow space, cowering, insensate.

Robin felt it turn and regard her. Guarded exhaustion came from the other mind in lieu of words, like the nonsense murmur of someone waking from a deep sleep after a long day. *It's me.* Robin smiled. *I'm here. I came back. I beat them and I'm here to get you out.*

The warmest light she'd ever felt poured from the presence as Annie recognized her.

It was love, it was love and sorrow and regret, and a vacant space in Robin's center filled up with such overwhelming affection that at first she could no longer speak, paralyzed with secondhand adoration. *It's okay,* she thought, *it's okay,* because she was sure she knew where the regret was coming from: her mother. *You didn't know what would happen when you summoned the demon, but it's okay, everything turned out okay for me.*

It wasn't only love that was filling her up, she gradually realized, it was Annie herself, her mother was moving toward her, *into* her, this consumed woman that had spent the last half-decade trapped in this spiritual sweat shop spinning straw into gold, spinning the town's prosperity into life-giving apples.

Robin enveloped the spirit as it stepped into her and suffused her with elation. She took the last fragment of her mother into her arms and held her until the dry well that had been her cell inside the tree was empty and cold.

"Oh," breathed Kenway at her side.

She opened her eyes and took her hands away from the now-cold bark, dimly aware that she'd been crying, *sobbing,* tears spilling down her face.

Her hands were soft and human again.

Both of them. She studied her left arm with astonishment and found it whole and functional. *New,* even—the scars that had littered her arms were gone without a trace. Robin's knees buckled and she sat on her ankles like a penitent in the dewy grass, holding herself, lost in a happiness so stunning and so savage it was almost grief.

Slipping his arms under Robin, Kenway lifted her, staggered up onto his titanium foot, and carried her out of the vineyard.

FRIDAY

Forty-Five

WAYNE WAS A ZOMBIE.

He spent the entirety of Halloween (and the two days before) piled up on the couch, mindlessly staring at a succession of horror movies on television and ignoring trick-or-treaters that rang at the doorbell every few minutes.

Where u at Dad

His cellphone was glued to his hand. In the hours and days since the assault on Lazenbury House had failed to turn up his father, he'd sent dozens and dozens of text messages to Leon's phone, waiting and listening for a response.

Where are u dad?

But none came. He refused to go to school, staying in bed until almost lunchtime, and he didn't sleep well at all, pacing quietly around the house after midnight, staring out the front window at the lights of downtown Blackfield like a soldier's wife.

They'd put in a missing-persons report at the police station, but Robin knew that if Cutty didn't want him to be found, he wouldn't be.

For her part, she drove Wayne around in her plumbing van all Wednesday night and all Thursday, looking for Leon in all the obvious places—the high school twice, the liquor store three times, the police-taped comic shop once, and 1168 no less than six times—but he was nowhere to be found.

Answer me dam it

Wayne was staying with Joel Ellis at his mother's uptown bungalow house, since it had a spare bedroom.

Robin spent Wednesday and Thursday night there, keeping vigil over the hollow-eyed Wayne and editing her videos for the MalusDomestica channel while Joel went back to work at Miguel's.

Since Kenway Griffin didn't have anything better to do, he hung around with her. On top of that, Ashe Armstrong came by in the evenings to talk with Joel about what they were going to do with Fisher's comic

412

shop, and ostensibly to console his best friend's brother, so except for Wayne, the house was alive with activity. Joel definitely appreciated the company, since the weekend's excitement was winding down and he'd finally had time to fully process his brother's death.

His decision to go back to work so soon wasn't made lightly. Miguel refused him at first, practically forcing him to go home and rest, and grieve, but Joel had insisted, saying he needed something to take his mind off of things, said he needed to stay busy.

Nothing made this more obvious than the way he'd been Wednesday afternoon; Armstrong had found him a drunken, sloppy mess splayed out in the kitchen floor with a beer, and he would have agreed to just about anything if it meant he wouldn't have to sit in his childhood home alone, listening to the wind lowing in the eaves, waiting for Cutty (or, he admitted, a resurrected Euchiss) to come finish him off.

Someone knocked at the front door. Robin tore her eyes away from the TV (*Night of the Living Dead,* of course) and answered it.

Instead of kids—she figured she'd probably handed out candy to at least thirty Spider-Men, Iron Men, and Batmen at this point—she found herself beholding the three magicians and their little dog, too. A feverish indigo sunset leapt across the sky behind them, making shadow-teeth of the city.

"Trick or treat." Sara was wearing her Murdercorn wig again. She must have rescued it from their demolished Suburban.

Robin was dressed as a witch, of course, green-faced and hook-nosed. In a fit of pique, she'd also painted her cleavage green to fill out the deep V of her black Lycra gown. "Nice," said Lucas Tiedeman. He was dressed in an Eastwood poncho and gambler hat, a cowboy revolver gleaming at his hip. "Super hot."

"Thanks," she said, dry but amused. "Come on in."

She stepped aside, eyeballing Gendreau's velvet top hat. With his navy waistcoat, he really *did* look like Willy Wonka.

Eduardo trotted between their feet and went into the living room. As soon as he saw Wayne sitting on the couch with his red eyes locked on the TV screen, the little dog clambered up onto the couch with him and pawed at his sleeve.

Noticing the dog, Wayne pulled Eduardo into his lap and wrapped his arms around him. Eddie licked his face consolingly.

Lucas smirked. "Eduardo Pendergast, the Boy Whisperer."

They filed into the kitchen and sat at Mama Ellis's table. The only light in the room came from the hood over the stove, casting a dim yellowish light at their feet. Somehow it gave the scene a desolate yet warm feel. Robin busied herself putting up the dishes in Joel's dish drain, and said over her shoulder, "I have a pot of coffee on, if anybody wants any."

"I'll take some," said Gendreau. His voice was the dusty, whispery croak of Death.

Robin eyed him. "How's your throat?"

"Getting better." The magician's pizzle cane looked odd without the pearl on top. "I owe you my life."

She smiled, searching the cabinet for a cup. She settled on a mug with a picture of a smiling macaw in front of a tropical vista. PANAMA CITY BEACH, it said across the bottom in slashy letters.

Sara opened the lid on the gravyboat in the middle of the table and peered inside. "Where's your boyfriend?" Whatever was in there must have been distasteful, because she grimaced and put it back down.

"I don't know," said Robin, pouring coffee. "He's been gone all day. He said he was trying to sell off his signage shop."

Sara grinned crookedly. "I take it he's made up his mind to go off with you, then."

"Yeah. He wants to be my 'cameraman'."

"If the van's a-rockin, don't come a-knockin," said Lucas, raising a fist for Sara to bump.

She scowled and opened the gravyboat, showing him the contents. "Pervert."

Lucas sat back. "Ew."

Handing off the coffee to Gendreau, Robin took off her floppy witch-hat and hung it on one of the posts of the fourth chair, then folded her arms and leaned against the stove.

"Thank you," he croaked.

"You're welcome."

"Oh, that reminds me." Gendreau reached into his jacket and took out a pocket watch, handing it to her. It was the busted pocket watch that had been hanging on Eduardo's collar like some kind of canine Flava Flav. "Eddie wanted you to have this."

"Is this his heart-road artifact?" Robin held it up to the hood-light and studied its cracked face-glass. It was genuine, but lacked the patina of an antique buffed by a thousand hands. She put it at less than twenty years old.

She could feel the power lying dormant inside, pulsing drowsily in time with the ticking clockwork.

Helping Annie into the afterlife had won her her humanity back, but she was still half-demon...and after the catalyzing effects of finally facing Andras, she supposed there were parts of her that were permanently stretched out of shape. She would never be fully normal again.

"I guess Eddie's hanging up his wizard hat," said Sara.

Lucas shrugged. "He really likes being a dog. Like, he *really* enjoys it. A forty-two-year-old dog. I think it's kind of creepy, to be honest, but to each their own, I guess."

"We should all be so lucky to find that kind of contentment," said Gendreau. "Perhaps *we* should give being a dog a try."

Lucas shook his head. "If I could lick my own nuts, I'd have to resign too."

414

Sara feigned a noisy dry-heave.

The back of Eduardo's watch screwed open. Robin took it off and examined the gears inside, where she found a lock of dark hair.

This was where the power she felt originated, a wellspring that darkled weakly but constantly, sending off the eerie signal of a long-dead radio station.

Hair in the watch…a tooth in the pearl…what *was* all this?

When she looked up at Gendreau, the question must have been plain on her face, because his own held an expectant solemnity. He looked twenty years older than he had when they'd met in her hospital room Tuesday; his bone-blond hair now seemed more silver than platinum, and his eyes were rimmed in shadow.

He took the tooth that had been inside the head of his cane out of his jacket pocket and put it on the table, sipping his coffee and regarding it as if he could divine the meaning of life from it.

Presently he asked, "Robin, have you ever heard of a 'teratoma'?"

"No."

"It's a type of tumor that contains a piece of foreign organic matter. Some teratomas have teeth in them…some contain hair, some skin cells, some bones, some even have entire body parts in them like hands and eyes."

"Well that's freaking *gross.*"

"Indeed." He picked up the tooth and held it at eye level. "Teratomas are rare, but not super-rare. One out of every forty thousand births. That doesn't sound like many, but it comes out to about five a day."

Robin couldn't help but be surprised. It sounded like the kind of nightmarish thing you'd only see maybe five times a year, if that. She remembered seeing something when she was studying in Heinrich's Texas stronghold…an article about children with oversized tumors that turned out to contain their unborn twin. Pale, gnarled, brain-dead hobgoblins wadded up in a pouch of skin, quietly and insidiously stealing their sibling's blood supply. Parasitic twin? She couldn't remember, and frankly she didn't want to. The concept was terrifying to think about, even in her current state. It was like something out of a Japanese horror movie.

"Anyway," Doc Gendreau continued, "the witches' *libbu-harrani* are teratoma, usually located around the heart."

"A cancer that channels ectoplasmic energy."

"Pretty much."

"Wait," said Robin, "you mean that when they do their ritual, the heart isn't actually replaced? It's still there?"

"You've never looked for yourself?"

She thought about it. "It's kind of hard to do an autopsy on a pile of ashes."

"Ah…yeah. I suppose it would be." He nodded. "But yes, the heart is still there. It just beats really slowly. The witch is—" he made air-quotes with his fingers, "—'undead'. This side of flatlining. A body on the brink of death, animated by the heart-road and kept from rotting by the dryad fruit."

Robin pushed away from the stove and paced slowly. "So it *is* possible to completely revert a witch to human form."

"Yes," wheezed Gendreau. She already knew this, but it was nice to get a second opinion, a rational confirmation…or at least, as rational as 'magic' could get.

"Cancers are not natural occurrences," he added. "They are… how shall I put this? …Attempts. Trespasses."

"Attempts at what?"

"Entry. Something's trying to use our bodies as doorways."

Robin's neck bristled. She stared at the curl of hair nestled inside the watch. "What is it?"

"We don't know. Ereshkigal? Whatever it is, it's trying to force its way into the material world…and the teratomas are the closest it can get. Teeth. Hair. Eyes." His eyes were dark and steely. "It's trying to use humanity to give birth to itself."

She closed the watch and slipped it into her pocket. "This wasn't completely Eduardo's idea, was it?"

Gendreau shook his head. "No. He only volunteered."

He took a deep sip of his coffee and placed it kindly back on the table with both hands, in a meditative fashion. "Consider the watch your enlistment bonus. If you'll join us. You've got the experience. You've got the power—"

"The po-*werrrrrr!*" sang Lucas, strumming an air guitar.

"—And if you'll accept my proposal, I can guarantee you that the warrants you've racked up in your adventures the past couple of years will …shall we say, get lost in red tape."

"Red taa-*aape!*" Lucas power-chorded.

The curandero gave him a disapproving scowl and continued.

"There are arson and murder cold cases out there, Robin. Breaking and entering charges floating in the legalsphere. Detectives still looking for a Caucasian woman in her late teens, early twenties. You're rocketing toward five million YouTube subscribers. You used to *never* use real names in your videos—your operation is going to shake to pieces because you're getting cocky. How long do you think it's going to be before the wrong person finds out about your videos and puts two and two together? We can *protect* you."

Robin sighed, feeling stupid and reckless. He had a point. Did she think she was going to be invisible forever? Did she think the goodwill of that handful of beat cops that lavished secret praise on her videos and offered allegiance in her page comments would continue into perpetuity?

Could she even be certain that they would still be on her side if they found out that the incidents in her videos were real?

"I don't do well with leashes."

"Trust me, it will be a long one." Gendreau gave her an earnest smile. "You will get to keep your videos, your van, your life ... for the most part. You saved mine. I will do everything in my power to make sure yours stays intact and that the worst analysis you'll have to endure is a cheek swab."

She swallowed, biting the inside of her cheek, looking at a tin sign nailed to the kitchen wall. DRINK COFFEE! DO STUPID THINGS FASTER!

"Can I have a couple days to think about it?"

Sara smiled. "And talk to Lover-Boy?"

Robin pulled a hand-towel out of the oven handle and chucked it at her face. Sara juked, but it landed on the table.

"I'm a little star-struck, if you want to know the truth," said Lucas. "I'm a big fan of your videos. Well, what I've seen of them this week, anyway."

"I uploaded the latest one today as a Halloween special. Almost an hour long. People are going apeshit for it. It's already got about ten thousand views."

The front door opened and closed. Kenway came into the kitchen, his keys jingling in his hand. "Looks like I'm missing a sweet party." He sidled around the crowded table and framed Robin's face with his big hands, kissing her on the forehead. "Hi you."

Her heart leapt. "...Hi."

Gendreau shotgunned the last of his coffee and pushed back his chair, rising.

Kenway started. "Don't let me run you guys off."

"Oh, we were just leaving," said the curandero, with a chastened smile. "I'd like to relax and find a good meal before we head home tomorrow. There's a Mongolian barbeque restaurant here in town and I've heard lovely things about those." He leaned on his headless cane.

"Happy Halloween, by the way," said Kenway.

"Happy Halloween," agreed Robin.

"Happy Halloween," the three Dog Stars echoed in unison.

"Thank you for the coffee," Gendreau told Robin, handing her the empty mug. As she reached for it, he locked eyes with her. "...And again, for saving my life."

She nodded meekly and turned to put the cup in the sink, staring out the window for a brief moment. Collecting herself.

Out front, a white Toyota Sienna waited by the curb, looking like an egg on wheels. Kenway and Robin stood on the front porch and watched the magicians march down the front walk. Sara wedged herself behind the wheel, grunted something about a 'fucking Oompa-Loompa', and readjusted the seat.

"You don't strike me as the minivan type," Robin told Gendreau.

The curandero paused to emulate sucking on a lemon. "I'm not," he rasped, tossing his cane in the back with Lucas. "But the rental selection here in Podunk leaves much to be desired. And thank the stars for good insurance, or we'd be *walking* back to Atlanta. Hertz isn't going to be pleased that the Suburban's little better than a box of parts now."

Eduardo scrabbled up into the van and Gendreau slid the side door shut with a *crump*.

He turned back to them, one hand tucked into a jacket pocket like a Napoleonic dandy. He tipped the blue velvet top hat, folding himself into the passenger seat. "I await your answer, Miss Martine."

Robin waved with a half-hearted smile.

The Sienna pulled away and rolled down the street, where it flashed its taillights at the stop sign, turned right, and disappeared.

"What was he talking about, an answer?" asked Kenway.

"Joining their Order thing. They probably want me to be their pet demon-girl or something." She sat on the front stoop, where the wind tugged and swept at her silky black wig. "Where have *you* been all day?"

"I got you a surprise."

"A *what?*" Robin's face burned. "You didn't have to do that."

"I know. But I wanted to."

"What is it?"

"If I told you, it wouldn't be a surprise, would it?"

She screwed up her face. "How *much* was it?"

"Some dollars."

She got up and slap-pushed him in the chest. "That's not a real answer, Hammer Boy."

He laughed and snagged her witch-gown, pulling her in and crushing her against him, and suddenly she was intoxicated by him, his cologne (was he even wearing it? she wasn't sure) making her dizzy. The wig tumbled down her back as he lifted her face and gave her a deep kiss.

Her hands balled into fists of their own accord, scrunching his shirt.

He broke away, then kissed her several more times all over her cheeks and forehead, slow and methodical. His beard was like being blessed with a loofah. "Come on," he told her, heading into the house to fetch Wayne. "We'll go check out your surprise."

Forty-Six

THEY DROVE SLOWLY UP Broad in Kenway's Chevy. Even after two days, the street was still littered with a rock-concert aftermath of trash and cast-off clothing. The city had towed away Doc Gendreau's overturned Suburban and the water company capped the broken fire hydrant outlet, but the amount of debris in the road was... well, the word "excessive" came to mind. Many of the shopfronts near the central plaza were busted out, leaving jagged-toothed mouths plundered of their contents.

Nobody could give the cops a straight answer as to why a riot had broken out in uptown Blackfield. But the prevailing theory, going on hearsay and conjecture, was that the car accident that kicked it off—the garbage truck running a red light and slamming into the Suburban—started with bystanders pulling the driver of the garbage truck out with the intent of beating him to death and it escalated through mob mentality and pure panic into a full-fledged riot.

They never learned who the driver of the truck actually was, or how he'd even gotten his hands on it...but the mutilated body of a man named Roy Euchiss (brother of renowned shitheel Owen Euchiss) had been found in the wreckage of Fisher Ellis's comic book shop, beaten to death. The acid damage to his skin seemed to corroborate Joel Ellis's story of what happened Sunday, and the fact that Michael DePalatis's (partner of renowned shitheel Owen Euchiss) body was found with Joel's stolen car seemed to link the brothers as accomplices.

The cops were still processing his fingerprints against prints found in Black Velvet, but Robin was sure they were eventually going to agree that the guy with the smashed face was the one and only Serpent that had been sending them creepy, taunting letters for the last couple of years.

She also had the feeling that the twin brothers might have even been sharing the Serpent name from time to time.

A deep sigh blew from the little boy beside her.

Robin took Wayne's hand and leaned over, looking into his eyes. *We'll find him.* The look of stony misery on his face broke her heart.

Kenway pulled into angle parking in front of his art shop, put the truck in gear, and turned it off.

He sat there so long that even Wayne looked over at him.

"You okay?" asked Robin.

"I sold the shop," said Kenway. One of his big hands came up and he scraped an eye with the heel of his hand.

She saw his face twist up and that was all it took to compel her from the truck and around to his side. She opened the driver door and took his arm, and Kenway turned in his seat, dropping his face into his hands. He started crying into them, *urgently,* a great shuddering-shaking that elicited deep, hitching gasps, *hup-hup-hup-hup-hup.*

Robin took his wrists. "Hey! What's wrong?"

"I sold the shop, Robin," he said between sobs. He let her pry his hands down. His face had turned a livid red and his eyes were bloodshot. Sitting sideways had tugged the cuff of his left pants leg up and the prosthetic foot clanked against the rail under his seat. "I sold it early this afternoon over *hup-hup-hup* lunch."

"I can't say that was the best of ideas," she said, "but why are you crying?"

"Because I'm letting him down again."

"Who? Let—"

Oh. *Ohhhh.*

She had figured it out, but she didn't need to, because he said, "Hendry. Chris. My old buddy."

"…Ah."

"I made breakfast and I let him d—" He cut himself off, and pain flashed across his face. "…I let him down, and now I'm sellin the shop and leavin town." With the last word, anguish tightened inside him and he squeezed his eyes shut, pressing the heel of his fist to his forehead.

Fresh tears rolled into his mustache. "I'm leavin, man…and it's like he's dead all over again."

Just seeing this big man crying his eyes out made Robin want to bawl too. She pushed his hair out of his face with her fingers and held his face. Veins thumped in his temples. "You're not letting him down, babe," she told him, her own eyes burning, "you're letting him go. You're lettin him go *on.* He's letting *you* go."

He shook his head, his fist still jammed against his eyebrow.

Wayne undid his seatbelt and got up on his knees, putting a hand on Kenway's back. She caught his eyes over the vet's shoulder and they traded a concerned vibe.

She let him cry it out for a little while.

"I did it because I needed to," he said.

"You did," she agreed.

"I need to quit…quit kicking around this town—"

"Quit kicking *yourself.*"

He nodded. "That too."

420

"You've got to stop blaming yourself for what he did." For a change, she took his face in her hands and kissed his forehead. "You did what you could, and he did what he felt like he had to do. None of that was on you. Okay?"

Kenway nodded, scrubbing the corners of his eyes with the collar of his shirt.

By now it was completely dark, and bright sharp stars glittered through holes in the gray tent of the sky. The Halloween night air was brisk and drafted down the street in damp, heavy canvas waves. A block down the street, a troupe of college-age trick-or-treaters walked by on their way to some party or other, screaming and laughing. Robin got her jacket out of the truck and put it on against the chill of the night's breeze. The hoodie looked anachronistic on top of the witch-gown.

When the knot in his chest finally loosened, Kenway dug in the door pocket for a handful of napkins and mopped his face with them. A sodium vapor streetlight behind them cast a dismal, rust-orange light over the scene.

"I'm probably ruinin your surprise, ain't I?" he asked, and blew his nose.

Robin couldn't help but chuckle. "No, no, not at all."

She stepped back to let him get out and he wadded the napkins into a ball, stuffing them into his pocket. Wayne got out and he shut the door.

"Come on," said Kenway, taking a shuddery breath. Heat lightning flickered silently across the pendulous clouds.

They followed him down the block to the little side parking lot reserved for the dentist's office and the Mexican restaurant. Robin's CONLIN PLUMBING van was no longer there—it was parked against the curb next to Joel's house—but parked in the slot where it had been was now a motorhome.

"Oh my God," said Robin, venturing closer. "You did not."

"1974 Winnebago Brave. I know a guy… he collects stuff like this. You should see his property, he lives on the road goin south out of town, across from the Methodist church. Old VW bugs all over the freaking place."

The Brave was one of the ugliest, boxiest things she'd ever seen. It resembled an ice cream truck, with a racing stripe down the side that bobbled near the front fender to form a heartbeat W. Kenway unlocked the door and opened it, and she climbed a tiny set of metal stairs into a wonderland of wood paneling. The inside of the motorhome was a cross between a treehouse and an armoire.

"I thought you might appreciate sleeping on a bed," he was saying, "even if it's an RV bed, a lot more than a sleeping bag in the back of a panel van."

Her throat closed up when she saw the sink full of ice and the bottle of champagne.

"That's for drinkin, not for smashin," Kenway said, climbing into the motorhome. The whole thing lurched to one side as he filled the narrow space with his bulk. "But if you *really* wanna christen it, I got a bottle of Boone's Farm some girl left in my fridge last Christmas after my Army unit party."

Wayne climbed in and sat in the dinner nook. "Cool," he said, listlessly staring around. His eyes were dim, bleak flashlights with old batteries. His hands rested on the table as if he couldn't remember what they were for.

Kenway stood in the galley gauging him. He opened the cupboard over the stove and took out a stack of clear party cups. "You know what, kid?" he said grimly, but encouragingly. "You need to take the edge off. How about you share this wine with us?"

"It's champagne."

"How about you share this champagne with us?"

Wayne stared into the back of the RV. "Yeah? Okay."

He checked his phone for the ten-thousandth time. A few moments ticked by as Kenway stood there with the bottle in his hand.

"Shit," he said, "I forgot to get a corkscrew. I'll be right back." He buried the bottle back in the ice and went outside, the motorhome shaking like a wet dog. There was a faint, metallic *clank* as he opened the toolbox on the back of his truck and then heavy raking noises as he rummaged through tools and other assorted detritus.

Wayne looked up from his phone. "I can't believe you guys are gonna sit in here and drink champagne while my dad's still out there somewhere. With that *witch.*"

Robin had forgotten she was dressed as one. The Lycra witch-dress hugged her slinky, boyish figure so tightly it began to make her self-conscious.

The windows flashed softly as heat lightning danced across the sky again. Sitting down in the breakfast nook across from him, she took his hands with her pasty green ones and looked into his face with deadly seriousness. "We're going to find them. I promise. I've found every witch I've looked for up til now...and this one won't get away either."

He watched her, the blinds-filtered light glinting on his glasses, the cellphone coloring his jaw a ghastly blue. The sky guttered the windows with lavender lightning.

"You hear me?" she reiterated. "We *will* find your dad."

He nodded, perhaps a bit dismissively, and went back to flipping through the apps on his phone.

"No. Listen." She leaned in and looked up at his face again.

He smouldered at her in irritation, but at least he was paying attention.

"I will turn every stone, I will burn down every house, I will fight every demon between here and Hell if that's what it takes." She sat back, letting her hands slide away from his. "I've killed to get where I am, and I ain't afraid to do it again. ... So don't count me out, little man."

In the reflection on Wayne's glasses, she saw an eerie green gleam in her own silhouette's eyes.

To his credit, he didn't flinch.

Kenway stepped into the Winnebago again, tilting it crazily. He held up a pair of channel-lock pliers. "Never leave home without em."

Robin shook her head. "You are such a redneck."

He picked up the champagne and clamped the parrothead of the pliers on the cork, twisting it like a stubborn bolt, and it came out with a heady *thoonk!*, gurgling white foam into the sink. He filled three cups with it and carried them to the table. Robin scooted over and let him sit down.

Wayne sipped at the champagne and wrinkled his nose. "Tastes kinda like ginger ale."

He finished it off. "I think I like beer better, honestly."

"Well, uhh!" Kenway tossed his back and slammed the cup on the table with a feeble clap of plastic. "I had no idea you was a grown-ass man, Mr Connoisseur!" The vet pushed himself to his feet and started to pour himself another, then decided to drink it straight from the bottle.

He gave a shudder. "Aight, maybe you got a point. I got some Terrapin and some Yuengling in my apartment." He pulled the plug on the sink to let the ice-water drain.

Robin took the bottle from him and pulled a swig. "I concur."

Kenway paused in the door to study her face.

"What do you think?" His face seemed to be asking, *Did I do good?*

She smiled widely. "I think you spent a hell of a lot of money and gambled your place away on a girl you barely know, but ... I do love it." The wooden cabinets and walls glowed a soft cheese-orange in the darkness. "I really do." She slid her arms around his neck and squeezed him tight. The bottle in her hand rolled across his back.

He pulled her against him and he gave her an earnest hug. "Thank you," he said, his face muffled by her jacket. "For understanding. For standin there and lettin me cry it out."

She pulled back and looked him in the face. The laugh-lines under his eyes were wet.

She scraped them with her thumb. "Of course."

They stepped down out of the Winnebago and Kenway locked it. Robin stood there, her eyes playing over his broad back, and she wondered what he was thinking, wondered how she'd let this man so easily slide into her crazy life where so many others before him had bounced right off. She thought about asking him if she was just his ticket out of town, but decided that the random crying jag over his friend and the fact that he actually had the money, and the means, to leave Blackfield whenever he wanted, must have meant that this was a conscious, deliberate decision on his part.

Was she, though? Was she just the means to an end? Was she an excuse to leave? Robin wrapped her arms around herself, feeling the cold a little bit more than usual. He did seem to have real feelings, but...if she let him in, was he going to stay?

"Are you *sure* you want to be my cameraman?" she finally blurted out. 'Cameraman', here, having evolved beyond its original platonic connotation.

Connotations, she thought, *isn't that where the magic is?*

Kenway turned, hope lighting up his red-rimmed eyes. "I don't think I've ever wanted anything more."

She realized it was the first time she'd seen anything like it since she'd met him. The even-keel Zen complacency she'd come to associate with him hadn't been contentment at all, it had been a... *lost-ness.* A sort of bleak one-foot-in-front-of-the-other dormancy. His perceived failure to save Chris Hendry had been a self-imposed prison cell.

"Even after what you've seen?" she asked.

Taking out a pack of cigarettes, he tapped one out and tucked it into his mouth. He produced a lighter. "Yeah. Hell, all that probably did the *opposite* of running me away." He cupped his hands around his face and lit the cigarette, putting the lighter away. They started up the sidewalk to his shop.

"Ever since I met you," he said, the cigarette's cherry flaring, "it's like... it's like...."

He pincered the cigarette away from his face, jetting a stream of blue-white smoke. "Well, lemme put it like this: do you have any idea how much body armor weighs in the Army?"

"I can't say I do."

"It's a Kevlar vest with ceramic impact plates capable of stopping assault rifle rounds. The Kevlar fabric by itself is like wearing a leather jacket, but with the plates in, it's forty pounds or more, especially with extra side plates, codpiece, helmet. It's heavy as balls, but if you wear it all day you kinda get used to it. But at the end of the day? When you take it off? Suddenly all that weight is magically gone. You feel like you're walking on the moon. Your step is *all* spring."

His beard parted with a broad smile. "Ever since I met you, it's like I took off my armor. I can breathe again. The gravity's so low I could jump right out of the atmosphere." An anxious hand crept up to rub his face. "And, you know, well, I don't ... really want to give that up. You know?"

The corner of Robin's mouth quirked up. "I know."

He unlocked the front door of his art shop, the cigarette cherry glowing in the dark shapes smeared across the glass, and pulled it open. The front area presented them with long smears of pale gray: the rollers and spools of his vinyl machines.

Robin and Wayne followed him through the shop and into the garage. Wayne's face was traced in blue by his cellphone screen. She could see that he was texting his father again. "I'll have to teach you how to play cornhole," Kenway told him, as they started up the stairs to the loft apartment. "You'll like it. Fun stuff."

"Mmm," Wayne grunted noncommittally.

An electronic *bink!* came from the top of the stairs.

Wayne froze, staring at Robin's face. His glasses were white squares, refracting the screen of his cellphone.

His thumb danced across his phone. They heard the *bink!* come from upstairs again. *"DAD?!"* Wayne screamed, scrambling up the stairs toward Kenway's apartment.

Robin lunged for his ankles and missed. *"No!"* she screamed after him. *"Don't go up there!"*

The boy reached the top of the staircase and disappeared over the crest. Robin and Kenway thundered up after him, his titanium foot clanking and thunking like a robot, the champagne sloshing in her hand. Rising into the lightless apartment, she scanned the dark shapes around them, trying to pick out something familiar, something human.

Wayne was in the open kitchen. The white-eyed shadow snatched up a square of light and waved it over his head. "It's his phone! It's Dad's phone!"

"Come on," Robin told him, her arms and neck prickling. "We need to get out of here, *now."*

He came over, holding up Leon's phone and his own. "Why is Dad's phone here? Is Dad here? Why would Dad be here? He's never even *been* here, has he?"

She took his wrist. "Come on, we got—"

"AAAH!" screamed Kenway, lurching forward onto one knee. The cigarette fell out of his mouth.

Robin spun, startled, to find Leon Parkin.

Both his hands were wrapped around the Osdathregar, and Leon had jammed it deep into Kenway's back. Heat lightning blued the clouds outside, briefly turning the windows overlooking the canal into a bank of television screens.

A strange silhouette, squat and angular, stood against the squares of dim light. The apartment plunged into darkness again.

We're screwed, Robin knew, *we waltzed right into this,* as Kenway crawled away on his clanking leg, the silver dagger jutting from his back. She moved toward the maniacally grinning Leon, clenching her fists and preparing for a hand-to-hand.

She still had the champagne; she'd break it over his head. *I got to take him out of commission first,* she decided, but Wayne's hands slammed into her chest.

"No!" the boy shrieked, *"don't kill him!"*

As soon as he shoved her, Wayne ran at his father. Leon threw his arms wide, his eyes and teeth flashing in the abyss of his black face. Wayne plowed into his belly and both of them teetered over the edge of the stairs, falling into the stairwell. The sound of them tumbling down the risers was a sickening drum solo of knees and elbows.

Leon snarled downstairs. Wayne screamed. The scuffling-smacking sounds of a fight carried up to her, and then everything was still and quiet.

Silent lightning illuminated the loft's windows, tracing the strange figure again. "It's so nice to finally meet you," the thing in the wheelchair said, with a voice that was like dry leaves blowing across a sidewalk.

"Morgan," said Robin.

"Morgan," said the Matron. "Sycorax. Circe. Cassandra of Apollo. Miss Cleo of the Psychic Hotline. One of those, I'm sure. I forget. You get to be my age, you forget a lot of things."

The light over the stove clicked on, bathing the apartment in a soft, slanting light.

Marilyn Cutty stood on the other side of Kenway's chopping block. "Happy Halloween, littlebird," said the witch, coming around the kitchen island at a stately pace.

Tearing her eyes away from Cutty, Robin peered at the wheelchair at the edge of the hoodlight and saw a thin, hunched creature, a hideous marionette swaddled in an old quilt. Her arms were twigs, hooked into drawn, papery fists. Her simian Yoda face pushed puggishly into the front of her skull. Eyes like manzanilla olives twitched in gaping sockets.

Perched in the valley between the Matron's hairy left ear and the knob of her left shoulder was a burden of sweat-slick flesh. It bulged and undulated like the egg of a giant snake.

"Ah, yes," rasped the antiquated troll, almost obscured under the tumor. Her face was a mask of stiff yellow skin. "Happy Halloween, my dear."

"Champagne," said Cutty. "Feeling festive, I see."

Robin bent carefully, cautiously, and stood the champagne bottle on the floor to free her hands. Her eyes flicked down to the Osdathregar sticking out of Kenway, and out of the corner of her eye she saw Cutty regard it as well.

Blood glistened between the veteran's lips. Was he dead? Her heart tumbled in her chest.

Robin lunged for the dagger, but she was too late. It leapt out of Kenway's back and whirled across the room, landing in Cutty's outstretched hand. Before Robin could react, Cutty gestured at her and an invisible force washed her up off the floor and across the apartment, where she hit the bedroom wall and hung there, suspended some eight feet in the air.

The impact knocked down several paintings in a card-flutter of canvas squares. The frames banged and slapped as they fell.

Cutty smiled as she paced slowly, inexorably, out of the kitchen. "Ereshkigal." She flourished the dagger. "We've been incubating her for

426

quite some time now. It takes time to resurrect a death-goddess, you know."

"*That's* why you settled in Blackfield and never left, never went nomad like the others," said Robin. The wall pressed against her back hard enough that she thought she would sink through the brick.

"Bingo." Cutty pointed the dagger like a magic wand.

The witch came around the front of the kitchen island and casually leaned against it. "The demon called you here, didn't it? The one Annie summoned, the one she infested her house with. It's been calling you. It brought you here."

"...Yes."

"Did it ever occur to you to wonder why?"

Robin stiffened. "It knew what you were doing! It knew—"

"—That the time was at hand." Cutty smiled. She gestured at the Matron and her fleshy, heaving tumor. "Hundreds of years, we've been working to bring Ereshkigal into the material world. Coddling it, feeding it life from the dryads. Mum's been eating for two for a very, *very* long time. And she's not the first...it's taken a lot of trial-and-error." The witch scoffed sadly. "Halloween. It's almost too on-the-nose, isn't it? Hokey. But I kinda like it."

Robin tried to push away from the wall, but no dice: she was glued down. She could move her hands, though, and as Cutty kept talking she slipped one into her jacket.

"Regretfully, I've missed a few of your birthdays, littlebird," said the witch, emphasizing every so often with the handle of the dagger. The blade rested in her hand. "What kind of a great-grandmother am I? So after your magician friends left, I thought, why don't I bring Mother to town and make a night of it? Throw you a surprise party? You and the goddess Ereshkigal can share a birthday party. Isn't that *neato-keen?*"

The top of the Matron's massive hunchback split open like a Jiffy-Pop bag—*splutch!*

But instead of popcorn, what volcanoed out was a river of ... at first Robin wasn't sure—it looked like crude oil, black and thick—then a nose-burning stench filled the apartment with fish and rotten eggs. Pus and blood and God knew what else sprayed straight up in the air and clattered to the floor around the wheelchair.

Even Cutty was surprised. "Oh, goodness me," she said, and tugged the collar of her sweater over her face.

Robin's fingers closed over the prize in the pocket of her jacket. She pulled out Eduardo's watch and flipped it upside down, pincering it with her thumbs to turn the back counterclockwise. The pewter plate came loose with a subtle click.

The shredded skin over the hunchback's colossal tumor spread like lips, and the whole thing tilted forward, spilling its contents.

A great gush of fibrous black matter poured out of the broken hump like a horse giving birth and hit the floor with a surprisingly solid, bony

427

weight. The empty sac flopped over the Matron's lap, covering her face with a parachute of loose skin. Soupy slime oozed down her shins.

Robin removed the watch's backplate and took out the teratoma hair inside. She focused on the lock of hair and found the energy lying latent inside. Eduardo's Gift of Manipulation spiraled up her arm and into her body. She put the watch back in her pocket.

"Hey, bitch," she said, pointing.

Preoccupied by the nauseating resurrection taking place in front of her, Cutty looked up.

"Happy Halloween." Robin put her index fingertip over the Osdathregar and stole it out of Cutty's hands as if she were dragging a file on a computer screen. The dagger whipped upward and hovered over the witch's head.

"The hell is this?" asked Cutty, staring up at it.

Robin whipped her hand down in a slashing motion. The Osdathregar arrowed down at the witch, but halted in mid-air as if it'd struck an invisible obstacle.

Cutty was pointing up at it, concentration on her face.

"Where did you learn to do *that*, littlebird?" she asked, grinning over her shoulder.

Robin pushed against her and the Osdathregar trembled, turning slowly in the air like the needle in a compass. "I get by with a little help from my friends." The dagger had become the ball in a game of will. She forced it but it wouldn't turn, and the bladepoint gradually, excruciatingly, rotated toward her.

"The Order?" Cutty cackled. "They're a bad influence on you." The witch thrust her finger, overpowering Robin, and the Osdathregar whipped across the room.

At the last instant Robin put up her hands in surprise and the dagger pierced her right palm, bursting from the back. The hilt slammed into the heel of her hand, the tip of the stiletto coming to a stop just a few inches from her face.

That's when it began to hurt, an incredible rush of pain. She could *feel* the blade between the bones of her hand. *"Aaaaaaah!"*

"I hate to do it, my sweet little demon, but you've got to be taught a lesson." Cutty stepped around to the kitchen island, selecting a filet knife from Kenway's dish drain. Then she went to the creature writhing on the floor and used it to pierce the caul covering its face.

Taking hold of the Osdathregar, Robin pulled it out of her hand, inviting a fresh round of agony. Blood ran down her arm. She flung it back at Cutty, who looked up just in time and put out a warning hand.

The dagger stopped in the air.

"You need new material," said Cutty, twirling her finger.

The Osdathregar tried to pivot again, but Robin pointed with both hands two-gun style. She howled with effort. *"Eeerrrrraaaah!"*

"Do you know what the definition of insanity is, dear?"

428

Robin pushed the dagger-tip away. Vivid red blood dribbled from her clenched fist. "I may not be insane," she growled from the wall, her entire body shaking with exertion, "but I'm pretty fuckin crazy."

The witch stepped away from the thing on the floor, redoubling her efforts, her teeth bared, eyes wide.

Figures coalesced to Robin's left and right, a pair of shadows made of cobwebs and a faint blue shine as if patched together from old memories. They marched toward the Osdathregar at a stately wedding pace.

A third one appeared between them, and Robin recognized her: Annie Martine, wearing the dress she'd died in.

Spirits. Ghosts. Robin swore to herself in shock.

The other two shades were a black man and an Asian woman. She supposed they must be Fisher Ellis and Wayne's mother Haruko.

"Wuh-what is this?" stammered Cutty.

Fisher and Haruko's gossamer hands rose and grasped the hilt of the Osdathregar, and it wheeled to point at the witch. Annie took up position directly behind it, and Cutty's fists balled into hard claws as they walked the dagger through her willpower like a trio of pallbearers.

A fourth ghost appeared, a bloody-faced man in a police uniform. Then a fifth and a sixth, two boys in black dress clothes. They all crowded around the hovering silver dagger, urging it forward.

Sweat trickled down Cutty's gray face. "No! *No!*"

As if she were bringing someone back to life with shock paddles, Robin punched forward with both fists. The spirits rushed forward and the Osdathregar caught Cutty in the solar plexus, lifting her.

Robin brought her fists down as if ending an orchestra piece and the dagger darted into the floor, nailing the witch to the hardwood planks.

"AAAARGH!"

As one, the ghosts faded, and the force that was pinning Robin to the wall let go. She dropped onto her hands and knees, barking her shin on Kenway's nightstand on the way down.

"Uuuuuuuhr," groaned the cadaverous horse-limbed thing on the floor.

Robin crawled to her feet and staggered toward it.

An angular shape moved restlessly inside a cloudy white caul. The rubbery sac was clear enough that she could see through it. Thick wisps of black hair clouded around pale limbs...an elbow...a hip...a hand... a face.

One bloody eye gazed through the membrane. A finger poked through and ripped the knife-hole wider.

Robin recoiled. Her ankle bumped something, and she found the bottle of champagne.

Getting an idea, she approached the thing currently tearing its way out of its amniotic sac. Her heart slammed a door in her chest over and over. Robin steeled herself and grabbed the reborn Ereshkigal. The death-goddess's flesh was like cold butter. Robin's fingers sank into clammy wax.

A thin, malformed face stared at her, eyes glassy and veiny under a scum of cold clear mucus. *"EEEEEEEEE!"*

Robin screamed back, terrified, *"Aaaaah!"* but she was already steamin' along and there wasn't no stoppin' *this* train. She rose, flexing, and lifted Ereshkigal by the upper arms. The wraith under the flapping caul screeched and kicked like a feral child.

A hard strange wind skirled through the apartment, rising and howling and stinking of rot and sulphur, and the paintings on the walls flapped and clacked in stiff wooden applause. Papers blew off their fridge-magnets and swirled on the air, plastering against the couch and cabinets. Robin's sexpot witch-gown ripped and flapped madly around her thighs.

Robin muscled the larval Ereshkigal over to the lifeless Matron in the wheelchair. There she dumped it on top of Morgan, or Sycorax, or whatever the ancient bitch wanted to call herself. Then she turned, grabbed up the bottle of champagne, and...

...remembered that champagne is not flammable.

"Shit. Shit!" she shouted into the building hurricane.

She dashed to the kitchen, threw the bottle into the sink (where it shattered) and hauled the refrigerator door open. Inside was a carton with one egg in it, a bottle of ketchup, a half-quart of milk, a box of Mexican leftovers, and enough liquor and beer to stock a tavern.

"Thank God for bachelors." She grabbed a bottle of Stolichnaya. Storming around the island (dodging Cutty's reaching hands on the way) she went over and poured Russian vodka all over the banshee.

"Nooooooo!" roared Cutty. Her face changed, became cavernous with teeth. A fell light shined in her eyes and she bucked ferociously against the dagger's hilt.

Robin found Kenway's cigarette and took a steep drag on it, sucking smoke.

The cherry throbbed orange.

She tossed the butt on the monster squirming in the wheelchair, where the Stolichnaya caught and went up in a bright splash of white flame. Ereshkigal shrieked and thrashed, gabbling nonsense. The wind caught the fire and whirled it into a helix of flame, worming toward the ceiling.

Rushing at the conflagration, Robin grabbed the arms of the wheelchair and ran it backwards. Flames licked at her face. Her eyebrows roasted, turning black, curling into ash.

The back of the wheelchair crashed through the window.

Robin found herself teetering on the edge of a three-story drop. Her arms windmilled as the wheelchair and its flaming payload somersaulted head over heels and crashed into the dry canal below in a shower of broken glass.

"You little bitch!" Cutty was screaming, still pinned to the floor by the Osdathregar.

Wind kicked across the side of the building, howling into the apartment through the broken window. Robin realized her jacket was on fire and wrestled it off, throwing it out into the canal.

"I'll kill you!"

She went over to where the witch was flailing around and picked up Wayne's phone, dialing 911.

"I'll tear your goddamn guts out!"

"Hello," the dispatcher said pleasantly. "What's your emergency?"

"My boyfriend's been stabbed."

Robin crouched next to Kenway. She frowned at the blood soaking through his shirt from the hole between his shoulder blades—what she could see of it through the tears in her eyes. "We're at 3210 Broad Avenue, Griffin's Art Shop. There's a big red picture of a gryphon on the front window. Please hurry."

Cutty snarled in a gutteral, blustering roar. *"I'll crack open your chest and eat your heart, girl!"*

The dispatcher sounded startled. "An ambulance is on the way?"

"Thanks," said Robin, hanging up.

The witch panted like a winded horse, slavering and coiling around the dagger in her chest. *"Get this thing out of me and I'll show you how to hurt! You'll wish Annie never pushed your sorry ass out of her rotten cunt!"*

"Keep talking."

Giving her a wide berth, Robin shut the refrigerator door. Then she braced her foot on the wall and hooked her fingers around the back of the fridge.

Six feet to her right, Cutty looked up, curious.

"What are you d—NO! *NOO!*"

Robin pried the fridge away from the wall and overturned it on top of Marilyn Cutty's face.

The Kenmore flattened the witch's skull with an impact heavy enough to vibrate the hardwood floor. Gray brains and skull fragments sprayed in a thin starburst.

Thin wisps of energy curled from underneath. Robin followed them and found Cutty's heart-road. She absorbed it. The spray of gore sizzled as if the floor were a griddle, and dissipated into black scum.

A few minutes later, Robin was finishing off the Stolichnaya and watching the thing in the canal burn, when the Parkins came trudging up the stairs. Wayne had one of Kenway's toluene paint markers and a deep scratch on his face. Leon had an *algiz* rune drawn on his forehead and he was cradling a blood-slick cat.

The three of them stared at each other with shell-shocked eyes.

A distant ambulance siren fell over them, growing to a caterwaul. "You look like you need a drink, Mr Parkin," said Robin, and she offered up the vodka bottle.

431

Leon smiled tiredly. "No thanks."

VALDEZ SUMMER WAS IN full swing as a 1974 Winnebago Brave trundled into the parking lot of Cap'n Joe's Tesoro gas station. The sky was a mystical, permeating fog that hovered at a height of about sixty feet. Emerald mountains crowded around the town, their peaks thrust into the low clouds as if jostling for a drink of rain.

Robin angled the RV underneath the awning (wincing in anticipation as the vehicle's brow just slipped under the eaves) and parked next to the pump at the end.

Satin gray ocean lapped at the shores of the bay across the road. She sat there for a moment, gazing absently, not really thinking.

Eventually she unclipped the seatbelt and climbed out of the driver's seat, squirreling into the living area. A trash bag full of clothes sat in the floor under the breakfast nook. She opened it and her lip curled at the coppery stink of blood and munge of wet ashes roiling up out of it. She tied it shut and opened the door, carrying it outside.

The parking lot was wet and seal-black, mottled with rain puddles. She clomped across them in her combat boots and threw the bag of clothes into a Dumpster, then went into the gas station.

She came back out with a little bag, glass clinking inside. She left the bag in the breakfast nook and went out to pump the gas.

Wind rolled in off the ocean, giant blundering warps of air that pushed waves across the puddles and made the aluminum sheeting in the awning bark metallically.

Robin gradually became aware of a presence standing at her left.

"Hi, Mom," she said, smiling over at a feminine figure as it coalesced from the cool Alaskan air.

Annie Martine smiled back. "Morning, love."

Robin's mother didn't talk much these days, but when she did, she spoke without the speech impediment of a scarred tongue. Her AM-radio voice was tinny and hollow, but her diction was razor sharp.

She wore a long flowing gown or sundress, or at least that's what Robin thought it was; the revenant was mostly diaphanous and gauzy, just coming into focus around the face and shoulders.

Only Robin could see and hear her. Ever since she'd pulled Annie out of the dryad and into herself, her mother appeared from time to time, as if checking in. She supposed she carried Annie in her heart now, or at least in some room of her mind. Or maybe it was a pleasant hallucination caused by going off her meds? She didn't know, but if so, this was the kind of delusion that she could live with, at least.

While she was standing there with a handful of nozzle, her mohawk whipping in the gale, a red pickup truck pulled in, paused as if in indecision, and then eased up to the other side of the last pump.

Robin eyed the bed of the pickup truck. A bundle of fishing poles, nets, a tackle box. A clutch of mashed beer cans.

The driver opened the door with a rusty *crack* and got out. She was mildly dismayed when she saw that he was dressed like some kind of farmer, in a dirty chambray shirt and even dirtier jeans. His face was a wild widower bristle of salt-and-pepper scruff. So it was a surprise when, instead of opening his mouth to reveal grungy chompers and a *Howdy, y'all*, he smiled with flawless eggshell teeth and said, "Guten morguen. Schönes Wetter, nicht wahr?" *Good morning. Lovely weather, isn't it?*

Robin blinked. "Uhh… Ja. Wenn Sie eine buh—Beerdigungen, v-vielleicht."

Yeah. If you like funerals, maybe.

The German laughed. "What brings a beautiful young woman like you out here to the middle of nowhere by herself?" he asked in a heavy accent. His eyes were hooded but clear. And they were gravitating to her ass. "And in such an unwieldy vehicle!"

"What a creepazoid," murmured the ghostly Annie.

Robin smiled patiently, glanced at the treeline, and whispered confidentially behind her hand, "Ich bin hier, um eine Hexe zu töten."

The German laughed even harder, throwing his head back. But when it began to fade, and he unscrewed his gascap, he looked up at her and saw something in her eyes that made his smile fall cold. If it were possible for a man's ears to lay flat back like a dog, Herr Fisherman's would have done so.

"Des Teufels Tochter—!" he said under his breath. He got back in his truck without putting the gascap back on, cranked it, and pulled around to the pump next to the store.

Then he sat and stared through the windshield.

His doors locked. *Clunk!*

Robin laughed. "You're gonna be waitin a while for *me* to leave, sucker," she said to herself. The meter on the pump had climbed to nine dollars. "This fat bitch is thirsty today."

She engaged the auto-cutoff and climbed into the Winnebago. Her Macbook sat on the breakfast nook table, a cord running up to the mobile

434

internet by the window. She opened the laptop and woke it up to find a couple of new emails buried in a mess of spam and Malus Domestica fan mail.

The first was from Anders Gendreau, asking her how Alaska was treating her. She typed up a quick answer and fired it off.

Hey Andy,

It's beautiful up here but hard to sleep with it daytime all the time. I'm done here for now, but I might spend a couple more days up here in the mountains before I take off back to the Lower 48, if you don't mind—I think I could use a little more nature in my life.

Looking forward to getting back to the States. Let me know if you guys want to get together for the Fourth.

—Robin

The second email was from Wayne Parkin.

Hi Robin!!!!!

I hope you're having fun and doing okay. Dad and I love the pictures you've been posting in Alaska and Canada. That moose you saw on the freeway was crazy!!!! I hope her and her calf are okay!!!

We miss you here. I dont know if you saw the pictures we put on Facebook but Joel Ellis and me fixed up the comic shop real good and with Fisher's fianceé Marissa's help, we got it up and running this week. Its doing great. I guess he made a will a couple years ago and left the shop to Joel. Him and Marissa are sharing ownership and thanks to all our ideas......especially Marissa coz she got a business degree.........Joel says the shop is "out of the hole" whatever that maens.

And it turned out that Miguel was the one that bought Kenway's art shop and turned it into another pizzeria......the Rocktown Cafe.........and since they're right down the street from the comic shop we share alot of business!!!

Anyway I just wanted to say hey and tell you that I'm doin real good in school. And thank you for kicking that demon out of our house. We sleep real good now. Dad had that symbol tattooed on our shoulders. At first the tattoo guy didn't want to do it but then Dad showed him your videos and told him what happened to him, and then the tattoo guy was all about some tattooing a kid. It hurt real bad but I didnt cry at all. Dad was proud of me.

Dad hasnt had a drink since we moved here. He misses Mom sometimes and he gets this look on his face when Mr Johnson messes up and offers him a beer but he never takes one.

435

So I'm real proud of him too.

Love you Ms Martine. You come see us when you get back.

PS. Joel decided to try his brothers "keto diet" after all. He had a hard time with it at first but now he looks like he's doin alright. He still cheats sometimes but he says he feels better than he has in a while. He says he's gonna get you on it when you come back.

Robin closed the Macbook, digging through the bag and coming up with a can of green tea. She opened it with a *snick!* and sat in the nook slurping and staring out the window, smiling.

She sighed.

"Get up, you lazy bastard," she groaned into the back. "I've been driving all night. It's your turn."

Kenway groaned back.

"Get uuuuup." Robin slurped tea.

"Uuuuuhhng."

She got up out of the nook and went into the back. The big vet was sprawled facedown on the bed in his underwear, the sheet sideways like a toga.

She pulled the sheet off and smacked him hard on the ass.

"Yo!" he shouted, scrambling to roll over. Grabbing her wrist, he dragged her into the bed and held her down until she was forced to pinch him, at which point it turned into a tickle-fight. He won by forfeit when he took her face in his hands and they kissed, an intoxication of slow gulping and lip-biting and tongue-licking.

"My devil-girl," he said, her cheeks cupped in his bear paws.

"The guy at the register in the gas station said that there are cruises out into Valdez Bay all day," she said, her breath gusting against his cheek. "There are sea lions and free danishes and all kinds of stuff. What do you think?"

He kissed her on the nose.

She looked down and feigned shock. "Looks like *somebody's* turned on by sea lions."

"No, but free danishes get me goin pretty good."

Not as good as he got *her* going. A potent warmth spread from the pit of her stomach.

Kenway got up and pulled an elastic sock over the end of his leg, then pushed it into his prosthetic foot and strapped it on. He lumbered through the Winnebago, pulled a can of coffee out of the bag, and opened it, slugging it back. Then he put on some jeans, a T-shirt, and a sandal, and went out to put up the petrol nozzle.

She watched him through the window. While they'd been necking in the back, another car had pulled up to the other side of the pump, a raggedy-looking station wagon.

A young woman was feeding gasoline into her car, her shoulders bunched up against the damp wind. Her eyes were rimmed with the dark circles of insomnia and she looked like she'd dressed in the dark.

Sitting in the back was a little boy. He seemed to recognize Kenway and rolled down his window...he said something, but it was so low Robin couldn't make it out.

The woman—his mother, assumedly—whirled on him and gave him an earful. He frowned and rolled the window back up. Before any further words could be exchanged, the boy's mother got in the car and drove away so fast that she skidded a bit when she stopped at the frontage.

"What was *that* about?" asked Robin as Kenway came back in and tucked his bulky self behind the wheel of the Winnebago.

"The little boy asked me if I was the guy from that Malus Domestica show on YouTube." He buckled his seatbelt and cranked the RV up, putting it in gear. "I told him I was. Then he said there's a witch that lives in the woods near his house. That she almost got his sister and now she's been prowling around all night trying to get *him*. The old fella at the general store calls her 'the Qalupalik', the Old Woman of the Sea."

"I take it his mom told him to shut up about the witches."

"Actually, she told him to shut up, shut up, *shut up about the goddamn witch.*"

He was already fording the parking lot, chasing after the station wagon. She staggered across the listing deck of the RV and plopped into the passenger seat. Catching a glimpse of the Dumpster she'd thrown the bag of clothes into, she realized that someone had spraypainted graffiti on the side of it.

"WELCOME TO ALASKA", it said, in two-foot-tall letters, the word ALASKA the largest of the three. What concerned Robin was the fact that the second A was the rune for *homelands*.

Witch territory.

A seagull cut the sky over the road and was gone. Robin leaned over to turn on the radio. A garble of static brought her to a station playing Halestorm's 'Daughters of Darkness'. Twist-tied to the sun visor was the old mosquito Mr. Nosy, smiling as he always did. She kissed her fingertips and tapped them to the stuffy's cheek.

"I thought you were taking a nap," Kenway said, pulling onto the highway as rock n' roll filled the Winnebago with sound and fury. Annie Martine stood behind the transmission hump, her hands on their headrests, smiling. As Robin watched, the shade vapored into nothing.

"Promises to keep, babe," she said, picking her fingernails with the Osdathregar, "and many witches to kill before I sleep."

THE END

About the Author

S. A. Hunt lives in Lyerly, Georgia. Sam's been writing and producing art for almost twenty years, and short stories and illustrations can be found at his website. If you liked the book, don't be shy! Feel free to go say hi! Keep up with the process by mailing list or by following my Twitter.

http://www.sahuntbooks.com/
http://www.twitter.com/authorsahunt

Other Books by S. A. Hunt

The Whirlwind in the Thorn Tree (The Outlaw King 1)
Law of the Wolf (The Outlaw King 2)
Ten Thousand Devils (The Outlaw King 3)
The Big Crunch (The Outlaw King 3.5), web exclusive

Short Stories
Chimneysweep
Talent Show
Pocket Change
The Hidden

THE OUTLAW ARMY

My books are also dedicated to everyone that have helped
bring it together, and everyone that always was and later
became my friends, kickstarters, moral (and immoral) support,
and street crew. You have been my rock.

Jessi Wagar
Chaser Spaeth
Jonathan Piacenti
Glenn Banton
Monica Hernandez
Christopher Ruz
Jan Berry
Tania Gunadi
Glenn James
Greg Benson (Mediocre Films)
Jeff Beesler
Danielle Waked
Nathan Tarantla
Chris Lason
Lucas Tiedeman
Cay Eli
Joe Donley
Nathaniel Gill
Dennis Koch
Se Lindley

Matthew Graybosch
Christopher Turner
Katie Fryhover
Evan Blackwell
KariAnn Ramadorai
Jenni Wiltz
Jon Wagner
Barbara Weaver
Phronk
Hilda Bowen
John Raymond Peterson
Theodros Haile
Levi Goddard
Mike Reeves-McMillan
Melinda LeBaron
Karen Conlin
A. D. "Bliss" Trask
Karen Schumacher
M. Todd Gallowglas
Mike DePalatis

Made in the USA
San Bernardino, CA
10 July 2017